D1121910

THE COLLECTED STORIES *of* RICHARD YATES

BY RICHARD YATES

Revolutionary Road

Eleven Kinds of Loneliness

A Special Providence

Disturbing the Peace

The Easter Parade

A Good School

Liars in Love

Young Hearts Crying

Cold Spring Harbor

The Collected Stories of Richard Yates

THE COLLECTED STORIES *of* RICHARD YATES

Introduction by Richard Russo

Methuen

10 9 8 7 6 5 4 3 2 1

Published in 2002
by Methuen Publishing Ltd
215 Vauxhall Bridge Rd, London SW1V 1EJ

First published in the USA in 2001 by
Henry Holt and Company, LLC

Copyright © 1957, 1961, 1962, 1974, 1976, 1978, 1980, 1981, 2001
by the Estate of Richard Yates

Introduction copyright © 2001 by Richard Russo

Methuen Publishing Limited Reg. No. 3543167

A CIP catalogue record for this book
is available from the British Library

ISBN 0 413 77125 3

These stories first appeared in *The Atlantic Monthly*, *Charm*, *Cosmopolitan*, *Esquire*, *Ploughshares*, *The New Yorker*, *Harper's Magazine*, and in the books *Eleven Kinds of Loneliness* and *Liars in Love*.

Printed and bound in Great Britain by
Creative Print and Design Ltd (Wales), Ebbw Vale

This book is sold subject to the condition that it shall not, by way of trade
or otherwise, be lent, resold, hired out, or otherwise circulated in any form of
binding or cover other than that in which it is published and without a similar
condition, including this condition, being imposed on the subsequent purchaser.

Contents

THE UNCOLLECTED STORIES

Editor's Note

"Evening on the Côte d'Azur" and "Thieves" were previously published in the journal *Ploughshares* in 1974 and 1976, respectively. The rest of Richard Yates's uncollected stories make their first appearance in this volume. Other than standard typographical corrections, the stories are published as Richard Yates wrote them.

The editor and Monica Shapiro, the author's daughter, would like to acknowledge Ronald J. Nelson of James Madison University for discovering the uncollected stories in the Richard Yates Collection at Boston University in 1996.

Introduction

Secret Hearts

by Richard Russo

Here is what I've come to think of as *my* Richard Yates story.

The main residential street of Gloversville, New York, where I grew up and where my parents and grandparents spent most of their adult lives (there and in neighboring Johnstown) is Kingsborough Avenue, and it's divided into "Upper" and "Lower." Upper Kingsborough is wide and bordered by mature maples and elms, and it's where the finest houses were built back when the glove shops and tanneries were still in operation and there was, at least for a select few, money. Lower Kingsborough Avenue is narrower, its houses more modest, mostly split-level ranches and tiny capes, built with money from the GI Bill by men and women of my parents' generation.

These days, when I return to Gloversville, my mother is often with me, because the purpose of our trip is usually to visit her sister, and when I turn onto Lower Kingsborough my mother always studies the small, well-maintained houses set closer to the street and to one another than the larger homes farther up, and she invariably remarks that all these little houses are "cute as a button." To own one of them had been a dream of hers when she was a young woman married to my father, who had himself just returned from the war at a time when the entire nation was flushed with both victory and optimism about the future. To my mother, one of these fresh, new little houses wasn't "pie in the sky," her phrase for big, impossible dreams (like owning one of the grand houses on Upper Kingsborough), which is why to this day she can't quite fathom how such a modest dream managed to elude her. The answer, though, is simple enough. My father—the man she chose to marry—had no intention of settling down. Not then, not ever.

Why I think of this as a Richard Yates story will be made clear by the twenty-seven *real* Richard Yates stories collected here for the first time under one cover. They have been too long out of print, and as a result an entire generation of readers will be coming to them for the first time, and for such readers it is my special honor and pleasure to introduce the fictional world of these stories, to suggest how and why they work on us, and to speculate upon what sort of man would usher them into the world. I'm confident that readers will not need me to tell them how great the stories are, or what a cause for celebration it is that they are finally restored in print, or that no library, private or public, that pretends interest in American literature of the highest order, or in the history of the contemporary short story, is complete without them. The beauty and symmetry of Yates's stories will send readers all the way back to Chekhov looking for antecedents, and they'll recognize the platform—the springboard really—these stories provide for Raymond Carver and just about every other writer of realistic fiction in America today. Teaching at the Iowa Writers' Workshop, Yates inspired a generation of talented young writers that included Andre Dubus, Theodore Weesner, and James Crumley, among others. And after almost a decade spent out of print, he continues to inspire almost fanatical devotion among writers. A couple of years ago, when a book tour took me to Iowa City, I happened to mention to my friend and former student, the writer John McNally, that I didn't have a copy of *Liars in Love*. He disappeared upstairs, returning moments later with a copy for me. When I asked how he happened to have an extra copy of a book that's so hard to find, he said that whenever he is in a strange city, he scours used bookstores for copies of Yates's books, buying up whatever he can find, in order to press them upon people who hadn't read him. How many had he given away in this fashion? McNally shrugged, grinning. Dozens? He didn't know, he'd lost track.

Yates has been described as a writer's writer by people who consider that a high compliment, but I suspect Yates himself would have understood that the phrase trails an unintended insult by suggesting that only other writers are sophisticated enough to appreciate his many gifts. The truth is that Richard Yates is not a sophisticated writer. He doesn't need to be; he's far too talented to have much use for either smoke or mirrors.

Astute readers will immediately be struck by how many of the stories collected here are about dreamers, and it is perhaps for this reason that it's hard to read them outside the context of that most famous American Dream story, *The Great Gatsby*. Yates admired no author more than Fitzgerald, as the writer-dreamer Jack Fields, the protagonist of Yates's autobiographical story "Saying Goodbye to Sally" suggests. Comparing Yates's dreamers to Fitzgerald's is immediately instructive. *Gatsby*, of course, is not so much the story of a great man as of an ordinary man with a great dream. Jimmy Gatz is determined not just to become rich and win Daisy Buchanan but, more audaciously, to negate the past and reinvent himself, even reshape the world, if need be. Fitzgerald set his novel in a world that is superficially similar to that of Yates's stories. In both cases, a world war had just concluded and America was victorious. Everything seemed possible except failure. But there were significant differences too. Perhaps because they have vivid memories not just of the war but also the Great Depression that preceded it, Yates's dreamers are less audacious, more cautious. They want things as badly as Jimmy Gatz, but they have less in the way of expectation. Living all but invisible lives, they're wary, unsure how much they have a right to hope for. Betty Meyers, a young mother and Navy wife with three kids, "trapped" on the Côte d'Azur, wants desperately to return home to Bayonne, New Jersey, a heartbreakingly modest and totally unironic ambition. In "A Wrestler with Sharks," Leon Sobel, who's written (but not published) nine books, wants a column and byline in a tiny trade union newspaper. Indeed, Yates wants us to understand, it may be the very modesty of such desires (for the little house, not the big one) that disguises their potential for life's most demoralizing failures. Yates understood that while we risk disappointment when we set for ourselves an ambitious goal and fail to achieve it, the challenge, in a sense, insulates us from the worst humiliation. Dream big and we're expected to fail. About the worst that can happen (Gatsby to the contrary notwithstanding) is that we'll be applauded for our pluck. Dream small, Yates seems to suggest, and we're expected to succeed. As a result, failure ensures not just disappointment, but humiliation, anguish, and, most dangerous of all, the impulse to dream smaller next time, thereby risking even greater failure. The characters we meet in Yates's stories are often already the victims of diminished expectation. Ken Platt, in "A Really Good Jazz Piano," assumes that when he and his best pal, Carson Wyler, meet two girls on the beach, he'll get the less attractive one, the "cute, freckled good-sport of a girl whose every cheerful glance and gesture showed she was used to taking second best."

Of course, not all of Yates's dreamers make the mistake of dreaming small. Cabby Bernie Silver in "Builders," a "poor, lost, brave little man, dreaming his huge and unlikely dream," clings tenaciously to a scheme that seems to the story's narrator, Bob Prentice, little more than a "pathetic delusion." Still, the story makes clear that while Bernie's dream of becoming the hero of a series of anecdotes about a wise, benevolent New York cabbie may be improbable, as Prentice suggests, "sillier things . . . have built empires in America." We realize, too, that the book of stories that keeps Bernie looking for the perfect writer masks a more modest goal that's shared by many of Yates's characters. Bernie would simply like to count for something, and his dogged pursuit of his dream, however improbable, keeps him heading somewhere, if only in his own imagination. And however improbable they may be, other people's dreams, as Prentice learns, have power. It's only when he buys into the little man's dream and writes a couple of Bernie's stories for him ("I took that little bastard of a story and I built the hell out of it") that Bob Prentice actually *becomes* a writer, a dream he's been toying with for a long time without really committing to it. By writing the stories and thereby indirectly acknowledging the validity of Bernie's far-fetched dream, Prentice finds himself closer to realizing his own.

But if dreams are necessary to a life that's worth living, if they are what give purpose and direction to otherwise mundane existences, why then do so many of Yates's dreamers seem doomed to fail? What are we to make of the fact that modest dreams are as likely to fail as grand ones? Is it our nature to dream unwisely? Yates seems to understand as clearly as Fitzgerald that the cruelest promise of democracy is that anybody can be anything. All men may be created equal, but they become unequal in a heartbeat, and in these stories large dreams are often paired with mediocre talents. Bill Grove's mother, Helen, a sculptor featured in two of Yates's finest stories ("Oh, Joseph, I'm So Tired" and "Regards at Home"), is not so much without talent as she is without *enough* talent to match her ambitions. Bernie Silver dreams of being special one day, but Helen assumes she already *is*, by virtue of her aspirations and superior sensibility. In "Joseph" she's commissioned to sculpt the head of the newly elected FDR, a stroke of luck she's determined to think of as her big chance, never suspecting that her meager talents cannot sustain her dream.

Indeed, it is luck that many of the Yates's characters blame for their failures. In "Jody Rolled the Bones" luck has a name—Jody—and it's Jody the young soldiers invoke when they call cadence during basic training: "Jody rolled the bones when yew left—RIGHT!" When you're drafted, it's Jody who gets to stay home and steal your girl and everything else that's rightfully yours. It's luck, they believe, that causes one man to be born rich, another to be placed in the path of live ammunition. But the story itself makes clear that, regardless of our inclination to believe in luck as the prime determiner of human destiny, both good and bad fortune are largely an illusion. For one thing, human beings seem uniquely designed to mistake good luck for bad and vice versa. The young soldiers in the story may believe they've been unlucky to be drafted and even unluckier to be in the hated Sergeant Reece's platoon, but at least in the latter they couldn't have been luckier, because it's Reece who will make men of them, something these boys want without knowing it. What they *think* they want—an easier life at boot camp—could be deadly where they're headed, a fact they're blind to until Jody rolls the bones again and Reece is transferred, leaving them under the command of Ruby, a "good Joe" who could well get them killed with kindness and incompetence. What good is luck, Yates seems to ask, if we are too stupid or blind to recognize it on the rare occasions it visits us?

Just as tellingly, luck is always relative, which is why the deck so often seems stacked against Yates's characters, even when it isn't. The veterans' hospital in "Out with the Old" is divided into two wings, causing the tuberculosis patients, who feel they've got the worst of things, to remark, "Those paraplegic bastards think they *own* the goddamn place." Nor do the luckless grasp that even those they consider the luckiest are themselves beset by the same gnawing self-doubts as everyone else. A famous actor in "Saying Goodbye to Sally" is so insecure he makes an elaborate show of having read George Bernard Shaw, while the director who criticizes the actor for his ignorance ("three years from now he'll discover the Communist Party") demonstrates his own lack of self-confidence by repeatedly asking Sally, an agent's secretary, what she thinks of his work.

No, it's not Jody rolling the bones that's causing all the problems, nor is it the fact that the world plays us false, as John Fallon, the B.A.R. man (whose wife wears falsies), believes. For Yates, human destiny is rooted not in chance but in character. Jack Fields, the writer in "Saying Goodbye to Sally," lives in a squalid flat in New York before Jody smiles on him and he's hired to write a screenplay for pay he describes as "dizzying" (the same thing happened to Yates himself when he was hired to write a screenplay for William Styron's *Lie Down in Darkness*), but the place he rents in L.A. turns out to be a dead ringer, squalor-wise, for the one he left in New York, causing Jack to wonder if his ex-wife might be right about his having a self-destructive personality. Yates's people not only don't understand what's happening to them, most also lack the ability to sort things out upon reflection afterwards, which makes them vulnerable to making the same mistakes again. Just as Gatsby dies without understanding what has befallen him, so do Yates's characters struggle in vain for self-knowledge. McIntyre, a father admitted to the tuberculosis ward in "Out with the Old," feeling both helpless and useless, wants desperately to relieve some of the burden borne by his young, pregnant daughter. "Your old dad may not be good for much any more," he writes to her, "but he does know a thing or two about life and especially one important thing, and that is . . ." Mac's inability to finish that sentence speaks eloquently to Yates's belief that our human inability to understand our experience is a basic design flaw. In this way our most potent and necessary dreams can derive from simple misunderstanding. Bill Grove, who over the years has become an expert on his mother's myriad failures of self-knowledge ("she never seemed to realize that if people could see her underpants they might not care what kind of hat she was wearing"), is much slower to comprehend his own motives, that his dream of going off to Europe and becoming a writer may mask a more urgent need—to escape his mother—that he's unwilling to confront.

Yates's characters not only don't understand the source of their own desires, they undervalue their own strengths and virtues, discounting their kindness and decency, as if they can't quite imagine that these qualities will get them anywhere in life. Nor do they recognize true worth in others. Miss Snell, the grade-school teacher in "Fun with a Stranger," offers each of her students a perfect gift of love in the form of an eraser, something they'll badly need in their mistake-filled adult lives, but her gift is unwanted by children too young to understand its nature or meaning. Yates writes brilliantly about children in many of these stories, partly, it seems to me, because he understands that in important ways most of us remain children all our lives, perpetually attracted to all the wrong things, taken in repeatedly by whatever is cheap and eye-catching and superficial. "A Glutton for Punishment"'s Walter Henderson, who discovers at the age of nine the intense pleasures inherent in defeat and who practices falling after he's shot playing cowboys and Indians, never quite grasps that he's patterned his entire adult life on this childish game. Failure will forever be his only grace. In other stories, Yates questions the ranking of what we generally regard as virtues. Honesty is demonstrated to be no substitute for compassion in "A Natural Girl," and intelligence is often revealed to be the tool of cruelty, as in "Trying Out for the Race," where Elizabeth Hogan Baker, who "was much too good for the kind of work she did," in a revealing gesture tosses aside *The New Republic* before ridiculing her best friend, Lucy Towers, whom she believes to be her intellectual inferior.

If the reason we're pulled into Richard Yates's stories so quickly has to do with our understanding of what his characters so desperately desire, what often keeps us turning pages is the more gradual revelation of those same characters' anxieties. The most primal of these, it seems, is loneliness, the fear of which causes the people in Yates's stories to endure terrible humiliations. As novelist Stewart O'Nan has observed in his fine, insightful essay on Yates in *The Boston Review* (which argues eloquently the need for this very volume of collected stories), much of Yates's power as a writer derives from his unwillingness to avert his eyes from his characters' most intense suffering. Grace, in "The Best of Everything," realizes by the end of the story that her impending marriage is a horrible mistake that will likely result in a life of searing regret for both herself and Ralph, her dim-witted fiancé. Her willingness to endure the humiliation of sexual rejection the night before her wedding can only be understood in terms of what she clearly understands to be her alternative—a solitary life. The long concluding scene in which she stands, vulnerable and nearly naked, both literally and metaphorically, as Ralph, utterly blind to her offer of love, impatiently explains how important his buddies are to him, is enough to make any reader squirm. Nor, Yates seems to say, are such torments reserved for the weak and the shy. Even the Carson Wylers of the world, who seem to have everything going for them, in the end, when their thin veneer of self-confidence is stripped away, reveal themselves to be as panic-stricken as the Ken Platts who idolize them:

> It wasn't what he said that mattered—for a minute it seemed that nothing Carson said would ever matter again—it was that his face was stricken with the uncannily familiar look of his own heart, the very face he himself, Lard-Ass Platt, had shown all his life to others: haunted and vulnerable and terribly dependent, trying to smile, a look that said Please don't leave me alone.

Indeed, Yates suggests, it may even be this worst of night terrors—of ending up alone in the world and trying to smile—that is responsible for our most tragic human blindness, our eager willingness to confuse what is true with what we want to be true. Take Paul Colby, the young soldier of "A Compassionate Leave," who manages, against very long odds, to remain a virgin despite his three-day pass to Paris at the end of the war. He would like to think it's Jody, rolling the bones against him, but finally, when he runs out of money during his last night in Paris and no longer can afford "even the most raucous of middle-aged whores," he has to admit that "he had probably arranged in his secret heart for this to be so." The need to conceal and to deny what's in our secret hearts is in the end what is responsible for the worst kind of dishonesty there is: self-deception, our willingness to sell ourselves a bill of goods. Bill Grove and his wife keep telling each other (and themselves) that they're in love, only to conclude years later that in reality "neither of us had anywhere else to go."

In the end I think it is Yates's relentless, unflinching investigation of our secret hearts, and his speaking to us in language as clear and honest and unadorned and unsentimental and uncompromising as his vision, that makes him such a great writer, and which makes the publication of these collected stories a literary event of such significance. Yates has been called the voice of his generation—that is, my parents' generation—and for me part of the fun of rereading the stories originally published in *Eleven Kinds of Loneliness* and *Liars in Love*, along with the other stories collected here, most published for the first time, was that doing so was like having a long, extended conversation with my father and mother on subjects we'd somehow managed to avoid all our lives. Still, I don't think that any writer gets to be the voice of his or her generation without transcending that generation, and that is what I believe these stories do. Because Richard Yates, in his quiet way, remains one of the most subversive writers I know. Critics have pointed out that Yates subverted the American character in his fiction, and it's true that there's much that the author found empty and even harmful in American institutions and American culture. But it's not just our "American" character that Yates lays bare in these stories. It's our deepest human nature. Peel away the carefully constructed layers of self-deception, and we discover that too often we're all simply horse traders, eager to move up in the world by swapping a shabby job, house, friend, spouse, even child, for a newer, better one. It's being traded, or knowing that we would be traded if we could be, that on occasion allows Yates's characters to see things in what one of them calls "the clear light of self-hatred."

Such brutal insight, I suspect, along with what Yates's former student and friend, the writer Robert Lacy, has referred to as his "seemingly congenital inability to sugarcoat," that may be the reason Yates never sold well in life and why, for a time, at least, his fiction has been allowed to slip out of print. And it's also probably the reason some critics have wistfully regretted the fact that these stories hold out so little hope, even accusing Yates of reveling in the failures his characters must endure. There may be some truth to the charge. There *is* perverse pleasure in pain, in suffering, even in humiliation. Bill Grove can't deny the enjoyment he gets when he takes his mother to get her teeth pulled, "hearing her grunt and shudder with the shock of each extraction." But his satisfaction has less to do with enjoying her pain than it does with the fact that what's happening to her is real, something she can't deny or (as is Helen's wont) make a romance out of. Perhaps, Yates suggests in "Builders," the need to make a romance out of ugly reality is a basic human craving, as is the accompanying need to disguise what we're doing from ourselves. The stories Bernie Silver wants Bob Prentice to tell about him are not so much lies as romances, realities seen in a certain light, and it is that light that Bernie is most insistent upon. The Bernie Silver of Prentice's stories is not an insignificant cabby, "his fingertips stained a shining gray from handling other people's coins and dollar bills all day," but rather a better, wiser Bernie, a Bernie that the little man still believes himself capable of becoming, a Bernie illuminated by the same light of hope that some of Yates's critics yearned for. "'Where are the windows?' [Bernie] demanded, spreading his hands. . . . 'Where does the light come in?'" Yet for Richard Yates, no matter how much he may have longed to bathe his characters in such light ("God knows," Prentice concedes, "there certainly ought to be a window around here somewhere, for all of us"), he believes this light to be a lie. The secret heart, in the end, is a windowless place, where light comes in "as best it can" through "cracks . . . left in the builder's faulty craftsmanship."

The excitement one feels reading these dark stories, I believe, is the exhilaration of encountering, recognizing, and embracing the truth. It's not a pretty truth? Too bad. That we recognize ourselves in the blindness, the neediness, the loneliness, even the cruelty of Yates's people, will have to suffice. And, in the end, Yates judges not the characters in these stories, nor us (we who recognize ourselves in them), nor himself, nor even God (that other faulty builder) too harshly. For me, one of the most enduring images in Richard Yates's stories is of the protagonist of "A Convalescent Ego," a man named Bill, who has recently come home from the hospital to recover from a serious operation. Physically diminished and feeling useless, he unwisely attempts to help his wife, who is supporting both of them during his convalescence, with the housework. Shaking the mop out the window, its head comes off, falling several stories into the courtyard below, leaving Bill "absurdly shaking the naked stick over the windowsill." Dignity would seem to be pretty much out of the question. Probably a lot of other things we want are out of the question too, including, perhaps, if we want it too badly, the modest little house on Lower Kingsborough.

—RR

September 2000

THE
Collected Stories of Richard Yates

FROM

Eleven Kinds of Loneliness

Doctor Jack-o'-Lantern

ALL MISS PRICE had been told about the new boy was that he'd spent most of his life in some kind of orphanage, and that the gray-haired "aunt and uncle" with whom he now lived were really foster parents, paid by the Welfare Department of the city of New York. A less dedicated or less imaginative teacher might have pressed for more details, but Miss Price was content with the rough outline. It was enough, in fact, to fill her with a sense of mission that shone from her eyes, as plain as love, from the first morning he joined the fourth grade.

He arrived early and sat in the back row—his spine very straight, his ankles crossed precisely under the desk and his hands folded on the very center of its top, as if symmetry might make him less conspicuous—and while the other children were filing in and settling down, he received a long, expressionless stare from each of them.

"We have a new classmate this morning," Miss Price said, laboring the obvious in a way that made everybody want to giggle. "His name is Vincent Sabella and he comes from New York City. I know we'll all do our best to make him feel at home."

This time they all swung around to stare at once, which caused him to duck his head slightly and shift his weight from one buttock to the other. Ordinarily, the fact of someone's coming from New York might have held a certain prestige, for to most of the children the city was an awesome, adult place that swallowed up their fathers every day, and which they themselves were permitted to visit only rarely, in their best clothes, as a treat. But anyone could see at a glance that Vincent

Sabella had nothing whatever to do with skyscrapers. Even if you could ignore his tangled black hair and gray skin, his clothes would have given him away: absurdly new corduroys, absurdly old sneakers and a yellow sweatshirt, much too small, with the shredded remains of a Mickey Mouse design stamped on its chest. Clearly, he was from the part of New York that you had to pass through on the train to Grand Central—the part where people hung bedding over their windowsills and leaned out on it all day in a trance of boredom, and where you got vistas of straight, deep streets, one after another, all alike in the clutter of their sidewalks and all swarming with gray boys at play in some desperate kind of ball game.

The girls decided that he wasn't very nice and turned away, but the boys lingered in their scrutiny, looking him up and down with faint smiles. This was the kind of kid they were accustomed to thinking of as "tough," the kind whose stares had made all of them uncomfortable at one time or another in unfamiliar neighborhoods; here was a unique chance for retaliation.

"What would you like us to call you, Vincent?" Miss Price inquired. "I mean, do you prefer Vincent, or Vince, or—or what?" (It was purely an academic question; even Miss Price knew that the boys would call him "Sabella" and that the girls wouldn't call him anything at all.)

"Vinny's okay," he said in a strange, croaking voice that had evidently yelled itself hoarse down the ugly streets of his home.

"I'm afraid I didn't hear you," she said, craning her pretty head forward and to one side so that a heavy lock of hair swung free of one shoulder. "Did you say 'Vince'?"

"Vinny, I said," he said again, squirming.

"Vincent, is it? All right, then, Vincent." A few of the class giggled, but nobody bothered to correct her; it would be more fun to let the mistake continue.

"I won't take time to introduce you to everyone by name, Vincent," Miss Price went on, "because I think it would be simpler just to let you learn the names as we go along, don't you? Now, we won't expect you to take any real part in the work for the first day or so; just take your time, and if there's anything you don't understand, why, don't be afraid to ask."

He made an unintelligible croak and smiled fleetingly, just enough to show that the roots of his teeth were green.

"Now then," Miss Price said, getting down to business. "This is Monday morning, and so the first thing on the program is reports. Who'd like to start off?"

Vincent Sabella was momentarily forgotten as six or seven hands went up, and Miss Price drew back in mock confusion. "Goodness, we do have a lot of reports this morning," she said. The idea of the reports—a fifteen-minute period every Monday in which the children were encouraged to relate their experiences over the weekend—was Miss Price's own, and she took a pardonable pride in it. The principal had commended her on it at a recent staff meeting, pointing out that it made a splendid bridge between the worlds of school and home, and that it was a fine way for children to learn poise and assurance. It called for intelligent supervision—the shy children had to be drawn out and the show-offs curbed—but in general, as Miss Price had assured the principal, it was fun for everyone. She particularly hoped it would be fun today, to help put Vincent Sabella at ease, and that was why she chose Nancy Parker to start off; there was nobody like Nancy for holding an audience.

The others fell silent as Nancy moved gracefully to the head of the room; even the two or three girls who secretly despised her had to feign enthrallment when she spoke (she was that popular), and every boy in the class, who at recess liked nothing better than to push her shrieking into the mud, was unable to watch her without an idiotically tremulous smile.

"Well—" she began, and then she clapped a hand over her mouth while everyone laughed.

"Oh, *Nancy*," Miss Price said. "You *know* the rule about starting a report with 'well.'"

Nancy knew the rule; she had only broken it to get the laugh. Now she let her fit of giggles subside, ran her fragile forefingers down the side seams of her skirt, and began again in the proper way. "On Friday my whole family went for a ride in my brother's new car. My brother bought this new Pontiac last week, and he wanted to take us all for a ride—you know, to try it out and everything? So we went into White Plains and had dinner in a restaurant there, and then we all wanted to go see this movie, *Doctor Jekyll and Mr. Hyde*, but my brother said it was too horrible and everything, and I wasn't old enough to enjoy it—oh, he made me so mad! And then, let's see. On Saturday I stayed home all day and helped my mother make my sister's wedding dress.

My sister's engaged to be married, you see, and my mother's making this wedding dress for her? So we did that, and then on Sunday this friend of my brother's came over for dinner, and then they both had to get back to college that night, and I was allowed to stay up late and say goodbye to them and everything, and I guess that's all." She always had a sure instinct for keeping her performance brief—or rather, for making it seem briefer than it really was.

"Very good, Nancy," Miss Price said. "Now, who's next?"

Warren Berg was next, elaborately hitching up his pants as he made his way down the aisle. "On Saturday I went over to Bill Stringer's house for lunch," he began in his direct, man-to-man style, and Bill Stringer wriggled bashfully in the front row. Warren Berg and Bill Stringer were great friends, and their reports often overlapped. "And then after lunch we went into White Plains, on our bikes. Only we *saw Doctor Jekyll and Mr. Hyde*." Here he nodded his head in Nancy's direction, and Nancy got another laugh by making a little whimper of envy. "It was real good too," he went on, with mounting excitement. "It's all about this guy who—"

"About a *man* who," Miss Price corrected.

"About a man who mixes up this chemical, like, that he drinks? And whenever he drinks this chemical, he changes into this real monster, like? You see him drink this chemical, and then you see his hands start to get all scales all over them, like a reptile and everything, and then you see his face start to change into this real horrible-looking face—with fangs and all? Sticking out of his mouth?"

All the girls shuddered in pleasure. "Well," Miss Price said, "I think Nancy's brother was probably wise in not wanting her to see it. What did you do *after* the movie, Warren?"

There was a general "*Aw-w-w!*" of disappointment—everyone wanted to hear more about the scales and fangs—but Miss Price never liked to let the reports degenerate into accounts of movies. Warren continued without much enthusiasm: all they had done after the movie was fool around Bill Stringer's yard until suppertime. "And then on Sunday," he said, brightening again, "Bill Stringer came over to *my* house, and my dad helped us rig up this old tire on this long rope? From a tree? There's this steep hill down behind my house, you see—this ravine, like?—and we hung this tire so that what you do is, you take the tire and run a little ways and then lift your feet, and you go swinging way, way out over the ravine and back again."

"That sounds like fun," Miss Price said, glancing at her watch.

"Oh, it's *fun*, all right," Warren conceded. But then he hitched up his pants again and added, with a puckering of his forehead, "'Course, it's pretty dangerous. You let go of that tire or anything, you'd get a bad fall. Hit a rock or anything, you'd probably break your leg, or your spine. But my dad said he trusted us both to look out for our own safety."

"Well, I'm afraid that's all we'll have time for, Warren," Miss Price said. "Now, there's just time for one more report. Who's ready? Arthur Cross?"

There was a soft groan, because Arthur Cross was the biggest dope in class and his reports were always a bore. This time it turned out to be something tedious about going to visit his uncle on Long Island. At one point he made a slip—he said "botormoat" instead of "motorboat"—and everyone laughed with the particular edge of scorn they reserved for Arthur Cross. But the laughter died abruptly when it was joined by a harsh, dry croaking from the back of the room. Vincent Sabella was laughing too, green teeth and all, and they all had to glare at him until he stopped.

When the reports were over, everyone settled down for school. It was recess time before any of the children thought much about Vincent Sabella again, and then they thought of him only to make sure he was left out of everything. He wasn't in the group of boys that clustered around the horizontal bar to take turns at skinning-the-cat, or the group that whispered in a far corner of the playground, hatching a plot to push Nancy Parker in the mud. Nor was he in the larger group, of which even Arthur Cross was a member, that chased itself in circles in a frantic variation of the game of tag. He couldn't join the girls, of course, or the boys from other classes, and so he joined nobody. He stayed on the apron of the playground, close to school, and for the first part of the recess he pretended to be very busy with the laces of his sneakers. He would squat to undo and retie them, straighten up and take a few experimental steps in a springy, athletic way, and then get down and go to work on them again. After five minutes of this he gave it up, picked up a handful of pebbles and began shying them at an invisible target several yards away. That was good for another five minutes, but then there were still five minutes left, and he could think of nothing to do but stand there, first with his hands in his pockets, then with his hands on his hips, and then with his arms folded in a manly way across his chest.

Miss Price stood watching all this from the doorway, and she spent the full recess wondering if she ought to go out and do something about it. She guessed it would be better not to.

She managed to control the same impulse at recess the next day, and every other day that week, though every day it grew more difficult. But one thing she could not control was a tendency to let her anxiety show in class. All Vincent Sabella's errors in schoolwork were publicly excused, even those having nothing to do with his newness, and all his accomplishments were singled out for special mention. Her campaign to build him up was painfully obvious, and never more so than when she tried to make it subtle; once, for instance, in explaining an arithmetic problem, she said, "Now, suppose Warren Berg and Vincent Sabella went to the store with fifteen cents each, and candy bars cost ten cents. How many candy bars would each boy have?" By the end of the week he was well on the way to becoming the worst possible kind of teacher's pet, a victim of the teacher's pity.

On Friday she decided the best thing to do would be to speak to him privately, and try to draw him out. She could say something about the pictures he had painted in art class—that would do for an opening—and she decided to do it at lunchtime.

The only trouble was that lunchtime, next to recess, was the most trying part of Vincent Sabella's day. Instead of going home for an hour as the other children did, he brought his lunch to school in a wrinkled paper bag and ate it in the classroom, which always made for a certain amount of awkwardness. The last children to leave would see him still seated apologetically at his desk, holding his paper bag, and anyone who happened to straggle back later for a forgotten hat or sweater would surprise him in the middle of his meal—perhaps shielding a hard-boiled egg from view or wiping mayonnaise from his mouth with a furtive hand. It was a situation that Miss Price did not improve by walking up to him while the room was still half full of children and sitting prettily on the edge of the desk beside his, making it clear that she was cutting her own lunch hour short in order to be with him.

"Vincent," she began, "I've been meaning to tell you how much I enjoyed those pictures of yours. They're really very good."

He mumbled something and shifted his eyes to the cluster of departing children at the door. She went right on talking and smiling, elaborating on her praise of the pictures; and finally, after the door had closed behind the last child, he was able to give her his attention. He did so tentatively at first; but the more she talked, the more he seemed to relax, until she realized she was putting him at ease. It was as simple and as gratifying as stroking a cat. She had finished with the pictures now and moved on, triumphantly, to broader fields of praise. "It's never easy," she was saying, "to come to a new school and adjust yourself to the—well, the new work, and new working methods, and I think you've done a splendid job so far. I really do. But tell me, do you think you're going to like it here?"

He looked at the floor just long enough to make his reply—"It's awright"—and then his eyes stared into hers again.

"I'm so glad. Please don't let me interfere with your lunch, Vincent. Do go ahead and eat, that is, if you don't mind my sitting here with you." But it was now abundantly clear that he didn't mind at all, and he began to unwrap a bologna sandwich with what she felt sure was the best appetite he'd had all week. It wouldn't even have mattered very much now if someone from the class had come in and watched, though it was probably just as well that no one did.

Miss Price sat back more comfortably on the desk top, crossed her legs and allowed one slim stockinged foot to slip part of the way out of its moccasin. "Of course," she went on, "it always does take a little time to sort of get your bearings in a new school. For one thing, well, it's never too easy for the new member of the class to make friends with the other members. What I mean is, you mustn't mind if the others seem a little rude to you at first. Actually, they're just as anxious to make friends as you are, but they're shy. All it takes is a little time, and a little effort on your part as well as theirs. Not too much, of course, but a little. Now for instance, these reports we have Monday mornings—they're a fine way for people to get to know one another. A person never feels he has to make a report; it's just a thing he can do if he wants to. And that's only one way of helping others to know the kind of person you are; there are lots and lots of ways. The main thing to remember is that making friends is the most natural thing in the world, and it's only a question of time until you have all the friends you want. And in the meantime, Vincent, I hope you'll consider *me* your friend, and feel free to call on me for whatever advice or anything you might need. Will you do that?"

He nodded, swallowing.

"Good." She stood up and smoothed her skirt over her long thighs. "Now I must go or I'll be late for *my* lunch. But I'm glad we had this little talk, Vincent, and I hope we'll have others."

It was probably a lucky thing that she stood up when she did, for if she'd stayed on that desk a minute longer Vincent Sabella would have thrown his arms around her and buried his face in the warm gray flannel of her lap, and that might have been enough to confuse the most dedicated and imaginative of teachers.

At report time on Monday morning, nobody was more surprised than Miss Price when Vincent Sabella's smudged hand was among the first and most eager to rise. Apprehensively she considered letting someone else start off, but then, for fear of hurting his feelings, she said, "All right, Vincent," in as matter-of-fact a way as she could manage.

There was a suggestion of muffled titters from the class as he walked confidently to the head of the room and turned to face his audience. He looked, if anything, too confident: there were signs, in the way he held his shoulders and the way his eyes shone, of the terrible poise of panic.

"Saturday I seen that pitcha," he announced.

"Saw, Vincent," Miss Price corrected gently.

"That's what I mean," he said; "I sore that pitcha. *Doctor Jack-o'-Lantern and Mr. Hide.*"

There was a burst of wild, delighted laughter and a chorus of correction: "Doctor *Jekyll*!"

He was unable to speak over the noise. Miss Price was on her feet, furious. "It's a *perfectly natural mistake*!" she was saying. "There's no reason for any of you to be so rude. Go on, Vincent, and please excuse this very silly interruption." The laughter subsided, but the class continued to shake their heads derisively from side to side. It hadn't, of course, been a perfectly natural mistake at all; for one thing it proved that he was a hopeless dope, and for another it proved that he was lying.

"That's what I mean," he continued. "*Doctor Jackal and Mr. Hide.* I got it a little mixed up. Anyways, I seen all about where his teet' start comin' outa his mout' and all like that, and I thought it was very good. And then on Sunday my mudda and fodda come out to see me in this car they got. This Buick. My fodda siz, 'Vinny, wanna go for a little ride?' I siz, 'Sure, where yiz goin'?' He siz, 'Anyplace ya like.' So I siz,

'Let's go out in the country a ways, get on one of them big roads and make some time.' So we go out—oh, I guess fifty, sixty miles—and we're cruisin' along this highway, when this cop starts tailin' us? My fodda siz, 'Don't worry, we'll shake him,' and he steps on it, see? My mudda's gettin' pretty scared, but my fodda siz, 'Don't worry, dear.' He's tryin' to make this turn, see, so he can get off the highway and shake the cop? But just when he's makin' the turn, the cop opens up and starts shootin', see?"

By this time the few members of the class who could bear to look at him at all were doing so with heads on one side and mouths partly open, the way you look at a broken arm or a circus freak.

"We just barely made it," Vincent went on, his eyes gleaming, "and this one bullet got my fodda in the shoulder. Didn't hurt him bad—just grazed him, like—so my mudda bandaged it up for him and all, but he couldn't do no more drivin' after that, and we had to get him to a doctor, see? So my fodda siz, 'Vinny, think you can drive a ways?' I siz, 'Sure, if you show me how.' So he showed me how to work the gas and the brake, and all like that, and I drove to the doctor. My mudda siz, 'I'm prouda you, Vinny, drivin' all by yourself.' So anyways, we got to the doctor, got my fodda fixed up and all, and then he drove us back home." He was breathless. After an uncertain pause he said, "And that's all." Then he walked quickly back to his desk, his stiff new corduroy pants whistling faintly with each step.

"Well, that was very—entertaining, Vincent," Miss Price said, trying to act as if nothing had happened. "Now, who's next?" But nobody raised a hand.

Recess was worse than usual for him that day; at least it was until he found a place to hide—a narrow concrete alley, blind except for several closed fire-exit doors, that cut between two sections of the school building. It was reassuringly dismal and cool in there—he could stand with his back to the wall and his eyes guarding the entrance, and the noises of recess were as remote as the sunshine. But when the bell rang he had to go back to class, and in another hour it was lunchtime.

Miss Price left him alone until her own meal was finished. Then, after standing with one hand on the doorknob for a full minute to gather courage, she went in and sat beside him for another little talk, just as he was trying to swallow the last of a pimento-cheese sandwich.

"Vincent," she began, "we all enjoyed your report this morning, but I think we would have enjoyed it more—a great deal more—if you'd told us something about your real life instead. I mean," she hurried on, "for instance, I noticed you were wearing a nice new windbreaker this morning. It *is* new, isn't it? And did your aunt buy it for you over the weekend?"

He did not deny it.

"Well then, why couldn't you have told us about going to the store with your aunt, and buying the windbreaker, and whatever you did afterwards. That would have made a perfectly good report." She paused, and for the first time looked steadily into his eyes. "You do understand what I'm trying to say, don't you, Vincent?"

He wiped crumbs of bread from his lips, looked at the floor, and nodded.

"And you'll remember next time, won't you?"

He nodded again. "Please may I be excused, Miss Price?"

"Of course you may."

He went to the boys' lavatory and vomited. Afterwards he washed his face and drank a little water, and then he returned to the classroom. Miss Price was busy at her desk now, and didn't look up. To avoid getting involved with her again, he wandered out to the cloakroom and sat on one of the long benches, where he picked up someone's discarded overshoe and turned it over and over in his hands. In a little while he heard the chatter of returning children, and to avoid being discovered there, he got up and went to the fire-exit door. Pushing it open, he found that it gave onto the alley he had hidden in that morning, and he slipped outside. For a minute or two he just stood there, looking at the blankness of the concrete wall; then he found a piece of chalk in his pocket and wrote out all the dirty words he could think of, in block letters a foot high. He had put down four words and was trying to remember a fifth when he heard a shuffling at the door behind him. Arthur Cross was there, holding the door open and reading the words with wide eyes. "Boy," he said in an awed half-whisper. "Boy, you're gonna get it. You're really gonna *get* it."

Startled, and then suddenly calm, Vincent Sabella palmed his chalk, hooked his thumbs in his belt and turned on Arthur with a menacing look. "Yeah?" he inquired. "Who's gonna squeal on me?"

"Well, nobody's gonna *squeal* on you," Arthur Cross said uneasily, "but you shouldn't go around writing—"

"Arright," Vincent said, advancing a step. His shoulders were slumped, his head thrust forward and his eyes narrowed, like Edward G. Robinson. "Arright. That's all I wanna know. I don't like squealers, unnastand?"

While he was saying this, Warren Berg and Bill Stringer appeared in the doorway—just in time to hear it and to see the words on the wall before Vincent turned on them. "And that goes fa you too, unnastand?" he said. "Both a yiz."

And the remarkable thing was that both their faces fell into the same foolish, defensive smile that Arthur Cross was wearing. It wasn't until they had glanced at each other that they were able to meet his eyes with the proper degree of contempt, and by then it was too late. "Think you're pretty smart, don'tcha, Sabella?" Bill Stringer said.

"Never mind what I think," Vincent told him. "You heard what I said. Now let's get back inside."

And they could do nothing but move aside to make way for him, and follow him dumfounded into the cloakroom.

It was Nancy Parker who squealed—although, of course, with someone like Nancy Parker you didn't think of it as squealing. She had heard everything from the cloakroom; as soon as the boys came in she peeked into the alley, saw the words and, setting her face in a prim frown, went straight to Miss Price. Miss Price was just about to call the class to order for the afternoon when Nancy came up and whispered in her ear. They both disappeared into the cloakroom—from which, after a moment, came the sound of the fire-exit door being abruptly slammed—and when they returned to class Nancy was flushed with righteousness, Miss Price very pale. No announcement was made. Classes proceeded in the ordinary way all afternoon, though it was clear that Miss Price was upset, and it wasn't until she was dismissing the children at three o'clock that she brought the thing into the open. "Will Vincent Sabella please remain seated?" She nodded at the rest of the class. "That's all."

While the room was clearing out she sat at her desk, closed her eyes and massaged the frail bridge of her nose with thumb and forefinger, sorting out half-remembered fragments of a book she had once read on the subject of seriously disturbed children. Perhaps, after all, she should never have undertaken the responsibility of Vincent Sabella's loneliness. Perhaps the whole thing called for the attention of a specialist. She took a deep breath.

"Come over here and sit beside me, Vincent," she said, and when he had settled himself, she looked at him. "I want you to tell me the truth. Did you write those words on the wall outside?"

He stared at the floor.

"Look at me," she said, and he looked at her. She had never looked prettier: her cheeks slightly flushed, her eyes shining and her sweet mouth pressed into a self-conscious frown. "First of all," she said, handing him a small enameled basin streaked with poster paint, "I want you to take this to the boys' room and fill it with hot water and soap."

He did as he was told, and when he came back, carrying the basin carefully to keep the suds from spilling, she was sorting out some old rags in the bottom drawer of her desk. "Here," she said, selecting one and shutting the drawer in a businesslike way. "This will do. Soak this up." She led him back to the fire exit and stood in the alley watching him, silently, while he washed off all the words.

When the job had been done, and the rag and basin put away, they sat down at Miss Price's desk again. "I suppose you think I'm angry with you, Vincent," she said. "Well, I'm not. I almost wish I could be angry—that would make it much easier—but instead I'm hurt. I've tried to be a good friend to you, and I thought you wanted to be my friend too. But this kind of thing—well, it's very hard to be friendly with a person who'd do a thing like that."

She saw, gratefully, that there were tears in his eyes. "Vincent, perhaps I understand some things better than you think. Perhaps I understand that sometimes, when a person does a thing like that, it isn't really because he wants to hurt anyone, but only because he's unhappy. He knows it isn't a good thing to do, and he even knows it isn't going to make him any happier afterwards, but he goes ahead and does it anyway. Then when he finds he's lost a friend, he's terribly sorry, but it's too late. The thing is done."

She allowed this somber note to reverberate in the silence of the room for a little while before she spoke again. "I won't be able to forget this, Vincent. But perhaps, just this once, we can still be friends—as long as I understand that you didn't mean to hurt me. But you must promise me that you won't forget it either. Never forget that when you do a thing like that, you're going to hurt people who want very much to like you, and in that way you're going to hurt yourself. Will you promise me to remember that, dear?"

The "dear" was as involuntary as the slender hand that reached out and held the shoulder of his sweatshirt; both made his head hang lower than before.

"All right," she said. "You may go now."

He got his windbreaker out of the cloakroom and left, avoiding the tired uncertainty of her eyes. The corridors were deserted, and dead silent except for the hollow, rhythmic knocking of a janitor's push-broom against some distant wall. His own rubber-soled tread only added to the silence; so did the lonely little noise made by the zipping-up of his windbreaker, and so did the faint mechanical sigh of the heavy front door. The silence made it all the more startling when he found, several yards down the concrete walk outside, that two boys were walking beside him: Warren Berg and Bill Stringer. They were both smiling at him in an eager, almost friendly way.

"What'd she do to ya, anyway?" Bill Stringer asked.

Caught off guard, Vincent barely managed to put on his Edward G. Robinson face in time. "Nunnya business," he said, and walked faster.

"No, listen—wait up, hey," Warren Berg said, as they trotted to keep up with him. "What'd she do, anyway? She bawl ya out, or what? Wait up, hey, Vinny."

The name made him tremble all over. He had to jam his hands in his windbreaker pockets and force himself to keep on walking; he had to force his voice to be steady when he said, "Nunnya *business*, I told ya. Lea' me alone."

But they were right in step with him now. "Boy, she must of given you the works," Warren Berg persisted. "What'd she say, anyway? C'mon, tell us, Vinny."

This time the name was too much for him. It overwhelmed his resistance and made his softening knees slow down to a slack, conversational stroll. "She din say nothin'," he said at last; and then after a dramatic pause he added, "She let the ruler do her talkin' for her."

"The *ruler*? Ya mean she used a *ruler* on ya?" Their faces were stunned, either with disbelief or admiration, and it began to look more and more like admiration as they listened.

"On the knuckles," Vincent said through tightening lips. "Five times on each hand. She siz, 'Make a fist. Lay it out here on the desk.' Then she takes the ruler and *Whop! Whop! Whop!* Five times. Ya think that don't hurt, you're crazy."

Miss Price, buttoning her polo coat as the front door whispered shut behind her, could scarcely believe her eyes. This couldn't be Vincent Sabella—this perfectly normal, perfectly happy boy on the sidewalk ahead of her, flanked by attentive friends. But it was, and the scene made her want to laugh aloud with pleasure and relief. He was going to be all right, after all. For all her well-intentioned groping in the shadows she could never have predicted a scene like this, and certainly could never have caused it to happen. But it was happening, and it just proved, once again, that she would never understand the ways of children.

She quickened her graceful stride and overtook them, turning to smile down at them as she passed. "Goodnight, boys," she called, intending it as a kind of cheerful benediction; and then, embarrassed by their three startled faces, she smiled even wider and said, "Goodness, it *is* getting colder, isn't it? That windbreaker of yours looks nice and warm, Vincent. I envy you." Finally they nodded bashfully at her; she called goodnight again, turned, and continued on her way to the bus stop.

She left a profound silence in her wake. Staring after her, Warren Berg and Bill Stringer waited until she had disappeared around the corner before they turned on Vincent Sabella.

"Ruler, my eye!" Bill Stringer said. "Ruler, my eye!" He gave Vincent a disgusted shove that sent him stumbling against Warren Berg, who shoved him back.

"Jeez, you lie about *everything*, don'tcha, Sabella? You lie about *everything*!"

Jostled off balance, keeping his hands tight in the windbreaker pockets, Vincent tried in vain to retain his dignity. "Think *I* care if yiz believe me?" he said, and then because he couldn't think of anything else to say, he said it again. "Think *I* care if yiz believe me?"

But he was walking alone. Warren Berg and Bill Stringer were drifting away across the street, walking backwards in order to look back on him with furious contempt. "Just like the lies you told about the policeman shooting your father," Bill Stringer called.

"Even *movies* he lies about," Warren Berg put in; and suddenly doubling up with artificial laughter he cupped both hands to his mouth and yelled, "Hey, Doctor Jack-o'-Lantern!"

It wasn't a very good nickname, but it had an authentic ring to it —

the kind of a name that might spread around, catch on quickly, and stick. Nudging each other, they both took up the cry:

"What's the matter, Doctor Jack-o'-Lantern?"

"Why don'tcha run on home with Miss Price, Doctor Jack-o'-Lantern?"

"So long, Doctor Jack-o'-Lantern!"

Vincent Sabella went on walking, ignoring them, waiting until they were out of sight. Then he turned and retraced his steps all the way back to school, around through the playground and back to the alley, where the wall was still dark in spots from the circular scrubbing of his wet rag.

Choosing a dry place, he got out his chalk and began to draw a head with great care, in profile, making the hair long and rich and taking his time over the face, erasing it with moist fingers and reworking it until it was the most beautiful face he had ever drawn: a delicate nose, slightly parted lips, an eye with lashes that curved as gracefully as a bird's wing. He paused to admire it with a lover's solemnity; then from the lips he drew a line that connected with a big speech balloon, and in the balloon he wrote, so angrily that the chalk kept breaking in his fingers, every one of the words he had written that noon. Returning to the head, he gave it a slender neck and gently sloping shoulders, and then, with bold strikes, he gave it the body of a naked woman: great breasts with hard little nipples, a trim waist, a dot for a navel, wide hips and thighs that flared around a triangle of fiercely scribbled pubic hair. Beneath the picture he printed its title: "Miss Price."

He stood there looking at it for a little while, breathing hard, and then he went home.

The Best of Everything

NOBODY EXPECTED GRACE to do any work the Friday before her wedding. In fact, nobody would let her, whether she wanted to or not.

A gardenia corsage lay in a cellophane box beside her typewriter—from Mr. Atwood, her boss—and tucked inside the envelope that came with it was a ten-dollar gift certificate from Bloomingdale's. Mr. Atwood had treated her with a special courtliness ever since the time she necked with him at the office Christmas party, and now when she went in to thank him he was all hunched over, rattling desk drawers, blushing and barely meeting her eyes.

"Aw, now, don't mention it, Grace," he said. "Pleasure's all mine. Here, you need a pin to put that gadget on with?"

"There's a pin that came with it," she said, holding up the corsage. "See? A nice white one."

Beaming, he watched her pin the flowers high on the lapel of her suit. Then he cleared his throat importantly and pulled out the writing panel of his desk, ready to give the morning's dictation. But it turned out there were only two short letters, and it wasn't until an hour later, when she caught him handing over a pile of Dictaphone cylinders to Central Typing, that she realized he had done her a favor.

"That's very sweet of you, Mr. Atwood," she said, "but I do think you ought to give me all your work today, just like any oth—"

"Aw, now, Grace," he said. "You only get married once."

The girls all made a fuss over her too, crowding around her desk and giggling, asking again and again to see Ralph's photograph ("Oh, he's *cute*!"), while the office manager looked on, nervously, reluctant to be a spoilsport but anxious to point out that it was, after all, a working day.

Then at lunch there was the traditional little party at Schrafft's—nine women and girls, giddy on their unfamiliar cocktails, letting their chicken à la king grow cold while they pummeled her with old times and good wishes. There were more flowers and another gift—a silver candy dish for which all the girls had whisperingly chipped in.

Grace said "Thank you" and "I certainly do appreciate it" and "I don't know what to say" until her head rang with the words and the corners of her mouth ached from smiling, and she thought the afternoon would never end.

Ralph called up about four o'clock, exuberant. "How ya doin', honey?" he asked, and before she could answer he said, "Listen. Guess what I got?"

"I don't know. A present or something? What?" She tried to sound excited, but it wasn't easy.

"A bonus. Fifty dollars." She could almost see the flattening of his lips as he said "fifty dollars" with the particular earnestness he reserved for pronouncing sums of money.

"Why, that's lovely, Ralph," she said, and if there was any tiredness in her voice be didn't notice it.

"Lovely, huh?" he said with a laugh, mocking the girlishness of the word. "Ya *like* that, huh, Gracie? No, but I mean I was really surprised, ya know it? The boss siz, 'Here, Ralph,' and he hands me this envelope. He don't even crack a smile or nothin', and I'm wonderin', what's the deal here? I'm getting fired here, or what? He siz, 'G'ahead, Ralph, open it.' So I open it, and then I look at the boss and he's grinning a mile wide." He chuckled and sighed. "Well, so listen, honey. What time ya want me to come over tonight?"

"Oh, I don't know. Soon as you can, I guess."

"Well listen, I gotta go over to Eddie's house and pick up that bag he's gonna loan me, so I might as well do that, go on home and eat, and then come over to your place around eight-thirty, nine o'clock. Okay?"

"All right," she said. "I'll see you then, darling." She had been calling him "darling" for only a short time—since it had become irrevocably clear that she was, after all, going to marry him—and the word still had an alien sound. As she straightened the stacks of stationery in her desk (because there was nothing else to do), a familiar little panic gripped her: she couldn't marry him—she hardly even *knew* him. Sometimes it occurred to her differently, that she couldn't marry him because she knew him too well, and either way it left her badly shaken, vulnerable to all the things that Martha, her roommate, had said from the very beginning.

"Isn't he funny?" Martha had said after their first date. "He says 'terlet.' I didn't know people really said 'terlet.'" And Grace had giggled, ready enough to agree that it *was* funny. That was a time when she had been ready to agree with Martha on practically anything—when it often seemed, in fact, that finding a girl like Martha from an ad in the *Times* was just about the luckiest thing that had ever happened to her.

But Ralph had persisted all through the summer, and by fall she had begun standing up for him. "What don't you *like* about him, Martha? He's perfectly nice."

"Oh, everybody's perfectly nice, Grace," Martha would say in her college voice, making perfectly nice a faintly absurd thing to be, and then she'd look up crossly from the careful painting of her fingernails. "It's just that he's such a little—a little *white worm*. Can't you see that?"

"Well, I certainly don't see what his *complexion* has to do with—"

"Oh God, *you* know what I mean. Can't you see what I *mean*? Oh, and all those friends of his, his Eddie and his Marty and his George with their mean, ratty little clerks' lives and their mean, ratty little . . . It's just that they're all *alike*, those people. All they ever say is 'Hey, wha' happen t'ya Giants?' and 'Hey, wha' happen t'ya Yankees?' and they all live way out in Sunnyside or Woodhaven or some awful place, and their mothers have those damn little china elephants on the mantelpiece." And Martha would frown over her nail polish again, making it clear that the subject was closed.

All that fall and winter she was confused. For a while she tried going out only with Martha's kind of men—the kind that used words like "amusing" all the time and wore small-shouldered flannel suits like a uniform; and for a while she tried going out with no men at all. She even tried that crazy business with Mr. Atwood at the office Christmas party. And all the time Ralph kept calling up, hanging around, waiting for her to make up her mind. Once she took him home to meet her parents in Pennsylvania (where she never would have dreamed of taking Martha), but it wasn't until Easter time that she finally gave in.

They had gone to a dance somewhere in Queens, one of the big American Legion dances that Ralph's crowd was always going to, and when the band played "Easter Parade" he held her very close, hardly moving, and sang to her in a faint, whispering tenor. It was the kind of thing she'd never have expected Ralph to do—a sweet, gentle thing—and it probably wasn't just then that she decided to marry him, but it always seemed so afterwards. It always seemed she had decided that minute, swaying to the music with his husky voice in her hair:

"I'll be all in clover
And when they look you over
I'll be the proudest fella
In the Easter Parade. . . ."

That night she had told Martha, and she could still see the look on Martha's face. "Oh, Grace, you're not—surely you're not *serious*. I mean, I thought he was more or less of a *joke*—you can't really mean you want to—"

"Shut up! You just shut up, Martha!" And she'd cried all night. Even now she hated Martha for it; even as she stared blindly at a row of filing cabinets along the office wall, half sick with fear that Martha was right.

The noise of giggles swept over her, and she saw with a start that two of the girls—Irene and Rose—were grinning over their typewriters and pointing at her. "*We* saw ya!" Irene sang. "*We* saw ya! Mooning again, huh Grace?" Then Rose did a burlesque of mooning, heaving her meager breasts and batting her eyes, and they both collapsed in laughter.

With an effort of will Grace resumed the guileless, open smile of a bride. The thing to do was concentrate on plans.

Tomorrow morning, "bright and early," as her mother would say, she would meet Ralph at Penn Station for the trip home. They'd arrive about one, and her parents would meet the train. "Good t'see ya, Ralph!" her father would say, and her mother would probably kiss him. A warm, homely love filled her: *they* wouldn't call him a white worm; *they* didn't have any ideas about Princeton men and "interesting" men and all the other kinds of men Martha was so stuck-up about. Then her father would probably take Ralph out for a beer and show him the paper mill where he worked (and at least Ralph wouldn't be snobby about a person working in a paper mill, either), and then Ralph's family and friends would come down from New York in the evening.

She'd have time for a long talk with her mother that night, and the next morning, "bright and early" (her eyes stung at the thought of her mother's plain, happy face), they would start getting dressed for the wedding. Then the church and the ceremony, and then the reception (Would her father get drunk? Would Muriel Ketchel sulk about not being a bridesmaid?), and finally the train to Atlantic City, and the hotel. But from the hotel on she couldn't plan any more. A door would lock behind her and there would be a wild, fantastic silence, and nobody in all the world but Ralph to lead the way.

"Well, Grace," Mr. Atwood was saying, "I want to wish you every happiness." He was standing at her desk with his hat and coat on, and all around here were the chattering and scraping-back of chairs that meant it was five o'clock.

"Thank you, Mr. Atwood." She got to her feet, suddenly surrounded by all the girls in a bedlam of farewell.

"All the luck in the world, Grace."

"Drop us a card, huh Grace? From Atlantic City?"

"So long, Grace."

"G'night, Grace, and listen: the best of everything."

Finally she was free of them all, out of the elevator, out of the building, hurrying through the crowds to the subway.

When she got home Martha was standing in the door of the kitchenette, looking very svelte in a crisp new dress.

"Hi, Grace. I bet they ate you alive today, didn't they?"

"Oh no," Grace said. "Everybody was—real nice." She sat down, exhausted, and dropped the flowers and the wrapped candy dish on a table. Then she noticed that the whole apartment was swept and dusted, and the dinner was cooking in the kitchenette. "Gee, everything looks wonderful," she said. "What'd you do all this for?"

"Oh, well, I got home early anyway," Martha said. Then she smiled, and it was one of the few times Grace had ever seen her look shy. "I just thought it might be nice to have the place looking decent for a change, when Ralph comes over."

"Well," Grace said, "it certainly was nice of you."

The way Martha looked now was even more surprising: she looked awkward. She was turning a greasy spatula in her fingers, holding it delicately away from her dress and examining it, as if she had something difficult to say. "Look, Grace," she began. "You do understand why I can't come to the wedding, don't you?"

"Oh, sure," Grace said, although in fact she didn't, exactly. It was something about having to go up to Harvard to see her brother before he went into the Army, but it had sounded like a lie from the beginning.

"It's just that I'd hate you to think I—well, anyway, I'm glad if you do understand. And the other thing I wanted to say is more important."

"What?"

"Well, just that I'm sorry for all the awful things I used to say about Ralph. I never had a right to talk to you that way. He's a very sweet boy and I—well, I'm sorry, that's all."

It wasn't easy for Grace to hide a rush of gratitude and relief when she said, "Why, that's all right, Martha, I—"

"The chops are on fire!" Martha bolted for the kitchenette. "It's all right," she called back. "They're edible." And when she came out to serve dinner all her old composure was restored. "I'll have to eat and run," she said as they sat down. "My train leaves in forty minutes."

"I thought it was *tomorrow* you were going."

"Well, it was, actually," Martha said, "but I decided to go tonight. Because you see, Grace, another thing—if you can stand one more apology—another thing I'm sorry for is that I've hardly ever given you and Ralph a chance to be alone here. So tonight I'm going to clear out." She hesitated. "It'll be a sort of wedding gift from me, okay?" And then she smiled, not shyly this time but in a way that was more in character—the eyes subtly averted after a flicker of special meaning. It was a smile that Grace—through stages of suspicion, bewilderment, awe, and practiced imitation—had long ago come to associate with the word "sophisticated."

"Well, that's very sweet of you," Grace said, but she didn't really get the point just then. It wasn't until long after the meal was over and the dishes washed, until Martha had left for her train in a whirl of cosmetics and luggage and quick goodbyes, that she began to understand.

She took a deep, voluptuous bath and spent a long time drying herself, posing in the mirror, filled with a strange, slow excitement. In her bedroom, from the rustling tissues of an expensive white box, she drew the prizes of her trousseau—a sheer nightgown of white nylon and a matching negligee—put them on, and went to the mirror again. She had never worn anything like this before, or felt like this, and the thought of letting Ralph see her like this sent her into the kitchenette for a glass of the special dry sherry Martha kept for cocktail parties. Then she turned out all the lights but one and, carrying her glass, went to the sofa and arranged herself there to wait for him. After a while she got up and brought the sherry bottle over to the coffee table, where she set it on a tray with another glass.

When Ralph left the office he felt vaguely let down. Somehow, he'd expected more of the Friday before his wedding. The bonus check had been all right (though secretly he'd been counting on twice that amount), and the boys had bought him a drink at lunch and kidded around in the appropriate way ("Ah, don't feel too bad, Ralph—worse things could happen"), but still, there ought to have been a real party. Not just the boys in the office, but Eddie, and *all* his friends. Instead there would only be meeting Eddie at the White Rose like every other night of the year, and riding home to borrow Eddie's suitcase and to eat, and then having to ride all the way back to Manhattan just to see Gracie for an hour or two. Eddie wasn't in the bar when he arrived, which sharpened the edge of his loneliness. Morosely he drank a beer, waiting.

Eddie was his best friend, and an ideal best man because he'd been in on the courtship of Gracie from the start. It was in this very bar, in fact, that Ralph had told him about their first date last summer: "Ooh, Eddie—what a paira *knockers*!"

And Eddie had grinned. "Yeah? So what's the roommate like?"

"Ah, you don't want the roommate, Eddie. The roommate's a dog. A snob too, I think. No, but this *other* one, this little *Gracie*—boy, I mean, she is *stacked*."

Half the fun of every date—even more than half—had been telling Eddie about it afterwards, exaggerating a little here and there, asking

Eddie's advice on tactics. But after today, like so many other pleasures, it would all be left behind. Gracie had promised him at least one night off a week to spend with the boys, after they were married, but even so it would never be the same. Girls never understood a thing like friendship.

There was a ball game on the bar's television screen and he watched it idly, his throat swelling in a sentimental pain of loss. Nearly all his life had been devoted to the friendship of boys and men, to trying to be a good guy, and now the best of it was over.

Finally Eddie's stiff finger jabbed the seat of his pants in greeting. "Whaddya say, sport?"

Ralph narrowed his eyes to indolent contempt and slowly turned around. "Wha' happen ta you, wise guy? Get lost?"

"Whaddya—in a hurry a somethin'?" Eddie barely moved his lips when he spoke. "Can't wait two minutes?" He slouched on a stool and slid a quarter at the bartender. "Draw one, there, Jack."

They drank in silence for a while, staring at the television. "Got a little bonus today," Ralph said. "Fifty dollars."

"Yeah?" Eddie said. "Good."

A batter struck out; the inning was over and the commercial came on. "So?" Eddie said, rocking the beer around in his glass. "Still gonna get married?"

"Why not?" Ralph said with a shrug. "Listen, finish that, willya? I wanna get a move on."

"Wait awhile, wait awhile. What's ya hurry?"

"C'mon, willya?" Ralph stepped impatiently away from the bar. "I wanna go pick up ya bag."

"Ah, bag schmagg."

Ralph moved up close again and glowered at him. "Look, wise guy. Nobody's gonna *make* ya loan me the goddamn bag, ya know. I don't wanna break ya *heart* or nothin'—"

"Arright, arright, arright. You'll getcha bag. Don't worry so much." He finished the beer and wiped his mouth. "Let's go."

Having to borrow a bag for his wedding trip was a sore point with Ralph; he'd much rather have bought one of his own. There was a fine one displayed in the window of a luggage shop they passed every night on their way to the subway—a big, tawny Gladstone with a zippered compartment on the side, at thirty-nine ninety-five—and Ralph had had his eye on it ever since Easter time. "Think I'll buy that," he'd told Eddie, in the same offhand way that a day or so before he had announced his engagement ("Think I'll marry the girl"). Eddie's response to both remarks had been the same: "Whaddya—crazy?" Both times Ralph had said, "Why not?" and in defense of the bag he had added, "Gonna get married, I'll *need* somethin' like that." From then on it was as if the bag, almost as much as Gracie herself, had become a symbol of the new and richer life he sought. But after the ring and the new clothes and all the other expenses, he'd found at last that he couldn't afford it; he had settled for the loan of Eddie's, which was similar but cheaper and worn, and without the zippered compartment.

Now as they passed the luggage shop he stopped, caught in the grip of a reckless idea. "Hey wait awhile, Eddie. Know what I think I'll do with that fifty-dollar bonus? I think I'll buy that bag right now." He felt breathless.

"Whaddya—crazy? Forty bucks for a bag you'll use maybe one time a year? Ya crazy, Ralph. C'mon."

"Ah—I dunno. Ya think so?"

"Listen, you better *keep* ya money, boy. You're gonna *need* it."

"Ah—yeah," Ralph said at last. "I guess ya right." And he fell in step with Eddie again, heading for the subway. This was the way things usually turned out in his life; he could never own a bag like that until he made a better salary, and he accepted it—just as he'd accepted without question, after the first thin sigh, the knowledge that he'd never possess his bride until after the wedding.

The subway swallowed them, rattled and banged them along in a rocking, mindless trance for half an hour, and disgorged them at last into the cool early evening of Queens.

Removing their coats and loosening their ties, they let the breeze dry their sweated shirts as they walked. "So what's the deal?" Eddie asked. "What time we supposed to show up in this Pennsylvania burg tomorra?"

"Ah, suit yourself," Ralph said. "Any time in the evening's okay."

"So whadda we do then? What the hell can ya do in a hillbilly town like that, anyway?"

"Ah, I dunno," Ralph said defensively. "Sit around and talk, I guess; drink beer with Gracie's old man or somethin'; I dunno."

"Jesus," Eddie said. "Some weekend. Big, big deal."

Ralph stopped on the sidewalk, suddenly enraged, his damp coat wadded in his fist. "Look, you bastid. Nobody's gonna *make* ya come, ya know—you or Marty or George or any a the rest of 'em. Get that straight. You're not doin' *me* no favors, unnastand?"

"Whatsa matta?" Eddie inquired. "Whatsa matta? Can'tcha take a joke?"

"Joke," Ralph said. "You're fulla jokes." And plodding sullenly in Eddie's wake, he felt close to tears.

They turned off into the block where they both lived, a double row of neat, identical houses bordering the street where they'd fought and loafed and played stickball all their lives. Eddie pushed open the front door of his house and ushered Ralph into the vestibule, with its homely smell of cauliflower and overshoes. "G'wan in," he said, jerking a thumb at the closed living-room door, and he hung back to let Ralph go first.

Ralph opened the door and took three steps inside before it hit him like a sock on the jaw. The room, dead silent, was packed deep with grinning, red-faced men—Marty, George, the boys from the block, the boys from the office—everybody, all his friends, all on their feet and poised motionless in a solid mass. Skinny Maguire was crouched at the upright piano, his spread fingers high over the keys, and when he struck the first rollicking chords they all roared into song, beating time with their fists, their enormous grins distorting the words:

"Fa he's a jally guh fella
Fa he's a jally guh fella
Fa he's a jally guh fell-ah
That nobody can deny!"

Weakly Ralph retreated a step on the carpet and stood there wide-eyed, swallowing, holding his coat. "*That nobody can deny!*" they sang, "*That nobody can deny!*" And as they swung into the second chorus Eddie's father appeared through the dining-room curtains, bald and beaming, in full song, with a great glass pitcher of beer in either hand. At last Skinny hammered out the final line:

"That—no—bod—dee—can—dee—nye!"

And they all surged forward cheering, grabbing Ralph's hand, pounding his arms and his back while he stood trembling, his own voice lost under the noise. "Gee, fellas—thanks. I—don't know what to—thanks, fellas. . . ."

Then the crowd cleaved in half, and Eddie made his way slowly down the middle. His eyes gleamed in a smile of love, and from his bashful hand hung the suitcase—not his own, but a new one: the big, tawny Gladstone with the zippered compartment on the side.

"*Speech!*" they were yelling. "*Speech! Speech!*"

But Ralph couldn't speak and couldn't smile. He could hardly even see.

At ten o'clock Grace began walking around the apartment and biting her lip. What if he wasn't coming? But of course he was coming. She sat down again and carefully smoothed the billows of nylon around her thighs, forcing herself to be calm. The whole thing would be ruined if she was nervous.

The noise of the doorbell was like an electric shock. She was halfway to the door before she stopped, breathing hard, and composed herself again. Then she pressed the buzzer and opened the door a crack to watch for him on the stairs.

When she saw he was carrying a suitcase, and saw the pale seriousness of his face as he mounted the stairs, she thought at first that he knew; he had come prepared to lock the door and take her in his arms. "Hello, darling," she said softly, and opened the door wider.

"Hi, baby." He brushed past her and walked inside. "Guess I'm late, huh? You in bed?"

"No." She closed the door and leaned against it with both hands holding the doorknob at the small of her back, the way heroines close doors in the movies. "I was just—waiting for you."

He wasn't looking at her. He went to the sofa and sat down, holding the suitcase on his lap and running his fingers over its surface. "Gracie," he said, barely above a whisper. "Look at this."

She looked at it, and then into his tragic eyes.

"Remember," he said, "I told you about that bag I wanted to buy? Forty dollars?" He stopped and looked around. "Hey, where's Martha? She in bed?"

"She's gone, darling," Grace said, moving slowly toward the sofa. "She's gone for the whole weekend." She sat down beside him, leaned close, and gave him Martha's special smile.

"Oh yeah?" he said. "Well anyway, listen. I said I was gonna borrow Eddie's bag instead, remember?"

"Yes."

"Well, so tonight at the White Rose I siz, 'C'mon, Eddie, let's go home pick up ya bag.' He siz, 'Ah, bag schmagg.' I siz, 'Whatsa matta?' but he don't say nothin', see? So we go home to his place and the living-room door's shut, see?"

She squirmed closer and put her head on his chest. Automatically he raised an arm and dropped it around her shoulders, still talking. "He siz, 'G'ahead, Ralph, open the door.' I siz, 'Whatsa deal?' He siz, 'Never mind, Ralph, open the door.' So I open the door, and oh Jesus." His fingers gripped her shoulder with such intensity that she looked up at him in alarm.

"They was all there, Gracie," he said. "All the fellas. Playin' the piana, singin', cheerin'—" His voice wavered and his eyelids fluttered shut, their lashes wet. "A big surprise party," he said, trying to smile. "Fa me. Can ya beat that, Gracie? And then—and then Eddie comes out and—Eddie comes out and hands me this. The very same bag I been lookin' at all this time. He bought it with his own money and he didn't say nothin', just to give me a surprise. 'Here, Ralph,' he siz. 'Just to let ya know you're the greatest guy in the world.'" His fingers tightened again, trembling. "I cried, Gracie," he whispered. "I couldn't help it. I don't think the fellas saw it or anything, but I was cryin'." He turned his face away and worked his lips in a tremendous effort to hold back the tears.

"Would you like a drink, darling?" she asked tenderly.

"Nah, that's all right, Gracie. I'm all right." Gently he set the suitcase on the carpet. "Only, gimme a cigarette, huh?"

She got one from the coffee table, put it in his lips and lit it. "Let me get you a drink," she said.

He frowned through the smoke. "Whaddya got, that sherry wine? Nah, I don't like that stuff. Anyway, I'm fulla beer." He leaned back and closed his eyes. "And then Eddie's mother feeds us this terrific meal," he went on, and his voice was almost normal now. "We had *steaks*; we had French-fried *potatas*"—his head rolled on the sofa-back with each item of the menu—"lettuce-and-tomata *salad, pickles, bread, butter*—everything. The works."

"Well," she said. "Wasn't that nice."

"And afterwards we had ice cream and coffee," he said, "and all the beer we could drink. I mean, it was a real spread."

Grace ran her hands over her lap, partly to smooth the nylon and partly to dry the moisture on her palms. "Well, that certainly was nice of them," she said. They sat there silent for what seemed a long time.

"I can only stay a minute, Gracie," Ralph said at last. "I promised 'em I'd be back."

Her heart thumped under the nylon. "Ralph, do you—do you like this?"

"What, honey?"

"My negligee. You weren't supposed to see it until—after the wedding, but I thought I'd—"

"Nice," he said, feeling the flimsy material between thumb and index finger, like a merchant. "Very nice. Wudga pay fa this, honey?"

"Oh—I don't know. But do you like it?"

He kissed her and began, at last, to stroke her with his hands. "Nice," he kept saying. "Nice. Hey, I like this." His hand hesitated at the low neckline, slipped inside and held her breast.

"I do love you, Ralph," she whispered. "You know that, don't you?"

His fingers pinched her nipple, once, and slid quickly out again. The policy of restraint, the habit of months was too strong to break. "Sure," he said. "And I love you, baby. Now you be a good girl and get ya beauty sleep, and I'll see ya in the morning. Okay?"

"Oh, Ralph. Don't go. Stay."

"Ah, I promised the fellas, Gracie." He stood up and straightened his clothes. "They're waitin' fa me, out home."

She blazed to her feet, but the cry that was meant for a woman's appeal came out, through her tightening lips, as the whine of a wife: "Can't they wait?"

"Whaddya—crazy?" He backed away, eyes round with righteousness. She would have to understand. If this was the way she acted before the wedding, how the hell was it going to be afterwards? "Have a heart, willya? Keep the fellas waitin' tonight? After all they done fa *me*?"

After a second or two, during which her face became less pretty than he had ever seen it before, she was able to smile. "Of course not, darling. You're right."

He came forward again and gently brushed the tip of her chin with his fist, smiling, a husband reassured. "'At's more like it," he said. "So I'll see ya, Penn Station, nine o'clock tomorra. Right, Gracie? Only, before I go—" he winked and slapped his belly. "I'm fulla beer. Mind if I use ya terlet?"

When he came out of the bathroom she was waiting to say goodnight, standing with her arms folded across her chest, as if for warmth. Lovingly he hefted the new suitcase and joined her at the door. "Okay, then, baby," he said, and kissed her. "Nine o'clock. Don't forget, now."

She smiled tiredly and opened the door for him. "Don't worry, Ralph," she said. "I'll be there."

Jody Rolled the Bones

SERGEANT REECE WAS a slim, quiet Tennessean who always managed to look neat in fatigues, and he wasn't exactly what we'd expected an infantry platoon sergeant to be. We learned soon enough that he was typical—almost a prototype—of the men who had drifted into the Regular Army in the thirties and stayed to form the cadres of the great wartime training centers, but at the time he surprised us. We were pretty naïve, and I think we'd all expected more of a Victor McLaglen—burly, roaring and tough, but lovable, in the Hollywood tradition. Reece was tough, all right, but he never roared and we didn't love him.

He alienated us on the first day by butchering our names. We were all from New York, and most of our names did require a little effort, but Reece made a great show of being defeated by them. His thin features puckered over the roster, his little mustache twitching at each unfamiliar syllable. "Dee—Dee Alice—" he stammered. "Dee Alice—"

"Here," D'Allessandro said, and it went like that with almost every name. At one point, after he'd grappled with Schacht, Scoglio, and Sizscovicz, he came to Smith. "Hey, Smith," he said, looking up with a slow, unengaging grin. "What the hell *yew* doin' heah 'mong all these gorillas?" Nobody thought it was funny. At last he finished and tucked the clipboard under his arm. "All right," he told us. "My name's Sahjint Reece and I'm your platoon sahjint. That means when I say do somethin', do it." He gave us a long, appraising glare. "P'toon!" he snapped, making his diaphragm jump. "Tetch—*hut!*" And his tyranny began. By the end of that day and for many days thereafter we had him firmly fixed in our minds as, to use D'Allessandro's phrase, a dumb Rebel bastard.

I had better point out here that we were probably not very lovable either. We were all eighteen, a confused, platoon-sized bunch of city kids determined to be unenthusiastic about Basic Training. Apathy in boys of that age may be unusual—it is certainly unattractive—but this was 1944, the war was no longer new, and bitterness was the fashionable mood. To throw yourself into Army life with gusto only meant you were a kid who didn't know the score, and nobody wanted to be that. Secretly we may have yearned for battle, or at least for ribbons, but on the surface we were shameless little wise guys about everything. Trying to make us soldiers must have been a staggering job, and Reece bore the brunt of it.

But of course that side of the thing didn't occur to us, at first. All we knew was that he rode us hard and we hated his guts. We saw very little of our lieutenant, a plump collegiate youth who showed up periodically to insist that if we played ball with him, he would play ball with us, and even less of our company commander (I hardly remember what he looked like, except that he wore glasses). But Reece was always there, calm and contemptuous, never speaking except to give orders and never smiling except in cruelty. And we could tell by observing the other platoons that he was exceptionally strict; he had, for instance, his own method of rationing water.

It was summer, and the camp lay flat under the blistering Texas sun. A generous supply of salt tablets was all that kept us conscious until nightfall; our fatigues were always streaked white from the salt of our sweat and we were always thirsty, but the camp's supply of drinking water had to be transported from a spring many miles away, so there was a standing order to go easy on it. Most noncoms were thirsty enough themselves to construe the regulation loosely, but Reece took it to heart. "If yew men don't learn nothin' else about soldierin'," he would say, "you're gonna learn water discipline." The water hung in Lister bags, fat canvas udders placed at intervals along the roads, and although it was warm and acrid with chemicals, the high point of every morning and every afternoon was the moment when we were authorized a break to fill our canteens with it. Most platoons would attack a Lister bag in a jostling wallowing rush, working its little steel teats until the bag hung limp and wrinkled, and a dark stain of waste lay spreading in the dust beneath it. Not us. Reece felt that half a canteenful at a time was enough for any man, and he would stand by the Lister bag in grim supervision, letting us at it in an orderly column of twos. When a man held his canteen too long under the bag, Reece would stop everything, pull the man out of line, and say, "Pour that out. All of it."

"I'll be *goddamned* if I will!" D'Allessandro shot back at him one day, and we all stood fascinated, watching them glare at each other in the dazzling heat. D'Allessandro was a husky boy with fierce black eyes who had in a few weeks become our spokesman; I guess he was the only one brave enough to stage a scene like this. "Whaddya think I am," he shouted, "a goddamn *camel*, like you?" We giggled.

Reece demanded silence from the rest of us, got it, and turned back to D'Allessandro, squinting and licking his dry lips. "All right," he said quietly, "drink it. All of it. The resta yew men keep away from that bag, keep your hands off your canteens. I want y'all to watch this. Go on, drink it."

D'Allessandro gave us a grin of nervous triumph and began to drink, pausing only to catch his breath with the water dribbling on his chest. "Drink it," Reece would snap each time he stopped. It made us desperately thirsty to watch him, but we were beginning to get the idea. When the canteen was empty Reece told him to fill it up again. He did, still smiling but looking a little worried. "Now drink that," Reece said. "Fast. Faster." And when he was finished, gasping, with the empty canteen in his hand, Reece said, "Now get your helmet and rifle. See that barracks over there?" A white building shimmered in the distance, a couple of hundred yards away. "You're gonna proceed on the double to that barracks, go around it and come back on the double. Meantime your buddies're gonna be waitin' here; ain't none of 'em gonna get nothin' to drink till yew get back. All right, now, move. *Move*. On the *double*."

In loyalty to D'Allessandro none of us laughed, but he did look absurd trotting heavily out across the drill field, his helmet wobbling. Before he reached the barracks we saw him stop, crouch, and vomit up the water. Then he staggered on, a tiny figure in the faraway dust, disappeared around the building, and finally emerged at the other side to begin the long trip back. At last he arrived and fell exhausted on the ground. "Now," Reece said softly. "Had enough to drink?" Only then were the rest of us allowed to use the Lister bag, two at a time.

When we were all through, Reece squatted nimbly and drew half a canteen for himself without spilling a drop.

That was the kind of thing he did, every day, and if anyone had suggested he was only doing his job, our response would have been a long and unanimous Bronx cheer.

I think our first brief easing of hostility toward him occurred quite early in the training cycle, one morning when one of the instructors, a strapping first lieutenant, was trying to teach us the bayonet. We felt pretty sure that in the big, modern kind of war for which we were bound we probably would not be called on to fight with bayonets (and that if we ever were it wouldn't make a hell of a lot of difference whether we'd mastered the finer points of parry and thrust), and so our lassitude that morning was even purer than usual. We let the instructor talk to us, then got up and fumbled through the various positions he had outlined.

The other platoons looked as bad as we did, and faced with such dreary incompetence on a company scale the instructor rubbed his mouth. "No," he said. "No, no, you men haven't got the idea at all. Fall back to your places and sit down. Sergeant Reece front and center, please."

Reece had been sitting with the other platoon sergeants in their customary bored little circle, aloof from the lecture, but he rose promptly and came forward.

"Sergeant, I'd like you to show these people what a bayonet is all about," the instructor said. And from the moment Reece hefted a bayoneted rifle in his hands we knew, grudgingly or not, that we were going to see something. It was the feeling you get at a ball game when a heavy hitter selects a bat. At the instructor's commands he whipped smartly into each of the positions, freezing into a slim statue while the officer crouched and weaved around him, talking, pointing out the distribution of his weight and the angles of his limbs, explaining that this was how it should be done. Then, to climax the performance, the instructor sent Reece alone through the bayonet course. He went through it fast, never off balance and never wasting a motion, smashing blocks of wood off their wooden shoulders with his rifle butt, driving his blade deep into a shuddering torso of bundled sticks and ripping it out to bear down on the next one. He looked good. It would be too much to say that he kindled our admiration, but there is an automatic pleasure in watching a thing done well. The other platoons were clearly impressed, and although nobody in our platoon said anything, I think we were a little proud of him.

But the next period that day was close-order drill, at which the platoon sergeants had full command, and within half an hour Reece had nagged us into open resentment again. "What the hell's he think," Schacht muttered in the ranks, "he's some kind of a big deal now, just because he's a hotshot with that stupid bayonet?" And the rest of us felt a vague shame that we had so nearly been taken in.

When we eventually did change our minds about him, it did not seem due, specifically, to any act of his, but to an experience that changed our minds about the Army in general, and about ourselves. This was the rifle range, the only part of our training we thoroughly enjoyed. After so many hours of drill and calisthenics, of droning lectures in the sun and training films run off in sweltering clapboard buildings, the prospect of actually going out and shooting held considerable promise, and when the time came it proved to be fun. There was a keen pleasure in sprawling prone on the embankment of the firing line with a rifle stock nestled at your cheek and the oily, gleaming clips of ammunition close at hand; in squinting out across a great expanse of earth at your target and waiting for the signal from a measured voice on the loudspeaker. "Ready on the right. Ready on the left. Ready on the firing line. . . . The flag is up. The flag is waving. The flag is down. Commence—*fire!*" There would be a blast of many rifles in your ears, a breathless moment as you squeezed the trigger, and a sharp jolt as you fired. Then you'd relax and watch the target slide down in the distance, controlled by unseen hands in the pit beneath it. When it reappeared a moment later a colored disk would be thrust up with it, waved and withdrawn, signaling your score. The man kneeling behind you with the scorecard would mutter, "Nice going" or "Tough," and you'd squirm in the sand and take aim again. Like nothing else we had found in the Army, this was something to rouse a competitive instinct, and when it took the form of wanting our platoon to make a better showing than the others, it brought us as close to a genuine *esprit de corps* as anything could.

We spent a week or so on the range, leaving early every morning and staying all day, taking our noon meal from a field kitchen that was in itself a refreshing change from the mess hall. Another good feature—at first it seemed the best of all—was that the range gave us a respite from Sergeant Reece. He marched us out there and back, and he supervised the cleaning of our rifles in the barracks, but for the bulk of the day he turned us over to the range staff, an impersonal, kindly crowd, much less concerned with petty discipline than with marksmanship.

Still, Reece had ample opportunity to bully us in the hours when he was in charge, but after a few days on the range we found he was easing up. When we counted cadence on the road now, for instance, he no longer made us do it over and over, louder each time, until our dry throats burned from yelling, "HUT, WHO, REEP, HOE!" He would quit after one or two counts like the other platoon sergeants, and at first we didn't know what to make of it. "What's the deal?" we asked each other, baffled, and I guess the deal was simply that we'd begun to do it right the first time, loud enough and in perfect unison. We were marching well, and this was Reece's way of letting us know it.

The trip to the range was several miles, and a good share of it was through the part of camp where marching at attention was required—we were never given route step until after we'd cleared the last of the company streets and buildings. But with our new efficiency at marching we got so that we almost enjoyed it, and even responded with enthusiasm to Reece's marching chant. It had always been his habit, after making us count cadence, to go through one of those traditional singsong chants calling for traditional shouts of reply, and we'd always resented it before. But now the chant seemed uniquely stirring, an authentic piece of folklore from older armies and older wars, with roots deep in the life we were just beginning to understand. He would begin by expanding his ordinary nasal "Left . . . left . . . left" into a mournful little tune: "Oh yew *had* a good *home* and yew *left*—" to which we would answer, "RIGHT!" as our right feet fell. We would go through several variations on this theme:

"Oh yew had a good job and yew left—"

"RIGHT!"

"Oh yew had a good gal and yew left—"

"RIGHT!"

And then he'd vary the tune a little: "Oh Jody rolled the bones when yew left—"

"RIGHT!" we'd yell in soldierly accord, and none of us had to wonder what the words meant. Jody was your faithless friend, the soft civilian to whom the dice-throw of chance had given everything you held dear; and the next verses, a series of taunting couplets, made it clear that he would always have the last laugh. You might march and shoot and learn to perfection your creed of disciplined force, but Jody was a force beyond control, and the fact had been faced by generations of proud, lonely men like this one, this splendid soldier who swung along beside our ranks in the sun and bawled the words from a twisted mouth: "Ain't no use in goin' home—Jody's got your gal and gone. Sound off—"

"HUT, WHO!"

"Sound off—"

"REEP, HOE!"

"Ever' time yew stand Retreat, Jody gets a piece of meat. Sound off—"

"HUT, WHO!"

"Sound off—"

"REEP, HOE!" It was almost a disappointment when he gave us route step on the outskirts of camp and we became individuals again, cocking back our helmets and slouching along out of step, with the fine unanimity of the chant left behind. When we returned from the range dusty and tired, our ears numb from the noise of fire, it was somehow bracing to swing into formal cadence again for the last leg of the journey, heads up, backs straight, and split the cooling air with our roars of response.

A good part of our evenings, after chow, would be spent cleaning our rifles with the painstaking care that Reece demanded. The barracks would fill with the sharp, good smells of bore cleaner and oil as we worked, and when the job had been done to Reece's satisfaction we would usually drift out to the front steps for a smoke while we waited our turns at the showers. One night a group of us lingered there more quietly than usual, finding, I think, that the customary small talk of injustice and complaint was inadequate, unsuited to the strange well-being we had all begun to feel these last few days. Finally Fogarty put the mood into words. He was a small, serious boy, the runt of the platoon and something of a butt of jokes, and I guess he had nothing much to lose by letting his guard down. "Ah, I dunno," he said, leaning back against the doorjamb with a sigh, "I dunno about you guys, but I like this—going out to the range, marching and all. Makes you feel like you're really soldiering, you know what I mean?"

It was a dangerously naïve thing to say—"soldiering" was Reece's favorite word—and we looked at him uncertainly for a second. But then D'Allessandro glanced deadpan around the group, defying anyone to laugh, and we relaxed. The idea of soldiering had become respectable, and because the idea as well as the word was inseparable in our minds from Sergeant Reece, he became respectable too.

Soon the change had come over the whole platoon. We were working with Reece now, instead of against him, trying instead of pretending to try. We wanted to be soldiers. The intensity of our effort must sometimes have been ludicrous, and might have caused a lesser man to suspect we were kidding—I remember earnest little choruses of "Okay, Sergeant" whenever he dispatched an order—but Reece took it all straight-faced, with that air of unlimited self-assurance that is the first requisite of good leadership. And he was as fair as he was strict, which must surely be the second requisite. In appointing provisional squad leaders, for example, he coolly passed over several men who had all but licked his shoes for recognition, and picked those he knew could hold our respect—D'Allessandro was one, and the others were equally well chosen. The rest of his formula was classically simple: he led by being excellent, at everything from cleaning a rifle to rolling a pair of socks, and we followed by trying to emulate him.

But if excellence is easy to admire it is hard to like, and Reece refused to make himself likable. It was his only failing, but it was a big one, for respect without affection can't last long—not, at least, where the sentimentality of adolescent minds is involved. Reece rationed kindness the way he rationed water: we might cherish each drop out of all proportion to its worth, but we never got enough or anything like enough to slake our thirst. We were delighted when he suddenly began to get our names right at roll call and when we noticed that he was taking the edge of insult off most of his reprimands, for we knew these signs to be acknowledgments of our growth as soldiers, but somehow we felt a right to expect more.

We were delighted too at the discovery that our plump lieutenant was afraid of him; we could barely hide our pleasure at the condescending look that came over Reece's face whenever the lieutenant appeared, or at the tone of the young officer's voice—uneasy, almost apologetic—when he said, "All right, Sergeant." It made us feel close to Reece in a proud soldierly alliance, and once or twice he granted us the keen compliment of a wink behind the lieutenant's back, but only once or twice. We might imitate his walk and his squinting stare, get the shirts of our suntans tailored skintight like his and even adopt some of his habits of speech, Southern accent and all, but we could never quite consider him a Good Joe. He just wasn't the type. Formal obedience, in working hours, was all he wanted, and we hardly knew him at all.

On the rare evenings when he stayed on the post he would sit either alone or in the unapproachable company of one or two other cadremen as taciturn as himself, drinking beer in the PX. Most nights and all weekends he disappeared into town. I'm sure none of us expected him to spend his free time with us—the thought would never have occurred to us, in fact—but the smallest glimpse into his personal life would have helped. If he had ever reminisced with us about his home, for instance, or related the conversations of his PX friends, or told us of a bar he liked in town, I think we would all have been touchingly grateful, but he never did. And what made it worse was that, unlike him, we had no real life outside the day's routine. The town was a small, dusty maze of clapboard and neon, crawling with soldiers, and to most of us it yielded only loneliness, however we may have swaggered down its avenues. There wasn't enough town to go around; whatever delights it held remained the secrets of those who had found them first, and if you were young, shy, and not precisely sure what you were looking for anyway, it was a dreary place. You could hang around the USO and perhaps get to dance with a girl long hardened against a callow advance; you could settle for the insipid pleasures of watermelon stands and penny arcades, or you could prowl aimlessly in groups through the dark back streets, where all you met as a rule were other groups of soldiers on the aimless prowl. "So whaddya wanna *do*?" we would ask each other impatiently, and the only answer was, "Ah, I dunno. Cruise around awhile, I guess." Usually we'd drink enough beer to be drunk, or sick, on the bus back to camp, grateful for the promise of an orderly new day.

It was probably not surprising, then, that our emotional life became ingrown. Like frustrated suburban wives we fed on each other's discontent; we became divided into mean little cliques and subdivided into jealously shifting pairs of buddies, and we pieced out our idleness with gossip. Most of the gossip was self-contained; for news from the extraplatoon world we relied largely on the company clerk, a friendly, sedentary man who liked to dispense rumors over a carefully balanced cup of coffee as he strolled from table to table in the mess hall. "I got this from Personnel," he would say in preface to some improbable hearsay about the distant brass (the colonel had syphilis; the stockade commander had weaseled out of a combat assignment; the training program had been cut short and we'd all be overseas in a month). But one Saturday noon he had something less remote; he had gotten it from his own company orderly room, and it sounded plausible. For weeks, he told us, the plump lieutenant had been trying to get Reece transferred; now it appeared to be in the works, and next week might well be Reece's last as a platoon sergeant. "His days are numbered," the clerk said darkly.

"Whaddya mean, transferred?" D'Allessandro asked. "Transferred where?"

"Keep your voice down," the clerk said, with an uneasy glance toward the noncoms' table, where Reece bent stolidly over his food. "I dunno. That part I dunno. Anyway, it's a lousy deal. You kids got the best damn platoon sergeant on the post, if you wanna know something. He's too *damn* good, in fact; that's his trouble. Too good for a half-assed second lieutenant to handle. In the Army it never pays to be that good."

"You're right," D'Allessandro said solemnly. "It never pays."

"Yeah?" Schacht inquired, grinning. "Is that right, Squad Leader? Tell us about it, Squad Leader." And the talk at our table degenerated into wisecracks. The clerk drifted away.

Reece must have heard the story about the same time we did; at any rate that weekend marked a sudden change in his behavior. He left for town with the tense look of a man methodically planning to get drunk, and on Monday morning he almost missed Reveille. He nearly always had a hangover on Monday mornings, but it had never before interfered with his day's work; he had always been there to get us up and out with his angry tongue. This time, though, there was an odd silence in the barracks as we dressed. "Hey, he isn't *here*," somebody called from the door of Reece's room near the stairs. "Reece isn't *here*." The squad leaders were admirably quick to take the initiative. They coaxed and prodded until we had all tumbled outside and into formation in the dark, very nearly as fast as we'd have done it under

Reece's supervision. But the night's CQ, in making his rounds, had already discovered Reece's absence and run off to rouse the lieutenant.

The company officers rarely stood Reveille, particularly on Mondays, but now as we stood leaderless in the company street our lieutenant came jogging around the side of the barracks. By the lights of the building we could see that his shirt was half buttoned and his hair wild; he looked puffy with sleep and badly confused. Still running, he called, "All right, you men, uh—"

All the squad leaders drew their breath to call us to attention, but they got no further than a ragged "Tetch—" when Reece emerged out of the gloaming, stepped up in front of the lieutenant, and said, "P'toon! Tetch—*hut!*" There he was, a little winded from running, still wearing the wrinkled suntans of the night before, but plainly in charge. He called the roll by squads; then he kicked out one stiff leg in the ornate, Regular Army way of doing an about-face, neatly executed the turn and ended up facing the lieutenant in a perfect salute. "All presen'accounted for, sir," he said.

The lieutenant was too startled to do anything but salute back, sloppily, and mumble "All right, Sergeant." I guess he felt he couldn't even say, "See that this doesn't happen again," since, after all, nothing very much had happened, except that he'd been gotten out of bed for Reveille. And I guess he spent the rest of the day wondering whether he should have reprimanded Reece for being out of uniform; he looked as if the question was already bothering him as he turned to go back to his quarters. Dismissed, our formation broke up in a thunderclap of laughter that he pretended not to hear.

But Sergeant Reece soon spoiled the joke. He didn't even thank the squad leaders for helping him out of a tight spot, and for the rest of the day he treated us to the kind of petty nagging we thought we had outgrown. On the drill field he braced little Fogarty and said, "When'd yew shave last?"

Like many of our faces, Fogarty's bore only a pale fuzz that hardly needed shaving at all. "About a week ago," he said.

"'Bout a week ago, *Sah*jint," Reece corrected.

"About a week ago, Sergeant," Fogarty said.

Reece curled back his thin lips. "Yew look lak a mangy ole mungrel bitch," he said. "Doan yew know you're s'posed to shave ever' day?"

"I wouldn't have nothing to *shave* every day."

"Wouldn't have nothin' to shave, *Sah*jint."

Fogarty swallowed, blinking. "Nothing to shave, Sergeant," he said.

We all felt badly let down. "What the hell's he think we are," Schacht demanded that noon, "a bunch of rookies?" And D'Allessandro grumbled in mutinous agreement.

A bad hangover might have excused Reece that day, but it could hardly have accounted for the next day and the day after that. He was bullying us without reason and without relief, and he was destroying everything he had built up so carefully in the many weeks before; the whole delicate structure of our respect for him crumbled and fell.

"It's final," the company clerk said grimly at supper Wednesday night. "The orders are cut. Tomorrow's his last day."

"So?" Schacht inquired. "Where's he going?"

"Keep your voice down," the clerk said. "Gonna work with the instructors. Spend part of his time out on the bivouac area and part on the bayonet course."

Schacht laughed, nudging D'Allessandro. "Hot damn," he said, "he'll eat that up, won't he? Specially the bayonet part. Bastard'll get to show off every day. He'll like that."

"Whaddya, *kidding*?" the clerk asked, offended. "Like it my ass. That guy loved his job. You think I'm kidding? He *loved* his job, and it's a lousy break. You kids don't know when you're well off."

D'Allessandro took up the argument, narrowing his eyes. "Yeah?" he said. "You think so? You oughta see him out there every day this week. Every day."

The clerk leaned forward so earnestly that some of his coffee spilled. "Listen," he said. "He's known about this all week—how the hellya *want* him to act? How the hell would *you* act if you knew somebody was screwing you out of the thing you liked best? Can'tcha see he's under a strain?"

But that, we all told him with our surly stares, was no excuse for being a dumb Rebel bastard.

"Some of you kids act too big for your pants," the clerk said, and went away in a sulk.

"Ah, don't believe everything you hear," Schacht said. "I'll believe he's transferred when I see it."

But it was true. That night Reece sat up late in his room, drinking morosely with one of his cronies. We could hear their low, blurred voices in the darkness, and the occasional clink of their whiskey bottle. The following day he was neither easy nor hard on us in the field, but brooding and aloof as if he had other things on his mind. And when he marched us back that evening he kept us standing in formation in front of the barracks for a few moments, at ease, before dismissing us. His restless glance seemed to survey all our faces in turn. Then he began to speak in a voice more gentle than any we had ever heard him use. "I won't be seein' yew men any more after today," he said. "I'm bein' transferred. One thing yew can always count on in th' Army, and that is, if yew find somethin' good, some job yew like, they always transfer your ass somewheres else."

I think we were all touched—I know I was; it was the closest he had ever come to saying he liked us. But it was too late. Anything he said or did now would have been too late, and our predominant feeling was relief. Reece seemed to sense this, and seemed to cut short the things he had planned to say.

"I know there ain't no call for me to make a speech," he said, "and I ain't gonna make one. Onliest thing I want to say is—" He lowered his eyes and stared at his dusty service shoes. "I want to wish all yew men a lot of luck. Y'all keep your nose clean, hear? And stay outa trouble?" The next words could scarcely be heard. "And doan let nobody push y'around."

A short, painful silence followed, as painful as the parting of disenchanted lovers. Then he drew himself straight. "P'toon! Tetch—*hut!*" He looked us over once more with hard and glittering eyes. "*Dismissed.*"

And when we came back from chow that night we found he had already packed his barracks bags and cleared out. We didn't even get to shake his hand.

Our new platoon sergeant was there in the morning, a squat jolly cab driver from Queens who insisted that we call him only by his first name, which was Ruby. He was every inch a Good Joe. He turned us loose at the Lister bags every chance he got, and confided with a giggle that, through a buddy of his in the PX, he often got his own canteen filled with Coca-Cola and crushed ice. He was a slack drillmaster, and on the road he never made us count cadence except when we passed an officer, never made us chant or sing anything except a ragged version of "Give My Regards to Broadway," which he led with fervor although he didn't know all the words.

It took us a little while to adjust to him, after Reece. Once when the lieutenant came to the barracks to give one of his little talks about playing ball, ending up with his usual "All right, Sergeant," Ruby hooked his thumbs in his cartridge belt, slouched comfortably, and said, "Fellas, I hope yez all listened and gave ya attention to what the lieutenant said. I think I can speak fa yez all as well as myself when I say, Lieutenant, we're *gonna* play ball wit' you, like you said, because this here is one platoon that knows a Good Joe when we see one."

As flustered by this as he had ever been by Reece's silent scorn, the lieutenant could only blush and stammer, "Well, uh—thank you, Sergeant. Uh—I guess that's all, then. Carry on." And as soon as the lieutenant was out of sight we all began to make loud retching noises, to hold our noses or go through the motions of shoveling, as if we stood knee-deep in manure. "Christ, Ruby," Schacht cried, "what the hella *you* buckin' for?"

Ruby hunched his shoulders and spread his hands, bubbling with good-natured laughter. "To stay alive," he said. "To stay alive, whaddya think?" And he defended the point vigorously over the mounting din of our ridicule. "Whatsa matta?" he demanded. "Whatsa matta? Don'tcha think he does it to the captain? Don'tcha think the captain does it up at Battalion? Listen, wise up, will yez? *Evvybody* does it! *Evvybody* does it! What the hellya think makes the Army *go*?" Finally he dismissed the whole subject with cab-driverly nonchalance. "Arright, arright, just stick around. *Yull* find out. Wait'll you kids got *my* time in the Army, *then* yez can talk." But by that time we were all laughing with him; he had won our hearts.

In the evenings, at the PX, we would cluster around him while he sat behind a battery of beer bottles, waving his expressive hands and talking the kind of relaxed, civilian language we all could understand. "Ah, I got this brother-in-law, a real smott bastid. Know how *he* got outa the Army? Know how *he* got out?" There would follow an involved, unlikely tale of treachery to which the only expected response was a laugh. "Sure!" Ruby would insist, laughing. "Don'tcha believe me? Don'tcha believe me? And this other guy I know, boy, talk about bein' *smott*—I'm tellin' ya, this bastid's *really* smott. Know how *he* got out?"

Sometimes our allegiance wavered, but not for long. One evening a group of us sat around the front steps, dawdling over cigarettes before we pushed off to the PX, and discussing at length—as if to convince ourselves—the many things that made life with Ruby so enjoyable. "Well yeah," little Fogarty said, "but I dunno. With Ruby it don't seem much like soldiering any more."

This was the second time Fogarty had thrown us into a momentary confusion, and for the second time D'Allessandro cleared the air. "So?" he said with a shrug. "Who the hell wants to soldier?"

That said it perfectly. We could spit in the dust and amble off toward the PX now, round-shouldered, relieved, confident that Sergeant Reece would not haunt us again. Who the hell wanted to soldier? "Not *me*," we could all say in our hearts, "not *this* chicken," and our very defiance would dignify the attitude. An attitude was all we needed anyway, all we had ever needed, and this one would always sit more comfortably than Reece's stern, demanding creed. It meant, I guess, that at the end of our training cycle the camp delivered up a bunch of shameless little wise guys to be scattered and absorbed into the vast disorder of the Army, but at least Reece never saw it happen, and he was the only one who might have cared.

No Pain Whatsoever

MYRA STRAIGHTENED HERSELF in the backseat and smoothed her skirt, pushing Jack's hand away.

"All right, baby," he whispered, smiling, "take it easy."

"You take it easy, Jack," she told him. "I mean it, now."

His hand yielded, limp, but his arm stayed indolently around her shoulders. Myra ignored him and stared out the window. It was early Sunday evening, late in December, and the Long Island streets looked stale; dirty crusts of snow lay shriveled on the sidewalk, and cardboard images of Santa Claus leered out of closed liquor stores.

"I still don't feel right about you driving me all the way out here," Myra called to Marty, who was driving, to be polite.

"'S all right," Marty grumbled. Then he sounded his horn and added, to the back of a slow truck, "Get that son of a bitch outa the way."

Myra was annoyed—why did Marty always have to be such a grouch?—but Irene, Marty's wife, squirmed around in the front seat with her friendly grin. "Marty don't mind," she said. "It's good for 'm, getting out on a Sunday insteada laying around the house."

"Well," Myra said, "I certainly do appreciate it." The truth was that she would much rather have taken the bus, alone, as usual. In the four years she had been coming out here to visit her husband every Sunday she had grown used to the long ride, and she liked stopping at a little cafeteria in Hempstead, where you had to change buses, for coffee and cake on the way home. But today she and Jack had gone over to Irene and Marty's for dinner, and the dinner was so late that Marty had to offer to drive her out to the hospital, and she had to accept. And then of course Irene had to come along, and Jack too, and they all acted as if they were doing her a favor. But you had to be polite. "It certainly is nice," Myra called, "to be riding out here in a car, instead of a—*don't* Jack!"

Jack said, "*Sh-h-h*, take it easy, baby," but she threw off his hand and twisted away. Watching them, Irene put her tongue between her teeth and giggled, and Myra felt herself blushing. It wasn't that there was anything to be ashamed of—Irene and Marty knew all about Jack and everything; most of her friends did, and nobody blamed her (after all, wasn't it almost like being a widow?)—it was just that Jack ought to know better. Couldn't he at least have the decency to keep his hands to himself now, of all times?

"There," Marty said. "Now we'll make some time." The truck had turned off and they were picking up speed, leaving the streetcar tracks and stores behind as the street became a road and then a highway.

"Care to hear the radio, kids?" Irene called. She clicked one of the dial tabs and a voice urged everyone to enjoy television in their own homes, now, tonight. She clicked another and a voice said, "Yes, your money buys more in a Crawford store!"

"Turn that son of a bitch off," Marty said, and sounding the horn again, he pulled out into the fast lane.

When the car entered the hospital grounds, Irene turned around in the front seat and said, "Say, this is a beautiful place. I mean it, isn't this a beautiful place? Oh, look, they got a Christmas tree up, with lights and all."

"Well," Marty said, "where to?"

"Straight ahead," Myra told him, "down to that big circle, where the Christmas tree is. Then you turn right, out around the Administration Building, and on out to the end of that street." He made the turn correctly, and as they approached the long, low TB building, she said, "Here it is, Marty, this one right here." He drew up to the curb and stopped, and she gathered together the magazines she had brought for her husband and stepped out on the thin gray snow.

Irene hunched her shoulders and turned around, hugging herself. "Oo-oo, it's *cold* out there, isn't it? Listen, honey, what time is it you'll be through, now? Eight o'clock, is it?"

"That's right," Myra said, "but listen, why don't you people go on home? I can just as soon take the bus back, like I always do."

"Whaddya think I am, crazy?" Irene said. "You think I want to drive all the way home with Jack moping there in the backseat?" She giggled and winked. "Be hard enough just trying to keep him happy while you're inside, let alone driving all the way home. No, listen, we'll cruise around a little, honey, maybe have a little drink or something, and then we'll come back here for you at eight o'clock sharp."

"Well okay, but I'd really just as soon—"

"Right here," Irene said. "We'll see you right here in front of the building at eight o'clock sharp. Now hurry up and shut the door before we all freeze to death."

Myra smiled as she slammed the door, but Jack, sulking, did not look up to smile back, or wave. Then the car rolled away and she walked up the path and the steps to the TB building.

The small waiting room smelled of steam heat and wet overshoes, and she hurried through it, past the door marked NURSES' OFFICE—CLEAN AREA and into the big, noisy center ward. There were thirty-six beds in the center ward, divided in half by a wide aisle and subdivided by shoulder-high partitions into open cubicles of six beds each. All the sheets and the hospital pajamas were dyed yellow, to distinguish them from uncontaminated linen in the hospital laundry, and this combined with the pale green of the walls made a sickly color scheme that Myra could never get used to. The noise was terrible too; each patient had a radio, and they all seemed to be playing different stations at once. There were clumps of visitors at some of the beds—one of the newer men lay with his arms around his wife in a kiss—but at other beds the men looked lonely, reading or listening to their radios.

Myra's husband didn't see her until she was right beside his bed. He was sitting up, cross-legged, frowning over something in his lap. "Hello, Harry," she said.

He looked up. "Oh, hi there, honey, didn't see you coming."

She leaned over and kissed him quickly on the cheek. Sometimes they kissed on the lips, but you weren't supposed to.

Harry glanced at his watch. "You're late. Was the bus late?"

"I didn't come on the bus," she said, taking off her coat. "I got a ride out. Irene, the girl that works in my office? She and her husband drove me out in their car."

"Oh, that's nice. Whyn't you bring 'em on in?"

"Oh, they couldn't stay—they had someplace else to go. But they both said to give you their regards. Here, I brought you these."

"Oh, thanks, that's swell." He took the magazines and spread them out on the bed: *Life*, *Collier's* and *Popular Science*. "That's swell, honey. Sit down and stay awhile."

Myra laid her coat over the back of the bedside chair and sat down. "Hello there, Mr. Chance," she said to a very long Negro in the next bed who was nodding and grinning at her.

"How're you, Mrs. Wilson?"

"Fine, thanks, and you?"

"Oh, no use complaining," Mr. Chance said.

She peered across Harry's bed at Red O'Meara, who lay listening to his radio on the other side. "Hi there, Red."

"Oh, hi, Mrs. Wilson. Didn't see you come in."

"Your wife coming in tonight, Red?"

"She comes Saturdays now. She was here last night."

"Oh," Myra said, "well, tell her I said hello."

"I sure will, Mrs. Wilson."

Then she smiled at the elderly man across the cubicle whose name she could never remember, who never had any visitors, and he smiled back, looking rather shy. She settled herself on the little steel chair, opening her handbag for cigarettes. "What's that thing on your lap, Harry?" It was a ring of blond wood a foot wide, with a great deal of blue knitting wool attached to little pegs around its edge.

"Oh, this?" Harry said, holding it up. "It's what they call rake-knitting. Something I got from occupational therapy."

"*What*-knitting?"

"Rake-knitting. See, what you do, you take this little hook and kind of pry the wool up and over each peg, like that, and you keep on doing that around and around the ring until you got yourself a muffler or a stocking cap—something like that."

"Oh, *I* see," Myra said. "It's like what we used to do when I was a kid, only we did it with a regular little spool, with nails stuck in it? You wind string around the nails and pull it through the spool and it makes sort of a knitted rope, like."

"Oh, yeah?" Harry said. "With a spool, huh? Yeah, I think my sister used to do that too, now that I think of it. With a spool. You're right, this is the same principle, only bigger."

"What're you going to make?"

"Oh, I don't know, I'm just fooling around with it. Thought I might make a stocking cap or something. I don't know." He inspected his work, turning the knitting-rake around in his hands, then leaned over and put it away in his bed stand. "It's just something to do."

She offered him the pack and he took a cigarette. When he bent forward to take the match the yellow pajamas gaped open and she saw his chest, unbelievably thin, partly caved-in on one side where the ribs were gone. She could just see the end of the ugly, newly healed scar from the last operation.

"Thanks, honey," he said, the cigarette wagging in his lips, and he leaned back against the pillows, stretching out his socked feet on the spread.

"How're you feeling, Harry?" she said.

"Feeling fine."

"You're looking better," she lied. "If you can gain a little weight now, you'll look fine."

"Pay up," said a voice over the din of the radios, and Myra looked around to see a little man coming down the center aisle in a wheelchair, walking the chair slowly with his feet, as all TB patients did to avoid the chest strain of turning the wheels with their hands. He was headed for Harry's bed, grinning with yellow teeth. "Pay up," he said again as the wheelchair came to a stop beside the bed. A piece of rubber tubing protruded from some kind of bandage on his chest. It coiled across his pajama top, held in place by a safety pin, and ended in a small rubber-capped bottle which rode heavily in his breast pocket. "Come on, come on," he said. "Pay up."

"Oh, yeah!" Harry said, laughing. "I forgot all about it, Walter." From the drawer of his bed stand he got out a dollar bill and handed it to the man, who folded it with thin fingers and put it in his pocket, along with the bottle.

"Okay, Harry," he said. "All squared away now, right?"

"Right, Walter."

He backed the wheelchair up and turned it around, and Myra saw that his chest, back and shoulders were crumpled and misshapen. "Sorry to butt in," he said, turning the sickly grin on Myra.

She smiled. "That's all right." When he had gone up the aisle again, she said, "What was that all about?"

"Oh, we had a bet on the fight Friday night. I'd forgotten all about it."

"Oh. Have I met him before?"

"Who, Walter? Sure, I think so, honey. You must've met him when I was over in surgery. Old Walter was in surgery more'n two years; they just brought him back here last week. Kid's had a rough time of it. He's got plenty of guts."

"What's that thing on his pajamas? That bottle?"

"He's draining," Harry said, settling back against the yellow pillows. "Old Walter's a good guy; I'm glad he's back." Then he lowered his voice, confidentially. "Matter of fact, he's one of the few really good guys left in this ward, with so many of the old crowd gone now, or over in surgery."

"Don't you like the new boys?" Myra asked, keeping her own voice low so that Red O'Meara, who was relatively new, wouldn't hear. "They seem perfectly nice to me."

"Oh, they're all right, I guess," Harry said. "I just mean, well, I get along better with guys like Walter, that's all. We been through a lot together, or something. I don't know. These new guys get on your nerves sometimes, the way they talk. For instance, there's not one of them knows anything about TB, and they all of them think they know it all; you can't tell them anything. I mean, a thing like that can get on your nerves."

Myra said she guessed she saw what he meant, and then it seemed that the best thing to do was change the subject. "Irene thought the hospital looked real pretty, with the Christmas tree and all."

"Oh, yeah?" Very carefully, Harry reached over and flicked his cigarette into the spotless ashtray on his bed stand. All his habits were precise and neat from living so long in bed. "How're things going at the office, honey?"

"Oh, all right, I guess. Remember I told you about that girl Janet that got fired for staying out too long at lunch, and we were all scared they'd start cracking down on that half-hour lunch period?"

"Oh, yeah," Harry said, but she could tell he didn't remember and wasn't really listening.

"Well, it seems to be all blown over now, because last week Irene and three other girls stayed out almost two hours and nobody said a word. And one of them, a girl named Rose, has been kind of expecting to get fired for a couple of months now, and they didn't even say anything to her."

"Oh, yeah?" Harry said. "Well, that's good."

There was a pause. "Harry?" she said.

"What, honey?"

"Have they told you anything new?"

"Anything new?"

"I mean, about whether or not you're going to need the operation on the other side."

"Oh, *no*, honey. I told you, we can't expect to hear anything on that for quite some time yet—I thought I explained all that." His mouth was smiling and his eyes frowning to show it had been a foolish question. It was the same look he always used to give her at first, long ago, when she would say, "But when do you *think* they'll let you come home?" Now he said, "Thing is, I've still got to get over this *last* one. You got to do one thing at a time in this business; you need a long postoperative period before you're really in the clear, especially with a record of breakdowns like I've had in the last—what is it, now—four years? No, what they'll do is wait awhile, I don't know, maybe six months, maybe longer, and see how this side's coming along. Then they'll decide about the other side. Might give me more surgery and they might not. You can't count on anything in this business, honey, you know that."

"No, of course, Harry, I'm sorry. I don't mean to ask stupid questions. I just meant, well, how're you feeling and everything. You still have any pain?"

"None at all, any more," Harry said. "I mean, as long as I don't go raising my arm too high or anything. When I do that it hurts, and sometimes I start to roll over on that side in my sleep, and that hurts too, but as long as I stay—you know—more or less in a normal position, why, there's no pain whatsoever."

"That's good," she said, "I'm awfully glad to hear that anyway."

Neither of them spoke for what seemed a long time, and in the noise of radios and the noise of laughing and coughing from other beds, their silence seemed strange. Harry began to riffle *Popular Science* absently with his thumb. Myra's eyes strayed to the framed picture on his bed stand, an enlarged snapshot of the two of them just before their marriage, taken in her mother's backyard in Michigan. She looked very young in the picture, leggy in her 1945 skirt, not knowing how to dress or even how to stand, knowing nothing and ready for anything with a child's smile. And Harry—but the surprising thing was that Harry looked older in the picture, somehow, than he did now. Probably it was the thicker face and build, and of course the clothes helped—the dark, decorated Eisenhower jacket and the gleaming boots. Oh, he'd been good-looking, all right, with his set jaw and hard gray eyes—much better looking, for instance, than a too stocky, too solid man like Jack. But now with the loss of weight there had been a softening about the lips and eyes that gave him the look of a thin little boy. His face had changed to suit the pajamas.

"Sure am glad you brought me this," Harry said of his *Popular Science*. "They got an article in here I want to read."

"Good," she said, and she wanted to say: Can't it wait until I've gone?

Harry flipped the magazine on its face, fighting the urge to read, and said, "How's everything else, honey? Outside of the office, I mean."

"All right," she said. "I had a letter from Mother the other day, kind of a Christmas letter. She sent you her best regards."

"Good," Harry said, but the magazine was winning. He flipped it over again, opened it to his article and read a few lines very casually—as if only to make sure it was the right article—and then lost himself in it.

Myra lighted a fresh cigarette from the butt of her last one, picked up the *Life* and began to turn the pages. From time to time she looked up to watch him; he lay biting a knuckle as he read, scratching the sole of one socked foot with the curled toe of the other.

They spent the rest of the visiting hour that way. Shortly before eight o'clock a group of people came down the aisle, smiling and trundling a studio piano on rubber-tired casters—the Sunday night Red Cross entertainers. Mrs. Balacheck led the procession; a kindly, heavyset woman in uniform, who played. Then came the piano, pushed by a pale young tenor whose lips were always wet, and then the female singers: a swollen soprano in a taffeta dress that looked tight under the arms and a stern-faced, lean contralto with a briefcase. They wheeled the piano close to Harry's bed, in the approximate middle of the ward, and began to unpack their sheet music.

Harry looked up from his reading. "Evening, Mrs. Balacheck."

Her glasses gleamed at him. "How're you tonight, Harry? Like to hear a few Christmas carols tonight?"

"Yes, ma'am."

One by one the radios were turned off and the chattering died. But just before Mrs. Balacheck hit the keys a stocky nurse intervened, thumping rubber-heeled down the aisle with a hand outstretched to ward off the music until she could make an announcement. Mrs. Balacheck sat back, and the nurse, craning her neck, called, "Visiting hour's over!" to one end of the ward and, "Visiting hour's over!" to the other. Then she nodded to Mrs. Balacheck, smiling behind her sterilized linen mask, and thumped away again. After a moment's whispered counsel, Mrs. Balacheck began to play an introductory "Jingle Bells," her cheeks wobbling, to cover the disturbance of departing visitors, while the singers retired to cough quietly among themselves; they would wait until their audience settled down.

"Gee," Harry said, "I didn't realize it was that late. Here, I'll walk you out to the door." He sat up slowly and swung his feet to the floor.

"No, don't bother, Harry," Myra said. "You lie still."

"No, that's all right," he said, wriggling into his slippers. "Will you hand me the robe, honey?" He stood up, and she helped him on with a corduroy VA bathrobe that was too short for him.

"Goodnight, Mr. Chance," Myra said, and Mr. Chance grinned and nodded. Then she said goodnight to Red O'Meara and the elderly man, and as they passed his wheelchair in the aisle, she said goodnight to Walter. She took Harry's arm, startled at its thinness, and matched his slow steps very carefully. They stood facing each other in the small awkward crowd of visitors that lingered in the waiting room.

"Well," Harry said, "take care of yourself now, honey. See you next week."

"Oo-oo," somebody's mother said, plodding hump-shouldered out the door, "it *is* cold tonight." She turned back to wave to her son, then grasped her husband's arm and went down the steps to the snow-blown path. Someone else caught the door and held it open for other visitors to pass through, filling the room with a cold draft, and then it closed again, and Myra and Harry were alone.

"All right, Harry," Myra said, "you go back to bed and listen to the music, now." He looked very frail standing there with his robe hanging open. She reached up and closed it neatly over his chest, took the dangling belt and knotted it firmly, while he smiled down at her. "Now you go on back in there before you catch cold."

"Okay. Goodnight, honey."

"Goodnight," she said, and standing on tiptoe, she kissed his cheek. "Goodnight, Harry."

At the door she turned to watch him walk back to the ward in the tight, high-waisted robe. Then she went outside and down the steps, turning up her coat collar in the sudden cold. Marty's car was not there; the road was bare except for the dwindling backs of the other visitors, passing under a streetlamp now as they made their way down to the bus stop near the Administration Building. She drew the coat more closely around her and stood close to the building for shelter from the wind.

"Jingle Bells" ended inside, to muffled applause, and after a moment the program began in earnest. A few solemn chords sounded on the piano, and then the voices came through:

"Hark, the herald angels sing,
Glory to the newborn King . . ."

All at once Myra's throat closed up and the streetlights swam in her eyes. Then half her fist was in her mouth and she was sobbing wretchedly, making little puffs of mist that floated away in the dark. It took her a long time to stop, and each sniffling intake of breath made a high sharp noise that sounded as if it could be heard for miles. Finally it was over, or nearly over; she managed to control her shoulders, to blow her nose and put her handkerchief away, closing her bag with a reassuring, businesslike snap.

Then the lights of the car came probing up the road. She ran down the path and stood waiting in the wind.

Inside the car a warm smell of whiskey hung among the cherry-red points of cigarettes, and Irene's voice squealed, "Oo-oo! Hurry up and shut the *door*!"

Jack's arms gathered her close as the door slammed, and in a thick whisper he said, "Hello, baby."

They were all a little drunk; even Marty was in high spirits. "Hold tight, everybody!" he called, as they swung around the Administration Building, past the Christmas tree, and leveled off for the straightaway to the gate, gaining speed. "Everybody hold tight!"

Irene's face floated chattering over the back of the front seat. "Myra, honey, listen, we found the most adorable little place down the road, kind of a roadhouse, like, only real inexpensive and everything? So listen, we wanna take you back there for a little drink, okay?"

"Sure," Myra said, "fine."

"'Cause I mean, we're way ahead of you now anyway, and anyway I want you to see this place . . . Marty, will you take it *easy*!" She laughed. "Honestly, anybody else driving this car with what he's had to drink in him, I'd be scared to death, you know it? But you never got to worry about old Marty. He's the best old driver in the world, drunk, sober, I don't care *what* he is."

But they weren't listening. Deep in a kiss, Jack slipped his hand inside her coat, expertly around and inside all the other layers until it held the flesh of her breast. "All over being mad at me, baby?" he mumbled against her lips. "Wanna go have a little drink?"

Her hands gripped the bulk of his back and clung there. Then she let herself be turned so that his other hand could creep secretly up her thigh. "All right," she whispered, "but let's only have one and then afterwards—"

"Okay, baby, okay."

"—and then afterwards, darling, let's go right home."

A Glutton for Punishment

FOR A LITTLE while when Walter Henderson was nine years old he thought falling dead was the very zenith of romance, and so did a number of his friends. Having found that the only truly rewarding part of any cops-and-robbers game was the moment when you pretended to be shot, clutched your heart, dropped your pistol and crumpled to the earth, they soon dispensed with the rest of it—the tiresome business of choosing up sides and sneaking around—and refined the game to its essence. It became a matter of individual performance, almost an art. One of them at a time would run dramatically along the crest of a hill, and at a given point the ambush would occur: a simultaneous jerking of aimed toy pistols and a chorus of those staccato throaty sounds—a kind of hoarse-whispered "*Pk-k-ew! Pk-k-ew!*"—with which little boys simulate the noise of gunfire. Then the performer would stop, turn, stand poised for a moment in graceful agony, pitch over and fall down the hill in a whirl of arms and legs and a splendid cloud of dust, and finally sprawl flat at the bottom, a rumpled corpse. When he got up and brushed off his clothes, the others would criticize his form ("Pretty good," or "Too stiff," or "Didn't look natural"), and then it would be the next player's turn. That was all there was to the game, but Walter Henderson loved it. He was a slight, poorly coordinated boy, and this was the only thing even faintly like a sport at which he excelled. Nobody could match the abandon with which he flung his limp body down the hill, and he reveled in the small acclaim it won him. Eventually the others grew bored with the game, after some older boys had laughed at them; Walter turned reluctantly to more wholesome forms of play, and soon he had forgotten about it.

But he had occasion to remember it, vividly, one May afternoon nearly twenty-five years later in a Lexington Avenue office building, while he sat at his desk pretending to work and waiting to be fired. He had become a sober, keen-looking young man now, with clothes that showed the influence of an Eastern university and neat brown hair that was just beginning to thin out on top. Years of good health had made him less slight, and though he still had trouble with his coordination it showed up mainly in minor things nowadays, like an inability to coordinate his hat, his wallet, his theater tickets and his change without making his wife stop and wait for him, or a tendency to push heavily against doors marked "Pull." He looked, at any rate, the picture of sanity and competence as he sat there in the office. No one could have told that the cool sweat of anxiety was sliding under his shirt, or that the fingers of his left hand, concealed in his pocket, were slowly grinding and tearing a book of matches into a moist cardboard pulp. He had seen it coming for weeks, and this morning, from the minute he got off the elevator, he had sensed that this was the day it would happen. When several of his superiors said, "Morning, Walt," he had seen the faintest suggestion of concern behind their smiles; then once this afternoon, glancing out over the gate of the cubicle where he worked, he'd happened to catch the eye of George Crowell, the department manager, who was hesitating in the door of his private office with some papers in his hand. Crowell turned away quickly, but Walter knew he had been watching him, troubled but determined. In a matter of minutes, he felt sure, Crowell would call him in and break the news—with difficulty, of course, since Crowell was the kind of boss who took pride in being a regular guy. There was nothing to do now but let the thing happen and try to take it as gracefully as possible.

That was when the childhood memory began to prey on his mind, for it suddenly struck him—and the force of it sent his thumbnail biting deep into the secret matchbook—that letting things happen and taking them gracefully had been, in a way, the pattern of his life. There was certainly no denying that the role of good loser had always held an inordinate appeal for him. All through adolescence he had specialized in it, gamely losing fights with stronger boys, playing football badly in the secret hope of being injured and carried dramatically off the field ("You got to hand it to old Henderson for *one* thing, anyway," the high-school coach had said with a chuckle, "he's a real little glutton for punishment"). College had offered a wider scope to his talent—there were exams to be flunked and elections to be lost—and later the Air Force had made it possible for him to wash out, honorably, as a flight cadet. And now, inevitably, it seemed, he was running true to form once more. The several jobs he'd held before this had been the beginner's kind at which it isn't easy to fail; when the opportunity for this one first arose it had been, in Crowell's phrase, "a real challenge."

"Good," Walter had said. "That's what I'm looking for." When he related that part of the conversation to his wife she had said, "Oh, wonderful!" and they'd moved to an expensive apartment in the East Sixties on the strength of it. And lately, when he started coming home with a beaten look and announcing darkly that he doubted if he could hold on much longer, she would enjoin the children not to bother him ("Daddy's very tired tonight"), bring him a drink and soothe him with careful, wifely reassurance, doing her best to conceal her fear, never guessing, or at least never showing, that she was dealing with a chronic, compulsive failure, a strange little boy in love with the attitudes of collapse. And the amazing thing, he thought—the really amazing thing—was that he himself had never looked at it that way before.

"Walt?"

The cubicle gate had swung open and George Crowell was standing there, looking uncomfortable. "Will you step into my office a minute?"

"Right, George." And Walter followed him out of the cubicle, out across the office floor, feeling many eyes on his back. Keep it dignified, he told himself. The important thing is to keep it dignified. Then the door closed behind them and the two of them were alone in the carpeted silence of Crowell's private office. Automobile horns blared in the distance, twenty-one stories below; the only other sounds were their breathing, the squeak of Crowell's shoes as he went to his desk and the creak of his swivel chair as he sat down. "Pull up a chair, Walt," he said. "Smoke?"

"No thanks." Walter sat down and laced his fingers tight between his knees.

Crowell shut the cigarette box without taking one for himself, pushed it aside and leaned forward, both hands spread flat on the plate-glass top of the desk. "Walt, I might as well give you this straight from the shoulder," he said, and the last shred of hope slipped away. The funny part was that it came as a shock, even so. "Mr. Harvey and I have felt for some time that you haven't quite caught on to the work here, and we've both very reluctantly come to the conclusion that the best thing to do, in your own best interests as well as ours, is to let you go. Now," he added quickly, "this is no reflection on you personally, Walt. We do a highly specialized kind of work here and we can't expect everybody to stay on top of the job. In your case particularly, we really feel you'd be happier in some organization better suited to your—abilities."

Crowell leaned back, and when he raised his hands their moisture left two gray, perfect prints on the glass, like the hands of a skeleton. Walter stared at them, fascinated, while they shriveled and disappeared.

"Well," he said, and looked up. "You put that very nicely, George. Thanks."

Crowell's lips worked into an apologetic, regular guy's smile. "Awfully sorry," he said. "These things just happen." And he began to fumble with the knobs of his desk drawers, visibly relieved that the worst was over. "Now," he said, "we've made out a check here covering your salary through the end of next month. That'll give you something in the way of—severance pay, so to speak—to tide you over until you find something." He held out a long envelope.

"That's very generous," Walter said. Then there was a silence, and Walter realized it was up to him to break it. He got to his feet. "All right, George. I won't keep you."

Crowell got up quickly and came around the desk with both hands held out—one to shake Walter's hand, the other to put on his shoulder as they walked to the door. The gesture, at once friendly and humiliating, brought a quick rush of blood to Walter's throat, and for a terrible second he thought he might be going to cry. "Well, boy," Crowell said, "good luck to you."

"Thanks," he said, and he was so relieved to find his voice steady that he said it again, smiling. "Thanks. So long, George."

There was a distance of some fifty feet to be crossed on the way back to his cubicle, and Walter Henderson accomplished it with style. He was aware of how trim and straight his departing shoulders looked to Crowell; he was aware too, as he threaded his way among desks whose occupants either glanced up shyly at him or looked as if they'd like to, of every subtle play of well-controlled emotion in his face. It was as if the whole thing were a scene in a movie. The camera had opened the action from Crowell's viewpoint and dollied back to take the entire office as a frame for Walter's figure in lonely, stately passage; now it came in for a long-held close-up of Walter's face, switched to other brief views of his colleagues' turning heads (Joe Collins looking worried, Fred Holmes trying to keep from looking pleased), and switched again to Walter's viewpoint as it discovered the plain, unsuspecting face of Mary, his secretary, who was waiting for him at his desk with a report he had given her to type.

"I hope this is all right, Mr. Henderson."

Walter took it and dropped it on the desk. "Forget it, Mary," he said. "Look, you might as well take the rest of the day off, and go see the personnel manager in the morning. You'll be getting a new job. I've just been fired."

Her first expression was a faint, suspicious smile—she thought he was kidding—but then she began to look pale and shaken. She was very young and not too bright; they had probably never told her in secretarial school that it was possible for your boss to get fired. "Why, that's *terrible*, Mr. Henderson. I—well, but why would they *do* such a thing?"

"Oh, I don't know," he said. "Lot of little reasons, I guess." He was opening and slamming the drawers of his desk, cleaning out his belongings. There wasn't much: a handful of old personal letters, a dry fountain pen, a cigarette lighter with no flint, and half of a wrapped chocolate bar. He was aware of how poignant each of these objects looked to her, as she watched him sort them out and fill his pockets, and he was aware of the dignity with which he straightened up, turned, took his hat from the stand and put it on.

"Doesn't affect you, of course, Mary," he said. "They'll have a new job for you in the morning. Well." He held out his hand. "Good luck."

"Thank you; the same to you. Well, then, g'night"—and here she brought her chewed fingernails up to her lips for an uncertain little giggle—"I mean, g'bye, then, Mr. Henderson."

The next part of the scene was at the water cooler, where Joe Collins's sober eyes became enriched with sympathy as Walter approached him.

"Joe," Walter said. "I'm leaving. Got the ax."

"No!" But Collins's look of shock was plainly an act of kindness; it couldn't have been much of a surprise. "Jesus, Walt, what the hell's the matter with these people?"

Then Fred Holmes chimed in, very grave and sorry, clearly pleased with the news: "Gee, boy, that's a damn shame."

Walter led the two of them away to the elevators, where he pressed the "down" button; and suddenly other men were bearing down on him from all corners of the office, their faces stiff with sorrow, their hands held out.

"Awful sorry, Walt . . ."

"Good luck, boy . . ."

"Keep in touch, okay, Walt? . . ."

Nodding and smiling, shaking hands, Walter said, "Thanks," and "So long," and "I certainly will"; then the red light came on over one of the elevators with its little mechanical *ding!* and in another few seconds the doors slid open and the operator's voice said, "Down!" He backed into the car, still wearing his fixed smile and waving a jaunty salute to their earnest, talking faces, and the scene found its perfect conclusion as the doors slid shut, clamped, and the car dropped in silence through space.

All the way down he stood with the ruddy, bright-eyed look of a man fulfilled by pleasure; it wasn't until he was out on the street, walking rapidly, that he realized how completely he had enjoyed himself.

The heavy shock of this knowledge slowed him down, until he came to a stop and stood against a building front for the better part of a minute. His scalp prickled under his hat, and his fingers began to fumble with the knot of his tie and the button of his coat. He felt as if he had surprised himself in some obscene and shameful act, and he had never felt more helpless, or more frightened.

Then in a burst of action he set off again, squaring his hat and setting his jaw, bringing his heels down hard on the pavement, trying to look hurried and impatient and impelled by business. A man could drive himself crazy trying to psychoanalyze himself in the middle of Lexington Avenue, in the middle of the afternoon. The thing to do was get busy now, and start looking for a job.

The only trouble, he realized, coming to a stop again and looking around, was that he didn't know where he was going. He was somewhere in the upper Forties, on a corner that was bright with florist shops and taxicabs, alive with well-dressed men and women walking in the clear spring air. A telephone was what he needed first. He hurried across the street to a drugstore and made his way through smells of toilet soap and perfume and ketchup and bacon to the rank of phone booths along the rear wall; he got out his address book and found the page showing the several employment agencies where his applications were filed; then he got his dimes ready and shut himself into one of the booths.

But all the agencies told him the same thing: no openings in his field at the moment; no point in his coming in until they called him. When he was finished he dug for the address book again, to check the number of an acquaintance who had told him, a month before, that there might soon be an opening in his office. The book wasn't in his inside pocket; he plunged his hands into the other pockets of his coat and then his pants, cracking an elbow painfully against the wall of the booth, but all he could find were the old letters and the piece of chocolate from his desk. Cursing, he dropped the chocolate on the floor and, as if it were a lighted cigarette, stepped on it. These exertions in the heat of the booth made his breathing rapid and shallow. He was feeling faint by the time he saw the address book right in front of him, on top of the coin box, where he'd left it. His finger trembled in the dial, and when he started to speak, clawing the collar away from his sweating neck with his free hand, his voice was as weak and urgent as a beggar's.

"Jack," he said. "I was just wondering—just wondering if you'd heard anything new on the opening you mentioned a while back."

"On the which?"

"The opening. You know. You said there might be a job in your—"

"Oh, that. No, haven't heard a thing, Walt. I'll be in touch with you if anything breaks."

"Okay, Jack." He pulled open the folding door of the booth and leaned back against the stamped-tin wall, breathing deeply to welcome the rush of cool air. "I just thought it might've slipped your mind or something," he said. His voice was almost normal again. "Sorry to bother you."

"Hell, that's okay," said the hearty voice in the receiver. "What's the matter, boy? Things getting a little sticky where you are?"

"*Oh* no," Walter found himself saying, and he was immediately glad of the lie. He almost never lied, and it always surprised him to discover how easy it could be. His voice gained confidence. "No. I'm all *right* here, Jack, it's just that I didn't want to—*you* know, I thought it might have slipped your mind, is all. How's the family?"

When the conversation was over, he guessed there was nothing more to do but go home. But he continued to sit in the open booth for a long time, with his feet stretched out on the drugstore floor, until a small, canny smile began to play on his face, slowly dissolving and changing into a look of normal strength. The ease of the lie had given him an idea that grew, the more he thought it over, into a profound and revolutionary decision.

He would not tell his wife. With luck he was sure to find some kind of work before the month was out, and in the meantime, for once in his life, he would keep his troubles to himself. Tonight, when she asked how the day had gone, he would say, "Oh, all right," or even "Fine." In the morning he would leave the house at the usual time and stay away all day, and he would go on doing the same thing every day until he had a job.

The phrase "Pull yourself together" occurred to him, and there was more than determination in the way he pulled himself together there in the phone booth, the way he gathered up his coins and straightened his tie and walked out to the street: there was a kind of nobility.

Several hours had to be killed before the normal time of his home-coming, and when he found himself walking west on Forty-second Street he decided to kill them in the Public Library. He mounted the wide stone steps importantly, and soon he was installed in the reading room, examining a bound copy of last year's *Life* magazines and going over and over his plan, enlarging and perfecting it.

He knew, sensibly, that there would be nothing easy about the day-to-day deception. It would call for the constant vigilance and cunning of an outlaw. But wasn't it the very difficulty of the plan that made it worthwhile? And in the end, when it was all over and he could tell her at last, it would be a reward worth every minute of the ordeal. He knew just how she would look at him when he told her—in blank dis-belief at first and then, gradually, with the dawning of a kind of respect he hadn't seen in her eyes for years.

"You mean you kept it to yourself all this *time*? But *why*, Walt?"

"Oh well," he would say casually, even shrugging, "I didn't see any point in upsetting you."

When it was time to leave the library he lingered in the main entrance for a minute, taking deep pulls from a cigarette and looking down over the five o'clock traffic and crowds. The scene held a special nostalgia for him, because it was here, on a spring evening five years before, that he had come to meet her for the first time. "Can you meet me at the top of the library steps?" she had asked over the phone that morning, and it wasn't until many months later, after they were married, that this struck him as a peculiar meeting place. When he asked her about it then, she laughed at him. "Of *course* it was inconvenient—that was the whole point. I wanted to pose up there, like a princess in a castle or something, and make you climb up all those lovely steps to claim me."

And that was exactly how it had seemed. He'd escaped from the office ten minutes early that day and hurried to Grand Central to wash and shave in a gleaming subterranean dressing room; he had waited in a fit of impatience while a very old, stout, slow attendant took his suit away to be pressed. Then, after tipping the attendant more than he could afford, he had raced outside and up Forty-second Street, tense and breathless as he strode past shoe stores and milk bars, as he winnowed his way through swarms of intolerably slow-moving pedestrians who had no idea of how urgent his mission was. He was afraid of being late, even half afraid that it was all some kind of a joke and she wouldn't be there at all. But as soon as he hit Fifth Avenue he saw her up there in the distance, alone, standing at the top of the library steps—a slender, radiant brunette in a fashionable black coat.

He slowed down, then. He crossed the avenue at a stroll, one hand in his pocket, and took the steps with such an easy, athletic nonchalance that nobody could have guessed at the hours of anxiety, the days of strategic and tactical planning this particular moment had cost him.

When he was fairly certain she could see him coming he looked up at her again, and she smiled. It wasn't the first time he had seen her smile that way, but it was the first time he could be sure it was intended wholly for him, and it caused warm tremors of pleasure in his chest. He couldn't remember the words of their greeting, but he remembered being quite sure that they were all right, that it was starting off well—that her wide shining eyes were seeing him exactly as he most wanted to be seen. The things he said, whatever they were, struck her as witty, and the things she said, or the sound of her voice when she said them, made him feel taller and stronger and broader of shoulder than ever before in his life. When they turned and started down the steps together he took hold of her upper arm, claiming her, and felt the light jounce of her breast on the backs of his fingers with each step. And the evening before them, spread out and waiting at their feet, seemed miraculously long and miraculously rich with promise.

Starting down alone, now, he found it strengthening to have one clear triumph to look back on—one time in his life, at least, when he had denied the possibility of failure, and won. Other memories came into focus when he crossed the avenue and started back down the gentle slope of Forty-second Street: they had come this way that evening too, and walked to the Biltmore for a drink, and he remembered how she had looked sitting beside him in the semidarkness of the cocktail lounge, squirming forward from the hips while he helped her out of the sleeves of her coat and then settling back, giving her long hair a toss and looking at him in a provocative sidelong way as she raised the glass to her lips. A little later she had said, "Oh, let's go down to the river—I love the river at this time of day," and they had left the hotel and walked there. He walked there now, down through the clangor of Third Avenue and up toward Tudor City—it seemed a much longer walk alone—until he was standing at the little balustrade, looking down over the swarm of sleek cars on the East River Drive and at the slow, gray water moving beyond it. It was on this very spot, while a tugboat moaned somewhere under the darkening skyline of Queens, that he had drawn her close and kissed her for the first time. Now he turned away, a new man, and set out to walk all the way home.

The first thing that hit him, when he let himself in the apartment door, was the smell of Brussels sprouts. The children were still at their supper in the kitchen: he could hear their high mumbled voices over the clink of dishes, and then his wife's voice, tired and coaxing. When the door slammed he heard her say, "There's Daddy now," and the children began to call, "Daddy! Daddy!"

He put his hat carefully in the hall closet and turned around just as she appeared in the kitchen doorway, drying her hands on her apron and smiling through her tiredness. "Home on time for once," she said. "How lovely. I was afraid you'd be working late again."

"No," he said. "No, I didn't have to work late." His voice had an oddly foreign, amplified sound in his own ears, as if he were speaking in an echo chamber.

"You do look tired, though, Walt. You look worn out."

"Walked home, that's all. Guess I'm not used to it. How's everything?"

"Oh, fine." But she looked worn out herself.

When they went together into the kitchen he felt encircled and entrapped by its humid brightness. His eyes roamed dolefully over the milk cartons, the mayonnaise jars and soup cans and cereal boxes, the peaches lined up to ripen on the windowsill, the remarkable frailty and tenderness of his two children, whose chattering faces were lightly streaked with mashed potato.

Things looked better in the bathroom, where he took longer than necessary over the job of washing up for dinner. At least he could be alone here, braced by splashings of cold water; the only intrusion was the sound of his wife's voice rising in impatience with the older child: "All right, Andrew Henderson. No story for *you* tonight unless you finish up all that custard *now*." A little later came the scraping of chairs and stacking of dishes that meant their supper was over, and the light scuffle of shoes and the slamming door that meant they had been turned loose in their room for an hour to play before bath time.

Walter carefully dried his hands; then he went out to the living-room sofa and settled himself there with a magazine, taking very slow, deep breaths to show how self-controlled he was. In a minute she came in to join him, her apron removed and her lipstick replenished, bringing the cocktail pitcher full of ice. "Oh," she said with a sigh. "Thank God that's over. Now for a little peace and quiet."

"I'll get the drinks, honey," he said, bolting to his feet. He had hoped his voice might sound normal now, but it still came out with echo-chamber resonance.

"You will not," she commanded. "You sit down. You deserve to sit still and be waited on, when you come home looking so tired. How did the day go, Walt?"

"Oh, all right," he said, sitting down again. "Fine." He watched her measuring out the gin and vermouth, stirring the pitcher in her neat, quick way, arranging the tray and bringing it across the room.

"There," she said, settling herself close beside him. "Will you do the honors, darling?" And when he had filled the chilled glasses she raised hers and said, "Oh, lovely. Cheers." This bright cocktail mood was a carefully studied effect, he knew. So was her motherly sternness over the children's supper; so was the brisk, no-nonsense efficiency with which, earlier today, she had attacked the supermarket; and so, later tonight, would be the tenderness of her surrender in his arms. The orderly rotation of many careful moods was her life, or rather, was what her life had become. She managed it well, and it was only rarely, looking very closely at her face, that he could see how much the effort was costing her.

But the drink was a great help. The first bitter, ice-cold sip of it seemed to restore his calm, and the glass in his hand looked reassuringly deep. He took another sip or two before daring to look at her again, and when he did it was a heartening sight. Her smile was almost completely free of tension, and soon they were chatting together as comfortably as happy lovers.

"Oh, isn't it nice just to sit down and unwind?" she said, allowing her head to sink back into the upholstery. "And isn't it lovely to think it's Friday night?"

"Sure is," he said, and instantly put his mouth in his drink to hide his shock. Friday night! That meant there would be two days before he could even begin to look for a job—two days of mild imprisonment in the house, or of dealing with tricycles and popsicles in the park, without a hope of escaping the burden of his secret. "Funny," he said. "I'd almost forgotten it was Friday."

"Oh, how *can* you forget?" She squirmed luxuriously deeper into the sofa. "I look forward to it all week. Pour me just a tiny bit more, darling, and then I must get back to the chores."

He poured a tiny bit more for her and a full glass for himself. His hand was shaking and he spilled a little of it, but she didn't seem to notice. Nor did she seem to notice that his replies grew more and more strained as she kept the conversation going. When she got back to the chores—basting the roast, drawing the children's baths, tidying up their room for the night—Walter sat alone and allowed his mind to slide into a heavy, gin-fuddled confusion. Only one persistent thought came through, a piece of self-advice that was as clear and cold as the drink that rose again and again to his lips: Hold on. No matter what she says, no matter what happens tonight or tomorrow or the next day, just hold on. Hold on.

But holding on grew less and less easy as the children's splashing bath-noises floated into the room; it was more difficult still by the time they were brought in to say goodnight, carrying their teddy bears and dressed in clean pajamas, their faces shining and smelling of soap. After that, it became impossible to stay seated on the sofa. He sprang up and began stalking around the floor, lighting one cigarette after another, listening to his wife's clear, modulated reading of the bedtime story in the next room ("You may go into the fields, or down the lane, but *don't* go into Mr. McGregor's garden . . .").

When she came out again, closing the children's door behind her, she found him standing like a tragic statue at the window, looking down into the darkening courtyard. "What's the matter, Walt?"

He turned on her with a false grin. "Nothing's the matter," he said in the echo-chamber voice, and the movie camera started rolling again. It came in for a close-up of his own tense face, then switched over to observe her movements as she hovered uncertainly at the coffee table.

"Well," she said. "I'm going to have one more cigarette and then I must get the dinner on the table." She sat down again—not leaning back this time, or smiling, for this was her busy, getting-the-dinner-on-the-table mood. "Have you got a match, Walt?"

"Sure." And he came toward her, probing in his pocket as if to bring forth something he had been saving to give her all day.

"God," she said. "Look at those matches. What *happened* to them?"

"These?" He stared down at the raddled, twisted matchbook as if it were a piece of incriminating evidence. "Must've been kind of tearing them up or something," he said. "Nervous habit."

"Thanks," she said, accepting the light from his trembling fingers, and then she began to look at him with wide, dead-serious eyes. "Walt, there *is* something wrong, isn't there?"

"Of course not. Why should there be anything wr—"

"Tell me the truth. Is it the job? Is it about—what you were afraid of last week? I mean, did anything happen today to make you think they might— Did Crowell say anything? Tell me." The faint lines on her face seemed to have deepened. She looked severe and competent and suddenly much older, not even very pretty anymore—a woman used to dealing with emergencies, ready to take charge.

He began to walk slowly away toward an easy chair across the room, and the shape of his back was an eloquent statement of impending defeat. At the edge of the carpet he stopped and seemed to stiffen, a wounded man holding himself together; then he turned around and faced her with the suggestion of a melancholy smile.

"Well, darling—" he began. His right hand came up and touched the middle button of his shirt, as if to unfasten it, and then with a great deflating sigh he collapsed backward into the chair, one foot sliding out on the carpet and the other curled beneath him. It was the most graceful thing he had done all day. "They got me," he said.

A Wrestler with Sharks

NOBODY HAD MUCH respect for *The Labor Leader*. Even Finkel and Kramm, its owners, the two sour brothers-in-law who'd dreamed it up in the first place and who somehow managed to make a profit on it year after year—even they could take little pride in the thing. At least, that's what I used to suspect from the way they'd hump grudgingly around the office, shivering the bile-green partitions with their thumps and shouts, grabbing and tearing at galley proofs, breaking pencil points, dropping wet cigar butts on the floor and slamming telephones contemptuously into their cradles. *The Labor Leader* was all either of them would ever have for a life's work, and they seemed to hate it.

You couldn't blame them: the thing was a monster. In format it was a fat biweekly tabloid, badly printed, that spilled easily out of your hands and was very hard to put together again in the right order; in policy it called itself "An Independent Newspaper Pledged to the Spirit of the Trade Union Movement," but its real pitch was to be a kind of trade journal for union officials, who subscribed to it out of union funds and who must surely have been inclined to tolerate, rather than to want or need, whatever thin sustenance it gave to them. The *Leader*'s coverage of national events "from the labor angle" was certain to be stale, likely to be muddled, and often opaque with typographical errors; most of its dense columns were filled with flattering reports on the doings of the unions whose leaders were on the subscription list, often to the exclusion of much bigger news about those whose leaders weren't. And every issue carried scores of simpleminded ads urging "Harmony" in the names of various small industrial firms that Finkel and Kramm had been able to beg or browbeat into buying space—a compromise that would almost certainly have hobbled a real labor paper but that didn't, typically enough, seem to cramp the *Leader*'s style at all.

There was a fast turnover on the editorial staff. Whenever somebody quit, the *Leader* would advertise in the help-wanted section of the *Times*, offering a "moderate salary commensurate with experience." This always brought a good crowd to the sidewalk outside the *Leader*'s office, a gritty storefront on the lower fringe of the garment district, and Kramm, who was the editor (Finkel was the publisher), would keep them all waiting for half an hour before he picked up a sheaf of application forms, shot his cuffs, and gravely opened the door—I think he enjoyed this occasional chance to play the man of affairs.

"All right, take your time," he'd say, as they jostled inside and pressed against the wooden rail that shielded the inner offices. "Take your time, gentlemen." Then he would raise a hand and say, "May I have your attention, please?" And he'd begin to explain the job. Half the applicants would go away when he got to the part about the salary structure, and most of those who remained offered little competition to anyone who was sober, clean and able to construct an English sentence.

That's the way we'd all been hired, the six or eight of us who frowned under the *Leader*'s sickly fluorescent lights that winter, and most of us made no secret of our desire for better things. I went to work there a couple of weeks after losing my job on one of the metropolitan dailies, and stayed only until I was rescued the next spring by the big picture magazine that still employs me. The others had other explanations, which, like me, they spent a great deal of time discussing: it was a great place for shrill and redundant hard-luck stories.

But Leon Sobel joined the staff about a month after I did, and from the moment Kramm led him into the editorial room we all knew he was going to be different. He stood among the messy desks with the look of a man surveying new fields to conquer, and when Kramm introduced him around (forgetting half our names) he made a theatrically solemn business out of shaking hands. He was about thirty-five, older than most of us, a very small, tense man with black hair that seemed to explode from his skull and a humorless thin-lipped face that was blotched with the scars of acne. His eyebrows were always in motion when he talked, and his eyes, not so much piercing as anxious to pierce, never left the eyes of his listener.

The first thing I learned about him was that he'd never held an office job before: he had been a sheet-metal worker all his adult life. What's more, he hadn't come to the *Leader* out of need, like the rest of us, but, as he put it, out of principle. To do so, in fact, he had given up a factory job paying nearly twice the money.

"What'sa matter, don'tcha believe me?" he asked, after telling me this.

"Well, it's not that," I said. "It's just that I—"

"Maybe you think I'm crazy," he said, and screwed up his face into a canny smile.

I tried to protest, but he wouldn't have it. "Listen, don't worry, McCabe. I'm called crazy a lotta times already. It don't bother me. My wife says, 'Leon, you gotta expect it.' She says, 'People never understand a man who wants something more outa life than just money.' And she's right! She's right!"

"No," I said. "Wait a second. I—"

"People think you gotta be one of two things: either you're a shark, or you gotta lay back and let the sharks eatcha alive—this is the world. Me, I'm the kinda guy's gotta go out and wrestle with the sharks. Why? I dunno why. This is crazy? Okay."

"Wait a second," I said. And I tried to explain that I had nothing whatever against his striking a blow for social justice, if that was what he had in mind; it was just that I thought *The Labor Leader* was about the least likely place in the world for him to do it.

But his shrug told me I was quibbling. "So?" he said. "It's a paper, isn't it? Well, I'm a writer. And what good's a writer if he don't get printed? Listen." He lifted one haunch and placed it on the edge of my desk—he was too short a man to do this gracefully, but the force of his argument helped him to bring it off. "Listen, McCabe. You're a young kid yet. I wanna tellya something. Know how many books I wrote already?" And now his hands came into play, as they always did sooner or later. Both stubby fists were thrust under my nose and allowed to shake there for a moment before they burst into a thicket of stiff, quivering fingers—only the thumb of one hand remained folded down. "Nine," he said, and the hands fell limp on his thigh, to rest until he needed them again. "Nine. Novels, philosophy, political theory—the entire gamut. And not one of 'em published. Believe me, I been around awhile."

"I believe you," I said.

"So finally I sat down and figured: What's the answer? And I figured this: the trouble with my books is, they tell the truth. And the truth is a funny thing, McCabe. People wanna read it, but they only wanna read it when it comes from somebody they already know their name. Am I right? So all right. I figure, I wanna write these books, first I gotta build up a name for myself. This is worth any sacrifice. This is the only way. You know something, McCabe? The last one I wrote took me two years?" Two fingers sprang up to illustrate the point, and dropped again. "Two years, working four, five hours every night and all day long on the weekends. And then you oughta seen the crap I got from the publishers. Every damn publisher in town. My wife cried. She says, 'But why, Leon? Why?'" Here his lips curled tight against his small, stained teeth, and the fist of one hand smacked the palm of the other on his thigh, but then he relaxed. "I told her, 'Listen, honey. You know why.'" And now he was smiling at me in quiet triumph. "I says, 'This book told the truth. That's why.'" Then he winked, slid off my desk and walked away, erect and jaunty in his soiled sport shirt and his dark serge pants that hung loose and shiny in the seat. That was Sobel.

It took him a little while to loosen up in the job: for the first week or so, when he wasn't talking, he went at everything with a zeal and a fear of failure that disconcerted everyone but Finney, the managing editor. Like the rest of us, Sobel had a list of twelve or fifteen union offices around town, and the main part of his job was to keep in touch with them and write up whatever bits of news they gave out. As a rule there was nothing very exciting to write about. The average story ran two or three paragraphs with a single-column head:

PLUMBERS WIN
3¢ PAY HIKE

or something like that. But Sobel composed them all as carefully as sonnets, and after he'd turned one in he would sit chewing his lips in anxiety until Finney raised a forefinger and said, "C'mere a second, Sobel."

Then he'd go over and stand, nodding apologetically, while Finney pointed out some niggling grammatical flaw. "Never end a sentence with a preposition, Sobel. You don't wanna say, 'gave the plumbers new grounds to bargain on.' You wanna say, 'gave the plumbers new grounds on which to bargain.'"

Finney enjoyed these lectures. The annoying thing, from a spectator's point of view, was that Sobel took so long to learn what everyone else seemed to know instinctively: that Finney was scared of his own shadow and would back down on anything at all if you raised your voice. He was a frail, nervous man who dribbled on his chin when he got excited and raked trembling fingers through his thickly oiled hair, with the result that his fingers spread hair oil, like a spoor of his personality, to everything he touched: his clothes, his pencils, his telephone and his typewriter keys. I guess the main reason he was managing editor was that nobody else would submit to the bullying he took from Kramm: their editorial conferences always began with Kramm shouting "Finney! Finney!" from behind his partition, and Finney jumping like a squirrel to hurry inside. Then you'd hear the relentless drone of Kramm's demands and the quavering sputter of Finney's explanations, and it would end with a thump as Kramm socked his desk. "*No*, Finney. No, no, *no*! What's the matter with you? I gotta draw you a picture? All right, all right, get outa here, I'll do it myself." At first you might wonder why Finney took it—nobody could need a job that badly—but the answer lay in the fact that there were only three bylined pieces in *The Labor Leader*: a boiler-plated sports feature that we got from a syndicate, a ponderous column called "LABOR TODAY, by Julius Kramm," that ran facing the editorial page, and a double-column box in the back of the book with the heading:

BROADWAY BEAT
BY WES FINNEY

There was even a thumbnail picture of him in the upper left-hand corner, hair slicked down and teeth bared in a confident smile. The text managed to work in a labor angle here and there—a paragraph on Actors' Equity, say, or the stagehands' union—but mostly he played it straight, in the manner of two or three real Broadway-and-nightclub columnists. "Heard about the new thrush at the Copa?" he would ask the labor leaders; then he'd give them her name, with a sly note about her bust and hip measurements and a folksy note about the state from which she "hailed," and he'd wind it up like this: "She's got the whole town talking, and turning up in droves. Their verdict, in which this department wholly concurs: the lady has class." No reader could have guessed that Wes Finney's shoes needed repair, that he got no complimentary tickets to anything and never went out except to take in a movie or to crouch over a liverwurst sandwich at the Automat. He wrote the column on his own time and got extra money for it—the figure I heard was fifty dollars a month. So it was a mutually satisfactory deal: for that small sum Kramm held his whipping boy in absolute bondage; for that small torture Finney could paste clippings in a scrapbook, with all the contamination of *The Labor Leader* sheared away into the wastebasket of his furnished room, and whisper himself to sleep with dreams of ultimate freedom.

Anyway, this was the man who could make Sobel apologize for the grammar of his news stories, and it was a sad thing to watch. Of course, it couldn't go on forever, and one day it stopped.

Finney had called Sobel over to explain about split infinitives, and Sobel was wrinkling his brow in an effort to understand. Neither of them noticed that Kramm was standing in the doorway of his office a few feet away, listening, and looking at the wet end of his cigar as if it tasted terrible.

"Finney," he said. "You wanna be an English teacher, get a job in the high school."

Startled, Finney stuck a pencil behind his ear without noticing that another pencil was already there, and both pencils clattered to the floor. "Well, I—" he said. "Just thought I'd—"

"Finney, this does not interest me. Pick up your pencils and listen to me, please. For your information, Mr. Sobel is not supposed to be a literary Englishman. He is supposed to be a literate American, and this I believe he is. Do I make myself clear?"

And the look on Sobel's face as he walked back to his own desk was that of a man released from prison.

From that moment on he began to relax; or almost from that moment—what seemed to clinch the transformation was O'Leary's hat.

O'Leary was a recent City College graduate and one of the best men on the staff (he has since done very well; you'll often see his byline in one of the evening papers), and the hat he wore that winter was of the waterproof cloth kind that is sold in raincoat shops. There was nothing very dashing about it—in fact its floppiness made O'Leary's face look too thin—but Sobel must secretly have admired it as a symbol of journalism, or of nonconformity, for one morning he showed up in an identical one, brand new. It looked even worse on him than on O'Leary, particularly when worn with his lumpy brown overcoat, but he seemed to cherish it. He developed a whole new set of mannerisms to go with the hat: cocking it back, with a flip of the index finger as he settled down to make his morning phone calls ("This is Leon Sobel, of *The Labor Leader* . . ."), tugging it smartly forward as he left the office on a reporting assignment, twirling it onto a peg when he came back to write his story. At the end of the day, when he'd dropped the last of his copy into Finney's wire basket, he would shape the hat into a careless slant over one eyebrow, swing the overcoat around his shoulders and stride out with a loose salute of farewell, and I used to picture him studying his reflection in the black subway windows all the way home to the Bronx.

He seemed determined to love his work. He even brought in a snapshot of his family—a tired, abjectly smiling woman and two small sons—and fastened it to his desktop with cellophane tape. Nobody else ever left anything more personal than a book of matches in the office overnight.

One afternoon toward the end of February, Finney summoned me to his oily desk. "McCabe," he said. "Wanna do a column for us?"

"What kind of a column?"

"Labor gossip," he said. "Straight union items with a gossip or a chatter angle—little humor, personalities, stuff like that. Mr. Kramm thinks we need it, and I told him you'd be the best man for the job."

I can't deny that I was flattered (we are all conditioned by our surroundings, after all), but I was also suspicious. "Do I get a byline?"

He began to blink nervously. "Oh, no, no byline," he said. "Mr. Kramm wants this to be anonymous. See, the guys'll give you any items they turn up, and you'll just collect 'em and put 'em in shape. It's just something you can do on office time, part of your regular job. See what I mean?"

I saw what he meant. "Part of my regular salary too," I said. "Right?"

"That's right."

"No thanks," I told him, and then, feeling generous, I suggested that he try O'Leary.

"Nah, I already asked him," Finney said. "He don't wanna do it either. Nobody does."

I should have guessed, of course, that he'd been working down the list of everyone in the office. And to judge from the lateness of the day, I must have been close to the tail end.

Sobel fell in step with me as we left the building after work that night. He was wearing his overcoat cloak-style, the sleeves dangling, and holding his cloth hat in place as he hopped nimbly to avoid the furrows of dirty slush on the sidewalk. "Letcha in on a little secret, McCabe," he said. "I'm doin' a column for the paper. It's all arranged."

"Yeah?" I said. "Any money in it?"

"Money?" He winked. "I'll tell y' about that part. Let's get a cuppa coffee." He led me into the tiled and steaming brilliance of the Automat, and when we were settled at a damp corner table he explained everything. "Finney says no money, see? So I said okay. He says no byline either. I said okay." He winked again. "Playin' it smart."

"How do you mean?"

"How do I mean?" He always repeated your question like that, savoring it, holding his black eyebrows high while he made you wait for the answer. "Listen, I got this Finney figured out. *He* don't decide these things. You think he decides anything around that place? You better wise up, McCabe. Mr. *Kramm* makes the decisions. And Mr. Kramm is an intelligent man, don't kid yourself." Nodding, he raised his coffee cup, but his lips recoiled from the heat of it, puckered, and blew into the steam before they began to sip with gingerly impatience.

"Well," I said, "okay, but I'd check with Kramm before you start counting on anything."

"Check?" He put his cup down with a clatter. "What's to check? Listen, Mr. Kramm wants a column, right? You think he cares if I get a byline or not? Or the money, either—you think if I write a good column he's gonna quibble over payin' me for it? Ya crazy. *Finney's* the one, don'tcha see? *He* don't wanna gimme a break because he's worried about losing his *own* column. Get it? So all right. I check with nobody until I got that column written." He prodded his chest with a stiff thumb. "On my own time. Then I take it to Mr. Kramm and we talk business. You leave it to me." He settled down comfortably, elbows on the table, both hands cradling the cup just short of drinking position while he blew into the steam.

"Well," I said. "I hope you're right. Be nice if it does work out that way."

"Ah, it may not," he conceded, pulling his mouth into a grimace of speculation and tilting his head to one side. "You know. It's a gamble." But he was only saying that out of politeness, to minimize my envy. He could afford to express doubt because he felt none, and I could tell he was already planning the way he'd tell his wife about it.

The next morning Finney came around to each of our desks with instructions that we were to give Sobel any gossip or chatter items we might turn up; the column was scheduled to begin in the next issue. Later I saw him in conference with Sobel, briefing him on how the column was to be written, and I noticed that Finney did all the talking: Sobel just sat there making thin, contemptuous jets of cigarette smoke.

We had just put an issue to press, so the deadline for the column was two weeks away. Not many items turned up at first—it was hard enough getting news out of the unions we covered, let alone "chatter." Whenever someone did hand him a note, Sobel would frown over it, add a scribble of his own and drop it in a desk drawer; once or twice I saw him drop one in the wastebasket. I only remember one of the several pieces I gave him: the business agent of a steamfitters' local I covered had yelled at me through a closed door that he couldn't be bothered that day because his wife had just had twins. But Sobel didn't want it. "So, the guy's got twins," he said. "So what?"

"Suit yourself," I said. "You getting much other stuff?"

He shrugged. "Some. I'm not worried. I'll tellya one thing, though—I'm not using a lotta this crap. This chatter. Who the hell's gonna read it? You can't have a whole column fulla crap like that. Gotta be something to hold it together. Am I right?"

Another time (the column was all he talked about now) he chuckled affectionately and said, "My wife says I'm just as bad now as when I was working on my books. Write, write, write. She don't care, though," he added. "She's really getting excited about this thing. She's telling everybody—the neighbors, everybody. Her brother come over Sunday, starts asking me how the job's going—you know, in a wise-guy kinda way? I just kept quiet, but my wife pipes up: 'Leon's doing a column for the paper now'—and she tells him all about it. Boy, you oughta seen his face."

Every morning he brought in the work he had done the night before, a wad of handwritten papers, and used his lunch hour to type it out and revise it while he chewed a sandwich at his desk. And he was the last one to go home every night; we'd leave him there hammering his typewriter in a trance of concentration. Finney kept bothering him—"How you coming on that feature, Sobel?"—but he always parried the question with squinted eyes and a truculent lift of the chin. "Whaddya worried about? You'll get it." And he would wink at me.

On the morning of the deadline he came to work with a little patch of toilet paper on his cheek; he had cut himself shaving in his nervousness, but otherwise he looked as confident as ever. There were no calls to make that morning—on deadline days we all stayed in to work on copy and proofs—so the first thing he did was to spread out the finished manuscript for a final reading. His absorption was so complete that he didn't look up until Finney was standing at his elbow. "You wanna gimme that feature, Sobel?"

Sobel grabbed up the papers and shielded them with an arrogant forearm. He looked steadily at Finney and said, with a firmness that he must have been rehearsing for two weeks: "I'm showing this to Mr. Kramm. Not you."

Finney's whole face began to twitch in a fit of nerves. "Nah, nah, Mr. Kramm don't need to see it," he said. "Anyway, he's not in yet. C'mon, lemme have it."

"You're wasting your time, Finney," Sobel said. "I'm waiting for Mr. Kramm."

Muttering, avoiding Sobel's triumphant eyes, Finney went back to his own desk, where he was reading proof on BROADWAY BEAT.

My own job that morning was at the layout table, pasting up the dummy for the first section. I was standing there, working with the unwieldly page forms and the paste-clogged scissors, when Sobel sidled up behind me, looking anxious. "You wanna read it, McCabe?" he asked. "Before I turn it in?" And he handed me the manuscript.

The first thing that hit me was that he had clipped a photograph to the top of page 1, a small portrait of himself in his cloth hat. The next thing was his title:

SOBEL SPEAKING
BY LEON SOBEL

I can't remember the exact words of the opening paragraph, but it went something like this:

> This is the "debut" of a new department in *The Labor Leader* and, moreover, it is also "something new" for your correspondent, who has never handled a column before. However, he is far from being a novice with the written word, on the contrary he is an "ink-stained veteran" of many battles on the field of ideas, to be exact nine books have emanated from his pen.
>
> Naturally in those tomes his task was somewhat different than that which it will be in this column, and yet he hopes that this column will also strive as they did to penetrate the basic human mystery, in other words, to tell the truth.

When I looked up I saw he had picked open the razor cut on his cheek and it was bleeding freely. "Well," I said, "for one thing, I wouldn't give it to him with your picture that way—I mean, don't you think it might be better to let him read it first, and then—"

"Okay," he said, blotting at his face with a wadded gray handkerchief. "Okay, I'll take the picture off. G'ahead, read the rest."

But there wasn't time to read the rest. Kramm had come in, Finney had spoken to him, and now he was standing in the door of his office, champing crossly on a dead cigar. "You wanted to see me, Sobel?" he called.

"Just a second," Sobel said. He straightened the pages of SOBEL SPEAKING and detached the photograph, which he jammed into his hip pocket as he started for the door. Halfway there he remembered to take off his hat, and threw it unsuccessfully at the hat stand. Then he disappeared behind the partition, and we all settled down to listen.

It wasn't long before Kramm's reaction came through. "*No*, Sobel. No, no, *no*! What *is* this? What are you tryna put *over* on me here?"

Outside, Finney winced comically and clapped the side of his head, giggling, and O'Leary had to glare at him until he stopped.

We heard Sobel's voice, a blurred sentence or two of protest, and then Kramm came through again: "'Basic human mystery'—this is gossip? This is chatter? You can't follow instructions? Wait a minute—Finney! Finney!"

Finney loped to the door, delighted to be of service, and we heard him making clear, righteous replies to Kramm's interrogation: Yes, he had told Sobel what kind of a column was wanted; yes, he had specified that there was to be no byline; yes, Sobel had been provided with ample gossip material. All we heard from Sobel was something indistinct, said in a very tight, flat voice. Kramm made a guttural reply, and even though we couldn't make out the words we knew it was all over. Then they came out, Finney wearing the foolish smile you sometimes see in the crowds that gape at street accidents, Sobel as expressionless as death.

He picked his hat off the floor and his coat off the stand, put them on, and came over to me. "So long, McCabe," he said. "Take it easy."

Shaking hands with him, I felt my face jump into Finney's idiot smile, and I asked a stupid question. "You leaving?"

He nodded. Then he shook hands with O'Leary—"So long, kid"—and hesitated, uncertain whether to shake hands with the rest of the staff. He settled for a little wave of the forefinger, and walked out to the street.

Finney lost no time in giving us all the inside story in an eager whisper: "The guy's *crazy*! He says to Kramm, 'You take this column or I quit'—just like that. Kramm just looks at him and says, 'Quit? Get outa here, you're fired.' I mean, what *else* could he say?"

Turning away, I saw that the snapshot of Sobel's wife and sons still lay taped to his desk. I stripped it off and took it out to the sidewalk. "Hey, Sobel!" I yelled. He was a block away, very small, walking toward the subway. I started to run after him, nearly breaking my neck on the frozen slush. "Hey *Sobel*!" But he didn't hear me.

Back at the office I found his address in the Bronx telephone directory, put the picture in an envelope and dropped it in the mail, and I wish that were the end of the story.

But that afternoon I called up the editor of a hardware trade journal I had worked on before the war, who said he had no vacancies on his staff but might soon, and would be willing to interview Sobel if he wanted to drop in. It was a foolish idea: the wages there were even lower than on the *Leader*, and besides, it was a place for very young men whose fathers wanted them to learn the hardware business—

Sobel would probably have been ruled out the minute he opened his mouth. But it seemed better than nothing, and as soon as I was out of the office that night I went to a phone booth and looked up Sobel's name again.

A woman's voice answered, but it wasn't the high, faint voice I'd expected. It was low and melodious—that was the first of my several surprises.

"Mrs. Sobel?" I asked, absurdly smiling into the mouthpiece. "Is Leon there?"

She started to say, "Just a minute," but changed it to "Who's calling, please? I'd rather not disturb him right now."

I told her my name and tried to explain about the hardware deal.

"I don't understand," she said. "What kind of a paper is it, exactly?"

"Well, it's a trade journal," I said. "It doesn't amount to much, I guess, but it's—*you* know, a pretty good little thing, of its kind."

"I see," she said. "And you want him to go in and apply for a job? Is that it?"

"Well I mean, if he *wants* to, is all," I said. I was beginning to sweat. It was impossible to reconcile the wan face in Sobel's snapshot with this serene, almost beautiful voice. "I just thought he might like to give it a try, is all."

"Well," she said, "just a minute, I'll ask him." She put down the phone, and I heard them talking in the background. Their words were muffled at first but then I heard Sobel say, "Ah, I'll talk to him—I'll just say thanks for calling." And I heard her answer, with infinite tenderness, "No, honey, why should you? He doesn't deserve it."

"McCabe's all right," he said.

"No he's not," she told him, "or he'd have the decency to leave you alone. Let me do it. Please. I'll get rid of him."

When she came back to the phone she said, "No, my husband says he wouldn't be interested in a job of that kind." Then she thanked me politely, said goodbye, and left me to climb guilty and sweating out of the phone booth.

Fun with a Stranger

ALL THAT SUMMER the children who were due to start third grade under Miss Snell had been warned about her. "Boy, you're gonna get it," the older children would say, distorting their faces with a wicked pleasure. "You're really gonna *get* it. Mrs. *Cleary's* all right" (Mrs. Cleary taught the other, luckier half of third grade) "—she's *fine*, but boy, that *Snell*—you better watch out." So it happened that the morale of Miss Snell's class was low even before school opened in September, and she did little in the first few weeks to improve it.

She was probably sixty, a big rawboned woman with a man's face, and her clothes, if not her very pores, seemed always to exude that dry essence of pencil shavings and chalk dust that is the smell of school. She was strict and humorless, preoccupied with rooting out the things she held intolerable: mumbling, slumping, daydreaming, frequent trips to the bathroom, and, the worst of all, "coming to school without proper supplies." Her small eyes were sharp, and when somebody sent out a stealthy alarm of whispers and nudges to try to borrow a pencil from somebody else, it almost never worked. "What's the trouble back there?" she would demand. "I mean you, John Gerhardt." And John Gerhardt—or Howard White or whoever it happened to be—caught in the middle of a whisper, could only turn red and say, "Nothing."

"Don't mumble. Is it a pencil? Have you come to school without a pencil again? Stand up when you're spoken to."

And there would follow a long lecture on Proper Supplies that ended only after the offender had come forward to receive a pencil from the small hoard on her desk, had been made to say, "Thank you,

Miss Snell," and to repeat, until he said it loud enough for everyone to hear, a promise that he wouldn't chew it or break its point.

With erasers it was even worse because they were more often in short supply, owing to a general tendency to chew them off the ends of pencils. Miss Snell kept a big, shapeless old eraser on her desk, and she seemed very proud of it. "This is *my* eraser," she would say, shaking it at the class. "I've had this eraser for five years. Five years." (And this was not hard to believe, for the eraser looked as old and gray and worn-down as the hand that brandished it.) "I've never played with it because it's not a toy. I've never chewed it because it's not good to eat. And I've never lost it because I'm not foolish and I'm not careless. I need this eraser for my work and I've taken good care of it. Now, why can't you do the same with *your* erasers? I don't know what's the matter with this class. I've never had a class that was so foolish and so careless and so *childish* about its supplies."

She never seemed to lose her temper, but it would almost have been better if she did, for it was the flat, dry, passionless redundance of her scolding that got everybody down. When Miss Snell singled someone out for a special upbraiding it was an ordeal by talk. She would come up to within a foot of her victim's face, her eyes would stare unblinking into his, and the wrinkled gray flesh of her mouth would labor to pronounce his guilt, grimly and deliberately, until all the color faded from the day. She seemed to have no favorites; once she even picked on Alice Johnson, who always had plenty of supplies and did nearly everything right. Alice was mumbling while reading aloud, and when she continued to mumble after several warnings Miss Snell went over and took her book away and lectured her for several minutes running. Alice looked stunned at first; then her eyes filled up, her mouth twitched into terrible shapes, and she gave in to the ultimate humiliation of crying in class.

It was not uncommon to cry in Miss Snell's class, even among the boys. And ironically, it always seemed to be during the lull after one of these scenes—when the only sound in the room was somebody's slow, half-stifled sobbing, and the rest of the class stared straight ahead in an agony of embarrassment—that the noise of group laughter would float in from Mrs. Cleary's class across the hall.

Still, they could not hate Miss Snell, for children's villains must be all black, and there was no denying that Miss Snell was sometimes nice in an awkward, groping way of her own. "When we learn a new word it's like making a friend," she said once. "And we all like to make friends, don't we? Now, for instance, when school began this year you were all strangers to me, but I wanted very much to learn your names and remember your faces, and so I made the effort. It was confusing at first, but before long I'd made friends with all of you. And later on we'll have some good times together—oh, perhaps a little party at Christmastime, or something like that—and then I know I'd be very sorry if I hadn't made that effort, because you can't very well have fun with a stranger, can you?" She gave them a homely, shy smile. "And that's just the way it is with words."

When she said something like that it was more embarrassing than anything else, but it did leave the children with a certain vague sense of responsibility toward her, and often prompted them into a loyal reticence when children from other classes demanded to know how bad she really was. "Well, not too bad," they would say uncomfortably, and try to change the subject.

John Gerhardt and Howard White usually walked home from school together, and often as not, though they tried to avoid it, they were joined by two of the children from Mrs. Cleary's class who lived on their street—Freddy Taylor and his twin sister Grace. John and Howard usually got about as far as the end of the playground before the twins came running after them out of the crowd. "Hey, wait up!" Freddy would call. "Wait up!" And in a moment the twins would fall into step beside them, chattering, swinging their identical plaid canvas schoolbags.

"Guess what we're gonna do next week," Freddy said in his chirping voice one afternoon. "Our whole class, I mean. Guess. Come on, guess."

John Gerhardt had already made it plain to the twins once, in so many words, that he didn't like walking home with a girl, and now he very nearly said something to the effect that one girl was bad enough, but two were more than he could take. Instead he aimed a knowing glance at Howard White and they both walked on in silence, determined not to answer Freddy's insistent "Guess."

But Freddy didn't wait long for an answer. "We're gonna take a field trip," he said, "for our class in Transportation. We're gonna go to Harmon. You know what Harmon is?"

"Sure," Howard White said. "A town."

"No, but I mean, you know what they *do* there? What they do is, that's where they change all the trains coming into New York from steam locomotives to electric power. Mrs. Cleary says we're gonna watch 'em changing the locomotives and everything."

"We're gonna spend practically the whole day," Grace said.

"So what's so great about that?" Howard White asked. "I can go there *any* day, if I feel like it, on my bike." This was an exaggeration—he wasn't allowed out of a two-block radius on his bike—but it sounded good, especially when he added, "I don't need any Mrs. Cleary to take me," with a mincing, sissy emphasis on the "Cleary."

"On a school day?" Grace inquired. "Can you go on a *school* day?"

Lamely Howard murmured, "Sure, if I feel like it," but it was a clear point for the twins.

"Mrs. Cleary says we're gonna take a lotta field trips," Freddy said. "Later on, we're gonna go to the Museum of Natural History, in New York, and a whole lotta other places. Too bad you're not in Mrs. Cleary's class."

"Doesn't bother me any," John Gerhardt said. Then he came up with a direct quotation from his father that seemed appropriate: "Anyway, I don't *go* to school to fool around. I go to school to work. Come on, Howard."

A day or two later it turned out that both classes were scheduled to take the field trip together; Miss Snell had just neglected to tell her pupils about it. When she did tell them it was in one of her nice moods. "I think the trip will be especially valuable," she said, "because it will be instructive and at the same time it will be a real treat for all of us." That afternoon John Gerhardt and Howard White conveyed the news to the twins with studied carelessness and secret delight.

But the victory was short-lived, for the field trip itself only emphasized the difference between the two teachers. Mrs. Cleary ran everything with charm and enthusiasm; she was young and lithe and just about the prettiest woman Miss Snell's class had ever seen. It was she who arranged for the children to climb up and inspect the cab of a huge locomotive that stood idle on a siding, and she who found out where the public toilets were. The most tedious facts about trains came alive when she explained them; the most forbidding engineers and switchmen became jovial hosts when she smiled up at them, with her long hair blowing and her hands plunged jauntily in the pockets of her polo coat.

Through it all Miss Snell hung in the background, gaunt and sour, her shoulders hunched against the wind and her squinted eyes roving, alert for stragglers. At one point she made Mrs. Cleary wait while she called her own class aside and announced that there would be no more field trips if they couldn't learn to stay together in a group. She spoiled everything, and by the time it was over the class was painfully embarrassed for her. She'd had every chance to give a good account of herself that day, and now her failure was as pitiful as it was disappointing. That was the worst part of it: she was pitiful—they didn't even want to look at her, in her sad, lumpy black coat and hat. All they wanted was to get her into the bus and back to school and out of sight as fast as possible.

The events of autumn each brought a special season to the school. First came Halloween, for which several art classes were devoted to crayoned jack-o'-lanterns and arching black cats. Thanksgiving was bigger; for a week or two the children painted turkeys and horns of plenty and brown-clad Pilgrim Fathers with high buckled hats and trumpet-barreled muskets, and in music class they sang "We Gather Together" and "America the Beautiful" again and again. And almost as soon as Thanksgiving was over the long preparations for Christmas began: red and green predominated, and carols were rehearsed for the annual Christmas Pageant. Every day the halls became more thickly festooned with Christmas trimmings, until finally it was the last week before vacation.

"You gonna have a party in your class?" Freddy Taylor inquired one day.

"Sure, prob'ly," John Gerhardt said, though in fact he wasn't sure at all. Except for that one vague reference, many weeks before, Miss Snell had said or hinted nothing whatever about a Christmas party.

"Miss Snell tell ya you're gonna have one, or what?" Grace asked.

"Well, she didn't exactly *tell* us," John Gerhardt said obscurely. Howard White walked along without a word, scuffing his shoes.

"Mrs. Cleary didn't tell us either," Grace said, "because it's supposed to be a surprise, but we know we're gonna have one. Some of the kids who had her last year said so. They said she always has this big party on the last day, with a tree and everything, and favors and things to eat. You gonna have all that?"

"Oh, I don't know," John Gerhardt said. "Sure, prob'ly." But later, when the twins were gone, he got a little worried. "Hey, Howard," he said, "you think she is gonna have a party, or what?"

"Search *me*," Howard White said, with a careful shrug. "*I* didn't say anything." But he was uneasy about it too, and so was the rest of the class. As vacation drew nearer, and particularly during the few anticlimactic days of school left after the Christmas Pageant was over, it seemed less and less likely that Miss Snell was planning a party of any kind, and it preyed on all their minds.

It rained on the last day of school. The morning went by like any other morning, and after lunch, like any other rainy day, the corridors were packed with chattering children in raincoats and rubbers, milling around and waiting for the afternoon classes to begin. Around the third-grade classrooms there was a special tension, for Mrs. Cleary had locked the door of her room, and the word soon spread that she was alone inside making preparations for a party that would begin when the bell rang and last all afternoon. "I peeked," Grace Taylor was saying breathlessly to anyone who would listen. "She's got this little tree with all blue lights, and she's got the room all fixed up and all the desks moved away and everything."

Others from her class tagged after her with questions—"*What'd* you see?" "All blue lights?"—and still others jostled around the door, trying to get a look through the keyhole.

Miss Snell's class pressed self-consciously against the corridor wall, mostly silent, hands in their pockets. Their door was closed too, but nobody wanted to see if it was locked for fear it might swing open and reveal Miss Snell sitting sensibly at her desk, correcting papers. Instead they watched Mrs. Cleary's door, and when it opened at last they watched the other children flock in. All the girls yelled, "Ooh!" in chorus as they disappeared inside, and even from where Miss Snell's class stood they could see that the room was transformed. There *was* a tree with blue lights—the whole room glowed blue, in fact—and the floor was cleared. They could just see the corner of a table in the middle, bearing platters of bright candy and cake. Mrs. Cleary stood in the doorway, beautiful and beaming, slightly flushed with welcome. She gave a kindly, distracted smile to the craning faces of Miss Snell's class, then closed the door again.

A second later Miss Snell's door opened, and the first thing they saw was that the room was unchanged. The desks were all in place, ready for work; their own workaday Christmas paintings still spotted the walls, and there was no other decoration except for the grubby red cardboard letters spelling "Merry Christmas" that had hung over the blackboard all week. But then with a rush of relief they saw that on Miss Snell's desk lay a neat little pile of red-and-white-wrapped packages. Miss Snell stood unsmiling at the head of the room, waiting for the class to get settled. Instinctively, nobody lingered to stare at the gifts or to comment on them. Miss Snell's attitude made it plain that the party hadn't begun yet.

It was time for spelling, and she instructed them to get their pencils and paper ready. In the silences between her enunciation of each word to be spelled, the noise of Mrs. Cleary's class could be heard—repeated laughter and whoops of surprise. But the little pile of gifts made everything all right; the children had only to look at them to know that there was nothing to be embarrassed about, after all. Miss Snell had come through.

The gifts were all wrapped alike, in white tissue paper with red ribbon, and the few whose individual shapes John Gerhardt could discern looked like they might be jackknives. Maybe it would be jackknives for the boys, he thought, and little pocket flashlights for the girls. Or more likely, since jackknives were probably too expensive, it would be something well-meant and useless from the dime store, like individual lead soldiers for the boys and miniature dolls for the girls. But even that would be good enough—something hard and bright to prove that she was human after all, to pull out of a pocket and casually display to the Taylor twins. ("Well, no, not a *party*, exactly, but she gave us all these little presents. Look.")

"John Gerhardt," Miss Snell said, "if you can't give your attention to anything but the . . . things on my desk, perhaps I'd better put them out of sight." The class giggled a little, and she smiled. It was only a small, shy smile, quickly corrected before she turned back to her spelling book, but it was enough to break the tension. While the spelling papers were being collected Howard White leaned close to John Gerhardt and whispered, "Tie clips. Bet it's tie clips for the boys and some kinda jewelry for the girls."

"Sh-sh!" John told him, but then he added, "Too thick for tie clips." There was a general shifting around; everyone expected the party to begin as soon as Miss Snell had all the spelling papers. Instead she called for silence and began the afternoon class in Transportation.

The afternoon wore on. Every time Miss Snell glanced at the clock they expected her to say, "Oh, my goodness—I'd almost forgotten." But she didn't. It was a little after two, with less than an hour of school left, when Miss Snell was interrupted by a knock on the door. "Yes?" she said irritably. "What is it?"

Little Grace Taylor came in, with half a cupcake in her hand and the other half in her mouth. She displayed elaborate surprise at finding the class at work—backing up a step and putting her free hand to her lips.

"Well?" Miss Snell demanded. "Do you want something?"

"Mrs. Cleary wants to know if—"

"Must you talk with your mouth full?"

Grace swallowed. She wasn't the least bit shy. "Mrs. Cleary wants to know if you have any extra paper plates."

"I have no paper plates," Miss Snell said. "And will you kindly inform Mrs. Cleary that this class is in session?"

"All right," Grace took another bite of her cake and turned to leave. Her eyes caught the pile of gifts and she paused to look at them, clearly unimpressed.

"You're holding up the class," Miss Snell said. Grace moved on. At the door she gave the class a sly glance and a quick, silent giggle full of cake crumbs, and then slipped out.

The minute hand crept down to two-thirty, passed it, and inched toward two-forty-five. Finally, at five minutes of three, Miss Snell laid down her book. "All right," she said, "I think we may all put our books away now. This is the last day of school before the holidays, and I've prepared a—little surprise for you." She smiled again. "Now, I think it would be best if you all stay in your places, and I'll just pass these around. Alice Johnson, will you please come and help me? The rest of you stay seated." Alice went forward, and Miss Snell divided the little packages into two heaps, using two pieces of drawing paper as trays. Alice took one paperful, cradling it carefully, and Miss Snell the other. Before they started around the room Miss Snell said, "Now, I think the most courteous thing would be for each of you to wait until everyone is served, and then we'll all open the packages together. All right, Alice."

They started down the aisle, reading the labels and passing out the gifts. The labels were the familiar Woolworth kind with a picture of Santa Claus and "Merry Christmas" printed on them, and Miss Snell had filled them out in her neat blackboard lettering. John Gerhardt's read: "To John G., From Miss Snell." He picked it up, but the moment he felt the package he knew, with a little shock, exactly what it was. There was no surprise left by the time Miss Snell returned to the head of the class and said, "All right."

He peeled off the paper and laid the gift on his desk. It was an eraser, the serviceable ten-cent kind, half white for pencil and half gray for ink. From the corner of his eye he saw that Howard White, beside him, was unwrapping an identical one, and a furtive glance around the room confirmed that all the gifts had been the same. Nobody knew what to do, and for what seemed a full minute the room was silent except for the dwindling rustle of tissue paper. Miss Snell stood at the head of the class, her clasped fingers writhing like dry worms at her waist, her face melted into the soft, tremulous smile of a giver. She looked completely helpless.

At last one of the girls said, "Thank you, Miss Snell," and then the rest of the class said it in ragged unison: "Thank you, Miss Snell."

"You're all very welcome," she said, composing herself, "and I hope you all have a pleasant holiday."

Mercifully, the bell rang then, and in the jostling clamor of retreat to the cloakroom it was no longer necessary to look at Miss Snell. Her voice rose above the noise: "Will you all please dispose of your paper and ribbons in the basket before you leave?"

John Gerhardt yanked on his rubbers, grabbed his raincoat, and elbowed his way out of the cloakroom, out of the classroom and down the noisy corridor. "Hey, Howard, wait up!" he yelled to Howard White, and finally both of them were free of school, running, splashing through puddles on the playground. Miss Snell was left behind now, farther behind with every step; if they ran fast enough they could even avoid the Taylor twins, and then there would be no need to think about any of it anymore. Legs pounding, raincoats streaming, they ran with the exhilaration of escape.

The B.A.R. Man

UNTIL HE GOT his name on the police blotter, and in the papers, nobody had ever thought much about John Fallon. He was employed as a clerk in a big insurance company, where he hulked among the file cabinets with a conscientious frown, his white shirt cuffs turned back to expose a tight gold watch on one wrist and a loose serviceman's identification bracelet, the relic of a braver and more careless time, on the other. He was twenty-nine years old, big and burly, with neatly combed brown hair and a heavy white face. His eyes were kindly except when he widened them in bewilderment or narrowed them in menace, and his mouth was childishly slack except when he tightened it to say something tough. For street wear, he preferred slick, gas-blue suits with stiff shoulders and very low-set buttons, and he walked with the hard, ringing cadence of steel-capped heels. He lived in Sunnyside, Queens, and had been married for ten years to a very thin girl named Rose who suffered from sinus headaches, couldn't have children, and earned more money than he did by typing eighty-seven words a minute without missing a beat on her chewing gum.

Five evenings a week, Sunday through Thursday, the Fallons sat at home playing cards or watching television, and sometimes she would send him out to buy sandwiches and potato salad for a light snack before they went to bed. Friday, being the end of the workweek and the night of the fights on television, was his night with the boys at the Island Bar and Grill, just off Queens Boulevard. The crowd there were friends of habit rather than of choice, and for the first half hour they would stand around self-consciously, insulting one another and jeering at each new arrival ("Oh Jesus, looka what just come in!"). But by the time the fights were over they would usually have joked and drunk themselves into a high good humor, and the evening would often end in song and staggering at two or three o'clock. Fallon's Saturday, after a morning of sleep and an afternoon of helping with the housework, was devoted to the entertainment of his wife: they would catch the show at one of the neighborhood movies and go to an ice-cream parlor afterwards, and they were usually in bed by twelve. Then came the drowsy living-room clutter of newspapers on Sunday, and his week began again.

The trouble might never have happened if his wife had not insisted, that particular Friday, on breaking his routine: there was a Gregory Peck picture in its final showing that night, and she said she saw no reason why he couldn't do without his prize fight, for once in his life. She told him this on Friday morning, and it was the first of many things that went wrong with his day.

At lunch—the special payday lunch that he always shared with three fellow clerks from his office, in a German tavern downtown—the others were all talking about the fights, and Fallon took little part in the conversation. Jack Kopeck, who knew nothing about boxing (he had called the previous week's performance "a damn good bout" when in fact it had been fifteen rounds of clinches and cream-puff sparring, with the mockery of a decision at the end), told the party at some length that the best all-around bout he'd ever seen was in the Navy. And that led to a lot of Navy talk around the table, while Fallon squirmed in boredom.

"So here *I* was," Kopeck was saying, jabbing his breastbone with a manicured thumb in the windup of his third long story, "my first day on a new ship, and nothing but these tailor-made dress blues to stand inspection in. Scared? Jesus, I was shakin' like a leaf. Old man comes around, looks at me, says, 'Where d'ya think *you're* at, sailor? A fancy-dress ball?'"

"Talk about inspections," Mike Boyle said, bugging his round comedian's eyes. "Lemme tell ya, *we* had this commander, he'd take this white glove and wipe his finger down the bulkhead? And brother, if that glove came away with a specka dust on it, you were dead."

Then they started getting sentimental. "Ah, it's a good life, though, the Navy," Kopeck said. "A clean life. The best part about the Navy is, you're somebody, know what I mean? Every man's got his own individual job to do. And I mean what the hell, in the Army all you do is walk around and look stupid like everybody else."

"Brother," said little George Walsh, wiping mustard on his knockwurst, "you can say that again. I had four years in the Army and, believe me, you can say that again."

That was when John Fallon's patience ran out. "Yeah?" he said "What parta the Army was that?"

"What part?" Walsh said, blinking. "Well, I was in the ordnance for a while, in Virginia, and then I was in Texas, and Georgia—how d'ya mean, what part?"

Fallon's eyes narrowed and his lips curled tight. "You oughta tried an infantry outfit, Mac," he said.

"Oh, well," Walsh deferred with a wavering smile.

But Kopeck and Boyle took up the challenge, grinning at him.

"The *infantry*?" Boyle said. "Whadda they got—specialists in the infantry?"

"You betcher ass they got specialists," Fallon said. "Every son of a bitch *in* a rifle company's a specialist, if you wanna know something. And I'll tellya *one* thing, Mac—they don't worry about no silk gloves and no tailor-made clothes, you can betcher ass on that."

"Wait a second," Kopeck said. "I wanna know one thing, John. What was your specialty?"

"I was a B.A.R. man," Fallon said.

"What's that?"

And this was the first time Fallon realized how much the crowd in the office had changed over the years. In the old days, back around 'forty-nine or 'fifty, with the old crowd, anyone who didn't know what a B.A.R. was would almost certainly have kept his mouth shut.

"The B.A.R.," Fallon said, laying down his fork, "is the Browning Automatic Rifle. It's a thirty-caliber, magazine-fed, fully-automatic piece that provides the major firepower of a twelve-man rifle squad. That answer your question?"

"How d'ya mean?" Boyle inquired. "Like a tommy gun?"

And Fallon had to explain, as if he were talking to children or girls, that it was nothing at all like a tommy gun and that its tactical function was entirely different; finally he had to take out his mechanical pencil and draw, from memory and love, a silhouette of the weapon on the back of his weekly pay envelope.

"So okay," Kopeck said, "tell me one thing, John. Whaddya have to know to shoot this gun? You gotta have special training, or what?"

Fallon's eyes were angry slits as he crammed the pencil and envelope back into his coat. "Try it sometime," he said. "Try walkin' twenty miles on an empty stomach with that B.A.R. and a full ammo belt on your back, and then lay down in some swamp with the water up over your ass, and you're pinned down by machine-gun and mortar fire and your squad leader starts yellin', 'Get that B.A.R. up!' and you gotta cover the withdrawal of the whole platoon or the whole damn company. *Try* it sometime, Mac—*you'll* find out whatcha gotta have." And he took too deep a drink of his beer, which made him cough and sputter into his big freckled fist.

"Easy, easy," Boyle said, smiling. "Don't bust a gut, boy."

But Fallon only wiped his mouth and glared at them, breathing hard.

"Okay, so you're a hero," Kopeck said lightly. "You're a fighting man. Tell me one thing, though, John. Did you personally shoot this gun in combat?"

"Whadda you think?" Fallon said through thin, unmoving lips.

"How many times?"

The fact of the matter was that Fallon, as a husky and competent soldier of nineteen, many times pronounced "a damn good B.A.R. man" by the others in his squad, had carried his weapon on blistered feet over miles of road and field and forest in the last two months of the war, had lain with it under many artillery and mortar barrages and jabbed it at the chests of many freshly taken German prisoners; but he'd had occasion to fire it only twice, at vague areas rather than men, had brought down nothing either time, and had been mildly reprimanded the second time for wasting ammunition.

"Nunnya goddamn business how many!" he said, and the others looked down at their plates with ill-concealed smiles. He glared at them, defying anyone to make a crack, but the worst part of it was that none of them said anything. They ate or drank their beer in silence, and after a while they changed the subject.

Fallon did not smile all afternoon, and he was still sullen when he met his wife at the supermarket, near home, for their weekend shopping. She looked tired, the way she always did when her sinus trouble was about to get worse, and while he ponderously wheeled the wire-mesh cart behind her he kept turning his head to follow the churning hips and full breasts of other young women in the store.

"Ow!" she cried once, and dropped a box of Ritz crackers to rub her heel in pain. "Can't you watch where you're *going* with that thing? You better let me push it."

"You shouldn't of stopped so sudden," he told her. "I didn't know you were gonna stop."

And thereafter, to make sure he didn't run the cart into her again, he had to give his full attention to her own narrow body and stick-thin legs. From the side view, Rose Fallon seemed always to be leaning slightly forward; walking, her buttocks seemed to float as an ungraceful separate entity in her wake. Some years ago, a doctor had explained her sterility with the fact that her womb was tipped, and told her it might be corrected by a course of exercises; she had done the exercises halfheartedly for a while and gradually given them up. Fallon could never remember whether her odd posture was supposed to be the cause or the result of the inner condition, but he did know for certain that, like her sinus trouble, it had grown worse in the years since their marriage; he could have sworn she stood straight when he met her.

"You want Rice Krispies or Post Toasties, John?" she asked him.

"Rice Krispies."

"Well, but we just had that last week. Aren't you tired of it?"

"Okay, the other, then."

"What are you mumbling for? I can't hear you."

"Post Toasties, I said!"

Walking home, he was puffing more than usual under the double armload of groceries. "What's the *matter*?" she asked, when he stopped to change his grip on the bags.

"Guess I'm outa shape," he said. "I oughta get out and play some handball."

"Oh, honestly," she said. "You're always saying that, and all you ever do is lie around and read the papers."

She took a bath before fixing the dinner, and then ate with a bulky housecoat roped around her in her usual state of post-bath dishevelment: hair damp, skin dry and porous, no lipstick and a smiling spoor of milk around the upper borders of her unsmiling mouth. "Where do you think you're going?" she said, when he had pushed his plate away and stood up. "Look at that—a full glass of milk on the table. Honestly, John, you're the one that makes me *buy* milk and then when I buy it you go and leave a full glass on the table. Now come back here and drink that up."

He went back and gulped the milk, which made him feel ill.

When her meal was over she began her careful preparations for the evening out; long after he had washed and dried the dishes she was still at the ironing board, pressing the skirt and blouse she planned to wear to the movies. He sat down to wait for her. "Be late to the show if you don't get a move on," he said.

"Oh, don't be silly. We've got practically a whole hour. What's the *matter* with you tonight, anyway?"

Her spike-heeled street shoes looked absurd under the ankle-length wrapper, particularly when she stooped over, splay-toed, to pull out the wall plug of the ironing cord.

"How come you quit those exercises?" he asked her.

"What exercises? What are you talking about?"

"You know," he said. "You know. Those exercises for your tipped utiyus."

"*Uterus*," she said. "You always say 'utiyus.' It's *uterus*."

"So what the hell's the difference? Why'd ya quit 'em?"

"Oh, honestly, John," she said, folding up the ironing board. "Why bring that up *now*, for heaven's sake?"

"So whaddya wanna do? Walk around with a tipped utiyus the resta ya life, or what?"

"Well," she said, "I certainly don't wanna get pregnant, if that's what you mean. May I ask where we'd be if I had to quit my job?"

He got up and began to stalk around the living room, glaring fiercely at the lamp shades, the watercolor flower paintings, and the small china figure of a seated, sleeping Mexican at whose back bloomed a dry cactus plant. He went to the bedroom, where her fresh underwear was laid out for the evening, and picked up a white brassiere containing the foam-rubber cups without which her chest was as meager as a boy's. When she came in he turned on her, waving it in her startled face, and said, "Why d'ya *wear* these goddamn things?"

She snatched the brassiere from him and backed against the door-jamb, her eyes raking him up and down. "Now, *look*," she said. "I've had *enough* of this. Are you gonna start acting decent, or not? Are we going to the movies, or not?"

And suddenly she looked so pathetic that he couldn't stand it. He grabbed his coat and pushed past her. "Do whatcha like," he said. "I'm goin' out." And he slammed out of the apartment.

It wasn't until he swung onto Queens Boulevard that his muscles began to relax and his breathing to slow down. He didn't stop at the Island Bar and Grill—it was too early for the fights anyway, and he was too upset to enjoy them. Instead, he clattered down the stairs to the subway and whipped through the turnstile, headed for Manhattan.

He had set a vague course for Times Square, but thirst overcame him at Third Avenue; he went up to the street and had two shots with a beer chaser in the first bar he came to, a bleak place with stamped-tin walls and a urine smell. On his right, at the bar, an old woman was waving her cigarette like a baton and singing "Peg o' My Heart," and on his left one middle-aged man was saying to another, "Well, my point of view is this: maybe you can argue with McCarthy's methods, but son of a bitch, you can't argue with him on principle. Am I right?"

Fallon left the place and went to another near Lexington, a chrome-and-leather place where everyone looked bluish green in the subtle light. There he stood at the bar beside two young soldiers with divisional patches on their sleeves and infantry braid on the PX caps that lay folded under their shoulder tabs. They wore no ribbons—they were only kids—but Fallon could tell they were no recruits: they knew how to wear their Eisenhower jackets, for one thing, short and skintight, and their combat boots were soft and almost black with polish. Both their heads suddenly turned to look past him, and Fallon, turning too, joined them in watching a girl in a tight tan skirt detach herself from a party at one of the tables in a shadowy corner. She brushed past them, murmuring, "Excuse me," and all three of their heads were drawn to watch her buttocks shift and settle, shift and settle until she disappeared into the ladies' room.

"Man, that's rough," the shorter of the two soldiers said, and his grin included Fallon, who grinned back.

"Oughta be a law against wavin' it around that way," the tall soldier said. "Bad for the troops."

Their accents were Western, and they both had the kind of blond, squint-eyed, country-boy faces that Fallon remembered from his old platoon. "What outfit you boys in?" he inquired. "I oughta reckanize that patch."

They told him, and he said, "Oh, yeah, sure—I remember. They were in the Seventh Army, right? Back in 'forty-four and -five?"

"Couldn't say for sure, sir," the short soldier said. "That was a good bit before our time."

"Where the hellya get that 'sir' stuff?" Fallon demanded heartily. "I wasn't no officer. I never made better'n pfc, except for a couple weeks when they made me an acting buck sergeant, there in Germany. I was a B.A.R. man."

The short soldier looked him over. "That figures," he said. "You got the build for a B.A.R. man. That old B.A.R.'s a heavy son of a bitch."

"You're right," Fallon said. "It's heavy, but, I wanna tellya, it's a damn sweet weapon in combat. Listen, what are you boys drinking? My name's Johnny Fallon, by the way."

They shook hands with him, mumbling their names, and when the girl in the tan skirt came out of the ladies' room they all turned to watch her again. This time, watching until she had settled herself at her table, they concentrated on the wobbling fullness of her blouse.

"Man," the short soldier said, "I mean, that's a pair."

"Probably ain't real," the tall one said.

"They're real, son," Fallon assured him, turning back to his beer with a man-of-the-world wink. "They're real. I can spot a paira falsies a mile away."

They had a few more rounds, talking Army, and after a while the tall soldier asked Fallon how to get to the Central Plaza, where he'd heard about the Friday night jazz; then they were all three rolling down Second Avenue in a cab, for which Fallon paid. While they stood waiting for the elevator at the Central Plaza, he worked the wedding ring off his finger and stuck it in his watch pocket.

The wide, high ballroom was jammed with young men and girls; hundreds of them sat listening or laughing around pitchers of beer; another hundred danced wildly in a cleared space between banks of tables. On the bandstand, far away, a sweating group of colored and white musicians bore down, their horns gleaming in the smoky light.

Fallon, to whom all jazz sounded the same, took on the look of a connoisseur as he slouched in the doorway, his face tense and glazed under the squeal of clarinets, his gas-blue trousers quivering with the slight, rhythmic dip of his knees and his fingers snapping loosely to the beat of the drums. But it wasn't music that possessed him as he steered the soldiers to a table next to three girls, nor was it music that made him get up, as soon as the band played something slow enough, and ask the best-looking of the three to dance. She was tall and well-built, a black-haired Italian girl with a faint shine of sweat on her brow, and as she walked ahead of him toward the dance floor, threading her way between the tables, he reveled in the slow grace of her twisting hips and floating skirt. In his exultant, beer-blurred mind he already knew how it would be when he took her home—how she would feel to his exploring hands in the dark privacy of the taxi, and how she would be later, undulant and naked, in some ultimate vague bedroom at the end of the night. And as soon as they reached the dance floor, when she turned around and lifted her arms, he crushed her tight and warm against him.

"Now, *look*," she said, arching back angrily so that the cords stood out in her damp neck. "Is that what you call *dancing*?"

He relaxed his grip, trembling, and grinned at her. "Take it easy, honey," he said. "I won't bite."

"Never mind the 'honey,' either," she said, and that was all she said until the dance was over.

But she had to stay with him, for the two soldiers had moved in on her lively, giggling girlfriends. They were all at the same table now, and for half an hour the six of them sat there in an uneasy party mood: one of the other girls (they were both small and blonde) kept shrieking with laughter at the things the short soldier was mumbling to her, and the other had the tall soldier's long arm around her neck. But Fallon's big brunette, who had reluctantly given her name as Marie, sat silent and primly straight beside him, snapping and unsnapping the clasp of the handbag in her lap. Fallon's fingers gripped the back of her chair with white-knuckled intensity, but whenever he let them slip tentatively to her shoulder she would shrug free.

"You live around here, Marie?" he asked her.

"The Bronx," she said.

"You come down here often?"

"Sometimes."

"Care for a cigarette?"

"I don't smoke."

Fallon's face was burning, the small curving vein in his right temple throbbed visibly, and sweat was sliding down his ribs. He was like a boy on his first date, paralyzed and stricken dumb by the nearness of her warm dress, by the smell of her perfume, by the way her delicate fingers worked on the handbag and the way the moisture glistened on her plump lower lip.

At the next table a young sailor stood up and bellowed something through cupped hands at the bandstand, and the cry was taken up elsewhere around the room. It sounded like "We want the saints!" but Fallon couldn't make sense of it. At least it gave him an opening. "What's that they're yellin'?" he asked her.

"'The Saints,'" she told him, meeting his eyes just long enough to impart the information. "They wanna hear 'The Saints.'"

"Oh."

After that they stopped talking altogether for a long time until Marie made a face of impatience at the nearest of her girlfriends. "Let's go, hey," she said. "C'mon. I wanna go home."

"Aw, *Marie*," the other girl said, flushed with beer and flirtation (she was wearing the short soldier's overseas cap now). "Don't be such a stupid." Then, seeing Fallon's tortured face, she tried to help him out. "Are you in the Army too?" she asked brightly, leaning toward him across the table.

"Me?" Fallon said, startled. "No, I—I used to be, though. I been outa the Army for quite a while now."

"Oh, yeah?"

"He used to be a B.A.R. man," the short soldier told her.

"Oh, yeah?"

"We want 'The Saints'!" "We want 'The Saints'!" They were yelling it from all corners of the enormous room now, with greater and greater urgency.

"C'mon, hey," Marie said again to her girlfriend. "Let's go, I'm tired."

"So *go* then," the girl in the soldier's hat said crossly. "*Go* if you want to, Marie. Can'tcha go home by yourself?"

"No, wait, listen—" Fallon sprang to his feet. "Don't go yet,

Marie—I'll tell ya what. I'll go get some more beer, okay?" And he bolted from the table before she could refuse.

"No more for me," she called after him, but he was already three tables away, walking fast toward the little ell of the room where the bar was. "Bitch," he was whispering. "Bitch. Bitch." And the images that tortured him now, while he stood in line at the makeshift bar, were intensified by rage: there would be struggling limbs and torn clothes in the taxi; there would be blind force in the bedroom, and stifled cries of pain that would turn to whimpering and finally to spastic moans of lust. Oh, he'd loosen her up! He'd loosen her up!

"C'mon, c'mon," he said to the men who were fumbling with pitchers and beer spigots and wet dollar bills behind the bar.

"We—want—'The Saints'!" "We—want—'The Saints'!" The chant in the ballroom reached its climax. Then, after the drums built up a relentless, brutal rhythm that grew all but intolerable until it ended in a cymbal smash and gave way to the blare of the brass section, the crowd went wild. It took some seconds for Fallon to realize, getting his pitcher of beer at last and turning away from the bar, that the band was playing "When the Saints Go Marching In."

The place was a madhouse. Girls screamed and boys stood yelling on chairs, waving their arms; glasses were smashed and chairs sent spinning, and four policemen stood alert along the walls, ready for a riot as the band rode it out.

When the saints
Go marching in
Oh, when the saints go marching in . . .

Fallon moved in jostled bewilderment through the noise, trying to find his party. He found their table, but couldn't be sure it was theirs—it was empty except for a crumpled cigarette package and a wet stain of beer, and one of its chairs lay overturned on the floor. He thought he saw Marie among the frantic dancers, but it turned out to be another big brunette in the same kind of dress. Then he thought he saw the short soldier gesturing wildly across the room, and made his way over to him, but it was another soldier with a country-boy face. Fallon turned around and around, sweating, looking everywhere in the dizzy crowd. Then a boy in a damp pink shirt reeled heavily against his elbow and the beer spilled in a cold rush on his hand and sleeve, and that was when he realized they were gone. They had ditched him.

He was out on the street and walking, fast and hard on his steel-capped heels, and the night traffic noises were appallingly quiet after the bedlam of shouting and jazz. He walked with no idea of direction and no sense of time, aware of nothing beyond the pound of his heels, the thrust and pull of his muscles, the quavering intake and sharp outward rush of his breath and the pump of his blood.

He didn't know if ten minutes or an hour passed, twenty blocks or five, before he had to slow down and stop on the fringe of a small crowd that clustered around a lighted doorway where policemen were waving the people on.

"Keep moving," one of the policemen was saying. "Move along, please. Keep moving."

But Fallon, like most of the others, stood still. It was the doorway to some kind of lecture hall—he could tell that by the bulletin board that was just visible under the yellow lights inside, and by the flight of marble stairs that led up to what must have been an auditorium. But what caught most of his attention was the picket line: three men about his own age, their eyes agleam with righteousness, wearing the blue-and-gold overseas caps of some veterans' organization and carrying placards that said:

SMOKE OUT THIS FIFTH AMENDMENT COMMIE
PROF. MITCHELL GO BACK TO RUSSIA
AMERICA'S FIGHTING SONS PROTEST MITCHELL

"Move along," the police were saying. "Keep moving."

"Civil rights, my ass," said a flat muttering voice at Fallon's elbow. "They oughta lock this Mitchell up. You read what he said in the Senate hearing?" And Fallon, nodding, recalled a fragile, snobbish face in a number of newspaper pictures.

"Look at there—" the muttering voice said. "Here they come. They're comin' out now."

And they were. Down the marble steps they came, past the bulletin board and out onto the sidewalk: men in raincoats and greasy tweeds, petulant, Greenwich Village–looking girls in tight pants, a few Negroes, a few very clean, self-conscious college boys.

The pickets were backed off and standing still now, holding their placards high with one hand and curving the other around their mouths to call, "Boo-oo! Boo-oo!"

The crowd picked it up: "Boo-oo!" "Boo-oo!" And somebody called, "Go back to Russia!"

"Keep moving," the cops were saying. "Move along, now. Keep moving."

"There he is," said the muttering voice. "There he comes now—that's Mitchell."

And Fallon saw him: a tall, slight man in a cheap double-breasted suit that was too big for him, carrying a briefcase and flanked by two plain women in glasses. There was the snobbish face of the newspaper pictures, turning slowly from side to side now, with a serene, superior smile that seemed to be saying, to everyone it met: *Oh, you poor fool. You poor fool.*

"KILL that bastard!"

Not until several people whirled to look at him did Fallon realize he was yelling; then all he knew was that he had to yell again and again until his voice broke, like a child in tears: *"KILL that bastard! KILL 'im! KILL 'im!"*

In four bucking, lunging strides he was through to the front of the crowd; then one of the pickets dropped his placard and rushed him, saying, "Easy, Mac! Take it *easy*—" But Fallon threw him off, grappled with another man and wrenched free again, got both hands on Mitchell's coat front and tore him down like a crumpled puppet. He saw Mitchell's face recoil in wet-mouthed terror on the sidewalk, and the last thing he knew, as the cop's blue arm swung high over his head, was a sense of absolute fulfillment and relief.

A Really Good Jazz Piano

BECAUSE OF THE midnight noise on both ends of the line there was some confusion at Harry's New York Bar when the call came through. All the bartender could tell at first was that it was a long-distance call from Cannes, evidently from some kind of nightclub, and the operator's frantic voice made it sound like an emergency. Then at last, by plugging his free ear and shouting questions into the phone, he learned that it was only Ken Platt, calling up to have an aimless chat with his friend Carson Wyler, and this made him shake his head in exasperation as he set the phone on the bar beside Carson's glass of Pernod.

"Here," he said. "It's for you, for God's sake. It's your buddy." Like a number of other Paris bartenders he knew them both pretty well: Carson was the handsome one, the one with the slim, witty face and the English-sounding accent; Ken was the fat one who laughed all the time and tagged along. They were both three years out of Yale and trying to get all the fun they could out of living in Europe.

"Carson?" said Ken's eager voice, vibrating painfully in the receiver. "This is Ken—I knew I'd find you there. Listen, when you coming down, anyway?"

Carson puckered his well-shaped brow at the phone. "You know when I'm coming down," he said. "I wired you, I'm coming down Saturday. What's the matter with you?"

"Hell, nothing's the matter with me—maybe a little drunk is all. No, but listen, what I really called up about, there's a man here named Sid plays a really good jazz piano, and I want you to hear him. He's a friend of mine. Listen, wait a minute, I'll get the phone over close so you can hear. Listen to this, now. Wait a minute."

There were some blurred scraping sounds and the sound of Ken laughing and somebody else laughing, and then the piano came through. It sounded tinny in the telephone, but Carson could tell it was good. It was "Sweet Lorraine," done in a rich traditional style with nothing commercial about it, and this surprised him, for Ken was ordinarily a poor judge of music. After a minute he handed the phone to a stranger he had been drinking with, a farm machinery salesman from Philadelphia. "Listen to this," he said. "This is first-rate."

The farm machinery salesman held his ear to the phone with a puzzled look. "What is it?"

"'Sweet Lorraine.'"

"No, but I mean what's the deal? Where's it coming from?"

"Cannes. Somebody Ken turned up down there. You've met Ken, haven't you?"

"No, I haven't," the salesman said, frowning into the phone. "Here, it's stopped now and somebody's talking. You better take it."

"Hello? Hello?" Ken's voice was saying. "Carson?"

"Yes, Ken. I'm right here."

"Where'd you go? Who was that other guy?"

"That was a gentleman from Philadelphia named—" he looked up questioningly.

"Baldinger," said the salesman, straightening his coat.

"Named Mr. Baldinger. He's here at the bar with me."

"Oh. Well listen, how'd you like Sid's playing?"

"Fine, Ken. Tell him I said it was first-rate."

"You want to talk to him? He's right here, wait a minute."

There were some more obscure sounds and then a deep middle-aged voice said, "Hello there."

"How do you do, Sid. My name's Carson Wyler, and I enjoyed your playing very much."

"Well," the voice said. "Thank you, thank you a lot. I appreciate it." It could have been either a colored or a white man's voice, but Carson assumed he was colored, mostly from the slight edge of self-consciousness or pride in the way Ken had said, "He's a friend of mine."

"I'm coming down to Cannes this weekend, Sid," Carson said, "and I'll be looking forward to—"

But Sid had evidently given back the phone, for Ken's voice cut in. "Carson?"

"What?"

"Listen, what time you coming Saturday? I mean what train and everything?" They had originally planned to go to Cannes together, but Carson had become involved with a girl in Paris, and Ken had gone on alone, with the understanding that Carson would join him in a week. Now it had been nearly a month.

"I don't know the exact train," Carson said, with some impatience. "It doesn't matter, does it? I'll see you at the hotel sometime Saturday."

"Okay. Oh and wait, listen, the other reason I called, I want to sponsor Sid here for the IBF, okay?"

"Right. Good idea. Put him back on." And while be was waiting he got out his fountain pen and asked the bartender for the IBF membership book.

"Hello again," Sid's voice said. "What's this I'm supposed to be joining here?"

"The IBF," Carson said. "That stands for International Bar Flies, something they started here at Harry's back in—I don't know. Long time ago. Kind of a club."

"Very good," Sid said, chuckling.

"Now, what it amounts to is this," Carson began, and even the bartender, for whom the IBF was a bore and a nuisance, had to smile with pleasure at the serious, painstaking way he told about it—how each member received a lapel button bearing the insignia of a fly, together with a printed booklet that contained the club rules and a listing of all other IBF bars in the world; how the cardinal rule was that when two members met they were expected to greet one another by brushing the fingers of their right hands on each other's shoulders and saying, "*Bzz-z-z, bzz-z-z!*"

This was one of Carson's special talents, the ability to find and convey an unashamed enjoyment in trivial things. Many people could not have described the IBF to a jazz musician without breaking off in an apologetic laugh to explain that it was, of course, a sort of sad little game for lonely tourists, a square's thing really, and that its very lack of sophistication was what made it fun; Carson told it straight. In much the same way he had once made it fashionable among some of the more literary undergraduates at Yale to spend Sunday mornings respectfully absorbed in the funny papers of the *New York Mirror*; more recently the same trait had rapidly endeared him to many chance acquaintances, notably to his current girl, the young Swedish art student for whom he had stayed in Paris. "You have beautiful taste in everything," she had told him on their first memorable night together. "You have a truly educated, truly original mind."

"Got that?" he said into the phone, and paused to sip his Pernod. "Right. Now if you'll give me your full name and address, Sid, I'll get everything organized on this end." Sid spelled it out and Carson lettered it carefully into the membership book, with his own name and Ken's as cosponsors, while Mr. Baldinger watched. When they were finished Ken's voice came back to say a reluctant goodbye, and they hung up.

"That must've been a pretty expensive telephone call," Mr. Baldinger said, impressed.

"You're right," Carson said. "I guess it was."

"What's the deal on this membership book, anyway? All this barfly business?"

"Oh, aren't you a member, Mr. Baldinger? I thought you were a member. Here, I'll sponsor you, if you like."

Mr. Baldinger got what he later described as an enormous kick out of it: far into the early morning he was still sidling up to everyone at the bar, one after another, and buzzing them.

Carson didn't get to Cannes on Saturday, for it took him longer than he'd planned to conclude his affair with the Swedish girl. He had expected a tearful scene, or at least a brave exchange of tender promises and smiles, but instead she was surprisingly casual about his leaving—even abstracted, as if already concentrating on her next truly educated, truly original mind—and this forced him into several uneasy delays that accomplished nothing except to fill her with impatience and him with a sense of being dispossessed. He didn't get to Cannes until the following Tuesday afternoon, after further telephone talks with Ken, and then, when he eased himself onto the station platform, stiff and sour with hangover, he was damned if he knew why he'd come at all. The sun assaulted him, burning deep into his gritty scalp and raising a quick sweat inside his rumpled suit; it struck blinding glints off the chromework of parked cars and motor scooters and made sickly blue vapors of exhaust rise up against pink buildings; it played garishly among the swarm of tourists who jostled him, showing him all their pores, all the tension of their store-new sports clothes, their clutched suitcases and slung cameras, all the anxiety of their smiling, shouting mouths. Cannes would be like any other resort town in the world, all hurry and disappointment, and why hadn't he stayed where he belonged, in a high cool room with a long-legged girl? Why the hell had he let himself be coaxed and wheedled into coming here?

But then he saw Ken's happy face bobbing in the crowd—"Carson!"—and there he came, running in his overgrown fat boy's thigh-chafing way, clumsy with welcome. "Taxi's over here, take your bag—boy, do you look beat! Get you a shower and a drink first, okay? How the hell are you?"

And riding light on the taxi cushions as they swung onto the Croisette, with its spectacular blaze of blue and gold and its blood-quickening rush of sea air, Carson began to relax. Look at the girls! There were acres of them; and besides, it was good to be with old Ken again. It was easy to see, now, that the thing in Paris could only have gotten worse if he'd stayed. He had left just in time.

Ken couldn't stop talking. Pacing in and out of the bathroom while Carson took his shower, jingling a pocketful of coins, he talked in the laughing, full-throated joy of a man who has gone for weeks without hearing his own voice. The truth was that Ken never really had a good time away from Carson. They were each other's best friends, but it had never been an equal friendship, and they both knew it. At Yale Ken would probably have been left out of everything if it hadn't been for his status as Carson's dull but inseparable companion, and this was a pattern that nothing in Europe had changed. What *was* it about Ken that put people off? Carson had pondered this question for years. Was it just that he was fat and physically awkward, or that he could be strident and silly in his eagerness to be liked? But weren't these essentially likable qualities? No, Carson guessed the closest he could come to a real explanation was the fact that when Ken smiled his upper lip slid back to reveal a small moist inner lip that trembled against his gum. Many people with this kind of mouth may find it no great handicap—Carson was willing to admit that—but it did seem to be the thing everyone remembered most vividly about Ken Platt, whatever more substantial-sounding reasons one might give for avoiding him; in any case it was what Carson himself was always most aware of, in moments of irritation. Right now, for example, in the simple business of trying to dry himself and comb his hair and put on fresh clothes, this wide, moving, double-lipped smile kept getting in his way. It was everywhere, blocking his reach for the towel rack, hovering too close over his jumbled suitcase, swimming in the mirror to eclipse the tying of his tie, until Carson had to clamp his jaws tight to keep from yelling, "All *right*, Ken—shut *up* now!"

But a few minutes later they were able to compose themselves in the shaded silence of the hotel bar. The bartender was peeling a lemon, neatly pinching and pulling back a strip of its bright flesh between thumb and knife blade, and the fine citric smell of it, combining with the scent of gin in the faint smoke of crushed ice, gave flavor to a full restoration of their ease. A couple of cold martinis drowned the last of Carson's pique, and by the time they were out of the place and swinging down the sidewalk on their way to dinner he felt strong again with a sense of the old camaraderie, the familiar, buoyant wealth of Ken's admiration. It was a feeling touched with sadness too, for Ken would soon have to go back to the States. His father in Denver, the author of sarcastic weekly letters on business stationery, was holding open a junior partnership for him, and Ken, having long since completed the Sorbonne courses that were his ostensible reason for coming to France, had no further excuse for staying. Carson, luckier in this as in everything else, had no need of an excuse: he had an adequate private income and no family ties; he could afford to browse around Europe for years, if he felt like it, looking for things that pleased him.

"You're still white as a sheet," he told Ken across their restaurant table. "Haven't you been going to the beach?"

"Sure." Ken looked quickly at his plate. "I've been to the beach a few times. The weather hasn't been too good for it lately, is all."

But Carson guessed the real reason, that Ken was embarrassed to display his body, so he changed the subject. "Oh, by the way," he said. "I brought along the IBF stuff, for that piano player friend of yours."

"Oh, swell." Ken looked up in genuine relief. "I'll take you over there soon as we're finished eating, okay?" And as if to hurry this prospect along he forked a dripping load of salad into his mouth and tore off too big a bite of bread to chew with it, using the remaining stump of bread to mop at the oil and vinegar in his plate. "You'll like him, Carson," he said soberly around his chewing. "He's a great guy. I really admire him a lot." He swallowed with effort and hurried on: "I mean hell, with talent like that he could go back to the States tomorrow and make a fortune, but he likes it here. One thing, of course, he's got a girl here, this really lovely French girl, and I guess he couldn't very well take her back with him—no, but really, it's more than that. People accept him here. As an artist, I mean, as well as a man. Nobody condescends to him, nobody tries to interfere with his music, and that's all he wants out of life. Oh, I mean he doesn't tell you all this—probably be a bore if he did—it's just a thing you sense about him. Comes out in everything he says, his whole mental attitude." He popped the soaked bread into his mouth and chewed it with authority. "I mean the guy's got *authentic* integrity," he said. "Wonderful thing."

"Did sound like a damn good piano," Carson said, reaching for the wine bottle, "what little I heard of it."

"Wait'll you really hear it, though. Wait'll he really gets going."

They both enjoyed the fact that this was Ken's discovery. Always before it had been Carson who led the way, who found the girls and learned the idioms and knew how best to spend each hour; it was Carson who had tracked down all the really colorful places in Paris where you never saw Americans, and who then, just when Ken was learning to find places of his own, had paradoxically made Harry's Bar become the most colorful place of all. Through all this, Ken had been glad enough to follow, shaking his grateful head in wonderment, but it was no small thing to have turned up an incorruptible jazz talent in the back streets of a foreign city, all alone. It proved that Ken's dependence could be less than total after all, and this reflected credit on them both.

The place where Sid played was more of an expensive bar than a nightclub, a small carpeted basement several streets back from the sea. It was still early, and they found him having a drink alone at the bar.

"Well," he said when he saw Ken. "Hello there." He was stocky and well-tailored, a very dark Negro with a pleasant smile full of strong white teeth.

"Sid, I'd like you to meet Carson Wyler. You talked to him on the phone that time, remember?"

"Oh yes," Sid said, shaking hands. "Oh yes. Very pleased to meet you, Carson. What're you gentlemen drinking?"

They made a little ceremony of buttoning the IBF insignia into the lapel of Sid's tan gabardine, of buzzing his shoulder and offering the shoulders of their own identical seersucker jackets to be buzzed in turn. "Well, this is fine," Sid said, chuckling and leafing through the booklet. "Very good." Then he put the booklet in his pocket, finished his drink and slid off the bar stool. "And now if you'll excuse me, I got to go to work."

"Not much of an audience yet," Ken said.

Sid shrugged. "Place like this, I'd just as soon have it that way. You get a big crowd, you always get some square asking for 'Deep in the Heart of Texas,' or some damn thing."

Ken laughed and winked at Carson, and they both turned to watch Sid take his place at the piano, which stood on a low spotlighted dais across the room. He fingered the keys idly for a while to make stray phrases and chords, a craftsman fondling his tools, and then he settled down. The compelling beat emerged, and out of it the climb and waver of the melody, an arrangement of "Baby, Won't You Please Come Home."

They stayed for hours, listening to Sid play and buying him drinks whenever he took a break, to the obvious envy of other customers. Sid's girl came in, tall and brown-haired, with a bright, startled-looking face that was almost beautiful, and Ken introduced her with a small uncontrollable flourish: "This is Jaqueline." She whispered something about not speaking English very well, and when it was time for Sid's next break—the place was filling now and there was considerable applause when he finished—the four of them took a table together.

Ken let Carson do most of the talking now; he was more than content just to sit there, smiling around this tableful of friends with all the serenity of a well-fed young priest. It was the happiest evening of his life in Europe, to a degree that even Carson would never have guessed. In the space of a few hours it filled all the emptiness of his past month, the time that had begun with Carson's saying, "*Go*, then. Can't you go to Cannes by yourself?" It atoned for all the hot miles walked up and down the Croisette on blistered feet to peek like a fool at girls who lay incredibly near naked in the sand; for the cramped, boring bus rides to Nice and Monte Carlo and St. Paul-de-Vence; for the day he had paid a sinister druggist three times too much for a pair of sunglasses only to find, on catching sight of his own image in the gleam of a passing shop window, that they made him look like a great blind fish; for the terrible daily, nightly sense of being young and rich and free on the Riviera—the Riviera!—and of having nothing to do.

Once in the first week he had gone with a prostitute whose canny smile, whose shrill insistence on a high price and whose facial flicker of distaste at the sight of his body had frightened him into an agony of impotence; most other nights he had gotten drunk or sick from bar to bar, afraid of prostitutes and of rebuffs from other girls, afraid even of striking up conversations with men lest they mistake him for a fairy. He had spent a whole afternoon in the French equivalent of a dime store, feigning a shopper's interest in padlocks and shaving cream and cheap tin toys, moving through the bright stale air of the place with a throatful of longing for home. Five nights in a row he had hidden himself in the protective darkness of American movies, just as he'd done years ago in Denver to get away from boys who called him Lard-Ass Platt, and after the last of these entertainments, back in the hotel with the taste of chocolate creams still cloying his mouth, he had cried himself to sleep. But all this was dissolving now under the fine reckless grace of Sid's piano, under the spell of Carson's intelligent smile and the way Carson raised his hands to clap each time the music stopped.

Sometime after midnight, when everyone but Sid had drunk too much, Carson asked him how long he had been away from the States. "Since the war," he said. "I came over in the Army and I never did go back."

Ken, coated with a film of sweat and happiness, thrust his glass high in the air for a toast. "And by God, here's hoping you never have to, Sid."

"Why is that, 'have to'?" Jaqueline said. Her face looked harsh and sober in the dim light. "Why do you say that?"

Ken blinked at her. "Well, I just mean—you know—that he never has to sell out, or anything. He never would, of course."

"What does this mean, 'sell out'?" There was an uneasy silence until Sid laughed in his deep, rumbling way. "Take it easy, honey," he said, and turned to Ken. "We don't look at it that way, you see. Matter of fact, I'm working on angles all the time to get back to the States, make some money there. We both feel that way about it."

"Well, but you're doing all right here, aren't you?" Ken said, almost pleading with him. "You're making enough money and everything, aren't you?"

Sid smiled patiently. "I don't mean a job like this, though, you see. I mean real money."

"You know who is Murray Diamond?" Jaqueline inquired, holding her eyebrows high. "The owner of nightclubs in Las Vegas?"

But Sid was shaking his head and laughing. "Honey, wait a minute—I keep telling you, that's nothing to count on. Murray Diamond happened to be in here the other night, you see," he explained. "Didn't have much time, but he said he'd try to drop around again some night this week. Be a big break for me. 'Course, like I say, that's nothing to count on."

"Well but *Jesus*, Sid—" Ken shook his head in bafflement; then, letting his face tighten into a look of outrage, he thumped the table with a bouncing fist. "Why prostitute yourself?" he demanded. "I mean damn it, you *know* they'll make you prostitute yourself in the States!"

Sid was still smiling, but his eyes had narrowed slightly. "I guess it's all in the way you look at it," he said.

And the worst part of it, for Ken, was that Carson came so quickly to his rescue. "Oh, I'm sure Ken doesn't mean that the way it *sounds*," he said, and while Ken was babbling apologies of his own ("No, of course not, all I meant was—*you* know . . .") he went on to say other things, light, nimble things that only Carson could say, until the awkwardness was gone. When the time came to say goodnight there were handshakes and smiles and promises to see each other soon.

But the minute they were out on the street, Carson turned on Ken. "Why did you have to get so damned sophomoric about that? Couldn't you see how embarrassing it was?"

"I know," Ken said, hurrying to keep pace with Carson's long legs, "I know. But hell, I *was* disappointed in him, Carson. The point is I never heard him *talk* like that before." What he omitted here, of course, was that he had never really heard him talk at all except in the one shy conversation that had led to the calling-up of Harry's Bar that other night, after which Ken had fled back to the hotel in fear of overstaying his welcome.

"Well but even so," Carson said. "Don't you think it's the man's own business what he wants to do with his life?"

"Okay," Ken said, "*okay*. I *told* him I was sorry, didn't I?" He felt so humble now that it took him some minutes to realize that, in a sense, he hadn't come off too badly. After all, Carson's only triumph tonight had been that of the diplomat, the soother of feelings; it was he, Ken, who had done the more dramatic thing. Sophomoric or not, impulsive or not, wasn't there a certain dignity in having spoken his mind that way? Now, licking his lips and glancing at Carson's profile as they walked, he squared his shoulders and tried to make his walk less of a waddle and more of a headlong, manly stride. "It's just that I can't help how I feel, that's all," he said with conviction. "When I'm disappointed in a person I show it, that's all."

"All right. Let's forget it."

And Ken was almost sure, though he hardly dared believe it, that he could detect a grudging respect in Carson's voice.

Everything went wrong the next day. The fading light of afternoon found the two of them slumped and staring in a bleak workingman's café near the railroad station, barely speaking to each other. It was a day that had started out unusually well too—that was the trouble.

They had slept till noon and gone to the beach after lunch, for Ken didn't mind the beach when he wasn't alone, and before long they had picked up two American girls in the easy, graceful way that Carson always managed such things. One minute the girls were sullen strangers, wiping scented oil on their bodies and looking as if any intrusion would mean a call for the police, the next minute they were weak with laughter at the things Carson was saying, moving aside their bottles and their zippered blue TWA satchels to make room for unexpected guests. There was a tall one for Carson with long firm thighs, intelligent eyes and a way of tossing back her hair that gave her a look of real beauty, and a small one for Ken—a cute, freckled good-sport of a girl whose every cheerful glance and gesture showed she was used to taking second best. Ken, bellying deep into the sand with his chin on two stacked fists, smiling up very close to her warm legs, felt almost none of the conversational tension that normally hampered him at times like this. Even when Carson and the tall girl got up to run splashing into the water he was able to hold her interest: she said several times that the Sorbonne "must have been fascinating," and she sympathized with his having to go back to Denver, though she said it was "probably the best thing."

"And your friend's just going to stay over here indefinitely, then?" she asked. "Is it really true what he said? I mean that he isn't studying or working or anything? Just sort of floating around?"

"Well—yeah, that's right." Ken tried a squinty smile like Carson's own. "Why?"

"It's interesting, that's all. I don't think I've ever met a person like that before."

That was when Ken began to realize what the laughter and the scanty French bathing suits had disguised about these girls, that they were girls of a kind neither he nor Carson had dealt with for a long time—suburban, middle-class girls who had dutifully won their parents' blessing for this guided tour; girls who said "golly Moses," whose campus-shop clothes and hockey-field strides would have instantly betrayed them on the street. They were the very kind of girls who had gathered at the punch bowl to murmur "Ugh!" at the way he looked in his first tuxedo, whose ignorant, maddeningly bland little stares of rejection had poisoned all his aching years in Denver and New Haven. They were squares. And the remarkable thing was that he felt so good. Rolling his weight to one elbow, clutching up slow, hot handfuls of sand and emptying them, again and again, he found his flow of words coming quick and smooth:

". . . no, really, there's a lot to see in Paris; shame you couldn't spend more time there; actually most of the places I like best are more or less off the beaten track; of course I was lucky in having a fairly good grasp of the language, and then I met so many congenial . . ."

He was holding his own; he was making out. He hardly even noticed when Carson and the tall girl came trotting back from their swim, as lithe and handsome as a couple in a travel poster, to drop beside them in a bustle of towels and cigarettes and shuddering jokes about how cold the water was. His only mounting worry was that Carson, who must by now have made his own discovery about these girls, would decide they weren't worth bothering with. But a single glance at Carson's subtly smiling, talking face reassured him: sitting tense at the tall girl's feet while she stood to towel her back in a way that made her breasts sway delightfully, Carson was plainly determined to follow through. "Look," he said. "Why don't we all have dinner together? Then afterwards we might—"

Both girls began chattering their regrets: they were afraid not, thanks anyway, they were meeting friends at the hotel for dinner and actually ought to be starting back now, much as they hated to— "God, look at the time!" And they really did sound sorry, so sorry that Ken, gathering all his courage, reached out and held the warm, fine-boned hand that swung at the small girl's thigh as the four of them plodded back toward the bathhouses. She even squeezed his heavy fingers, and smiled at him.

"Some other night, then?" Carson was saying. "Before you leave?"

"Well, actually," the tall girl said, "our evenings do seem to be pretty well booked up. Probably run into you on the beach again though. It's been fun."

"Goddamn little snot-nosed New Rochelle bitch," Carson said when they were alone in the men's bathhouse.

"*Sh-h-h!* Keep your *voice* down, Carson. They can *hear* you in there."

"Oh, don't be an idiot." Carson flung his trunks on the duckboards with a sandy slap. "I hope they do hear me—what the hell's the matter with you?" He looked at Ken as if he hated him. "Pair of goddamn teasing little professional virgins. *Christ*, why didn't I stay in Paris?"

And now here they were, Carson glowering, Ken sulking at the sunset through flyspecked windows while a pushing, garlic-smelling bunch of laborers laughed and shouted over the pinball machine. They went on drinking until long past the dinner hour; then they ate a late, upleasant meal together in a restaurant where the wine was corky and there was too much grease on the fried potatoes. When the messy plates were cleared away Carson lit a cigarette. "What do you want to do tonight?" he said.

There was a faint shine of grease around Ken's mouth and cheeks. "I don't know," he said. "Lot of good places to go, I guess."

"I suppose it would offend your artistic sensibilities to go and hear Sid's piano again?"

Ken gave him a weak, rather testy smile. "You still harping on that?" he said. "Sure I'd like to go."

"Even though he may prostitute himself?"

"Why don't you lay off that, Carson?"

They could hear the piano from the street, even before they walked into the square of light that poured up from the doorway of Sid's place. On the stairs the sound of it grew stronger and richer, mixed now with the sound of a man's hoarse singing, but only when they were down in the room, squinting through the blue smoke, did they realize the singer was Sid himself. Eyes half closed, head turned to smile along his shoulder into the crowd, he was singing as he swayed and worked at the keys.

"Man, she got a pair of eyes. . . ."

The blue spotlight struck winking stars in the moisture of his teeth and the faint thread of sweat that striped his temple.

"I mean they're brighter than the summer skies
And when you see them you gunna realize
Just why I love my sweet Lorraine. . . ."

"Damn place is packed," Carson said. There were no vacancies at the bar, but they stood uncertainly near it for a while, watching Sid perform, until Carson found that one of the girls on the bar stools directly behind him was Jaqueline. "Oh," he said. "Hi. Pretty good crowd tonight."

She smiled and nodded and then craned past him to watch Sid.

"I didn't know he sang too," Carson said. "This something new?"

Her smile gave way to an impatient little frown and she put a forefinger against her lips. Rebuffed, he turned back and moved heavily from one foot to the other. Then he nudged Ken. "You want to go or stay? If you want to stay let's at least sit down."

"*Sh-h-h!*" Several people turned in their chairs to frown at him. "*Sh-h-h!*"

"Come on, then," he said, and he led Ken sidling and stumbling through the ranks of listeners to the only vacant table in the room, a small one down in front, too close to the music and wet with spilled drink, that had been pushed aside to make room for larger parties. Settled there, they could see now that Sid wasn't looking into the crowd at large. He was singing directly to a bored-looking couple in evening clothes who sat a few tables away, a silver-blonde girl who could have been a movie starlet and a small, chubby bald man with a deep tan, a man so obviously Murray Diamond that a casting director might have sent him here to play the part. Sometimes Sid's large eyes would stray to other parts of the room or to the smoke-hung ceiling, but they seemed to come into focus only when he looked at these two people. Even when the song ended and the piano took off alone on a long, intricate variation, even then he kept glancing up to see if they were watching. When he finished, to a small thunderclap of applause, the bald man lifted his face, closed it around an amber cigarette holder and clapped his hands a few times.

"Very nice, Sam," he said.

"My name's Sid, Mr. Diamond," Sid said, "but I thank you a lot just the same. Glad y'enjoyed it, sir." He was leaning back, grinning along his shoulder while his fingers toyed with the keys. "Anything special you'd like to hear, Mr. Diamond? Something old-time? Some more of that real old Dixieland? Maybe a little boogie, maybe something a little on the sweet side, what we call a commercial number? Got all kind of tunes here, waitin' to be played."

"Anything at all, uh, Sid," Murray Diamond said, and then the blonde leaned close and whispered something in his ear. "How about 'Stardust,' there, Sid?" he said. "Can you play 'Stardust'?"

"Well, now, Mr. Diamond. If I couldn't play 'Stardust' I don't guess I'd be in business very long, France or any other country." His grin turned into a deep false laugh and his hands slid into the opening chords of the song.

That was when Carson made his first friendly gesture in hours, sending a warm blush of gratitude into Ken's face. He hitched his chair up close to Ken's and began to speak in a voice so soft that no one could have accused him of making a disturbance. "You know something?" he said. "This is disgusting. My God, I don't care if he wants to go to Las Vegas. I don't even care if he wants to suck *around* for it. This is something else. This is something that turns my stomach." He paused, frowning at the floor, and Ken watched the small wormlike vein moving in his temple. "Putting on this phony accent," Carson said. "All this big phony Uncle Remus routine." And then he went into a little popeyed, head-tossing, hissing parody of Sid. "Yassuh, Mr. Dahmon' suh. Wudg'all lak t'heah, Mr. Dahmon' suh? Got awl *kine* a toons heah, jes' waitin' to played, and yok, yok, yok, and shet ma mouf!" He finished his drink and set the glass down hard. "You know damn well he doesn't have to talk that way. You know damn well he's a perfectly bright, educated guy. My God, on the phone I couldn't even tell he was colored."

"Well yeah," Ken said. "It is sort of depressing."

"Depressing? It's degrading." Carson curled his lip. "It's degenerate."

"I know," Ken said. "I guess that may be partly what I meant about prostituting himself."

"You were certainly right, then. This is damn near enough to make you lose faith in the Negro race."

Being told he was right was always a tonic to Ken, and it was uncommonly bracing after a day like this. He knocked back his drink, straightened his spine and wiped the light mustache of sweat from his upper lip, pressing his mouth into a soft frown to show that his faith, too, in the Negro race was badly shaken. "Boy," he said. "I sure had him figured wrong."

"No," Carson assured him, "you couldn't have known."

"Listen, let's go, then, Carson. The hell with him." And Ken's mind was already full of plans: they would stroll in the cool of the Croisette for a long, serious talk on the meaning of integrity, on how rare it was and how easily counterfeited, how its pursuit was the only struggle worthy of a man's life, until all the discord of the day was erased.

But Carson moved his chair back, smiling and frowning at the same time. "Go?" he said. "What's the matter with you? Don't you want to stay and watch the spectacle? I do. Doesn't it hold a certain horrible fascination for you?" He held up his glass and signaled for two more cognacs.

"Stardust" came to a graceful conclusion and Sid stood up, bathed in applause, to take his break. He loomed directly over their table as he came forward and stepped down off the dais, his big face shining with sweat; he brushed past them, looking toward Diamond's table, and paused there to say, "Thank you, sir," though Diamond hadn't spoken to him, before he made his way back to the bar.

"I suppose he thinks he didn't see us," Carson said.

"Probably just as well," Ken said. "I wouldn't know what to say to him."

"Wouldn't you? I think I would."

The room was stifling, and Ken's cognac had taken on a faintly repellent look and smell in his hand. He loosened his collar and tie with moist fingers. "Come on, Carson," he said. "Let's get out of here. Let's get some air."

Carson ignored him, watching what went on at the bar. Sid drank something Jaqueline offered and then disappeared into the men's room. When he came out a few minutes later, his face dried and composed, Carson turned back and studied his glass. "Here he comes. I think we're going to get the big hello, now, for Diamond's benefit. Watch."

An instant later Sid's fingers brushed the cloth of Carson's shoulder. "*Bzz-z-z, bzz-z-z!*" he said. "How're you tonight?"

Very slowly, Carson turned his head. With heavy eyelids he met Sid's smile for a split second, the way a man might look at a waiter who had accidentally touched him. Then he turned back to his drink.

"Oh-oh," Sid said. "Maybe I didn't do that right. Maybe I got the wrong shoulder here. I'm not too familiar with the rules and regulations yet." Murray Diamond and the blonde were watching, and Sid winked at them, thumbing out the IBF button in his lapel as he moved in sidling steps around the back of Carson's chair. "This here's a club we belong to, Mr. Diamond," he said. "Barflies club. Only trouble is, I'm not very familiar with the rules and regulations yet." He held the attention of nearly everyone in the room as he touched Carson's other shoulder. "*Bzz-z-z, bzz-z-z!*" This time Carson winced and drew his jacket away, glancing at Ken with a perplexed little shrug as if to say, Do you know what this man wants?

Ken didn't know whether to giggle or vomit; both desires were suddenly strong in him, though his face held straight. For a long time afterwards he would remember how the swabbed black plastic of the table looked between his two unmoving hands, how it seemed the only steady surface in the world.

"Say," Sid said, backing away toward the piano with a glazed smile. "What *is* this here? Some kinda conspiracy here?"

Carson allowed a heavy silence to develop. Then with an air of sudden, mild remembrance, seeming to say, Oh yes, of course, he rose and walked over to Sid, who backed up confusedly into the spotlight. Facing him, he extended one limp finger and touched him on the shoulder. "Buzz," he said. "Does that take care of it?" He turned and walked back to his seat.

Ken prayed for someone to laugh—anyone—but no one did. There was no movement in the room but the dying of Sid's smile as he looked at Carson and at Ken, the slow fleshy enclosing of his teeth and the widening of his eyes.

Murray Diamond looked at them too, briefly—a tough, tan little face—then he cleared his throat and said, "How about 'Hold Me,' there, Sid? Can you play 'Hold Me'?" And Sid sat down and began to play, looking at nothing.

With dignity, Carson nodded for the check and laid the right number of thousand- and hundred-franc notes on the saucer. It seemed to take him no time at all to get out of the place, sliding expertly between the tables and out to the stairs, but it took Ken much longer. Lurching, swaying in the smoke like a great imprisoned bear, he was caught and held by Jaqueline's eyes even before he had cleared the last of the tables. They stared relentlessly at the flabby quaver of his smile, they drilled into his back and sent him falling upstairs. And as soon as the sobering night air hit him, as soon as he saw Carson's erect white suit retreating several doors away, he knew what he wanted to do. He wanted to run up and hit him with all his strength between the shoulder blades, one great chopping blow that would drop him to the street, and then he would hit him again, or kick him—yes, kick him—and he'd say, goddamn you! goddamn you, Carson! The words were already in his mouth and he was ready to swing when Carson stopped and turned to face him under a streetlamp.

"What's the trouble, Ken?" he said. "Don't you think that was funny?"

It wasn't what he said that mattered—for a minute it seemed that nothing Carson said would ever matter again—it was that his face was stricken with the uncannily familiar look of his own heart, the very face he himself, Lard-Ass Platt, had shown all his life to others: haunted and vulnerable and terribly dependent, trying to smile, a look that said Please don't leave me alone.

Ken hung his head, either in mercy or shame. "Hell, I don't know, Carson," he said. "Let's forget it. Let's get some coffee somewhere."

"Right." And they were together again. The only problem now was that they had started out in the wrong direction: in order to get to the Croisette they would have to walk back past the lighted doorway of Sid's place. It was like walking through fire, but they did it quickly and with what anyone would have said was perfect composure, heads up, eyes front, so that the piano only came up loud for a second or two before it diminished and died behind them under the rhythm of their heels.

Out with the Old

BUILDING SEVEN, THE TB building, had grown aloof from the rest of Mulloy Veterans' Hospital in the five years since the war. It lay less than fifty yards from Building Six, the paraplegic building—they faced the same flagpole on the same windswept Long Island plain—but there had been no neighborliness between them since the summer of 1948, when the paraplegics got up a petition demanding that the TB's be made to stay on their own lawn. This had caused a good deal of resentment at the time ("Those paraplegic bastards think they *own* the goddamn place"), but it had long since ceased to matter very much; nor did it matter that nobody from Building Seven was allowed in the hospital canteen unless he hid his face in a sterile paper mask.

Who cared? After all, Building Seven was different. The hundred-odd patients of its three yellow wards had nearly all escaped the place at least once or twice over the years, and had every hope of escaping again, for good, as soon as their X rays cleared up or as soon as they had recovered from various kinds of surgery; meanwhile, they did not think of it as home or even as life, exactly, but as a timeless limbo between spells of what, like prisoners, they called "the outside." Another thing: owing to the unmilitary nature of their ailment, they didn't think of themselves primarily as "veterans" anyway (except perhaps at Christmastime, when each man got a multigraphed letter of salutation from the President and a five-dollar bill from the *New York Journal-American*) and so felt no real bond with the wounded and maimed.

Building Seven was a world of its own. It held out a daily choice between its own kind of virtue—staying in bed—and its own kind of vice: midnight crap games, AWOL, and the smuggling of beer and whiskey through the fire-exit doors of its two latrines. It was the stage for its own kind of comedy—the night Snyder chased the charge nurse into the fluoroscopy room with a water pistol, for instance, or the time the pint of bourbon slipped out of old Foley's bathrobe and smashed at Dr. Resnick's feet—and once in awhile its own kind of tragedy—the time Jack Fox sat up in bed to say, "Chrissake, open the *window*," coughed, and brought up the freak hemorrhage that killed him in ten minutes, or the other times, two or three times a year, when one of the men who had been wheeled away to surgery, smiling and waving to cries of "Take it easy!" and "Good luck t'ya, boy!" would never come back. But mostly it was a world consumed by its own kind of boredom, where everyone sat or lay amid the Kleenex and the sputum cups and the clangor of all-day radios. That was the way things were in C Ward on the afternoon of New Year's Eve, except that the radios were swamped under the noise of Tiny Kovacs's laughter.

He was an enormous man of thirty, six and a half feet tall and broad as a bear, and that afternoon he was having a private talk with his friend Jones, who looked comically small and scrawny beside him. They would whisper together and then laugh—Jones with a nervous giggle, repeatedly scratching his belly through the pajamas, Tiny with his great guffaw. After a while they got up, still flushed with laughter, and made their way across the ward to McIntyre's bed.

"Hey, Mac, listen," Jones began, "Tiny'n I got an idea." Then he got the giggles and said, "Tell him, Tiny."

The trouble was that McIntyre, a fragile man of forty-one with a lined, sarcastic face, was trying to write an important letter at the time. But they both mistook his grimace of impatience for a smile, and Tiny began to explain the idea in good faith.

"Listen, Mac, tonight around twelve I'm gonna get all undressed, see?" He spoke with some difficulty because all his front teeth were missing; they had gone bad soon after his lungs, and the new plate the hospital had ordered for him was long overdue. "I'll be all naked except I'm gonna wear this towel, see? Like a diaper? And then look, I'm gonna put this here acrost my chest." He unrolled a strip of four-inch bandage, a yard long, on which he or Jones had written "1951" in big block numerals, with marking ink. "Get it?" he said. "A big fat baby? No teef? And then listen, Mac, you can be the old year, okay? You can put this here on, and this here. You'll be perfect." The second bandage said "1950," and the other item was a false beard of white cotton wool that they'd dug up from a box of Red Cross supplies in the dayroom—it had evidently belonged to an old Santa Claus costume.

"No, thanks," McIntyre said. "Find somebody else, okay?"

"Aw, jeez, you gotta do it, Mac," Tiny said. "Listen, we thought of evvybody else in the building and you're the only one—don'tcha see? Skinny, bald, a little gray hair? And the best part is you're like me, you got no teef *eiver*." Then, to show no offense was meant, he added, "Well, I mean, at lease you could take 'em out, right? You could take 'em out for a couple minutes and put 'em back in *after*—right?"

"Look, Kovacs," McIntyre said, briefly closing his eyes, "I already said no. Now will the both a you please take off?"

Slowly Tiny's face reshaped itself into a pout, blotched red in the cheeks as if he'd been slapped. "Arright," he said with self-control, grabbing the beard and the bandages from McIntyre's bed. "Arright, the hell wiv it." He swung around and strode back to his own side of the ward, and Jones trotted after him, smiling in embarrassment, his loose slippers flapping on the floor.

McIntyre shook his head. "How d'ya like them two for a paira idiot bastards?" he said to the man in the next bed, a thin and very ill Negro named Vernon Sloan. "You hear all that, Vernon?"

"I got the general idea," Sloan said. He started to say something else but began coughing instead, reaching out a long brown hand for his sputum cup, and McIntyre went to work on his letter again.

Back at his own bed, Tiny threw the beard and the bandages in his locker and slammed it shut. Jones hurried up beside him, pleading. "Listen, Tiny, we'll get another guy, is all. We'll get Shulman, or—"

"Ah, Shulman's too fat."

"Well, or Johnson, then, or—"

"Look, forget it, willya, Jones?" Tiny exploded. "Piss on it. I'm through. Try thinkin' up somethin' to give the guys a little laugh on New Year's, and that's whatcha get."

Jones sat down on Tiny's bedside chair. "Well, hell," he said after a pause, "it's still a good idea, isn't it?"

"Ah!" Tiny pushed one heavy hand away in disgust. "Ya think any a these bastids 'ud appreciate it? Ya think there's one sunuvabitchin' bastid in this building 'ud appreciate it? Piss on 'em all."

It was no use arguing; Tiny would sulk for the rest of the day now. This always happened when his feelings were hurt, and they were hurt fairly often, for his particular kind of jollity was apt to get on the other men's nerves. There was, for instance, the business of the quacking rubber duck he had bought in the hospital canteen shortly before Christmas, as a gift for one of his nephews. The trouble that time was that in the end he had decided to buy something else for the child and keep the duck for himself; quacking it made him laugh for hours on end. After the lights were out at night he would creep up on the other patients and quack the duck in their faces, and it wasn't long before nearly everyone told him to cut it out and shut up. Then somebody—McIntyre, in fact—had swiped the duck from Tiny's bed and hidden it, and Tiny had sulked for three days. "You guys think you're so smart," he had grumbled to the ward at large. "Actin' like a buncha kids."

It was Jones who found the duck and returned it to him; Jones was about the only man left who thought the things Tiny did were funny. Now his face brightened a little as he got up to leave. "Anyway, I got my bottle, Tiny," he said. "You'n *me'll* have some fun tonight." Jones was not a drinking man, but New Year's Eve was special and smuggling was a challenge: a few days earlier he had arranged to have a pint of rye brought in and had hidden it, with a good deal of giggling, under some spare pajamas in his locker.

"Don't tell nobody *else* you got it," Tiny said. "I wouldn't tell these bastids the time a day." He jerked a cigarette into his lips and struck the match savagely. Then he got his new Christmas robe off the hanger and put it on—careful, for all his temper, to arrange the fit of the padded shoulders and the sash just right. It was a gorgeous robe, plum-colored satin with contrasting red lapels, and Tiny's face and manner assumed a strange dignity whenever be put it on. This look was as new, or rather, as seasonal, as the robe itself: it dated back to the week before, when he'd gotten dressed to go home for his Christmas pass.

Many of the men were a revelation in one way or another when they appeared in their street clothes. McIntyre had grown surprisingly humble, incapable of sarcasm or pranks, when he put on his scarcely worn accounting clerk's costume of blue serge, and Jones had grown surprisingly tough in his old Navy foul-weather jacket. Young Krebs, whom everybody called Junior, had assumed a portly maturity with his double-breasted business suit, and Travers, who most people had forgotten was a Yale man, looked oddly effete in his J. Press flannels and his button-down collar. Several of the Negroes had suddenly become Negroes again, instead of ordinary men, when they appeared in their sharply pegged trousers, draped coats and huge Windsor knots, and they even seemed embarrassed to be talking to the white men on the old familiar terms. But possibly the biggest change of all had been Tiny's. The clothes themselves were no surprise—his family ran a prosperous restaurant in Queens, and he was appropriately well-turned-out in a rich black overcoat and silk scarf—but the dignity they gave him was remarkable. The silly grin was gone, the laugh silenced, the clumsy movements overcome. The eyes beneath his snap-brim hat were not Tiny's eyes at all, but calm and masterful. Even his missing teeth didn't spoil the effect, for he kept his mouth shut except to mutter brief, almost curt Christmas wishes. The other patients looked up with a certain shy respect at this new man, this dramatic stranger whose hard heels crashed on the marble floor as he strode out of the building—and later, when he swung along the sidewalks of Jamaica on his way home, the crowds instinctively moved aside to make way for him.

Tiny was aware of the splendid figure he cut, but by the time he was home he'd stopped thinking about it; in the circle of his family it was real. Nobody called him Tiny there—he was Harold, a gentle son, a quiet hero to many round-eyed children, a rare and honored visitor. At one point, in the afterglow of a great dinner, a little girl was led ceremoniously up to his chair, where she stood shyly, not daring to meet his eyes, her fingers clasping the side seams of her party dress. Her mother urged her to speak: "Do you want to tell Uncle Harold what you say in your prayers every night, Irene?"

"Yes," the little girl said. "I tell Jesus please to bless Uncle Harold and make him get well again soon."

Uncle Harold smiled and took hold of both her hands "That's swell, Irene," he said huskily. "But you know, you shunt *tell* Him. You should *ask* Him."

She looked into his face for the first time. "That's what I mean," she said. "I ask Him."

And Uncle Harold gathered her in his arms, putting his big face over her shoulder so she couldn't see that his eyes were blurred with tears. "That's a good girl," he whispered. It was a scene nobody in Building Seven would have believed.

He remained Harold until the pass was over and he strode away from a clinging family farewell, shrugging the great overcoat around his shoulders and squaring the hat. He was Harold all the way to the bus terminal and all the way back to the hospital, and the other men still looked at him oddly and greeted him a little shyly when he pounded back into C Ward. He went to his bed and put down his several packages (one of which contained the new robe), then headed for the latrine to get undressed. That was the beginning of the end, for when he came out in the old faded pajamas and scuffed slippers there was only a trace of importance left in his softening face, and even that disappeared in the next hour or two, while he lay on his bed and listened to the radio. Later that evening, when most of the other returning patients had settled down, he sat up and looked around in the old, silly way. He waited patiently for a moment of complete silence, then thrust his rubber duck high in the air and quacked it seven times to the rhythm of "shave-and-a-haircut, two-bits," while everybody groaned and swore. Tiny was back, ready to start a new year.

Now, less than a week later, he could still recapture his dignity whenever he needed it by putting on the robe, striking a pose and thinking hard about his home. Of course, it was only a question of time before the robe grew rumpled with familiarity, and then it would all be over, but meanwhile it worked like a charm.

Across the aisle, McIntyre sat brooding over his unfinished letter. "I don't know, Vernon," he said to Sloan. "I felt sorry for you last week, having to stay in this dump over Christmas, but you know something? You were lucky. I wish they wouldn't of let me go home either."

"That so?" Sloan said. "How do you mean?"

"Ah, I don't know," McIntyre said, wiping his fountain pen with a piece of Kleenex. "I don't know. Just that it's a bitch, having to come back afterwards, I guess." But that was only part of it; the other part, like the letter he'd been trying to write all week, was his own business.

McIntyre's wife had grown fat and bewildered in the last year or two. On the alternate Sunday afternoons when she came out to visit him she never seemed to have much on her mind but the movies she had seen, or the television shows, and she gave him very little news of their two children, who almost never came out. "Anyway, you'll be seein' them Christmas," she would say. "We'll have a lot of fun. Only listen, Dad, are you sure that bus trip isn't gonna tire you out?"

"'Course not," he had said, a number of times. "I didn't have no trouble last year, did I?"

Nevertheless he was breathing hard when he eased himself off the bus at last, carrying the packages he had bought in the hospital canteen, and he had to walk very slowly up the snow-crusted Brooklyn street to his home.

His daughter, Jean, who was eighteen now, was not there when he came in.

"Oh, sure," his wife explained, "I thought I told you she'd prob'ly be out tonight."

"No," he said. "You didn't tell me. Where'd she go?"

"Oh, out to the movies is all, with her girlfriend Brenda. I didn't think you'd mind, Dad. Fact, I told her to go. She needs a little night off once in a while. *You* know, she's kind of run-down. She gets nervous and everything."

"What's she get nervous about?"

"Well, *you* know. One thing, this job she's got now's very tiring. I mean she likes the work and everything, but she's not used to the full eight hours a day, you know what I mean? She'll settle down to it. Come on, have a cuppa coffee, and then we'll put the tree up. We'll have a lot of fun."

On his way to wash up he passed her empty room, with its clean cosmetic smell, its ragged teddy bear and framed photographs of singers, and he said, "It sure seems funny to be home."

His boy, Joseph, had still been a kid fooling around with model airplanes the Christmas before; now he wore his hair about four inches too long and spent a great deal of time working on it with his comb, shaping it into a gleaming pompadour with upswept sides. He was a heavy smoker too, pinching the cigarette between his yellow-stained thumb and forefinger and cupping the live end in his palm. He hardly moved his lips when he spoke, and his only way of laughing was to make a brief snuffling sound in his nose. He gave one of these little snorts during the trimming of the Christmas tree, when McIntyre said something about a rumor that the Veterans Administration might soon increase disability pensions. It might have meant nothing, but to McIntyre it was the same as if he had said, "Who you tryna kid, Pop? We know where the money's coming from." It seemed an unmistakable, wise-guy reference to the fact that McIntyre's brother-in-law, and not his pension, was providing the bulk of the family income. He resolved to speak to his wife about it at bedtime that night, but when the time came all he said was, "Don't he ever get his hair cut anymore?"

"All the kids are wearing it that way now," she said. "Why do you have to criticize him all the time?"

Jean was there in the morning, slow and rumpled in a loose blue wrapper. "Hi, sweetie," she said, and gave him a kiss that smelled of sleep and stale perfume. She opened her presents quietly and then lay for a long time with one leg thrown over the arm of a deep upholstered chair, her foot swinging, her fingers picking at a pimple on her chin.

McIntyre couldn't take his eyes off her. It wasn't just that she was a woman—the kind of withdrawn, obliquely smiling woman that had filled him with intolerable shyness and desire in his own youth—it was something more disturbing even than that.

"Whaddya looking at, Dad?" she said, smiling and frowning at once. "You keep *lookin'* at me all the time."

He felt himself blushing. "I always like to look at pretty girls. Is that so terrible?"

"'Course not." She began intently plucking at the broken edge of one of her fingernails, frowning down at her hands in a way that made her long eyelashes fall in delicate curves against her cheeks. "It's just—you know. When a person keeps looking at you all the time it makes you nervous, that's all."

"Honey, listen." McIntyre leaned forward with both elbows on his skinny knees. "Can I ask you something? What's all this business about being nervous? Ever since I come home, that's all I heard. 'Jean's very nervous. Jean's very nervous.' So listen, will you please tell me something? What's there to be so nervous about?"

"Nothing," she said. "I don't know, Dad. Nothing, I guess."

"Well, because the reason I ask—" he was trying to make his voice deep and gentle, the way he was almost sure it had sounded long ago, but it came out scratchy and querulous, short of breath—"the reason I ask is, if there's something bothering you or anything, don't you think you ought to tell your dad about it?"

Her fingernail tore deep into the quick, which caused her to shake it violently and pop it into her mouth with a little whimper of pain, and suddenly she was on her feet, red-faced and crying. "Dad, willya lea' me alone? Willya just please lea' me *alone*?" She ran out of the room and upstairs and slammed her door.

McIntyre had started after her, but instead he stood swaying and glared at his wife and son, who were examining the carpet at opposite ends of the room.

"What's the matter with her, anyway?" he demanded. "Huh? What the hell's going on around here?" But they were as silent as two guilty children. "C'mon," he said. His head made a slight involuntary movement with each suck of air into his frail chest. "C'mon, goddamn it, *tell* me."

With a little wet moan his wife sank down and spread herself among the sofa cushions, weeping, letting her face melt. "All right," she said. "All right, you asked for it. We all done our best to give you a nice Christmas, but if you're gonna come home and snoop around and drive everybody crazy with your questions, all right—it's your funeral. She's four months pregnant—there, now are you satisfied? Now willya please quit bothering everybody?"

McIntyre sat down in an easy chair that was full of rattling Christmas paper, his head still moving with each breath.

"Who was it?" he said at last. "Who's the boy?"

"*Ask* her," his wife said. "Go on, ask her and see. She won't tell you. She won't tell anybody—that's the whole trouble. She wouldn't even of let on about the *baby* if I hadn't found out, and now she won't even tell her own mother the boy's name. She'd rather break her mother's heart—yes, she would, and her brother's too."

Then he heard it again, a little snuffle across the room. Joseph was standing there smirking as he stubbed out a cigarette. His lower lip moved slightly and he said, "Maybe she don't *know* the guy's name."

McIntyre rose very slowly out of the rattling paper, walked over to his son and hit him hard across the face with the flat of his hand, making the long hair jump from his skull and fall around his ears, making his face wince into the face of a hurt, scared little boy. Then blood began to run from the little boy's nose and dribble on the nylon shirt he had gotten for Christmas, and McIntyre hit him again, and that was when his wife screamed.

A few hours later he was back in Building Seven with nothing to do. All week he ate poorly, talked very little, except to Vernon Sloan, and spent a great deal of time working on a letter to his daughter that was still unfinished on the afternoon of New Year's Eve.

After many false starts, which had ended up among the used Kleenex tissues in the paper bag that hung beside his bed, this was what he had written:

> JEAN HONEY,
>
> I guess I got pretty excited and made a lot of trouble when I was home. Baby it was only that I have been away so long it is hard for me to understand that your a grown up woman and that is why I kind of went crazy that day. Now Jean I have done some thinking since I got back here and I want to write you a few lines.
>
> The main thing is try not to worry. Remember your not the first girl that's made a mistake and
>
> *(p. 2)*
> gotten into trouble of this kind. Your mom is all upset I know but do not let her get you down. Now Jean it may seem that you and I don't know each other very well any more but this is not so. Do you remember when I first come out of the army and you were about 12 then and we used to take a walk in Prospect Pk. sometimes and talk things over. I wish I could have a talk like that
>
> *(p. 3)*
> with you now. Your old dad may not be good for much any more but he does know a thing or two about life and especially one important thing, and that is

That was as far as the letter went.

Now that Tiny's laughter was stilled, the ward seemed unnaturally quiet. The old year faded in a thin yellow sunset behind the west windows; then darkness fell, the lights came on and shuddering rubber-wheeled wagons of dinner trays were rolled in by masked and gowned attendants. One of them, a gaunt, bright-eyed man named Carl, went through his daily routine.

"Hey, you guys heard about the man that ran over himself?" he asked, stopping in the middle of the aisle with a steaming pitcher of coffee in his hand.

"Just pour the coffee, Carl," somebody said.

Carl filled a few cups and started across the aisle to fill a few more, but midway he stopped again and bugged his eyes over the rim of his sterile mask. "No, but listen—you guys heard about the man that ran over himself? This is a new one." He looked at Tiny, who usually was more than willing to play straight man for him, but Tiny was moodily buttering a slice of bread, his cheeks wobbling with each stroke of the knife. "Well, anyways," Carl said at last, "this man says to this kid, 'Hey kid, run acrost the street and get me a packa cigarettes, willya?' Kid says, 'No,' see? So the man ran over him*self*!" He doubled up and pounded his thigh. Jones groaned appreciatively; everyone else ate in silence.

When the meal was over and the trays cleared away, McIntyre tore up the old beginning of page 3 and dropped it in the waste bag. He resettled his pillows, brushed some food crumbs off the bed, and wrote this:

> *(p. 3)*
> with you now.
> So Jean please write and tell me the name of this boy. I promise I

But he threw that page away too, and sat for a long time writing nothing, smoking a cigarette with his usual careful effort to avoid inhaling. At last he took up his pen again and cleaned its point very carefully with a leaf of Kleenex. Then he began new page:

> *(p. 3)*
> with you now.
> Now baby I have got an idea. As you know I am now waiting to have another operation on the left side in February but if all goes well maybe I could take off out of this place by April 1. Of course I would not get a discharge but I could take a chance like I did in 1947 and hope for better luck this time. Then we could go away to the country someplace just you and I and I could take a part time job and we could

The starched rustle and rubber-heeled thump of a nurse made him look up; she was standing beside his bed with a bottle of rubbing alcohol. "How about you, McIntyre?" she said. "Back rub?"

"No thanks," he said. "Not tonight."

"My goodness." She peered just a little at the letter, which he shielded just a little with his hand. "You still writing letters? Every time I come past here you're writing letters. You must have a lot of people to write to. I wish I had the time to catch up on my letters."

"Yeah," he said. "Well, that's the thing, see. I got plenty of time."

"Well, but how can you think of so many things to write about?" she said. "That's my trouble. I sit down and I get all ready to write a letter and then I can't think of a single thing to write about. It's terrible."

He watched the shape of her buttocks as she moved away down the aisle. Then he read over the new page, crumpled it, and dropped it in the bag. Closing his eyes and massaging the bridge of his nose with thumb and forefinger, he tried to remember the exact words of the first version. At last he wrote it out again as well as he could:

> *(p. 3)*
> with you now.
>
> Baby Jean your old dad may not be good for much any more but he does know a thing or two about life and especially one important thing, and that is

But from there on, the pen lay dead in his cramped fingers. It was as if all the letters of the alphabet, all the combinations of letters into words, all the infinite possibilities of handwritten language had ceased to exist.

He looked out the window for help, but the window was a black mirror now and gave back only the lights, the bright bedsheets and pajamas of the ward. Pulling on his robe and slippers, he went over to stand with his forehead and cupped hands against the cold pane. Now he could make out the string of highway lights in the distance and, beyond that, the horizon of black trees between the snow and the sky. Just above the horizon, on the right, the sky was suffused with a faint pink blur from the lights of Brooklyn and New York, but this was partly hidden from view by a big dark shape in the foreground that was a blind corner of the paraplegic building, a world away.

When McIntyre turned back from the window to blink in the yellow light, leaving a shriveling ghost of his breath on the glass, it was with an oddly shy look of rejuvenation and relief. He walked to his bed, stacked the pages of his manuscript neatly, tore them in halves and in quarters and dropped them into the waste bag. Then he got his pack of cigarettes and went over to stand beside Vernon Sloan, who was blinking through his reading glasses at *The Saturday Evening Post*.

"Smoke, Vernon?" he said.

"No thanks, Mac. I smoke more'n one or two a day, it only makes me cough."

"Okay," McIntyre said, lighting one for himself. "Care to play a little checkers?"

"No thanks, Mac, not right now. I'm a little tired—think I'll just read awhile."

"Any good articles in there this week, Vernon?"

"Oh, pretty good," he said. "Couple pretty good ones." Then his mouth worked into a grin that slowly disclosed nearly all of his very clean teeth. "Say, what's the matter with you, man? You feelin' good or somethin'?"

"Oh, not too bad, Vernon," he said, stretching his skinny arms and his spine. "Not too bad."

"You finish all your writin' finally? Is that it?"

"Yeah, I guess so," he said. "My trouble is, I can't think of anything to write about."

Looking across the aisle to where Tiny Kovacs's wide back sat slumped in the purple amplitude of the new robe, he walked over and laid a hand on one of the enormous satin shoulders. "So?" he said.

Tiny's head swung around to glare at him, immediately hostile. "So what?"

"So where's that beard?"

Tiny wrenched open his locker, grabbed out the beard and thrust it roughly into McIntyre's hands. "Here," he said. "You want it? Take it."

McIntyre held it up to his ears and slipped the string over his head. "String oughta be a little tighter," he said. "There, how's that? Prob'ly look better when I get my teeth out."

But Tiny wasn't listening. He was burrowing in his locker for the strips of bandage. "Here," he said. "Take this stuff too. I don't want no part of it. You wanna do it, you get somebody else."

At that moment Jones came padding over, all smiles. "Hey, you gonna do it, Mac? You change your mind?"

"Jones, talk to this big son of a bitch," McIntyre said through the wagging beard. "He don't wanna cooperate."

"Aw, *jeez*, Tiny," Jones implored. "The whole *thing* depends on you. The whole *thing* was your idea."

"I already told ya," Tiny said. "I don't want no part of it. You wanna do it, you find some other sucker."

After the lights went out at ten nobody bothered much about hiding their whiskey. Men who had been taking furtive nips in the latrines all evening now drank in quietly jovial groups around the wards, with the unofficial once-a-year blessing of the charge nurse. Nobody took particular notice when, a little before midnight, three men from C Ward slipped out to the linen closet to get a sheet and a towel, then to the kitchen to get a mop handle, and then walked the length of the building and disappeared into the A Ward latrine.

There was a last-minute flurry over the beard: it hid so much of McIntyre's face that the effect of his missing teeth was spoiled. Jones solved the problem by cutting away all of it but the chin whiskers, which he fastened in place with bits of adhesive tape. "There," he said, "that does it. That's perfect. Now roll up your pajama pants, Mac, so just your bare legs'll show under the sheet? Get it? Now where's your mop handle?"

"Jones, it don't *work*!" Tiny called tragically. He was standing naked except for a pair of white woolen socks, trying to pin the folded towel around his loins. "The son of a bitch won't stay *up*!"

Jones hurried over to fix it, and finally everything was ready. Nervously, they killed the last of Jones's rye and dropped the empty bottle into a laundry hamper; then they slipped outside and huddled in the darkness at the head of A Ward.

"Ready?" Jones whispered. "Okay. . . . Now." He flicked on the overhead lights, and thirty startled faces blinked in the glare.

First came 1950, a wasted figure crouched on a trembling staff, lame and palsied with age; behind him, grinning and flexing his muscles, danced the enormous diapered baby of the New Year. For a second or two there was silence except for the unsteady tapping of the old man's staff, and then the laughter and the cheers began.

"*Out wivvie old!*" the baby bellowed over the noise, and he made an elaborate burlesque of hauling off and kicking the old man in the seat of the pants, which caused the old man to stagger weakly and rub one buttock as they moved up the aisle. *"Out wivvie old! In wivva new!"*

Jones ran on ahead to turn on the lights of B Ward, where the ovation was even louder. Nurses clustered helplessly in the doorway to watch, frowning or giggling behind their sterile masks as the show made its way through cheers and catcalls.

"Out wivvie old! In wivva new!"

In one of the private rooms a dying man blinked up through the window of his oxygen tent as his door was flung open and his light turned on. He stared bewildered at the frantic toothless clowns who capered at the foot of his bed; finally he understood and gave them a yellow smile, and they moved on to the next private room and the next, arriving at last in C Ward, where their friends stood massed and laughing in the aisle.

There was barely time for the pouring of fresh drinks before all the radios blared up at once and Guy Lombardo's band broke into "Auld Lang Syne"; then all the shouts dissolved into a great off-key chorus in which Tiny's voice could be heard over all the others:

"Should old acquaintance be forgot
And never brought to mind? . . . "

Even Vernon Sloan was singing, propped up in bed and holding a watery highball, which he slowly waved in time to the music. They were all singing.

"For o-o-old lang syne, my boys,
For o-o-old lang syne . . . "

And when the song was over the handshaking began.

"Good luck t'ya, boy."

"Same to you, boy—hope you make it this year."

All over Building Seven men wandered in search of hands to shake; under the noise of shouts and radios the words were repeated again and again: "Good luck t'ya. . . ." "Hope you make it this year, boy. . . ." And standing still and tired by Tiny Kovacs's bed, where the purple robe lay thrown in careless wads and wrinkles, McIntyre raised his glass and his bare-gummed smile to the crowd, with Tiny's laughter roaring in his ear and Tiny's heavy arm around his neck.

Builders

WRITERS WHO WRITE about writers can easily bring on the worst kind of literary miscarriage; everybody knows that. Start a story off with "Craig crushed out his cigarette and lunged for the typewriter," and there isn't an editor in the United States who'll feel like reading your next sentence.

So don't worry: this is going to be a straight, no-nonsense piece of fiction about a cabdriver, a movie star, and an eminent child psychologist, and that's a promise. But you'll have to be patient for a minute, because there's going to be a writer in it too. I won't call him "Craig," and I can guarantee that he won't get away with being the only Sensitive Person among the characters, but we're going to be stuck with him right along and you'd better count on his being as awkward and obtrusive as writers nearly always are, in fiction or in life.

Thirteen years ago, in 1948, I was twenty-two and employed as a rewrite man on the financial news desk of the United Press. The salary was fifty-four dollars a week and it wasn't much of a job, but it did give me two good things. One was that whenever anybody asked me what I did I could say, "Work for the UP," which had a jaunty sound; the other was that every morning I could turn up at the *Daily News* building wearing a jaded look, a cheap trench coat that had shrunk a size too small for me, and a much-handled brown fedora ("Battered" is the way I would have described it then, and I'm grateful that I know a little more now about honesty in the use of words. It was a handled hat, handled by endless nervous pinchings and shapings and reshapings; it wasn't battered at all). What I'm getting at is that just for those few minutes each day, walking up the slight hill of the last hundred yards between the subway exit and the *News* building, I was Ernest Hemingway reporting for work at the *Kansas City Star*.

Had Hemingway been to the war and back before his twentieth birthday? Well, so had I; and all right, maybe there were no wounds or medals for valor in my case, but the basic fact of the matter was there. Had Hemingway bothered about anything as time-wasting and career-delaying as going to college? Hell, no; and me neither. Could Hemingway ever really have cared very much about the newspaper business? Of course not; so there was only a marginal difference, you see, between his lucky break at the *Star* and my own dismal stint on the financial desk. The important thing, as I knew Hemingway would be the first to agree, was that a writer had to begin somewhere.

"Domestic corporate bonds moved irregularly higher in the moderately active trading today. . . ." That was the kind of prose I wrote all day long for the UP wire, and "Rising oil shares paced a lively curb market," and "Directors of Timken Roller Bearing today declared"—hundreds on hundreds of words that I never really understood (What in the name of God are puts and calls, and what is a sinking fund debenture? I'm still damned if I know), while the teletypes chugged and rang and the Wall Street tickers ticked and everybody around me argued baseball, until it was mercifully time to go home.

It always pleased me to reflect that Hemingway had married young; I could go right along with him there. My wife, Joan, and I lived as far west as you can get on West Twelfth Street, in a big three-window room on the third floor, and if it wasn't the Left Bank it certainly wasn't our fault. Every evening after dinner, while Joan washed the dishes, there would be a respectful, almost reverent hush in the room, and this was the time for me to retire behind a three-fold screen in the corner where a table, a student lamp and a portable typewriter were set up. But it was here, of course, under the white stare of that lamp, that the tenuous parallel between Hemingway and me endured its heaviest strain. Because it wasn't any "Up in Michigan" that came out of my machine; it wasn't any "Three Day Blow" or "The Killers"; very often, in fact, it wasn't really anything at all, and even when it was something Joan called "marvelous," I knew deep down that it was always, always something bad.

There were evenings too when all I did behind the screen was goof off—read every word of the printing on the inside of a matchbook, say, or all the ads in the back of the *Saturday Review of Literature*—and it was during one of those times, in the fall of the year, that I came across these lines:

> Unusual free-lance opportunity for talented writer. Must have imagination. Bernard Silver.

—and then a phone number with what looked like a Bronx exchange.

I won't bother giving you the dry, witty, Hemingway dialogue that took place when I came out from behind the screen that night and Joan turned around from the sink, with her hands dripping soapsuds on the open magazine, and we can also skip my cordial, unenlightening chat with Bernard Silver on the phone. I'll just move on ahead to a couple of nights later, when I rode the subway for an hour and found my way at last to his apartment.

"Mr. Prentice?" he inquired. "What's your first name again? Bob? Good, Bob, I'm Bernie. Come on in, make yourself comfortable."

And I think both Bernie and his home deserve a little description here. He was in his middle or late forties, a good deal shorter than me and much stockier, wearing an expensive-looking pale blue sport shirt with the tails out. His head must have been half again the size of mine, with thinning black hair washed straight back, as if he'd stood face-up in the shower; and his face was one of the most guileless and self-confident faces I've ever seen.

The apartment was very clean, spacious and cream-colored, full of carpeting and archways. In the narrow alcove near the coat closet ("Take your coat and hat; good. Let's put this on a hanger here and we'll be all set; good"), I saw a cluster of framed photographs showing World War I soldiers in various groupings, but on the walls of the living room there were no pictures of any kind, only a few wrought-iron lamp brackets and a couple of mirrors. Once inside the room you weren't apt to notice the lack of pictures, though, because all your attention was drawn to a single, amazing piece of furniture. I don't know what you'd call it—a credenza?—but whatever it was it seemed to go on forever, chest-high in some places and waist-high in others, made of at least three different shades of polished brown veneer. Part of it was a television set, part of it was a radio-phonograph; part of it thinned out into shelves that held potted plants and little figurines; part of it, full of chromium knobs and tricky sliding panels, was a bar.

"Ginger ale?" he asked. "My wife and I don't drink, but I can offer you a glass of ginger ale."

I think Bernie's wife must always have gone out to the movies on nights when he interviewed his writing applicants; I did meet her later, though, and we'll come to that. Anyway, there were just the two of us that first evening, settling down in slippery leatherette chairs with our ginger ale, and it was strictly business.

"First of all," he said, "tell me, Bob. Do you know *My Flag Is Down*?" And before I could ask what he was talking about he pulled it out of some recess in the credenza and handed it over—a paperback book that you still see around the drugstores, purporting to be the memoirs of a New York taxicab driver. Then he began to fill me in, while I looked at the book and nodded and wished I'd never left home.

Bernard Silver was a cab driver too. He had been one for twenty-two years, as long as the span of my life, and in the last two or three of these years he had begun to see no reason why a slightly fictionalized version of his own experiences shouldn't be worth a fortune. "I'd like you to take a look at this," he said, and this time the credenza yielded up a neat little box of three-by-five-inch file cards. Hundreds of experiences, he told me; all different; and while he gave me to understand that they might not all be strictly true, he could assure me there was at least a kernel of truth in every last one of them. Could I imagine what a really good ghostwriter might do with a wealth of material like that? Or how much that same writer might expect to salt away when his own fat share of the magazine sales, the book royalties and the movie rights came in?

"Well, I don't know, Mr. Silver. It's a thing I'd have to think over. I guess I'd have to read this other book first, and see if I thought there was any—"

"No, wait awhile. You're getting way ahead of me here, Bob. In the first place I wouldn't want you to read that book because you wouldn't learn anything. That guy's all gangsters and dames and sex and drinking and that stuff. I'm completely different." And I sat swilling ginger ale as if to slake a gargantuan thirst, in order to be able to leave as soon as possible after he'd finished explaining how completely different he was. Bernie Silver was a warm person, he told me; an ordinary, everyday guy with a heart as big as all outdoors and a real philosophy of life; did I know what he meant?

I have a trick of tuning out on people (it's easy; all you do is fix your eyes on the speaker's mouth and watch the rhythmic, endlessly changing shapes of lips and tongue, and the first thing you know you can't hear a word), and I was about to start doing that when he said:

"And don't misunderstand me, Bob. I never yet asked a writer to do a single word for me on spec. You write for me, you'll be paid for everything you do. Naturally it can't be very big dough at this stage of the game, but you'll be paid. Fair enough? Here, let me fill up your glass."

This was the proposition. He'd give me an idea out of the file; I'd develop it into a first-person short story by Bernie Silver, between one and two thousand words in length, for which immediate payment was guaranteed. If he liked the job I did, there would be plenty of others where it came from—an assignment a week, if I could handle that much—and in addition to my initial payment, of course, I could look forward to a generous percentage of whatever subsequent income the material might bring. He chose to be winkingly mysterious about his plans for marketing the stories, though he did manage to hint that the *Reader's Digest* might be interested, and he was frank to admit he didn't yet have a publisher lined up for the ultimate book they would comprise, but he said he could give me a couple of names that would knock my eye out. Had I ever heard, for example, of Manny Weidman?

"Or maybe," he said, breaking into his all-out smile, "maybe you know him better as Wade Manley." And this was the shining name of a movie star, a man about as famous in the thirties and forties as Kirk Douglas or Burt Lancaster today. Wade Manley had been a grammar-school friend of Bernie's right here in the Bronx. Through mutual friends they had managed to remain sentimentally close ever since, and one of the things that kept their friendship green was Wade Manley's oft-repeated desire to play the role of rough, lovable Bernie Silver, New York Hackie, in any film or television series based on his colorful life. "Now I'll give you another name," he said, and this time he squinted cannily at me while pronouncing it, as if my recognizing it or not would be an index of my general educational level. "Dr. Alexander Corvo."

And luckily I was able not to look too blank. It wasn't a celebrity name, exactly, but it was far from obscure. It was one of those *New York Times* names, the kind of which tens of thousands of people are dimly aware because they've been coming across respectful mentions of them in the *Times* for years. Oh, it might have lacked the impact of "Lionel Trilling" or "Reinhold Niebuhr," but it was along that line; you could probably have put it in the same class with "Huntington Hartford" or "Leslie R. Groves," and a good cut or two above "Newbold Morris."

"The whaddyacallit man, you mean?" I said. "The childhood-tensions man?"

Bernie gave me a solemn nod, forgiving this vulgarity, and spoke the name again with its proper identification. "I mean Dr. Alexander Corvo, the eminent child psychologist."

Early in his rise to eminence, you see, Dr. Corvo had been a teacher at the very same grammar school in the Bronx, and two of the most unruly, dearly loved little rascals in his charge there had been Bernie Silver and Manny What's-his-name, the movie star. He still retained an incurable soft spot for both youngsters, and nothing would please him more today than to lend whatever influence he might have in the publishing world to furthering their project. All the three of them needed now, it seemed, was to find that final element, that elusive catalyst, the perfect writer for the job.

"Bob," said Bernie, "I'm telling you the truth. I've had one writer after another working on this, and none of them's been right. Sometimes I don't trust my own judgment; I take their stuff to Dr. Corvo and he shakes his head. He says, 'Bernie, try again.'

"Look, Bob." He came earnestly forward in his chair. "This isn't any fly-by-night idea here; I'm not stringing anybody along. This thing is building. Manny, Dr. Corvo and myself—we're *building* this thing. Oh, don't worry, Bob, I *know*—what, do I look that stupid?—I know they're not building the way *I'm* building. And why should they? A big movie star? A distinguished scholar and author? You think they haven't got plenty of things of their own to build? A lot more important things than this? Naturally. But Bob, I'm telling you the truth: they're interested. I can show you letters, I can tell you times they've sat around this apartment with their wives, or Manny has anyway, and we've talked about it hours on end. They're interested, nobody has to worry about that. So do you see what I'm telling you, Bob? I'm telling you the truth. This thing is building." And he began a slow, two-handed building gesture, starting from the carpet, setting invisible blocks into place until they'd made a structure of money and fame for him, money and freedom for both of us, that rose to the level of our eyes.

I said it certainly did sound fine, but that if he didn't mind I'd like to know a little more about the immediate payment for the individual stories.

"And now I'll give you the answer to that one," he said. He went to the credenza again—part of it seemed to be a kind of desk—and after sorting out some papers he came up with a personal check. "I won't just tell you," he said. "I'll show you. Fair enough? This was my last writer. Take it and read it."

It was a canceled check, and it said that Bernard Silver had paid, to the order of some name, the sum of twenty-five dollars and no cents. "Read it!" he insisted, as if the check were a prose work of uncommon merit in its own right, and he watched me while I turned it over to read the man's endorsement, which had been signed under some semilegible words of Bernie's own about this being advance payment in full, and the bank's rubber stamp. "Look all right to you?" he inquired. "So that's the arrangement. All clear now?"

I guessed it was as clear as it would ever be, so I gave him back the check and said that if he'd show me one of the file cards now, or whatever, we might as well get going.

"Way-*hait* a minute, now! Hold your *horses* a minute here." His smile was enormous. "You're a pretty fast guy, you know that, Bob? I mean I like you, but don't you think I'd have to be a little bit of a dope to go around making out checks to everybody walked in here saying they're a writer? I know you're a newspaperman. Fine. Do I know you're a writer yet? Why don't you let me see what you got there in your lap?"

It was a manila envelope containing carbon copies of the only two halfway presentable short stories I had ever managed to produce in my life.

"Well," I said. "Sure. Here. Of course these are a very different kind of thing than what *you're*—"

"Never mind, never mind; naturally they're different," he said, opening the envelope. "You just relax a minute, and let me take a look."

"What I mean is, they're both very kind of—well, literary, I guess you'd say. I don't quite see how they'll give you any real idea of my—"

"Relax, I said."

Rimless glasses were withdrawn from the pocket of his sport shirt and placed laboriously into position as he settled back, frowning, to read. It took him a long time to get through the first page of the first story, and I watched him, wondering if this might turn out to be the very lowest point in my literary career. A *cab* driver, for Christ's sake. At last the first page turned, and the second page followed so closely after it that I could tell he was skipping. Then the third and the fourth—it was a twelve- or fourteen-page story—while I gripped my empty, warming ginger ale glass as if in readiness to haul off and throw it at his head.

A very slight, hesitant, then more and more judicial nodding set in as he made his way toward the end. He finished it, looked puzzled, went back to read over the last page again; then he laid it aside and picked up the second story—not to read it, but only to check it for length. He had clearly had enough reading for one night. Off came the glasses and on came the smile.

"Well, very nice," he said. "I won't take time to read this other one now, but this first one's very nice. 'Course, naturally, as you said, this is a very different kind of material you got here, so it's a little hard for me to—*you* know—" and he dismissed the rest of this difficult sentence with a wave of the hand. "I'll tell you what, though, Bob. Instead of just reading here, let me ask you a couple of questions about writing. For example." He closed his eyes and delicately touched their lids with his fingers, thinking, or more likely pretending to think, in order to give added weight to his next words. "For example, let me ask you this. Supposing somebody writes you a letter and says, 'Bob, I didn't have time to write you a short letter today, so I had to write you a long one instead.' Would you know what they meant by that?"

Don't worry, I played this part of the evening pretty cool. I wasn't going to let twenty-five bucks get away from me without some kind of struggle; and my answer, whatever sober-sided nonsense it was, could have left no doubt in his mind that this particular writing candidate knew something of the difficulty and the value of compression in prose. He seemed gratified by it, anyway.

"Good. Now let's try a different angle. I mentioned about 'building' a while back; well, look. Do you see where writing a story is building something too? Like building a house?" And he was so pleased with his own creation of this image that he didn't even wait to take in the careful, congratulatory nod I awarded him for it. "I mean a house has got to have a roof, but you're going to be in trouble if you build your roof first, right? Before you build your roof you got to build your walls. Before you build your walls you got to lay your foundation—and I mean all the way down the line. Before you lay your foundation you got to bulldoze and dig yourself the right kind of hole in the ground. Am I right?"

I couldn't have agreed with him more, but he was still ignoring my rapt, toadying gaze. He rubbed the flange of his nose with one wide knuckle; then he turned on me triumphantly again.

"So all right, supposing you build yourself a house like that. Then what? What's the first question you got to ask yourself about it when it's done?"

But I could tell he didn't care if I muffed this one or not. *He* knew what the question was, and he could hardly wait to tell me.

"Where are the windows?" he demanded, spreading his hands. "That's the question. Where does the light come in? Because do you see what I mean about the light coming in, Bob? I mean the—the *philosophy* of your story; the *truth* of it; the—"

"The illumination of it, sort of," I said, and he quit groping for his third noun with a profound and happy snap of the fingers.

"That's it. That's it, Bob. You got it."

It was a deal, and we had another ginger ale to clinch it as he thumbed through the idea file for my trial assignment. The "experience" he chose was the time Bernie Silver had saved a neurotic couple's marriage, right there in the cab, simply by sizing them up in his rearview mirror as they quarreled and putting in a few well chosen words of his own. Or at least, that was the general drift of it. All it actually said on the card was something like:

> High class man & wife (Park Ave.) start fighting in cab, very upset, lady starts yelling divorce. I watch them in rear view and put my 2 cents worth in & soon we are all laughing. Story about marriage, etc.

But Bernie expressed full confidence in my ability to work the thing out.

In the alcove, as he went through the elaborate business of getting my trench coat out of the closet and helping me on with it, I had time for a better look at the World War I photographs—a long company lineup, a number of framed yellow snapshots showing laughing men with their arms around each other, and one central picture of a lone bugler on a parade ground, with dusty barracks and a flag high in the distance. It could have been on the cover of an old American Legion magazine, with a caption like "Duty"—the perfect soldier, slim and straight at attention, and Gold Star Mothers would have wept over the way his fine young profile was pressed in manly reverence against the mouth of his simple, eloquent horn.

"I see you like my boy there," Bernie said fondly. "I bet you'd never guess who that boy is today."

Wade Manley? Dr. Alexander Corvo? Lionel Trilling? But I suppose I really did know, even before I glanced around at his blushing, beaming presence, that the boy was Bernie himself. And whether it sounds silly or not, I'll have to tell you that I felt a small but honest-to-God admiration for him. "Well, I'll be damned, Bernie. You look—you look pretty great there."

"Lot skinnier in those days, anyway," he said, slapping his silken paunch as he walked me to the door, and I remember looking down into his big, dumb, flabby face and trying to find the bugler's features somewhere inside it.

On my way home, rocking on the subway and faintly belching and tasting ginger ale, I grew increasingly aware that a writer could do a hell of a lot worse than to pull down twenty-five dollars for a couple of thousand words. It was very nearly half what I earned in forty miserable hours among the domestic corporate bonds and the sinking fund debentures; and if Bernie liked this first one, if I could go on doing one a week for him, it would be practically the same as getting a 50 percent raise. Seventy-nine a week! With that kind of dough coming in, as well as the forty-six Joan brought home from her secretarial job, it would be no time at all before we had enough for Paris (and maybe we wouldn't meet any Gertrude Steins or Ezra Pounds there, maybe I wouldn't produce any *Sun Also Rises*, but the earliest possible expatriation was nothing less than essential to my Hemingway plans). Besides, it might even be fun—or at least it might be fun to tell people about: I would be the hackie's hack, the builder's builder.

In any case I ran all the way down West Twelfth Street that night, and if I didn't burst in on her, laughing and shouting and clowning around, it was only because I forced myself to stand leaning against the mailboxes downstairs until I'd caught my breath and arranged my face into the urbane, amused expression I planned to use for telling her about it.

"Well, but who do you suppose is putting up all the money?" she asked. "It can't be out of his own pocket, can it? A cab driver couldn't afford to pay out twenty-five a week for any length of time, could he?"

It was one aspect of the thing that hadn't occurred to me—and it was just like her to come up with so dead-logical a question—but I did my best to override her with my own kind of cynical romanticism. "Who knows? Who the hell cares? Maybe Wade Manley's putting up the money. Maybe Dr. Whaddyacallit's putting it up. The point is, it's there."

"Well," she said, "good, then. How long do you think it'll take you to do the story?"

"Oh, hell, no time at all. I'll knock it off in a couple hours over the weekend."

But I didn't. I spent all Saturday afternoon and evening on one false start after another; I kept getting hung up in the dialogue of the quarreling couple, and in technical uncertainties about how much Bernie could really see of them in his rearview mirror, and in doubts about what any cabdriver could possibly say at such a time without the man's telling him to shut up and keep his eyes on the road.

By Sunday afternoon I was walking around breaking pencils in half and throwing them into the wastebasket and saying the hell with it; the hell with everything; apparently I couldn't even be a goddamn ghostwriter for a goddamn ignorant slob of a driver of a goddamn taxicab.

"You're *trying* too hard," Joan said. "Oh, I knew this would happen. You're being so insufferably *literary* about it, Bob; it's ridiculous. All you have to do is think of every corny, tear-jerking thing you've ever read or heard. Think of Irving Berlin."

And I told her I'd give her Irving Berlin right in the mouth in about a minute, if she didn't lay off me and mind her own goddamn business.

But late that night, as Irving Berlin himself might say, something kind of wonderful happened. I took that little bastard of a story and I built the hell out of it. First I bulldozed and dug and laid myself a real good foundation; then I got the lumber out and bang, bang, bang—up went the walls and on went the roof and up went the cute little chimney top. Oh, I put plenty of windows in it too—big, square ones—and when the light came pouring in it left no earthly shadow of a doubt that Bernie Silver was the wisest, gentlest, bravest and most lovable man who ever said "folks."

"It's perfect," Joan told me at breakfast, after she'd read the thing. "Oh, it's just perfect, Bob. I'm sure that's just exactly what he wants."

And it was. I'll never forget the way Bernie sat with his ginger ale in one hand and my trembling manuscript in the other, reading as I'd still be willing to bet he'd never read before, exploring all the snug and tidy wonders of the little home I'd built for him. I watched him discovering each of those windows, one after another, and saw his face made holy with their light. When he was finished he got up—we both got up—and he shook my hand.

"Beautiful," he said. "Bob, I had a feeling you'd do a good one, but I'll tell you the truth. I didn't know you'd do as good a one as this. Now you want your check, and I'll tell you something. You're not getting any check. For this you get cash."

Out came his trusty black cabdriver's wallet. He thumbed through its contents, picked out a five-dollar bill and laid it in my hand. He evidently wanted to make a ceremony out of presenting me with one bill after another, so I stood smiling down at it and waiting for the next one; and I was still standing there with my hand out when I looked up and saw him putting the wallet away.

Five bucks! And even now I wish I could say that I shouted this, or at least that I said it with some suggestion of the outrage that gripped my bowels—it might have saved an awful amount of trouble later—but the truth is that it came out as a very small, meek question: "Five bucks?"

"Right!" He was rocking happily back on his heels in the carpet.

"Well, but Bernie, I mean what's the deal? I mean, you showed me that check, and I—"

As his smile dwindled, his face looked as shocked and hurt as if I'd spat into it. "Oh, Bob," he said. "Bob, what is this? Look, let's not play any games here. I know I showed you that check; I'll show you that check again." And the folds of his sport shirt quivered in righteous indignation as he rummaged in the credenza and brought it out.

It was the same check, all right. It still read twenty-five dollars and no cents; but Bernie's cramped scribbling on the other side, above the other man's signature and all mixed up with the bank's rubber stamp, was now legible as hell. What it said, of course, was: "In full advance payment, five write-ups."

So I hadn't really been robbed—conned a little, maybe, that's all—and therefore my main problem now, the sick, ginger-ale-flavored feeling that I was certain Ernest Hemingway could never in his life have known, was my own sense of being a fool.

"Am I right or wrong, Bob?" he was asking. "Am I right or wrong?" And then he sat me down again and did his smiling best to set me straight. How could I possibly have thought he meant twenty-five a time? Did I have any idea what kind of money a hackie took home? Oh, some of your owner-drivers, maybe it was a different story; but your average hackie? Your fleet hackie? Forty, forty-five, maybe sometimes fifty a week if they were lucky. Even for a man like himself, with no kids and a wife working full time at the telephone company, it was no picnic. I could ask any hackie if I didn't believe him; it was no picnic. "And I mean you don't think anybody *else* is picking up the tab for these write-ups, do you? Do you?" He looked at me incredulously, almost ready to laugh, as if the very idea of my thinking such a thing would remove all reasonable doubt about my having been born yesterday.

"Bob, I'm sorry there was any misunderstanding here," he said, walking me to the door, "but I'm glad we're straight on it now. Because I mean it, that's a beautiful piece you wrote, and I've got a feeling it's going to go places. Tell you what, Bob, I'll be in touch with you later this week, okay?"

And I remember despising myself because I didn't have the guts to tell him not to bother, any more than I could shake off the heavy, fatherly hand that rode on my neck as we walked. In the alcove, out in front of the young bugler again, I had a sudden, disturbing notion that I could foretell an exchange of dialogue that was about to take place. I would say, "Bernie, were you really a bugler in the army, or was that just for the picture?"

And with no trace of embarrassment, without the faintest flickering change in his guileless smile, he would say, "Just for the picture."

Worse still: I knew that the campaign-hatted head of the bugler himself would turn then, that the fine tense profile in the photograph would slowly loosen and turn away from the mouthpiece of a horn through which its dumb, no-talent lips could never have blown a fart, and that it would wink at me. So I didn't risk it. I just said, "See you, Bernie," and got the hell out of there and went home.

Joan's reaction to the news was surprisingly gentle. I don't mean she was "kind" to me about it, which would have damn near killed me in the shape I was in that night; it was more that she was kind to Bernie.

Poor, lost, brave little man, dreaming his huge and unlikely dream—that kind of thing. And could I imagine what it must have cost him over the years? How many of these miserably hard-earned five-dollar payments he must have dropped down the bottomless maw of second- and third- and tenth-rate amateur writers' needs? How lucky for him, then, through whatever dissemblings with his canceled check, to have made contact with a first-rate professional at last. And how touching, and how "sweet," that he had recognized the difference by saying, "For this you get cash."

"Well, but for Christ's sake," I told her, grateful that it could for once be me instead of her who thought in terms of the deadly practicalities. "For Christ's sake, you know *why* he gave me cash, don't you? Because he's going to sell that story to the *Reader's* goddamn *Digest* next week for a hundred and fifty thousand dollars, and because if I had a photostated check to prove I wrote it he'd be in trouble, that's why."

"Would you like to bet?" she inquired, looking at me with her lovely, truly unforgettable mixture of pity and pride. "Would you like to bet that if he does sell it, to the *Reader's Digest* or anywhere else, he'll insist on giving you half?"

"Bob Prentice?" said a happy voice on the telephone, three nights later. "Bernie Silver. Bob, I've just come from Dr. Alexander Corvo's home, and listen. I'm not going to tell you *what* he told me, but I'll tell you this. Dr. Alexander Corvo thinks you're pretty good."

Whatever reply I made to this—"Does he really?" or "You mean he really likes it?"—it was something bashful and telling enough to bring Joan instantly to my side, all smiles. I remember the way she plucked at my shirtsleeve as if to say, There—what did I tell you? And I had to brush her away and wag my hand to keep her quiet during the rest of the talk.

"He wants to show it to a couple of his connections in the publishing field," Bernie was saying, "and he wants me to get another copy made up to send out to Manny on the Coast. So listen, Bob, while we're waiting to see what happens on this one, I want to give you some more assignments. Or wait—listen." And his voice became enriched with the dawning of a new idea. "Listen. Maybe you'd be more comfortable working on your own. Would you rather do that? Would you rather just skip the card file, and use your own imagination?"

Late one rainy night, deep in the Upper West Side, two thugs got into Bernie Silver's cab. To the casual eye they might have looked like ordinary customers, but Bernie had them spotted right away because "Take it from me, a man doesn't hack the streets of Manhattan for twenty-two years without a little specialized education rubbing off."

One was a hardened-criminal type, of course, and the other was little more than a frightened boy, or rather "just a punk."

"I didn't like the way they were talking," Bernie told his readers through me, "and I didn't like the address they gave me—the lowest dive in town—and most of all I didn't like the fact that they were riding in my automobile."

So do you know what he did? Oh, don't worry, he didn't stop the cab and step around and pull them out of the backseat and kick them one after the other in the groin—none of that *My-Flag-Is-Down* nonsense. For one thing, he could tell from their talk that they weren't making a getaway; not tonight, at least. All they'd done tonight was case the joint (a small liquor store near the corner where he'd picked them up); the job was set for tomorrow night at eleven. Anyway, when they got to the lowest dive in town the hardened criminal gave the punk some money and said, "Here, kid; you keep the cab, go on home and get some sleep. I'll see you tomorrow." And that was when Bernie knew what he had to do.

"That punk lived way out in Queens, which gave us plenty of time for conversation, so I asked him who he liked for the National League pennant." And from there on, with deep folk wisdom and consummate skill, Bernie kept up such a steady flow of talk about healthy, clean-living milk-and-sunshine topics that he'd begun to draw the boy out of his hard delinquent shell even before they hit the Queensboro

Bridge. They barreled along Queens Boulevard chattering like a pair of Police Athletic League enthusiasts, and by the time the ride was over, Bernie's fare was practically in tears.

"I saw him swallow a couple of times when he paid me off" was the way I had Bernie put it, "and I had a feeling something had changed in that kid. I had a hope of it, anyway, or maybe just a wish. But I knew I'd done all I could for him." Back in town, Bernie called the police and suggested they put a couple of men around the liquor store the following night.

Sure enough, a job was attempted on that liquor store, only to be foiled by two tough, lovable cops. And sure enough, there was only one thug for them to carry off to the pokey—the hardened-criminal one. "I don't know where the kid was that night," Bernie concluded, "but I like to think he was home in bed with a glass of milk, reading the sports page."

There was the roof and there was the chimney top of it; there were all the windows with the light coming in; there was another approving chuckle from Dr. Alexander Corvo and another submission to the *Reader's Digest*; there was another whisper of a chance for a Simon and Schuster contract and a three-million-dollar production starring Wade Manley; and there was another five in the mail for me.

A small, fragile old gentleman started crying in the cab one day, up around Fifty-ninth and Third, and when Bernie said, "Anything I can help with, sir?" there followed two and a half pages of the most heart-tearing hard-luck story I could imagine. He was a widower; his only daughter had long since married and moved away to Flint, Michigan; his life had been an agony of loneliness for twenty-two years, but he'd always been brave enough about it until now because he'd had a job he loved—tending the geraniums in a big commercial greenhouse. And now this morning the management had told him he would have to go: too old for that kind of work.

"And only then," according to Bernie Silver, "did I make the connection between all this and the address he'd given me—a corner near the Manhattan side of the Brooklyn Bridge."

Bernie couldn't be sure, of course, that his fare planned to hobble right on out to the middle of the bridge and ease his old bones over the railing; but he couldn't take any chances, either. "I figured it was time for me to do some talking" (and he was right about that: another heavy half-page of that tiresome old man's lament and the story would have ruptured the hell out of its foundation). What came next was a brisk page and a half of dialogue in which Bernie discreetly inquired why the old man didn't go and live with his daughter in Michigan, or at least write her a letter so that maybe she'd invite him; but oh, no, he only keened that he couldn't possibly be a burden on his daughter and her family.

"'Burden?' I said, acting like I didn't know what he meant. 'Burden? How could a nice old gentleman like you be a burden on anybody?'"

"'But what else would I be? What can I offer them?'"

"Luckily we were stopped at a red light when he asked me that, so I turned around and looked him straight in the eye. 'Mister,' I said, 'don't you think that family'd like having somebody around the place that knows a thing or two about growing geraniums?'"

Well, by the time they got to the bridge the old man had decided to have Bernie let him off at a nearby Automat instead, because he said he felt like having a cup of tea, and so much for the walls of the damn thing. This was the roof: six months later, Bernie received a small, heavy package with a Flint, Michigan, postmark, addressed to his taxi fleet garage. And do you know what was in that package? Of course you do. A potted geranium. And here's your chimney top: there was also a little note, written in what I'm afraid I really did describe as a fine old spidery hand, and it read, simply, "Thank you."

Personally, I thought this one was loathsome, and Joan wasn't sure about it either; but we mailed it off anyway and Bernie loved it. And so, he told me over the phone, did his wife Rose.

"Which reminds me, Bob, the other reason I called; Rose wants me to find out what evening you and your wife could come up for a little get-together here. Nothing fancy, just the four of us, have a little drink and a chat. You think you might enjoy that?"

"Well, that's very nice of you, Bernie, and of course we'd enjoy it very much. It's just that offhand I don't quite know when we could arrange to—hold on a second." And I covered the mouthpiece and had an urgent conference about it with Joan in the hope that she'd supply me with a graceful excuse.

But she wanted to go, and she had just the right evening in mind, so all four of us were hooked.

"Oh, good," she said when I'd hung up. "I'm glad we're going. They sound sweet."

"Now, *look*." And I aimed my index finger straight at her face. "We're not going at all if you plan to sit around up there making them both aware of how 'sweet' they are. I'm not spending any evenings as gracious Lady Bountiful's consort among the lower classes, and that's final. If you want to turn this thing into some goddamn Bennington girls' garden party for the servants, you can forget about it right now. You hear me?"

Then she asked me if I wanted to know something, and without waiting to find out whether I did or not, she told me. She told me I was just about the biggest snob and biggest bully and biggest all-around loud-mouthed jerk she'd ever come across in her life.

One thing led to another after that; by the time we were on the subway for our enjoyable get-together with the Silvers we were only barely on speaking terms, and I can't tell you how grateful I was to find that the Silvers, while staying on ginger ale themselves, had broken out a bottle of rye for their guests.

Bernie's wife turned out to be a quick, spike-heeled, girdled and bobby-pinned woman whose telephone operator's voice was chillingly expert at the social graces ("How do you do? So nice to meet you; do come in; please sit down; Bernie, help her, she can't get her coat off"); and God knows who started it, or why, but the evening began uncomfortably with a discussion of politics. Joan and I were torn between Truman, Wallace, and not voting at all that year; the Silvers were Dewey people. And what made it all the worse, for our tender liberal sensibilities, was that Rose sought common ground by telling us one bleak tale after another, each with a more elaborate shudder, about the inexorable, menacing encroachment of colored and Puerto Rican elements in this part of the Bronx.

But things got jollier after a while. For one thing they were both delighted with Joan—and I'll have to admit I never met anyone who wasn't—and for another the talk soon turned to the marvelous fact of their knowing Wade Manley, which gave rise to a series of proud reminiscences. "Bernie never takes nothing off him, though, don't worry," Rose assured us. "Bernie, tell them what you did that time he was here and you told him to sit down and shut up. He did! He did! He kind of gave him a push in the chest—this *movie* star!—and he said,

'Ah, siddown and sheddep, Manny. *We* know who you are!' Tell them, Bernie."

And Bernie, convulsed with pleasure, got up to reenact the scene. "Oh, we were just kind of kidding around, you understand," he said, "but anyway, that's what I did. I gave him a shove like this, and I said, 'Ah, siddown and sheddep, Manny. *We* know who you are!'"

"He did! That's the God's truth! Pushed him right down in that chair over there! Wade Manley!"

A little later, when Bernie and I had paired off for a man-to-man talk over the freshening of drinks, and Rose and Joan were cozily settled in the love seat, Rose directed a roguish glance at me. "I wouldn't want to give this husband of yours a swelled head, Joanie, but do you know what Dr. Corvo told Bernie? Shall I tell her, Bernie?"

"Sure, tell her! Tell her!" And Bernie waved the bottle of ginger ale in one hand and the bottle of rye in the other, to show how openly all secrets could be bared tonight.

"Well," she said. "Dr. Corvo said your husband is the finest writer Bernie's ever had."

Later still, when Bernie and I were in the love seat and the ladies were at the credenza, I began to see that Rose was a builder too. Maybe she hadn't built that credenza with her own hands, but she'd clearly done more than her share of building whatever heartfelt convictions were needed to sustain the hundreds on hundreds of dollars its purchase must be costing them on the installment plan. A piece of furniture like that was an investment in the future; and now, as she stood fussing over it and wiping off little parts of it while she talked to Joan, I could have sworn I saw her arranging a future party in her mind. Joan and I would be among those present, that much was certain ("This is Mr. Robert Prentice, my husband's assistant, and Mrs. Prentice"), and the rest of the guest list was almost a foregone conclusion too: Wade Manley and his wife, of course, along with a careful selection of their Hollywood friends; Walter Winchell would be there, and Earl Wilson and Toots Shor and all that crowd; but far more important, for any person of refinement, would be the presence of Dr. and Mrs. Alexander Corvo and some of the people who comprised their set. People like the Lionel Trillings and the Reinhold Niebuhrs, the Huntington Hartfords and the Leslie R. Groveses—and if anybody on the order of Mr. and Mrs. Newbold Morris wanted to come, you could be damn sure they'd have to do some pretty fancy jockeying for an invitation.

It was, as Joan admitted later, stifling hot in the Silvers' apartment that night; and I cite this as a presentable excuse for the fact that what I did next—and it took me a hell of a lot less time to do it in 1948 than it does now, believe me—was to get roaring drunk. Soon I was not only the most vociferous but the only talker in the room; I was explaining that, by Jesus God, we'd all four of us be millionaires yet.

And wouldn't we have a ball? Oh, we'd be slapping Lionel Trilling around and pushing him down into every chair in this room and telling him to shut up—"And you too, Reinhold Niebuhr, you pompous, sanctimonious old fool! Where's *your* money? Why don't you put your money where your mouth is?"

Bernie was chuckling and looking sleepy, and Joan was looking humiliated for me, and Rose was smiling in cool but infinite understanding of how tiresome husbands could sometimes be. Then we were all out in the alcove trying on at least half a dozen coats apiece, and I was looking at the bugler's photograph again wondering if I dared to ask my burning question about it. But this time I wasn't sure which I feared more: that Bernie might say, "Just for the picture," or that he might say, "Sure I was!" and go rummaging in the closet or in some part of the credenza until he'd come up with the tarnished old bugle itself, and we'd all have to go back and sit down again while Bernie put his heels together, drew himself erect, and sounded the pure, sad melody of taps for us all.

That was in October. I'm a little vague on how many "By Bernie Silver" stories I turned out during the rest of the fall. I do remember a comic-relief one about a fat tourist who got stuck at the waist when he tried to climb up through the skyview window of the cab for better sight-seeing, and a very solemn one in which Bernie delivered a lecture on racial tolerance (which struck a sour note with me, considering the way he'd chimed in with Rose's views on the brown hordes advancing over the Bronx); but mostly what I remember about him during that period is that Joan and I could never seem to mention him without getting into some kind of an argument.

When she said we really ought to return his and Rose's invitation, for example, I told her not to be silly. I said I was sure they wouldn't expect it, and when she said "Why?" I gave her a crisp, impatient briefing on the hopelessness of trying to ignore class barriers, of pretending that the Silvers could ever really become our friends, or that they'd ever really want to.

Another time, toward the end of a curiously dull evening when we'd gone to our favorite premarital restaurant and failed for an hour to find anything to talk about, she tried to get the conversation going by leaning romantically toward me across the table and holding up her wineglass. "Here's to Bernie's selling your last one to the *Reader's Digest.*"

"Yeah," I said. "Sure. Big deal."

"Oh, don't be so gruff. You know perfectly well it could happen any day. We might make a lot of money and go to Europe and everything."

"Are you kidding?" It suddenly annoyed me that any intelligent, well-educated girl in the twentieth century could be so gullible; and that such a girl should actually be my wife, that I would be expected to go on playing along with this kind of simpleminded innocence for years and years to come, seemed, for the moment, an intolerable situation. "Why don't you grow up a little? You don't really think there's ever been a chance of his selling that junk, do you?" And I looked at her in a way that must have been very much like Bernie's own way of looking at me, the night he asked if I'd really thought he meant twenty-five a time. "Do you?"

"Yes, I do," she said, putting her glass down. "Or at least, I did. I thought you did too. If you don't, it seems sort of cynical and dishonest to go on working for him, doesn't it?" And she wouldn't talk to me all the way home.

The real trouble, I guess, was that we were both preoccupied with two far more serious matters by this time. One was our recent discovery that Joan was pregnant, and the other was that my position at the United Press had begun to sink as steadily as any sinking fund debenture.

My time on the financial desk had become a slow ordeal of waiting for my superiors to discover more and more of how little I knew about what I was doing; and now however pathetically willing I might be to learn all the things I was supposed to know, it had become much too ludicrously late to ask. I was hunching lower and lower over my clattering typewriter there all day and sweating out the ax—the kind, sad dropping of the assistant financial editor's hand on my shoulder ("Can I speak to you inside a minute, Bob?")—and each day that it didn't happen was a kind of shabby victory.

Early in December I was walking home from the subway after one of those days, dragging myself down West Twelfth Street like a seventy-year-old, when I discovered that a taxicab had been moving beside me at a snail's pace for a block and a half. It was one of the green-and-white kind, and behind its windshield flashed an enormous smile.

"Bob! What's the matter, there, Bob? You lost in thought or something? This where you live?"

When he parked the cab at the curb and got out, it was the first time I'd even seen him in his working clothes: a twill cap, a buttoned sweater and one of those columnar change-making gadgets strapped to his waist; and when we shook hands it was the first time I'd seen his fingertips stained a shiny gray from handling other people's coins and dollar bills all day. Close up, smiling or not, he looked as worn out as I felt.

"Come on in, Bernie." He seemed surprised by the crumbling doorway and dirty stairs of the house, and also by the whitewashed, poster-decorated austerity of our big single room, whose rent was probably less than half of what he and Rose were paying uptown, and I remember taking a dim Bohemian's pride in letting him notice these things; I guess I had some snobbish notion that it wouldn't do Bernie Silver any harm to learn that people could be smart and poor at the same time.

We couldn't offer him any ginger ale and he said a glass of plain water would be fine, so it wasn't much of a social occasion. It troubled me afterwards to remember how constrained he was with Joan—I don't think he looked her full in the face once during the whole visit—and I wondered if this was because of our failure to return that invitation. Why is it that wives are nearly always blamed for what must at least as often as not be their husbands' fault in matters like that? But maybe it was just that he was more conscious of his cab driver's costume in her presence than in mine. Or maybe he had never imagined that such a pretty and cultivated girl could live in such stark surroundings, and was embarrassed for her.

"I'll tell you what I dropped by about, Bob. I'm trying a new angle." And as he talked I began to suspect, more from his eyes than his words, that something had gone very wrong with the long-range building program. Maybe a publishing friend of Dr. Corvo's had laid it on the line at last about the poor possibilities of our material; maybe Dr. Corvo himself had grown snappish; maybe there had been some crushing final communication from Wade Manley, or, more crushingly, from Wade Manley's agency representative. Or it might have been simply that Bernie was tired after his day's work in a way that no glass of plain water would help; in any case he was trying a new angle.

Had I ever heard of Vincent J. Poletti? But he gave me this name as if he knew perfectly well it wouldn't knock my eye out, and he followed it right up with the information that Vincent J. Poletti was a Democratic State Assemblyman from Bernie's own district in the Bronx.

"Now, this man," he said, "is a man that goes out of his way to help people. Believe me, Bob, he's not just one of your cheap vote-getters. He's a real public servant. What's more, he's a comer in the Party. He's going to be our next Congressman. So here's the idea, Bob. We get a photograph of me—I have this friend of mine'll do it for nothing—we get it taken from the backseat of the cab, with me at the wheel kind of turning around and smiling like this, get it?" He turned his body away from his smiling head to show me how it would look. "And we print this picture on the cover of a booklet. The title of the booklet"— and here he sketched a suggestion of block lettering in the air—"the title of the booklet is 'Take It from Bernie.' Okay? Now. Inside the booklet we have a story—just exactly like the others you wrote except this time it's a little different. This time I'm telling a story about why Vincent J. Poletti is the man we need for Congress. I don't mean just a bunch of political talk, either, Bob. I mean a real little story."

"Bernie, I don't see how this is going to work. You can't have a 'story' about why anybody is the man we need for Congress."

"Who says you can't?"

"And anyway I thought you and Rose were Republicans."

"On the national level, yes. On the local level, no."

"Well, but hell, Bernie, we just had an election. There won't be another election for two years."

But he only tapped his head and made a faraway gesture to show that in politics it paid a man to think ahead.

Joan was over in the kitchen area of the room, cleaning up the breakfast dishes and getting the dinner started, and I looked to her for help, but her back was turned.

"It just doesn't sound right, Bernie. I don't know anything about politics."

"So? Know, schmow. What's to know? Do you know anything about driving a cab?"

No; and I sure as hell didn't know anything about Wall Street, either—Wall Street, Schmall Street!—but that was another depressing little story. "I don't know, Bernie; things are very unsettled right now. I don't think I'd better take on any more assignments for the time being. I mean for one thing I may be about to—" But I couldn't bring myself to tell him about my UP problem, so I said, "For one thing Joan's having a baby now, and everything's sort of—"

"Wow! Well, isn't that something!" He was on his feet and shaking my hand. "Isn't—that—something! Congratulations, Bob, I think this is—I think this is really wonderful. Congratulations, there, Joanie!" And it seemed a little excessive to me at the time, but maybe that's the way such news will always strike a middle-aged, childless man.

"Oh, listen, Bob," he said when we settled down again. "This Poletti thing'll be duck soup for you; and I'll tell you what. Seeing as this is just a one-shot and there won't be any royalties, we'll make it ten instead of five. Is that a deal?"

"Well, but wait a second, Bernie. I'm going to need some more information. I mean what exactly does this guy do for people?"

And it soon became clear that Bernie knew very little more about Vincent J. Poletti than I did. He was a real public servant, that was all; he went out of his way to help people. "Oh, Bob, listen. What's the difference? Where's your imagination? You never needed any help before. Listen. What you just told me gives me one idea right off the bat. I'm driving along; these two kids hail me out in front of the maternity hospital, this young veteran and his wife. They got this little-biddy baby, three days old, and they're happy as larks. Only here's the trouble. This boy's got no job or anything. They only just moved here, they don't know anybody, maybe they're Puerto Ricans or something, they got a week's rent on their room and that's it. Then they're broke. So I'm taking them home, they live right in my neighborhood, and we're chatting away, and I say, 'Listen, kids. I think I'll take you to see a friend of mine.'"

"Assemblyman Vincent J. Poletti."

"Naturally. Only I don't tell them his name yet. I just say 'this friend of mine.' So we get there and I go in and tell Poletti about it and he comes out and talks to the kids and gives them money or something. See? You got a good share of your story right there."

"Hey, yeah, and wait a minute, Bernie." I got up and began dramatically pacing the floor, the way people in Hollywood story conferences are supposed to do. "Wait a minute. After he gives them money, he gets into your cab and you take off with him down the Grand Concourse, and those two Puerto Rican kids are standing there on the sidewalk kind of looking at each other, and the girl says, 'Who *was* that man?' And the boy looks very serious and he says, 'Honey, don't you know? Didn't you notice he was wearing a mask?' And she says, 'Oh no, it couldn't be the—' And he says, 'Yes, yes, it was. Honey, that was the Lone Assemblyman.' And then listen! You know what happens next? Listen! Way off down the block they hear this voice, and you know what the voice is calling?" I sank to the floor on one trembling knee to deliver the punch line. "It's calling 'Hi-yo, Bernie *Sil*ver—away!"

And it may not look very funny written down, but it almost killed me. I must have laughed for at least a minute, until I went into a coughing fit and Joan had to come and pound me on the back; only very gradually, coming out of it, did I realize that Bernie was not amused. He had chuckled in bewildered politeness during my seizure, but now he was looking down at his hands and there were embarrassing blotches of pink in his sober cheeks. I had hurt his feelings. I remember resenting it that his feelings could be hurt so easily, and resenting it that Joan had gone back to the kitchen instead of staying to help me out of this awkward situation, and then beginning to feel very guilty and sorry, as the silence continued, until I finally decided that the only decent way of making it up to him was to accept the assignment. And sure enough, he brightened instantly when I told him I'd give it a try.

"I mean you don't necessarily have to use that about the Puerto Rican kids," he assured me. "That's just one idea. Or maybe you could start it off that way and then go on to other things, the more the better. You work it out any way you like."

At the door, shaking hands again (and it seemed that we'd been shaking hands all afternoon), I said, "So that's ten for this one, right, Bernie?"

"Right, Bob."

"Do you really think you should have told him you'd do it?" Joan asked me the minute he'd gone.

"Why not?"

"Well, because it *is* going to be practically impossible, isn't it?"

"Look, will you do me a favor? Will you please get off my back?"

She put her hands on her hips. "I just don't understand you, Bob. Why *did* you say you'd do it?"

"Why the hell do you think? Because we're going to need the ten bucks, that's why."

In the end I built—oh, built, schmilt. I put page one and then page two and then page three into the old machine and I *wrote* the son of a bitch. It did start off with the Puerto Rican kids, but for some reason I couldn't get more than a couple of pages out of them; then I had to find other ways for Vincent J. Poletti to demonstrate his giant goodness.

What does a public servant do when he really wants to go out of his way to help people? Gives them money, that's what he does; and pretty soon I had Poletti forking over more than he could count. It got so that anybody in the Bronx who was even faintly up against it had only to climb into Bernie Silver's cab and say, "The Poletti place," and their troubles were over. And the worst part of it was my own grim conviction that it was the best I could do.

Joan never saw the thing, because she was asleep when I finally managed to get it into an envelope and into the mail. And there was no word from Bernie—or about him, between the two of us—for nearly a week. Then, at the same hour as his last visit, the frayed-out end of the day, our doorbell rang. I knew there was going to be trouble as soon as I opened the door and found him smiling there, with spatters of rain on his sweater, and I knew I wasn't going to stand for any nonsense.

"Bob," he said, sitting down, "I hate to say it, but I'm disappointed in you this time." He pulled my folded manuscript out of his sweater. "This thing is—Bob, this is nothing."

"It's six and a half pages. That's not nothing, Bernie."

"Bob, please don't give me six and a half pages. I know it's six and a half pages, but it's nothing. You made this man into a fool, Bob. You got him giving his dough away all the time."

"You told me he gave dough, Bernie."

"To the Puerto Rican kids I said yes, sure, maybe he could give a little, fine. And now you come along and you got him going around spending here like some kind of—some kind of drunken sailor or something."

I thought I might be going to cry, but my voice came out very low and controlled. "Bernie, I did ask you what else he could do. I did tell you I didn't know what the hell else he could do. If you wanted him to do something else, you should've made that clear."

"But *Bob*," he said, standing up for emphasis, and his next words have often come back to me as the final, despairing, everlasting cry of the Philistine. "Bob, *you're* the one with the imagination!"

I stood up too, so that I could look down at him. *I* knew I was the one with the imagination. I also knew I was twenty-two years old and as tired as an old man, that I was about to lose my job, that I had a baby on the way and wasn't even getting along very well with my wife; and now every cab driver, every two-bit politician's pimp and phony bugler in the city of New York was walking into my house and trying to steal my money.

"Ten bucks, Bernie."

He made a helpless gesture, smiling. Then he looked over into the kitchen area, where Joan was, and although I meant to keep my eyes on him, I must have looked there too, because I remember what she was doing. She was twisting a dish towel in her hands and looking down at it.

"Listen, Bob," he said. "I shouldn't of said it was nothing. You're right! Who could take a thing six and a half pages long and say it's nothing? Probably a lot of good stuff in this thing, Bob. You want your ten bucks; all right, fine, you'll get your ten bucks. All I'm asking is this. First take this thing back and change it a little, that's all. Then we can—"

"Ten bucks, Bernie. Now."

His smile had lost its life, but it stayed right there on his face while he took the bill out of his wallet and handed it over, and while I went through a miserable little show of examining it to make goddamn sure it was a ten.

"Okay, Bob," he said. "We're all square, then. Right?"

"Right."

Then he was gone, and Joan went swiftly to the door and opened it and called, "Goodnight, Bernie!"

I thought I heard his footsteps pause on the stairs, but I didn't hear any answering "Goodnight" from him, so I guessed that all he'd done was to turn around and wave to her, or blow her a kiss. Then from the window I saw him move out across the sidewalk and get into his taxicab and drive away. All this time I was folding and refolding his money, and I don't believe I've ever held anything in my hand that I wanted less.

The room was very quiet with only the two of us moving around in it, while the kitchen area steamed and crackled with the savory smells of a dinner that I don't think either of us felt like eating. "Well," I said. "That's that."

"Was it really necessary," she inquired, "to be so dreadfully unpleasant to him?"

And this, at the time, seemed clearly to be the least loyal possible thing she could have said, the unkindest cut of all. "Un*pleasant* to him! Un*pleasant* to him! Would you mind telling me just what the hell I'm supposed to do? Am I supposed to sit around being 'pleasant' while some cheap, lying little parasitic leech of a *cab* driver comes in here and bleeds me *white*? Is that what you want? Huh? Is *that* what you want?"

Then she did what she often used to do at moments like that, what I sometimes think I'd give anything in life never to have seen her do: she turned away from me and closed her eyes and covered her ears with both hands.

Less than a week later the assistant financial editor's hand did fall on my shoulder at last, right in the middle of a paragraph about domestic corporate bonds in moderately active trading.

It was still well before Christmas, and I got a job to tide us over as a demonstrator of mechanical toys in a Fifth Avenue dimestore. And I think it must have been during that dimestore period—possibly while winding up a little tin-and-cotton kitten that went "Mew!" and rolled over, "Mew!" and rolled over, "Mew!" and rolled over—it was along in there sometime, anyway, that I gave up whatever was left of the idea of building my life on the pattern of Ernest Hemingway's. Some construction projects are just plain out of the question.

After New Year's I got some other idiot job; then in April, with all the abruptness and surprise of spring, I was hired for eighty dollars a week as a writer in an industrial public-relations office, where the question of whether or not I knew what I was doing never mattered very much because hardly any of the other employees knew what they were doing either.

It was a remarkably easy job, and it allowed me to save a remarkable amount of energy each day for my own work, which all at once began to go well. With Hemingway safely abandoned, I had moved on to an F. Scott Fitzgerald phase; then, the best of all, I had begun to find what seemed to give every indication of being my own style. The winter was over, and things seemed to be growing easier between Joan and me too, and in the early summer our first daughter was born.

She caused a one- or two-month interruption in my writing schedule, but before long I was back at work and convinced that I was going from strength to strength: I had begun to bulldoze and dig and lay the foundation for a big, ambitious, tragic novel. I never did finish the book—it was the first in a series of more unfinished novels than I like to think about now—but in those early stages it was fascinating work, and the fact that it went slowly seemed only to add to its promise of eventual magnificence. I was spending more and more time each night behind my writing screen, emerging only to pace the floor with a headful of serene and majestic daydreams. And it was late in the year, all the way around to fall again, one evening when Joan had gone out to the movies, leaving me as baby-sitter, when I came out from behind the screen to pick up a ringing phone and heard: "Bob Prentice? Bernie Silver."

I won't pretend that I'd forgotten who he was, but it's not too much to say that for a second or two I did have trouble realizing that I'd ever really worked for him—that I could ever really have been involved, at first hand, in the pathetic delusions of a taxicab driver. It gave me pause, which is to say that it caused me to wince and then to sheepishly grin at the phone, to duck my head and smooth my hair with my free hand in a bashful demonstration of *noblesse oblige*—this accompanied by a silent, humble vow that whatever Bernie Silver might want from me now, I would go out of my way to avoid any chance of hurting his feelings. I remember wishing Joan were home, so that she could witness my kindness.

But the first thing be wanted to know about was the baby. Was it a boy or a girl? Wonderful! And who did she look like? Well, of course, naturally, they never did look like anybody much at that age. And how did it feel to be a father? Huh? Feel pretty good? Good! Then he took on what struck me as a strangely formal, cap-holding tone, like that of a long-discharged servant inquiring after the lady of the house. "And how's Mrs. Prentice?"

She had been "Joan" and "Joanie" and "Sweetheart" to him in his own home, and I somehow couldn't believe he'd forgotten her name; I could only guess that he hadn't heard her call out to him on the stairs that night after all—that maybe, remembering only the way she'd stood there with her dish towel, he had even blamed her as the instigator of my own intransigence over the damned ten bucks. But all I could do now was to tell him she was fine. "And how've you people been, Bernie?"

"Well," he said, "*I've* been all right," and here his voice fell to the shocked sobriety of hospital-room conferences. "But I almost lost Rose, a couple of months back."

Oh, it was okay now, he assured me, she was much better and home from the hospital and feeling well; but when he started talking about "tests" and "radiology" I had the awful sense of doom that comes when the unmentionable name of cancer hangs in the air.

"Well, Bernie," I said, "I'm terribly sorry she's been ill, and please be sure to give her our—"

Give her our what? Regards? Best wishes? Either one, it suddenly seemed to me, would carry the unforgivable taint of condescension. "Give her our love," I said, and immediately chewed my lip in fear that this might sound the most condescending of all.

"I will! I will! I'll certainly do that for you, Bob," he said, and so I was glad I'd put it that way. "And now, what I called you about is this." And he chuckled. "Oh, don't worry, no politics. Here's the thing. I've got this really terrifically talented boy working for me now, Bob. This boy's an artist."

And great God, what a sickly, intricate thing a writer's heart is! Because do you know what I felt when he said that? I felt a twinge of jealousy. "Artist," was he? I'd show them who the hell the artist was around *this* little writing establishment.

But right away Bernie started talking about "strips" and "layouts," so I was able to retire my competitive zeal in favor of the old, reliable ironic detachment. What a relief!

"Oh, an *artist*, you mean. A *comic*-strip artist."

"Right. Bob, you ought to see the way this boy can draw. You know what he does? He makes me look like me, but he makes me look a little bit like Wade Manley too. Do you get the picture?"

"It sounds fine, Bernie." And now that the old detachment was working again, I could see that I'd have to be on my guard. Maybe he wouldn't be needing any more stories—by now he probably had a whole credenzaful of manuscripts for the artist to work from—but he'd still be needing a writer to do the "continuity," or whatever it's called, and the words for the artist's speech balloons, and I would now have to tell him, as gently and gracefully as possible, that it wasn't going to be me.

"Bob," he said, "this thing is really building. Dr. Corvo took one look at these strips and he said to me, 'Bernie, forget the magazine business, forget the book business. You've found the solution.'"

"Well. It certainly does sound good, Bernie."

"And Bob, here's why I called. I know they keep you pretty busy down there at the UP, but I was wondering if you might have time to do a little—"

"I'm not working for the UP anymore, Bernie." And I told him about the publicity job.

"Well," he said. "That sounds like you're really coming up in the world there, Bob. Congratulations."

"Thanks. Anyway, Bernie, the point is I really don't think I'd have time to do any writing for you just now. I mean I'd certainly like to, it isn't that; it's just that the baby does take up a lot of time here, and then I've got my own work going—I'm doing a novel now, you see—and I really don't think I'd better take on anything else."

"Oh. Well, okay, then, Bob; don't worry about it. All I meant, you see, is that it really would've been a break for us if we could of made use of your—*you* know, your writing talent in this thing."

"I'm sorry too, Bernie, and I certainly do wish you luck with it."

You may well have guessed by now what didn't occur to me, I swear, until at least an hour after I'd said goodbye to him: that this time Bernie hadn't wanted me as a writer at all. He'd thought I was still at the UP, and might therefore be a valuable contact close to the heart of the syndicated comic-strip business.

I can remember exactly what I was doing when this knowledge came over me. I was changing the baby's diaper, looking down into her round, beautiful eyes as if I expected her to congratulate me, or thank me, for having once more managed to avoid the terrible possibility of touching her skin with the point of the safety pin—I was doing that, when I thought of the way his voice had paused in saying, "We could of made use of your—"

During that pause he must have abandoned whatever elaborate building plans might still have lain in saying "your connections there at the UP" (and he didn't know I'd been fired; for all he knew I might still have as many solid connections in the newspaper business as Dr. Corvo had in the child psychology field or Wade Manley had in the movies), and had chosen to finish it off with "your writing talent" instead. And so I knew that for all my finicking concern over the sparing of Bernie's feelings in that telephone conversation, it was Bernie, in the end, who had gone out of his way to spare mine.

I can't honestly say that I've thought very much about him over the years. It might be a nice touch to tell you that I never get into a taxicab without taking a close look at the driver's neck and profile, but it wouldn't be true. One thing that is true, though, and it's just now occurred to me, is that very often in trying to hit on the right wording for some touchy personal letter, I've thought of: "I didn't have time to write you a short letter today, so I had to write you a long one instead."

Whether I meant it or not when I wished him luck with his comic strip, I think I started meaning it an hour later. I mean it now, wholeheartedly, and the funny part is that he might still be able to build it into something, connections or not. Sillier things than that have built empires in America. At any rate I hope he hasn't lost his interest in the project, in one form or another; but more than anything I hope to God—and I'm not swearing this time—I hope to whatever God there may be that he hasn't lost Rose.

Reading all this over, I can see that it hasn't been built very well. Its beams and joists, its very walls are somehow out of kilter; its foundation feels weak; possibly I failed to dig the right kind of hole in the ground in the first place. But there's no point in worrying about such things now, because it's time to put the roof on it—to bring you up to date on what happened to the rest of us builders.

Everybody knows what happened to Wade Manley. He died unexpectedly a few years later, in bed; and the fact that it was the bed of a young woman not his wife was considered racy enough to keep the tabloids busy for weeks. You can still see reruns of his old movies on television, and whenever I see one I'm surprised all over again to find that he was a good actor—much too good, I expect, ever to have gotten caught in any cornball role as a cab driver with a heart as big as all outdoors.

As for Dr. Corvo, there was a time when everybody knew what happened to him too. It happened in the very early fifties, whichever year it was that the television companies built and launched their most massive advertising campaigns. One of the most massive of all was built around a signed statement by Dr. Alexander Corvo, eminent child psychologist, to the effect that any boy or girl in our time whose home lacked a television set would quite possibly grow up emotionally deprived. Every other child psychologist, every articulate liberal, and very nearly every parent in the United States came down on Alexander Corvo like a plague of locusts, and when they were done with him there wasn't an awful lot of eminence left. Since then, I'd say offhand that the *New York Times* would give you half a dozen Alexander Corvos for a single Newbold Morris any day of the week.

That takes the story right on up to Joan and me, and now I'll have to give you the chimney top. I'll have to tell you that what she and I were building collapsed too, a couple of years ago. Oh, we're still friendly—no legal battles over alimony, or custody, or anything like that—but there you are.

And where are the windows? Where does the light come in?

Bernie, old friend, forgive me, but I haven't got the answer to that one. I'm not even sure if there *are* any windows in this particular house. Maybe the light is just going to have to come in as best it can, through whatever chinks and cracks have been left in the builder's faulty craftsmanship, and if that's the case you can be sure that nobody feels worse about it than I do. God knows, Bernie; God knows there certainly ought to be a window around here somewhere, for all of us.

FROM

Liars in Love

Oh, Joseph, I'm So Tired

WHEN FRANKLIN D. ROOSEVELT was President-elect there must have been sculptors all over America who wanted a chance to model his head from life, but my mother had connections. One of her closest friends and neighbors, in the Greenwich Village courtyard where we lived, was an amiable man named Howard Whitman who had recently lost his job as a reporter on the *New York Post*. And one of Howard's former colleagues from the *Post* was now employed in the press office of Roosevelt's New York headquarters. That would make it easy for her to get in—or, as she said, to get an entrée—and she was confident she could take it from there. She was confident about everything she did in those days, but it never quite disguised a terrible need for support and approval on every side.

She wasn't a very good sculptor. She had been working at it for only three years, since breaking up her marriage to my father, and there was still something stiff and amateurish about her pieces. Before the Roosevelt project her specialty had been "garden figures"—a life-size little boy whose legs turned into the legs of a goat at the knees and another who knelt among ferns to play the pipes of Pan; little girls who trailed chains of daisies from their upraised arms or walked beside a spread-winged goose. These fanciful children, in plaster painted green to simulate weathered bronze, were arranged on homemade wooden pedestals to loom around her studio and to leave a cleared space in the middle for the modeling stand that held whatever she was working on in clay.

Her idea was that any number of rich people, all of them gracious and aristocratic, would soon discover her: they would want her sculpture to decorate their landscaped gardens, and they would want to make her their friend for life. In the meantime, a little nationwide publicity as the first woman sculptor to "do" the President-elect certainly wouldn't hurt her career.

And, if nothing else, she had a good studio. It was, in fact, the best of all the studios she would have in the rest of her life. There were six or eight old houses facing our side of the courtyard, with their backs to Bedford Street, and ours was probably the showplace of the row because the front room on its ground floor was two stories high. You went down a broad set of brick steps to the tall front windows and the front door; then you were in the high, wide, light-flooded studio. It was big enough to serve as a living room too, and so along with the green garden children it contained all the living-room furniture from the house we'd lived in with my father in the suburban town of Hastings-on-Hudson, where I was born. A second-floor balcony ran along the far end of the studio, with two small bedrooms and a tiny bathroom tucked away upstairs; beneath that, where the ground floor continued through to the Bedford Street side, lay the only part of the apartment that might let you know we didn't have much money. The ceiling was very low and it was always dark in there; the small windows looked out underneath an iron sidewalk grating, and the bottom of that street cavity was thick with strewn garbage. Our roach-infested kitchen was barely big enough for a stove and sink that were never clean, and for a brown wooden icebox with its dark, ever-melting block of ice; the rest of that area was our dining room, and not even the amplitude of the old Hastings dining-room table could brighten it. But our Majestic radio was in there too, and that made it a cozy place for my sister Edith and me: we liked the children's programs that came on in the late afternoons.

We had just turned off the radio one day when we went out into the studio and found our mother discussing the Roosevelt project with Howard Whitman. It was the first we'd heard of it, and we must have interrupted her with too many questions because she said, "Edith? Billy? That's enough, now. I'll tell you all about this later. Run out in the garden and play."

She always called the courtyard "the garden," though nothing grew there except a few stunted city trees and a patch of grass that never had a chance to spread. Mostly it was bald earth, interrupted here and there by brick paving, lightly powdered with soot and scattered with the droppings of dogs and cats. It may have been six or eight houses long, but it was only two houses wide, which gave it a hemmed-in, cheerless look; its only point of interest was a dilapidated marble fountain, not much bigger than a birdbath, which stood near our house. The original idea of the fountain was that water would drip evenly from around the rim of its upper tier and tinkle into its lower basin, but age had unsettled it; the water spilled in a single ropy stream from the only inch of the upper tier's rim that stayed clean. The lower basin was deep enough to soak your feet in on a hot day, but there wasn't much pleasure in that because the underwater part of the marble was coated with brown scum.

My sister and I found things to do in the courtyard every day, for all of the two years we lived there, but that was only because Edith was an imaginative child. She was eleven at the time of the Roosevelt project, and I was seven.

"Daddy?" she asked in our father's office uptown one afternoon. "Have you heard Mommy's doing a head of President Roosevelt?"

"Oh?" He was rummaging in his desk, looking for something he'd said we might like.

"She's going to take his measurements and stuff here in New York," Edith said, "and then after the Inauguration, when the sculpture's done, she's going to take it to Washington and present it to him in the White House." Edith often told one of our parents about the other's more virtuous activities; it was part of her long, hopeless effort to bring them back together. Many years later she told me she thought she had never recovered, and never would, from the shock of their breakup: she said Hastings-on-Hudson remained the happiest time of her life, and that made me envious because I could scarcely remember it at all.

"Well," my father said. "That's really something, isn't it." Then he found what he'd been looking for in the desk and said, "Here we go; what do you think of these?" They were two fragile perforated sheets of what looked like postage stamps, each stamp bearing the insignia of an electric lightbulb in vivid white against a yellow background, and the words "More light."

My father's office was one of many small cubicles on the twenty-third floor of the General Electric building. He was an assistant regional sales manager in what was then called the Mazda Lamp

Division—a modest job, but good enough to have allowed him to rent into a town like Hastings-on-Hudson in better times—and these "More light" stamps were souvenirs of a recent sales convention. We told him the stamps were neat—and they were—but expressed some doubt as to what we might do with them.

"Oh, they're just for decoration," he said. "I thought you could paste them into your schoolbooks, or—you know—whatever you want. Ready to go?" And he carefully folded the sheets of stamps and put them in his inside pocket for safekeeping on the way home.

Between the subway exit and the courtyard, somewhere in the West Village, we always walked past a vacant lot where men stood huddled around weak fires built of broken fruit crates and trash, some of them warming tin cans of food held by coat-hanger wire over the flames. "Don't stare," my father had said the first time. "All those men are out of work, and they're hungry."

"Daddy?" Edith inquired. "Do you think Roosevelt's good?"

"Sure I do."

"Do you think all the Democrats are good?"

"Well, most of 'em, sure."

Much later I would learn that my father had participated in local Democratic Party politics for years. He had served some of his political friends—men my mother described as dreadful little Irish people from Tammany Hall—by helping them to establish Mazda Lamp distributorships in various parts of the city. And he loved their social gatherings, at which he was always asked to sing.

"Well, of course, you're too young to remember Daddy's singing," Edith said to me once after his death in 1942.

"No, I'm not; I remember."

"But I mean really remember," she said. "He had the most beautiful tenor voice I've ever heard. Remember 'Danny Boy'?"

"Sure."

"Ah, God, that was something," she said, closing her eyes. "That was really—that was really something."

When we got back to the courtyard that afternoon, and back into the studio, Edith and I watched our parents say hello to each other. We always watched that closely, hoping they might drift into conversation and sit down together and find things to laugh about, but they never did. And it was even less likely than usual that day because my mother had a guest—a woman named Sloane Cabot who was her best friend in the courtyard, and who greeted my father with a little rush of false, flirtatious enthusiasm.

"How've you been, Sloane?" he said. Then he turned back to his former wife and said, "Helen? I hear you're planning to make a bust of Roosevelt."

"Well, not a bust," she said. "A head. I think it'll be more effective if I cut it off at the neck."

"Well, good. That's fine. Good luck with it. Okay, then." He gave his whole attention to Edith and me. "Okay. See you soon. How about a hug?"

And those hugs of his, the climax of his visitation rights, were unforgettable. One at a time we would be swept up and pressed hard into the smells of linen and whiskey and tobacco; the warm rasp of his jaw would graze one cheek and there would be a quick moist kiss near the ear; then he'd let us go.

He was almost all the way out of the courtyard, almost out in the street, when Edith and I went racing after him.

"Daddy! Daddy! You forgot the stamps!"

He stopped and turned around, and that was when we saw he was crying. He tried to hide it—he put his face nearly into his armpit as if that might help him search his inside pocket—but there is no way to disguise the awful bloat and pucker of a face in tears.

"Here," he said. "Here you go." And he gave us the least convincing smile I had ever seen. It would be good to report that we stayed and talked to him—that we hugged him again—but we were too embarrassed for that. We took the stamps and ran home without looking back.

"Oh, aren't you excited, Helen?" Sloane Cabot was saying. "To be meeting him, and talking to him and everything, in front of all those reporters?"

"Well, of course," my mother said, "but the important thing is to get the measurements right. I hope there won't be a lot of photographers and silly interruptions."

Sloane Cabot was some years younger than my mother, and strikingly pretty in a style often portrayed in what I think are called Art Deco illustrations of that period: straight dark bangs, big eyes, and a big mouth. She too was a divorced mother, though her former husband had vanished long ago and was referred to only as "that bastard" or "that cowardly son of a bitch." Her only child was a boy of Edith's age named John, whom Edith and I liked enormously.

The two women had met within days of our moving into the courtyard, and their friendship was sealed when my mother solved the problem of John's schooling. She knew a Hastings-on-Hudson family who would appreciate the money earned from taking in a boarder, so John went up there to live and go to school, and came home only on weekends. The arrangement cost more than Sloane could comfortably afford, but she managed to make ends meet and was forever grateful.

Sloane worked in the Wall Street district as a private secretary. She talked a lot about how she hated her job and her boss, but the good part was that her boss was often out of town for extended periods: that gave her time to use the office typewriter in pursuit of her life's ambition, which was to write scripts for the radio.

She once confided to my mother that she'd made up both of her names: "Sloane" because it sounded masculine, the kind of name a woman alone might need for making her way in the world, and "Cabot" because—well, because it had a touch of class. Was there anything wrong with that?

"Oh, Helen," she said. "This is going to be wonderful for you. If you get the publicity—if the papers pick it up, and the newsreels—you'll be one of the most interesting personalities in America."

Five or six people were gathered in the studio on the day my mother came home from her first visit with the President-elect.

"Will somebody get me a drink?" she asked, looking around in mock helplessness. "Then I'll tell you all about it."

And with the drink in her hand, with her eyes as wide as a child's, she told us how a door had opened and two big men had brought him in.

"Big men," she insisted. "Young, strong men, holding him up under the arms, and you could see how they were straining. Then you saw this *foot* come out, with these awful metal braces on the shoe, and then the *other* foot. And he was sweating, and he was panting for breath, and his face was—I don't know—all bright and tense and horrible." She shuddered.

"Well," Howard Whitman said, looking uneasy, "he can't help being crippled, Helen."

"Howard," she said impatiently, "I'm only trying to tell you how *ugly* it was." And that seemed to carry a certain weight. If she was an authority on beauty—on how a little boy might kneel among ferns to play the pipes of Pan, for example—then surely she had earned her credentials as an authority on ugliness.

"*Any*way," she went on, "they got him into a chair, and he wiped most of the sweat off his face with a handkerchief—he was still out of breath—and after a while he started talking to some of the other men there; I couldn't follow that part of it. Then finally he turned to me with this smile of his. Honestly, I don't know if I can describe that smile. It isn't something you can see in the newsreels; you have to be there. His eyes don't change at all, but the corners of his mouth go up as if they're being pulled by puppet strings. It's a frightening smile. It makes you think: this could be a dangerous man. This could be an evil man. Well anyway, we started talking, and I spoke right up to him. I said, 'I didn't vote for you, Mr. President.' I said, 'I'm a good Republican and I voted for President Hoover.' He said, 'Why are you here, then?' or something like that, and I said, 'Because you have a very interesting head.' So he gave me the smile again and he said, 'What's interesting about it?' And I said, 'I like the bumps on it.'"

By then she must have assumed that every reporter in the room was writing in his notebook, while the photographers got their flashbulbs ready; tomorrow's papers might easily read:

GAL SCULPTOR TWITS FDR
ABOUT "BUMPS" ON HEAD

At the end of her preliminary chat with him she got down to business, which was to measure different parts of his head with her calipers. I knew how that felt: the cold, trembling points of those clay-encrusted calipers had tickled and poked me all over during the times I'd served as model for her fey little woodland boys.

But not a single flashbulb went off while she took and recorded the measurements, and nobody asked her any questions; after a few nervous words of thanks and goodbye she was out in the corridor again among all the hopeless, craning people who couldn't get in. It must have been a bad disappointment, and I imagine she tried to make up for it by planning the triumphant way she'd tell us about it when she got home.

"Helen?" Howard Whitman inquired, after most of the other visitors had gone. "Why'd you tell him you didn't vote for him?"

"Well, because it's true. I *am* a good Republican; you know that."

She was a storekeeper's daughter from a small town in Ohio; she had probably grown up hearing the phrase "good Republican" as an index of respectability and clean clothes. And maybe she had come to relax her standards of respectability, maybe she didn't even care much about clean clothes anymore, but "good Republican" was worth clinging to. It would be helpful when she met the customers for her garden figures, the people whose low, courteous voices would welcome her into their lives and who would almost certainly turn out to be Republicans too.

"I believe in the aristocracy!" she often cried, trying to make herself heard above the rumble of voices when her guests were discussing Communism, and they seldom paid her any attention. They liked her well enough: she gave parties with plenty of liquor, and she was an agreeable hostess if only because of her touching eagerness to please; but in any talk of politics she was like a shrill, exasperating child. She believed in the aristocracy.

She believed in God too, or at least in the ceremony of St. Luke's Episcopal Church, which she attended once or twice a year. And she believed in Eric Nicholson, the handsome middle-aged Englishman who was her lover. He had something to do with the American end of a British chain of foundries: his company cast ornamental objects into bronze and lead. The cupolas of college and high-school buildings all over the East, the lead casement windows for Tudor-style homes in places like Scarsdale and Bronxville—these were some of the things Eric Nicholson's firm had accomplished. He was always self-deprecating about his business, but ruddy and glowing with its success.

My mother had met him the year before, when she'd sought help in having one of her garden figures cast into bronze, to be "placed on consignment" with some garden-sculpture gallery from which it would never be sold. Eric Nicholson had persuaded her that lead would be almost as nice as bronze and much cheaper; then he'd asked her out to dinner, and that evening changed our lives.

Mr. Nicholson rarely spoke to my sister or me, and I think we were both frightened of him, but he overwhelmed us with gifts. At first they were mostly books—a volume of cartoons from *Punch*, a partial set of Dickens, a book called *England in Tudor Times* containing tissue-covered color plates that Edith liked. But in the summer of

1933, when our father arranged for us to spend two weeks with our mother at a small lake in New Jersey, Mr. Nicholson's gifts became a cornucopia of sporting goods. He gave Edith a steel fishing rod with a reel so intricate that none of us could have figured it out even if we'd known how to fish, a wicker creel for carrying the fish she would never catch, and a sheathed hunting knife to be worn at her waist. He gave me a short ax whose head was encased in a leather holster and strapped to my belt—I guess this was for cutting firewood to cook the fish—and a cumbersome net with a handle that hung from an elastic shoulder strap, in case I should be called upon to wade in and help Edith land a tricky one. There was nothing to do in that New Jersey village except take walks, or what my mother called good hikes; and every day, as we plodded out through the insect-humming weeds in the sun, we wore our full regalia of useless equipment.

That same summer Mr. Nicholson gave me a three-year subscription to *Field & Stream*, and I think that impenetrable magazine was the least appropriate of all his gifts because it kept coming in the mail for such a long, long time after everything else had changed for us: after we'd moved out of New York to Scarsdale, where Mr. Nicholson had found a house with a low rent, and after he had abandoned my mother in that house—with no warning—to return to England and to the wife from whom he'd never really been divorced.

But all that came later; I want to go back to the time between Franklin D. Roosevelt's election and his Inauguration, when his head was slowly taking shape on my mother's modeling stand.

Her original plan had been to make it life-size, or larger than life-size, but Mr. Nicholson urged her to scale it down for economy in the casting, and so she made it only six or seven inches high. He persuaded her too, for the second time since he'd known her, that lead would be almost as nice as bronze.

She had always said she didn't mind at all if Edith and I watched her work, but we had never much wanted to; now it was a little more interesting because we could watch her sift through many photographs of Roosevelt cut from newspapers until she found one that would help her execute a subtle plane of cheek or brow.

But most of our day was taken up with school. John Cabot might go to school in Hastings-on-Hudson, for which Edith would always yearn, but we had what even Edith admitted was the next best thing: we went to school in our bedroom.

During the previous year my mother had enrolled us in the public school down the street, but she'd begun to regret it when we came home with lice in our hair. Then one day Edith came home accused of having stolen a boy's coat, and that was too much. She withdrew us both, in defiance of the city truant officer, and pleaded with my father to help her meet the cost of a private school. He refused. The rent she paid and the bills she ran up were already taxing him far beyond the terms of the divorce agreement; he was in debt; surely she must realize he was lucky even to have a job. Would she ever learn to be reasonable?

It was Howard Whitman who broke the deadlock. He knew of an inexpensive, fully accredited mail-order service called The Calvert School, intended mainly for the homes of children who were invalids. The Calvert School furnished weekly supplies of books and materials and study plans; all she would need was someone in the house to administer the program and to serve as a tutor. And someone like Bart Kampen would be ideal for the job.

"The skinny fellow?" she asked. "The Jewish boy from Holland or wherever it is?"

"He's very well educated, Helen," Howard told her. "And he speaks fluent English, and he'd be very conscientious. And he could certainly use the money."

We were delighted to learn that Bart Kampen would be our tutor. With the exception of Howard himself, Bart was probably our favorite among the adults around the courtyard. He was twenty-eight or so, young enough so that his ears could still turn red when he was teased by children; we had found that out in teasing him once or twice about such matters as that his socks didn't match. He was tall and very thin and seemed always to look startled except when he was comforted enough to smile. He was a violinist, a Dutch Jew who had emigrated the year before in the hope of joining a symphony orchestra, and eventually of launching a concert career. But the symphonies weren't hiring then, nor were lesser orchestras, so Bart had gone without work for a long time. He lived alone in a room on Seventh Avenue, not far from the courtyard, and people who liked him used to worry that he might not have enough to eat. He owned two suits, both cut in a way that must have been stylish in the Netherlands at the time: stiff, heavily padded shoulders and a nipped-in waist; they would probably have looked better on someone with a little more meat on his bones. In shirtsleeves, with the cuffs rolled back, his hairy wrists and forearms looked even more fragile than you might have expected, but his long hands were shapely and strong enough to suggest authority on the violin.

"I'll leave it entirely up to you, Bart," my mother said when he asked if she had any instructions for our tutoring. "I know you'll do wonders with them."

A small table was moved into our bedroom, under the window, and three chairs placed around it. Bart sat in the middle so that he could divide his time equally between Edith and me. Big, clean, heavy brown envelopes arrived in the mail from The Calvert School once a week, and when Bart slid their fascinating contents onto the table it was like settling down to begin a game.

Edith was in the fifth grade that year—her part of the table was given over to incomprehensible talk about English and History and Social Studies—and I was in the first. I spent my mornings asking Bart to help me puzzle out the very opening moves of an education.

"Take your time, Billy," he would say. "Don't get impatient with this. Once you have it you'll see how easy it is, and then you'll be ready for the next thing."

At eleven each morning we would take a break. We'd go downstairs and out to the part of the courtyard that had a little grass. Bart would carefully lay his folded coat on the sidelines, turn back his shirt cuffs, and present himself as ready to give what he called airplane rides. Taking us one at a time, he would grasp one wrist and one ankle; then he'd whirl us off our feet and around and around, with himself as the pivot, until the courtyard and the buildings and the city and the world were lost in the dizzying blur of our flight.

After the airplane rides we would hurry down the steps into the studio, where we'd usually find that my mother had set out a tray bearing three tall glasses of cold Ovaltine, sometimes with cookies on the side and sometimes not. I once overheard her telling Sloane Cabot she thought the Ovaltine must be Bart's first nourishment of the day—and I think she was probably right, if only because of the way his hand would tremble in reaching for his glass. Sometimes she'd forget to prepare the tray and we'd crowd into the kitchen and fix it ourselves; I can never see a jar of Ovaltine on a grocery shelf without remembering those times. Then it was back upstairs to school again. And during that year, by coaxing and prodding and telling me not to get impatient, Bart Kampen taught me to read.

It was an excellent opportunity for showing off. I would pull books down from my mother's shelves—mostly books that were the gifts of Mr. Nicholson—and try to impress her by reading mangled sentences aloud.

"That's wonderful, dear," she would say. "You've really learned to read, haven't you."

Soon a white-and-yellow "More light" stamp was affixed to every page of my Calvert First Grade Reader, proving I had mastered it, and others were accumulating at a slower rate in my arithmetic workbook. Still other stamps were fastened to the wall beside my place at the school table, arranged in a proud little white-and-yellow thumb-smudged column that rose as high as I could reach.

"You shouldn't have put your stamps on the wall," Edith said.

"Why?"

"Well, because they'll be hard to take off."

"Who's going to take them off?"

That small room of ours, with its double function of sleep and learning, stands more clearly in my memory than any other part of our home. Someone should probably have told my mother that a girl and boy of our ages ought to have separate rooms, but that never occurred to me until much later. Our cots were set foot-to-foot against the wall, leaving just enough space to pass alongside them to the school table, and we had some good conversations as we lay waiting for sleep at night. The one I remember best was the time Edith told me about the sound of the city.

"I don't mean just the loud noises," she said, "like the siren going by just now, or those car doors slamming, or all the laughing and shouting down the street; that's just close-up stuff. I'm talking about something else. Because you see there are millions and millions of people in New York—more people than you can possibly imagine, ever—and most of them are doing something that makes sound. Maybe talking, or playing the radio, maybe closing doors, maybe putting their forks down on their plates if they're having dinner, or dropping their shoes if they're going to bed—and because there are so many of them, all those little sounds add up and come together in a kind of hum. But it's so faint—so very, very faint—that you can't hear it unless you listen very carefully for a long time."

"Can you hear it?" I asked her.

"Sometimes. I listen every night, but I can only hear it sometimes. Other times I fall asleep. Let's be quiet now, and just listen. See if you can hear it, Billy."

And I tried hard, closing my eyes as if that would help, opening my mouth to minimize the sound of my breathing, but in the end I had to tell her I'd failed. "How about you?" I asked.

"Oh, I heard it," she said. "Just for a few seconds, but I heard it. You'll hear it too, if you keep trying. And it's worth waiting for. When you hear it, you're hearing the whole city of New York."

The high point of our week was Friday afternoon, when John Cabot came home from Hastings. He exuded health and normality; he brought fresh suburban air into our bohemian lives. He even transformed his mother's small apartment, while he was there, into an enviable place of rest between vigorous encounters with the world. He subscribed to both *Boys' Life* and *Open Road for Boys*, and these seemed to me to be wonderful things to have in your house, if only for the illustrations. John dressed in the same heroic way as the boys shown in those magazines, corduroy knickers with ribbed stockings pulled taut over his muscular calves. He talked a lot about the Hastings high-school football team, for which he planned to try out as soon as he was old enough, and about Hastings friends whose names and personalities grew almost as familiar to us as if they were friends of our own. He taught us invigorating new ways to speak, like saying "What's the diff?" instead of "What's the difference?" And he was better even than Edith at finding new things to do in the courtyard.

You could buy goldfish for ten or fifteen cents apiece in Woolworth's then, and one day we brought home three of them to keep in the fountain. We sprinkled the water with more Woolworth's granulated fish food than they could possibly need, and we named them after ourselves: "John," "Edith," and "Billy." For a week or two Edith and I would run to the fountain every morning, before Bart came for school, to make sure they were still alive and to see if they had enough food, and to watch them.

"Have you noticed how much bigger Billy's getting?" Edith asked me. "He's huge. He's almost as big as John and Edith now. He'll probably be bigger than both of them."

Then one weekend when John was home he called our attention to how quickly the fish could turn and move. "They have better reflexes than humans," he explained. "When they see a shadow in the water, or anything that looks like danger, they get away faster than you can blink. Watch." And he sank one hand into the water to make a grab for the fish named Edith, but she evaded him and fled. "See that?" he asked. "How's that for speed? Know something? I bet you could shoot an arrow in there, and they'd get away in time. Wait." To prove his point he ran to his mother's apartment and came back with the handsome bow and arrow he had made at summer camp (going to camp every summer was another admirable thing about John); then he knelt at the rim of the fountain like the picture of an archer, his bow steady in one strong hand and the feathered end of his arrow tight against the bowstring in the other. He was taking aim at the fish named Billy. "Now, the velocity of this arrow," he said in a voice weakened by his effort, "is probably more than a car going eighty miles an hour. It's probably more like an airplane, or maybe even more than that. Okay; watch."

The fish named Billy was suddenly floating dead on the surface, on his side, impaled a quarter of the way up the arrow with parts of his pink guts dribbled along the shaft.

I was too old to cry, but something had to be done about the shock and rage and grief that filled me as I ran from the fountain, heading blindly for home, and halfway there I came upon my mother. She stood looking very clean, wearing a new coat and dress I'd never seen before and fastened to the arm of Mr. Nicholson. They were either just going out or just coming in—I didn't care which—and Mr. Nicholson frowned at me (he had told me more than once that boys of my age went to boarding school in England), but I didn't care about that either. I bent my head into her waist and didn't stop crying until long after I'd felt her hands stroking my back, until after she had assured me that goldfish didn't cost much and I'd have another one soon, and that John was sorry for the thoughtless thing he'd done. I had discovered, or rediscovered, that crying is a pleasure—that it can be a pleasure beyond all reckoning if your head is pressed in your mother's waist and her hands are on your back, and if she happens to be wearing clean clothes.

There were other pleasures. We had a good Christmas Eve in our house that year, or at least it was good at first. My father was there, which obliged Mr. Nicholson to stay away, and it was nice to see how relaxed he was among my mother's friends. He was shy, but they seemed to like him. He got along especially well with Bart Kampen.

Howard Whitman's daughter, Molly, a sweet-natured girl of about my age, had come in from Tarrytown to spend the holidays with him, and there were several other children whom we knew but rarely saw. John looked very mature that night in a dark coat and tie, plainly aware of his social responsibilities as the oldest boy.

After awhile, with no plan, the party drifted back into the dining-room area and staged an impromptu vaudeville. Howard started it: he brought the tall stool from my mother's modeling stand and sat his daughter on it, facing the audience. He folded back the opening of a brown paper bag two or three times and fitted it on to her head; then he took off his suit coat and draped it around her backwards, up to the chin; he went behind her, crouched out of sight, and worked his hands through the coatsleeves so that when they emerged they appeared to be hers. And the sight of a smiling little girl in a paper-bag hat, waving and gesturing with huge, expressive hands, was enough to make everyone laugh. The big hands wiped her eyes and stroked her chin and pushed her hair behind her ears; then they elaborately thumbed her nose at us.

Next came Sloane Cabot. She sat very straight on the stool with her heels hooked over the rungs in such a way as to show her good legs to their best advantage, but her first act didn't go over.

"Well," she began, "I was at work today—you know my office is on the fortieth floor—when I happened to glance up from my typewriter and saw this big old man sort of crouched on the ledge outside the window, with a white beard and a funny red suit. So I ran to the window and opened it and said, 'Are you all right?' Well, it was Santa Claus, and he said, 'Of course I'm all right; I'm used to high places. But listen, miss: can you direct me to number seventy-five Bedford Street?'"

There was more, but our embarrassed looks must have told her we knew we were being condescended to; as soon as she'd found a way to finish it she did so quickly. Then, after a thoughtful pause, she tried something else that turned out to be much better.

"Have you children ever heard the story of the first Christmas?"

she asked. "When Jesus was born?" And she began to tell it in the kind of hushed, dramatic voice she must have hoped might be used by the narrators of her more serious radio plays.

". . . And there were still many miles to go before they reached Bethlehem," she said, "and it was a cold night. Now, Mary knew she would very soon have a baby. She even knew, because an angel had told her, that her baby might one day be the savior of all mankind. But she was only a young girl"—here Sloane's eyes glistened, as if they might be filling with tears—"and the traveling had exhausted her. She was bruised by the jolting gait of the donkey and she ached all over, and she thought they'd never, ever get there, and all she could say was 'Oh, Joseph, I'm so tired.'"

The story went on through the rejection at the inn, and the birth in the stable, and the manger, and the animals, and the arrival of the three kings; when it was over we clapped a long time because Sloane had told it so well.

"Daddy?" Edith asked. "Will you sing for us?"

"Oh well, thanks, honey," he said, "but no; I really need a piano for that. Thanks anyway."

The final performer of the evening was Bart Kampen, persuaded by popular demand to go home and get his violin. There was no surprise in discovering that he played like a professional, like something you might easily hear on the radio; the enjoyment came from watching how his thin face frowned over the chin rest, empty of all emotion except concern that the sound be right. We were proud of him.

Some time after my father left a good many other adults began to arrive, most of them strangers to me, looking as though they'd already been to several other parties that night. It was very late, or rather very early Christmas morning, when I looked into the kitchen and saw Sloane standing close to a bald man I didn't know. He held a trembling drink in one hand and slowly massaged her shoulder with the other; she seemed to be shrinking back against the old wooden icebox. Sloane had a way of smiling that allowed little wisps of cigarette smoke to escape from between her almost-closed lips while she looked you up and down, and she was doing that. Then the man put his drink on top of the icebox and took her in his arms, and I couldn't see her face anymore.

Another man, in a rumpled brown suit, lay unconscious on the dining-room floor. I walked around him and went into the studio, where a good-looking young woman stood weeping wretchedly and three men kept getting in each other's way as they tried to comfort her. Then I saw that one of the men was Bart, and I watched while he outlasted the other two and turned the girl away toward the door. He put his arm around her and she nestled her head in his shoulder; that was how they left the house.

Edith looked jaded in her wrinkled party dress. She was reclining in our old Hastings-on-Hudson easy chair with her head tipped back and her legs flung out over both the chair's arms, and John sat cross-legged on the floor near one of her dangling feet. They seemed to have been talking about something that didn't interest either of them much, and the talk petered out altogether when I sat on the floor to join them.

"Billy," she said, "do you realize what time it is?"

"What's the diff?" I said.

"You should've been in bed hours ago. Come on. Let's go up."

"I don't feel like it."

"Well," she said, "I'm going up, anyway," and she got laboriously out of the chair and walked away into the crowd.

John turned to me and narrowed his eyes unpleasantly. "Know something?" he said. "When she was in the chair that way I could see everything."

"Huh?"

"I could see everything. I could see the crack, and the hair. She's beginning to get hair."

I had observed these features of my sister many times—in the bathtub, or when she was changing her clothes—and hadn't found them especially remarkable; even so, I understood at once how remarkable they must have been for him. If only he had smiled in a bashful way we might have laughed together like a couple of regular fellows out of *Open Road for Boys*, but his face was still set in that disdainful look.

"I kept looking and looking," he said, "and I had to keep her talking so she wouldn't catch on, but I was doing fine until you had to come over and ruin it."

Was I supposed to apologize? That didn't seem right, but nothing else seemed right either. All I did was look at the floor.

When I finally got to bed there was scarcely time for trying to hear the elusive sound of the city—I had found that a good way to keep from thinking of anything else—when my mother came blundering in. She'd had too much to drink and wanted to lie down, but instead of going to her own room she got into bed with me. "Oh," she said. "Oh, my boy. Oh, my boy." It was a narrow cot and there was no way to make room for her; then suddenly she retched, bolted to her feet, and ran for the bathroom, where I heard her vomiting. And when I moved over into the part of the bed she had occupied my face recoiled quickly, but not quite in time, from the slick mouthful of puke she had left on her side of the pillow.

For a month or so that winter we didn't see much of Sloane because she said she was "working on something big. Something really big." When it was finished she brought it to the studio, looking tired but prettier than ever, and shyly asked if she could read it aloud.

"Wonderful," my mother said. "What's it about?"

"That's the best part. It's about us. All of us. Listen."

Bart had gone for the day and Edith was out in the courtyard by herself—she often played by herself—so there was nobody for an audience but my mother and me. We sat on the sofa and Sloane arranged herself on the tall stool, just as she'd done for telling the Bethlehem story.

"There is an enchanted courtyard in Greenwich Village," she read. "It's only a narrow patch of brick and green among the irregular shapes of very old houses, but what makes it enchanted is that the people who live in it, or near it, have come to form an enchanted circle of friends.

"None of them have enough money and some are quite poor, but they believe in the future; they believe in each other, and in themselves.

"There is Howard, once a top reporter on a metropolitan daily newspaper. Everyone knows Howard will soon scale the journalistic heights again, and in the meantime he serves as the wise and humorous sage of the courtyard.

"There is Bart, a young violinist clearly destined for virtuosity on the concert stage, who just for the present must graciously accept all lunch and dinner invitations in order to survive.

"And there is Helen, a sculptor whose charming works will someday grace the finest gardens in America, and whose studio is the favorite gathering place for members of the circle."

There was more like that, introducing other characters, and toward the end she got around to the children. She described my sister as "a lanky, dreamy tomboy," which was odd—I had never thought of Edith that way—and she called me "a sad-eyed, seven-year-old philosopher," which was wholly baffling. When the introduction was over she paused a few seconds for dramatic effect and then went into the opening episode of the series, or what I suppose would be called the "pilot."

I couldn't follow the story very well—it seemed to be mostly an excuse for bringing each character up to the microphone for a few lines apiece—and before long I was listening only to see if there would be any lines for the character based on me. And there were, in a way. She announced my name—"Billy"—but then instead of speaking she put her mouth through a terrible series of contortions, accompanied by funny little bursts of sound, and by the time the words came out I didn't care what they were. It was true that I stuttered badly—I wouldn't get over it for five or six more years—but I hadn't expected anyone to put it on the radio.

"Oh, Sloane, that's marvelous," my mother said when the reading was over. "That's really exciting."

And Sloane was carefully stacking her typed pages in the way she'd probably been taught to do in secretarial school, blushing and smiling with pride. "Well," she said, "it probably needs work, but I do think it's got a lot of potential."

"It's perfect," my mother said. "Just the way it is."

Sloane mailed the script to a radio producer and he mailed it back with a letter typed by some radio secretary, explaining that her material had too limited an appeal to be commercial. The radio public was not yet ready, he said, for a story of Greenwich Village life.

Then it was March. The new President promised that the only thing we had to fear was fear itself, and soon after that his head came packed in wood and excelsior from Mr. Nicholson's foundry.

It was a fairly good likeness. She had caught the famous lift of the chin—it might not have looked like him at all if she hadn't—and everyone told her it was fine. What nobody said was that her original plan had been right, and Mr. Nicholson shouldn't have interfered: it was too small. It didn't look heroic. If you could have hollowed it out and put a slot in the top, it might have made a serviceable bank for loose change.

The foundry had burnished the lead until it shone almost silver in the highlights, and they'd mounted it on a sturdy little base of heavy black plastic. They had sent back three copies: one for the White House presentation, one to keep for exhibition purposes, and an extra one. But the extra one soon toppled to the floor and was badly damaged—the nose mashed almost into the chin—and my mother might have burst into tears if Howard Whitman hadn't made everyone laugh by saying it was now a good portrait of Vice President Garner.

Charlie Hines, Howard's old friend from the *Post* who was now a minor member of the White House staff, made an appointment for my mother with the President late on a weekday morning. She arranged for Sloane to spend the night with Edith and me; then she took an evening train down to Washington, carrying the sculpture in a cardboard box, and stayed at one of the less expensive Washington hotels. In the morning she met Charlie Hines in some crowded White House anteroom, where I guess they disposed of the cardboard box, and he took her to the waiting room outside the Oval Office. He sat with her as she held the naked head in her lap, and when their turn came he escorted her in to the President's desk for the presentation. It didn't take long. There were no reporters and no photographers.

Afterwards Charlie Hines took her out to lunch, probably because he'd promised Howard Whitman to do so. I imagine it wasn't a first-class restaurant, more likely some bustling, no-nonsense place favored by the working press, and I imagine they had trouble making conversation until they settled on Howard, and on what a shame it was that he was still out of work.

"No, but do you know Howard's friend Bart Kampen?" Charlie asked. "The young Dutchman? The violinist?"

"Yes, certainly," she said. "I know Bart."

"Well, Jesus, there's *one* story with a happy ending, right? Have you heard about that? Last time I saw Bart he said, 'Charlie, the Depression's over for me,' and he told me he'd found some rich, dumb, crazy woman who's paying him to tutor her kids."

I can picture how she looked riding the long, slow train back to New York that afternoon. She must have sat staring straight ahead or out the dirty window, seeing nothing, her eyes round and her face held in a soft shape of hurt. Her adventure with Franklin D. Roosevelt had come to nothing. There would be no photographs or interviews or feature articles, no thrilling moments of newsreel coverage; strangers would never know of how she'd come from a small Ohio town, or of how she'd nurtured her talent through the brave, difficult, one-woman journey that had brought her to the attention of the world. It wasn't fair.

All she had to look forward to now was her romance with Eric Nicholson, and I think she may have known even then that it was faltering—his final desertion came the next fall.

She was forty-one, an age when even romantics must admit that youth is gone, and she had nothing to show for the years but a studio crowded with green plaster statues that nobody would buy. She believed in the aristocracy, but there was no reason to suppose the aristocracy would ever believe in her.

And every time she thought of what Charlie Hines had said about Bart Kampen—oh, how hateful; oh, how hateful—the humiliation came back in wave on wave, in merciless rhythm to the clatter of the train.

She made a brave show of her homecoming, though nobody was there to greet her but Sloane and Edith and me. Sloane had fed us, and she said, "There's a plate for you in the oven, Helen," but my mother said she'd rather just have a drink instead. She was then at the onset of a long battle with alcohol that she would ultimately lose; it must have seemed bracing that night to decide on a drink instead of dinner. Then she told us "all about" her trip to Washington, managing to make it sound like a success. She talked of how thrilling it was to be actually inside the White House; she repeated whatever small, courteous thing it was that President Roosevelt had said to her on receiving the head. And she had brought back souvenirs: a handful of note-size White House stationery for Edith, and a well-used briar pipe for me. She explained that she'd seen a very distinguished-looking man smoking the pipe in the waiting room outside the Oval Office; when his name was called he had knocked it out quickly into an ashtray and left it there as he hurried inside. She had waited until she was sure no one was looking; then she'd taken the pipe from the ashtray and put it in her purse. "Because I knew he must have been somebody important," she said. "He could easily have been a member of the Cabinet, or something like that. Anyway, I thought you'd have a lot of fun with it." But I didn't. It was too heavy to hold in my teeth and it tasted terrible when I sucked on it; besides, I kept wondering what the man must have thought when he came out of the President's office and found it gone.

Sloane went home after awhile, and my mother sat drinking alone at the dining-room table. I think she hoped Howard Whitman or some of her other friends might drop in, but nobody did. It was almost our bedtime when she looked up and said, "Edith? Run out in the garden and see if you can find Bart."

He had recently bought a pair of bright tan shoes with crepe soles. I saw those shoes trip rapidly down the dark brick steps beyond the windows—he seemed scarcely to touch each step in his buoyancy—and then I saw him come smiling into the studio, with Edith closing the door behind him. "Helen!" he said. "You're back!"

She acknowledged that she was back. Then she got up from the table and slowly advanced on him, and Edith and I began to realize we were in for something bad.

"Bart," she said, "I had lunch with Charlie Hines in Washington today."

"Oh?"

"And we had a very interesting talk. He seems to know you very well."

"Oh, not really; we've met a few times at Howard's, but we're not really—"

"And he said you'd told him the Depression was over for you because you'd found some rich, dumb, crazy woman who was paying you to tutor her kids. Don't interrupt me."

But Bart clearly had no intention of interrupting her. He was backing away from her in his soundless shoes, retreating past one stiff green garden child after another. His face looked startled and pink.

"I'm not a rich woman, Bart," she said, bearing down on him. "And I'm not dumb. And I'm not crazy. And I can recognize ingratitude and disloyalty and sheer, rotten viciousness and *lies* when they're thrown in my face."

My sister and I were halfway up the stairs, jostling each other in our need to hide before the worst part came. The worst part of these things always came at the end, after she'd lost all control and gone on shouting anyway.

"I want you to get out of my house, Bart," she said. "And I don't ever want to see you again. And I want to tell you something. All my life I've hated people who say 'Some of my best friends are Jews.' Because *none* of my friends are Jews, or ever will be. Do you understand me? *None* of my friends are Jews, or ever will be."

The studio was quiet after that. Without speaking, avoiding each other's eyes, Edith and I got into our pajamas and into bed. But it wasn't more than a few minutes before the house began to ring with our mother's raging voice all over again, as if Bart had somehow been brought back and made to take his punishment twice.

". . . And I said '*None* of my friends are Jews, or ever will be. . . .'"

She was on the telephone, giving Sloane Cabot the highlights of the scene, and it was clear that Sloane would take her side and comfort her. Sloane might know how the Virgin Mary felt on the way to Bethlehem, but she also knew how to play my stutter for laughs. In a case like this she would quickly see where her allegiance lay, and it wouldn't cost her much to drop Bart Kampen from her enchanted circle.

When the telephone call came to an end at last there was silence downstairs until we heard her working with the ice pick in the icebox: she was making herself another drink.

There would be no more school in our room. We would probably never see Bart again—or if we ever did, he would probably not want to see us. But our mother was ours; we were hers; and we lived with that knowledge as we lay listening for the faint, faint sound of millions.

A Natural Girl

IN THE SPRING of her sophomore year when she was twenty, Susan Andrews told her father very calmly that she didn't love him anymore. She regretted it, or at least the tone of it, almost at once, but it was too late: he sat looking stunned for a few seconds and then began to cry, all hunched over to hide his face from her, trying with one unsteady hand to get a handkerchief out of his dark suit. He was one of the five or six most respected hematologists in the United States, and nothing like this had happened to him for a great many years.

They were alone in Susan's dormitory room at a small, celebrated liberal arts college called Turnbull, in Wisconsin. She had worn a demure yellow dress that day because it seemed appropriate for his visit, but now she felt constricted by the primness of it and the way it obliged her to keep her narrow, pretty knees pressed together. She would much rather have been wearing faded jeans and a man's shirt with the top two buttons unfastened, as she did on most other days. Her brown eyes were big and sorrowful and her long hair was almost black. She had recently been told many times, in ardor and with justice, that she was a lovely girl.

She knew that if she'd made her declaration in anger or in tears there might now be some way to take it back, but she wasn't really sorry to have that option closed. She had come to learn the value and the price of honesty in all things: if you dealt cleanly with the world there was never any taking of anything back. Still, this was the first time she had ever seen her father cry, and it brought a heaviness of blood to her own throat.

"All right," Dr. Andrews said in a broken voice, still hanging his head. "All right, you don't love me. But tell me this much, dear. Tell me why."

"There *is* no why," Susan said, grateful that her voice came out in a normal way. "There's no more why to not loving than there is to loving. I think most intelligent people understand that."

And he got slowly to his feet, looking ten years older than he'd looked a few minutes before. He had to get home to St. Louis, and the drive would be an agony of distance. "Well," he said, "I'm sorry I cried. Guess I'm turning into some kind of maudlin old man or something. Anyway, I'd better be getting started. I'm sorry. I'm sorry about everything."

"I wish you wouldn't apologize; I'm sorry too. Wait, I'll walk you out to the car."

And all the way back to the sun-dazzled parking lot, past very old, neat college buildings and clusters of boisterously laughing kids—had anybody ever dreamed there would be this many *kids* in the world?—Edward Andrews tried to plan his parting words. He didn't want to say he was sorry again, but couldn't think of anything else. At last he said, "I know your mother'd like to hear from you, Susan, and so would your sisters. Why don't you call home tonight, if you're not too busy."

"Okay, sure," she said. "I'm glad you reminded me. Well. Drive carefully." Then she was gone, and he was on the road.

Edward Andrews had seven daughters, and he liked being known as a family man. It often pleased him to consider that all his girls were nice-looking and most of them smart: the oldest was long married to a deep-thinking professor of philosophy who might have been intimidating if he hadn't continued over the years to be a shy and vulnerable boy; the second was rarely seen because her husband was an admirably steady lawyer in Baltimore who didn't like to travel, and the third was in evidence perhaps a little too much—a sweetly dopey girl, knocked-up in high school and quickly married to a nice, bumbling kid for whom jobs had frequently to be found. And there were the three little girls still living at home, all of them solemn about hair styling and menstrual cycles, and all an exasperating joy to have around the house.

But there was only one Susan. She was the middle child, born soon after he'd come back from the war, and he would always associate her birth with the first high hopes of world peace. Framed photographs on the walls at home showed her reverently kneeling as a six-year-old Christmas angel, with gauze-and-wire wings, or seated with far more decorum than anyone else at a birthday-party table. And he couldn't even flip through the family snapshot albums without having his heart stopped, every time, by those big, sorrowful eyes. I know who I am, she seemed to be saying in each picture; do you know who you are?

"I don't like *Alice in Wonderland*," she had told him once when she was eight.

"You don't? Why?"

"Because it's like a fever dream."

And he had never again been able to read a page of either of those books, or to look at the famous Tenniel illustrations, without seeing what she meant and agreeing with her.

Making Susan laugh had never been easy unless you had something really funny to say, but it was always well worth the effort if you did. He could remember staying late in the office, when she was ten or twelve—or, hell, right on up through her high-school years, for that matter—in order to sort out all the funny things that came into his head and to save only one, the best, for trying out on Susan when he got home.

Oh, she had been a marvelous child. And although it had seemed to surprise her, it was no surprise at all to him when she was accepted into one of the finest colleges in the country. *They* knew an exceptional person when they found one.

But how could anyone have guessed she would fall in love with her history teacher, a divorced man of twice her age, and that she would then insist on going with the man to his new job at a state university, even though it meant forfeiting the Turnbull tuition that had been paid in full?

"Dear, look," he had said in the dormitory this afternoon, trying to reason with her, "I want you to understand this: It isn't the money. That's not important, apart from its being a little on the irresponsible side. The point is simply that your mother and I feel you're not old enough to make a decision like this."

"Why bring Mother into it?" she said. "Why do you always need Mother to support whatever it is you want?"

"I don't," he said. "I'm not doing that. But we're both deeply concerned—or I'll put it this way, if you like: *I'm* deeply concerned."

"Why?"

"Because I love you. Do you love me?"

And so he had walked right into it, like a comedian walking into a thrown custard pie.

He knew she might not really have meant it, even if she'd thought she did. Girls of that age were so busy being overwhelmed by romance and sex that they didn't even know what they were saying half the time. Still, there it was—the last thing he had ever expected to hear from his favorite child.

And he was ready to crumple up and cry all over again as he held the car down to the speed limit on the Interstate, but he fought back the tears because he had to keep his eyes clear, and because his wife and the younger girls were waiting at home, and because everything else that made sense in his life would be waiting there too; and besides, no civilized man would go to pieces twice in the same day.

As soon as she was alone, Susan hurried to David Clark's apartment and into his arms, where she cried for a long time—surprising herself, because she hadn't meant to cry at all.

"Oh, baby," he said, stroking her shuddering back. "Oh, now, baby, it can't have been all that bad. Come and have a drink and we'll talk it over."

David Clark was neither strong nor handsome, but the bewildered look that had blighted his boyhood was long submerged now in a face that suggested intelligence and humor. For years he had made it a point of honor not to mess around with the girls in the classes he taught. "There isn't any sport in it," he would explain to other teachers. "It's taking unfair advantage. It's shooting fish in a barrel." It was shyness too, and a terrible fear of rejection, though he didn't usually mention those aspects of the matter.

But the whole of that argument had vanished some months ago when he found he could get through a lecture only by letting his gaze go back time and again, like that of a man seeking nourishment, to Miss Andrews in the front row.

"Oh, Jesus Christ Almighty," he told her during their first night together. "Oh, baby, you're like nothing else I've ever known. You're like—you're like—oh, Jesus God, you're extraordinary."

And she told him, in whispers, that he had opened a whole new world for her. She told him he had brought her to life.

Within a very few days she moved in with him, leaving only enough of her belongings in the dormitory room to make it "presentable," and so began the happiest time in David Clark's memory. There was never an awkward or a disappointing moment. He couldn't stop marveling at how young she was, because she was never silly and often wise. He loved to watch her walk around his place, naked or dressed, because the look on her sweet, grave face made clear that she felt at home.

"Oh, don't go away . . ." That was the cry, or the plea, that had broken from David Clark's mouth as if wholly beyond his control with almost all the women he'd known since his divorce. Several girls had seemed to find it endearing, others had been baffled by it, and one sharp-tongued woman had called it "an unmanly thing to say."

But after the first few nights with Susan he rarely fell back on that line. This magnificently young, long-legged girl, whose flesh held the very pulse and rhythm of love, was here to stay.

"Hey, Susan?" he said once. "Know what?"

"What?"

"You make me feel calm. That may not sound like a very big deal, but the point is I've wanted to be calm all my life, and nobody else has ever made me feel that way."

"Well, that's certainly a nice compliment, David," she said, "but I think I can top it."

"How?"

"You make me feel I know who I am."

On the afternoon of her father's visit, when she tried to explain how she'd felt on seeing her father cry, David did his best to soothe and comfort her. But before long she withdrew from him to grieve in solitude, in another room, and the silence went on a little too long for his liking.

"Look," he told her. "Why don't you write him a letter. Take three or four days over it, if you want, to make it nice. Then you'll be able to put the whole thing behind you. That's what people do, haven't you noticed? People learn to put things behind them."

They were married a year and a half later, in a Presbyterian church near the vast university campus where David was then employed. They had a spacious old apartment that visitors frequently found "interesting," and for a while they felt little need of anything to do except take pleasure in each other.

But soon David began to worry long and hard about the outrage of the war in Vietnam. He lectured angrily about it in the classroom; he helped to circulate petitions and to organize campus rallies; and he got quietly drunk over it a few times, alone, stumbling to bed at two or three in the morning and muttering incomprehensibly until he passed out in the warmth of Susan's sleep.

"You know something?" he asked her one evening in the kitchen, when he was helping her wash the dishes. "I think Eugene McCarthy is going to emerge as the greatest political hero of the second half of this century. He makes the Kennedy brothers look sick."

And later that night he began to complain that he'd never liked academic life in the first place. "Teachers simply aren't plugged *in* to the world," he told her as he walked dramatically around the living room with a drink in his hand. She was curled up on the sofa with her sewing basket, mending a torn seam in a pair of his pants.

"Christ's sake," he said, "we read about the world and we talk about it, but we're never a part of it. We're locked safe away somewhere else, off on the sidelines or up in the clouds. We don't *act*. We don't even know *how* to act."

"It's always seemed to me that you do," Susan said. "You apply professional skills to sharing your knowledge with others, and so you help to broaden and enrich people's minds. Isn't that acting?"

"Ah, I don't know," he said, and he was almost ready to pull back from the whole discussion. Disparaging his work might only undermine the very foundation of her respect for him. And this was an even more chilling thought: there might have been a hint, when she'd said "Isn't that acting?" that she meant "acting" in the theatrical sense, as if all those lectures back at Turnbull, when he'd paced the head of the classroom to the music of his own voice, pausing again and again to turn and look at her—as if all that had been nothing more than what an actor is expected to do.

He sat quietly for a while, until it occurred to him that this too might be considered an act: a man with a drink in the lamplight, brooding. Then he was on his feet and in motion again.

"Okay," he said, "but look. I'm forty-three. In ten more years I'll be wearing carpet slippers. I'll be watching *The Merv Griffin Show* and getting peevish from wishing you'd hurry up with the popcorn—do you see what I'm trying to say? And the point is, this whole McCarthy thing is enormously attractive to me. I'd really like to be mixed up in something like that—if not with McCarthy himself, then at least with *some*body who's on our side, *some*body who knows the world's going to fall apart unless we can wake people up and make them—help them to see their—oh, shit, baby, I want to get into politics."

Many carefully worded letters went out over the next few weeks, and many nervous phone calls. Old acquaintances were revived, some of them leading to new acquaintances; there were interviews and lunches, in various cities, with men who could either help him or not and who often kept their secret until the moment of the parting handshake.

In the end, when it was too late to do any useful work for the McCarthy campaign anyway, David was hired to write speeches for a handsome, vigorous Democrat named Frank Brady, who was then running for Governor of a heavily industrial Middle Western state and had been acclaimed in several national magazines for his "charisma." And when Frank Brady won the election, David was retained in the State House as a member of the Governor's inner circle.

"Oh, it isn't just writing speeches," he explained to his wife when they were settled with their belongings in the drab suburban metropolis of the state's capital city. "The speeches are only the gravy. A lot more of my time is spent in things like—well, like getting up position papers and keeping them fresh."

"What are position papers?" Susan asked.

"Well, Frank has to be ready with well-reasoned opinions on all the issues—issues like Vietnam and civil rights, of course, but a lot of other stuff too: farm prices, labor-management relations, the environment and all that. So I do some research—oh, and there's a really good staff of research people in the office to make it easy for me—and I put together four or five typewritten pages, something Frank can read and digest in a few minutes, and that's his—that's his position paper. It becomes the position he'll take on whatever issue it is, whenever it's being discussed."

"Oh," Susan said. While listening to him talk she had decided that their sofa and coffee table didn't look right where they were, against the far wall of this unfamiliar, oddly proportioned room. By moving them over here, and by putting these chairs over there, it might be possible to restore the pleasing order of their old "interesting" place. But she didn't have much hope for her plan: the new arrangement probably wouldn't look right either. "Well," she said, "I see. Or at least I think I see. It means that apart from writing every word that comes out of the man's mouth—except of course for the television talk-shows, when all he does is mumble and grin at movie stars—apart from that, you do his thinking for him too. Right?"

"Oh, now, come on," he said, and he gestured widely to show how foolish and how wrong she was. He wished they weren't in chairs, because if they'd been on the sofa he would have taken her in his arms. "Baby, come on. Look. Frank Brady is a man who came up out of nowhere, who made his own way without owing anybody anything, who then waged a strong and inspiring campaign, and who's been freely elected Governor. Millions of people trust him, and believe in him, and look to him for leadership. On the other hand, all I am is an employee—one of his aides, or what I guess is called a 'special counsel.' Is it really so terrible that I feed him words?"

"I don't know; I guess not. And I mean that's good, that's fine, everything you've said; only, listen: I'm really tired out. Could we sort of go to bed now?"

When she became pregnant, Susan was pleased to discover that she liked it. She had heard any number of women talk of pregnancy as a slow ordeal to be endured, but now from month to month she felt only a peaceful ripening. Her appetite was good, she slept well, she was hardly ever nervous, and toward the end she was willing to acknowledge that she enjoyed the deference of strangers in public places.

"I almost wish this could go on forever," she said to David. "It does slow you down a little, but it makes you feel—it really makes your body feel good."

"Good," he said. "I knew it would. You're a natural girl. Everything you do is so—so natural. I think that's what I've always liked best about you."

Their daughter, who they named Candace, caused substantial changes in their lives. They had suddenly relinquished their privacy;

they were jittery all day; everything looked fragile and smelled sour. But they both knew better than to complain, and so by finding ways to encourage and console each other they got through the early, most difficult months without making any mistakes.

Several times a year David traveled to a distant Eastern town to visit the children of his first marriage, and those were never happy occasions.

The boy was sixteen now and failing all his courses in high school—failing too, it seemed, in all attempts at making friends. He was mostly silent and evasive around the house, cringing away from his mother's tactful suggestions about "professional counseling" and "getting help," rousing himself only to laugh at the silliest jokes on television. It seemed clear that he would soon leave home to join the floating world of hippies, where brains didn't count for much and friendship was held to be as universal as love.

The girl was twelve and much more promising, though her sweet face was blotched with bad skin and seemed set forever in a melancholy look, as if she couldn't stop contemplating the nature of loss.

And their mother, once a girl on whom David Clark had believed his very life depended ("But it's true; I mean it; I can't live without you, Leslie . . ."), had become a harried, absentminded, stout and pathetically pleasant creature of middle age.

He always felt he had blundered into a house of strangers. Who are these people? he kept asking himself, looking around. Are these people supposed to have something to do with me? Or I with them? Who's this wretched boy, and what's the matter with this sad little girl? Who's this clumsy woman, and why doesn't she do something about her clothes and her hair?

When he smiled at them he could feel the small muscles around his mouth and eyes performing the courteous ritual of each smile. When he had dinner with them he might as well have been eating in some old and honorable cafeteria where tables were shared for convenience, but where all customers, hunched over their plates, respected one another's need to be alone.

"Well, I wouldn't be alarmed about it, David," his former wife said once, when he'd taken her aside to discuss their son. "It's an ongoing problem, and we'll simply have to deal with it on those terms."

Toward the end of that visit he began counting the hours. Three hours; two hours; oh, Jesus, one hour more—until finally, gulping fresh air on the street, he was free. All the way back on the plane that night, riding over half of America as he munched dry-roasted peanuts and drank bourbon, he did his best to empty his mind of everything and to keep it that way.

And at last, trembling with fatigue at three in the morning, he carried his suitcase up the steps of his own house and into the living room, where he felt along the wall for the light switch. He meant to tiptoe quickly through the rooms and go to bed, but found instead that he had to stand a long time in the brightness, looking around, stunned by a sense of having never seen this place before.

Who lived here? And he started down the shadowed hall to find out. The door of the baby's room was only partly open and there wasn't much light, but he could see the tall white crib. And between the slender bars of it, deep in the scents of talcum powder and sweet piss, he could see a lump that occupied hardly any space but seemed to give off energy in its very stillness. Someone alive was in there. Someone was in there who would grow up soon, and who might turn out to be anybody at all.

He hurried to the other dark bedroom, where he allowed himself just enough light from the hall for guidance.

"David?" Susan said, half asleep, turning heavily in the bedclothes. "Oh, I'm so glad you're home."

"Yeah," he told her. "Oh, Jesus, baby, so am I."

And in her arms he discovered that his life wasn't over yet, after all.

Susan found little to like in the capital city: it went on for miles, everywhere you looked, without ever really becoming a city at all. There were many trees—that was nice—but the rest of it seemed to be all shopping malls and gas stations and gleaming fast-food franchises. When the baby was old enough to ride in a stroller she hoped she might explore new parts of town and find better things, but that turned out to be as futile as wishing David hadn't gone to work for Frank Brady in the first place.

One warm afternoon, having ventured too far from home for comfort, she was on her way back, pushing the stroller, when it began to seem that she might not make it. There were only about three blocks to go, but in the shimmering haze of the day they looked like five or six, or more. She stopped to rest, breathing hard, and became very much aware of her heart—the approximate size and shape and weight of it, the feel of it, as well as its beating and its terrible mortality. The baby turned in the plastic seat to look up and to ask, with round eyes, why they had stopped, and Susan did her best to answer that look with a reassuring smile.

"We're okay, Candace," she said, as if Candace could understand. "We're okay. We'll be home in just a minute."

And she made the distance. She even made the stairs, which were the worst part. She got Candace bedded down, got the contraption of the stroller folded flat and put away; then she lay on the living-room sofa until her heart came back to normal—until the big thumping threat of it receded and was absorbed once again into the body that had been made to feel so good in pregnancy.

She was still on the sofa, wondering whether or not to take a nap, when David came home from work.

"Wow," he said, sinking into one of the chairs across the room from her. "Jesus. Talk about a hard day at the office. I want to tell you, baby, this one was a bitch. . . ."

As she listened, or rather as she tried to listen while watching him talk, it occurred to Susan that he looked older than his age. He had taken to wearing a short beard, at her suggestion—it was she who trimmed it for him every three weeks or so—but she wasn't sure she would have suggested it if she'd known it would be white. And she didn't know if she would ever get used to his new hair, which had been entirely his own idea. As long as she'd known him his straight brown hair had been heavily streaked with gray, and she'd always found that attractive, but some months ago he had decided to let it grow because he didn't want to be the only man in the State House with a nineteen-fifties haircut, and now in luxuriance it was far more gray than brown. It was long enough in back to hide the collars of his shirt and his coat, long and heavy enough on the sides to cover his ears and to swing against his cheeks when he leaned forward, and it hung cropped in carefully irregular bangs across his forehead in the manner of the actress Jane Fonda.

That wasn't all: his legs, which she would have described as "lean" only a few years ago, looked so thin now in their neat gray flannel trousers as to suggest that he wouldn't be able to ride a bicycle without wobbling and veering slowly all over the street.

". . . And there are times," he was saying, delicately rubbing his closed eyelids with thumb and forefinger, "there are times when I wish Frank Brady would just go away and get lost. You can't imagine what the pressure's like in that sweatshop. Well. Get you a drink?"

"Sure," she said. "Thanks." And she watched him walk out of the room to the kitchen. She heard the soft slam of the big refrigerator door and the breaking open of an ice tray, and then came something unexpected and frightening: a burst of high, wild laughter that didn't sound like David at all. It went on and on, rising into falsetto and falling only part of the way down as he gasped for breath, and he was still in the grip of its convulsions when he came weakly back into the room with a very dark bourbon and water rocking and clinking in his hand.

"Baby, listen," he said as soon as he was able to speak. "I've just thought of the perfect revenge to take on Frank Brady. Listen. Staple—" But he got no further than that before the laughter hit him again. When he'd recovered he took a deep breath, made a sober face, and said, "Staple his lower lip to his desk."

She achieved a smile, but it wasn't enough to please him.

"Oh, shit," he said, looking hurt. "You don't think that's funny."

"Sure I do. It's pretty funny, when you picture it."

Then they were sitting close together on the sofa, and he was taking greedy swigs of his drink as if this rich, good whiskey was the main thing he had waited for all day.

"Could I have one too?" she asked.

"Have one what?"

"You know; a drink."

"Oh, Jesus, I'm sorry," he said as he got up to lunge for the kitchen again. "I'm sorry, dear. I meant to fix you one and I just forgot, that's all. I'm getting absentminded in my old age, that's all."

And she waited, still smiling, hoping he wouldn't want to talk about his old age anymore. He wasn't yet forty-seven.

Another time, late one night when they were alone and cleaning up after having several people in for dinner, David remarked sourly of one guest that he was a pompous, humorless young twerp.

"Oh, I wouldn't say that," Susan said. "I think he's nice."

"Oh, yeah, 'nice.' That word covers just about everything for you, doesn't it. Well, fuck it. Fuck 'nice.'" And he slammed out of the room and down the hall as if he meant to go straight to bed. There was a good deal of thumping and banging in the bedroom for a minute or two; then he came back and faced her again, trembling. "'Nice,'" he said. "'Nice.' Is that what you want? You want the world to be 'nice'? Because listen, baby. Listen, sweetheart. The world is about as nice as shit. The world is struggle and rape and humiliation and death. The world is no fucking place for dreamy little rich girls from St. Louis, do you understand me? Go *home*, for Christ's sake. Get outa here and go home to your fucking *father* if you want to find 'nice.'"

While he stood shouting at her, with all that gray and white hair shaking around his almost eclipsed, almost forgotten face, it was like watching a child's tantrum enacted in the person of a crazy old man.

But it didn't last long. It was over quickly when he sat down in shame and silence to hold his elaborate head in his hands. Then, soon enough, came his choked-out, abject apology. "Oh, Jesus, Susan, I'm sorry," he said. "I don't know what gets into me when I'm like that."

"It's all right," she told him. "Let's just—let's just sort of go easy on each other for a while."

And going easy on each other turned out to be almost a pleasure. The gentleness and quiet of it, the temperance of it, permitted them both to shy away from the heat of each other's concerns without ever seeming to flinch, yet it permitted them the old intimacy too, when they both felt like it, and so they got along.

Through the difficulties of two more years there were times of peace, times of exultant companionship and other times of exasperation and bickering, or of silence; it all seemed to settle out into what David called a good marriage.

"Hey, Susan?" he would ask now and then, affecting a boyish bashfulness. "Think we'll make it?"

"Sure," she would say.

Not long after his nation's withdrawal from the war that had impelled him to change his life, David Clark made arrangements to go back to his teaching job. He then wrote a letter of resignation to Governor Brady, an act that made him feel "wonderful," and he urged his wife not to worry about the future. These years away from the classroom, he explained, had simply been a mistake—not a bad or a costly mistake, perhaps even one he could ultimately find profit in—but a mistake nonetheless. He was a school man. He had always been a school man, and would probably always be.

"Unless," he said, looking suddenly shy, "unless you think of all this as kind of—going backwards or something."

"Why would I think that?"

"I don't know. Sometimes it's hard to tell what you're thinking. It always has been."

"Well," she said, "I suppose that's something I can't help, isn't it."

And they both fell silent. It was a warm afternoon at the end of summer. They were sitting with iced-tea glasses in which the ice had melted and the watery tea was almost gone.

"Oh, baby, listen—" he began, and he reached over to clasp her thigh for emphasis but hesitated and drew his hand back. "Listen," he said again. "Let me tell you something: we'll be all right."

After a long pause, examining her warm glass, she said, "No we won't."

"Huh?"

"I said no we won't. We haven't been all right for a long time and we aren't all right now and it isn't going to get any better. I'm sorry if this comes as a surprise but it really shouldn't, and it wouldn't if you'd ever known me as well as you think you do. It's over, that's all. I'm leaving. I'll be taking Candace to California as soon as I can get our stuff packed, probably in a day or two. I'll call my parents tonight and tell them, and then my whole family will know. Once everybody knows, I imagine it'll be easier for you to accept."

All the blood seemed to have gone out of David's face, and all the moisture out of his mouth. "I don't believe this," he said. "I don't believe I'm sitting in this chair."

"Well, you'll believe it soon enough. And nothing you can say is going to stop me."

He set his empty glass on the floor and got quickly to his feet, as he always did for shouting, but he didn't shout. Instead he peered very closely at her face, as if trying to penetrate the surface of it, and said, "My God, you really mean this, don't you. I've really lost you, haven't I. You don't—love me anymore."

"That's right," she said. "Exactly. I don't love you anymore."

"Well, but for Christ's sake, Susan, why? Can you tell me why?"

"There *is* no why," she said. "There's no more why to not loving than there is to loving. Isn't that something most intelligent people understand?"

In an excellent residential suburb of St. Louis, a place of broad lawns and of deep, cool houses set back among shade trees, Edward Andrews sat alone in his study, trying to finish an article he'd been asked to write for a medical journal. He thought he had most of it right, but he couldn't find a way to work up the final paragraphs into a real conclusion, and every time he tried something different it seemed to get worse. The thing kept coming to a stop, rather than to an end.

"Ed?" his wife called from the hallway. "That was Susan on the phone. She's on the Interstate, and she'll be here with Candace in half an hour. You want to get dressed or anything?"

He certainly did. He wanted to take a quick hot shower too, and to stand at the mirror solemnly combing and recombing his hair until he got it parted just the right way. A clean shirt then, with the cuffs folded back two turns, and a fresh pair of lightweight flannels—all this to prove that at sixty-three he could still be spruce and vigorous for Susan.

When she arrived there were huggings and kissings in the front hall—Dr. Andrews's lips brushed the cool lobe of an ear—and there were happy exclamations at how much Candace had grown, how different she looked, since the last time her grandparents had seen her.

Alone in the kitchen, preparing drinks and coming to an abrupt, nervous decision that he'd better have a quick one now, here, before taking the tray into the living room, Dr. Andrews wondered once again what it was that could make him tremble in the presence of this dearest child, this particular girl. She was always so calm and so competent, for one thing. She had probably never done an incompetent or irresponsible thing in her life, except for wasting her Turnbull College tuition that time—and that, now that he thought of it, was nothing at all compared to the way millions of other children had behaved in those years, with their flowers and their love beads, their fuzzy-headed Eastern religions and their mindless pursuit of drug-induced derangement. Maybe David Clark could be thanked, after all, for having steered her away from all that; but no, that wasn't right. The credit couldn't go to Clark because it belonged to Susan herself. She was too intelligent ever to have been a vagabond, just as she was too honest to go on living with a man she no longer loved.

"So what are your plans, Susan?" he asked as he brought the bright tinkling tray of drinks into the room. "California's kind of a big place. Kind of a scary place too."

"Scary? How do you mean?"

"Oh, well, I don't know," he said, and he was ready to back down on anything now if it meant avoiding an argument. "All I meant was—you know—judging from some of the stuff you read in magazines, and so forth. I don't really have any firsthand information at all."

Susan explained, then, that she had a few friends in Marin County—"that's up north of San Francisco"—so she wouldn't be starting out among strangers. She would find a place to live, and then she'd look for some kind of work.

"What kind?" he asked. "I mean, is there anything in particular you'd like to do?"

"I don't really know yet," she said. "I'm pretty good with children; I might work in a nursery school or a day-care center; otherwise I'll look for something else." She crossed her narrow, pretty knees under the hem of an attractive tweed skirt, and he wondered if she had changed into fresh clothes in some motel room on the road in order to look nice for this homecoming.

"Well, dear," he said. "I hope you know I'll be happy to help out in any way I can if you're—"

"No, no, Daddy, that's okay. We can get along easily on what David sends us. We'll be all right."

And it was such a fine thing to hear her say "Daddy" that he allowed himself to sit back, silent and almost relaxed. He didn't even ask the one question foremost in his mind: How *is* David, Susan? How's he taking all this?

He had met and talked with David Clark only a few times—first at the wedding, and on four or five occasions since then—and he'd been surprised each time to discover that he liked the man. Once, tentatively, they had begun to discuss politics, until David said, "Well, Doctor, I guess I've always been a bleeding-heart liberal," and Edward Andrews found that appealing—the humor and the self-deprecation of it, if not the way it might apply to current issues. He had even decided not to mind David's being twenty years older than Susan, or his having another, earlier family far away, because all that seemed to suggest he wasn't likely to make any more mistakes; he would devote the prime of his middle age to his second marriage. And the best part, the thing that seemed to make nothing else matter, was that this shy, courteous, sometimes bewildered-looking stranger could never take his eyes away from Susan in any gathering. Couldn't everybody see he was in love with her? And wasn't that the first thing to look for in a son-in-law? Well, sure it was. Of course it was. And so, therefore, what now? What was the poor son of a bitch going to do with the rest of his life?

Susan and her mother were talking of family matters. All three of the younger girls were living away from home now, two of them married, and there were other bits of news to be exchanged about the older girls. Then after awhile—inevitably, it seemed—they took up the subject of childbearing.

Agnes Andrews would be sixty before very long, and for many years she had been obliged to wear spectacles with lenses so thick that it wasn't easy to see the expression in her eyes: you had to rely on the smile or the frown or the patient, neutral look of her mouth. And her husband had to acknowledge that the rest of her was rapidly aging too. There wasn't much left of her once-lustrous hair except what the hairdresser could salvage and primp; her body sagged in some places and was bloated in others. She looked like what she was: a woman who'd been called Mother in shrill, hungering voices for most of her life.

Long ago, almost beyond memory, she had been a neat, crisp, surprisingly passionate young nurse whose flesh he had been wholly unable to resist. The only minor deterrent, easily ignored from their first night right on up through the night he'd proposed to her ("I love you, Agnes; oh, I love you, and I need you. I need you . . ."), the only qualifying aspect of his love had been his knowledge that some people—his mother, for one—might think it strange of him to marry a girl of the working class.

". . . Well, Judy was my easiest," she was saying. "I never knew a thing. I went into the hospital and they put me under, and when I woke up it was all over. She was born, I was full of painkillers so I felt all right, and somebody gave me a bowl of Rice Krispies. No, but some of the others were a lot harder—you, for instance. Yours was a difficult birth. Still, I think my worst times were with the younger girls, probably because I was getting older. . . ."

Agnes rarely talked at such length—whole days could pass without her saying a word—but this had come to be her favorite topic. She sat leaning forward, her forearms on her knees and her clasped hands rolling this way and that to emphasize the points she was making.

". . . And you see Dr. Palmer thought I was unconscious—they all did—but the anesthetic wasn't working. I could feel everything, and I could hear every word they said. I heard Dr. Palmer say, 'Watch out for that uterus: it's thin as paper.'"

"God," Susan said. "Weren't you frightened?"

And Agnes gave a tired little laugh that made her glasses gleam in the fading afternoon light. "Well," she said, "when you've been through it as many times as I have, I guess you don't really think much about being frightened anymore."

Candace, who had been given a glass of ginger ale with a cherry in it, went over to stand and stare out of the big windows that faced west, almost as if she were trying to gauge the distance to California. "Mommy?" she called, turning back. "Are we staying here tonight, or what?"

"Oh no, honey," Susan told her. "We can only stay a little while. We've got a long drive ahead."

Out in the kitchen again, Edward Andrews broke open a tray of ice cubes with more force and noise than necessary, hoping it might stifle his mounting rage, but it didn't. He had to turn away and press his forehead hard against the heel of one trembling hand, like a goddamned actor in a tragedy.

Girls. Would they always drive you crazy? Would their smiles of rejection always drop you into despair and their smiles of welcome lead only into new, worse, more terrible ways of breaking your heart? Were you expected to listen forever to one of them bragging about how paper-thin her womb was, or to another saying, "We can only stay a little while"? Oh, dear Christ, how in the whole of a lifetime can anybody understand girls?

After a minute or two he achieved a semblance of composure. He carried the fresh drinks back into the living room with an almost stately bearing, determined that for this next, last little while he would keep everything down and quiet inside him so that neither of these girls, these women, would sense his anguish.

Half an hour later, in the early dusk, they were all out in the driveway. Candace was seated and belted in on the passenger side of the car, and Susan, with the car keys out and ready in her hand, was embracing her mother. Then she stepped over to give her father a hug, but it wasn't really much of a hug at all; it was more like an agreeable gesture of dismissal.

"Drive carefully, dear," he said into the softness of her dark, fragrant hair. "And listen—"

She drew away from him with a pleasant, attentive look, but he had swallowed whatever it was or might have been that he wanted her to know, and all he said instead was "Listen: keep in touch, okay?"

Trying Out for the Race

ELIZABETH HOGAN BAKER, who liked to have it known that both her parents were illiterate Irish immigrants, wrote feature stories for a chain of Westchester County newspapers through all the years of the Depression. Her home office was in New Rochelle but she was on the road every day in a rusty, quivering Model A Ford that she drove fast and carelessly, often squinting in the smoke of a cigarette held in one corner of her lips. She was a handsome woman, blond, sturdy, and still young, with a full-throated laugh for anything she found absurd, and this wasn't the life she had planned for herself at all.

"Can you figure it out?" she would ask, usually at night and after a few drinks. "Bring myself up from peasant stock, put myself through college, take a lousy little job on a suburban paper because it seemed a good-enough way to mark time for a year or two, and now look. Look. Can you figure it out?"

Nobody could. Her friends—and she always had admiring friends—could only agree that she'd had rotten luck. Elizabeth was much too good for the kind of work she did and for the inhibiting, stifling environment it had forced on her.

Back in the twenties, as a girl and a daydreaming reporter on the New Rochelle *Standard-Star*, she had looked up from her desk one day to see a tall, black-haired, shy-looking young man being shown around the office, a new staff member named Hugh Baker. "And the minute he walked in," she would say later, many times, "I thought, There's the man I'm going to marry." It didn't take long. They were married within a year and had a daughter two years later; then, soon, everything fell apart in ways Elizabeth never cared to discuss. Hugh Baker moved alone to New York, where he eventually became a feature writer for one of the evening dailies and was often praised for what the editors called his light touch. And even Elizabeth never disparaged that: over the years, embittered or not, she always said Hugh Baker was the only man she had ever known who could really make her laugh. But now she was thirty-six, with nothing to do at the end of most days but go home to an upstairs apartment in New Rochelle and pretend to take pleasure in her child.

A stout middle-aged woman named Edna, whose slip seemed always to hang at least an inch below the hem of her dress all the way around, was working at the kitchen stove when Elizabeth let herself in.

"Everything seems to be under control, Mrs. Baker," Edna said. "Nancy's eaten her supper, and I was just putting this on the low heat so you can have it whenever you're ready. I made a nice casserole; it turned out very nice."

"Good, Edna, that's fine." And Elizabeth pulled off her worn leather driving gloves. She always did this with an unconscious little flourish, like that of a cavalry officer just dismounted and removing his gauntlets after a long, hard ride.

Nancy appeared to be ready for bed when they looked in on her: she was in her pajamas and fooling around on the floor of her room in some aimless game that involved the careful alignment of a few old toys. She was nine, and she would be tall and dark like her father. Edna had recently cut out the soles of the feet in her Dr. Denton pajamas to give her more freedom—she was growing out of everything—but Elizabeth thought the pouches of excess cloth at her ankles looked funny; besides, she was fairly sure that children of nine weren't supposed to wear that kind of pajamas anymore. "How was your day?" she inquired from the doorway.

"Oh, okay." And Nancy looked up only briefly at her mother. "Daddy called."

"Oh?"

"And he said he's coming out to see me Saturday after next and he's got tickets for *The Pirates of Penzance* at the County Center."

"Well, that's nice," Elizabeth said, "isn't it."

Then Edna stepped crouching into the room with her arms held wide. Nancy scrambled up eagerly, and they stood hugging for a long time. "See you tomorrow, then, funny-face," Edna said against the child's hair.

It often seemed to Elizabeth that the best part of the day was when she was alone at last, curled up on the sofa with a drink, with her spike-heeled shoes cast off and tumbled on the carpet. Perhaps a sense of well-earned peace like this was the best part of life itself, the part that made all the rest endurable. But she had always tried to know enough not to kid herself—self-deception was an illness—and so after a couple of drinks she was willing to acknowledge the real nature of these evenings alone: she was waiting for the telephone to ring.

Some months ago she had met an abrupt, intense, sporadically dazzling man named Judd Leonard. He ran his own small public-relations firm in New York and would snarl at anyone who didn't know the difference between public relations and publicity. He was forty-nine and twice divorced; he was often weak with ambition and anger and alcohol, and Elizabeth had come to love him. She had spent three or four weekends in his chaotic apartment in the city; once he had shown up here in New Rochelle, laughing and shouting, and they'd talked for hours and he'd taken her on this very sofa, and he'd been nicely obedient about getting out of the place before Nancy woke up in the morning.

But Judd Leonard hardly ever called her now—or rather, hardly ever called her when he was able to speak coherently—and so Elizabeth had begun to wait here, one night after another.

When the phone rang at last she was dozing off on the sofa, having just decided to let the casserole dry out in the oven and to sleep right here, in her clothes—the hell with it—but it wasn't Judd.

It was Lucy Towers, one of her most admiring friends, and this meant she would be on the damned phone for at least an hour.

". . . Well, sure, Lucy," she said. "Just give me a second to sort of pull myself together, okay? I was taking a nap."

"Oh. Well, of course; I'm sorry. I'll wait." Lucy was a few years older than Elizabeth, and if self-deception was an illness she was well into its advanced stages. She described herself as being "in real estate," which meant she had worked in various real-estate offices around the county, but she seemed unable or unwilling to hold those jobs and was often idle for long periods; she lived mostly on what her former husband sent her every month. She had a daughter of thirteen or so and a son of Nancy's age. And she had groundless social aspirations—social pretensions—that Elizabeth found silly. Still, Lucy was sweet and comforting, and they had been friends for years.

When she'd made a new drink and settled into a weary sitting position, Elizabeth picked up the phone again. "Okay," she said. "I'm fine now, Lucy."

"I'm sorry if I called at the wrong time," Lucy Towers said, "but the thing is I simply couldn't wait to tell you this marvelous *idea* I have. First of all, do you know those houses along the Post Road in Scarsdale? Oh, I mean it's *Scars*dale, I know, but none of those houses have much market value because they're on the Post Road, you see, so most of them are rental properties and one or two of them are really very nice. . . ."

This was the idea: if Elizabeth and Lucy were to pool their resources, they could share one of those houses—and Lucy thought she had just the right place picked out already, though of course Elizabeth would have to inspect it first. There'd be plenty of room to combine both households—the children would love every minute of it—and with the money they'd save they could even hire a maid.

"Oh, and besides," Lucy concluded, coming to the real point at last, "besides, I'm awfully tired of living alone, Elizabeth. Aren't you?"

The house, on a highway that bore steady traffic even in 1935, was bulky and glistening in the autumn sun. It was a jumble of architectural styles and materials: much of it was mock-Tudor but there were other expanses of fieldstone and still others of pink stucco, as if several things had gone wrong with the building plans and the men had been obliged to finish the job as best they could. It might not be much to look at, the rental agent conceded, but it was sound and clean, it was "tight," and at a rent like this it was certainly a bargain.

Lucy Towers and her children were the first to arrive on the appointed day of occupancy. The girl, Alice, who would be starting junior high school next week, wanted everything to look as nice as possible, and so she was a great help to her mother in moving their old furniture around into new and "interesting" arrangements to suit the unfamiliar rooms.

"Russell, will you get out of my *way*, please?" she said to her brother, who had found an old rubber ball in one of the packing boxes and was bouncing it moodily on the floor. "He keeps getting in my way and getting in my *way*," Alice explained, "just when I'm trying to—ugh!"

"All right." And Lucy Towers swept back her hair in an exasperated gesture that revealed a coating of house dust on the inside of her forearm, runneled with several clean, dry streaks from when she had last washed her hands. "Dear, if you're not going to work with us you'd better go outside," she told her son. "Please."

So Russell Towers stuffed the ball in his pocket and went down the short slope of weedy, uncropped grass to the edge of the highway with nothing to do but stand there, watching the cars. The Bakers would soon be coming along in their old Ford, either before or after their moving van, and he decided it might be nice to have them find him here, like a courteous sentinel posted at the driveway.

Russell's family had changed houses and towns many times, and he'd never liked moving, but this new venture was the least promising yet. He had occasionally been pressed into acquaintance with Nancy Baker since they'd both been six, but he'd always shied away from her, or she from him, because they both understood it was their mothers who were friends. Now, and perhaps for years to come, Nancy's bedroom and his own would be along the same short corridor, with a single bathroom; they would eat their meals together and might easily be stuck with nobody else for company the rest of the time. They had been assigned to separate sections of the third grade—a plan the principal had said was "wise"—but even so, there were bound to be other difficulties. If he ever brought somebody home from school (assuming he would make any friends at all, which was something he couldn't bring himself to think about yet), Nancy's presence in the house would be all but impossible to explain.

When the Model A did pull up and make its shuddering turn into the driveway, Mrs. Baker got out first and asked Russell to wait here until the van came, because she wasn't sure if the driver would know which house it was. Then Nancy got out of the car and came around to wait with him, carrying a suitcase and a small, grubby-looking teddy bear. She smiled uncertainly, Russell looked quickly down, and they both watched with apparent interest as Mrs. Baker ground out a cigarette with her shoe and made her way up to the kitchen door.

"Know why they call it the Post Road?" he asked, squinting off into the distance of it. "Because it goes all the way up to Boston. You're really supposed to call it the Boston Post Road, and I think the 'post' part is because they carry the mail on it."

"Oh," Nancy said. "Well, no, I didn't know that." Then she held up her teddy bear and said, "His name's George. He's slept with me every night of my life since I was four years old."

"Oh yeah?"

Russell didn't see the van coming until it had slowed down to negotiate the turn. He waved vigorously anyway, but the driver didn't notice, or need to.

Within a very few weeks Nancy Baker turned out to be impossible. She was stubborn and sulky and a terrible crybaby; the empty feet of her mutilated Dr. Dentons were ludicrous, and one of her prominent front teeth crookedly overlapped another in a way appropriate only to homely, tiresome little girls. She was shameless in her pursuit of Alice Towers, even after Alice had tactfully discouraged her time and again ("Not *now*, Nancy, I *told* you, I'm *busy* with something"). And although Lucy Towers made occasional formal efforts to be kind, she too seemed always dismayed by her. "Nancy isn't a very—attractive child, is she?" she remarked once, thoughtfully, to her son. Russell needed no further evidence to know how awful Nancy was, but there was ample further evidence anyway: her own mother seemed to find her impossible too.

There were mornings when the Towers family had to sit embarrassed at breakfast and hear the noise of mother and daughter locked in quarreling upstairs. "*Nan*cy!" Elizabeth would cry, with the same stagey lilt in her voice that she sometimes used for reciting Irish poetry. "*Nan*cy! I'm not putting up with this another *mo*ment. . . ." And through it all came the sound of Nancy's voice in tears. There would be a thump or two and a slamming of doors, and then the sharp, heavy tread of Elizabeth alone, coming downstairs in her spike-heeled pumps.

"Sometimes," she intoned through clenched teeth as she came into the dining room one morning, "sometimes I wish that child were at the bottom of the sea." She pulled out her chair and sat down with enough authority to suggest she was glad she'd said that, and would say it again. "Do you know what it was this time? It was shoelaces."

"Will you want something, Mrs. Baker?" asked the Negro maid, whose presence here was still a source of surprise to everyone.

"No, thanks, Myra, there isn't time. I'll just have coffee. If I don't have coffee I won't be responsible for my actions. Well. First it was shoelaces," Elizabeth went on. "She has only one flat shoelace and one round one, you see, and she's ashamed to go to school that way. Can you imagine? Can you imagine that? When half the children in the United States aren't getting enough to eat? Oh, and that was only the beginning. She then said she misses Edna. She wants Edna. So can someone please tell me what I'm expected to do? Am I expected to go over to New Rochelle and *get* the wretched woman and *bring* her here? And take her *home* again? Besides, I think she's working in the radio-tube factory now—a point I was *wholly* unable to get across."

Elizabeth took her coffee as if it were medicine and trudged out to the car. By then it was time for Alice and Russell to leave for school, and Lucy Towers found something to do in her bedroom. Nobody was there when Nancy came down at last to eat nothing, to put on her coat and hurry out between the borders of other people's lawns, through a broken fence and then along a gently curving suburban lane to the school building, where a frowning teacher would mark her "tardy" one more time.

But there was worse trouble by now in that Russell Towers had found himself ill-equipped to serve, even if only symbolically, as man of the house. There wasn't anything quiet or self-assured or dignified about him. He too, like Nancy, could throw dreadful fits of temper and crying that made him feel humiliated even while they were going on. When his mother came to his room one evening to announce that she was "going out to dinner in White Plains" with a man he had met only once before, a big, bald, red-faced man who had called him Champ and who was probably listening at the foot of the stairs right now, ready to learn in head-shaking wonderment what a snot-nosed little mother's boy he was, Russell went all the way. He faked a collapse on the floor as if tantrums were a form of epileptic seizure, then he faked a collapse on the bed, and he was appalled at the shrillness of his own voice: "You *can't* go! You *can't* go!"

". . . Oh, please," Lucy was saying. "Please, Russell. Listen. Listen. I'll bring you something nice, I promise, and you'll find it when you wake up, and that'll let you know I'm home."

". . . Ah! Oh! Oh! . . ."

"Please, now, Russell. Please . . ."

On waking ashamed the next morning he found a small, well-made stuffed toy in the form of a lamb beside his pillow—a gift for a baby, or a girl. He took it to the wooden chest against the wall that contained all the other toys he had outgrown, put it inside, and closed the lid. He was a mother's boy, all right, and at times like this it seemed useless ever to deny it.

"You sure made a racket last night," Nancy said to him later that day.

"Yeah, well, I've heard you make a lot of racket too. Plenty of times."

He might have added that he'd even heard Harry Snyder make a racket, and Harry was a year older, but she hadn't been present at Harry's tantrum and so would probably not have believed it, or even have cared.

School had as yet produced no real friends for Russell, and he worried about that, but Harry Snyder was the boy next door, and so a casual, loafing kind of friendship had been easy to achieve with him. One day they were intently hunkered down over many tin soldiers in the basement of Harry's house when Mrs. Snyder came to the stairs and called down, "Russell, you'll have to go home now. Harry has to come up and get ready because we're all going for a drive to Mount Vernon."

"Aw, Mom, *now*? You mean *now*?"

"Certainly I mean 'now.' Your father wanted to get started an hour ago."

And that was when Harry went into action. In three swift, merciless kicks he sent soldiers flying in all directions, ruining formations that had been all afternoon in the making, and he howled and flailed and cried like someone half his age, while Russell looked away in a wincing smile of embarrassment.

"Harry!" Mrs. Snyder called. "Harry, I want you to stop this right now. Do you hear me?"

But he didn't stop until long after she'd come down and led him tragically upstairs; when Russell crept out for home he could still hear the terrible sound of it ringing across the yellow grass.

Even so, there was an important difference. Harry had cried because he wanted his mother to leave him alone; Russell had cried because he didn't—and therein lay the very definition of a mother's boy.

On some winter evenings Elizabeth would set up her typewriter in the living room and be lost in concentration for hours, hammering out her newspaper features or trying for something more substantial that she might submit to a magazine. She sat as straight as a stenographer at her work, her spine never touching the back of the chair, and she wore horn-rimmed glasses. Sometimes a lock of her pretty blond hair would dislodge itself and fall over one eye, and she'd put it back with impatient fingers—often the same fingers that held a short, burning cigarette. There was always a full ashtray on one side of her machine; on the other, near the paper supply, a big block of milk chocolate lay carefully broken apart in its torn-open wrapper—the kind of Hershey bar that cost almost fifty cents. Everyone understood, though, that this chocolate wasn't for passing around: it was the fuel Elizabeth needed when she wasn't drinking.

There were long intervals between spells of typing, when she would hunch over a pencil to revise and correct her pages, and then the silence was broken only by the occasional *whack-whack-whack* of a car's loose tire chain whipping the underside of its fender along the packed snow and ice of the Post Road. During one such lull, on a night of heavy snowfall, the telephone rang for the first time in what seemed many weeks.

"I'll get it!" Alice Towers cried in headlong eagerness for the social life of junior high, but then she turned back and said, "It's for you, Mrs. Baker." And they all listened as Elizabeth murmured and laughed into the phone in a way that could only have meant it was a man.

"My God," she told Lucy when she'd hung up, "I think Judd Leonard is insane. He's at the Hartsdale station and he says he'll be here in a taxi in ten minutes. Can you imagine anybody coming all the way out here on a night like this?" But moving uncertainly back toward her scattered worktable, then turning and taking off her glasses, she couldn't hide a shy, pleased look that transformed her suddenly into a girl. "Well, Jesus, Lucy, is my hair all right?" she said. "Are my clothes all right? Do you think there's time to wash up and change?"

Judd Leonard arrived with gusts of laughter and a great stamping-off of snow in the vestibule. His thin city shoes weren't used to stuff like this and even his expensive overcoat looked forlorn, but he triumphantly displayed a heavy, snow-flecked paper bag that clinked with bottles of liquor. He gave Lucy Towers a kiss on the cheek to prove he had heard what a nice woman she was, and he was attentive to the children: he explained to them that he was an old broken-down word man and a very dear friend of Nancy's mother.

Everybody stayed up late that night. Lucy seemed to do most of the talking at first, telling Westchester anecdotes; then Elizabeth held forth at enthusiastic length on Communism, and Judd Leonard went right along with her. Even though he earned his living in private enterprise, he said, he'd be happy to see every vestige of it down the drain if that meant humanity might then have a chance. These were times of inevitable change; only a fool could fail to recognize that. Long after the children were in bed upstairs his rolling, thunderous voice filled the snowbound house. They listened as long as they could, comprehending or not, until they fell asleep in the rhythms of it.

When the snow had stopped the following afternoon, Elizabeth and Judd departed quietly by taxi for the Hartsdale station. As they rode together on the train to New York he said, "Your roommate's an imbecile. Give her three drinks and all she wants to talk about is garden parties."

"Oh, Lucy's all right," Elizabeth said. "She just takes a little getting used to. Besides, it's a nice arrangement, sharing that house. It suits me."

"Ah, funny little Irish Scarsdale Bolshevik," he said fondly, putting his arm around her. "You're really not a hell of a lot smarter than she is, you know that?"

By the third or fourth day of Elizabeth's absence, Lucy assumed she was staying with Judd in New York for a while, commuting out to New Rochelle for work and back to the city each night. But wouldn't it have been only considerate to let people know her plans? Wasn't it a little thoughtless not even to have told Nancy?

Russell Towers found it amazing that Nancy didn't know where her mother was and gave no sign of being eaten alive with worry—seemed, in fact, not even to care. He hung around the open door of her room one day, after Elizabeth had been gone for a week or more, watching Nancy work on the floor with some art paper taken from school and with a colored-pencil set of her own.

At last he said, "Heard from your mother yet?"

"Nope," she said.

"Any idea where she is or anything?"

"Nope."

He knew the next question might easily make him a fool in her eyes, but couldn't hold it back. "You worried about it?"

And Nancy looked up at him in a frank, thoughtful way. "No," she said. "I know she'll come back. She always does."

That was impressive. As he slouched away to his own room, Russell knew that an attitude like that was exactly what he needed in his own life. But he knew too, sitting on his bed to think it over, that it was out of the question. It was as far-fetched as trying to compare himself to the athletes shown on the backs of breakfast-cereal boxes. He was an anxious, skinny little kid, forever too young for his age, and anyone opening the lid of his toy chest would only find sickening proof of it.

Alice Towers was once again the first to reach the phone when it rang a few nights later. "Oh, sure," she said, and then, "It's for you, Nancy. It's your mother."

Nancy took the call standing up, with her back to the Towers family. After the opening "Hi" her words were indistinct; then she was silent, listening, holding her shoulders in a high, unnatural way. At last, she turned and held out the phone to Lucy, who took it up quickly.

"Well, E*liz*abeth. Are you all right? We've all been a little—concerned about you."

"Lucy, I need my child," Elizabeth said in the old Irish-poetry voice. "I want you to send me my child tonight."

"Oh. Well, look. For one thing the last train's probably been gone for hours, and besides, I—"

"The last train leaves there at ten-thirty-something," Elizabeth said. "Judd looked it up on the timetable. That gives her plenty of time to get ready."

"Well, but Elizabeth, I really don't think this is a very good idea. Has she ever taken a train alone before? And at night?"

"Oh, nonsense. It's only a forty-minute ride, and Judd and I'll be there to meet her, or at least I will. She knows that. I've told her, all she has to do when she gets off the train is follow the crowd."

And Lucy hesitated. "Well," she said, "I suppose if you can promise to be there when she—"

"'Promise'? Am I expected to make a 'promise'? To you? About something like this? You're beginning to make me tired, Lucy."

Russell thought his mother looked hurt and bewildered and a little foolish after she'd hung up the phone, but she recovered quickly, and from then on she did everything right. In a tone that came out as a nice mixture of authority and affection, she sent Nancy upstairs to change her clothes and to pack. Then she called for a station taxicab, explaining that a nine-year-old girl would be traveling alone and asking if the driver could see her safely aboard the train.

When Nancy came down in a fresh dress, with her winter coat and her overnight bag, Lucy Towers said, "Oh, good. You look very nice, dear." And Russell couldn't be sure, but he thought it was the first time he had ever heard his mother call her "dear."

"Oh, wait," Nancy said, "I forgot." And she ran upstairs again and came back with her grubby-looking teddy bear.

"Oh, well, of course," Lucy said. "And I'll tell you what we'll do." She took the small suitcase on her lap and unfastened the clasps of it. "We'll open this up and we'll put old George right in there on top; that way you'll know exactly where he is at all times." And the best part of that, which Nancy's bashful smile only confirmed, was that Lucy had remembered the teddy bear's name.

"Now," Lucy said, and busied herself with her purse. "Let's see about money. I only have about a dollar and a half over the price of your ticket, but I'm sure that'll be enough. Your mother'll be waiting in Grand Central, so there won't really be any need for money at all. You've been in Grand Central before, haven't you?"

"Yes."

"Well, the thing to remember when you're alone is that all you have to do is follow the crowd. There'll be a long platform and then a long ramp going up; then you'll come out inside the station and that's where your mother'll be."

"Okay."

The cab's horn sounded in the driveway then, and all three members of the Towers family went out over slick crusted snow, in a freezing wind, to wish Nancy goodbye.

She was gone for well over a week, and there were no telephone calls. When she came back, alone, having somehow arranged for her own taxi home from the Hartsdale station (and that in itself was something Russell wasn't at all sure he'd have known how to do), she didn't tell much about her trip.

"Did you have a nice time in the city, Nancy?" Lucy Towers asked at dinner, while the maid moved softly around the table with plates of spaghetti and meat sauce.

"It was cold most of the time," Nancy said. "One day it was warm enough to go up and sit on the roof, so I did that, but I was only up there about an hour—one hour—before I was covered with soot. My hands, my face, my clothes, everything. Black."

"Mm, yes," Lucy said, winding too thick a load of spaghetti onto her fork. "Well, the air in New York does get—very dirty."

Harry Snyder's tantrum over the tin soldiers had never been mentioned, but the long aftermath of it seemed to have made him a little testy in Russell's presence. He had become hard to please and quick to find fault, and he stood around a lot looking "tough" with his thumbs hooked into the belt of his corduroy knickers.

"Whaddya got in there?" he asked one afternoon in Russell's room, indicating the toy chest.

"Nothing much. Just old stuff my mother hasn't thrown away."

But that didn't stop Harry from going over and opening the thing. "Jeez," he said. "You like stuff like this? You play with stuff like this?"

"'Course not," Russell said. "I told you, it's just that my mother hasn't ever gotten around to throwing—"

"So why don't you throw it away yourself, if you don't like it? Huh? How come you have to wait for your mother to do it?"

It was a bad moment, and the only thing to do was get Harry out of the room at once. But there was no getting him downstairs and outside, because he seemed to think it might be more interesting to stand for a while at the doorway of Nancy's room, looking in.

"Whaddya doing, Nancy?" he asked her.

"Nothing; just putting my programs away."

"Your what?"

"These, look. Theater programs. I've been to five different Gilbert and Sullivan operettas with my father, and I always save the programs. The next one we're going to see is *The Mikado*."

"The McWhat?"

"It means the emperor of Japan," she explained. "It's supposed to be very good. But my favorite so far is *The Pirates of Penzance*, and I think that's Daddy's favorite too. He sent me all the sheet music for it, the whole score."

Russell had never known her to be this talkative and high-spirited except when she brought a girl home from school, and even then what little could be heard of the conversation seemed mostly to be uncontrolled giggles. Now she was summarizing the libretto to the best of her ability, careful not to dwell on any aspect of it that might hamper Harry's grasp of the whole. Early in her monologue she had made some slight gesture of welcome to the boys, and soon they were in virtual possession of her room: Harry seated in the only chair with the sheaf of theater programs on his lap, Russell standing near the window with his thumbs in his belt.

". . . And I think the best part," she was saying, "the best part is this minor character of a policeman. He's very stiff and gruff." She paced a few steps and turned, pantomiming stiffness and gruffness. "He's wonderful, and he sings this wonderful song."

And she took up the song, trying for a deep male voice and a Cockney accent, trying mightily not to smile:

"When a felon's not engaged in his employment
—his employment"

"Oh, I forgot to tell you that part," she said, smoothing her hair with a nervous hand. "There's this whole chorus of people on the stage, you see, and they always come in and repeat the end of each line like that":

"—his employment
Or maturing his felonious little plans
—little plans
His capacity for innocent enjoyment
—cent enjoyment
Is just as great as any honest man's
—honest man's
Our feelings we with difficulty smother
—culty smother
When constabulary duty's to be done
—to be done
Ah, taking one consideration with another—"

Harry Snyder distorted his face and made a slow, loud retching sound, as if this were the worst and most nauseating song he had ever heard, and to simulate vomiting he spilled all the theater programs onto the floor with a splat. That won him a tense little laugh of complicity from Russell, and then there was silence in the room.

The surprise and hurt in Nancy's face lasted only a few seconds before she was furious. She might cry later, but she certainly wasn't crying yet. "All right, out," she said. "Get out of here. Both of you. Now."

And they could only stumble deliriously from the room like clowns, shoving each other and mugging, making it look like a mock retreat in order to make a mockery of her anger. She slammed the door behind them so hard that flakes of paint fell from the hallway ceiling, and for the rest of the afternoon they found nothing to do but fool around in the backyard, avoiding each other's eyes, until it was time for Harry to go home.

When Elizabeth finally came back she looked "awful"—that was how Lucy described it to Alice.

"You think it's all over, then?" Alice asked. "With Judd?" She had come to rely on her mother for interpretations of adult behavior, because there was no one else to ask, but it wasn't always profitable: last month a girl in the ninth grade had dropped out of school because she was pregnant, and Lucy's revulsion at the news had precluded any interpretation at all.

"Oh, well, I don't know about *that*," Lucy said now, "and I hope you won't start asking personal questions or anything, because it's really none of our—"

"Personal questions? Why would I do that?"

"Oh, well, it's just that you're always so inquisitive, dear, about other people's private business."

And Alice looked wounded, an expression even more frequent on her face lately than on her mother's, or her brother's.

The Towers family shied away from Elizabeth most of the time, and so did Nancy; it was like having a stranger in the house. Coming heavily downstairs in her spike heels, standing at the front windows to stare out at the Post Road as if in deep thought, picking at whatever food was set before her and drinking a lot after dinner as she paged impatiently through many magazines, Elizabeth didn't even seem to notice how uncomfortable she made everyone feel.

Then one night, long after the children were in bed, she cast aside *The New Republic* and said, "Lucy, I don't think this is working out. I'm sorry, because it did seem like a good idea, but I think we both ought to start looking for other places to live."

Lucy was stunned. "Well, but we signed a two-year lease," she said.

"Oh, come on. I've broken leases before and so have you. People break leases all the time. I don't think you and I are well suited to living like this, that's all, and the kids don't like it either, so let's call it off."

Lucy felt as if a man were leaving her. After a brief, intense effort to keep from crying—she knew it would be ridiculous to cry over something like this—she said, hesitantly, "Will you be moving into the city, then? With Judd?"

"Oh, *Jesus*, no." Elizabeth got up and began pacing the rug. "That loudmouth. That overbearing, posturing, drunken son of a bitch—and anyway, he broke off with me." She gave a harsh little laugh. "You ought to've *seen* the way he broke off with me. You ought to've *heard* it. No, I'll look for something like I had before, or maybe better, where I can just be quiet and go about my—go about my business alone."

"Well, Elizabeth, I wish you'd think it over. I know you've had a difficult time this winter, but it doesn't really seem fair of you to—oh, look: wait a few weeks or a month; then decide. Because there *are* advantages for you here, or can be, and besides, you and I are friends."

Elizabeth let the word "friends" hang in the air for a while, as if to examine it.

"Well," Lucy said, qualifying it, "I mean we certainly have a lot in common, and we—"

"No, we don't." And Elizabeth's eyes took on a glint of cruelty that Lucy had never seen in them before. "We don't have anything in common at all. I'm a Communist and you'll probably vote for Alf Landon. I've worked all my life and you've scarcely lifted a finger. I've never even *believed* in alimony, and you live on it."

There was nothing for Lucy Towers to do then but sweep out of the room in silence, climb the stairs, get into bed and wait for convulsions of weeping to overcome her. But she fell asleep before it happened, probably because she too had drunk a good deal that night.

By then it was early spring. They had been together in the house for six months, and now the end of it was in the air. It wasn't discussed much, but the days took on a quality of last times for everyone.

On one side of the house, away from the side where Harry Snyder lived, lay a vacant lot that made a good theater for war games: some of its weeds were tall enough to hide in, and there were trails and open spaces of packed dirt for the enactment of infantry combat. Russell was fooling around the lot alone one afternoon, perhaps because it might be the last time he'd be able to, but there wasn't much point in it without Harry. He was on his way home when he looked up and found Nancy watching him from the back porch.

"What were you *doing* out there?" she asked him.

"Nothing."

"Looked like you were walking around in circles and talking to yourself."

"Oh, I was," he said, pulling a goofy face. "I do that all the time. Doesn't everybody?"

And to his great relief she seemed to think that was funny; she even rewarded him with an agreeable little laugh.

In no time at all they were strolling the vacant lot together while he pointed out the landmarks of recent military action. Here was the clump of weeds where Harry Snyder had concealed his machine-gun emplacement; here was the trail down which Russell had led a phantom patrol, and the first burst of fire had caught him right across the chest.

To recapture the scene he reeled back in shock and crumpled to the dirt, lying still. "There's nothing much you can do if you get it in the chest that way," he explained as he got up to brush off his clothes. "But the worst thing is taking a grenade in the belly." And that called for another performance of agony and dusty sprawling.

After the third time he died for her, she looked at him thoughtfully. "You really like the falling down part, don't you," she said.

"Huh?"

"Well, I mean the best part of it for you is getting killed, right?"

"No," he said defensively, because her tone had implied something unwholesome in such a preference. "No, I just—I don't know."

That took the edge off the pleasure, though they remained on cordial terms as they walked back to the house; still, it couldn't be denied that for a little while they had been companions.

And it was on the strength of that, during their lunch break from school the following day, that Russell came thumping in from the back porch with something important to tell her.

She had gotten home first; she was settled back in the cushions of the living-room sofa, gazing out a window wrapping a lock of her black hair around her index finger.

"Hey," he said, "this is pretty funny. You know that real big guy in your class? Carl Shoemaker?"

"Sure," she said. "I know him."

"Well, I was coming out of school just now and Carl Shoemaker was there on the playground with these two other guys and he called me over. He said, 'Hey, Towers, you gonna try out for the race?'

"I said, 'What race?'

"He said, 'The human race. But I better warn you, they don't let sissies in.'

"I said, 'So who's the sissy?'

"And he said, 'Aren't you one? I heard you were. That's why I'm warning you.'

"So I said, 'Look, Shoemaker. Find somebody else to warn, okay?' I said, 'You want somebody to warn, you better keep looking.'"

It was a fairly accurate rendering of the dialogue, and Nancy seemed to have followed it with interest. But the last line of it now had an inconclusive ring, as if leaving open a chance that there might be further trouble when he went back to school. "So then after that," he told her, "after that they just sort of smiled and walked away, Shoemaker and the two other guys. I don't think they'll mess with me anymore. But I mean the whole thing was, really kind of—kind of funny."

He wondered now why he had told her about it at all, instead of finding other things to discuss. Watching her there on the sofa, in the noon light, he could see how she would probably look when she grew up and got pretty.

"Said he'd heard you were a sissy, uh?" she said.

"Well, that's what he said he'd *heard*, but I think I—"

And she gave him a long, infuriatingly sly look. "Well," she said. "I wonder where he ever heard that."

The thumbs came out of Russell's belt as he backed slowly away from her across the rug, round-eyed, aghast at her betrayal. Just before he reached the doorway he saw the slyness in her face give way to fear, but it was too late: they both knew what he would do next, and there was no stopping him.

At the foot of the stairs he called, "Mom? Mom?"

"What *is* it, dear?" Lucy Towers appeared on the landing, looking unsettled and wearing what she called her tea dress.

"Nancy told Carl Shoemaker I'm a sissy and he told a lot of other guys and now everybody's saying it and it's a lie. It's a lie."

In a stately manner appropriate to the tea dress, Lucy came downstairs. "Oh," she said. "Well. This is something we can discuss at lunch."

Elizabeth never came home for lunch and Alice ate in the junior-high-school cafeteria, so there were only the three of them at the table: Russell and his mother on one side, Nancy on the other. There was nobody to deflect the force of Lucy's slow, impassioned, relentless voice.

"I'm surprised at what you did, Nancy, and I'm deeply troubled by it. People don't do things like that. People don't spread malicious gossip and lies about their friends behind their backs. It's as bad as stealing, or cheating. It's disgusting. Oh, I suppose there are people who behave that way, but they aren't the kind of people I'd want to sit at a table with, or live in a house with, or ever have as friends of my own. Do you understand me, Nancy?"

The maid came in with their plates—there would be small portions of veal, mashed potatoes and peas today—and she lingered to give Lucy a look of veiled reproach before going back to the kitchen. She had never worked in a house like this before, and didn't want to again. A nice lady, a crazy lady, and three sad-looking kids: what kind of a house was that? Well, it would most likely be over soon—she had already put the agency on the lookout for a new job—but meanwhile, somebody ought to shut that crazy lady's mouth before she scolded that little girl to death.

"Russell is your friend, Nancy," Lucy Towers was saying, "and he's a person you share your home with. When you spread vicious lies about him at school, behind his back, you're inflicting great damage. Oh, I'm sure you know that; you've known it from the start. But I wonder if you ever stopped to think of me. Because do you want to know something, Nancy? *I* found this house. *I* asked your mother to join me in it, so we could all live together. *I* was the one who kept hoping and hoping there'd be a little peace and harmony in our lives here—yes, and I went on hoping even after I knew there wouldn't be. So you see it isn't only Russell you've hurt, Nancy; it's me. It's me. You've hurt me terribly, Nancy. . . ."

There was more, and it came to an end exactly as Russell knew it would. All through the upbraiding Nancy had sat silent, with a rigid face and downcast eyes—she had even managed to eat a little, as if to show she was above all this—but eventually her mouth began to fall apart. There were telltale twitches of the lips, increasingly difficult to control; then it came open and was locked in a shape of despair around two partly chewed green peas, and she was crying wretchedly but making no sound.

They were both late for school that afternoon, though Nancy had a head start of at least a hundred yards. Walking out between the borders of other people's lawns and through the broken fence and then along the gently curving lane, Russell could catch only an occasional glimpse of her far ahead, a tall, slim girl with a way of walking that suggested she was older than nine. She would grow up and get pretty; she would get married and have boys and girls of her own; so it was probably a dumb and even a sissy thing to be afraid she would always remember what Russell Towers had done to her today. Still, there would now be no way of knowing, ever, if she would forget it.

"Well, I don't see any point in prolonging this," Elizabeth said the next day, setting two packed suitcases on the living-room floor. "Nancy and I'll go up to White Plains and stay in a hotel for a few days; then when we're settled somewhere I'll send back for the rest of our stuff."

"You're putting me in a very awkward position," Lucy said solemnly.

"Oh, come on; I don't see that at all. Here, look, I'll leave you an extra month's rent, okay?" She sat briefly at her old worktable with her checkbook, and scribbled on it. "There," she said when it was done. "That ought to take care of the suffering." And she and Nancy carried their bags out to the Model A.

None of the Towers family went to the front windows to wave goodbye, but it didn't matter because neither of the Bakers looked back.

"Know something?" Elizabeth said when she and Nancy were heading north on the Post Road. "I couldn't really afford to write that check. It won't bounce, but it's going to give us a tight month. Still, maybe there are times when you have to buy your way out of something whether you can afford it or not."

After another mile or so she glanced from the road to Nancy's serious profile and said, "Well, Jesus, can't we even have a couple of laughs in this car? Why don't you sing me Gilbert and Sullivan or something?"

And Nancy gave her a brief, shy smile before turning away again. Slowly, Elizabeth removed the driving glove from her right hand. She reached across her daughter's lap, clasped the outer thigh and brought her sliding over, careful to keep her small knees clear of the shuddering gear shift. She held the child's thighs pressed fast against her own for a long time; then, in a voice so soft it could scarcely be heard over the sound of the car, she said, "Listen, it'll be all right, sweetheart. It'll be all right."

Liars in Love

WHEN WARREN MATHEWS came to live in London, with his wife and their two-year-old daughter, he was afraid people might wonder at his apparent idleness. It didn't help much to say he was "on a Fulbright" because only a few other Americans knew what that meant; most of the English would look blank or smile helpfully until he explained it, and even then they didn't understand.

"Why tell them anything at all?" his wife would say. "Is it any of their business? What about all the Americans living here on *private* incomes?" And she'd go back to work at the stove, or the sink, or the ironing board, or at the rhythmic and graceful task of brushing her long brown hair.

She was a sharp-featured, pretty girl named Carol, married at an age she often said had been much too young, and it didn't take her long to discover that she hated London. It was big and drab and unwelcoming; you could walk or ride a bus for miles without seeing anything nice, and the coming of winter brought an evil-smelling sulphurous fog that stained everything yellow, that seeped through closed windows and doors to hang in your rooms and afflict your wincing, weeping eyes.

Besides, she and Warren hadn't been getting along well for a long time. They may both have hoped the adventure of moving to England might help set things right, but now it was hard to remember whether they'd hoped that or not. They didn't quarrel much—quarreling had belonged to an earlier phase of their marriage—but they hardly ever enjoyed each other's company, and there were whole days when they seemed unable to do anything at all in their small, tidy basement flat without getting in each other's way. "Oh, sorry," they would mutter after each clumsy little bump or jostle. "Sorry . . ."

The basement flat had been their single stroke of luck: it cost them only a token rent because it belonged to Carol's English aunt, Judith, an elegant widow of seventy who lived alone in the apartment upstairs and who often told them, fondly, how "charming" they were. She was very charming too. The only inconvenience, carefully discussed in advance, was that Judith required the use of their bathtub because there wasn't one in her own place. She would knock shyly at their door in the mornings and come in, all smiles and apologies, wrapped in a regal floor-length robe. Later, emerging from her bath in billows of steam with her handsome old face as pink and fresh as a child's, she would make her way slowly into the front room. Sometimes she'd linger there to talk for a while, sometimes not. Once, pausing with her hand on the knob of the hallway door, she said, "Do you know, when we first made this living arrangement, when I agreed to sublet this floor, I remember thinking, Oh, but what if I don't *like* them? And now it's all so marvelous, because I do like you both so very much."

They managed to make pleased and affectionate replies; then, after she'd gone, Warren said, "That was nice, wasn't it."

"Yes; very nice." Carol was seated on the rug, struggling to sink their daughter's heel into a red rubber boot. "Hold still, now, baby," she said. "Give Mommy a break, okay?"

The little girl, Cathy, attended a local nursery school called The Peter Pan Club every weekday. The original idea of this had been that it would free Carol to find work in London, to supplement the Fulbright income; then it turned out there was a law forbidding British employers to hire foreigners unless it could be established that the foreigner offered skills unavailable among British applicants, and Carol couldn't hope to establish anything like that. But they'd kept Cathy enrolled in the nursery school anyway because she seemed to like it, and also—though neither parent quite put it into words—because it was good to have her out of the house all day.

And on this particular morning Carol was especially glad of the prospect of the time alone with her husband: she had made up her mind last night that this was the day she would announce her decision to leave him. He must surely have come to agree, by now, that things weren't right. She would take the baby home to New York; once they were settled there she would get a job—secretary or receptionist or something—and make a life of her own. They would keep in touch by mail, of course, and when his Fulbright year was done they could—well, they could both think it over and discuss it then.

All the way to The Peter Pan Club with Cathy chattering and clinging to her hand, and all the way back, walking alone and faster, Carol tried to rehearse her lines just under her breath; but when the time came it proved to be a much less difficult scene than she'd feared. Warren didn't even seem very surprised—not, at least, in ways that might have challenged or undermined her argument.

"Okay," he kept saying gloomily, without quite looking at her. "Okay . . ." Then after awhile he asked a troubling question. "What'll we tell Judith?"

"Well, yes, I've thought of that too," she said, "and it *would* be awkward to tell her the truth. Do you think we could just say there's an illness in my family, and that's why I have to go home?"

"Well, but your family is *her* family."

"Oh, that's silly. My father was her brother, but he's dead. She's never even met my mother, and anyway they'd been divorced for God knows how many years. And there aren't any other lines of—you know—lines of communication, or anything. She'll never find out."

Warren thought about it. "Okay," he said at last, "but I don't want to be the one to tell her. You tell her, okay?"

"Sure. Of course I'll tell her, if it's all right with you."

And that seemed to settle it—what to tell Judith, as well as the larger matter of their separation. But late that night, after Warren had sat staring for a long time into the hot blue-and-pink glow of the clay filaments in their gas fireplace, he said "Hey, Carol?"

"What?" She was flapping and spreading clean sheets on the couch, where she planned to sleep alone.

"What do you suppose he'll be like, this man of yours?"

"What do you mean? *What* man of mine?"

"You know. The guy you're hoping to find in New York. Oh, I know he'll be better than me in about thirteen ways, and he'll certainly be an awful lot richer, but I mean what'll he be like? What'll he *look* like?"

"I'm not listening to any of this."

"Well, okay, but tell me. What'll he look like?"

"I don't know," she said impatiently. "A dollar bill, I guess."

Less than a week before Carol's ship was scheduled to sail, The Peter Pan Club held a party in honor of Cathy's third birthday. It was a fine occasion of ice cream and cake for "tea," as well as the usual fare of bread and meat paste, bread and jam, and cups of a bright fluid that was the English equivalent of Kool-Aid. Warren and Carol stood together on the sidelines, smiling at their happy daughter as if to promise her that one way or another they would always be her parents.

"So you'll be here alone with us for a while, Mr. Mathews," said Marjorie Blaine, who ran the nursery school. She was a trim, chain-smoking woman of forty or so, long divorced, and Warren had noticed a few times that she wasn't bad. "You must come round to our pub," she said. "Do you know Finch's, in the Fulham Road? It's rather a scruffy little pub, actually, but all sorts of nice people go there."

And he told her he would be sure to drop by.

Then it was the day of the sailing, and Warren accompanied his wife and child as far as the railroad station and the gate to the boat train.

"Isn't Daddy coming?" Cathy asked, looking frightened.

"It's all right, dear," Carol told her. "We have to leave Daddy here for now, but you'll see him again very soon." And they walked quickly away into the enclosing crowd.

One of the presents given to Cathy at the party was a cardboard music box with a jolly yellow duck and a birthday-card message on the front, and with a little crank on one side: when you turned the crank it played a tinny rendition of "Happy Birthday to You." And when Warren came back to the flat that night he found it, among several other cheap, forgotten toys, on the floor beneath Cathy's stripped bed. He played it once or twice as he sat drinking whiskey over the strewn books and papers on his desk; then, with a child's sense of pointless experiment, he turned the crank the other way and played it backwards, slowly. And once he'd begun doing that he found he couldn't stop, or didn't want to, because the dim, rude little melody it made suggested all the loss and loneliness in the world.

Dum dee *dum da da-da*
Dum dee *dum da da-da* . . .

He was tall and very thin and always aware of how ungainly he must look, even when nobody was there to see—even when the whole of his life had come down to sitting alone and fooling with a cardboard toy, three thousand miles from home. It was March of 1953, and he was twenty-seven years old.

"Oh, you poor man," Judith said when she came down for her bath in the morning. "It's so *sad* to find you all alone here. You must miss them terribly."

"Yeah, well, it'll only be a few months."

"Well, but that's awful. Isn't there someone who could sort of look after you? Didn't you and Carol meet any young people who might be company for you?"

"Oh, sure, we met a few people," he said, "but nobody I'd want to—you know, nobody I'd especially want to have around or anything."

"Well then, you ought to get out and make *new* friends."

Soon after the first of April, as was her custom, Judith went to live in her cottage in Sussex, where she would stay until September. She would make occasional visits back to town for a few days, she explained to Warren, but "Don't worry; I'll always be sure to ring you up well in advance before I sort of *descend* on you again."

And so he was truly alone. He went to the pub called Finch's one night with a vague idea of persuading Marjorie Blaine to come home with him and then of having her in his own and Carol's bed. And he found her alone at the crowded bar, but she looked old and fuddled with drink.

"Oh, I say, Mr. Mathews," she said. "Do come and join me."

"Warren," he said.

"What?"

"People call me Warren."

"Ah. Yes, well, this is England, you see; we're all dreadfully formal here." And a little later she said, "I've never quite understood what it is you do, Mr. Mathews."

"Well, I'm on a Fulbright," he said. "It's an American scholarship program for students overseas. The government pays your way, and you—"

"Yes, well of course America is quite good about that sort of thing, isn't it. And I should imagine you must have a very clever mind." She gave him a flickering glance. "People who haven't lived often do." Then she cringed, to pantomime evasion of a blow. "Sorry," she said quickly, "sorry I said that." But she brightened at once. "Sarah!" she called. "Sarah, do come and meet young Mr. Mathews, who wants to be called Warren."

A tall, pretty girl turned from a group of other drinkers to smile at him, extending her hand, but when Marjorie Blaine said, "He's an American," the girl's smile froze and her hand fell.

"Oh," she said. "How nice." And she turned away again.

It wasn't a good time to be an American in London. Eisenhower had been elected and the Rosenbergs killed; Joseph McCarthy was on the rise and the war in Korea, with its reluctant contingent of British troops, had come to seem as if it might last forever. Still, Warren Mathews suspected that even in the best of times he would feel alien and homesick here. The very English language, as spoken by natives, bore so little relation to his own that there were far too many opportunities for missed points in every exchange. Nothing was clear.

He went on trying, but even on better nights, in happier pubs than Finch's and in the company of more agreeable strangers, he found only a slight lessening of discomfort—and he found no attractive, unattached girls. The girls, whether blandly or maddeningly pretty, were always fastened to the arms of men whose relentlessly witty talk could leave him smiling in bafflement. And he was dismayed to find how many of these people's innuendoes, winked or shouted, dwelt on the humorous aspects of homosexuality. Was all of England obsessed with that topic? Or did it haunt only this quiet, "interesting" part of London where Chelsea met South Kensington along the Fulham Road?

Then one night he took a late bus for Piccadilly Circus. "What do you want to go *there* for?" Carol would have said, and almost half the ride was over before he realized that he didn't have to answer questions like that anymore.

In 1945, as a boy on his first furlough from the Army after the war, he had been astonished at the nightly promenade of prostitutes then called Piccadilly Commandos, and there had been an unforgettable quickening of his blood as he watched them walk and turn, walk and turn again: girls for sale. They seemed to have become a laughingstock among more sophisticated soldiers, some of whom liked to slump against buildings and flip big English pennies onto the sidewalk at their feet as they passed, but Warren had longed for the courage to defy that mockery. He'd wanted to choose a girl and buy her and have her, however she might turn out to be, and he'd despised himself for letting the whole two weeks of his leave run out without doing so.

He knew that a modified version of that spectacle had still been going on as recently as last fall, because he and Carol had seen it on their way to some West End theater. "Oh, I don't believe this," Carol said. "Are they really all whores? This is the saddest thing I've ever seen."

There had lately been newspaper items about the pressing need to "clean up Piccadilly" before the impending Coronation, but the police must have been lax in their efforts so far, because the girls were very much there.

Most of them were young, with heavily made-up faces; they wore bright clothes in the colors of candy and Easter eggs, and they either walked and turned or stood waiting in the shadows. It took him three straight whiskeys to work up the nerve, and even then he wasn't sure of himself. He knew he looked shabby—he was wearing a gray suit coat with old Army pants, and his shoes were almost ready to be thrown away—but no clothes in the world would have kept him from feeling naked as he made a quick choice from among four girls standing along Shaftesbury Avenue and went up to her and said, "Are you free?"

"Am I free?" she said, meeting his eyes for less than a second. "Honey, I've been free all my life."

The first thing she wanted him to agree on, before they'd walked half a block, was her price—steep, but within his means; then she asked if he would mind taking a short cab ride. And in the cab she explained that she never used the cheap hotels and rooming houses around here, as most of the other girls did, because she had a six-month-old daughter and didn't like to leave her for long.

"I don't blame you," he said. "I have a daughter too." And he instantly wondered why he'd felt it necessary to tell her that.

"Oh yeah? So where's your wife?"

"Back in New York."

"You divorced then, or what?"

"Well, separated."

"Oh yeah? That's too bad."

They rode in an awkward silence for a while until she said, "Listen, it's all right if you want to kiss me or anything, but no big feely-feely in the cab, okay? I really don't go for that."

And only then, kissing her, did he begin to find out what she was like. She wore her bright yellow hair in ringlets around her face—it was illuminated and darkened again with each passing streetlamp; her eyes were pleasant despite all the mascara; her mouth was nice; and though he tried no big feely-feely his hands were quick to discover she was slender and firm.

It wasn't a short cab ride—it went on until Warren began to wonder if it might stop only when they met a waiting group of hoodlums who would haul him out of the backseat and beat him up and rob him and take off in the cab with the girl—but it came to an end at last on a silent city block in what he guessed was the northeast of London. She took him into a house that looked rude but peaceful in the moonlight; then she said, "Shh," and they tiptoed down a creaking linoleum corridor and into her room, where she switched on a light and closed the door behind them.

She checked the baby, who lay small and still and covered-up in the center of a big yellow crib against one wall. Along the facing wall, not six feet away, stood the reasonably fresh-looking double bed in which Warren was expected to take his pleasure.

"I just like to make sure she's breathing," the girl explained, turning back from the crib; then she watched him count out the right number of pound and ten-shilling notes on the top of her dresser. She turned off the ceiling light but left a small one on at the bedside as she began to undress, and he managed to watch her while nervously taking off his own clothes. Except that her cotton-knit underpants looked pitifully cheap, that her brown pubic hair gave the lie to her blond head, that her legs were short and her knees a little thick, she was all right. And she was certainly young.

"Do you ever enjoy this?" he asked when they were clumsily in bed together.

"Huh? How do you mean?"

"Well, just—you know—after a while it must get so you can't really—" and he stopped there in a paralysis of embarrassment.

"Oh, no," she assured him. "Well, I mean it depends on the *guy* a lot, but I'm not—I'm not a block of ice or anything. You'll find out."

And so, in wholly unexpected grace and nourishment, she became a real girl for him.

Her name was Christine Phillips and she was twenty-two. She came from Glasgow, and she'd been in London for four years. He knew it would be gullible to believe everything she told him when they sat up later that night over cigarettes and a warm quart bottle of beer; still, he wanted to keep an open mind. And if much of what she said was predictable stuff—she explained, for example, that she wouldn't have to be on the street at all if she were willing to take a job as a "hostess" in a "club," but that she'd turned down many such offers because "all those places are clip joints"—there were other, unguarded remarks that could make his arm tighten around her in tenderness, as when she said she had named her baby Laura "because I've always thought that's the most beautiful girl's name in the world. Don't you?"

And he began to understand why there was scarcely a trace of Scotch or English accent in her speech: she must have known so many Americans, soldiers and sailors and random civilian strays, that they had invaded and plundered her language.

"So what do you do for a living, Warren?" she asked. "You get money from home?"

"Well, sort of." And he explained, once again, about the Fulbright program.

"Yeah?" she said. "You have to be smart for that?"

"Oh, not necessarily. You don't have to be very smart for anything in America anymore."

"You kidding me?"

"Not wholly."

"Huh?"

"I mean I'm only kidding you a little."

And after a thoughtful pause she said, "Well, I wish *I* could've had more schooling. I wish I was smart enough to write a book, because I'd have a hell of a book to write. Know what I'd call it?" She narrowed her eyes, and her fingers sketched a suggestion of formal lettering in the air. "I'd call it *This Is Piccadilly*. Because I mean people don't really *know* what goes on. Ah, Jesus, I could tell you things that'd make your—well, never mind. Skip it."

". . . Hey, Christine?" he said later still, when they were back in bed.

"Uh-huh?"

"Want to tell each other the stories of our lives?"

"Okay," she said with a child's eagerness, and so he had to explain again, shyly, that he was only kidding her a little.

The baby's cry woke them both at six in the morning, but Christine got up and told him he could go back to sleep for a while. When he awoke again he was alone in the room, which smelled faintly of cosmetics and piss. He could hear several women talking and laughing nearby, and he didn't know what he was expected to do but get up and dressed and find his way out of here.

Then Christine came to the door and asked if he would like a cup of tea. "Whyn't you come on out, if you're ready," she said as she carefully handed him the hot mug, "and meet my friends, okay?"

And he followed her into a combination kitchen and living room whose windows overlooked a weed-grown vacant lot. A stubby woman in her thirties stood working at an ironing board with the electrical cord plugged into a ceiling fixture, and another girl of about Christine's age lay back in an easy chair, wearing a knee-length robe and slippers, with her bare, pretty legs ablaze in morning sunlight. A gas fireplace hissed beneath a framed oval mirror, and the good smells of steam and tea were everywhere.

"Warren, this is Grace Arnold," Christine said of the woman at the ironing board, who looked up to say she was pleased to meet him, "and this is Amy." Amy licked her lips and smiled and said, "Hi."

"You'll probably meet the kids in a minute," Christine told him. "Grace has six kids. Grace and *Alfred* do, I mean. Alfred's the man of the house."

And very gradually, as he sipped and listened, mustering appropriate nods and smiles and inquiries, Warren was able to piece the facts together. Alfred Arnold was an interior housepainter, or rather a "painter and decorator." He and his wife, with all those children to raise, made ends meet by renting out rooms to Christine and Amy in full knowledge of how both girls earned their living, and so they had all become a kind of family.

How many polite, nervous men had sat on this sofa in the mornings, watching the whisk and glide of Grace Arnold's iron, helplessly intrigued with the sunny spectacle of Amy's legs, hearing the talk of these three women and wondering how soon it would be all right to leave? But Warren Mathews had nothing to go home to, so he began to hope this pleasant social occasion might last.

"You've a nice name, Warren," Amy told him, crossing her legs. "I've always liked that name."

"Warren?" Christine said. "Can you stay and have something to eat with us?"

Soon there was a fried egg on buttered toast for each of them, served with more tea around a clean kitchen table, and they all ate as daintily as if they were in a public place. Christine sat beside him, and once during the meal she gave his free hand a shy little squeeze.

"If you don't have to rush off," she said, while Grace was stacking the dishes, "we can get a beer. The pub'll be open in half an hour."

"Good," he said. "Fine." Because the last thing he wanted to do was rush off, even when all six children came clamoring in from their morning's play down the street, each of them in turn wanting to sit on his lap and poke fun at him and run jam-stained fingers through his hair. They were a shrill, rowdy crowd, and they all glowed with health. The oldest was a bright girl named Jane who looked oddly like a Negro—light-skinned, but with African features and hair—and who giggled as she backed away from him and said, "Are you Christine's fella?"

"I sure am," he told her.

And he did feel very much like Christine's fella when he took her out alone to the pub around the corner. He liked the way she walked—she didn't look anything at all like a prostitute in her fresh tan raincoat with the collar turned up around her cheeks—and he liked her sitting close beside him on a leather bench against the wall of an old brown room where everything, even the mote-filled shafts of sunlight, seemed to be steeped in beer.

"Look, Warren," she said after awhile, turning her bright glass on the table. "Do you want to stay over another night?"

"Well, no, I really—the thing is I can't afford it."

"Oh, I didn't mean that," she said, and squeezed his hand again. "I didn't mean for money. I meant—just stay. Because I want you to."

Nobody had to tell him what a triumph of masculinity it was to have a young whore offer herself to you free of charge. He didn't even need *From Here to Eternity* to tell him that, though he would always remember how that novel came quickly to mind as he drew her face up closer to his own. She had made him feel profoundly strong. "Oh, that's nice," he said huskily, and he kissed her. Then, just before kissing her again, he said, "Oh, that's awfully nice, Christine."

And they both made frequent use of the word *nice* all afternoon. Christine seemed unable to keep away from him except for brief intervals when she had to attend to the baby; once, when Warren was alone in the living room, she came dancing slowly and dreamily across the floor, as if to the sound of violins, and fell into his arms like a girl in the movies. Another time, curled fast against him on the sofa, she softly crooned a popular song called "Unforgettable" to him, with a significant dipping of her eyelashes over the title word whenever the lyrics brought it around.

"Oh, you're nice, Warren," she kept saying. "You know that? You're really nice."

And he would tell her, again and again, how nice she was too.

When Alfred Arnold came home from work—a compact and tired and bashfully agreeable-looking man—his wife and young Amy were quick to busy themselves in the ritual of making him welcome: taking his coat, readying his chair, bringing his glass of gin. But Christine held back, clinging to Warren's arm, until the time came to take him up for a formal introduction to the man of the house.

"Pleased to meet you, Warren," Alfred Arnold said. "Make yourself at home."

There was corned beef with boiled potatoes for supper, which everyone said was very good, and in the afterglow Alfred fell to reminiscing in a laconic way about his time as prisoner of war in Burma. "Four years," he said, displaying the fingers of one hand with only the thumb held down. "Four years."

And Warren said it must have been terrible.

"Alfred?" Grace said. "Show Warren your citation."

"Oh no, love; nobody wants to bother with that."

"Show him," she insisted.

And Alfred gave in. A thick black wallet was shyly withdrawn from his hip pocket; then from one of its depths came a stained, much-folded piece of paper. It was almost falling apart at the creases, but the typewritten message was clear: it conveyed the British Army's recognition that Private A. J. Arnold, while a prisoner of war of the Japanese in Burma, had been commended by his captors as a good and steady worker on the construction of a railroad bridge in 1944.

"Well," Warren said. "That's fine."

"Ah, you know the women," Alfred confided, tucking the paper back where it came from. "The women always want you to show this stuff around. I'd rather forget the whole bloody business."

Christine and Warren managed to make an early escape, under Grace Arnold's winking smile, and as soon as the bedroom door was shut they were clasped and writhing and breathing heavily, eager and solemn in lust. The shedding of their clothes took no time at all but seemed a terrible hindrance and delay; then they were deep in bed and reveling in each other, and then they were joined again.

"Oh, Warren," she said. "Oh, God. Oh, Warren. Oh, I love you."

And he heard himself saying more than once, more times than he cared to believe or remember, that he loved her too.

Sometime after midnight, as they lay quiet, he wondered how those words could have spilled so easily and often from his mouth. And at about the same time, when Christine began talking again, he became aware that she'd had a lot to drink. A quarter-full bottle of gin stood on the floor beside the bed, with two cloudy, finger-printed glasses to prove they had both made ample use of it, but she seemed to be well ahead of him now. Pouring herself still another one, she sat back in comfort against the pillows and the wall and talked in a way that suggested she was carefully composing each sentence for dramatic effect, like a little girl pretending to be an actress.

"You know something, Warren? Everything I ever wanted was taken away from me. All my life. When I was eleven I wanted a bicycle more than anything in the world, and my father finally bought me one. Oh, it was only secondhand and cheap, but I loved it. And then that same summer he got mad and wanted to punish me for something—I can't even remember what—and he took it away. I never saw it again."

"Yeah, well, that must've felt bad," Warren said, but then he tried to steer the talk along less sentimental lines. "What kind of work does your father do?"

"Oh, he's a pen-pusher. For the gas works. We don't get along at all, and I don't get along with my mother either. I never go home. No, but it's true what I said: everything I ever wanted was—you know—

taken away from me." She paused there, as if to bring her stage voice back under control, and when she began to speak again, with greater confidence, it was in the low, hushed tones appropriate for an intimate audience of one.

"Warren? Would you like to hear about Adrian? Laura's father? Because I'd really like to tell you, if you're interested."

"Sure."

"Well, Adrian's an American Army officer. A young major. Or maybe he's a lieutenant colonel by now, wherever he is. I don't even know where he is, and the funny part is I don't care. I really don't care at all anymore. But Adrian and I had a wonderful time until I told him I was pregnant; then he froze up. He just froze up. Oh, I suppose I didn't really think he'd ask me to marry him or anything—he had this rich society girl waiting for him back in the States; I knew that. But he got very cold and he told me to get an abortion, and I said no. I said, 'I'm going to have this baby, Adrian.' And he said, 'All right.' He said, 'All right, but you're on your own, Christine. You'll have to raise this child any way you can.' That was when I decided to go and see his commanding officer."

"His commanding officer?"

"Well, *somebody* had to help," she said. "*Somebody* had to make him see his responsibility. And God, I'll never forget that day. The regimental commander was this very dignified man named Colonel Masters, and he just sat there behind his desk and looked at me and listened, and he nodded a few times. Adrian was there with me, not saying a word; there were just the three of us in the office. And in the end Colonel Masters said, 'Well, Miss Phillips, as far as I can see it comes down to this. You made a mistake. You made a mistake, and you'll have to live with it.'"

"Yeah," Warren said uneasily. "Yeah, well, that must've been—"

But he didn't have to finish that sentence, or to say anything else that might let her know he hadn't believed a word of the story, because she was crying. She had drawn up her knees and laid the side of her rumpled head on them as the sobs began; then she set her empty glass carefully on the floor, slid back into bed, and turned away from him, crying and crying.

"Hey, come on," he said. "Come on, baby, don't cry." And there was nothing to do but turn her around and take her in his arms until she was still.

After a long time she said, "Is there any more gin?"

"Some."

"Well, listen, let's finish it, okay? Grace won't mind, or if she wants me to pay her for it, I'll *pay* her for it."

In the morning, with her face so swollen from emotion and sleep that she tried to hide it with her fingers, she said, "Jesus. I guess I got pretty drunk last night."

"That's okay; we both drank a lot."

"Well, I'm sorry," she said in the impatient, almost defiant way of people accustomed to making frequent apologies. "I'm sorry." She had taken care of the baby and was walking unsteadily around the little room in a drab green bathrobe. "Anyway, listen. Will you come back, Warren?"

"Sure. I'll call you, okay?"

"No, there's no telephone here. But will you come back soon?" She followed him out to the front door, where he turned to see the limpid appeal in her eyes. "If you come in the daytime," she said, "I'll always be home."

For a few days, idling at his desk or wandering the streets and the park in the first real spring weather of the year, Warren found it impossible to keep his mind on anything but Christine. Nothing like this could ever have been expected to happen in his life: a young Scotch prostitute in love with him. With a high, fine confidence that wasn't at all characteristic of him, he had begun to see himself as a rare and privileged adventurer of the heart. Memories of Christine in his arms whispering, "Oh, I love you," made him smile like a fool in the sunshine, and at other moments he found a different, subtler pleasure in considering all the pathetic things about her—the humorless ignorance, the cheap, drooping underwear, the drunken crying. Even her story of "Adrian" (a name almost certainly lifted from a women's magazine) was easy to forgive—or would be, once he'd found some wise and gentle way of letting her know he knew it wasn't true. He might eventually have to find a way of telling her he hadn't really meant to say he loved her too, but all that could wait. There was no hurry, and the season was spring.

"Know what I like most about you, Warren?" she asked very late in their third or fourth night together. "Know what I really love about you? It's that I feel I can trust you. All my life, that's all I ever wanted:

somebody to trust. And you see I keep making mistakes and making mistakes because I trust people who turn out to be—"

"Shh, shh," he said, "it's okay, baby. Let's just sleep now."

"Well, but wait a second. Listen a minute, okay? Because I really do want to tell you something, Warren. I knew this boy Jack. He kept saying he wanted to marry me and everything, but this was the trouble: Jack's a gambler. He'll always be a gambler. And I suppose you can guess what that meant."

"What'd it mean?"

"It meant money, that's what it meant. Staking him, covering his losses, helping him get through the month until payday—ah, Christ, it makes me sick just to think of all that now. For almost a year. And do you know how much of it I ever got back? Well, you won't believe this, but I'll tell you. Or no, wait—I'll show you. Wait a second."

She got up and stumbled and switched on the ceiling light in an explosion of brilliance that startled the baby, who whimpered in her sleep. "It's okay, Laura," Christine said softly as she rummaged in the top drawer of her dresser; then she found what she was looking for and brought it back to the bed. "Here," she said. "Look. Read this."

It was a single sheet of cheap ruled paper torn from a tablet of the kind meant for schoolchildren, and it bore no date.

> Dear Miss Phillips:
>
> Enclosed is the sum of two pounds ten shillings. This is all I can afford now and there will be no more as I am being shipped back to the U.S. next week for discharge and separation from the service.
>
> My Commanding Officer says you telephoned him four times last month and three times this month and this must stop as he is a busy man and can not be bothered with calls of this kind. Do not call him again, or the 1st Sgt. either, or anyone else in this organization.
>
> Pfc. John F. Curtis

"Isn't that the damnedest thing?" Christine said. "I mean really, Warren, isn't that the goddamnedest thing?"

"Sure is." And he read it over again. It was the sentence beginning "My Commanding Officer" that seemed to give it all away, demolishing "Adrian" at a glance and leaving little doubt in Warren's mind that John F. Curtis had fathered her child.

"Could you turn the light off now, Christine?" he said, handing the letter back to her.

"Sure, honey. I just wanted you to see that." And she had undoubtedly wanted to see if he'd be dumb enough to swallow the story too.

When the room was dark again and she lay curled against his back, he silently prepared a quiet, reasonable speech. He would say, Baby, don't get mad, but listen. You mustn't try to put these stories over on me anymore. I didn't believe the one about Adrian and I don't believe Jack the Gambler either, so how about cutting this stuff out? Wouldn't it be better if we could sort of try to tell each other the truth?

What stopped his mouth, on thinking it over, was that to say all that would humiliate her into wrath. She'd be out of bed and shouting in an instant, reviling him in the ugliest language of her trade until long after the baby woke up crying, and then there would be nothing but wreckage.

There might still be an appropriate moment for inquiring into her truthfulness—there would have to be, and soon—but whether it made him feel cowardly or not he had to acknowledge, as he lay facing the wall with her sweet arm around his ribs, that this wasn't the time.

A few nights later, at home, he answered the phone and was startled to hear her voice: "Hi, honey."

"Christine? Well, hi, but how'd you—how'd you get this number?"

"You gave it to me. Don't you remember? You wrote it down."

"Oh, yeah, sure," he said, smiling foolishly into the mouthpiece, but this was alarming. The phone here in the basement flat was only an extension of Judith's phone upstairs. They rang simultaneously, and when Judith was home she always picked up her receiver on the first or second ring.

"So listen," Christine was saying. "Can you come over Thursday instead of Friday? Because it's Jane's birthday and we're having a party. She'll be nine. . . ."

After he'd hung up he sat hunched for a long time in the attitude of a man turning over grave and secret questions in his mind. How could he have been dumb enough to give her Judith's number? And soon he remembered something else, a second dumb thing that brought him to his feet for an intense, dramatic pacing of the floor: she knew his address too. Once in the pub he had run out of cash and been unable to pay for all the beer, so he'd given Christine a check to cover it.

"Most customers find it's a convenience to have their street addresses printed beneath their names on each check," an assistant bank manager had explained when Warren and Carol opened their checking account last year. "Shall I order them that way for you?"

"Sure, I guess so," Carol had said. "Why not?"

He was almost all the way to the Arnolds' house on Thursday before he realized he'd forgotten to buy a present for Jane. But he found a sweetshop and kept telling the girl at the counter to scoop more and more assorted hard candies into a paper bag until he had a heavy bundle of the stuff that he could only hope might be of passing interest to a nine-year-old.

And whether it was or not, Jane's party turned out to be a profound success. There were children all over that bright, ramshackle apartment, and when the time came for them to be seated at the table—three tables shoved together—Warren stood back smiling and watching with his arm around Christine, thinking of that other party at The Peter Pan Club. Alfred came home from work with a giant stuffed panda bear that he pressed into Jane's arms, laughing and then crouching to receive her long and heartfelt hug. But soon Jane was obliged to bring her delirium under control because the cake was set before her. She frowned, closed her eyes, made a wish and blew out all nine candles in a single heroic breath as the room erupted into full-throated cheers.

There was plenty to drink for the grown-ups after that, even before the last of the party guests had gone home and all the Arnold children were in bed. Christine left the room to put her baby down for the night, carrying a drink along with her. Grace had begun fixing supper with apparent reluctance, and when Alfred excused himself to have a bit of a rest she turned the gas burners down very low and abandoned the stove to join him.

That left Warren alone with Amy, who stood meticulously applying her makeup at the oval mirror above the mantelpiece. She was really a lot better looking than Christine, he decided as he sat on the sofa with a drink in his hand, watching her. She was tall and long-legged and flawlessly graceful, with a firm slender ass that made you ache to clasp it and with plump, pointed little breasts. Her dark hair hung to her shoulder blades, and this evening she had chosen to wear a narrow black skirt with a peach-colored blouse. She was a proud and lovely girl, and he didn't want to think about the total stranger who would have her for money at the end of the night.

Amy had finished with her eyes and begun to work on her mouth, drawing the lipstick slowly along the yielding shape of each full lip until it glistened like marzipan, then pouting so that one lip could caress and rub the other, then parting them to inspect her perfect young teeth for possible traces of red. When she was finished, when she'd put all her implements back into a little plastic case and snapped it shut, she continued to stand at the mirror for what seemed at least half a minute, doing nothing, and that was when Warren realized she knew he'd been staring at her in all this privacy and silence, all this time. At last she turned around in such a quick, high-shouldered way, and with such a look of bravery conquering fear, that it was as if he might be halfway across the floor to make a grab for her.

"You look very nice, Amy," he said from the sofa.

Her shoulders slackened then and she let out a breath of relief, but she didn't smile. "Jesus," she said. "You scared the shit out of me."

When she'd put on her coat and left the house, Christine came back into the room with the languorous, self-indulgent air of a girl who has found a good reason for staying home from work.

"Move over," she said, and sat close beside him. "How've you been?"

"Oh, okay. You?"

"Okay." She hesitated then, as if constrained by the difficulty of making small talk. "Seen any good movies?"

"No."

She took his hand and held it in both of her own. "You miss me?"

"I sure did."

"The hell you did." And she flung down his hand as if it were something vile. "I went around to your place the other night, to surprise you, and I saw you going in there with a girl."

"No you didn't," he told her. "Come on, Christine, you know you didn't do that at all. Why do you always want to tell me these—"

Her eyes narrowed in menace and her lips went flat. "You calling me a liar?"

"Oh, Jesus," he said, "don't be like that. Why do you want to be like that? Let's just drop it, okay?"

She seemed to be thinking it over. "Okay," she said. "Look: It was dark and I was across the street; I could've had the wrong house; it could've been somebody else I saw with the girl, so okay, we'll drop it. But I want to tell you something: don't ever call me a liar, Warren. I'm warning you. Because I swear to God"—and she pointed emphatically toward her bedroom—"I swear on that baby's life I'm not a liar."

"Ah, look at the lovebirds," Grace Arnold called, appearing in the doorway with her arm around her husband. "Well, you're not making *me* jealous. Me and Alfred are lovebirds too, aren't we, love? Married all these years and still lovebirds."

There was supper then, much of it consisting of partly burned beans, and Grace held forth at length on the unforgettable night when she and Alfred had first met. There'd been a party; Alfred had come alone, all shy and strange and still wearing his army uniform, and from the moment Grace spotted him across the room she'd thought, Oh, him. Oh, yes, he's the one. They had danced for a while to some phonograph records, though Alfred wasn't much of a dancer; then they'd gone outside and sat together on a low stone wall and talked. Just talked.

"What'd we talk about, Alfred?" she asked, as if trying in vain to remember.

"Oh, I don't know, love," he said, pink with pleasure and embarrassment as he pushed his fork around in his beans. "Don't suppose it could've been much."

And Grace turned back to address her other listeners in a lowered, intimate voice. "We talked about—well, about everything and nothing," she said. "You know how that can be? It was like we both knew—you know?—like we both knew we were made for each other." This last statement seemed a little sentimental even for Grace's taste, and she broke off with a laugh. "Oh, and the funny part," she said, laughing, "the funny part was, these friends of mine left the party a little after we did because they were going to the pictures? So they went up to the pictures and stayed for the whole show, then they went round to the pub afterwards and stayed there till closing time, and it was practically morning when they came back down that same road and found me and Alfred still sitting on the wall, still talking. Ah, God, they still tease me about that, my friends do when I see them, even now. They say 'Whatever were you two *talking* about, Grace?' And I just laugh. I say, 'Oh, never mind. We were talking, that's all.'"

A respectful hush fell around the table.

"Isn't that wonderful?" Christine asked quietly. "Isn't it wonderful when two people can just—find each other that way?"

And Warren said it certainly was.

Later that night, when he and Christine sat naked on the edge of her bed to drink, she said, "Well, I'll tell you one thing, anyway: I wouldn't half mind having Grace's life. The part of it that came *after* she met Alfred, I mean; not the part before." And after a pause she said, "I don't suppose you'd ever guess it, from the way she acts now—I don't suppose you'd ever guess she was a Piccadilly girl herself."

"Was she?"

"Ha, 'was she.' You better bet she was. For years, back during the war. Got into it because she didn't know any better, like all the rest of us; then she had Jane and didn't know how to get out." And Christine gave him a little glancing smile with a wink in it. "Nobody knows where Jane came from."

"Oh." And if Jane was nine years old today it meant she had been conceived and born in a time when tens of thousands of American Negro soldiers were quartered in England and said to be having their way with English girls, provoking white troops into fights and riots that ended only when everything went under in the vast upheaval of the Normandy Invasion. Alfred Arnold would still have been a prisoner in Burma then, with well over a year to wait for his release.

"Oh, she's never tried to deny it," Christine said. "She's never lied about it; give her credit for that. Alfred knew what he was getting, right from the start. She probably even told him that first night they met, because she would've known she couldn't hide it—or maybe he knew already because maybe that whole *party* was Piccadilly girls; I don't know. But I know he knew. He took her off the street and he married her, and he adopted her child. You don't find very many men like that. And I mean Grace is my best friend and she's done a lot for me, but sometimes she acts like she doesn't even know how lucky she is. Sometimes—oh, not tonight; she was showing off for you tonight—but sometimes she treats Alfred like dirt. Can you imagine that? A man like Alfred? That really pisses me off."

She reached down to fill their glasses, and by the time she'd settled back to sip he knew what his own next move would have to be.

"Well, so I guess you're sort of looking for a husband too, aren't you, baby," he said. "That's certainly understandable, and I'd like you to know I wish I could—you know—ask you to marry me, but the fact is I can't. Just can't."

"Sure," she said quietly, looking down at an unlighted cigarette in her fingers. "That's okay; forget it."

And he was pleased with the way this last exchange had turned out—even with the whopping lie of the "wish" in his part of it. His bewildering, hazardous advance into this strange girl's life was over, and now he could prepare for an orderly withdrawal. "I know you'll find the right guy, Christine," he told her, warm in the kindness of his own voice, "and it's bound to happen soon because you're such a nice girl. In the meantime, I want you to know that I'll always—"

"Look, I said *forget* it, okay? Jesus Christ, do you think *I* care? You think I give a shit about you? Listen." She was on her feet, naked and strong in the dim light, wagging one stiff forefinger an inch away from his wincing face. "Listen, skinny. I can get anybody I want, any time, and you better get that straight. You're only here because I felt sorry for you, and you better get that straight too."

"Felt sorry for me?"

"Well, *sure*, with all that sorrowful shit about your wife taking off, and your little girl. I felt sorry for you and I thought, Well, why not? That's my trouble; I never learn. Sooner or later I always think, Why not? and then I'm shit outa luck. Listen: Do you have any idea how much money I could've made all this time? Huh? No, you never even thought about that part of it, didja. Oh, no, you were all hearts and flowers and sweet-talk and bullshit, weren'tcha. Well, you know what I think you are? I think you're a ponce."

"What's a 'ponce'?"

"I don't know what it is where you come from," she said, "but in this country it's a man who lives off the earnings of a—ah, never mind. The hell with it. Fuck it. I'm tired. Move over, okay? Because I mean if all we're gonna do is sleep, let's sleep."

But instead of moving over he got up in the silent, trembling dignity of an insulted man and began to put his clothes on. She seemed either not to notice or not to care what he was doing as she went heavily back to bed, but before very long, when he was buttoning his shirt, he could tell she was watching him and ready to apologize.

"Warren?" she said in a small, fearful voice. "Don't go. I'm sorry I called you that, and I'll never say it again. Just please come back and stay with me, okay?"

That was enough to make his fingers pause in the fastening of shirt buttons; then, soon, it was enough to make him begin unfastening them again. Leaving now, with nothing settled, might easily be worse than staying. Besides, there was an undeniable advantage in being seen as a man big enough to be capable of forgiveness.

". . . Oh," she said when he was back in bed. "Oh, this is better. This is better. Oh, come closer and let me—there. There. Oh. Oh, I don't think anybody in the whole world ever wants to be alone at night. Do you?"

It was a fragile, pleasant truce that lasted well into the morning, when he made an agreeable if nervous departure.

But all the way home on the Underground he regretted having made no final statement to her. He went over the openings of several final statements in his mind as he rode—"Look, Christine, I don't think this is working out at all. . . ." or "Baby, if you're going to think of me as a ponce, and stuff like that, I think it's about time we . . ."—until he realized, from the uneasy, quickly averted glances of other passengers on the train, that he was moving his lips and making small, reasonable gestures with his hands.

"Warren?" said Judith's old, melodious voice on the telephone that afternoon, calling from Sussex. "I thought I might run up to town on Tuesday and stay for a week or two. Would that be a terrible nuisance for you?"

He told her not to be silly and said he'd be looking forward to it, but he'd scarcely hung up the phone before it rang again and Christine said, "Hi, honey."

"Oh, hi. How are you?"

"Well, okay, except I wasn't very nice to you last night. I get that way sometimes. I know it's awful, but I do. Can I make it up to you, though? Can you come over Tuesday night?"

"Well, I don't know, Christine, I've been thinking. Maybe we'd better sort of—"

Her voice changed. "You coming or not?"

He let her wait through a second or two of silence before he agreed to go—and he agreed then only because he knew it would be better to make his final statement in person than on the phone.

He wouldn't spend the night. He would stay only as long as it took to make himself clear to her; if the house was crowded he would take her around to the pub, where they could talk privately. And he resolved not to rehearse any more speeches: he would find the right words when the time came, and the right tone.

But apart from its having to be final, the most important thing about his statement—the dizzyingly difficult thing—was that it would have to be nice. If it wasn't, if it left her resentful, there might be any amount of trouble later on the phone—a risk that could no longer be taken, with Judith home—and there might be worse events even than that. He could picture Christine and himself as Judith's guests at afternoon tea in her sitting room ("Do bring your young friend along, Warren"), just as Carol and he had often been in the past. He could see Christine waiting for a conversational lull, then setting down her cup and saucer firmly, for emphasis, and saying, "Listen, lady. I got news for you. You know what this big sweet nephew of yours is? Huh? Well, I'll tell you. He's a ponce."

He had planned to arrive well after supper, but they must have gotten a late start tonight because they were all still at the table, and Grace Arnold offered him a plate.

"No thanks," he said, but he sat down beside Christine anyway, with a drink, because it would have seemed rude not to.

"Christine?" he said. "When you've finished eating, want to come around to the pub with me for a while?"

"What for?" she asked with her mouth full.

"Because I want to talk to you."

"We can talk here."

"No we can't."

"So what's the big deal? We'll talk later, then."

And Warren felt his plans begin to slide away like sand.

Amy seemed to be in a wonderful mood that night. She laughed generously at everything Alfred and Warren said; she sang a chorus of "Unforgettable" with at least as much feeling as Christine had brought to it; she backed away into the middle of the room, stepped out of her shoes, and favored her audience with a neat, slow little hip-switching dance to the theme music of the movie *Moulin Rouge*.

"How come you're not going out tonight, Amy?" Christine inquired.

"Oh, I don't know; I don't feel like it. Sometimes all I want to do is stay home and be quiet."

"Alfred?" Grace called. "See if there's any lime juice, because if there's lime juice we can have gin and lime."

They found dance music on the radio and Grace melted into Alfred's arms for an old-fashioned waltz. "I love a waltz," she explained. "I've always loved a waltz"—but it stopped abruptly when they waltzed into the ironing board and knocked it over, which struck everyone as the funniest thing they had ever seen.

Christine wanted to prove she could jitterbug, perhaps in rivalry with Amy's dance, but Warren made a clumsy partner for her: he hopped and shuffled and worked up a sweat and didn't really know how to send her whirling out to their arms' length and bring her whirling back, the way it was supposed to be done, so their performance too dissolved into awkwardness and laughter.

". . . Oh, isn't it nice that we're all such good friends," Grace Arnold said, earnestly breaking the seal on a new bottle of gin. "We can just be here and enjoy ourselves tonight and nothing else matters in the world as long as we're together, right?"

Right. Sometime later, Alfred and Warren sat together on the sofa discussing points of difference and similarity in the British and American armies, a couple of old soldiers at peace; then Alfred excused himself to get another drink, and Amy sank smiling into the place he had left, lightly touching Warren's thigh with her fingertips to establish the opening of a new conversation.

"Amy," Christine said from across the room. "Take your hands off Warren or I'll kill you."

And everything went bad after that. Amy sprang to her feet in heated denial of any wrongdoing, Christine's rebuttal was loud and foul, Grace and Alfred stood with the weak smiles of spectators at a street accident, and Warren wanted to evaporate.

"You're *always* doing that," Christine shouted. "Ever since I got you *in*to this house you've been waving it around and rubbing it up against every man I bring home. You're cheap; you're a tart; you're a little slut."

"And you're a *whore*," Amy cried, just before bursting into tears. She lurched for the door then, but didn't make it: she was obliged to turn back with her fist in her mouth, her eyes bright with terror, in order to witness what Christine was saying to Grace Arnold.

"All right, Grace, listen." Christine's voice was high and perilously steady. "You're my best friend and you always will be, but you've got to make a choice. It's her or me. I mean it. Because I swear on that baby's life"—and one arm made a theatrical sweep in the direction of her bedroom—"I swear on that baby's life I'm not staying in this house another day if she stays too."

"Oh," Amy said, advancing on her. "Oh, that was a rotten thing to do. Oh, you're a filthy—"

And the two girls were suddenly locked in combat, wrestling and punching, or trying to punch, tearing clothes and pulling hair. Grace tried to separate them, a shrill, quivering referee, but she only got pummeled and pushed around herself until she fell down, and that was when Alfred Arnold moved in.

"Shit," he said. "Break it up. Break it *up*." He managed to pull Christine away from Amy's throat and shove her roughly aside, then he prevented Amy from any further action by throwing her down full-length on the sofa, where she covered her face and wept.

"Cows," Alfred said as he stumbled and righted himself. "Fucking cows."

"Put some coffee on," Grace suggested from the chair she had crawled to, and Alfred blundered to the stove and set a pan of water on the gas. He fumbled around for a bottle of instant-coffee syrup and put a spoonful of the stuff into each of five clean cups, breathing hard; then he began stalking the room with the wide and glittering eyes of a man who never thought his life would turn out like this.

"Fucking cows," he said again. "Cows." And with all his strength he smashed his right fist against the wall.

"Well, I knew Alfred was upset," Christine said later, when she and Warren were in bed, "but I didn't think he'd go and hurt his hand that way. That was awful."

"Can I come in?" Grace asked with a timid knock on the door, and she came in looking happy and disheveled. She was still wearing her dress but had evidently removed her garter belt, for her black nylon stockings had fallen into wrinkles around her ankles and her shoes. Her naked legs were pale and faintly hairy.

"How's Alfred's hand?" Christine inquired.

"Well, he's got it soaking in hot water," Grace said, "but he keeps taking it out and trying to put it in his mouth. He'll be all right. Anyway, listen, though, Christine. You're right about Amy. She's no good. I've known that ever since you brought her here. I didn't want to say anything because she was your friend, but that's the God's truth. And I just want you to know you're my favorite, Christine. You'll always be my favorite."

Lying and listening, with the bedclothes pulled up to his chin, Warren longed for the silence of home.

". . . Remember the time she lost all the dry-cleaning tickets and lied about it?"

"Oh, and remember when you and me were getting ready to go to the pictures that day?" Grace said. "And there wasn't time to fix sandwiches so we had egg on toast instead because it was quicker? And she kept hanging around saying, 'What're you making *eggs* for?' She was so mad and jealous because we hadn't asked her to come along to the pictures she was acting like a little kid."

"Well, she *is* a little kid. She doesn't have any—doesn't have any maturity at all."

"Right. You're absolutely right about that, Christine. And I'll tell you what I've decided to do: I'll tell her first thing in the morning. I'll simply say, 'I'm sorry, Amy, but you're no longer welcome in my home. . . .'"

Warren got out of the house before dawn and tried to sleep in his own place, though he couldn't hope for more than an hour or two because he had to be up and dressed and smiling when Judith came down for her bath.

"I must say you're certainly *looking* well, Warren," Judith told him. "You look as calm and fit as a man thoroughly in charge of his life. There isn't a *trace* of that haggard quality that used to worry me about you sometimes."

"Oh?" he said. "Well, thanks, Judith. You're looking very well too, but then of course you always do."

He knew the phone was going to ring, and he could only hope it would be silent until noon. That was when Judith went out to lunch—or, on days when she'd decided to economize, it was the time she went out to do her modest grocery shopping. She would carry a string bag around the neighborhood to be filled by deferential, admiring shopkeepers—Englishmen and women schooled for generations to know a lady when they saw one.

At noon, from the front windows, he watched her stately old figure descend the steps and move slowly down the street. And it seemed no more than a minute after that when the phone burst into ringing, his nerves making it sound much louder than it was.

"You sure took off in a hurry," Christine said.

"Yeah. Well, I couldn't sleep. How'd it go with Amy this morning?"

"Oh, that's okay now. That's all over. The three of us had a long talk, and in the end I talked Grace into letting her stay."

"Well, good. Still, I'm surprised she'd *want* to stay."

"Are you kidding? Amy? You think she has anywhere else to go? Jesus, if you think *Amy* has anywhere else to go you're outa your mind. And I mean you know me, Warren: I get all upset sometimes, but I couldn't ever just turn somebody out on the street." She paused, and he could hear the faint rhythmic click of her chewing gum. He hadn't known, until then, that she ever chewed gum.

For a moment it occurred to him that having her in this placid, rational, gum-chewing frame of mind might be his best opportunity yet for breaking off with her, over the telephone or not, but he hadn't quite organized his opening remarks before she was talking again.

"So listen, honey, I don't think I'll be able to see you for a while. Tonight's out, and tomorrow night too, and all through the weekend." And she gave a quietly harsh little laugh. "I've got to make *some* money, don't I?"

"Well, *sure*," he said. "*Sure* you do; I know that." And not until those agreeable words were out of his mouth did he realize they were exactly the kind of thing a ponce might say.

"I might be able to come around to your place some afternoon, though," Christine suggested.

"No, don't do that," he said quickly. "I'm—I'm almost always out at the library in the afternoons."

They settled on an evening in the following week, at her place, at five; but something in her voice made him suspect even then that she wouldn't be there—that intentionally failing to keep this appointment would be her inarticulate way of getting rid of him, or at least of making a start at it: nobody's ponce could expect to last forever. And so, when the day and the hour came, he wasn't surprised to find her gone.

"Christine's not here, Warren," Grace Arnold explained, backing politely away from the door to let him come in. "She said to tell you she'd call. She had to go up to Scotland for a few days."

"Oh? Is there—trouble at home, then?"

"How do you mean 'trouble'?"

"Well, I just mean is there an—" And Warren found himself mouthing the same lame alibi that Carol and he had once agreed would be good enough for Judith, in what now seemed another life. "Is there an illness in her family, or something like that?"

"That's right, yes." Grace was visibly grateful for his help. "There's an illness in her family."

And he said he was sorry to hear it.

"Can I get you something, Warren?"

"No thanks. I'll see you, Grace." Turning to leave, he found that the words for a cool, final exit line were already forming themselves in his mind. But he hadn't yet reached the door when Alfred came in from work, looking embarrassed, with his forearm encased in a heavy plaster cast from the elbow to the tips of the splinted fingers and hung in a muslin sling.

"Jesus," Warren said, "that sure looks uncomfortable."

"Ah, you get used to it," Alfred said, "like everything else."

"Know how many bones he broke, Warren?" Grace asked, almost as if she were boasting. "Three. Three bones."

"Wow. Well, but how can you do any work, Alfred, with a hand like that?"

"Oh, well." And Alfred managed a small, self-deprecating smile. "They give me all the cushy jobs."

At the door, holding the knob in readiness, Warren turned back and said, "Tell Christine I stopped by, Grace, okay? And you might tell her too that I don't believe a word of anything you said about Scotland. Oh, and if she wants to call me, tell her I said not to bother. So long."

Riding home, he kept assuring himself that he would probably never hear from Christine again. He might have wished for a more satisfactory conclusion; still, perhaps no satisfactory conclusion would ever have been possible. And he was increasingly pleased with the last thing he'd said: "If she wants to call me, tell her I said not to bother." That, under the circumstances, had been just the right message, delivered in just the right way.

It was very late at night when the phone rang the next time; Judith was almost certainly asleep, and Warren sprang to pick it up before it could wake her.

"Listen," Christine said, her voice empty of all affection and even of all civility, like that of an informer in a crime movie. "I'm just calling because this is something you ought to know. Alfred's mad at you. I mean really mad."

"He is? Why?"

And he could almost see the narrowing of her eyes and lips. "Because you called his wife a liar."

"Oh, come on. I don't believe—"

"You don't believe me? All right, wait and see. I'm just telling you for your own good. When a man like Alfred feels his wife has been insulted, that's trouble."

The next day was Sunday—the man of the house would be home—and it took Warren most of the morning to decide that he'd better go there and talk to him. It seemed a silly thing to do, and he dreaded meeting Christine; still, once it was done he could put all of them out of his mind.

But he didn't have to go near the house. Turning the corner into the last block he met Alfred and the six children walking up the street, all dressed up for some Sunday outing, possibly to the zoo. Jane seemed glad to see him: she was holding Alfred's good left hand and wearing a bright pink ribbon in her African hair. "Hi, Warren," she said as the younger ones came to a stop and clustered around.

"Hi, Jane. You look really nice." And then he faced the man. "Alfred, I understand I owe you an apology."

"Apology? What for?"

"Well, Christine said you were angry with me for what I said to Grace."

Alfred looked puzzled, as if contemplating issues too complex and subtle ever to be sorted out. "No," he said. "No, there was nothing like that."

"Okay, then. Good. But I wanted to tell you I didn't mean any—you know."

With a slight grimace, Alfred hitched his cast into a better position in the sling. "Piece of advice for you, Warren," he said. "You don't ever want to listen to the women too much." And he winked like an old comrade.

When Christine called him again it was in a rush of girlish ebullience, as if nothing had ever gone wrong between them—but Warren would never know what brought about the change, nor ever need to weigh its truth or falsehood.

"Honey, listen," she said, "I think it's mostly all blown over at home now—I mean he's all calmed down and everything—so if you want to come over tomorrow night, or the next night or whenever you can, we can have a nice—"

"Now, wait a minute," he told her. "You just listen to me a minute, sweetheart—oh, and by the way I think it's about time we cut out all the 'honey' and the 'sweetheart' stuff, don't you? Listen to me."

He had gotten to his feet for emphasis, standing his ground, with the telephone cord snaked tight across his shirt and his free hand clenched into a fist that shook as rhythmically in the air as that of an impassioned public speaker as he made his final statement.

"Listen to me. Alfred didn't even know what the hell I meant when I tried to apologize. Didn't even know what the hell I was talking about, do you understand me? All right. That's one thing. Here's the other thing. I've had enough. Don't be calling me anymore, Christine, do you understand me? Don't be *calling* me anymore."

"Okay, honey," she said in a quick, meek voice that was almost lost in the sound of her hanging up.

And he was still gripping the phone at his cheek, breathing hard, when he heard the slow and careful deposit of Judith's receiver into its cradle upstairs.

Well, all right, and who cared? He walked over to a heavy cardboard box full of books and kicked it hard enough to send it skidding three or four feet away and release a shuddering cloud of dust; then he looked around for other things to kick, or to punch, or to smash and break, but instead he went back and sat bouncingly on the couch again and socked one fist into the palm of the other hand. Yeah, yeah, well, the hell with it. So what? Who cared?

After awhile, as his heart slowed down, he found he could think only of the way Christine's voice had flickered to nothingness with the words "Okay, honey." There had never been anything to fear. All this time, if he had ever before taken a stern tone with her, she would have vanished from his life in an instant—"Okay, honey"—even, perhaps, with an obliging, cowering smile. She was only a dumb little London streetwalker, after all.

A few days later there was a letter from his wife that changed everything. She had mailed hasty, amicable letters once a week or so since she'd been back in New York, typed on the rattling stationery of the business office where she'd found her job, but this one was in handwriting, on soft blue paper, and gave every sign of having been carefully composed. It said she loved him, that she missed him terribly and wanted him to come home—though it added quickly that the choice would have to be entirely his own.

". . . When I think back over our time together I know the trouble was more my fault than yours. I used to mistake your gentleness for weakness—that must have been my worst mistake because it's the most painful to remember, but oh there were so many others . . ."

Characteristically, she devoted a long paragraph to matters of real estate. The apartment shortage in New York was terrible, she explained, but she'd found a fairly decent place: three rooms on the second floor in a not-bad neighborhood, and the rent was surprisingly . . .

He hurried through the parts about the rent and the lease and the dimensions of the rooms and windows, and he lingered over the end of her letter.

"The Fulbright people won't object to your coming home early if you *want* to, will they? Oh, I do hope you will—that you'll want to, I mean. Cathy keeps asking me when her daddy is coming home, and I keep saying, 'Soon.'"

"I have a terrible confession," Judith said over tea in her sitting room that afternoon. "I listened in to your talk on the phone the other night—and then of course I made the silly mistake of hanging up before you did, so you certainly must have known I was there. I'm frightfully sorry, Warren."

"Oh," he said. "Well, that doesn't matter."

"No, I don't suppose it does, really. If we're going to live in close quarters, I suppose there'll always be these small invasions of privacy. But I did want you to know I'm—well, never mind. You know." Then after a moment she gave him a sly, teasing look. "I wouldn't have expected you to have such a temper, Warren. So harsh. So loud and domineering. Still, I must say I didn't much care for the girl's voice. She sounded a bit vulgar."

"Yeah. Well, it's a long story." And he looked down at his teacup, aware that he was blushing, until he felt it would be all right to look up again and change the subject. "Judith, I think I'll be going home pretty soon. Carol's found a place for us to live in New York, so as soon as I—"

"Oh, then you've settled it," Judith said. "Oh, that's marvelous."

"Settled what?"

"Whatever it was that was making you both so miserable. Oh, I'm so glad. You didn't ever really think I believed the nonsense about the illness in the family, did you? Has any young wife ever crossed the ocean alone for a reason like that? I was even a little annoyed with Carol for *assuming* I'd believe it. I kept wanting to say, Oh, tell me, dear. Tell me. Because you see when you're old, Warren—" Her eyes began to leak and she wiped them ineffectually with her hand. "When you're old, you want so much for the people you love to be happy."

On the night before his sailing, with his bags packed and with the basement flat as clean as a whole day's scrubbing could make it, Warren set to work on the final task of clearing his desk. Most of the books could be thrown away and all the necessary papers could be stacked and made to fit the last available suitcase space—Christ, he was getting out of here; Oh, Christ, he was going home—but when he gathered up the last handful of stuff it uncovered the little cardboard music box.

He took the time to play it backwards, slowly, as if to remind himself forever of its dim and melancholy song. He allowed it to call up a vision of Christine in his arms whispering, "Oh, I love you," because he would want to remember that too, and then he let it fall into the trash.

A Compassionate Leave

NOTHING EVER SEEMED to go right for the 57th Division. It had come overseas just in time to take heavy casualties in the Battle of the Bulge; then, too-quickly strengthened with masses of new replacements, it had plodded through further combat in eastern France and in Germany, never doing badly but never doing especially well, until the war was over in May.

And by July of that year, when service with the Army of Occupation had begun to give every promise of turning into the best time of their lives—there were an extraordinary number of unattached girls in Germany then—all the men of the luckless 57th were loaded into freight trains and hauled back to France.

Many of them wondered if this was their punishment for having been indifferent soldiers. Some of them even voiced that question, during the tedious ride in the boxcars, until others told them to shut up about it. And there was little hope of welcome or comfort in their destination: the people of France were famous, at the time, for detesting Americans.

When the train carrying one battalion came to a stop at last in a sunny field of weeds near Rheims, which nobody even wanted to learn how to pronounce, the men dropped off and struggled with their equipment into trucks that drove them to their new place of residence—an encampment of olive-drab squad tents hastily pitched a few days before, where they were told to stuff muslin mattress covers with the clumps of straw provided for that purpose, and to cradle their empty rifles upside down in the crotches formed by the crossed wooden legs of their canvas cots. Captain Henry R. Widdoes, a gruff and hard-drinking man who commanded C company, explained everything the next morning when he addressed his assembled men in the tall yellow grass of the company street.

"Way I understand it," he began, taking the nervous little backward and forward steps that were characteristic of him, "this here is what they call a redeployment camp. They got a good many of 'em going up all through this area. They'll be moving men out of Germany according to the point system and bringing 'em through these camps for processing on their way home. And what we're gonna do, we're gonna do the whaddyacallit, the processing. We're the permanent party here. I don't know what our duties'll be, mostly supply work and clerical work, I imagine. Soon as I have more information I'll let you know. Okay."

Captain Widdoes had been awarded the Silver Star for leading an attack through knee-deep snow last winter; the attack had gained him an excellent tactical advantage and lost him nearly half a platoon. Even now, many of the men in the company were afraid of him.

A few weeks after their arrival in the camp, when their straw mattresses had flattened out and their rifles were beginning to speckle with rust from the dew, there was a funny incident in one of the squad tents. A buck sergeant named Myron Phelps, who was thirty-three but looked much older, and who had been a soft-coal miner in civilian life, delicately tapped the ash from a big PX cigar and said, "Ah, I wish you kids'd quit talking about Germany. I'm tired of all this Germany, Germany, Germany." Then he stretched out on his back, causing his flimsy cot to wobble on the uneven earth. He folded one arm under his head to suggest a world of peace, using the other to gesture lazily with the cigar. "I mean what the hell would you be doing if you *was* in Germany? Huh? Well, you'd be out getting laid and getting the clap and getting the syphilis and getting the blue balls, that's all, and you'd be drinking up all that schnapps and beer and getting soft and getting out of shape. Right? Right? Well, if you ask me, this here is a whole lot better. We got fresh air, we got shelter, we got food, we got discipline. This is a *man's* life."

And at first everybody thought he was kidding. It seemed to take at least five seconds, while they gaped at Phelps and then at each other and then at Phelps again, before the first thunderclap of laughter broke.

"Jee-sus *Christ*, Phelps, 'a man's life,'" somebody cried, and somebody else called, "Phelps, you're an asshole. You've always *been* an asshole."

Phelps had struggled upright under the attack; his eyes and mouth were pitiably angry, and there were pink blotches of embarrassment in both cheeks.

". . . How about your fucking *coal* mine, Phelps? Was that 'a man's life' too? . . ."

He looked helpless, trying to speak and not being heard, and soon he began to look wretched. It was clear in his face that he knew the phrase "a man's life" would now be passed around to other tents, to other explosions of laughter, and that it would haunt him as long as he stayed in this company.

Private First Class Paul Colby was still laughing along with the others when he left the tent that afternoon on his way to an appointment with Captain Widdoes, but he wasn't sorry when the laughter dwindled and died behind him. Poor old Myron Phelps had made buck sergeant because he'd been one of the only two men left in his squad after the Bulge, and he would almost certainly lose the stripes soon if he went on making a fool of himself.

And there was more to it than that. Whether Paul Colby was quite able to admit it to himself or not, he had agreed with at least one element in Phelps's outburst: he too had come to like the simplicity, the order and the idleness of life in these tents in the grass. There was nothing to prove here.

Colby had been one of the many replacements who joined the company in Belgium last January, and the few remaining months of the war had taken him through pride and terror and fatigue and dismay. He was nineteen years old.

At Captain Widdoes's desk in the orderly room tent, Colby came to attention, saluted, and said, "Sir, I want to request permission to apply for a compassionate leave."

"For a what?"

"For a compassionate—"

"At ease."

"Thank you, sir. The thing is, back in the States you could sometimes get a compassionate leave if you had trouble at home—if there'd been a death, or if somebody was very sick or something like that. And now over here, since the war ended, they've been giving them out for guys just to visit close relatives in Europe—I mean nobody has to be sick or anything."

"Oh, yeah?" Widdoes said. "Yeah, I think I read that. You got relatives here?"

"Yes, sir. My mother and my sister, in England."

"You English?"

"No, sir. I'm from Michigan; that's where my father lives."

"Well, then, I don't get it. How come your—"

"They're divorced, sir."

"Oh." And Widdoes's frown made clear that he still didn't quite get it, but he began writing on a pad. "Okay, uh, Colby," he said at last. "Now, you write down your—you know—your mother's name here, and her address, and I'll get somebody to put the rest of the shit together. You'll be informed if it comes through, but I better tell you, all the paperwork's so fucked up throughout this area I don't think you better count on it."

So Colby decided not to count on it, which brought a slight easing of pressure in his conscience. He hadn't seen his mother or sister since he was eleven, and knew almost nothing of them now. He had applied for the leave mostly from a sense of duty, and because there had seemed no alternative. But now there were two possibilities, each mercifully beyond his control:

If it came through there might be ten days of excessive politeness and artificial laughter and awkward silences, while they all tried to pretend he wasn't a stranger. There might be slow sight-seeing tours of London in order to kill whole afternoons; they might want to show him "typically English" things to do, like nibbling fish and chips out of twisted newspaper, or whatever the hell else it was that typically English people did, and there would be repeated expressions of how nice everything was while they all counted the days until it was over.

If it didn't come through he might never see them again; but then he had resigned himself to that many years ago, when it had mattered a great deal more—when it had, in fact, amounted to an almost unendurable loss.

"Well, your mother was one of these bright young English girls who come over to America thinking the streets are paved with gold," Paul Colby's father had explained to him, more than a few times, usually walking around the living room with a drink in his hand. "So we got married, and you and your sister came along, and then pretty soon I guess she started wondering, well, where's the great promise of this country? Where's all the happiness? Where's the gold? You follow me, Paul?"

"Sure."

"So she started getting restless—damn, she got restless, but I'll spare you that part of it—and pretty soon she wanted a divorce. Well, okay, I thought, that's in the cards, but then by Jesus she said, 'I'll take the children.' And I told her, I said, 'Way-*hait* a minute.' I said, 'Hold your *horses* a minute here, Miss Queen of England; let's play *fair*.'

"Well, fortunately, I had this great friend of mine at the time, Earl Gibbs, and Earl was a crackerjack lawyer. He told me, 'Fred, she wouldn't have a leg to stand on in a custody dispute.' I said, 'Earl, just get me the kids.' I said, 'Let me have the kids, Earl, that's all I ask.' And he tried. Earl did his best for me, but you see by then she'd moved down to Detroit and she had both of you there with her, so it wasn't easy. I went down there once to take you both to a ballgame, but your sister said she didn't like baseball and wasn't feeling very well anyway—Christ, what grief a little thing like that can cause! So it was just you and me went out to Briggs Stadium that day and watched the Tigers play—do you remember that? Do you remember that, Paul?"

"Sure."

"And then afterwards I brought you back up here to stay with me. Well, your mother threw a fit. That's the only word for it. She was wholly irrational. She already had boat tickets to England, you see, for the three of you, and she came storming up here in this rattletrap little Plymouth that she didn't even know how to drive, and she started yelling and screaming that I'd 'kidnapped' you. Do you remember?"

"Yes."

"Well, that was one god-awful afternoon. Earl Gibbs and his wife happened to be here with me at the time, and that saved the day—or half-saved it, I guess. Because once we'd all managed to get your mother calmed down a little, Earl went to her and talked to her for a long time, and in the end he said, 'Vivien, count your blessings. Settle for what you can get.'

"So you see, she had no choice. She drove away in that crummy car with your sister riding beside her, and I guess a couple weeks later they were in London, and that was it. That was it.

"Well, but the point I'm trying to make here, Paul, is that things did work out pretty much for the best after all. I was fortunate enough to meet your stepmother, and we're right for each other. Anybody can see we're right for each other, right? As for your mother, I know she was never happy with me. Any man, Paul—*any* man—oughta know when a woman isn't happy with him. And what the hell, life's too short: I forgave her long ago for the pain she caused me as my wife. There's only one thing I can't forgive her for. Ever. She took away my little girl."

Paul Colby's sister, Marcia, was almost exactly a year younger than he. At five, she had taught him how to blow steady bubbles in bath-water; at eight, she had kicked over his electric train in order to persuade him that paper dolls could be more entertaining, which was true; a year or so after that, trembling in fear together, they had dared each other to jump from a high limb of a maple tree, and they'd done it, though he would always remember that she went first.

On the afternoon of their parents' hysteria, and of the lawyer's sonorous entreaties for order in the living room, he had watched Marcia from the house as she waited in the passenger seat of the mud-spattered Plymouth in the driveway. And because he was fairly sure nobody would notice his absence, he went out to visit with her.

When she saw him coming she rolled down her window and said, "What're they doing in there, anyway?"

"Well, they're—I don't know. There's a lot of—I don't really know what they're doing. I guess it'll be okay, though."

"Yeah, well, I guess so too. Only, you better get back inside, Paul, okay? I mean I don't think Daddy'd want to see you out here."

"Okay." On his way to the house he stopped and looked back, and they exchanged quick, shy waves.

At first there were frequent letters from England—jolly, sometimes silly, hastily written ones from Marcia, careful and increasingly stilted ones from his mother.

During the "Blitz" of 1940, when every American radio news commentator implied that all London was in rubble and on fire, Marcia wrote at some length to suggest that perhaps the reports might be exaggerated. Things were certainly terrible in the East End, she said, which was "cruel" because that was where most of the poor people lived, but there were "very extensive areas" of the city that hadn't been touched. And the suburb where she and their mother were, eight miles out, had been "perfectly safe." She was thirteen when she wrote that, and it stayed in his mind as a remarkably intelligent, remarkably thoughtful letter for someone of that age.

Over the next few years she drifted out of the habit of writing, except for Christmas and birthday cards. But his mother's letters continued with dogged regularity, whether he'd answered the last one or not, and it became an effort of will to read them—an effort even to open the flimsy blue envelopes and unfold the notepaper. Her strain in the writing was so clear that it could only make for strain in the reading; her final, pointedly cheerful paragraph always came as a relief, and he could sense her own relief at having brought it off. She had married again within a year or two after going back to England; she and her new husband soon had a son, "your little half brother," of whom she said Marcia was "enormously fond." In 1943 she wrote that Marcia was "with the American Embassy in London now," which seemed a funny thing to say about a sixteen-year-old girl, and there were no supporting details.

He had written to his sister from Germany once, managing to work in a few deft references to his combat infantry service, and had received no reply. It could have been because military mail was unreliable at the time, but it could also have meant she'd simply neglected to write back—and that had left a small, still-open wound in his feelings.

Now, after leaving the orderly room, he wrote a quick letter to his mother explaining his helplessness in the matter of the leave; when it was done and mailed, he felt he could easily afford to stretch out on his cot in the drowsing, mildewed, half-deserted tent. He wasn't far across the aisle of trampled dirt from where poor old Myron Phelps lay sleeping off his shame—or, more likely, still ashamed and so pretending to sleep.

The big news of the following month was that three-day passes to Paris would now be issued in C company, a few at a time, and the tents began to ring with shrill and lubricious talk. Sure, the French hated Americans—everybody knew that—but everybody knew what "Paris" meant too. All you had to do in Paris, it was said, was walk up to a girl on the street—well-dressed, high-class-looking, *any* kind of girl—and say, "Are you in business, baby?" If she wasn't she'd smile and say no; if she was—or maybe even if she wasn't but just sort of happened to feel like it—then oh, Jesus God.

Paul Colby arranged to take his pass with George Mueller, a quiet, thoughtful boy who had become his best friend in the rifle squad. Several nights before they went to Paris, in one of the soft-voiced conversations that were characteristic of their friendship, he haltingly confided to George Mueller what he'd never told anyone else and didn't even want to think about: he had never gotten laid in his life.

And Mueller didn't laugh. He'd been a virgin too, he said, until one night in a bunker with a German girl a week before the war ended. And he wasn't even sure if that counted: the girl had kept laughing and laughing—he didn't know what the hell she was laughing about—and he'd been so nervous that he didn't really get inside her before he came, and then she'd pushed him away.

Colby assured him that it did count—it certainly counted a great deal more than any of his own dumb fumblings. And he might have told Mueller about a few of those, but decided they were better kept to himself.

Not long before they'd left Germany, C company had been placed in charge of two hundred Russian "displaced persons"—civilian captives whom the Germans had put to work as unpaid laborers in a small-town plastics factory. On Captain Widdoes's orders, the newly freed Russians were soon quartered in what looked like the best residential section of town—neat, attractive houses on a hill well away from the factory—and the Germans who'd lived up there (those, at least, who hadn't fled the advancing army days or weeks before) were assigned to the barracks in the old slave-laborers' compound.

There wasn't much for the riflemen to do in that pleasant, partially bombed-out town but stroll in the gentle spring weather and make occasional gestures at keeping things, as Widdoes said, "under control." Paul Colby was on guard duty alone at the very top of the residential hill one afternoon at sunset when a Russian girl came out and smiled at him, as though she'd been watching him from a window. She was seventeen or so, slim and pretty, wearing the kind of cheap, old, wash-ruined cotton dress that all the Russian women wore, and her breasts looked as firm and tender as ripe nippled peaches. Apart from knowing he would absolutely have to get his hands on her, he didn't know what to do. Far down the hill, and on either side, there was no one else in sight.

He made what he hoped was a courtly little bow and shook hands with her—that seemed an appropriate opening for an acquaintance that would have to take place without language—and she gave no sign of thinking it silly or puzzling. Then he bent to put his rifle and helmet on the grass, straightened up again and took her in his arms—she felt marvelous—and kissed her mouth, and there was a thrilling amount of tongue in the way she kissed back. Soon he had one splendid breast naked in his hand (he fondled it as impersonally as if it *were* a nippled peach) and blood was flowing heavily in him; but then the old, inevitable shyness and the terrible awkwardness set in, as they'd set in with every girl he had ever touched.

And as always before, he was quick to find excuses: he couldn't take her back into the house because it would be crowded with other Russians—or so he imagined—and he couldn't have her out here because someone would be sure to come along; it was almost time for the guard truck to pick him up anyway.

There seemed nothing to do, then, but release the girl from their clasping embrace and stand close beside her, one arm still around her, so they could gaze together down the long hill at the sunset. It occurred to him, as they lingered and lingered in that position, that they might make an excellent scene for the final fadeout of some thunderous Soviet-American movie called *Victory over the Nazis*. And when the guard truck did come for him, he couldn't even lie to himself that he felt anger and frustration: he was relieved.

There was a taciturn, illiterate rifleman in the second squad named Jesse O. Meeks—one of the four or five men in the platoon who had to mark *X* instead of signing the payroll every month—and within two days after the fadeout of the great Soviet-American movie, Jesse O. Meeks took full possession of that sweet girl.

"Ain't no use lookin' around for old Meeks tonight," somebody said in the platoon quarters. "No use lookin' for him tomorra, either, or the day after that. Old Meeks got himself shacked up re-eal fine."

But here in France, on a morning bright with promise, Colby and George Mueller presented themselves at the first sergeant's desk to claim their three-day passes. At the left-hand edge of the desk, on a metal base screwed into the wood, stood an ample rotary dispenser of linked, foil-wrapped condoms: you could reel off as many as you thought you might need. Colby let Mueller go first, in order to watch how many he took—six—then he self-consciously took six himself and stuffed them into his pocket, and they set out together for the motor pool.

They wore their brand-new Eisenhower jackets, with their modest display of ribbons and the handsome blue-and-silver panels of their Combat Infantry Badges, and they had carefully darkened and shined their combat boots. They walked clumsily, though, because each of them carried two cartons of stolen PX cigarettes inside his trouser legs: cigarettes were said to bring twenty dollars a carton on the Paris black market.

Coming into the city was spectacular. The Eiffel Tower, the Arch of Triumph—there it all was, just the way it looked in *Life* magazine, and it went on for miles in all directions: there was so much of it that you couldn't stop turning and looking, turning and looking again.

The truck let them off at the American Red Cross Club, which would serve as a homely base of operations. It provided dormitories and showers and regular meals, and there were rooms for Ping-Pong and for drowsing in deep upholstered chairs. Only some kind of a twerp would want to spend much time in this place, when there was such a wealth of mystery and challenge beyond its doors, but Colby and Mueller agreed to have lunch here anyway, because it was lunch-time.

And the next thing, they decided, was to get rid of the cigarettes. It was easy. A few blocks away they met a small, tight-faced boy of about fourteen who led them upstairs to a triple-locked room that was packed to the ceiling with American cigarettes. He was so intimidating in his silence and so impatient to conclude the deal, paying them off from a huge roll of lovely French banknotes, as to suggest that in three or four more years he might be an important figure in the European underworld.

George Mueller had brought his camera and wanted snapshots to send to his parents, so they took a guided bus tour of major landmarks that went on until late in the afternoon.

"We ought to have a map," Mueller said when they were rid of the boring, chattering tour guide at last. "Let's get a map." There were shabby old men everywhere selling maps to soldiers, as if selling toy balloons to children; when Colby and Mueller opened the many folds of theirs and spread it flat against the side of an office building, jabbing their forefingers at different parts of it and both talking at once, it was their first discord of the day.

Colby knew, from having read *The Sun Also Rises* in high school, that the Left Bank was where everything nice was most likely to happen. Mueller had read that book too, but he'd been listening to the guys in the tent for weeks, and so he favored the area up around the Place Pigalle.

"Well, but it's all prostitutes up there, George," Colby said. "You don't want to settle for some prostitute right away, do you? Before we've even tried for something better?" In the end they reached a compromise: they would try the Left Bank first—there was plenty of time—and then the other.

"Wow," Mueller said in the Metro station; he had always been good at figuring things out. "See how this works? You push the button where you are and the one where you want to go, and the whole fucking route lights up. You'd have to be an idiot to get lost in this town."

"Yeah."

And Colby soon had to admit that Mueller was right about the Left Bank. Even after a couple of hours its endless streets and boulevards failed to suggest that anything nice might happen. You could see hundreds of people sitting, bright with talk and laughter in each of the long, deep sidewalk cafés, with plenty of good-looking girls among them, but their cool and quickly averted glances established at once their membership in the majority of French who detested Americans. And if you did occasionally see a pretty girl walking alone and tried to catch her eye, however bashfully, she looked capable of pulling a police whistle out of her purse and blowing it, hard, on being asked if she was in business.

But oh, Jesus God, the area up around the Place Pigalle. It throbbed in the new-fallen darkness with the very pulse of sex; it had a decidedly sinister quality too, in the shadows and in the guarded faces of everyone you saw. Steam rose from iron manhole lids in the street and was instantly turned red and blue and green in the vivid lights of gas and electric signs. Girls and women were everywhere, walking and waiting, among hundreds of prowling soldiers.

Colby and Mueller took their time, watching everything, seated at a café table and nursing highballs of what the waiter had promised was "American whiskey." Dinner was out of the way—they had made a quick stop at the Red Cross to wash up and to eat, and Mueller had left his camera there (he didn't want to took like some tourist tonight)—so there was nothing to do for a while but watch.

"See the girl coming out of the door with the guy across the street?" Mueller inquired, narrowing his eyes. "See 'em? The girl in the blue? And the guy's walking away from her now?"

"Yeah."

"I swear to God it wasn't five minutes ago I saw them going *in* that door. Son of a bitch. She gave him five minutes—*less* than five minutes—and she probably charged him twenty bucks."

"Jesus." And Colby took a drink to help him sort out a quick profusion of ugly pictures in his mind. What could be accomplished in five minutes? Wouldn't it take almost that long just to get undressed and dressed again? How miserably premature could a premature ejaculation be? Maybe she had blown him, but even that, according to exhaustive discourse in the tent, was supposed to take a hell of a lot longer than five minutes. Or maybe—this was the possibility that brought a chill around his heart—maybe the man had been stricken with panic up there in the room. Maybe, watching her get ready, he had suddenly known he couldn't do what was expected—known it beyond all hope of trying or even of pretending to try—and so had blurted some apology in high-school French and shoved money into her hands, and she'd followed him closely downstairs talking all the way (Coarse? Contemptuous? Cruel?) until they were free to separate in the street.

For himself, Colby decided it would be best not to go with a streetwalker—even one he might spend a long time choosing for qualities of youth and health and the look of a gentle nature. The thing to do was find a girl in a bar—this bar or one of the others—and talk with her for a while, however brokenly, and go through the pleasant ritual of buying drinks. Because even if the girls in the bars *were* only streetwalkers at rest (or could they be whores of a higher caliber, with higher prices? And how could you possibly find out about distinctions like that?)—even so, you might at least have some sense of acquaintance before arriving at the bed.

It took Colby a minute or two to catch the waiter's eye for another round, and when he turned back he found George Mueller conversing with a woman who sat alone at the next table, a few inches away. The woman—you couldn't call her a girl—was trim and pleasant-looking, and from the stray phrases Colby overheard she seemed to be speaking mostly in English. Mueller had turned his chair away for talking, so his face was partly obscured, but Colby could see the heavy blush of it and the tense, shy smile. Then he saw the woman's hand moving slowly up and down Mueller's thigh.

"Paul?" Mueller said when he and the woman got up to leave. "Look, I may not see you again tonight, but I'll see you back in the whaddyacallit in the morning, okay? The Red Cross. Or maybe not in the morning, but you know. We'll work it out."

"Sure; that's okay."

In no other bar of the entire area around the Place Pigalle could a girl or a woman be found sitting alone. Paul Colby made certain of that because he tried them all—tried several of them twice or three times—and he drank so much in the course of his search that he wandered miles from where he'd started; he was in some wholly separate part of Paris when the sound of a rollicking piano brought him in off the street to a strange little American-style bar. There he joined five or six other soldiers, most of them apparently strangers to one another; they stood with their arms around each other's Eisenhower jackets and sang all ten choruses of "Roll Me Over" at the top of their lungs, with the piano thumping out the melody and the flourishes. Somewhere in the sixth or seventh verse it struck Colby that this might be considered a fairly memorable way to conclude your first night in Paris, but by the time it ended he knew better—and so, plainly, did all the other singers.

George Mueller had said you would have to be an idiot to get lost in this town, but Paul Colby stood for half an hour in some Metro station, pushing buttons, making more and more elaborate route patterns light up in many colors, until a very old man came along and told him how to get to the Red Cross Club. And there, where everybody knew that only some kind of a twerp would want to spend much time, he crawled into his dormitory bed as if it were the last bed in the world.

Things were even worse the next day. He was too sick with a hangover to get his clothes on until noon; then he crept downstairs and looked into each of the public rooms for George Mueller, knowing he wouldn't find him. And he walked the streets for hours, on sore feet, indulging himself in the bleak satisfactions of petulance. What the hell was supposed to be so great and beautiful about Paris anyway? Had anybody ever had the guts to say it was just another city like Detroit or Chicago or New York, with too many pale, grim men in business suits hurrying down the sidewalks, and with too much noise and gasoline exhaust and too much plain damned uncivilized rudeness? Had anybody yet confessed to being dismayed and bewildered and bored by this whole fucking place, and lonely as a bastard too?

Late in the day he discovered white wine. It salved and dispelled his hangover; it softened the rasp of his anger into an almost pleasant melancholy. It was very nice and dry and mild and he drank a great deal of it, slowly, in one quietly obliging café after another. He found various ways to compose himself at the different tables, and soon he began to wonder how he must look to casual observers; that, for as long as he could remember, had been one of his most secret, most besetting, least admirable habits of mind. He imagined, as the white wine wore on and on, that he probably looked like a sensitive young man in wry contemplation of youth and love and death—an "interesting" young man—and on that high wave of self-regard he floated home and hit the sack again.

The final day was one of stunted thought and shriveled hope, of depression so thick that all of Paris lay awash and sinking in it while his time ran out.

Back in the Place Pigalle at midnight and drunk again—or more likely feigning drunkenness to himself—he found he was almost broke. He couldn't afford even the most raucous of middle-aged whores now, and he knew he had probably arranged in his secret heart for this to be so. There was nothing left to do but make his way to the dark part of the city where the Army trucks were parked.

You weren't really expected to make the first truck; you could even miss the last truck, and nobody would care very much. But those unspoken rules of conduct no longer applied to Paul Colby: he was very likely the only soldier in Europe ever to have spent three days in Paris without getting laid. And he had learned beyond question now that he could no longer attribute his trouble to shyness or awkwardness: it was fear. It was worse than fear: it was cowardice.

"How come you didn't pick up my messages?" George Mueller asked him in the tent the next day. Mueller had left three notes for Colby on the Red Cross message board, he said—one on the morning after they'd split up that first night, and two others later.

"I guess I didn't even notice there was a message board."

"Well, Christ, it was right there in the front room, by the desk," Mueller said, looking hurt. "I don't see how you could've missed it."

And Colby explained, despising himself and turning away quickly afterwards, that he hadn't really spent all that much time in the Red Cross Club.

Less than a week later he was summoned to the orderly room and told that the papers for his compassionate leave were ready. And a very few days after that, abruptly deposited somewhere in London, he checked into a murmurous, echoing Red Cross Club that was almost a duplicate of the one in Paris.

He spent a long time in the shower and changed meticulously into his other, wholly clean uniform—stalling and stalling; then, with his finger trembling in the dial of a cumbersome British coin telephone, he called his mother.

"Oh, my dear," her voice said. "Is this really you? Oh, how very strange . . ."

It was arranged that he would visit her that afternoon, "for tea," and he rode out to her suburb on a clattering commuters' train.

"Oh, well, how nice!" she said in the doorway of her tidy, semi-detached house. "And how fine you are in your marvelous American uniform. Oh, my dear; oh, my dear." As she pressed the side of her head against the ribbons and the Combat Badge she seemed to be weeping, but he couldn't be sure. He said it certainly was good to see her too, and they walked together into a small living room.

"Well, my goodness," she said, having apparently dried her tears. "How can I possibly hope to entertain a great big American soldier in a scruffy little house like this?"

But soon they were comfortable—at least as comfortable as they would ever be—sitting across from each other in upholstered chairs while the clay filaments popped and hissed and turned blue and orange in a small gas fireplace. She told him her husband would soon be home, as would their son, who was now six and "dying" to meet him.

"Well, good," he said.

"And I did try to reach Marcia on the phone, but I was a fraction of a second too late at the Embassy switchboard; then later I rang her flat but there was no answer, so I expect they're both out. She's been sharing a flat with another girl for a year or so now, you see"—and here his mother sniffed sharply through one nostril and turned her face partly away, a mannerism that brought her suddenly alive from his memory—"she's quite the young woman of the world these days. Still, we can try again later in the evening, and perhaps we'll—"

"No, that's okay," he said. "I'll call her tomorrow."

"Well, whatever you wish."

And it was whatever he wished for the rest of that rapidly darkening afternoon, even after her husband had come home—a drained-looking man in middle age whose hat left a neat ridge around the crown of his flat, well-combed hair, and who ventured almost no conversational openings—and their little boy, who seemed far from dying to meet him as he peered from hiding and stuck out his tongue.

Would Paul like another bread-and-butter sandwich with his tea? Good. Would he like a drink? Oh, good. And was he sure he wouldn't stay a while longer and have some sort of scrappy little supper with them—baked beans on toast sort of thing—and spend the night? Because really, there was plenty of room. It was whatever he wished.

He could hardly wait to get out of the house, though he kept assuring himself, on the train back into town, that he hadn't been rude.

And he awoke barely able to face breakfast in his nervousness about calling the American Embassy.

"Who?" said a switchboard operator. "What department is that, please?"

"Well, I don't know; I just know she works there. Isn't there some way you can—"

"Just a moment . . . yes, here: we do have a Miss Colby, Marcia, in Disbursements. I'll connect you." And after several buzzings and clickings, after a long wait, a voice came on the line as clear as a flute and happy to hear from him—a sweet-sounding English girl.

". . . Well, that'd be marvelous," she was saying. "Could you come round about five? It's the first building over from the main one, just to the left of the FDR statue if you're coming up from Berkeley Square; you can't miss it; and I'll be there in half a minute if you're waiting, or—you know—I'll be waiting there if you're late."

It took him awhile to realize, after hanging up the phone, that she hadn't once spoken his name; she had probably been shy too.

There was an overheated shop in the Red Cross basement where two sweating, jabbering Cockneys in undershirts would steam-press your whole uniform for half a crown, while many soldiers waited in line for the service, and Colby chose to kill part of the afternoon down there. He knew his clothes didn't really need pressing, but he wanted to look nice tonight.

Then he was coming up from Berkeley Square, trying in every stride to perfect what he hoped would be a devil-may-care kind of walk. There was the FDR statue, and there was her office building; and there in the corridor, straggling alone behind a group of other women and girls, came a hesitant, large-eyed, half-smiling girl who could only have been Marcia.

"Paul?" she inquired. "Is it Paul?"

He rushed forward and enwrapped her in a great hug, pinning her arms and nuzzling her hair, hoping to swing her laughing off her feet—and he brought it off well, probably from his self-tutelage in the devil-may-care walk; by the time her shoes hit the floor again she *was* laughing, with every sign of having liked it.

". . . Well!" she said. "Aren't you something."

"So are you," he said, and offered her his arm for walking.

In the first place they went to, which she'd described as "a rather nice, smallish pub not far from here," he kept secretly congratulating himself on how well he was doing. His talk was fluent—once or twice he even made her laugh again—and his listening was attentive and sympathetic. Only one small thing went wrong: he had assumed that English girls liked beer, but she changed her order to "pink gin," which made him feel dumb for having failed to ask her; apart from that he couldn't find anything the matter with his performance.

If there had been a mirror behind the bar he would certainly have sneaked a happy glance into it on his way to the men's room; he had stamped twice on the old floor in the regulation manner for making his trouser legs "blouse down" over his boots, then walked away from her through the smoke-hung crowd in the new devil-may-care style, and he hoped she was watching.

". . . What does Disbursements mean?" he asked when he got back to their table.

"Oh, nothing much. In a business firm I suppose you'd call it the payroll office. I'm a payroll clerk. Ah, I know," she said then, with a smile that turned wittily sour, "Mother's told you I'm 'with the American Embassy.' God. I heard her saying that to people on the phone a few times, when I was still living there; that was about the time I decided to move out."

He had been so concerned with himself that he didn't realize until now, offering a light for her cigarette, what a pretty girl she was. And it wasn't only in the face; she was nice all the way down.

". . . I'm afraid our timing's been rather awkward, Paul," she was saying. "Because tomorrow's the last day before my vacation and I had no idea you were coming, you see, so I arranged to spend the week with a friend up in Blackpool. But we can get together again tomorrow night, if you like—could you come up to the flat for supper or something?"

"Sure. That'd be fine."

"Oh, good. Do come. It won't be much, but we can sort of fortify ourselves by having a real dinner tonight. Jesus, I'm hungry, aren't you?" And he guessed that a lot of English girls had learned to say "Jesus" during the war.

She took him to what she called "a good black-market restaurant," a warm, closed-in, upstairs room that did look fairly clandestine; they sat surrounded by American officers and their women, forking down rich slices of what she told him was horsemeat steak. They were oddly shy with each other there, like children in a strange house, but soon afterwards, in the next pub they visited, they got around to memories.

"It's funny," she said. "I missed Daddy terribly at first, it was like a sickness, but then it got so I couldn't really remember him very well. And lately, I don't know. His letters seem so—well, sort of loud and empty. Sort of vapid."

"Yeah. Well, he's a very—yeah."

"And once during the war he sent me a Public Health Service pamphlet about venereal disease. That wasn't really a very tactful thing to do, was it?"

"No. No, it wasn't."

But she remembered the electric train and the paper dolls. She remembered the terrifying jump from the maple tree—the worst part, she said, was that you had to clear another horrible big branch on the way down—and yes, she remembered waiting alone in the car that afternoon while their parents shouted in the house. She even remembered that Paul had come out to the car to say goodbye.

At the end of the evening they settled into still another place, and that was where she started talking about her plans. She might go back to the States and go to college next year—that was what their father wanted her to do—but then there was also a chance that she might go back and get married.

"Yeah? No kidding? Who to?"

The little smile she gave him then was the first disingenuous look he had seen in her face. "I haven't decided," she said. "Because you see there've been any number of offers—well, *almost* any number." And out of her purse came a big, cheap American wallet of the kind with many hinged plastic frames for photographs. There was one smiling or frowning face after another, most of them wearing their overseas caps, a gallery of American soldiers.

". . . and this is Chet," she was saying, "he's nice; he's back in Cleveland now. And this is John, he'll be going home soon to a small town in east Texas; and this is Tom; he's nice; he's . . ."

There were probably five or six photographs, but there seemed to be more. One was a decorated 82nd Airborne man who looked impressive, but another was a member of service and support personnel—a "Blue-Star Commando"—and Colby had learned to express a veiled disdain for those people.

"Well, but what does that matter?" she inquired. "I don't care what he 'did' or didn't 'do' in the war; what's *that* got to do with anything?"

"Okay; I guess you're right," he said while she was putting the wallet away, and he watched her closely. "But look: are you in love with any of these guys?"

"Oh, well, certainly, I suppose so," she said. "But then, that's easy, isn't it?"

"What is?"

"Being in love with someone, if he's nice and you like him."

And that gave him much to think about, all the next day.

The following night, when he'd been asked to "come up for supper or something," he gravely inspected her white, ill-furnished apartment and met her roommate, whose name was Irene. She looked to be in her middle thirties, and it was clear from her every glance and smile that she enjoyed sharing a place with someone so much younger. She made Colby uneasy at once by telling him what a "nice-looking boy" he was; then she hovered and fussed over Marcia's fixing the drinks, which were a cheap brand of American blended whiskey and soda, with no ice.

The supper turned out to be even more perfunctory than he'd

imagined—a casserole of Spam and sliced potatoes and powdered milk—and while they were still at the table Irene laughed heartily at something Colby said, something he hadn't meant to be all that funny. Recovering, her eyes shining, she turned to Marcia and said, "Oh, he's sweet, your brother, isn't he—and d'you know something? I think you're right about him. I think he *is* a virgin."

There are various ways of enduring acute embarrassment: Colby might have hung his blushing head, or he might have stuck a cigarette in his lips and lighted it, squinting, looking up at the woman with still-narrowed eyes and saying, "What makes you think that?" but what he did instead was burst out laughing. And he went on laughing and laughing long after the time for showing what a preposterous assumption they had made; he was helpless in his chair; he couldn't stop.

". . . *Irene!*" Marcia was saying, and she was blushing too. "I don't know what you're *talking* about—*I* never said that."

"Oh, well, sorry; sorry; my fault," Irene said, but there was still a sparkle in her eye across the messy table when he pulled himself together at last, feeling a little sick.

Marcia's train would leave at nine, from some station far in the north of London, so she had to hurry. "Look, Paul," she said over the hasty packing of her suitcase, "there's really no need for you to come along all that way; I'll just run up there by myself."

But he insisted—he wanted to get away from Irene—and so they rode nervously together, without speaking, on the Underground. But they got off at the wrong stop—"Jesus, that was foolish," she said; "now we'll have to walk"—and when they were walking they began to talk again.

"I'll never know what possessed Irene to say such a silly thing," she said.

"That's okay. Forget it."

"Because I only said you seemed very young. Was that such a terrible thing to say?"

"I guess not."

"I mean who ever minded being *young*, for God's sake—isn't that what everyone wants to be?"

"I guess so."

"Oh, you guess not and you guess so. Well, it's true—everyone does want to be young. I'm eighteen now, and sometimes I wish I were *six*teen again."

"Why?"

"Oh, so I could do things a little more intelligently, I suppose; try not to go chasing after uniforms quite so much—British *or* American; I don't know."

So she had been laid at sixteen, either by some plucky little RAF pilot or some slavering American, and probably by several of both.

He was tired of walking and of carrying the suitcase; it took an effort of will to remind himself that he was an infantry soldier. Then she said, "Oh, look: we've made it!" and they ran the last fifty yards into the railroad station and across its echoing marble floor. But her train had gone, and there wasn't another one due to leave for an hour. They sat uncomfortably on an old bench for a while; then they went out to the street again to get the fresh air.

She took the suitcase from him, placed it against the base of a lamppost and seated herself prettily on it, crossing her nice legs. Her knees were nice too. She looked thoroughly composed. She would leave tonight knowing he was a virgin—she would know it forever, whether she ever saw him again or not.

"Paul?" she said.

"Yeah?"

"Look, I was only sort of teasing you about those boys in the photographs—I don't know why I did that, except to be silly."

"Okay. I knew you were teasing." But it was a relief to hear her say it, even so.

"They were just boys I met when I used to go to the Red Cross dances at Rainbow Corner. None of them ever really did propose to me except Chet, and that was only a kidding-around sort of thing because he said I was pretty. If I ever took him up on it he'd die."

"Okay."

"And it was silly just now to tell you about chasing uniforms when I was sixteen—God, I was *terrified* of boys at sixteen. Have you any idea what it is that makes people of our age want to claim more knowledge of—of sex and so forth than they really have?"

"No. No, I don't." He was beginning to like her more and more, but he was afraid that if he let her go on she would soon insist she was a virgin too, to make him feel better; that would almost certainly be a condescending lie, and so would only make him feel worse.

"Because I mean we have our whole *lives*," she said, "isn't that right? Take you: you'll be going home soon and going to college and there'll be girls coming in and out of your life for years; then eventually you'll fall in love with someone, and isn't that what makes the world go around?"

She was being kind to him; he didn't know whether to be grateful or to sink even further into wretchedness.

"And then me, well I'm in love with someone now," she said, and this time there appeared to be no teasing in her face. "I've wanted to tell you about him ever since we met, but there hasn't been time. He's the man I'm going up to spend the week with in Blackpool. His name is Ralph Kovacks and he's twenty-three. He was a waist-gunner on a B-17 but he only flew thirteen missions because his nerves fell apart and he's been in and out of hospitals ever since. He's sort of small and funny-looking and all he wants to do is sit around in his underwear reading great books, and he's going to be a philosopher and I've sort of come to think I can't live without him. I may not go to the States at all next year; I may go to Heidelberg because that's where Ralph wants to go; the whole question is whether or not he'll let me stay with him."

"Oh," Colby said. "I see."

"What d'you mean, you 'see'? You really aren't much of a conversationalist, you know that? You 'see.' What can you possibly 'see' from what little I've told you? Jesus, how can you see anything at all with those big, round, virginal eyes of yours?"

He was walking away from her, head down, because there seemed nothing else to do, but he hadn't gone far before she came running after him, her little high-heeled shoes clicking on the sidewalk. "Oh, Paul, don't go away," she called. "Come back; please come back. I'm terribly sorry."

So they went back together to where the suitcase stood against the lamppost, but this time she didn't sit down. "I'm terribly sorry," she said again. "And look, don't come to the train with me; I want to say goodbye here. Only, listen. Listen. I know you'll be all right. We'll both be all right. It's awfully important to believe that. Well; God bless."

"Okay, and you too," he said. "You too, Marcia."

Then her arms went up and around his neck and the whole slender weight of her was pressed against him for a moment, and in a voice broken with tears she said, "Oh, my brother."

He walked a great distance alone after that, and there wasn't anything devil-may-care about it. The heels of his boots came down in a calm, regular cadence, and his face was set in the look of a practical young man with a few things on his mind. Tomorrow he would telephone his mother and say he'd been called back to France, "for duty," a phrase she would neither understand nor ever question; then all that would be finished. And with seven days left in this vast, intricate, English-speaking place, there was every reason to expect he would have a girl.

Regards at Home

"WELL, I KNOW it seems funny," the young man said, getting up from his drawing board, "but I don't think we've been formally introduced. My name's Dan Rosenthal." He was tall and heavy, and his face suggested the pain of shyness.

"Bill Grove," I told him as we shook hands, and then we could both pretend to settle down. We had just been hired at Remington Rand and assigned to share a glassed-in cubicle in the bright, murmurous maze of the eleventh floor; this was in the spring of 1949, in New York.

Dan Rosenthal's job was to design and illustrate the company's "external house organ," a slick and unreadable monthly magazine called *Systems*; mine was to write and edit the copy for it. He seemed able to talk and listen while executing even the subtlest parts of his work, and I soon fell to neglecting mine for hours and days at a time, so there began an almost steady flow of conversation over the small space between his immaculate drawing board and the ever-more dismaying clutter of my desk.

I was twenty-three that year; Dan was a year or so older, and there was a gruff, rumbling gentleness in his voice that seemed to promise he would always be good company. He lived with his parents and his younger brother in Brooklyn, "just around the corner from Coney Island, if that gives you a picture," and he was a recent graduate of the art school at Cooper Union—a school that charges no tuition but is famous for being highly selective. I'd heard that only one out of ten applicants is accepted there; when I asked him if that was true he said he didn't know.

"So where'd *you* go to school, Bill?" he asked, and that was always an awkward question.

I had come out of the Army with the wealth of the GI Bill of Rights at my disposal, but hadn't taken advantage of it—and I will never wholly understand why. It was partly fear: I'd done poorly in high school, the Army had assessed my IQ at 109, and I didn't want the risk of further failure. And it was partly arrogance: I planned to become a professional writer as soon as possible, and that made four years of college seem a wasteful delay. There was a third factor too—one that took too much explaining for comfort, but could in a greatly simplified form be easier to tell than all the fear-and-arrogance stuff—and this had become the reply I gave most often on being asked why I hadn't gone to college. "Well," I would say, "I had my mother to take care of."

"Oh, that's too bad," Dan Rosenthal said, looking concerned. "I mean, it's too bad you had to miss out on college." He seemed to be thinking it over for a while, trailing a delicate paintbrush back and forth under the clean scent of banana oil that always hung in his side of the cubicle. Then he said, "Still, if the GI Bill gives allotments for dependent wives and children, how come they wouldn't do it for a dependent mother?"

That was something I had never looked into; worse, it was something that had never occurred to me. But whatever lame and evasive reply I made didn't matter much because he had already moved on to find another marshy place in the dark field of my autobiography.

"And you're married now?" he said.

"Uh-huh."

"Well, so who's taking care of Mother? You still doing that too?"

"No, she's—well, she's pretty much back on her feet now," I said, and that was a lie.

I knew he wouldn't press me on it, and he didn't. Office friendships don't work that way. But I knew too, as I fingered nervously through the *Systems* copy, that I had better watch my mouth around Dan Rosenthal from now on.

My mother, who had lived on alimony payments as long as I could remember, had been left with nothing after my father died in 1942.

At first she'd taken a few harsh and degrading jobs—working in a lens-grinding shop, working in the cheap loft factories that make department-store mannequins—but work like that was pitifully wrong for a bewildered, rapidly aging, often hysterical woman who had always considered herself a sculptor with at least as much intensity as I brought to the notion of myself as a writer. During my time in the Army she had collected something from her status as a "Class A Dependent," but it couldn't have been much. For a while she lived with my older sister and her family in the Long Island suburbs, but the clash of personalities in that unhappy house soon brought her back to New York—and to me. My sister wrote me a letter about it, as if it were too delicate a matter for discussion on the phone, explaining that her husband's "views" on sharing his home with in-laws were "sound in theory, though terribly difficult in practice," and saying she was sure I would understand.

That was how it started. My mother and I lived on what little I earned at apprentice jobs, first on a trade journal and later as a rewrite man for the United Press, and we shared an apartment she had found on Hudson Street. Except for a nagging sense that this wasn't a very adventurous or attractive way for a young man to live, I was comfortable there at first. We got along surprisingly well; but then, we always had.

All through childhood I had admired the way she made light of money troubles—that, perhaps even more than the art she doggedly aspired to or the love she so frequently invoked, was what had made her uncommon and fine for me. If we were occasionally evicted from our rented homes, if we seldom had presentable clothes and sometimes went hungry for two or three days while waiting for my father's monthly check, those hardships only enhanced the sweet poignance of her reading *Great Expectations* aloud to my sister and me in her bed. She was a free spirit. *We* were free spirits, and only a world composed of creditors or of "people like your father" could fail to appreciate the romance of our lives.

Now, she often assured me that this new arrangement was only temporary—she would surely find some way to get "back on her feet" in no time at all—but as the months wore on she made no effort, or any reasonable plans, and so I began to lose patience. This wasn't making any sense. I didn't want to listen to her torrential talk anymore or join in her laughter; I thought she was drinking too much; I found her childish and irresponsible—two of my father's words—and I didn't even want to look at her: small and hunched in tasteful clothes that were never quite clean, with sparse, wild, yellow-gray hair and a soft mouth set in the shape either of petulance or of hilarity.

Her teeth had been bad for years. They were unsightly, and they'd begun to hurt. I took her to the Northern Dispensary, an antique little triangular brick landmark of the Village that was said to be the oldest free dental clinic in New York. A pleasant young dentist examined her and told us that all her teeth would have to be removed.

"Oh, no," she cried.

The work couldn't be done here in the clinic, he explained, but if she came to his private office in Queens he would do it there, equip her with dentures, and charge us only half his normal fee because she was a clinic patient.

It was a deal. We took a train out to Jamaica and I sat with her through it all, hearing her grunt and shudder with the shock of each extraction, watching the dentist drop one ugly old tooth after another onto his little porcelain tray. It made my toes clench and my scalp prickle; it was a terrible but oddly satisfying thing to watch. There, I thought as each tooth fell bloody on the tray. There . . . there . . . there. How could she make a romance out of this? Maybe now, at last, she would come to terms with reality.

All the way home that afternoon, with the lower half of her face so fallen-in that she wouldn't let anyone see it, she rode staring out the train window and pressed a wad of Kleenex to her mouth. She seemed utterly defeated. That night, when worse pain set in, she thrashed and moaned in her bed and pleaded with me for a drink.

"Well, I don't think that's too good an idea," I told her. "I mean alcohol warms your blood, and when you're bleeding, you see, it'll only make it worse."

"Call him up," she commanded. "Call what's-his-name, the dentist. Get the Queens information operator. I don't care what time it is. I'm dying. Do you understand me? I'm dying."

And I obeyed her. "I'm sorry to bother you at home, Doctor," I began, "but the thing is I wondered if it would be all right for my mother to have something to drink."

"Oh, certainly," he said. "Fluids are the best thing. Fruit juices, iced tea, any of the popular sodas and soft drinks; that'll be fine."

"No, I meant—you know—whiskey. Alcohol."

"Oh." And he explained, tactfully, that alcohol would not be advisable at all.

In the end I gave her a couple of drinks anyway and had three or four myself, standing alone and slumped at the window in a melodramatic posture of despair. I thought I would never get out of that place alive.

After she got her new teeth, and after the first discomfort of wearing them was over, she seemed to shed twenty years. She smiled and laughed frequently and spent a lot of time at the mirror. But she was afraid everyone would know they were false teeth, and that made her shy.

"Can you hear me clacking when I talk?" she would ask me.

"No."

"Well, *I* can hear it. And do you see this awful little *crease* under my nose, where they fit in? Is that very noticeable?"

"No, of course not. Nobody's going to notice that."

In her days as a sculptor she had joined three art organizations that required the paying of dues: the National Sculpture Society, the National Association of Women Artists, and something called Pen and Brush, which was a local Village women's club—a relic, I think, of the old, old Village of smocks and incense and monogrammed Egyptian cigarettes and Edna St. Vincent Millay. At my urging she had reluctantly agreed to let her dues lapse at the two uptown enterprises, but she clung to Pen and Brush because it was "socially" important for her.

That was all right with me; it didn't cost much, and they sometimes held group exhibitions of painting and sculpture—awful afternoons of tea and sponge cake, of heavily creaking wooden floors and clustering ladies in funny hats—at which a small, old, finger-smudged piece of my mother's sculpture might win an Honorable Mention.

"And you see, it's only recently that they've let sculptors *in*to Pen and Brush," she explained, far more often than necessary. "It was always just writers and painters before that, and of course they can't change the *name* of it now, to include the sculptors, but we call ourselves 'the chiselers.'" And that always struck her as so funny that she'd laugh and laugh, either trying to hide her old teeth with her fingers or, later, happily displaying the gleam of her new ones.

I met almost nobody of my own age during that time, except by hanging around Village bars and trying to figure out what was going on; then once I was taken to a small party and met a girl named Eileen who turned out to be as lonely as I was, though she was better at concealing it. She was tall and slender with rich dark red hair and a pretty, bony face that could sometimes look warily stern, as if the world were trying to put something over on her. She too had come from what she called a "shabby-genteel" background (I had never heard that phrase before and added it at once to my vocabulary); her parents too had been long divorced; she hadn't gone to college either; and, again like me, she earned her living as a white-collar employee. She was a secretary in a business office. An important difference here was that she insisted she liked her work because it was "a good job," but I imagined there would be plenty of time for talking her out of that.

From the beginning, and for the whole of the next year, we were hardly ever apart except during working hours. It may not have been love, but we couldn't have been persuaded of that because we kept telling each other, and telling ourselves, that it was. If we often quarreled, the movies had proved time and again that love was like that. We couldn't keep away from each other, though I think we both came to suspect, after awhile, that this might be because neither of us had anywhere else to go.

Eileen wanted to meet my mother, and I knew it would be a mistake but couldn't think of an acceptable way to say no. And my mother, predictably, didn't like her. "Well, she's a pleasant girl, dear," she said later, "but I don't see how you can find her so at*trac*tive."

Then once when Eileen was telling me about a boring middle-aged man who lived in her building, she said, "He's been on the fringes of art for so many years, talking and talking about it, that he's come to expect all the prerogatives of being an artist without ever doing the work. I mean he's an *art* bum, like your mother."

"An art bum?"

"Well, you know. When you fool around with it all your life, trying to impress people with something that isn't really there and never really was—don't you think that's tiresome? Don't you think it's a waste of everybody's time?"

From old loyalty I tried to defend my mother against the art-bum charge, but it came out weak and lame and overstated, and there might have been yet another quarrel if we hadn't found some way to change the subject.

Some mornings when I'd come home after daylight, with barely time to put on a clean shirt for work, my mother would greet me with a tragic stare—and once or twice she said, as if I were the girl, "Well, I certainly hope you know what you're doing." Then one evening late in the year she went into one of her uncontrollable rages and referred to Eileen as "that cheap little Irish slut of yours." But that wasn't really so bad because it enabled me to get up in a disdainful silence and walk out of the place and shut the door, leaving her to wonder if I would ever come back.

That winter I came down with pneumonia, which seemed only in keeping with the general run of our bad luck. And during my recovery in the hospital there was a time when my mother and Eileen, who had skillfully avoided each other until then, found themselves riding in the same elevator and came into the ward together for the afternoon visiting hour. They took chairs on opposite sides of the high steel bed and made hesitant conversation across my chest, while I turned my head on the pillow from one to the other of their remarkably different faces, the old and the new, trying to muster appropriate expressions for each of them.

Then Eileen pulled open one side of my hospital gown, peered beneath it, and began massaging the flesh on my ribs with her hand. "Isn't he a nice color?" she inquired with a bright false trill in her voice.

"Well, yes, I've always thought so," my mother said quietly.

"Do you know what the best part is, though?" Eileen said. "The best part is, he's the same color all over."

And it might have been funny if my mother hadn't chosen to take it in silence, slightly lowering her eyelids and lifting her chin, like a dowager obliged to confront an impudent scullery maid; all Eileen could do was put her hand back in her lap and look down at it.

I was released from the ward a few days later, though not before a mild and conscientious-looking doctor lectured me on the virtues of adequate nutrition and regular hours. "You're underweight," he explained as if I didn't know it, as if being skinny hadn't been a terrible source of embarrassment all my life. "And you've had several lung ailments, and your general physical type suggests a susceptibility to TB."

I didn't know what to make of that as I rode home on the subway with my grubby little brown paper bag of toilet articles, but I knew it was something that would have to wait. For now, and for God only knew how long a time to come, there were other troubles.

And the most dreaded, the worst conceivable trouble came within a month or two, one warm night in Eileen's apartment when she said she wanted to break off with me. We had been "courting"—her word—for a year, and there didn't seem to be any future in it. She said she was "still interested in other men," and when I said, "*What* other men?" she looked away and made some enigmatic reply that told me I was losing the argument.

I knew I had a point—she didn't know any other men; still, she had a good point too. She wanted the freedom to be lonely again, to wait at her telephone until somebody asked her to some place where there would *be* other men, and then from among several candidates she would choose one. He would probably be older than me, and better-looking and better-dressed, with a few dollars in the bank and some idea of where his life was going, and he certainly wouldn't have a mother on his hands.

So it was over; and for a little while, taking a tragic view of my situation, I thought I would probably die. I wasn't yet as old as John Keats, another ill-nourished tubercular type, but then I hadn't yet established any claim to genius, either, and so my death might well be poignant in its very obscurity—a youth consumed before his time, an unknown soldier mourned by no one, ever, except perhaps by a single girl.

But I was still expected to hammer out United Press copy eight hours a day, and to ride the subway and pay attention to where the hell I was walking on the street, and it doesn't take long to discover that you have to be alive to do things like that.

One evening I came home and found my mother barely able to suppress the joy of something she had to tell me. For a moment of unreasoning hope, looking into her happy face, I thought the good news might be that she'd found some decent work, but that wasn't it.

There was going to be an evening's entertainment at Pen and Brush, she said, and a party afterwards. Each category of the club's membership would present a humorous song or skit or something, and she had been chosen to do the turn for the sculpture contingent.

There was a mindless little commercial jingle on the radio then, advertising bananas. A girl with a South American accent would come on and sing, to a Latin beat:

I'm Chiquita Banana and I've—come to say
Bananas have to ripen in a—certain way . . .

And this was my mother's parody of it, composed for the pleasure of the Pen and Brush ladies and performed, with bright eyes and a brisk little hopping around on the floor of our wretched home, for me:

Oh, we are the sculptors and we've—come to say
You have to treat the sculptors in a—certain way . . .

She was fifty-seven years old. It had often occurred to me that she was crazy—there had been people who said she was crazy as long as I could remember—but I think it must have been that night, or very soon afterwards, that I decided to get out.

I borrowed three hundred dollars from the bank, gave it to my mother, explained that I would make all the payments on it, and told her, in so many words, that she was on her own.

Then I hurried to Eileen's place—hurried as if in fear that "other men" might get there first—and asked her if she would marry me right away, and she said yes.

"It's funny about us," she said later. "We're nothing alike, we don't really have any common interests or anything, but there certainly is a—chemical affinity, isn't there."

"Yeah."

And on chemical affinity alone, it seemed, in a crumbling apartment at the quiet waterfront edge of the Village, we survived the summer of 1948.

There were times when my mother would call up in meekness and urgency to ask me for twenty, or ten, or five, until Eileen and I came to dread the ringing of the phone; then before very long she began to earn most of her own living. She was sculpting the heads for department-store mannequins on a freelance basis, working at home—at least there would be no more factory employment—but she wanted me to know that something much better might soon come through for her. She had learned that the National Association of Women Artists planned to hire an administrative and public-relations person. Wouldn't that be a wonderful kind of job? There was no requirement that the person be able to type, which was a blessing, but the trouble was they would probably want her to work as a volunteer for a while before they'd put her on a salary. And if she had to spend several months working full-time there without pay, how could she get her mannequin heads done? Wasn't it ironic how things never seemed to work out quite right?

Yeah.

Late that fall I was fired from the United Press—for general incompetence, I think, though that word wasn't used in the cordial little firing speech—and there were a few tense weeks until I found work on a labor union newspaper. Then in the spring I was hired at Remington Rand, and so began my time of sloth and talk in that dry little glassed-in cubicle with Dan Rosenthal.

Once I'd learned not to tell him too much about myself, we got along very well. And it became very important for me to earn and keep his good opinion.

Much of his talk was about his family. He told me his father was a cutter in the men's clothing industry and had "done a remarkable amount in the way of self-education," but then he said, "Ah, shit. It's impossible to say something like that without demeaning the man. You get a picture of some funny little guy hunched over a machine all day and then talking Kierkegaard all night. That's not what I mean at all. Know something? When you're close to someone, when you love someone, you can only make a goddamn fool of yourself trying to explain it. Same with my mother."

And he was greatly proud of his brother, Phil, who was then in one of the several city high schools established for gifted students. "I ordered him," he said once. "When I was seven years old I told my parents I wanted a kid brother and wouldn't take no for an answer. They had no choice. So they came through for me, and that was fine, but the trouble was I hadn't realized it'd be years before I could play with him, or talk to him, or teach him anything, or do anything at *all* with him, and that was hard to take. Still, ever since he was about six I haven't had many complaints. We got a piano in the house and Phil was playing classical music in a couple of months. I'm not kidding. When it was time for high school he had his pick of the finest schools in the city. He's still very shy with girls, and I think he worries about that, but the girls sure as hell aren't shy with him. The damn phone rings every night. Girls. Just calling up to have a little time with Phil. Oh, son of a bitch, this kid's got everything."

Several times Dan said he guessed he was about ready to move into a place of his own, and he asked me in a tentative way about rents in different parts of the Village, but these plans implied no difficulty with his family. It seemed rather that moving away was what he thought the world might now expect of him, in view of his age and education. He wanted to do the right thing.

Then one morning he called in to the office, hoarse with shock and lack of sleep, and said, "Bill? Listen, I won't be in for a few days. I don't know how many days. My father died last night."

When he came back to work he was very pale and seemed to have shrunk a little. He said "fuck" a great many times in muttering over office problems; then after a week or so he wanted to tell me about his father's life.

"You know what a cutter does?" he asked. "Well, he operates a little machine all day. The machine's got an automatic blade, sort of like a jigsaw; the man takes maybe twenty-five layers of cloth—flannel or worsted or whatever the hell it happens to be—and he works the blade around through that whole stack of stuff according to some pattern, like maybe a sleeve or a lapel or a coat pocket. And there's lint everywhere. It gets up into your nose; it gets into your throat. You're living your whole life in fucking *lint*. And can you imagine a man of high intelligence—a man of high intelligence doing that kind of work for thirty-five years? For no better reason than that he's never had time to be trained in anything else? Ah, shit. Shit. It's enough to break your fucking heart. Fifty-two years old."

Dan took up cigars that summer, always carrying a cluster of them in his shirt pocket, chewing and smoking them all day as he bent over his work. It seemed to me that he didn't really enjoy them much—they sometimes drove him into coughing fits—but it was as if they were a necessary part of his preparation for the thick, premature middle age he had assigned himself at twenty-five.

"You know this guy in the office I've told you about?" I said to Eileen one night. "The artist? Dan Rosenthal? I think he's getting into practice for being an old man."

"Oh? How do you mean?"

"Well, he's getting so—ah, I can't explain it. I'm not even sure if I've got it right."

She could seldom explain anything to me about people in her office, either. Our conversations often dissolved into admissions that we weren't even sure if we had it right, and then there would be silence until a quarrel broke out over something else.

We weren't an ideal couple. We had been married at ages we both now considered too young, and for reasons we both now considered inadequate. There were times when we could talk long and pleasantly, as if to prove we were good companions; still, even then, some of her speech mannerisms made me wince. Instead of "yeah" she said "yaw," often while squinting against the smoke of a cigarette; she said "as per usual" too—an accounting-department witticism, I think—and instead of "everything" she often said "the works." That was the way smart, no-nonsense New York secretaries talked, and a smart, no-nonsense New York secretary was all she had ever allowed herself to want to be.

Well, almost ever. During the previous winter, to my great surprise, she had enrolled in an acting class at the New School. She would come home breathless with what she was learning, eager to talk without any secretarial rhetoric at all; those were the best of our times together. Nobody could have guessed, on those nights, that this sweet student of the dramatic arts devoted forty hours a week to toiling in the office of a fabric manufacturer called Botany Mills.

At the end of the New School year all members of her class performed, for an audience composed mostly of relatives and friends, in a dusty old theater on Second Avenue. There were two- and three-character scenes taken from familiar American plays; other students had chosen to act alone, as Eileen did. She had picked something light but not insubstantial—a long, subtle, self-contained monologue from *Dream Girl* by Elmer Rice—and everybody let her know she was wonderful to watch and to hear.

She did so well that night that the New School offered her a scholarship for the following year. And that was when the trouble began. She thought it over for a few days—there were long silences in the apartment while she peeled potatoes or worked at the ironing board—and then she announced that she'd decided to turn down the scholarship. Going to school at night was too tiring after a full day's work. Oh, it had been all right this year—it had been "fun"—but to go on with it would be foolish: even if it was free, it would cost too much in other ways. Besides, nobody could learn much about acting from these little adult-education courses. If she really wanted to learn, in any professional sense, she would have to study full-time; and that, of course, was out of the question.

"Why?"

"What do you mean, 'why?' "

"Well, Jesus, Eileen, you don't need that job. You could quit that dumb little job tomorrow. *I* can take care of—"

"Oh, you can take care of *what*?" And she turned to face me with both small fists on her hips, a gesture that always meant we were in for a bad one.

I loved the girl who'd wanted to tell me all about "the theater," and the girl who'd stood calm and shy in the thunderclap of applause that followed her scene from *Dream Girl*. I didn't much like the dependable typist at Botany Mills, or the grudging potato peeler, or the slow, tired woman who frowned over the ironing board to prove how poor we were. And I didn't want to be married to anyone, ever, who said things like, "Oh, you can take care of *what*?"

It was a bad one, all right. It went on until after we'd waked the neighbors, and it was never resolved, as none of our worst fights ever were. Our lives, by that time, seemed to be all torn nerves and open wounds; I think we might have broken up that summer, and maybe for good, if we hadn't learned that Eileen was pregnant.

Dan Rosenthal rose happily from his drawing board to shake hands on hearing there was a baby on the way. But after that brief ceremony, when we'd both sat down again, he peered at me reflectively. "How can you be a father," he asked, "when you still look like a son?"

One weekend soon after that, on one of the first chilly days of fall, I was out gathering scrap lumber in a vacant lot near the river. Our apartment house was very old and badly kept, but we had a fireplace that "worked." I chose only boards that could be split and broken down to fireplace size, and when I had enough to last a few days I pitched them over the high wire fence that surrounded the lot. From a distance that fence might have looked difficult to scale, but there were enough sagging places in it to make easy footholds. I went up and over it, and had just dropped to the street when I saw Dan Rosenthal walking toward me.

"Well," he said. "You looked pretty good there, coming over the fence. You looked very nimble."

That was a pleasure. I remember being pleased too that he'd found me wearing an old Army field jacket and blue jeans. He was dressed in a suit and tie and a light, new-looking topcoat.

As we walked back to the house with the load of wood—Dan carried part of it, holding it carefully away from his coat—he explained that he'd come over to the city today to visit a Cooper Union friend; then he'd found he had a few hours on his hands, so he'd just been walking around the Village. He hoped I didn't mind his dropping by.

"Hell, no," I told him. "This is great, Dan. Come on up; I'd like you to meet my wife."

Except that we lived there, Eileen and I weren't really Village people at all. Bohemians made us nervous. The very word *hip* held vaguely frightening overtones for us, as did the idea of smoking pot—or "tea," as I think it was usually called then—and what few parties we went to were most often composed of other young office workers as square as ourselves.

Even so, when I brought Dan Rosenthal into the house and upstairs that afternoon, I found I was doing my best to slouch and mumble and squint for him. And Eileen couldn't have been more helpful if she'd tried: we discovered her reclining on the big studio couch, wearing her black turtleneck sweater and black slacks. I had always loved that outfit because it was vastly becoming, with her long red hair, and also because it seemed to loosen all her joints. She had worn it to the acting class sometimes, and she nearly always wore it on evenings when we'd sit quietly for hours in the San Remo or some other locally famous bar, trying to conquer our uneasiness among young men who slouched and mumbled and squinted with their pale, long-haired girls, whole crowds of them erupting now and then into roars of laughter over matters we were fairly sure we would never understand.

If you're young enough, there can be exhilaration in pretending to be something you're not. And if I'd been nimble in vaulting the fence, if I'd been a little hip on the stairs, it was time to be rugged now. Crouching, and with a good deal more force than necessary, I smashed and split those boards over the ringing iron knob of an andiron hauled from the fireplace; then, when they'd been reduced to manageable sticks, I broke each stick in half, or into thirds, one after another, against one straining knee. Some of the lumber had held rows of rusty nails, and Dan said, "Watch those nails," but I told him without words that I could look out for myself. Hadn't I done stuff like this all my life? Hadn't I been a rifleman in the Army? Did he think I'd always been some indoor kind of business-office guy in a white shirt? Hell, there wasn't much you couldn't learn in knocking around the world; how else did he think I had won this stunning girl, from whom he seemed almost wholly unable to take his eyes?

Soon I had a nice fire going. Dan removed his suit coat and loosened his tie; the three of us sat around in attitudes of comfort, drinking beer, and my posturing entered a quiet, "interesting" new phase. Well, no, I told him, aiming a sad smile into the flames, I'd decided to shelve the novel I'd been working on since last spring. It didn't feel right. "And if a thing doesn't feel right," I explained, "you're better off leaving it alone." I always tried to use short, cryptic phrases in discussing the craft.

"Yeah," he said.

"I imagine it's the same in painting, in a different way."

"Well, sort of."

"Besides, I've got a few old stories I want to fix up and send around. You have to fix them up, you know. You have to keep taking 'em apart and putting 'em together. They don't write themselves."

"Uh-huh."

I held forth at some length, then, on how hard it was to get any real writing done when you were stuck in a full-time job. We'd been trying to save a little money so we could live in Europe, I explained, but now, with the baby coming, there wasn't much chance of that.

"You want to live in Europe?" he asked.

"Well, it's a thing we've always talked about. Paris, mostly."

"Why?"

Like some of his other questions, this one was disquieting. There weren't any real reasons. Part of it was the legend of Hemingway, and that of Joyce; the other part was that I wanted to put three thousand miles of sea between my mother and myself. "Oh, well," I said, "it's mostly just that the cost of living's much lower there; we could probably get by on a lot less, and I'd have more time to work."

"You speak any French?"

"No; still, I suppose we could learn. Ah, hell, it's just—you know—the whole thing's probably just a daydream." From the very sound of my voice I could tell I was faltering, so I stopped talking as soon as I could.

"Dan?" Eileen inquired, and her face in the firelight was a masterpiece of innocent flirtation. Nobody ever had to tell her when she'd made a conquest. "Is it true that only one applicant out of ten is accepted at Cooper Union?"

"Well, you hear different figures," he said bashfully, not quite meeting her eyes, "but it's something like that."

"That's wonderful. I mean that's really impressive. It must have made you very proud to go there."

She had thoroughly destroyed my act, if not the whole of my weekend; even so, their talk gave me the beginnings of what seemed a pretty good idea.

There was a lot more talk, and more beer; then she said, "Will you stay and have supper with us, Dan?"

"Oh, that's a very nice thought," he said, "but maybe it'd better wait for another time; I should've been home long ago. Mind if I use your phone?"

He called his mother and talked agreeably for a few minutes; later, after he'd left with many thanks and apologies and promises to come again soon, Eileen said the phone call had sounded like a husband talking to his wife.

"Yeah, well, that's the thing, you see," I told her. "Ever since his father died he's been acting sort of as if his mother *were* his wife. And he's got a younger brother, seven or eight years younger, and now he acts as if the brother were their son."

"Oh," she said. "Well, that's sort of sad, isn't it. Does he have a girl?"

"I don't think so. If so, he never mentions her."

"I really like him a lot, though," she said as she began to clatter pots and pans in the kitchen area of the room, getting dinner started. "I like him better than anyone I've met in a long time. He's very—kind."

It was such a carefully chosen word that I wondered why she'd chosen it, and I was quick to assume it was because that particular word could not, very readily, be applied to me.

But the hell with it. I could hardly wait to get into the alcove formed by a folding screen in the corner, where my worktable was. The partly typed, partly scribbled abortion of my novel lay there, as did the several stories I planned to take apart and put together, to fix up and send around. My new idea, though, had nothing to do with writing at all.

I had always had a knack for drawing simple cartoons, and that night I filled many sheets of typing paper with caricatures of people who worked on the eleventh floor at Remington Rand. They were people Dan and I had to be patient with and nice to every day, and I was almost certain, as I chuckled over a few of the better ones, that the pictures would appeal to him.

It took me several more nights to weed out the crude ones, and to clean up the better ones; then one morning, as casually as possible, I dropped the finished stack of them on his drawing board.

"What's this?" he said. "Oh, I get it: Arch Davenport. And poor old Gus Hoffman. And who's this? Jack Sheridan, right? Oh, and I guess this is Mrs. Jorgensen in the typing pool. . . ."

When he'd inspected them all he said, "Well, these are clever, Bill." But I'd heard him use "clever" in a disparaging sense too many times to take it as a compliment.

"Ah, they're nothing much," I assured him. "I just thought they might—you know—give you a laugh."

The truth was that I'd hoped they might do a great deal more. I had worked out a scheme in which these drawings were only the opening move, and now his lukewarm response seemed to prohibit telling him the rest of it. But my reticence didn't last long. Before the day was over—even before lunch, I think—I'd spelled out the whole damned thing for him.

There were hundreds of Americans now enrolled in art schools in Paris on the GI Bill, I explained. Many of them were serious artists, of course, but many others weren't artists at all: they met few if any academic requirements; they were openly exploiting the GI Bill to subsidize their lives in Paris. And the art schools didn't care, because they were happy to have steady money coming in from the United States government. I had read about this in *Time* magazine, and the article had singled out one art school, by name, as being "perhaps the most casual of all in its handling of the matter."

I had now decided to apply for admission to that school as a way of getting on with my writing, I told Dan Rosenthal, but I would need a letter of recommendation. So here was the thing: Would he write the letter?

He looked puzzled and faintly displeased. "I don't get it," he said. "Me write the letter? They're supposed to've heard of me?"

"No. But you can be damn sure they've heard of Cooper Union."

It didn't go over very well—I'd have had to be blind not to see that—but he agreed. He wrote the letter quickly, using one of his drawing pencils, and passed it over to me for typing.

He had told the school authorities that I was a friend whose ability at line drawing showed promise, and that he wished to support my application; he had saved his Cooper Union credentials for the second and final paragraph.

"Well, this is fine, Dan," I said. "Thanks a lot. Really. There's just one thing: when you say I'm a 'friend,' don't you think that might tend to weaken the whole—"

"Ah, shit," he said without looking up, and I may have been wrong but I thought his neck was a darker pink than usual. "Shit, Bill. Come on. I said you were a friend. I didn't say we were brothers under the skin."

If he disliked me then, and I think he probably did, it wasn't a thing he allowed to show. After that first embarrassing day it began to appear that everything was all right between us again.

And now that he'd met my wife there was a new litany in the ritual of our acquaintance. Every night, or at least on nights when we left the building together and walked to the street corner where we'd have to separate for our different kinds of public transit, he would give me a shy little wave and say, "Well. Regards at home."

He said it on so many nights that after awhile he seemed to feel a need for variation: with a mock scowl he would say, "How about some regards?" or "Let's have some regards there, huh?" But those weren't very satisfactory alternatives, so he went back to the original line. I would always thank him and wave back and call, "Same here," or "You too, Dan," and that small exchange came to seem a fitting conclusion to the day.

I never heard from the "casual" Paris art school—they didn't even acknowledge receipt of my application—so I was left to assume that the *Time* story must have brought them an avalanche of letters from other no-talent applicants all over America, misfits and losers and unhappy husbands for whom "Paris" had come to mean the last bright hope.

Dan came home with me for dinner several times during the next few months, and Eileen soon discovered he could make her laugh. That was nice, but I could almost never make her laugh myself—hadn't, it seemed, since the very early days of our time together—and so I was jealous. Then late one night after he'd gone and our place had grown uncomfortably quiet with only the two of us there, she pointed out that we had never really given a party. And she said she wanted to do it right away, before she got "too big," so we went through with it—both of us, I think, in terror of doing everything wrong.

Dan brought along one of his Cooper Union friends, an impeccably courteous young man named Jerry, who in turn brought a lovely, dead-silent girl. The party was all right—at least it was noisy and rapidly revolving—so Eileen and I were able to tell each other afterwards that it had been fine. A week or two later, in the office, Dan said, "Know something? Jerry and his girl are getting married. And you want to know something else? It was your party that did the trick. I'm not kidding. Jerry told me they both thought the two of you were so—I don't know; who knows?—so romantic, I guess, that they figured what the hell; let's do it. And they're doing it. Jerry's taken a job I don't think he ever would've considered otherwise, working for some commercial-art school way the hell up in the northern part of British Columbia. I don't know what the hell he'll be doing up there—teaching Eskimos how to hold a T-square, I guess—but there's no turning back now. It's done. The die is fucking cast."

"Well, that's great," I said. "Tell him congratulations for me."

"Yeah, I will; I will." Then he turned his chair away from his drawing board—he didn't often do that—and sat looking grave and thoughtful, examining the wet end of his cigar. "Well, hell, I'd like to get married too," he said. "I mean I'm not really *immune* to it or anything, but there are a few obstacles. Number one, I haven't met the right girl. Number two, I've got too many other responsibilities. Number three—or wait, come to think of it, who the hell needs number three?"

Soon after the year turned into 1950, and a few weeks before the baby was due, the National Association of Women Artists agreed at last to hire my mother at a starting salary of eighty a week. "Oh, Jesus, what a relief," Eileen said, and I couldn't have agreed more. Except for the smiling boredom entailed in having her over for dinner once, "to celebrate," it seemed now that we could stop thinking about her almost indefinitely.

Then our daughter was born. Dan Rosenthal paid a surprise visit to Eileen in the hospital afterwards, bringing flowers, and that made her blush. I walked him out into the corridor for a window-view of the baby, whom he solemnly pronounced a beauty; then we went back and sat at Eileen's bedside for half an hour or so.

"Oh, Dan,"' she said when he got up to leave, "it was *so* nice of you to come."

"My pleasure," he told her. "Entirely my pleasure. I'm very big on maternity wards."

The famous Long Island housing development called Levittown had recently been opened for business, and some of the younger married men around the eleventh floor began discussing at length—each of them explaining to the others, as if to convince himself—the many things that made it a good deal.

Then Dan told me he too had decided to buy into Levittown, and I might have said, But you're not even *married*, if I hadn't checked myself in time. He and his mother and brother had gone out there last weekend.

What had won him over to Levittown was that the basement of the house they inspected was remarkably big and bright. "It might as well've been *designed* as a studio," he said. "I walked around that basement and all I could think was Wow. I'm gonna paint my ass off down here. And I can even make prints, set up a lithograph stone, whatever the hell I want. You know all this stuff about the perils of suburbia? How your life's supposed to fall apart when you move out of the city? I don't believe any of that. If your life's ready to fall apart, it'll fall apart anywhere."

Another time he said, "You know anything about Harvard?"

"Harvard? No."

"Well, I think Phil's got a fairly good chance of getting in there, maybe even on a scholarship. It sounds fine; still, all I know about Harvard is the reputation, you know?—the outside view. And that's sort of like the Empire State Building, right? You see it from a distance, maybe at sunset, and it's this majestic, beautiful thing. Then you get inside, you walk around a couple of the lower floors, and it turns out to be one of the sleaziest office buildings in New York: there's nothing in there but small-time insurance agencies and costume-jewelry wholesalers. There isn't any *reason* for the tallest building in the world. So you ride all the way up to the top and your eardrums hurt and you're out there at the parapet looking out, looking down, and even that's a disappointment because you've seen it all in photographs so many times. Or take Radio City Music Hall, if you're a kid of about thirteen—same thing. I took Phil there once when I was home from the service, and we both knew it was a mistake. Oh, it's pretty nice to see seventy-eight good-looking girls come out and start kicking their legs up in unison—even if they're half a mile away, even if you happen to know they're all married to airline pilots and living in Rego Park—but I mean all you ever personally *find* in Radio City Music Hall is a lot of wrinkled old chewing gum stuck up underneath the arms of your fucking chair. Right? So I don't know; I think Phil and I'd better go up to Harvard for a couple of days and kind of snoop around."

And they did. Mrs. Rosenthal went along too. Dan came back to the office overflowing with enthusiasm for everything about Harvard, including the very sound of its name. "You can't imagine it, Bill," he told me. "You have to be there; you have to walk around and look, and listen, and take it all in. It's amazing: right there in the middle of a commercial city, this whole little world of ideas. It's like about twenty-seven Cooper Unions put together."

So it was arranged that Phil would be enrolled as a Harvard freshman the following fall, and Dan remarked more than a few times that the kid would certainly be missed at home.

One evening when we left the building together he held our walk down to a stroll in order to get something off his chest that seemed to have been bothering him all day.

"You know all this 'need help' talk you hear around?" he inquired. "'He needs help'; 'She needs help'; 'I need help'? Seems like almost everybody I know is taking up psychotherapy as if it were the new national craze, like Monopoly back in the thirties. And I've got this friend of mine from school—bright guy, good artist, married, holding down a pretty good job. Saw him last night and he told me he wants to be psychoanalyzed but can't afford it. Said he applied to this free clinic up at Columbia, had to take a lot of tests and write some half-assed essay about himself, and they turned him down. He said, 'I guess they didn't think I was interesting enough.' I said, 'Whaddya mean?' And he said, 'Well, I got the impression they're up to their ass in overmothered Jewish boys.' Can you understand something like that?"

"No." We were strolling in the dusk past brilliant storefronts—a travel agency, a shoe store, a lunch counter—and I remember studying each one as if it might help me keep my brains together.

"Because I mean what's the deal on being 'interesting' in the first place?" Dan demanded. "Are we all supposed to lie on a couch and spill our guts to prove how 'interesting' we are? That's a degree of sophistication I don't care to attain. Well." We were at the corner now, and just before he moved away he waved his cigar at me. "Well. Regards at home."

I had felt terrible all that spring, and it was getting worse. I coughed all the time and had no strength; I knew I was losing weight because my pants seemed ready to fall off; my sleep was drenched in sweat; all I wanted during the day was to find a place to lie down, and there was no place like that in the whole of Remington Rand. Then one lunch hour I went to a free X-ray service near the office and learned I had advanced tuberculosis. A bed was found for me in a veterans' hospital on Staten Island, and so I retired from the business world, if not from the world itself.

I have since read that TB is high on the list of "psychosomatic" illnesses: people are said to come down with it while proving how hard they have tried under impossibly difficult circumstances. And there may be a lot of truth in that, but all I knew then was how good it felt to be encouraged—even to be ordered, by a grim ex-Army nurse wearing a sterile mask—to lie down and stay there.

It took eight months. In February of 1951 I was released as an outpatient and told I could get continuing treatment at VA-approved clinics "anywhere in the world." That phrase had a nice ring to it, and this was the best part: I was told my illness had qualified as a "service-connected disability," allowing me to collect two hundred dollars a month until my lungs were clean, and that there was a retroactive clause in the deal providing two thousand dollars in cash.

Eileen and I had never known such a glow of success. Late one night I was trying to make plans, wondering aloud whether to go back to Remington Rand or look for a better job, when Eileen said, "Oh, listen: let's do it."

"Do what?"

"You know. Go to Paris. Because I mean if we don't do it now, while we're young enough and brave enough, when are we ever going to do it at all?"

I could scarcely believe she'd said that. She looked, then, very much the way she'd looked acknowledging the applause after her scene from *Dream Girl*—and there was a touch of the old secretarial "toughness" in her face too, suggesting that she might well turn out to be a sturdy traveler.

Because everything happened so fast after that, the next thing I remember clearly is the cramped farewell party in our cabin, or tourist-class "stateroom," aboard the SS *United States*. Eileen was trying to change the baby's diaper on an upper berth, but it wasn't easy because so many people were crowded into the small room. My mother was there, seated on the edge of a lower berth and talking steadily, telling everyone about the National Association of Women Artists. Several employees of Botany Mills were there, and several other random acquaintances, and Dan Rosenthal was there too. He had brought a bottle of champagne and an expensive-looking hand puppet, in the form of a tiger, which the baby wouldn't appreciate for another two years.

This tense gathering was what I'd heard Eileen describe on the phone a few times as "our little shipboard *soignée*"—I didn't think that word was right but didn't know enough French to correct her. There was plenty of liquor flowing, but most of it seemed to be going down my mother's throat. She wore a nice spring suit, with a rich little feathered hat that had probably been bought for the occasion.

". . . Well, but you see we're the only national organization in the country; our membership is up in the thousands now, and of course each member has to submit proof of professional standing as an artist before we'll even consider their application, so we're really a very . . ." And the deeper she settled into her monologue the farther she allowed her knees to move apart, with a forearm on each one, until the shadowy pouch of her underpants was visible to all guests seated across from her. That was an old failing: she never seemed to realize that if people could see her underpants they might not care what kind of hat she was wearing.

Dan Rosenthal was the first to leave, even before the first warning horn had sounded. He said it had been very nice to meet my mother, shaking hands with her; then he gravely turned to Eileen with both arms held out.

She had finished with the diapering—finished too, it seemed, with all concern for any of the other visitors. "Oh, *Dan*," she cried, looking sad and lovely, and she melted fast against him. I saw his heavy fingers clap the small of her back three or four times.

"Take care of my friend the promising writer," he said.

"Well, sure, but *you* take care, Dan, okay? And promise to write?"

"Of course," he told her. "Of course. That goes without saying."

Then he let her go, and I sprang to his service as an escort upstairs to the main deck and the gangplank. We were both quickly winded in climbing, so we took our time on the sharply curving, paint-smelling staircase, but he talked a lot anyway.

"So you're gonna send back a whole bunch of stories, right?" he asked me.

"Right." And only dimly aware of paraphrasing his Levittown plans, I said, "I'm gonna write my ass off over there."

"Well, good," he said. "So it turns out you didn't need that shitty little art school after all. You'll never have to sneak around pretending to be an artist and playing hooky all day, and conspiring with a bunch of very 'casual' Frenchmen to rob the United States. That's good. That's fine. You'll be doing this whole thing on your own, with money you've earned from your fucked-up lungs, and I'm proud of you. I mean it."

We were up on the open deck now, facing each other in the cluster of people near the gangplank.

"So okay," he said as we shook hands. "Keep in touch. Only, listen: do me a favor." He stepped back to pull on his topcoat, which flapped in the light wind, and to shrug and settle it around his neck; then he came up close and looked at me in stern admonishment. "Do me a favor," he said again. "Don't piss it all away."

I didn't know what he meant, even after he'd winked to show he was mostly kidding, until it occurred to me that I had everything he must ever have wanted—everything he'd resigned himself, since his father's death, never to wish for again. I had luck, time, opportunity, a young girl for a wife, and a child of my own.

A great, deep ship's horn blew then, frightening dozens of seagulls into the sky. It was the sound of departure and of voyage, a sound that can make the walls of your throat fill up with blood whether you have anything to cry about or not. From the railing I saw his thick back descending slowly toward the pier. He wasn't yet far away: I could still call some final pleasantry that would oblige him to turn and smile and wave, and I thought of calling, Hey, Dan? Regards at home! But for once I managed to keep my mouth shut, and I've always been glad of that. All I did was watch him walk away between fenced-off crowds and into the heavy shadows of the pier until he was gone.

Then I hurried back down those newly painted, seaworthy stairs to get my mother off the boat—there wouldn't be many more warning horns—and to take up the business of my life.

Saying Goodbye to Sally

JACK FIELDS'S FIRST novel took him five years to write, and it left him feeling reasonably proud but exhausted almost to the point of illness. He was thirty-four then, and still living in a dark, wretchedly cheap Greenwich Village cellar that had seemed good enough for holing-up to get his work done after his marriage fell apart. He assumed he'd be able to find a better place and perhaps even a better life when his book came out, but he was mistaken: though it won general praise, the novel sold so poorly that only a scant, brief trickle of money came in during the whole of its first year in print. By that time Jack had taken to drinking heavily and not writing much—not even doing much of the anonymous, badly paid hackwork that had provided his income for years, though he still managed to do enough of that to meet his alimony payments—and he had begun to see himself, not without a certain literary satisfaction, as a tragic figure.

His two small daughters frequently came in from the country to spend weekends with him, always wearing fresh, bright clothes that were quick to wilt and get dirty in the damp and grime of his terrible home, and one day the younger girl announced in tears that she wouldn't take showers there anymore because of the cockroaches in the shower stall. At last, after he'd swatted and flushed away every cockroach in sight, and after a lot of coaxing, she said she guessed it would be okay if she kept her eyes shut—and the thought of her standing blind in there behind the mildewed plastic curtain, hurrying, trying not to shift her feet near the treacherously swarming drain as she soaped and rinsed herself, made him weak with remorse. He knew he ought to get out of here. He'd have had to be crazy not to know that—maybe he was crazy already, just for being here and continuing to inflict this squalor on the girls—but he didn't know how to begin the delicate, difficult task of putting his life back in order.

Then in the early spring of 1962, not long after his thirty-sixth birthday, there came a wholly unexpected break: he was assigned to write a screenplay based on a contemporary novel that he greatly admired. The producers would pay his way to Los Angeles to meet with the director, and it was recommended that he remain "out there" until he finished the script. It probably wouldn't take more than five months, and that first phase of the project alone, not to mention the dizzying prospect of subsequent earnings, would bring him more money than he'd made in any previous two or three years put together.

When he told his daughters about it, the older girl asked him to send her an inscribed photograph of Richard Chamberlain; the younger one had no requests.

In someone else's apartment a jolly, noisy party was held for him, closely attuned to the jaunty image of himself that he always hoped to convey to others, with a big hand-lettered banner across one wall:

GOODBYE BROADWAY
HELLO GRAUMAN'S CHINESE

And two nights later he sat locked alone and stiff with alcohol among strangers in the long, soft, murmurous tube of his very first jet plane. He slept most of the way across America and didn't wake up until they were floating low over the miles upon miles of lights in the darkness of outer Los Angeles. It occurred to him then, as he pressed his forehead against a small cold window and felt the fatigue and anxiety of the past few years beginning to fall away, that what lay ahead of him—good or bad—might easily turn out to be a significant adventure: F. Scott Fitzgerald in Hollywood.

For the first two or three weeks of his time in California, Jack lived as a guest in the sumptuous Malibu home of the director, Carl Oppenheimer, a dramatic, explosive, determinedly tough-talking man of thirty-two. Oppenheimer had gone straight from Yale into New York television during the years when there were still strictly disciplined "live" plays for the evening audience. When reviewers began to use the word "genius" in writing about his work on those shows he'd been summoned to Hollywood, where he'd turned down many more movie projects than he accepted, and where his pictures rapidly made a name for him as one of what somebody had decided to call The New Breed.

Like Jack Fields, Oppenheimer was a father of two and divorced, but he was never alone. A bright and pretty young actress named Ellis lived with him, prided herself on finding new ways to please him every day, often gave him long, rapturous looks that he seemed not to notice, and habitually called him "My love"—softly, with the stress on "my." And she managed to be an attentive hostess too.

"Jack?" she inquired at sunset one afternoon as she handed their guest a drink in a heavy, costly glass. "Did you ever hear what Fitzgerald did when he lived out here at the beach? He put up a sign outside his house that said 'Honi Soit Qui Malibu.'"

"Oh yeah? No, I'd never heard that."

"Isn't that wonderful? God, wouldn't it have been fun to be around then, when all the real—"

"Ellie!" Carl Oppenheimer called from across the room, where he was bent over and slamming cabinet doors behind a long, well-stocked bar of rich blond wood and leather. "Ellie, can you check the kitchen and find out what the fuck's happened to all the bouillon?"

"Well, certainly, my love," she said, "but I thought it was in the *mornings* that you liked bullshots."

"Sometimes yes," he told her, straightening up and smiling in a way that suggested exasperation and self-control. "Sometimes no. As it happens, I feel like making up a batch of them now. And the point is simply that I'd like to know how the fuck I can make bullshots without any fucking bouillon, you follow me?"

And as Ellis hurried obediently away, both men turned to watch the movement of firm, quivering buttocks in her skintight slacks.

By then Jack had grown eager to find a place of his own, and perhaps even a girl of his own, and so as soon as the screenplay was outlined—as soon as they'd agreed on what Oppenheimer called the thrust of it—he moved out.

A few miles down the coast highway, in the part of Malibu that looks from the road like nothing more than a long row of weather-beaten shacks pressed together, he rented the lower half of a very small two-story beach house. It had a modest picture window overlooking the ocean and a sandy little concrete porch, but that was practically all it had. He didn't realize until after moving in—and after paying the required three months' rent in advance—that the place was very nearly as dismal and damp as his cellar in New York. Then, in a long-familiar pattern, he began to worry about himself: maybe he was incapable of finding light and space in the world; maybe his nature would always seek darkness and confinement and decay. Maybe—and this was a phrase then popular in national magazines—he was a self-destructive personality.

To rid himself of those thoughts he came up with several good reasons why he ought to drive into town and see his agent right away; and once he was out in the afternoon sun, with his rented car purring along past masses of bright tropical foliage, he began to feel better.

The agent's name was Edgar Todd, and his office was near the top of a new high-rise building at the edge of Beverly Hills. Jack had been in to talk with him three or four times—the first time, when he asked how to go about getting the inscribed photograph of Richard Chamberlain, it had turned out to be a matter that Edgar Todd could settle with a single quick, casual phone call—and each time he'd grown more and more aware that Edgar's secretary, Sally Baldwin, was a strikingly attractive girl.

At first glance she might not quite have fallen into the "girl" category because her carefully coiffed hair was gray, with silver streaks, but the shape and texture of her face suggested she wasn't more than thirty-five, and so did the slender, supple, long-legged way she moved around. She had told him once that she "loved" his book and was certain it would make a wonderful movie some day; another time, as he was leaving the office, she'd said, "Why don't we see more of you? Come back and visit us."

But today she wasn't there. She wasn't at her trim secretarial desk in the carpeted hall outside Edgar's office, nor was she anywhere else in sight. It was Friday afternoon; she had probably gone home early, and he felt a chill of disappointment until he saw that the door of Edgar's office was ajar. He knocked lightly, twice, then shoved it open and went inside—and there she was, lovelier than ever, seated at Edgar's enormous desk with the spines of at least a thousand shelved, bright-covered novels forming a backdrop to her sweet face. She was reading.

"Hello, Sally," he said.

"Oh, hi. Nice to see you."

"Edgar gone for the day?"

"Well, he said it was lunch, but I don't think we'll see him again till next week. It's nice to be interrupted though; I've been reading the worst novel of the year."

"You do Edgar's reading for him?"

"Well, most. He doesn't have the time, and anyway he hates to read. So I type up little one- and two-page summaries of the books that come in, and he reads those."

"Oh. Well, listen, Sally, how about coming out for a drink with me?"

"I'd love to," she said, closing the book. "I was beginning to think you'd never ask."

And in something less than two hours later, at a small shadowed table in the bar of a famous hotel, they were shyly but firmly holding hands because it was clear and settled that she would come home with him tonight—and, by implication, for the whole weekend. Looking at her, Jack Fields had begun to feel as calm and strong and full of blood as if the notion of his being a self-destructive personality had never occurred to him. He was all right. The world was still intact, and everybody knew what made it go around.

"Only, look, Jack," she said. "Could we make another stop first? Here in Beverly? Because I'll have to pick up a few things, and anyway I'd like you to see where I live."

And she directed his driving up the shallow grade that forms the first residential part of Beverly Hills, before the steeper slopes begin. He discovered that all the roads there were arranged in graceful curves, as if their designers had been unable to bear the thought of straight lines, and that there were very tall, elegantly slender palm trees at precisely measured intervals. Some of the big houses along those roads were handsome, some were plain, and some were ugly, but they all suggested wealth beyond the comprehension of an ordinary man.

"Now if you take your next left," Sally said, "we're practically home. Good. . . . Here."

"You live *here*?"

"Yup. I can explain everything."

It was a vast white mansion of the Old South, with at least six columns rising from its porch to its lofty portico, with a great many sun-bright windows, with a long extension of itself in the form of a wing on one side, and, beyond a swimming pool, with several connected outbuildings of the same color and style.

"We always go in this way, past the pool," Sally said. "Nobody ever uses the front door."

And the ample room she led him into from the pool terrace was what he guessed would be called a den, though it might easily have been a library if she had somehow contrived to bring Edgar Todd's thousand novels home from the office. Its high walls were paneled in pleasingly dark wood, there were deep leather sofas and armchairs, and there was a fireplace with small flames fluttering in it, though the day was mild. An arrangement of leather-padded wrought-iron benches was built out around the hearth, and on one of the benches sat a pale, sad boy of about thirteen, facing away from the fire and holding his clasped hands between his thighs, looking as though he had come to sit here because there was nothing else to do.

"Hi, Kick," Sally said to him. "Kicker, I'd like you to meet Jack Fields. This is Kicker Jarvis."

"Hello, Kicker."

"Hi."

"You watch the Dodger game today?" Sally asked him.

"No."

"Oh? Why not?"

"I don't know; didn't feel like it."

"Where's your lovely mother?"

"I don't know. Getting dressed, I guess."

"Kicker's lovely mother is an old friend of mine," Sally explained. "She's the one who owns this tremendous place; I just live here."

"Oh?"

And when the boy's mother came into the room a minute later, Jack thought she *was* lovely—as tall and graceful as Sally and even better looking, with long black hair and with blue eyes that lighted up in automatic flirtation at the sound of her name: Jill.

But he didn't really want to meet a woman more desirable than Sally tonight—Sally would be plenty for the time being, even in Hollywood—so he looked closely enough at Jill Jarvis to find something blank or stunned in her heart-shaped face, though he scarcely had time to inspect it before she turned away.

"Sally, look at this," she said, and she thrust a heavy paperback book into Sally's hands. "Isn't it marvelous? I mean isn't it marvelous? I sent away for it weeks and weeks ago and I'd about given up, but it finally came in the mail today." Courteously peering, Jack saw that its title was *The Giant Crossword Puzzle Solving Book*. "Look how *thick* it is," Jill insisted. "I'll *never* get stuck in a puzzle again."

"Wonderful," Sally said, giving it back to her. Then she said, "Excuse me a couple of seconds, Jack, okay?" She hurried into the living room, which looked as wide as a lake, and he watched her pretty legs running up a soundless staircase in a shaft of pale afternoon light.

Jill Jarvis told him to sit down and went away somewhere to "get drinks," leaving him alone with Kicker in what seemed an increasingly awkward silence.

"You go to school around here?" Jack inquired.

"Yeah."

And that was the end of their talk. The funny-paper section from last Sunday's *Los Angeles Times* lay on the hearth bench and the boy turned sideways to hunch and stare at it, but Jack was fairly sure he wasn't reading or even looking at the pictures; he was only waiting for his mother to come back.

Above the fireplace, in a space plainly meant for some heavy old portrait or landscape, there hung instead a small painting on black velvet, in harshly bright colors, showing the face of a circus clown with a melancholy expression; the artist's signature, so prominently written in white that it might have been the title, read "Starr of Hollywood." It was the kind of picture you can find on the walls of third-rate bars and lunch counters all over the United States, and in the airless waiting rooms of failing doctors and dentists; it looked so foolishly out of place in this room as to suggest that someone had stuck it there as a joke—but then, so did *The Giant Crossword Puzzle Solving Book*, which now lay displayed alone on a coffee table that must have cost two thousand dollars.

"I can't imagine what's keeping Woody," Jill said as she carried a liquor tray into the room.

"Want me to call the studio?" Kicker asked her.

"No, don't bother; he'll be along. You know Woody."

Then Sally came downstairs again with a Mexican straw satchel that looked pleasingly full—she *did* plan to spend the weekend with him—and said, "Let's just have one drink, Jack, and then we'll go."

But they had two, because Woody came smiling home during their first one and insisted that they stay for another. He was about Jack's age or younger, of medium height and lightly built, wearing jeans, fringed Indian moccasins, and a complicated shirt that fastened with metal snaps instead of buttons. He moved in a very limber way with a frequent dipping of the knees, and his face showed an unguarded eagerness to be liked.

"Well, it's certainly very nice out at Malibu," he said when he had come to rest at last in one of the armchairs. "I had a place out there for a few years—a small place, but very nice. Still, I've really come to love it here in Beverly. I feel at home here, that's the only way to put it, and you know a funny thing? I've never felt that way about any other place in my life. Get you a refill?"

"No thanks," Jack said. "We'd better be getting started."

"When'll we look for you, Sally?" Jill inquired.

"Oh, I don't know," Sally called back as she and Jack made for the terrace door, with Jack carrying the Mexican bag. "I'll give you a call sometime tomorrow, okay?"

"I won't let you take her away forever, Jack," Woody called. "You gotta promise you'll bring her back soon, okay?"

"Okay," Jack told him. "I promise."

And they were free, just the two of them, hurrying out past the swimming pool and down to the driveway and into his waiting car. All the way home—and the ride seemed to take no time at all in the new-fallen darkness of this still and fragrant night—he wanted to laugh aloud because this was the way things should always have been in his life; this was pretty nice: good money coming in, a weekend coming up, and a girl coming out to love him at the shore of the Pacific Ocean.

"Oh, I think it's sort of—cute," Sally said of his apartment. "Of course it's small, but you could really do a lot with it."

"Yeah, well, I probably won't be here long enough to do much. Can I get you a drink?"

"No thanks. Why don't you just—" She turned from her scrutiny of the black picture window to smile at him, looking bold and shy at the same time and then subtly averting her eyes. "Why don't you just come over here so we can sort of fall all over each other."

No other woman he'd known had made a more graceful passage from acquaintance to intimacy. There was nothing embarrassed in the way she undressed, and nothing of the show-off either: the clothes fell and were flung from her as if she'd waited all day to be rid of them; then she slipped into his bed and turned to welcome him with a look of desire that was as pretty as anything he'd ever seen in the movies. Her long body was strong and tender, and so was the pride she took in knowing what men believe a woman's flesh is for. It was a very long time before he could possibly have thought of any other woman, or girl, even if he'd wanted to.

"Oh, listen to the surf," she said later, when they were nestled together in peace. "Isn't that a wonderful sound?"

"Yeah."

But Jack Fields, curled close at her back with his arm around her and with one of her fine tits alive in his hand, wasn't paying attention to the surf at all. He was too happy and sleepy to accomplish more than a single coherent, mercifully private thought: F. Scott Fitzgerald meets Sheilah Graham.

Sally Baldwin had grown up as Sally Munk—"Jesus, I couldn't *wait* to get rid of that name"—in an industrial California town where her father had worked as an electrician until his early death, and her mother had then worked for many years as a seamstress in a department-store fitting room. In high school Sally had been chosen as a supporting actress in a series of grade-B movies about adolescent life—"sort of like the old Andy Hardy pictures, only nowhere near as good; still, they were a lot better than all this dumb little beach-ball bikini stuff they're fobbing off on the kids nowadays"—but her contract had expired when she grew too tall for the roles expected of her. She had put herself through college on what was left of her movie earnings, and later by working as a waitress. "Cocktail waitressing is the worst kind," she explained. "Pays the best, but it can be really—really demoralizing work."

"Did you wear those hip-length black net stockings?" he asked, thinking she must have looked terrific. "And those little—"

"Yeah, yeah, all that," she said impatiently. "And then pretty soon I got married. Lasted about nine years. He was a lawyer—is a lawyer, I mean. You know how they say never marry a lawyer because you'll never win an argument? Lot of truth in that. We didn't have any children—at first he kept saying he didn't want any, then later it turned out I couldn't have any anyway. I have a whaddyacallit, a fibroid."

And it was early afternoon, when they were lying back in canvas deck chairs on his sandy little porch, before Sally brought the story around to Jill Jarvis and her mansion.

". . . Well, I don't really *know* where all the money comes from," she said. "I know she gets an awful lot of it from her father, someplace in Georgia, and I know his family's had an awful lot of it down there for an awful long time, but I mean I don't really know where it *comes* from. Cotton or something, I guess. And of course Frank Jarvis is rich too, so she came out of that marriage with quite a nice settlement, as well as the house. So then you see when *my* marriage broke up she asked me to come and live there, and I was sort of—thrilled. I'd always loved that house—still do; probably always will. Besides, I didn't really have anywhere else to go. I knew the best I could do alone, on my salary, would've been some neat little place out in the Valley, and that's my definition of spiritual suicide. I'd rather eat worms than live in the Valley.

"Oh, and Jill really went out of her way to make it nice for me too. She hired a professional decorator to do my apartment, and God, you ought to see it, Jack. Well, you will see it. It's really only one big room but it's about as big as three rooms put together, and it's all bright and sunny and you can see green things all around. I love it. I love going in there after a day at the office and taking off my shoes and sort of dancing around for a minute thinking Wow. Look at me. Gawky Sally What's-her-name from No-place, California."

"Yeah," he said, "that does sound nice."

"Then after awhile I began to figure out that she'd wanted me there mostly for—well, for protective coloration, sort of. She was living with a college boy then, or graduate student, I guess he was, and she seemed to think it'd sort of look better if there were two women in the house. I finally found a way to ask her about that once, and she was surprised I'd even had to ask—she thought I'd understood from the beginning. Made me feel a little—I don't know—made me feel funny."

"Yeah; I can see that."

"Anyway, the college boy only stuck around for a year or two, and since then there's been quite a parade. I'll just give you the highlights. There was a lawyer who was a friend of her ex-husband's—a friend of my ex-husband's too, which was a little uncomfortable—and there was a man from Germany named Klaus who runs a Volkswagen agency in town. He was nice, and he was very good with Kicker."

"How do you mean, 'good' with him?"

"Well, he'd take him to ball games, or to the movies, and he'd talk to him a lot. That's important for a boy without a father."

"Does he see much of his father?"

"No. It's hard to explain, but no—not at all. Because you see Frank Jarvis has always said he doesn't think he *is* Kicker's father, so he's never wanted anything to do with him."

"Oh."

"Well, you hear of situations like that; it's not uncommon. *Any*way, Klaus moved out after a while, and now Woody's the man in residence. Did you happen to notice the dopey little clown up over the fireplace? That's him—I mean he painted it. Woody Starr. Starr of Hollywood. And I mean of course you can't call him an artist, unless you want to be as dumb about it as Jill is. He's just kind of an amiable guy trying to make a few dollars out of the tourist trade. He has a shop down on Hollywood Boulevard—he always calls it 'the studio'—with his corny little sign hung out over the sidewalk; oh, and he doesn't just do clowns—he does black velvet moonlit lakes and black velvet winter scenes and black velvet mountains with waterfalls and God only knows what the hell else. So anyway, Jill wandered in there one day and thought all that black velvet trash was beautiful. It's always amazing to find out what crummy taste she has, in everything but clothes. And I guess she thought Woody Starr was beautiful too, because she brought him home the same night. That was about three years ago.

"And the funny part is he *is* sort of lovable. He can make you laugh. He's even—interesting, in his own way: been all over the world in the Merchant Marine, knows a lot of stories. I don't know. Woody grows on you. And it's really touching to watch him with Kicker: I think Kicker loves him even more than he loved Klaus."

"Where'd he get that name?"

"What name? Starr?"

"No, the boy."

"'Kicker'? Oh, Jill started that. She used to say he almost kicked her to death before he was born. His real name's Alan, but you'd better not try calling him Al, or anything. Call him Kicker."

By the time Jack got up and went into the house for more drinks he'd decided it would be much better if Sally lived in a regular apartment, like a regular secretary. Still, maybe they could arrange to spend most of their time together out here at the beach; besides, it was too early to worry about stuff like that. All his life, it now seemed, he had spoiled things for himself by worrying too soon.

"Know what, Sally?" he said, carrying their full, cold glasses back outdoors, and he was going to say, "You've got really great legs," but went back to the old topic instead. "It's beginning to sound like you live in a pretty fucked-up household."

"Oh, I know," she said. "Somebody else I knew called it 'degenerate.' That seemed too strong a word, but later I could see what he meant."

It was the first time she had made any reference to "somebody else I knew," or "he," and as Jack sipped at his clicking whiskey he gave in to a sulk of irrational jealousy. How many guys had she met in Edgar Todd's office and gone laughingly out for drinks with, over the years? And she had probably said, to each of them, "Could we make another stop first? Here in Beverly? Because I'll have to pick up a few things, and anyway I'd like you to see where I live." Worse: after thrashing and moaning in each man's bed all night she had probably told him, as she'd told Jack Fields in the small hours of this very morning, that he was "wonderful."

Had they all been writers? If so, what the hell were their names? Oh, there had probably been a few movie directors in there too, and movie technicians, and different kinds of people who had to do with the "packaging" of television shows.

He was making himself feel terrible, and the only way to stop it was to start talking again. "You know, you really look a lot younger than thirty-six, Sally," he said. "I mean except for the—"

"I know; except for the hair. I hate it. It's been gray since I was twenty-four and I used to dye it, but that didn't look right either."

"No, listen, it looks great. I didn't mean—" And hunching earnestly toward her on the lower part of his deck chair he launched into an apology that carried him helplessly from one lame line to another. He said her hair had been the first thing that attracted him, and when her look told him she knew that was a lie he dropped it quickly and tried something else. He said he'd always thought prematurely gray hair could make a pretty girl "interesting" and "mysterious"; he said he was surprised a lot of girls didn't *dye* their hair gray, and that was when she started laughing.

"God, you really like to apologize, don't you. If I let you go on with this, you'd probably go on and on."

"Well, okay," he said, "but listen: let me tell you something else." He moved over to her deck chair, placed one haunch on the edge of it, and began massaging one of her warm, firm thighs with his hand. "I think you've got just about the greatest legs I've ever seen."

"Oh, that feels nice," she said, and her eyelids lowered very slightly. "That really feels nice. You know what, though, Jack? We're going to waste practically the whole afternoon if we don't get up pretty soon and go back in the house and play."

On Monday morning, sore-eyed and jittery from lack of sleep as he drove her back to Edgar Todd's office, he began to be afraid they would never have such a good time again. All future days and nights might wither under the strain of trying to recapture this first weekend. They would discover unpleasant, unattractive things in each other; they would seek and find small grievances; they would quarrel; they would get bored.

He licked his lips. "Can I call you?"

"Whaddya mean, can you call me?" she said. "If you don't, I'll never let you hear the end of it."

She spent several nights of that week with him, and the whole of the next weekend and much of the following week. Not until the end of that time was he obliged to visit Jill Jarvis's house again, and then it was only because Sally insisted that she wanted him to see her apartment upstairs.

"Give me five minutes to get it looking decent, Jack, okay?" she told him in the den. "You wait here and talk to Woody, and I'll come down and get you when I'm ready." So he was left alone and smiling with Woody Starr, who seemed nervous too.

"Well, my only quarrel with you, Jack," Woody said as they sat down in leather armchairs, partly facing each other, "is that you've been keeping Sally away too much. We miss her. It's like losing a member of the family. Whyn't you bring her home more often?" Then, without waiting for an answer, he hurried on as if steady talking were the best-known remedy for shyness. "No, but seriously, though, Sally's one of my favorite people. I think the world of her. She hasn't had an easy life, but nobody'd ever guess it. She's one of the finest human beings I know."

"Yeah," Jack said, making the leather creak as he shifted his weight. "Yeah, she's pretty nice, all right."

Then Kicker came hurrying in from the pool terrace for an intense, animated discussion with Woody Starr about a broken bicycle.

"Well, if the trouble's in the sprocket itself, Kick," Woody said when he'd sorted out the facts, "we'll have to take it into the shop. Be better to let those guys handle it than mess with it ourselves, right?"

"But the shop's *closed*, Woody."

"Well, it's closed for today, but we can take it in tomorrow. What's the big hurry?"

"Oh, I dunno. I was—gonna go down to the firehouse, is all. Some of the guys from school hang around there."

"Hell, I'll run you down there, Kick; no problem."

And the boy seemed to think it over for a few seconds, looking at the rug, before he said, "No, that's okay, Woody. I can go tomorrow, or some other time."

"Ready?" Sally called from the doorway. "Now, if you'll just step this way, sir, I'll take you up and show you my very own professionally decorated apartment."

She led him out into the main living room—all he could see of it was an acre of waxed floor, with mounds of cream-colored upholstery seeming to float in the pink evening light of tall windows—and up the elegant staircase. She took him down a second-story hallway past three or four closed doors; then she opened the final door, whirled inside with a theatrical flourish, and stood beaming there to welcome him.

It *was* as big as three rooms put together, and the ceiling was uncommonly high. The walls were a subtle shade of pale blue that the professional decorator must have considered "right" for Sally, though much of the wall space was given over to glass: huge gilt-framed mirrors on one side and an L-shaped display of French windows along two others, with heavy curtains poised to glide and sweep across their panes. There were two double beds, which Jack thought a little excessive even by professional-decorator standards, and on various chests or end tables around the expanse of deep white carpet stood big pottery lamps whose fabric shades were three or four feet tall. In one corner, at the far end of the room, was a very low, round, black-lacquered table with a floral centerpiece, and with cushions placed at intervals on the floor around it as if in readiness for a Japanese meal; in another, near the entrance, a ceramic umbrella stand held a bouquet of giant peacock feathers.

"Yeah," Jack murmured, turning around and squinting slightly in an effort to take it all in. "Yeah, this is really nice, honey. I can see why you like it."

"Go in and look at the bathroom," she commanded. "You've never seen such a bathroom in your life."

And after inspecting the flawless gleam and splendor of the bathroom, he came back and said, "No, that's really true. You're right. I never have."

He stood peering down at the Japanese table for a moment; then he said, "You ever use this?"

"'Use' it?"

"Oh, well, I just thought you might call up five or six very close friends once in a while, get 'em all up here in their socks and sit 'em cross-legged around this thing, turn down the lights and break out the chopsticks and have yourselves a swell little evening in Tokyo."

There was a silence. "You're making fun of me, Jack," she said, "and I think you're going to find that's not a very good idea."

"Aw, baby, come on. I was only—"

"The *dec*orator put it there," she said. "I wasn't consulted on anything he did because Jill wanted the whole apartment to be a surprise for me. Besides, I've never thought it was funny at all. I think it makes a very nice deco*ra*tion."

And they hadn't yet recovered from that unpleasantness when they went back downstairs and found that a new guest had come to join in the cocktail hour. He was a short, stocky, faintly Oriental-looking young man named Ralph who gathered Sally close in a hug to which she responded with rapture, though she had to stoop for it, and who then held out a stubby hand and told Jack it was nice to meet him.

Ralph was an engineer, Jill Jarvis explained, pronouncing the word as if it were a title of rare distinction, and he'd just been telling of how he'd gone to work for a "marvelous" firm—still a small firm, but growing fast because they were bringing in "wonderful" new contracts. Wasn't that exciting?

"Well, it's my boss who makes it exciting," Ralph said, going back to his chair and his drink. "Cliff Myers. He's a dynamo. Founded the company eight years ago when he was fresh out of the Navy after the Korean war. Began with a couple of routine little Navy contracts, started branching out, and since then there's been no stopping him. Remarkable man. Oh, he drives his people hard, no question about that, but he drives himself harder than any man I've ever known. Give him two or three more years and he'll be the most prominent engineering executive in L.A., if not in all of California."

"Wonderful," Jill said. "And he's still young?"

"Well, thirty-eight; that's pretty young in this business."

"I always love to see that," Jill said fervently, narrowing her eyes. "I love to see a man go out and get what he's after."

And Woody Starr gazed down at his drink with a little smile of self-deprecation, suggesting that he knew perfectly well he hadn't ever gone out after much, or gotten much, except a dumb little souvenir shop on Hollywood Boulevard.

"Is he married?" Jill inquired discreetly.

"Oh yeah, very nice wife; no kids. They have a very nice home out in Pacific Palisades."

"Why don't you bring them over sometime, Ralph? You think they'd enjoy that? Because really, I'd love to meet them."

"Well, sure, Jill," Ralph said, though his face betrayed a flicker of embarrassment. "I'm sure they'd like that a lot."

The talk went on to other things, then—or rather it sank for at least an hour into joshing and banter about nothing at all, or insiders' references to hilarious old times that Jack was unable to follow. He kept looking for opportunities to get Sally up and out of there, but she was so clearly enjoying herself, going along with the laughs, that he could only set his bite and smile to prove his patience.

"Hey, Jill?" Kicker said from the dining-room doorway, and that was the first time Jack noticed that the boy called his mother by her first name. "We ever gonna eat?"

"You go ahead, Kick," she told him. "Ask Nippy to fix you a plate. We'll be along in a while."

". . . And they go through that same dopey routine about dinner every *night*," Sally said later, when she and Jack were alone in his car on the way out to the beach. "Kicker always says, 'We ever gonna eat?' and she always gives him that exact same answer, as if they're *both* trying to pretend it doesn't happen all the time. Sometimes it's ten-thirty or eleven before she feels like eating, and all the food's ruined, but by then everybody's so smashed they don't care. If you could *see* the beautiful cuts of meat that go to waste in that kitchen. Ah, God, if only she could have a little more—I don't know. It's just that I wish—well, never mind. I wish a lot of things."

"I know you do," he said, and reached over with one hand to hold her tense thigh. "So do I."

They rode in silence for what seemed a long time; then she said, "No, but did you like Ralph, Jack?"

"I don't know; hardly had a chance to talk to him."

"Well, I hope you'll get to know him better. Ralph and I've been friends for years. He's a very—a very dear person."

And Jack winced in the darkness. He hadn't heard her use that phrase before, or any of its fudgy little show-business equivalents—"a very sweet man"; "a very gutsy lady." Still, she had been born and raised on the fringes of Hollywood; she had worked for years in a Hollywood agency, hearing Hollywood people talk all day. Was it any wonder that some of their language had seeped into her own?

"Ralph's a Hawaiian," she was saying. "He was a college friend of the other boy I told you about, the one Jill was living with when I moved in. And I think Jill felt sorry for him, this painfully shy Hawaiian kid who never seemed to have any fun. Then it turned out he needed a place to live, so she let him have the big ground-floor apartment in the main outbuilding—you know the one with all the French doors? Facing the pool? Well, wow, talk about having fun. It changed his life. He told me once—this was years later, after he'd moved away—he said, 'Oh, it'd usually be like pulling teeth to get girls to go out with me, because I guess that's what you have to expect if you're a funny-looking little guy with the wrong kind of clothes, but once they saw where I lived, once they saw that *place*, it was magic.' He said, 'Get two or three drinks into a girl and she'd be out skinny-dipping in the pool with me every time. And after that,' he said, 'after that, all the rest of it was a piece of cake.'" And Sally's voice dissolved in a rich little peal of lewd laughter.

"Yeah, well, that's nice," Jack said. "That's a nice story."

"And then," Sally went on, "then he told me, he said, 'Oh, I always knew it was phony. I knew that whole setup at Jill's was phony. But I used to say to myself, Ralph, if you're gonna be a phony, you might as well be a *real* phony.' Isn't that sweet? I mean in its own kind of awkward, funny way, isn't that sweet?"

"Yeah. Sure is."

But later that night, lying awake while Sally slept, listening to the heavy gathering and pound and rumble and hiss of each wave on the beach, time and again, he wondered if Sheilah Graham had ever referred to someone as being "a very dear person." Well, maybe, or maybe she had used whatever other Hollywood jargon was current in her time, and Fitzgerald probably hadn't minded at all. *He* knew she would never be Zelda; that was one of the ways he knew he loved her. Holding himself together every day for her, dying for a drink but staying away from it, putting what little energy he had into those sketchy opening chapters of *The Last Tycoon*, he must have been humbly grateful just to have her there.

For weeks they were as domestic as a married couple. Except during her hours in the office they were always together at his place. They took long walks on the beach, finding new beachside places to have a drink when they were tired. They talked for hours—"You could *never* bore me," she said, making his lungs feel deeper than they'd felt in years—and he found he was making much better progress on the screenplay. He could look up from his manuscript after dinner and see her curled on the plastic sofa in the lamplight, knitting—she was making a heavy sweater for Kicker's birthday—and that vision never failed to please his sense of order and peace.

But it didn't last. Before the summer was half over, he was startled one evening to find her watching him in a keen, sad, bright-eyed way.

"What's the matter?"

"I can't stay here anymore, Jack, that's all. I mean it. It's gotten so I absolutely can't bear this place. It's cramped and dark and damp—Jesus, it's not damp, it's *wet*."

"*This* room's always dry," he said defensively, "and it's always light too, in the daytime. Sometimes it gets so bright I have to close the—"

"Well, but this room's only about five feet *square*," she said, standing up for emphasis, "and the rest of it's a rotten old tomb. You know what I found on the floor of the shower stall this morning? I found this terrible little pale, transparent worm, sort of like a snail only without any shell, and I accidentally stepped on it about four times before

I realized what the hell I was doing. Jesus!" She gave a profound shudder, letting the ragged gray clump of her knitting fall to the floor as she clasped and held herself with both arms, and Jack was reminded of his daughter in that other loathsome shower stall, back in New York.

"And the bedroom!" Sally said. "That mattress is about a hundred years old and it's all sour and it reeks of mildew. And no matter where I hang my clothes they're always clammy when I put them on in the morning. So I've had it, Jack, that's all. I'm never going into the office again wearing wet clothes and having to squirm around and *scratch* myself all day, and that's final."

And from the way she bustled around getting her things together after that speech, packing the Mexican bag and a small suitcase too, it was clear that she didn't even plan to stay for the night. Jack sat biting his lip, trying to think of something to say; then he got to his feet because that seemed better than sitting.

"I'm going home, Jack," she said. "You're perfectly welcome to come with me, and in fact I'd really like you to, but that part of it's entirely up to you."

It didn't take him long to make up his mind. He argued with her a little and feigned exasperation, for the sake of his rapidly diminishing pride, but in less than half an hour he was riding tense at the wheel of his car and following the taillights of hers at a respectful distance. He had even brought along the stacked pages of his screenplay and a supply of fresh paper and pencils, because she'd assured him there were any number of big, clean, well-appointed rooms in Jill's house where he could work all day in total privacy, if that was what he might decide he wanted to do. "And I mean really, wouldn't it be better to spend the rest of our time together at my place?" she'd said. "Come on. You know it would. And how much time do we have left anyway? Seven weeks or something? Six?"

So it happened that Jack Fields became, briefly, a resident of that Greek Revival mansion in Beverly Hills. Giving more thanks than he felt, he accepted the use of an upstairs room to work in—it even had a bathroom that was nearly as opulent as Sally's—and their nights together were spent in her "apartment," where neither of them ever mentioned the Japanese dinner table again.

During the cocktail hour each day it was necessary to associate with Jill Jarvis and to be drawn, however reluctantly, into her world, but at first, after a drink or two and an exchange of winks, they would manage to escape to a restaurant and an evening of their own. Later, though, more and more often and to Jack's increasing annoyance, Sally would go on drinking and talking with whatever guests of Jill's were there until they'd find themselves caught up in the ritual of the late, late dinner at home—until the plump uniformed Negro maid named Nippy appeared in the doorway saying, "Miz Jarvis? There isn't gonna be nothing left of this meat at all unless you folks come and eat it pretty soon."

Stiff and swaying, their eyes barely able to focus on their plates, the party would pick at blackened steak and shrunken, wrinkled vegetables until, as if in acknowledgment of a common revulsion, they would leave most of their dinner untouched and go back to the den to drink again. And the worst part was that Jack too, by this time, would find he wanted nothing more than more to drink. He and Sally, on some of those nights, were too drunk for anything but sleep as they climbed the reeling stairs; he would crawl alone into her bed and pass out, waking many hours later to lie listening to the slow rasp of her breath, discovering more than once that it came from the other double bed.

He had learned that he didn't much like Sally when she drank. Her eyes would grow startlingly bright, her upper lip would loosen and bloat, and she'd laugh as stridently as an unpopular schoolgirl over things he didn't think were funny at all.

Late one afternoon the young Hawaiian, Ralph, dropped in again, but this time, despite happy cries of greeting and welcome from the girls, he was a solemn bearer of terrible news as he eased himself into a leather chair.

"You know the head of my firm I was telling you about?" he said. "Cliff Myers? His wife died this morning. Heart attack. Collapsed in the bathroom. Thirty-five years old." And lowering his eyes he took a hesitant sip of scotch as if it were a funereal sacrament.

Jill and Sally came urgently forward in their cushions to stare at him, their eyes round and their mouths instantly shaped for the syllable "Oh!" that burst from them in unison. Then Sally said, "My God!" and Jill, slumping weakly with one wrist against her lovely forehead, said, "Thirty-five years old. Oh, the poor man. The poor man."

Neither Jack nor Woody Starr had yet joined in the grief, but after quick self-conscious glances at each other they were able to murmur appropriate things.

"Was there any history of heart trouble at *all*?" Sally demanded.

"None at all," Ralph assured her. "None at all."

And for once, in these endless cocktail times, they had something substantial to talk about. Cliff Myers was a man of iron, Ralph told them. If he hadn't proved that in his professional career—and God knew he certainly had—then he'd proved it this morning. First he had tried and failed to administer mouth-to-mouth resuscitation on the bathroom floor; then he'd wrapped his wife in a blanket, carried her out to the car and driven her to the hospital, knowing she was probably dead all the way. The doctors there wanted to give him a sedative after they'd broken the news, but you didn't just go around giving sedatives to a man like Cliff Myers. He had driven home alone, and by nine-fifteen—nine-fifteen!—he had called the office to explain why he wouldn't be in for work today.

"Oh!" Sally cried. "Oh, God, I can't bear this. I can't bear this"—and she got up and ran from the room in tears.

Jack followed her quickly into the living room but she wouldn't let him put his arms around her, and he realized at once that he didn't really mind the refusal.

"Hey, come on, Sally," he said, standing several feet apart from her with his hands in his pockets while she wept, or seemed to weep. "Come on. Take it easy."

"Well, but things like this up*set* me, that's all; I can't help it. I'm *sen*sitive, that's all."

"Yeah, well, okay; okay."

"A girl with everything to live for," she said in a quavering voice, "and her whole life going out like that—click—and then *whump* on the bathroom floor; oh, God. Oh, God."

"Well, but look," he said. "Don't you think you're overdoing this a little? I mean you didn't even know the girl and you don't know the man either, so it's really like something you've read in the paper, right? And the point is you can read stuff like this in the paper every day, over your chicken-salad sandwich, and it doesn't necessarily make you—"

"Oh, Jesus, chicken-salad sandwich," she said with loathing, looking him harshly up and down as she backed away. "You really are a cold bastard, aren't you. You know something? You know what I've just begun to figure out about you? You're a cold, unfeeling son of a bitch and you don't care about anything in the world but yourself and your rotten self-indulgent scribbling and no *wonder* your wife couldn't stand the sight of you."

And she was halfway up the stairs before he decided that his best reply was to make no reply at all. He went back into the den to finish his drink and try to figure things out, and he was doing that when Kicker came in with a lumpy, badly rolled sleeping bag on his shoulder.

"Hey, Woody?" the boy said. "You ready?"

"Sure, Kick." Woody got quickly to his feet and knocked back his whiskey, and they left the house together. Jill, huddled with Ralph in an intense discussion of Cliff Myers's tragedy, barely glanced up to wish them good night.

After awhile Jack went upstairs, walked on mincing tiptoe past Sally's closed door and struck off down an adjoining hall to gather up the screenplay and the other personal stuff that had accumulated in "his" room; then he went back downstairs and made a nervous departure past Jill and Ralph, who paid him no attention.

He would wait a few days before calling Sally at the office. If they could make it up, that would be fine, though probably never as fine as before. And if not, well, hell, weren't there plenty of other girls in Los Angeles? Weren't there girls much younger than Sally who cavorted in marvelously scanty bathing suits on the sand beyond his window every day? Or couldn't he ask Carl Oppenheimer to introduce him to one of the many, many girls Carl Oppenheimer seemed to know? Besides, there were only a few weeks left before he'd be done with the script and back in New York, so who the hell cared?

But as his car hummed through the darkness toward Malibu he knew that line of reasoning was nonsense. Drunken and foolish or not, gray-haired or not, Sally Baldwin was the only woman in the world.

Until an hour before dawn that night he sat drinking in his chill, damp bedroom, hearing the surf and breathing the mildew from his hundred-year-old mattress, allowing himself to entertain the thought that he might be a self-destructive personality after all. What saved him, enabling him to lie down and cover himself with sleep at last, was his knowledge that any number of sanctimonious people had agreed to hang that bleak and terrible label on F. Scott Fitzgerald too.

Sally called up two days later and said, in a shy and guarded voice, "You still mad at me?"

And he assured her that he wasn't, while his right hand gripped the phone as if for life and his left made wide, mindless gestures in the air to prove his sincerity.

"Well, okay, I'm glad," she said. "And I'm sorry, Jack. Really. I know I drink too much and everything. And I've felt awful since you left, and I miss you an awful lot. So look: You think you might come in this afternoon and meet me at the Beverly Wilshire? You know? Where we had our first drink together, way back whenever it was?"

And all the way to that well-remembered bar he made heartfelt plans for the kind of reconciliation that might make them both feel young and strong again. If she could get a little time off from work they could take a trip together—up to San Francisco or down to Mexico—or else he could move out of the damned beach house and find a better place to stay with her in town.

But almost from the moment Sally sat down with him, when they were holding hands as tightly on the table as they'd done that other time, it was clear that Sally had other ideas.

"Well, I'm furious with Jill," she began. "Absolutely furious. It's been one ridiculous thing after another. First of all we went to the hairdresser yesterday—we always do that together—and on the way home she said she thought we ought to stop going places together. I said, 'What do you mean? What're you talking about, Jill?' And she said, 'I think people think we're lesbians.' Well, it made me sick, that's all. Made me sick.

"And then last night she called Ralph and asked him—oh, and in this very low, suggestive voice too—asked him to invite Cliff Myers over for dinner tonight. Can you believe that? I said, 'Jill, that's tasteless.' I said, 'Look: a month or two from now it might be a thoughtful gesture, but the man's wife's only been dead two *days*. Can't you see how—how tasteless that is?' And she said, 'I don't care if it is.' She said, 'I've got to meet that man. I'm helplessly attracted to everything that man stands for.'

"Oh, and it's even worse than that, Jack. Because you see Woody Starr has this lousy little apartment in the back of his studio? Where he used to live before he moved in with Jill? And I think it's against the law—I mean I think there's a city ordinance that merchants aren't supposed to sleep in their shops—but anyway, sometimes he takes Kicker down there to bunk in for a night or two with him, and they cook breakfast for themselves and stuff; I guess it's sort of like camping out. So they've spent the past couple of nights there, and today Jill called me at the office in this terrible fit of giggles—she sounded about sixteen—and said, 'Guess what. I've just conned Woody into keeping Kicker in the studio another night. Isn't that neat?' I said, 'What do you mean?' And she said, 'Oh, don't be dense, Sally. Now they won't be here to spoil everything when Cliff *Myers* comes over.' I said, 'Well, in the first place, Jill, what makes you think he'll come over at all?' And she said, 'Didn't I tell you? Ralph called this morning and confirmed it. He's bringing Cliff Myers to the house at six o'clock.'"

"Oh," Jack said.

"And so listen, Jack. It'll probably be awful, watching her try to seduce that poor guy, but will you—will you come home with me? Because the point is I don't want to go through it alone."

"Why go through it at all? We can get a room somewhere—hell, we can get a room right here, if you like."

"And not even have clean clothes in the morning?" she said. "Go to work in this same terrible dress? No thanks."

"That's dumb, Sally. Make a quick run up to the house, get your clothes and come back, and then we'll—"

"Look, Jack. If you don't want to come along with me you certainly don't have to, but I'm going anyway. I mean everything may be sick and degenerate or whatever you want to call it in that house, but it's my home."

"Oh, shit, you know better than that. Whaddya mean 'home,' for Christ's sake? That fucking menagerie couldn't be *any*body's home."

She looked at him in an offended, willfully humorless way, like someone whose religion has been held up to ridicule. "It's the only home I have, Jack," she said quietly.

"*Balls!*" And several people at neighboring tables looked quickly up and around at him, with startled faces. "I mean goddamnit, Sally," he said, trying and failing to lower his voice, "if it gives you some kind of perverse pleasure to lie back and let Jill fucking Jarvis parade her depravity through your life, that's something you really ought to take up with some fucking psy*chi*atrist instead of me."

"Sir," a waiter said at his elbow, "I'll have to ask you to keep your voice down and watch your language. You can be heard all over this room."

"It's all right," Sally told the waiter. "We're leaving."

On the way out of the place, torn between more reckless shouting and abject apologies for having shouted at all, Jack hung his head and walked stiffly, in silence.

"Well," she said when they reached her parked car in the dazzling afternoon sun, "you were really attractive in there, weren't you? You really gave a memorable performance, didn't you? How can I ever go *in* there again without getting funny looks from the waiters and everyone else?"

"Yeah, well, you can write it all down in your memory book."

"Oh, good. And my memory book is getting so wonderfully full, isn't it? What a pleasure it'll be when I'm sixty years old. Look, Jack. You coming or staying?"

"I'll follow you," he said, and he wondered at once, as he moved away to his own car, why he hadn't had the guts to say, "Staying."

Then he was following her among the slender palms of the first shallow rise of Beverly Hills, and then they were bringing their cars to a halt in Jill's big driveway, where the cars of two other visitors were already parked. Sally slammed her car door a little harder than necessary and stood waiting, ready to deliver a smiling speech that she'd probably prepared and rehearsed during the short drive from the hotel.

"Well, if nothing else," she said, "this should be interesting. I mean wouldn't any woman want to meet a man like Cliff Myers? He's young, he's rich, he's going places, and he's available. Wouldn't it be funny if I snare him away from Jill before she even gets her hands on him?"

"Ah, come on, Sally."

"Whaddya mean, 'come on'? Whadda *you* got to say about it? You really take a hell of a lot for granted, you know that?" They had made their way up onto the pool terrace and were approaching the big French doors of the den. "I mean in four more weeks you'll have gone back to wherever the hell you came from, so what am I supposed to do in the meantime? Am I really supposed to sit around and *knit* while every halfway decent man in the world passes me by?"

"Sally and Jack," Jill said solemnly from a leather sofa, "I'd like you to meet Cliff Myers." And Cliff Myers rose from his place close beside her to accept the introductions. He was tall and thick, in a rumpled suit, and his short hair stood upright in the blond bristles of a crew cut that made him look like a big, blunt-faced boy. Sally went to him first and told him of her sorrow for his terrible loss; Jack hoped a similar message might be conveyed in the dead-serious way he shook hands.

"Well, as I was just telling Jill," Cliff Myers said when they were all settled, "I've sure been racking up a lot of sympathy points. Walked into the office yesterday and a couple of the secretaries started crying; stuff like that. Went out to lunch with a client today and I thought the maiter dee was gonna start crying on me too. The waiter too. Funny business, this sympathy-getting bit. Too bad you can't put it in the bank, right? 'Course, it prob'ly won't last, so I may as well enjoy it while I can, right? Hey, Jill? Mind if I help myself to a little more of the Grand-dad?"

She told him to sit still, and she made the fixing and serving of his drink into a little ceremony of selfless admiration. When he took the first sip she watched carefully to make sure it was just to his liking.

Then Ralph came staggering into the room on rubber legs, comically exaggerating the heaviness of a load of firewood he held against his chest. "Hey, know what?" he said. "This really takes me back to old times. Jill used to work the hell out of me when I lived here, you see, Cliff," he explained as he crouched and dropped the wood in a neat pile on the hearth. "That was how I paid my rent. And I swear to God, you'd never guess how much work there is to do around a place like this."

"Oh, I can imagine," Cliff Myers said. "You got a really big—a really big place here."

Ralph straightened up and brushed shreds of bark from his rep tie and Oxford shirt, then from the lapels and sleeves of his trim hopsack jacket. He might still be a funny-looking little guy, but he no longer wore the wrong kind of clothes. Dusting his hands, he smiled shyly at his employer. "Nice, though, isn't it, Cliff?" he said. "I knew you'd like it here."

And Cliff Myers assured him that it was very nice, very fine indeed.

"I suppose it may seem funny to have a fire in the summertime," Jill said, "but it does get chilly here at night."

"Oh, yeah," Cliff said. "Out on the Palisades we used to light fires in the evening all year round. My wife always liked to have a fire." And Jill conspicuously squeezed his heavy hand.

Dinner was on time that night, but Jack Fields ate almost nothing. He brought a full drink to the table and went back once or twice to replenish it; as soon as the unusually elaborate meal was over he sank into a shadowed corner of the den, well away from the party, and went on drinking. He knew this was his third or fourth consecutive night of drunkenness, but he could worry about that some other time. He couldn't rid himself of Sally's saying, "He's young, he's rich, he's going places, and he's available," and whenever he looked up now he could see the profile of her pretty head on its elegant neck, glowing in the firelight, smiling or laughing or saying, "Oh, that's marvelous," in response to whatever dumb, dumb remark this bereaved stranger, this asshole Cliff Myers, had just made.

Soon he found he couldn't even watch her anymore because a heavy dark mist had closed in on all four sides of his vision, causing his head to droop and hang until the only thing he could see at all—and he saw it with the terrible clarity of self-hatred—was his own left shoe on the carpet.

". . . Hey, uh, Jack?"

"Uh?"

"I said wanna gimme a hand?" It was Ralph's voice. "Come on."

"Uh. Uh. Wai' second. Okay." And with energy that came from nowhere, or from the desperate last reserves of shame, he forced himself up and followed Ralph rapidly out into the kitchen and down the cellar stairs, nearly falling, until they came to a heap of firewood against the cellar wall. Off to one side, by itself, lay a log cut to fireplace length that must have been two feet thick: it looked like a sawed-off segment of telephone pole, and it held the full weight of Jack's drunken scrutiny. "Son of a bitch," he said.

"What'sa matter?"

"That's the biggest fucking log I ever saw in my life."

"Yeah, well, never mind that," Ralph said. "We just want the little stuff." And with double armloads of the little stuff piled to their chins they went back upstairs, all the way up to the second floor and into the high, wide emptiness of Jill's bedroom, or Jill's and Woody Starr's bedroom, which Jack had never seen before. At the far end of it, well away from the hearth where Ralph squatted to unload the wood, many yards of white cloth were hung from the ceiling and draped partly around the borders of a great "Hollywood" bed to form a bower that might have been dreamed by an adolescent girl as the last word in luxury and romance.

"Okay," Ralph said. "That'll do the job." And though he was plainly drunk himself, swaying on his haunches, he began the meticulous task of building and lighting a fire between the polished brass andirons.

Jack did his best to leave the room quickly but kept veering sideways against the near wall; then he decided it might be helpful to use the wall for support and guidance, letting one shoulder slide heavily along it while he gave his whole attention to lifting and placing his feet in the deep champagne-colored carpet. He knew dimly that Ralph had finished at the fireplace, had lurched past him muttering, "Come on," and gone away into the hall, leaving him alone in this treacherously unstable but mercifully open room; he could see too that the bright doorway was very near now—only a few more steps—but his knees had begun to soften and buckle. He thought he could feel his shoulder sliding down the wall, rather than along it; then the tilting yellow carpet came slowly closer until it offered itself up as a logical, necessary surface for his hands, and for the side of his face.

Sometime later the sounds of low voices and laughter brought him awake. He lay staring at the open door and calculating whether he'd be able to make a run for it, knowing suddenly that Jill Jarvis and Cliff Myers were huddled together on this same carpet at the fireplace, ten or fifteen feet behind his head.

"So what's with this character on the floor?" Cliff Myers inquired. "He live here too?"

"Well, sort of," Jill said, "but he's harmless. He belongs to Sally. She'll come get him out in a minute, or else Ralph will, or else he'll get himself out. Don't worry about it."

"Hell, I'm not worried about anything. Just wondering how I can get this log settled in there without burning my mitts, is all. Sit back a second. There. That's got it."

And Jack took drunken, disdainful notice of Cliff Myers's saying "mitts" instead of hands. Only a dumb son of a bitch would say that, even when constricted with the shyness of flirtation, even if still in shock over his wife's death.

"Know something?" Jill said quietly. "You're quite a guy, Cliff."

"Yeah? Well, you're quite a girl."

There then began moist little sounds of kissing, and pleased, purring moans that suggested he was feeling her up. A zipper raced open (The back of her dress? The front of his pants?) and that was the last thing Jack Fields heard as he clambered to his feet and got the hell out of there and shut the door behind him.

He wasn't yet in good enough shape to find his way to Sally's room; all he could do was sit at the top of the stairs with his head in his hands, waiting for balance. After a few minutes he felt the whole staircase shuddering, and Ralph's voice called, "Coming through! Coming through, please!" The sturdy little Hawaiian was climbing the stairs with remarkable speed and agility. His straining face gleamed with happiness, and in his arms he carried the single giant log from the cellar. "Coming through, please!" he called again as Jack made way for him, and without pausing to knock at the bedroom door he shouldered it open and lunged inside. There was just enough light to show that Jill Jarvis and Cliff Myers had left the fireplace; they were evidently in the bed. "Sorry, miss!" Ralph called as he hurried with his burden to the hearthside, "Sorry, sir! Compliments of the Company Commander!" And he dumped the great log onto the fire with a terrible thump that made the andirons ring and sent up a multitude of orange sparks.

"Oh, Ralph, you *idiot*!" Jill cried from within her bower. "Get *outa* here now!"

But Ralph was already leaving as quickly as he'd come, giggling at how funny it must have looked, and he was followed by rich, hearty peals of baritone laughter from the bed—the laughter of a man who might soon be the most prominent engineering executive in all of California, and who had always prided himself on knowing how to spot real talent in the young fellows he put on his payroll.

"Well, I guess neither of us were exactly at our best," Sally said the next morning, trying to do something about her hair at the mirror of her dressing table. It was Saturday: she wouldn't have to go to work, but she said she didn't know what else she wanted to do.

Jack was still in bed and wondering if it might be wise to drink nothing but beer, in moderation, for the rest of his life. "I guess I'll go back to the beach," he said. "Try and get some work done."

"Okay." She got up and drifted aimlessly to one of her many French windows. "Oh, Jesus, come and look at this," she said. "I mean really. Come and look." And he struggled up to join her at the window, which overlooked the swimming pool. Cliff Myers lay floating in the water, on his back, wearing a pair of maroon trunks that must surely have belonged to Woody Starr. Jill stood at the edge of the pool in a stunningly brief bikini, apparently calling to him, holding out a bright cocktail glass in either hand.

"Brandy Alexanders," Sally explained. "When I went down to the kitchen for coffee, Nippy gave me this big worried look and said, 'Sally? You know how to make a brandy Alexander?' She said, 'Miz Jarvis told me to make up a whole batch of 'em, and the trouble is I don't know how. We got a book on it somewhere?'" And Sally sighed. "Well, so everything worked out nicely, didn't it. Mr. Myers and Mrs. Jarvis are seen enjoying their breakfast cocktails at poolside, on the third morning after the late Mrs. Myers's death." After a silence she said, "Still, I suppose this is a little healthier for Jill than the way she's spent all her *other* mornings as long as I've known her—lying in bed till noon with her coffee and her cigarettes and her endless, mindless fucking *cross*word puzzles."

"Yeah, well, look, Sally. You want to come home with me?"

And she answered him without taking her eyes from the window. "I don't know; I don't think so. We'd just start fighting again. I'll call you, Jack, okay?"

"Okay."

"Besides," she said, "I ought to be here when Woody and Kicker come home. I think I might be able to help. Oh, not Woody, of course, but Kicker. I mean Kicker loves me—or at least he used to. Sometimes he used to call me his 'proxy mother.'" She lingered silent at the window for a long time, looking jaded, her upper lip beginning to loosen the way it did when she was drunk. "Have you any idea," she asked, "of what it means to be a woman unable to have a child? Even if you don't necessarily want one, it's a terrible thing to discover you can't; and sometimes—oh, God, I don't know. Sometimes I think having a child is all I've ever really wanted in my whole life."

On his unsteady way out of the house, Jack went into the kitchen and said, "Hey, uh, Nippy? Think you could find me a beer?"

"Well, I believe that can be arranged, Mr. Fields," the maid said. "Sit right here at the table." When he was settled with the beer she sat

And with her door locked against any possibility of blundering intrusion, they spent the whole afternoon being as nice to each other as either of them had ever learned to be. Only after the long bank of Sally's western windows had gone from gold to crimson to dark blue did they rouse themselves at last to take showers, and to put on their clothes.

Then, before very long, Sally went back to the inexhaustible topic of Jill's behavior. She paced the carpet on her slim, stockinged feet as she talked, and Jack thought she had never looked prettier. But he let most of her talk go past his hearing, nodding or shaking his head at whatever intervals seemed appropriate, usually after she had whirled to stare at him in mute appeal for endorsement of her dismay. He began paying attention only when she got around to what she called the worst part.

". . . Because I mean really, Jack, the worst part of all this is what it's doing to Kick. Jill thinks he doesn't know what's going on, but she's crazy. He does. He mopes around the house all day looking pale and wretched and as if he's about to—I don't know. And he won't even let me talk to him. He won't let me comfort him or be friends with him or anything. And for the past two nights you know what he's done? He's taken off alone on his bike and spent the night with Woody, down in the studio. I don't think Jill even noticed he was gone, either time."

"Yeah, well, that's—that's too bad."

"Oh, and he hates Cliff. Absolutely hates him. Whenever Cliff says anything to him he freezes up—and I don't blame him. Because you know something else, Jack? You were right about Cliff from the start and I was wrong, that's all. He's nothing but a big, dumb—he's a dullard."

On Jill's instructions, Nippy had fed the boy at least an hour before the adults' dinner was served. She had also equipped the big dining-room table with two matching silver candleholders, each bearing three new candles, and she'd turned out the lights so that everything was bathed in a flickering glow of romance.

"Isn't this nice?" Jill inquired. "I always forget about candles. I think we ought to have candles every night." And the way she was dressed suggested other forgotten things well worth remembering, perhaps her own swift and careless girlhood as a privileged daughter of the South. She wore a simple, expensive-looking black dress with a neckline low enough to show the beginnings of her small, firm breasts, and a single strand of pearls that she twisted nervously at her throat with her free hand while toying with her food.

Cliff Myers was flushed and jovial with Old Grand-dad. He told one smiling, self-aggrandizing anecdote after another about his engineering firm, with Jill pronouncing each story "wonderful" in turn; then he said, "No, but listen, another thing, Jill. This you gotta hear. First of all, I find I get some of my best thinking done when I'm driving the freeway to work. Don't know why that's true, but I've learned to trust it. So. Know what I thought up this morning?" He efficiently sliced open his baked potato and lowered his face to savor the rising heat of it, making his audience wait. He heavily buttered and salted it, forked up a slice of lamb chop, and looked happily reflective as he chewed; then, talking around the meat, he said, "How's this for openers?" And he swallowed. "We've got this very high-grade industrial glue in the lab. You wouldn't believe it. Paint that stuff on any metal surface, touch it, and I swear to God you can't get your hand loose. Try soap and water, try any kinda detergent, try alcohol, or you name it. Can't get loose. So look." Almost half a chop went into his mouth, but he was scarcely able to chew because he had begun to laugh. "Look: supposing I get this little truck." He broke off, helpless with laughter, one hand spanning his forehead while he struggled for composure. Of his three listeners, only Jill was smiling.

"So okay," Cliff Myers said at last, and his mouth was apparently clear. "Supposing I get one of our company panel trucks. Supposing I dress up in one of our drivers' uniforms—they wear these kind of cream-colored coveralls with the insignia on the front pocket and the company name spelled out across the back? With these visor caps? And of course the truck's got the company name on it too, you follow me? 'Myers'? So I come driving up here with this aluminum tub fulla roses—three, four dozen American Beauties, the very best—and of course when I bring it out I'll be real careful to hold it by the dry part, so *my* mitts'll be free; then your little friend Woody'll come out there on the terrace to see what's up, and I'll say, 'Mr. Starr?' And I'll shove that slick, glued-up tub into his hands and say, 'Flowers, sir. Flowers for Mrs. Jarvis. Compliments of Cliff Myers.' And I'll get back into the truck and take off, or maybe I'll stay just long enough to kind of wink at him, and old Starr of Hollywood'll just *be* there. He'll just *be* there, you follow me? It'll take him maybe thirty seconds to figure out he's *stuck* to the son of a bitch, and maybe five or ten minutes more to realize he's been had, he's been faked out, somebody's pulled a fast one on him, and I swear to God, Jill, I'd bet money—I'd bet *money* the little bastard'll never bother you again."

Jill had looked enraptured through the latter part of his recital; now she squeezed his hand on the table with both of her own and said, "Marvelous. Oh, that's marvelous, Cliff," and they laughed together, looking each other up and down with bright eyes.

"Jill," Sally said from across the table, after awhile. "This is just a joke, isn't it."

"Well, of *course* it is," Jill said impatiently, as if reproving a slow child. "It's an absolutely inspired idea for a practical joke. The men in Cliff's firm play practical jokes on each other all the time—I think it's a delightful way to survive all the dull and boring parts of life, don't you?"

"Well, but I mean, you'd certainly never agree to going through with a thing like that, would you."

"Oh, I don't know," Jill said in a light, teasing voice. "Maybe; maybe not. But don't you think it's a delightfully wicked idea?"

"I think you're out of your mind," Sally told her.

"Oh, I think so too," she said with an attractive little wrinkling of her nose. "I think Cliff is too. Isn't that what it means to be in love?"

Later that night, when Jack and Sally were alone, she said, "I don't even want to talk about it. I don't want to talk about it or think about it or anything, okay?"

And it certainly was. Any time Sally was unwilling to talk or think about Jill Jarvis was perfectly okay with Jack.

The following night he took her to a restaurant for dinner, and then out for an evening at the home of Carl Oppenheimer.

"Jesus," she said as they drove up the coast highway toward the better part of Malibu, "I'm really a little scared to meet him, you know?"

"Why?"

"Well, because of who he *is*. He's one of the few major—"

"Come on, Sally. There isn't anything 'major' about him. He's only a movie director and he's only thirty-two years old."

"Are you out of your mind? He's brilliant. He's one of the two or three top directors in the industry. Have you any idea how lucky you are to be working with him?"

"Well, okay, but then, does he have any idea how lucky he is to be working with me?"

"God," she said. "You've got an ego that nobody'd believe. Tell me something: If you're so great, how come your clothes are all falling apart? And how come you've got snails in your shower stall? Huh? And how come your bed smells like death?"

"Jack!" Carl Oppenheimer called from the bright doorway of his house, after they'd walked the long, heavily leaf-shadowed path from the place where they'd left the car. "And you're Sally," he said with an earnest frown. "*Really* nice to meet you."

She said it was certainly an honor to meet him too, and they went inside to where young Ellis stood smiling in welcome, wearing a floor-length dress. She looked lovely, and she rose on tiptoe to give Jack an eager little kiss of old acquaintance, which he hoped Sally would notice; then, as they moved chatting pleasantly into the big room overlooking the ocean, where the liquor was, she turned to Sally again and said, "I love your hair. Is that the natural color, or do you—"

"No, it's natural," Sally told her. "I just get it streaked."

"Sit down, sit down!" Oppenheimer commanded, but he chose to remain standing himself, or rather walking, slowly treading the floor of this ample and excellent room with a heavy glass of bourbon tinkling in one hand while the other made large gestures to accompany his talk. He was telling of his frustrations over the past few weeks in trying to finish a movie that was well behind schedule, and of how "impossible" it was to work with its star—an actor so famous that the very mention of his name was a kind of conversational triumph.

". . . And then today," he said, "today everything on the set had to stop dead—cameras, sound, everything—while he took me off in a corner and sat me down to discuss what he called Dramatic Theory, and he asked me if I was familiar with the work of a playwright named George Bernard Shaw. You think anybody'd believe that? You think anybody in America'd believe how dumb the son of a bitch is? Christ's sake, this year he's discovered Shaw; three years from now he'll discover the Communist Party."

Oppenheimer seemed to tire of his monologue after awhile; he came heavily to rest in a deep sofa and put his arm around Ellis, who nestled close to him; then he asked Sally if she was an actress too.

"Oh, no," she said quickly, brushing invisible specks of cigarette ash off her lap, "but thanks anyway. I don't really do anything very—I'm only—I'm a secretary. I work for Edgar Todd, the agent."

"Well, hell, that's fine with me," Oppenheimer said expansively. "Some of my best friends are secretaries." And as if aware that this last line might not have been wholly successful, he hurried on to ask her how long she'd worked for Edgar, and how she liked her job, and where she lived.

"I live in Beverly," she told him. "I have an apartment in the home of a friend there; it's very nice."

"Yeah, well, that's—nice," he said. "I mean Beverly's very nice."

For the last hour or so of that evening in Oppenheimer's house, Jack found himself perched cozily with Ellis on two of the tall, leather-topped stools along the bar that occupied one side of the room. She told him at length of her childhood in Pennsylvania, of the summer stock company that had provided her first real "experience of theater," and of the wonderfully lucky sequence of events that had led to her meeting Carl. And Jack was so pleased with her youth and prettiness, and so flattered by her attention, that he only dimly realized he had heard the whole story before, during the time he'd stayed here.

Across the room, Carl and Sally were engaged in a steady and intense discussion. Jack couldn't hear much of it, in the several times he tried to listen, beyond the insistent, dead-serious rumble of Carl's voice, though once he heard Sally say, "Oh, no, I loved it. Really. I loved it all the way through."

"Well, this's been great," Carl Oppenheimer said when it was time for them to leave. "Sally. Wonderful meeting you; good talking to you. Jack: we'll be in touch."

And then came the long, drink-fuddled ride back to town. For what seemed twenty minutes there was silence in the car, until Sally said, "They've sort of—got everything, haven't they. I mean they're young, they're in love, and everybody knows he's a brilliant man so it doesn't really matter whether she's got any talent or not because she's a cute little sexpot anyway. What could ever go wrong in a house like that?"

"Oh, I don't know; I can think of a couple of things that might go wrong."

"You know what I really didn't like about him, though?" she said. "I didn't like the way he kept asking me what I thought of his movies.

He'd mention one picture after another and ask me if I'd seen it, and then he'd say, 'So what'd you think? Did you like it?' Or he'd say, 'Didn't you think it kind of fell apart in the second half?' Or 'Didn't you feel so-and-so was a little miscast as the girl?' And I mean really, Jack. Isn't that a bit much?"

"Why?"

"Well, because who am *I*?" She rolled her window half open and snapped her cigarette away into the wind. "I mean Jesus, after all, who am *I*?"

"Whaddya mean, who are you?" he said. "I know who you are, and so does Oppenheimer, and so do you. You're Sally Baldwin."

"Yeah, yeah," she said quietly, facing the black window. "Yeah, yeah, yeah, yeah."

When they walked into the Beverly Hills house, Jack was startled to find Woody Starr instead of Cliff Myers sitting with Jill, until he remembered Sally's telling him that Cliff had agreed to stay away for a night or two so that Jill could sensibly and permanently disengage herself from Woody. And the way Woody looked now as he rose from the sofa to greet them—drawn, shamefaced, seeming to apologize for his very presence—made it clear that Jill had already broken the news.

"Well, hey, Sally," he said. "Hello, Jack. We're just having a—can I get you a drink?"

"No thanks," Sally told him. "Good to see you, though, Woody. How've you been?"

"Oh, can't complain. Not much business at the studio, but apart from that I've been—you know—staying out of trouble."

"Well, good," she said. "We'll see you, Woody." And she led Jack smiling through the clumps of leather furniture and out into the living room and up the grand staircase. Only when she had closed and locked her own door behind them did she allow herself to speak again. "God," she said. "Did you see his face?"

"Well, he didn't look very—"

"He looked dead," she said. "He looked like a man with all the life gone out of him."

"Well, okay, but look: this happens all the time. Women get tired of men; men get tired of women. You can't go around letting your heart get broken over all the losers."

"Ah, you're in a mellow philosophical mood tonight, aren't you," she said, leaning forward and reaching back to unfasten the hooks of her dress. "Very mature, very wise—it must've come over you when you were all cuddled up with Ellis What's-her-name at Oppenheimer's bar."

But within an hour, after she had cried out for love of him and after they'd then fallen apart to lie waiting for sleep, her voice was very small and shy. "Jack? How much time is there now? Two more weeks? Less?"

"Oh, I dunno, baby. I may stay around a little longer, though, just for—"

"Just for what?" And all her bitterness came back. "For me? Oh, Jesus, no, don't do that. You think I want you doing *me* any favors?"

Early the next morning, when she brought their coffee up to the room, she could barely wait to put the tray on a table before telling him what she'd found downstairs in the den. Woody Starr was still there, lying asleep in his clothes on the sofa. He didn't even have a blanket or a pillow. Wasn't that the damnedest thing?

"Why?"

"Well, why didn't he leave last *night*, for God's sake?"

"Maybe he wants to say goodbye to the boy."

"Oh," she said. "Well, yes, I suppose you're right. It's probably that. It's probably because of Kick."

When they went downstairs and caught a glimpse of Woody and Kicker talking quietly together, they withdrew quickly into the kitchen to socialize with Nippy and to wait in hiding until it would be time for Kicker to leave for school. They didn't know, and Jill Jarvis wouldn't remember until later, that this was a school holiday.

"Oh, Jesus, Nip," Sally said, wilting onto a kitchen chair. "I really don't feel like going to work today."

"*Don't*, then," Nippy said. "Know something, Sally? I've never seen you take a day off the whole time I've been in this house. Listen, that old office can get along without you once in a while. Why don't you and Mr. Fields do something nice today? Go someplace nice for lunch, take in a good movie or something. Or take a drive; it's beautiful weather out. You could go down to San Juan Capistrano or something nice like that. You know how they say in the song about when the swallows come back to Capistrano? Well, if I'm not mistaken, it's just about that time of year. You could go down there and watch the swallows coming back and all; wouldn't that be nice?"

"Ah, I don't know, Nippy," Sally said. "It'd be nice, but I think I'd better at least put in an appearance at the office or Edgar'll be eating his arm. And I'm practically fifteen minutes late as it is."

Leaving the kitchen at last, when Sally said it would be "safe" to face the den, they were relieved to find themselves alone. Jack noticed too, in passing, that the black velvet painting of the clown had been removed from the wall above the fireplace. But then, through the sunny panes of the French doors, they saw Woody and Kicker out on the pool terrace, standing close together and still talking.

"Oh, why can't he just *go*?" Sally said. "How long does it take *any*body to say goodbye?"

Woody Starr's luggage was heaped on the terrace beside him: an old Army duffel bag that he'd probably used in the Merchant Marine, a suitcase, and a couple of well-filled paper shopping bags, bright with department-store advertising and heavily reinforced with brown twine. He bent over to divide the load, and he and Kicker carried all the stuff down from the terrace and stowed it in his car. Then they came back up, Woody with his arm around the boy's shoulders, and walked up close to the house for their final parting.

Jack and Sally retreated well back into the den to avoid being seen watching, and they watched. They saw Woody Starr put both arms around the boy and gather him up into an abrupt, tight, clinging embrace. After that, Woody started to walk away and Kicker made for the house—but Kicker stopped and turned, and then they saw what had caught his eye: a small cream-colored delivery truck coming swiftly up the driveway with MYERS emblazoned in brown letters on its side.

"Oh, I can't bear this," Sally said, going limp and pressing her face into Jack's shirt. "I can't bear this."

The truck came to a stop a few yards beneath the place where Woody waited on the terrace and Cliff Myers got out, red-faced, with a self-conscious little smile, into the sunshine. He hurried around to the rear of the truck in his coveralls, which were several sizes too small for him, brought out his glistening metal tub with its massed and wobbling heads of a great many roses, carried it up to Woody Starr, and thrust it into his hands. He appeared to be talking as he did this—seemed, in fact, to have been talking steadily and perhaps mindlessly since his arrival, as though compelled to do so by an unexpected spasm of embarrassment—but once the tub of roses was in Woody's possession he was able to stop. He drew himself exaggeratedly straight, touched two fingers to the neat visor of his cap, and made his getaway to the truck in a stiff-legged run that was almost certainly faster and clumsier than he'd planned it to be.

Kicker had missed none of it. He went back across the terrace to join Woody, who had squatted to set the tub down, and now they were both huddled low over it in conference.

"It's okay, baby," Jack said into Sally's hair. "It's okay now. He's gone."

"I know," she said. "I saw the whole thing."

"Well, look: you think we could find something in the house for his hands? Think Nippy could find something?"

"Like what, though? Some kind of detergent, or solvent, or what?"

But it wasn't necessary to find anything in the house. After a minute or two Woody and Kicker moved away together with the bright roses riding between them, and with Jack Fields following at a stranger's distance. They went into the shadows of the big garage, where Kicker carefully poured gasoline from a five-gallon can down the surface of the tub and over Woody's hands until Woody was able to work them free. That was all it took. Then Kicker used the heel of his shoe to shove the tub raspingly across the floor of the garage and hard against the wall, where it would stay until long after the glue had dried to harmlessness and the roses were dead.

Alan B. ("Kicker") Jarvis enrolled in what his mother described as the finest boys' boarding school in the West, and he left home to take up residence there almost at once.

Later in the same week Jill and Cliff went to Las Vegas to be married—she said she had always wanted to be married in one of the "adorable" little wedding chapels of that city. Their honeymoon plans, at the time they left Los Angeles, were still indefinite: they hadn't yet decided whether to spend a month in Palm Springs, a month in the Virgin Islands, or a month in France and Italy. "Or maybe," she confided to Sally, "maybe we'll say the hell with it, take three months and go to *all* those places."

Jack Fields's screenplay had been finished and accepted and quarreled over and finished and accepted again; then Carl Oppenheimer fervently shook hands with him. "I think we'll have a picture, Jack," he said. "I think we'll have a picture." And Ellis rose to give him a quick, sweet kiss.

He talked long and jovially on the phone with his daughters about the fine times they'd be having in New York very soon, and he spent a day buying gifts for them. With Sally's advisory help, he also bought two new suits of clothes at the Los Angeles Brooks Brothers in order to go home looking like a success. And at Sally's suggestion, secretly wincing at the cost of it, he bought quart bottles of brandy, bourbon, scotch, and vodka and arranged for them all to be gift-wrapped, packed in a gift box, and delivered to Jill's house with a brief, carefully worded note about her "hospitality."

When he'd closed out his occupancy of the beach place, he and Sally drove down to spend four days of a prolonged holiday weekend in an oceanside motel near San Diego that Sally recommended as being "wonderful." He would have liked to know when and with whom she had learned how wonderful it was, but with so little time left he knew better than to ask.

On the way back to Los Angeles they stopped at the Mission of San Juan Capistrano and walked slowly around and through it among many other cordially shuffling tourists, each with a handful of tourist brochures, but there were no swallows in sight.

"Looks like they've all taken off this year," Sally said, "instead of coming back."

That gave Jack what seemed a pretty funny idea, and when they were out at the car again he backed away from her into the roadside weeds with the nimble steps of an entertainer. He knew he looked all right in his new clothes and he'd always been able to sing a little, or at least to fake the sound of singing. "Hey listen, baby," he said. "How's this?" And he sang from a straight-standing crooner's posture, with both arms rising slightly from his sides, palms out, to convey sincerity.

"When the swallows take off from Capistrano,
That's when I'll be taking off from you . . . "

"Oh, that's sensational," Sally said before he could even go on to the next line. "That's really socko, Jack. You really do have a great sense of humor, you know that?"

On their last evening, seated in what Edgar Todd had solemnly promised them was the finest restaurant in Los Angeles, she looked disconsolate as she picked at her crabmeat Imperial. "This is kind of dumb, isn't it?" she said. "Spending all this money when you'll be on the plane in a couple of hours anyway?"

"Doesn't seem dumb to me; I thought it might be nice." He had thought too that it might be the kind of thing F. Scott Fitzgerald would have done at a time like this, but he kept that part of it to himself. He had tried for years to prevent anyone from knowing the full extent of his preoccupation with Fitzgerald, though a girl in New York had once uncovered it in a relentless series of teasing, bantering questions that left him with nothing to hide.

"Well, okay," Sally said. "We'll sit here and be elegant and witty and sad together and smoke about forty-five cigarettes apiece." But her sarcasm wasn't really convincing, because she'd met him at the office that afternoon wearing a new, expensive-looking blue dress that he could have sworn she'd bought in the hope of being taken to a place like this.

"Can't get over that dress of yours," he told her. "I think it's just about the best-looking dress I've ever seen."

"Thank you," she said. "And I'm glad I've got it. Might be useful in helping me trap the *next* counterfeit F. Scott Fitzgerald who comes stumbling out to Movieland."

Driving her home to Beverly Hills, he risked two or three glances at her face and was pleased to find it calm and reflective.

"I guess I've had sort of an idle, aimless life, when you think about it," she said after a while. "Work my way through college and never use it, never do anything I could be proud of or even enjoy; never even adopt a child when I had the chance."

And a few more miles of illuminated city went by before she moved close to him and touched his arm with both hands. "Jack?" she said shyly. "That wasn't just kidding around, was it? About how we can write a whole lot of letters to each other and talk on the phone sometimes?"

"Aw, Sally. Why would I want to kid around about that?"

He took her up to where the shallow steps of the pool terrace began and they got out of the car for their leave-taking: they sat together on a lower step and kissed as self-consciously as children.

"Well, okay," she said. "Goodbye. Know something funny? We've really been saying goodbye all along, since the very first time I went out with you. Because I mean we've always known there wasn't much time, so it's been a saying goodbye kind of deal from the start, right?"

"I guess so. Anyway, listen: take care, baby."

They got up quickly, in embarrassment, and he watched her make her way up onto the terrace—a tall, supple, oddly gray-haired girl in the best-looking dress he had ever seen.

He had just started back for the car when he heard her calling, "Jack! Jack!"

And she came clattering down the steps again and into his arms. "Oh, wait," she said breathlessly. "Listen. I forgot to tell you something. You know the heavy sweater I've been knitting all summer for Kicker? Well, that was a lie—I'm pretty sure it's the only lie I ever told you. It was never for Kicker; it's for you. I took the measurements from the only ratty old sweater I could find in your place, and the whole plan was to get it finished before you left, only now it's too late. But I'll finish it, Jack, I swear. I'll work on it every day and I'll mail it to you, okay?"

He held her with what seemed all his strength, feeling her tremble, and said against her hair that he'd be very, very glad to have it.

"Oh, Jesus, I hope it'll fit," she said. "Wear it—wear it in health, okay?"

And she was hurrying back up toward the door, where she turned to wave, using her free hand to wipe quickly at one and then the other of her eyes.

He stood watching until after she'd gone inside, and until the tall windows of one room after another cast their sudden light into the darkness. Then more lights came on and more, room upon room, as Sally ventured deeper into the house she had always loved and probably always would—having it now, for the first time and at least for a little while, all to herself.

THE
Uncollected Stories

The Canal

"WAIT A MINUTE—wasn't that the same division you were in, Lew?" Betty Miller turned on her husband, almost spilling her drink, her eyes wide and ready for a priceless coincidence. She had interrupted Tom Brace in the middle of a story, and now everyone had to wait for Lew Miller's reply.

"No it wasn't, darling," he told her, "I'm sorry. It was a pretty big army." He put his arm around her slim waist and felt the pleasant response of her hand slipping around his own. What an awful bore this party was; they had been cornered for nearly an hour with the Braces, whom they knew only slightly—Tom Brace was an account executive in the advertising agency where Miller wrote copy—and there seemed to be no escape. The backs of Miller's legs had begun to ache from standing, and he wanted to go home. "Go on, Tom," he said.

"Yes," Betty said. "I'm sorry, Tom, please go on. You were just about to cross a canal, seven years ago this week."

Tom Brace laughed and winked, forgiving the interruption, understanding about women and their silly questions. "No, but seriously, Lew," he said, "what *was* your outfit?" Miller told him, and while Betty was saying, "Oh yes, of course," Brace stared at the ceiling, repeating the numerals. Then he said, "Why, by God, Lew! You guys were right on our left in that very job I've been telling you about—the canal deal? March of '45? I remember distinctly."

Miller had been vaguely afraid all along that it might turn out to be the same canal, and now there was nothing to do but agree that yes, as a matter of fact, that was right, in March of '45.

"Why isn't that marvelous," Nancy Brace said, twisting her pearls with an elegant index finger.

Brace was flushed with excitement. "I remember distinctly," he said, "you guys crossed the canal a good deal further north than we did, up to our left, and then we circled back and met each other in a kind of pincer movement a couple days later. Remember? Well, Jesus, boy, this calls for a drink." He handed around fresh cocktails while the hostess's maid held the tray. Miller took a martini gratefully and drank off too much of it on the first swallow. It was necessary, now, for the two husbands to pair off briefly to discuss details of terrain and hours of attack, while the wives got together to agree that it certainly was marvelous.

Watching Brace and nodding, but listening to the women, Miller heard Nancy Brace say, "Honestly, I don't know how they lived through it—any of it," and she shuddered. "But I never get tired of Tom's war stories; he makes it all so *vivid* for me, somehow—sometimes I feel I'd been over there myself."

"I envy you," Betty Miller said softly, in a tone that Miller knew was calculated for dramatic effect, "Lew never talks about the war." And Miller realized uneasily that for Betty there was a special kind of women's-magazine romanticism in having a husband who never talked about the war—a faintly tragic, sensitive husband, perhaps, or at any rate a charmingly modest one—so that it really didn't matter if Nancy Brace's husband *was* more handsome, more solid in his Brooks Brothers suit and, once, more dashing in his trim lieutenant's uniform. It was ludicrous, and the worst part of it was that Betty knew better. She knew perfectly well he had seen almost nothing of the war compared with a man like Brace, that he'd spent most of his service at a public-relations desk in North Carolina until they transferred him to the infantry in 1944. Secretly he was pleased, of course—it only meant that she loved him—but he would have to tell her later, when they were alone, that he wished she'd stop making him a hero whenever anybody mentioned the war. Suddenly he was aware that Brace had asked him a question. How's that, Tom?"

"I said, how'd you have it going across? What kind of resistance they give you?"

"Artillery fire," Miller told him. "No small arms to speak of; you see, we'd been covered by a good-sized barrage of our own, and I guess whatever German infantry there was had been driven back away from the canal before we got started. But their artillery was still working and we ran into plenty of that. Eighty-eights."

"No machine guns up along that opposite bank?" With his free hand Brace fingered his neat Windsor knot and thrust his jaw up and out to free another inch of neck.

"No," Miller said, "as I remember it there weren't any."

"If there were," Brace assured him, winking grimly, "you'd remember it. That was our trouble, right from the start. 'Member how that canal was? Probably less than fifty yards wide? Well, right from the minute we climbed into those goddamn little boats we were covered by these two Jerry machine guns up on the opposite bank, maybe a hundred yards apart. They held their fire until we were out in the middle of the drink—I was in the first boat—and then they cut loose."

"My God," Betty Miller said. "In a *boat*. Weren't you *terrified*?"

Tom Brace's face broke into a shy, boyish grin. "Never been so scared in my life," he said softly.

"Did you have to go in a boat too, darling?" Betty asked.

"No I didn't. I was just going to say, Tom, that up where we were we didn't need boats. There was this little footbridge that was only partly blown out, and we just used that and waded the rest of the way."

"A bridge?" Brace said. "Jesus, that must've been a break. Get your vehicles and stuff across?"

"Oh no," Miller said, "not on this bridge; it was only a little wooden footbridge, and as I say it was partly in the water. There'd been a previous attempt to cross the canal that day, you see, and the bridge had been partly destroyed. Actually, my memory of the bridge itself is very vague—it might even have been something our own engineers had tried to put up, come to think of it, although that doesn't seem likely." He smiled. "It was a long time ago, and the fact of it is I just don't remember, Tom. I've got a pretty poor memory, to tell the truth."

To tell the truth—but to tell the truth, Miller thought, would be to say, Poor memory, hell. I've forgotten only what I didn't care about, and all I cared about that night was running in the dark, first on the concrete of a road, then on dirt, then on boards that trembled underfoot, sloping down, and then in the water. Then we were on the other side and there were some ladders to climb. There was a great deal of noise. I remember that, all right.

"Well," Tom Brace said, "if it was at night and you were under artillery fire I guess you weren't paying much attention to the damn bridge; I don't blame you."

But Miller knew that he did blame him; it was inexcusable not to have remembered about the bridge. Tom Brace would never have forgotten a thing like that because too much would have depended on his knowing. He would have had a plastic-covered map stuck in his field jacket, under the grimy webbing straps, and when the men in his platoon asked breathless questions he would have known, coolly and without excitement, the whole tactical situation.

"What kind of a unit were you in, Lew?"

"Rifle company."

"What'd you have, a platoon?" It was Brace's way of asking if he had been an officer.

"Oh no," Miller said. "I didn't have any rank."

"Yes you did too," Betty Miller said. "You were some kind of a sergeant."

Miller smiled. "I'd had a T-4 rating in the States," he explained to Brace, "in public relations, but it didn't amount to anything when they kicked me into the infantry. I went over as a rifleman replacement, a pfc."

"Tough break," Brace said. "But anyway—"

"Isn't a T-4 the same thing as a sergeant?" Betty asked.

"Not exactly, darling," Miller told her. "I've explained all that to you before."

"Anyway," Brace said, "you say somebody else had tried to cross the canal that day and been thrown back? And you guys had to make the second try at night? That must've been a sour deal."

"It was," Miller said. "As a matter of fact it was particularly sour because that afternoon we'd been put back in regimental reserve, our battalion was supposed to get a few days' rest, and just about the time we got our sacks unrolled we got word to move up to the line again."

"Oh Jesus," Brace said. "That used to happen to us all the time too. Wasn't that a bitch? So of course your men's morale was all shot to hell before you even got started."

"Well," Miller said, "I don't think our morale was ever very high anyway. We didn't have that kind of an outfit." And to tell the truth would have been to say that the worst part of the afternoon was an incident about the loss of a raincoat. Kavic, the squad leader, scrawny, intensely competent, nineteen years old, had said: "Okay, everybody check their equipment. I don't want to see nothing left behind," and with tired eyes and fingers Miller checked his equipment. But later, on the road, he was touched on the shoulder blade by Wilson, the assistant squad leader, a portly Arkansas farmer. "Don't see your raincoat there on your belt, Miller. Lose it?"

And there was nothing to say, after a moment's slapping of the cartridge belt, feeling the loss, but, "Yeah, I guess I must have."

Kavic turned around from the head of the column. "What's the trouble back there?"

"Miller lost his raincoat."

And Kavic stopped in the road and waited, livid, for Miller to come abreast of him. "Goddamn it, Miller, can't you hold on to anything?"

"I'm sorry, Kavic, I thought I had it."

"Goddamn right you're sorry. Next time it rains you're gonna be sorrier 'n hell. You know goddamn well what the supply situation is—now why can't you hold on to anything?"

And there was nothing to do but walk, shamefaced, with a face grown used to shame. That was the worst part of the afternoon, to tell the truth.

"What the hell happened to that maid?" Tom Brace said. "Do you see her, honey?"

"I think she's in the kitchen," his wife said. "I'll go root her out," and she strode away, hips twitching prettily in an expensive cocktail dress.

"Tell her we're all dying of thirst," Brace called after her. Then he turned back to Miller. "So what happened, Lew? This is really interesting to me, finding out what went on up in your sector that night. Did your company make the assault, or what?"

"No, one of the other companies was the first to cross," Miller said, "but it amounted to the same thing for my squad, I mean the squad I was in, because we were farmed out to work for the battalion wire section that night carrying spools of communications wire across the canal, and we followed right after the first company."

"I see," Brace said.

"But actually it was a good deal, because all we had to worry about was getting the wire over and staying out of trouble, and then after the crossing we got to hang around while the battalion CP was set up. We goofed off all the next day before we joined our own company again."

"Wait a minute now, you're getting ahead of the story," Brace said. "I want to hear about the crossing itself. You said you had artillery on you when you crossed?"

"Started before we crossed," Miller said. There was no avoiding it now. "As I remember it, the artillery started coming in when we were still a couple hundred yards from the canal, on the road."

"Was this at night?" Betty asked.

"That's right."

"Eighty-eights, were they?" Brace said.

"That's right." And now it was all there. The seven years dissolved and it was all there—the dark gray road lined with black trees, the shuffling columns of men on either side. The familiar pain of bandoliers and straps of webbing gripped his shoulders and neck, and there was a new pain cutting the flesh of his hand: a looped and knotted strand of communications wire from which hung, heavily, a big steel spool. Some of the spools had handles, but Miller had drawn one that didn't, and there was no way to carry it without cutting his hand. "Stay together now," Wilson urged in a hoarse whisper, "everybody stay together." The only way to stay together in the dark, five paces apart, was to concentrate on the dim blur of the next man's back, Shane's. Shane's back was short and square, the helmet rode low on its shoulders. Whenever it grew too dim Miller hurried a few steps to catch up; when it seemed too close he held back, trying always to keep the five paces. There was a quick fluttering rush of air and a—*Slam!*—somewhere on the other side of the road. Like great collapsing centipedes both columns of men rolled into the ditches. Miller fell flat on his belly—it was a good, deep ditch—and the spool banged into his kidneys. Then there was another fluttering rush and another—*Slam!*—closer this time, and in the shocked silence before the next one there were the inevitable voices: "Eighty-eights" and "Keep moving, men, keep moving." Miller had raised his head just enough to see Shane's boots sprawled in the dirt ahead of him, and to touch them with his fingers. When the boots moved, he would move too. The next one was much louder—*Slam!*—and Miller felt something clink on his helmet and spatter across his back. From across the road there was a tremulous, almost apologetic voice: "Medic? Medic?"

"Where? Where are ya?"

"Over here, here he is."

"Keep moving, men."

Shane's boots moved and Miller followed, scrambling to his feet and running crouched over, rifle in one hand and spool in the other. At the next fluttering rush Shane and Miller both hit the dirt in time—*Slam!*—and then they got up quickly and ran again. Everybody was running now. Across the road a new voice broke from baritone to wild falsetto: "Oh-oh-oh! Oh! Oh! The blood's coming out it's coming out it's coming out *it's coming out!*"

"Quiet!"

"Shut that bastard up!"

"*S'coming out! S'coming* OUT!"

"Where? Where *are* ya?"

"Keep moving, men. Keep moving."

Shane's back ran on in the darkness, swerved to the right, up onto the bald surface of the road again, and then went straight ahead, faster. Miller lost it, ran faster and found it. But was it the same back? Wasn't this one too tall? There was another fluttering rush, the back sprawled out on the road and Miller fell beside it—*Slam!*—and then he grabbed its shoulder. "Shane?"

"Wrong man, Mac."

Miller started to run again. At the next rush of air he ducked convulsively without changing his stride—*Slam!*—and went on running. "Shane? Shane?" He slowed down to keep in step with a short figure—a lieutenant, he saw by the white smear on the helmet—who was jogging along calling, "Keep moving, men," over his shoulder. With absurd politeness he said, "Pardon me, sir, can you tell me where the wire crew is?" "I'm afraid not, soldier. Sorry." At least the lieutenant, too, was rattled enough to be absurdly polite. "Keep moving, men."

Miller pulled ahead of him, then cut out across the road. At the top of the road's crown there was another fluttering rush, and he dove for the other side like a ballplayer sliding home, just in time—*Slam!* A figure lay prone in the ditch. "Hey Mac, you seen the wire squad?" There was no answer. "Hey Mac—" Still no answer; dead, maybe, or maybe just scared half to death. Miller ran again, and it wasn't until much later that he thought:—or maybe wounded. My God, I should have stopped and felt his heart—called a medic. But he ran, back across the road again, only ducking for the shells now—*Slam!*—and sometimes not even ducking, thinking: my God, I'm brave—look at me, I'm on my feet and everybody else is falling down. He was sure he had never run so fast in his life. The road ended—turned right or something—and he ran with the crowd straight ahead, down a wide slope of muddy earth. The barrage was mostly behind him now, or seemed to be. Then there was the bridge, with men jostling and crowding—"Take it easy, you guys . . . take it *easy*"—and then the sudden cold shock of water up his legs. Just ahead of him a man fell headlong with a heavy splash and two or three others stopped to help him up. The shore was like the other shore at first, sloping mud, but then came a retaining wall, stone or concrete, fifteen or twenty feet high in the darkness. Somebody muttered, "Ladders . . . ladders," and Miller, groping, found the dark wooden rungs against the wall. He slung his rifle and clumsily thrust the other arm through the spool's carrying wire, to free both hands, and then he began to climb, vaguely aware of other ladders on either side of him and other men climbing them. A boot stepped on his fingers and he felt the squirm of other fingers under his own boot. The rungs ended short of the top and there was an instant of wild teetering without a handhold until a pair of arms reached down to help him up. "Thanks," he said, kneeling on the edge of the embankment, and the man ran off. Miller turned back and reached down to grab the next man's hands, and the next man said, "Thanks." All along the top of the embankment there was a babble of voices, excited, out of breath: ". . . this way . . ." ". . . which way? . . ." ". . . over here . . ." ". . . where the hell do we go now? . . ." They were in a plowed field; the uneven earth gave like soft sponge under Miller's boots. He followed the sounds and shadows into the field, running again, while the shells rushed over his head to explode well behind him—*Slam . . . Slam . . . Slam . . .*—back on the other side of the canal. And it was there in the field that Wilson's voice said, "Miller? That you?"

"Wilson? Jesus, thank God!"

"Where the hellya been?"

"Where've *I* been—my God, I've been looking all over hell for *you*!"

"Keep your voice down. Got your spool?"

"Sure I've got it."

"Hang on to it. And for Christ's sake stay with us this time. Come on."

"So what happened," Tom Brace said, "after you got to the other side?"

Miller closed his eyes and passed his hand over them. "Well," he said, "after we climbed the retaining wall we were in a plowed field."

"Retaining wall? You mean you had a goddamn *wall* to climb? We didn't have anything like that down where we were."

"Well it wasn't bad," Miller said, "because there were these ladders running up the face of it."

Brace frowned, picturing it. "Ladders? Seems funny the Jerries wouldn't've knocked them down, though, doesn't it?" he said. "Couldn't they have been something your own people put up?"

"Well I guess they could have been, at that, now that I think of it," Miller said. "I'm afraid I just don't remember." Uncertain about the bridge; uncertain about the ladders—this was quite a night for uncertainties. "Anyway," he went on, "we went across this big plowed field, and as I remember it we didn't run into any more trouble until we got to this little town that was our objective for the night, on the other side of the field. There was some small-arms fire there, more or less of a rearguard action, I guess."

"I see," Brace said.

"But as I said, all my squad had to worry about was those spools of wire; after that we had nothing to do but find a place to goof off."

In the first thin blue of daylight they were crouched in the shelter of a wall, listening to the stutter of machine guns down the street and waiting to be dismissed from the wire detail. That was when Wilson said, "Kavic wants to see you, Miller," and Miller scuttled up to the place where Kavic sat waiting against the wall, his face gaunt with fatigue, his helmet cocked rakishly on his thin skull.

"Miller, what the hell happened to you back there on the canal?"

"I lost sight of Shane during the shelling."

"Well why'n the name of Christ can't you keep up?"

"It wasn't a question of keeping *up*, Kavic, I—"

"All right, never mind all that, Miller. I'll put it this way: you give me more goddamn trouble than all the rest of the men in this squad put together. You're more goddamn trouble than you're worth. You got an answer for that?"

"As I remember it," he told Tom Brace, "we found an empty house and went to sleep in it. Slept for about twenty-four straight hours, except for taking turns standing guard, and when we woke up the town was all cleared. It was the Battalion CP and our own company was a couple miles up the road."

"I see," Brace said.

"Here you are, gentlemen," Nancy Brace called. "On the house." She was bringing a tray with four martinis on it.

"Good deal," Brace said. "Thanks a lot, honey."

Miller drank greedily, hoping to put the image of Kavic back where it belonged.

"Did I miss the best part of the story?" Nancy asked.

"Oh, there wasn't any story, as usual," Betty said. "It seems my husband went to sleep for twenty-four straight hours." She put her pretty lips to the glass and took a sip. Then she said brightly, "But what happened to *you* on that canal, Tom? The last we heard from you was where you were bobbing around in a boat, getting shot at. Don't tell me *you* went to sleep."

"Well," Brace said, "not for a little while, anyway. That was a bad night. We didn't have any artillery on us, we were luckier than you there, Lew, and we didn't have any walls to climb either, but as I said there were these two Jerry machine guns up on the bank, and that seemed plenty bad enough at the time. How we ever made it to the other side I'll never know. One thing, I had this damn good B.A.R. man. He got that old B.A.R. into action in about one second flat, right from the boat. That way nobody got panicky, even though two—no, three of the kids were hit, two of them killed. In the boat behind ours they all panicked and went over the side, all their damn equipment strapped to their backs and everything. Some of them drowned and the rest weren't fit for anything when they did get ashore. The third boat had it a little easier, because by that time our own people back on shore had a couple machine guns firing and they were able to provide some cover. But let me tell you, when we finally did get to the other side it was a lonely damn place to be."

"What on earth did you *do*?" Betty asked.

"Had to get those damn guns some way," Brace said. "What we needed was mortar fire, but I couldn't call for any because our goddamn radio was on the blink, either that or the radio man was too scared to operate it right. 'Course, I figured the people back there had sense enough to start putting down some mortar fire anyway, without being asked, but where we were, exposed and all, we didn't feel much like waiting around for them to make up their minds." Brace paused and put his empty glass on the low table behind him. He pulled out a pack of cigarettes, shook one loose and stuck it in his lips, leaning forward to accept a light from his wife. "It was one of those moments," he said, "when you have to do some damn-fool thing before you even think about it, just to keep your men from losing their heads completely. Thing is, you have to *act* like you're in command of the situation. So what I did was this: we were right close to one of the Jerry guns, and I could see from the tracers it was pretty busy defending itself against the fire from the other side, so I had that B.A.R. man I told you about keep laying it on the other gun, further down the line—he didn't need much coaxing; he was a damn good man—and I crawled up to within about fifty feet of the near gun and started pitching grenades. Luck? I want to tell you, I've never been so lucky in my life. The gun quit after the second grenade, and we found these two Jerries deader'n hell. Then about that time our mortars started in on the other gun, and all we had to do was lie low and sweat it out till the rest of our people got across."

"My *God*," Betty said.

"Wasn't that the time they gave you the Silver Star, darling?" Nancy Brace asked.

Brace laughed, winking at Miller. "Isn't that just like a woman?" he said. "That's the only part of the story she cares about."

"My God," Betty said, "it sounds to me as though you should have gotten *several* Silver Stars."

"What are you people doing," the hostess said, appearing suddenly through veils of cigarette smoke, "fighting the war all over again? Or are you planning the next one?"

"We're still on the last one," Nancy Brace said, "only now it's VE Day and it's time to go home." She slipped her arm through her husband's, bracelets jingling, and smiled up at him. "How about it, Lieutenant?"

"But you can't leave," the hostess said. "You have to stay and plan the next one. What's the point of fighting the last war if you're not going to stay and plan the next one?" She had taken several too many of her own martinis.

"Guess this is what you call a strategic withdrawal," Brace said.

"Right, honey? No, but listen, it's been a great party but we've really got to go. I'll get the coats, honey."

"Oh, look what *time* it is," Betty said. "I think we'd better think about going too, darling. Will you get our things?"

"You mean you're *all* going?" the hostess said. "But who's going to stay and help me plan the next war?"

Miller smiled and nodded, backing away, and then turned to follow Brace into a dark bedroom, where the coats of guests lay ensnarled on the bed. Brace already had his own coat on and his wife's furs over his arm, and as Miller came into the room he straightened up from the bed and turned around. "This yours, Lew?" he asked, holding up Miller's gabardine topcoat. It looked somehow forlorn, rumpled and not quite clean, hanging there from Brace's hand.

"Yes," Miller said, "that's it. That's my hat next to it, and that's Betty's coat over there, near the foot. There, that one. Thanks, Tom."

When they came out the two wives were waiting by the front door. "The nice things have all been said," Nancy Brace told them, "so all we have to do is get out of here."

"Good girl," Brace said.

They went out and down several flights of neat, carpeted stairs to the street. "Oh it's raining," Betty Miller moaned as they stood huddled in the doorway. "We'll never find a taxi."

Tom Brace trotted up the three wet steps to the sidewalk, turning up his coat collar and peering both ways down the gleaming dark street. "Here's one," he said. "*Taxi!*"

"Oh, you're wonderful, Tom," Betty Miller said.

As the cab swerved to the curb Brace sprang for its door, wrenched it open and called, "You people take this one, Lew. I'll run up to the avenue and grab one for us."

"Oh no," Miller said, "there's no need for that, I—" But Brace was already gone, sprinting up the street with the easy grace of an athlete. "Goodnight," he called back. Miller turned to Nancy Brace. "No, look, there's no reason why you people shouldn't—"

"Oh don't be silly," she said. "Go on now, hurry up."

Betty was already in the cab. "Come *on*, Lew," she said, "for heaven's *sake*."

"Well I guess there's nothing I—" he laughed stupidly. "Goodnight." Then he ran across the sidewalk into the cab and shut the door.

He gave the address and settled back beside his wife as the cab started up.

"Oh God," Betty said tiredly, "I've been to some dull parties, but *that* one! That one takes the all-time cake." She sighed and leaned against the cushions, her eyes closed.

"Those damn conceited Brace people. Darling, *why* do you let an ass like that eclipse you so in a conversation?" Her head was off the cushions now, her eyes were fixed angrily on him in the darkness. "I've never seen it fail. You just stand there completely silent and let some awful show-off Tom Brace talk us both to death. You let those people *eclipse* you so."

"Betty," Miller said. "Will you do me a favor?" And he watched her frown turn to a look of hurt in the light of a passing streetlamp. "Will you shut up? Will you please for God's sake shut up?"

A Clinical Romance

THE NEW PATIENT was a big, thick-chested man, twenty-three or so, and he didn't look sick at all. But the moment he tiptoed into the admitting ward and headed for the empty bed beside Frank Garvey's, during Quiet Hour one June afternoon, Garvey could tell he was a repeat case. First-time patients looked shy in the hospital pajamas as they walked or were wheeled into the long, high room. They would glance about uneasily at the rows of horizontal men in tousled sheets, the sputum cups and Kleenex boxes and photographs of wives, before they yielded, tentatively, to the fresh bed that was to be their own, and usually they started asking questions right away ("How long've *you* been here? Eighteen *months*? No, but I mean, how long is it for the *average* cure?").

But this one knows his way around; a couple of the old-timers in the rear of the ward were waving and grinning at him, which proved it. Observing the rules of the Quiet Hour, he put his folded clothes in the bed stand with elaborate care to avoid noise. Then, seeing Garvey was awake, he offered his hand across the space between their beds. "No point waiting for a formal introduction," he said in a whisper, and with a boy's smile that broke the tight Irish toughness of his face. "My name's Tom Lynch."

"Frank Garvey; glad to know you. Been here before?"

"Fifteen months the first time; then I got fed up and signed out. That was five months ago." He smiled again. "I had a five-month vacation."

Miss Baldridge, the charge nurse, broke it up with a shrill command from the door that jolted several other men awake. "All right, Lynch, let's cut the talking and get into that sack. You *know* better than to come blabbing around making noise before three."

Lynch swung his bulk around to face her, outraged. "Listen, we weren't making any—" She stopped him with an explosive "Sh-sh-sh!," advanced into the room and aimed a stiff finger at his bed. "Inside, boy!"

Slowly he scraped off his slippers and climbed under the sheet. Miss Baldridge stood there watching him, hands on hips, ready to give the ultimate shout—"You're on Report!"—at the next sign of impertinence. She was a former Army major, devoted to nursely discipline and critical of any nurse on her present staff, notably a pretty young blonde named Miss Kovarsky, who called the patients Mr. or listened to their complaints at any length, and she was in top form today. This morning she had commanded the radios to be silent while she paced the center aisle and delivered a lecture on luckiness to all the twenty-odd men in the ward. If you had to get tuberculosis, she felt, you were lucky to have the Veterans Administration taking care of you, and luckier still to be in this particular hospital, so close to New York, with its first-rate medical staff. Therefore, she had pointed out, her small eyes triumphant over the rim of her regulation linen mask, the least you could do was *cooperate*. Garvey, who was a former English instructor and spent most of his time reading, was singled out on two counts—the disorderly pile of books on his windowsill (he was lucky to be allowed *any* books) and the cigarette ashes on the floor near his bed (he was lucky to be allowed to smoke; in most TB hospitals it was against the rules). And though Garvey was unwilling to be contrite he was equally unwilling to smile foolishly at her, or to lose his temper, either of which would only have made it worse. There was no defense, he had decided grimly, just as there was no defense for this hulking, amiable stranger in the next bed who knew better than to come blabbing around before three, and who now lay sweating on his back, controlling himself. There were no sounds except breathing, and, beyond drawn venetian blinds, the sound of insects charging the window screens, buzzing and bumping against them in a fury of frustration before they zipped away.

Satisfied, Miss Baldridge turned on her rubber sole and started toward the door.

"Tune in tomorrow," said a low voice across the aisle, in the fruity tones of a radio announcer, "for another heartwarming chapter in the life of—Pru Baldridge, Girl Army Officer." She paused only for a split second in her prim departure, but that was enough to make it clear that she had been stung, then abandoned her impulse to attack in favor of a quick retreat, pretending she hadn't hear. As she neared the door the voice became louder, joined now by a chorus of badly suppressed laughter from all over the ward: "Can a girl soldier find happiness in a veterans' hospital?" It was Costello, an ex-salesman and former Air Force gunner, and he had scored a clean victory, a rout. The laughter rose jubilantly around him; he sat up in bed and went through the burlesque of taking a bow.

"Thanks," Lynch called across the aisle in a stage whisper.

"Don't mention it," Costello said. "Any time." He was a slight, dark man of thirty whose face was prematurely creased with laugh wrinkles. Though he had been here only a few months, his record of quitting or being expelled from one hospital after another dated back to the end of the war.

Coyne, a big, pimpled boy whose bed was next to Costello's and who always appreciated Costello's jokes whether they were funny or not, was almost unconscious with laughter now, his face beet red, his bed trembling. At three o'clock, when Miss Baldridge reappeared to signal the end of Quiet Hour, he was still grinning. "Hey, Miss Baldridge," he asked her, "can a girl soldier find happiness in a veterans' hospital?"

"Oh, Coyne," she said, "for heaven's sake grow up." And she began snatching open the venetian blinds, admitting the blaze of afternoon. A moody attendant followed her, passing out a thermometer to each man, and Miss Kovarsky moved gracefully from bed to bed taking pulses.

"How are you today, Mr. Garvey?" Miss Kovarsky's voice was low, her fingers small and cool on Garvey's wrist.

"Fine, thanks."

She smiled at him, or at least her eyes narrowed above the white mask, and then she went on to Lynch's bed.

In a minute the radios were on again with the accounts of several ball games, and the coughing, laughing and chattering of the ward was resumed. Most of the afternoon revolved around Lynch; it was necessary for those who knew him to welcome him back, and for those who didn't to assimilate him into the crowd. First he was surrounded by the old-timers, elderly men who had lived in the admitting ward for years and whose memories were long. After they had brought him up to date on hospital gossip, chuckling and scratching themselves with weak fingers, and while one of them, old Mr. Mueller, shuffled off to spread the news of his return through the other wards, Lynch exchanged names and information with Costello, Coyne and some of the other younger men who had arrived since his time. Then Mr. Mueller came back with an enthusiastic group of ambulant patients, strangers to Garvey, some of whom wore convalescent uniforms of green cotton gabardine. They all said they were sorry to see Lynch back, and that it must be tough to be here in the admitting ward, right back where he had started from, and then they settled down to talk of old times, of beer parties in the latrine and of stolen visits (the wards were on the ground floor, and there were fire exits in the latrines) to neighborhood bars. They talked of innumerable good guys who had been kicked out, or were doing well or badly, or were as crazy as ever, or were "over in surgery now," and of one or two good guys who had died. Garvey put on his glasses and began to read.

Shortly before supper, Miss Baldridge scattered the crowd. "All right, get back where you belong," she said. "All of you." When they had gone, Lynch shook out a cigarette and offered the pack to Garvey.

"How long you been here, Frank?"

First names were almost never used in the admitting ward, and Garvey felt a surprising glow of pleasure at the boy's friendliness. "Three months," he said, "I'm just starting out."

"You been through the worst part," Lynch assured him. "I know that was the worst part for me. After that the time goes by faster. You get used to the life; you get to know different guys."

"Any idea how long you'll be here this time? Have they told you anything?"

"Told me I got a new cavity and I turned positive again, and that means they'll want to give me a lobe job. Probably keep me here on bed rest for two or three months, and then take me over to surgery. After that there's no telling. A year; maybe more."

A lobe job means a lobectomy, the removal of a section of lung and the ribs around it; that was all Garvey knew about it, except that it usually left a man with a partly crumpled chest and a perpetually half-shrugged shoulder, and that it often led to complications. There was some chance that Garvey's own disease might require surgery, and he didn't like to think about it. "Well," he said, "I certainly hope you make it soon. What did you say your first name was?"

"Tom."

During supper and for the rest of the evening they talked; if the time went by faster when you got to know different guys, Garvey decided, it might be well to get to know them. They compared stories about the hospital staff, agreeing that Miss Baldridge was a tough customer but that most of the other nurses and attendants were all right, though Lynch took exception to one of the night attendants, a small, roguishly effeminate man named Cianci, who, he said, had tried to make a pass at him once. "I told him, 'Look, Buster, if you want to play games, you picked the wrong boy, understand? I think you better keep outa my way from now on.'" Then they talked of the outside and Lynch told about his father who had retired from the fire department and his kid brother who wanted to be a professional middleweight. He asked Garvey about teaching and said he had always wanted to go in for that kind of work himself; as a kid he had thought about joining the Jesuits, and later about qualifying for the regular board of education, but of course it was too late now. What he should have done, he said, was use his GI Bill for college after the Navy, instead of fooling around as he had, working in a supermarket and playing semipro football on Saturdays, until the disease caught up with him.

But it became increasingly clear, as Lynch led up to the subject, touched on it, paused shyly and studied his cigarette, that what he really wanted to talk about was his girl. "I just started going with her when I was home this time," he said, after Garvey had helped him along. "Started getting pretty serious. I know it sounds corny, but I never knew I could get that crazy about any girl. She's all I think about, all the time. I don't know, she's—" Gently he smoothed the sheet with the palm of his hand, finding, perhaps, that there were no words delicate enough for the thing he was trying to say. Then he grinned. "Anyway, all I want to do now is get married. Soon as I get out of here the right way, with an arrested case, I'm going to collect that pension, maybe get myself some kind of easy, part-time job, and then I'm going to get married. You're married, aren't you, Frank?"

Garvey said he was, and that he had two children.

"Boys?"

"Boy and a girl."

"That's nice, a boy and a girl. They come here to see you?"

"My wife does; they don't let the kids in. She'll be here tomorrow," he added. "You'll meet her. And maybe I'll get to meet your girl."

Lynch looked up quickly. "No," he said, "she won't be coming here. That's impossible."

"Too far?"

"No, she just lives over in Jersey, it's not that. It's just impossible, that's all. "There was an embarrassed pause. "Look, I'm not trying to be mysterious or anything; don't get me wrong. I'll explain it to you some other time."

Awkwardly, they talked of other things for a while, and then Lynch got out his stationery box and began to write a letter. He was still working on it, tearing up pages and starting them again, when the lights went out at ten o'clock, and he had to strike a match for light to put his writing things away. It must have been after midnight when Garvey was awakened by a harsh, repeated, strangely muffled sound; in his dream it had been a dog barking far away. He opened his eyes and listened. It was the sound of weeping, desperately stifled as if by a pillow, and it came from Lynch's bed.

Garvey was permitted to share the secret about the girl a week or so later, one evening when the climate between them seemed right for confidences. And after that, for the rest of the long summer of waiting for Lynch's lobe job, the shared secret brought Garvey into a special kinship, gave him a special responsibility.

He had seen it coming all through supper. When the trays were cleared away, Lynch came over to sit on the chair between their beds, and that was when it came out. "Look, Frank, this is just between you and me, understand? I figure I'll go nuts if I don't tell somebody." He drew the chair closer. "This girl I've been telling you about. It's Kovarsky."

"Who?"

"Miss Kovarsky. You know, the nurse."

"Well, I'll be damned, Tom," Garvey said. "Congratulations."

"Now, listen, don't let on about this, whatever you do, understand?"

"Oh, hell, don't worry; I understand."

"I started dating her after I got home," Lynch went on in his half-whisper. "I never messed around with her here. Thing is, see, there's some kind of a regulation against nurses having personal contacts with the patients, and old Baldridge has it in for Mary anyway. She could lose her job if we're not careful. Hell, I wanted to tell everybody. I felt kind of proud about it, you know what I mean?"

Garvey started to speak, but Lynch said, "Sh-sh-sh," for Costello was sauntering across the aisle, followed by Coyne.

"Lynch, old man," Costello said. "We need a pair of pants. The lad here turned in his clothes like a good boy, and now he needs a pair of pants. You still got that suit in your stand, haven't you?"

"Coyne?" Lynch said. "What the hell, Coyne, you mean *you're* going out?" Garvey was surprised too. This was old stuff for Costello, but Coyne had been taking the cure conscientiously until now.

"Ah, just for a couple beers," Coyne said. "We'll get back in time for the bed check at eleven."

"Well, look, Coyne, you're welcome to the pants," Lynch said, "whole suit if you want it, but I'd think twice about this going-out crap if I were you. I mean, you go out tonight, then you'll want to go out tomorrow night, and pretty soon—"

"Pretty soon he'll be just like me," Costello broke in. "Right, Lynch? One foot in the grave and the other on a banana peel." He clapped Lynch on the shoulder and laughed. Coyne laughed with him, self-consciously, and so did Lynch, shaking his head. "Ah, don't worry, Lynch, I'll take care of the lad. Bring him back just like new, and that's a promise. You got Professor Garvey here for a witness. Right, Professor?"

Then they had gone toward the latrine, Coyne hugging Lynch's blue trousers furtively under his arm. Lynch shook his head again. "Guess I sound like some kind of an old lady, preaching that way, but that bothers me. I mean, a single guy, all right, let him kill himself if he wants to, but Coyne's married and he's got a few responsibilities. I can't see it. And that goes for you too, you bastard. I catch you goofing off, with that pretty wife of yours, I'll break your head." He laughed. "How about that—and I'm the guy that used to raise all the hell around here, on Report all the time. But you see? That's what Mary's done for me. It's like I was married to her already."

"That's fine," Garvey said, "except for the business of having to keep it a secret. Must be pretty hard to take, when she's around every day."

"It's not too bad. For one thing she's not around every day; half the time she works the other wards. And when she's here we kind of wink at each other and whisper a little bit, like when she's giving me a sponge bath or something. And then we write a lot of letters and I call her up when she's home. Not on this portable phone here in the ward, you get no privacy on that bastard. I use the booth down the hall, you know? The one that's supposed to be for the staff? I wait till nobody's around and then duck in there. It *is* a pain in the neck in some ways, though. Like this week, she's on the midnight-to-eight shift, you know? So a couple nights ago I thought I'd go into the nurse's office around one, maybe get to see her alone. Jesus, fourteen different guys coming in for sleeping pills and aspirins; we never had a chance."

"You going to try it again?"

"Ah, what's the use. Be the same story. Besides, I got no business running around after midnight. I'm taking the cure this time, and anyway, after tonight she goes back on days." He yawned and stretched his big arms, and then he leaned back with a reflective look. "Only thing that really bothers me, is the way some of these wise guys talk about her. *You* know the way a guy talks about a nurse—'Boy, I'd like to get into *her* pants'; stuff like that. Sometimes I want to stand up and say, 'Look, you bastards, lay off. That's mine.' You know what I mean?"

After lights out, he went on whispering about his girl and their five months together. From the start they had found they could sit for hours over a couple of beers, just talking, and have a wonderful time, which was something he'd never been able to do with a girl before. And there were times, long afternoons on a sand dune, for instance, and nights in the rich, dark secrecy of her parked automobile, when Lynch felt almost sick because he knew he had never been so happy. He had not taken her "all the way," however. "I could have," he said. "I could have twenty different times, we were so close to it—I'm not saying that to brag or anything, I just mean I could have very easily—but I didn't, and I think that was one of the things she liked about me at first. I guess all the other guys she'd been out with had knocked themselves out trying for it, and she got fed up with that stuff. I said, 'Honey, I can wait. I know when something's worth waiting for,' and I think she liked that."

Coyne and Costello did not get back for the eleven o'clock bed check, but fortunately there were several other empty beds then, and many voices in the latrine, so the five-to-eleven nurse, Mrs. Fosdick, let it go with a familiar cry through the latrine door: "I want everybody out of there in five minutes." But when she came back again just before her shift ended, an hour later, she meant business. Her flashlight was trained on Coyne's empty bed this time, and Lynch tried to cover for him. "Coyne's in the latrine, Mrs. Fosdick."

"Oh, yeah? How about Costello?"

"I think he's in there too."

"Well, they *better* be," she said, and the flashlight went away. Mrs. Fosdick was a squat middle-aged widow who did her job exactly the way Miss Baldridge liked it, and everybody said she would be the next charge nurse if Miss Baldridge went back into the Army. "Coyne?" she called. "Costello? You in there?"

There were muffled cries of "Yeah" and "Sure thing," and a moment later the two of them came in to bed, giggling and weaving through the dark ward. "Jesus, that was a close call," Coyne whispered to Lynch, tiptoeing across the aisle. "We just barely got in there, taking off our clothes, when she comes to the door and hollers in. Oh Jesus, I'm half loaded." He sat down on the foot of Garvey's bed and told them all about it, giggling and filling the air with his sharp breath. They had taken the bus to some gin mill about a mile down the road and started off with beer, but then they met these two broads—kind of old, he said, but not too bad—and Costello started buying shots all around. "He's telling them his name's Costello and mine's Abbott," Coyne said. "Jesus, that guy's a million laughs when he's half crocked. So anyway, here we are, drinking shots and having a big time, and all of a sudden I see it's eleven o'clock. I says, 'Jesus, Costello, we better shove off.' He says, 'Ah, don't worry so much.' Well anyway, I finally get him outa there, and he tells the broads we'll be back at twelve-thirty."

"So you're going out again?" Lynch asked him.

"Sure, soon as that little Polak nurse, what's-her-name, comes on duty. Kovarsky. Costello says he can fix it up with her." He stood up and peered across the dark aisle.

"Guess he's in the office now, talking to her. Oh Jesus, what a night." Then he loped over to his own bed and lay down to wait, and Garvey tried to sleep. But half an hour later he heard someone stumbling around Lynch's bed again. "Lynch," Coyne was saying, "You awake?"

"Yeah."

"Here's your pants. Guess we're staying in."

"What happened?"

"Ah, my boy Costello. Now I can't get him outa the *nurse's* office. He's been in there for an hour, got his arm kinda halfway around her, and every time I go to the door he gives me this big wink and makes a sign for me to leave 'em alone. Guess he's really giving her the business."

"Oh, yeah?" Lynch said, with what seemed to Garvey exactly the right degree of disinterest. "How's he making out?"

"Ah, Christ," Coyne said. "I don't think he's getting to first base."

Lynch put the pants away, turned over and settled himself for sleep.

The next afternoon he came back from a visit to the forbidden telephone booth with a confidential grin. "I just heard all about Costello last night," he told Garvey. "Said she couldn't get rid of him till almost two. He was in there all that time trying to promote a date for himself." He cocked one foot on the chair and rested a forearm on his meaty knee. "I got half a notion to take him aside and tell him he's wasting his time."

"Why don't you?"

"I'm trying to keep this thing quiet, remember?" The feet came down and he straightened his back, hitching up his pajama pants. "First place, he'd never believe me, and in the second place he'll find out soon enough, if he keeps it up. She'll tell him if she has to."

About a week later his confidence seemed badly shaken. The portable ward telephone, a coin-operated instrument on a wheeled platform that could be plugged in beside the beds, was a constant source of quarrels among the patients; its users were always accused of hogging it. Costello began hogging it more than anyone else, but after the first few arguments it became a standing ward joke, especially among the men on his side of the aisle, who started calling him Lover Boy. He would lie in bed and talk very low into the phone for an hour at a time, sometimes shielding the mouthpiece with his hand.

"You know who he's talking to, don't you, Frank?" Lynch asked one evening, half-smiling but looking annoyed. "You know who he calls up all the time?"

"Oh, hell," Garvey said. "How can you be sure? Could be a different girl every night."

"Look; when I tried to call her last night the line was busy until just about the time he got done over there. So tonight I listened real close when he made the call. It's her number he gave."

"You mean just from the sound of the dial? You can't tell anything from that."

"You don't dial numbers in Jersey, you give them to the operator. And it's her number he gave, right down to the *J* on the end."

They both watched Costello mumbling and grinning into the telephone. "Well," Garvey said, "you'll notice he does all the talking."

"Oh, sure, I know that. I know he isn't making *out* or anything, don't get me wrong. Just makes me a little sore, that's all. I wonder what he *talks* about all that time."

As soon as Costello hung up, Lynch walked out to the telephone booth. When he came back he lay down and listened to his radio for a while. Then quite suddenly he snapped it off and came over to Garvey's bed. "You know a funny thing, Frank? When I called her up I said—just a little sarcastic, you know, not sore or anything—I said, 'Honey, you're a pretty busy girl.' Didn't want to come right out and say I knew it was Costello, you know what I mean? Might sound like I was jealous. And I figured she'd tell me about it, like she did before, but she didn't. Said it was her *sister* using the phone. So what could I say? Call her a liar? I don't know what the hell to think."

"I wouldn't worry about it," Garvey said. "Probably just that she was afraid you *might* be jealous; might get upset over nothing."

"Well, yeah," Lynch said doubtfully, "I guess you're right." He didn't want to talk about it any more, and all the next morning he was silent and brooding until the mail came. But when he read the letter he received, and it looked as though he read it several times, he seemed relieved and pleased.

Garvey caught his eye. "She still love you?"

Lynch smiled, half embarrassed and half proud, and said yes, he guessed so. And that afternoon, when Mary Kovarsky took the pulses after Quiet Hour, she gave Lynch a look that sent the color rising flagrantly in his thick neck. Even with the mask covering half her face, it was a look conveying all the reassurance in the world.

Everything seemed all right, then. Lynch had no further trouble getting his calls through, and Costello no longer hogged the portable telephone; apparently he had given up. Any traces of doubt were removed a month later, when it became evident that Costello had, as Coyne put it, gotten himself shacked up with something in the neighborhood, possibly one of the girls they had met that night in the bar, when Costello had been a million laughs. This was indicated—proven to Coyne—by the fact that he had begun going out three or four nights a week, sometimes taking Coyne along but always leaving him after the first few beers to go off alone. Soon he stopped taking Coyne altogether, and it was regularly reported that the headlights of a car came up to within a hundred yards of the latrine's fire exit, where the car apparently picked Costello up and drove him away. Once he returned a white shirt he had borrowed from old Mr. Mueller, who held it up with comic chagrin to show it was smeared with lipstick. "Damn shirt's been in my stand for two years," he whined, surrounded by laughter, "and all *I* ever got on it was *dust*." And Coyne, examining Costello's bare back when he stripped to the waist in the heat of that same afternoon, swore he could see scratches, evidence that frenzied fingers had clawed him. "Damn, boy," he said, "she really must've given you the business."

By now it was late summer, heavy and hot in the ward, and except during visiting hours the men would lie half-naked on stripped beds, too hot to read or write or play cards, while the radios droned. (". . . It's a high, high fly ball out to left field; Woodling's under it—a-and—takes it, to retire the side. Say, men: Want a shave that leaves your face feeling like a million dollars? . . .") Electric fans had been shelved at either end of the room, but their lolling wire faces barely stirred the sickroom air, barely lifted and let fall the dangling corner of a sheet. In order to survive the afternoon it was almost essential to have some promise of an evening's reward, so beer parties in the latrine had become more frequent, arranged by telephoning a local delicatessen whose delivery boy had standing instructions to wait outside the fire exit until a patient slipped out to meet him. It was on just such a day, with a party planned, that Lynch received his final letter in the afternoon mail. He came over to Garvey's bed with that odd, incongruous little smile that plays on the lips of the very shy when they announce a death. "It's all over, Frank. She wants to call the whole thing off."

"Christ, Tom, what do you mean? Just like that? Out of a clear sky?"

"Wasn't exactly a clear sky," he said. "Seems that way now, but I guess I've known for a couple of weeks she was acting kind of funny—" He broke off, as if bewildered, far from satisfied with what he had said. "Ah, I don't know, I don't know, it just don't sound natural. You want to read it?"

"Not unless you want me to."

"Go ahead."

"You sure?"

"Sure I'm sure. Go ahead—see if it sounds natural to *you*."

Mary Kovarsky's handwriting was a blend of lifelessly even grammar-school scripts and girlish affectations. Some of her *i's* were dotted with little circles.

Dear Tom,

I've been trying to write this letter for a long time but I guess I was afraid. I'm not as brave as you are about a lot of things. But I guess the only thing to do is write it and get it over with. If we go on this way one of us is bound to get hurt.

I don't want you to call me up any more or write me any more letters, Tom. I've thought about it again and again until I think I will go crazy or something if I think about it any more, and that is the way it's got to be. If I ever wanted to get married to anybody it was you, Tom, but I guess I just don't want to get married. Not yet anyway. I don't feel sure enough of myself.

After tomorrow I am being transferred to one of the Gen'l Med. Wards, so you won't be seeing me any more and I think that will make it easier. I will send your letters and your foto back as I guess you will want them. You can throw mine away if you like. I wish you a lot of luck in getting well soon.

Sincerely,
Mary

The party shaped up about nine. Two cases had been ordered and when Garvey and Lynch joined the group in the latrine the delivery boy had just arrived. Coyne brought the first case through the fire-exit door, and then old Mueller wrestled the second one inside, his scrawny back bent painfully. Costello gave him a hand, and they stowed both cartons in the shower stall, where they would be out of sight in case an angry nurse opened the door or an unfriendly attendant walked through. The parties always began the same way; after the hiding of the beer and a search for can openers, the first round of cans would be punctured with careful noiselessness, and the men would settle down to talk, very quietly at first, about the nurses on duty that night—whether they were good skates or could be counted on to make trouble. It was a big, ugly room of yellow-brown tile, staringly lighted by two big globes in the ceiling. The only places to sit down were the open toilet bowls that stood in facing rows against two of the walls, two or three steel chairs from the ward that had been left here from previous parties, and an overturned wastebasket.

Tonight it developed that a reasonably good skate, a Miss Berger, was on duty until midnight, but that they'd have to watch their step after that because old Fosdick had the twelve-to-eight shift. Coyne did most of the talking, his chair tilted back against the tiles and his pajama pants hiked to the knee while he scratched a white leg. "Hell, I don't think we got to worry about old Fosdick, long as we keep the noise down. She's been pretty good lately."

"You want to watch her, though," Costello said. "She's all right as long as she thinks you're scared of her, but she won't take any crap."

"Well," Coyne said, grinning over at Garvey and Lynch, "I guess our boy Costello's the expert on *that* subject all right. Ha-ha-ha goddamn! Any of us tried raising the kind of hell he does around here we'd be on Report five times a week." Costello chuckled, pleased, and swilled the beer around in his half-empty can. "Ah, it's all in knowing the angles, lad. Some things can't be taught, that's all."

Lynch looked all alone, hunched on one of the toilet bowls in his faded pajamas, staring at the floor. He had eaten almost none of the supper, drank the coffee and nibbled at the cake that was for dessert, that was about all. Garvey was trying to think of something to say, trying to get him to talk.

"What's the matter with old Lynch over there," Coyne demanded. "He sick or something? Got a slight case of TB or something?"

"I think he needs a new beer," Garvey said. "That's his trouble."

"By God, Professor," Costello said, "that's my trouble too." And he went to the shower stall.

By the time the first case was gone the party had divided into two groups; Mueller and several other old-timers at one end of the room, comparing reminiscences of hospitals they had known, and Lynch, Garvey, Coyne and Costello at the other end, talking about homosexuality. Garvey didn't know how the subject came up; he hadn't been listening to all of it. The beer had numbed his senses a little and he had removed and wiped his glasses several times before he realized they weren't really misted; he was getting drunk.

"—So when he said that," Coyne was saying, "about coming up to his room, I figured 'oh-oh, I don't want no part of this,' so I told him no thanks, I had to go, and I took off. But it was a funny thing, to look at him you'd never think he was any different from you and me." It was the end of a long story, Coyne's contribution.

"Sure," Costello said. "That's the way a lot of them are. Look and act just like anybody else."

"That's the kind you want to look out for," Lynch said. "I hate them sneaky bastards." He bore down heavily on the opener, piercing a fresh can, and the foam slopped over his fingers onto the floor.

"No reason to hate 'em," Costello said, shrugging.

"Oh, no?" Lynch glared at him. He looked tough sitting there, his pajama top open across his chest, a tiny religious medallion swinging on its damp silver chain among the hairs. "Well, I do. I hate their guts, every one of 'em. Like that Cianci bastard, that attendant. 'Member, Frank? I told you about him. Comes creeping around one night when I'm taking a shower, starts talking about how lonely the boys must get here, giving me that goddamned smile of his. 'You lonely, Lynch?' he says. I told him, 'Look, Jack—you want to play games, you picked the wrong boy. Think you better keep outa my way from now on.' That's the only way to talk to them bastards. I hate 'em all."

"Oh, what the hell," Costello said. "They're psycho cases, that's all."

"Oh, yeah?" Lynch said. "Oh, yeah? Well if you like 'em so goddamn much I'll fix you up with Cianci."

Costello laughed softly. "Jesus, he gets nasty when he's drunk, doesn't he? I didn't know you were one of these nasty drunks, Lynch."

"I want everybody out of there in five minutes," Mrs. Fosdick called through the door.

"Okay, Mrs. Fosdick," Costello called back. "Just breaking it up now." The old-timers began tiptoeing to the shower stall to deposit their empty cans.

"Damn," Coyne whispered. "We still got half a case in there."

"So?" Costello said, yawning and getting to his feet. "Go in and lay down for half an hour, then come back and finish it up if you want to. Me, I'm going to sleep."

"Well, Christ, we can't let it go to waste," Coyne said. "How about you, Garvey?"

"I think I've had enough too."

"Lynch?"

"What?"

"Want to come back?"

"Hell," Lynch said. "I'm just beginning."

They filed out and felt their way to bed in the darkness. Garvey lay down gratefully and closed his eyes, but opened them quickly when he felt a sudden rush of dizziness. For a long time it was necessary to lie with the pillow folded tight under the back of his neck and concentrate on the dim white outline of the foot of his bed. Whenever he closed his eyes or lost sight of the outline, the sickly dizziness returned. His concentration was so intense that he scarcely noticed when Lynch got up, whispering to Coyne, and the two of them went back to the latrine. Sleep settled over him in uneasy, fitful waves, each heavier than the last. He fought them off at first and then gave in, like a man drowning.

"—Garvey. Garvey." It was Coyne's voice, low and urgent. "Garvey." Something was digging into his shoulder; Coyne's hand. The folded pillow was a painful lump under his skull, and there was another streak of pain over his eyes. "Garvey." His mouth felt swollen, too dry for speaking. "What time is it?" he said at last.

"Jesus, I don't know." Coyne's voice had a sharp whiskey smell. "About four, I guess."

"Four?" he said, tying to make it mean something.

"Listen, your boy Lynch is in bad shape. We been out to a couple gin mills and he's loaded. Sitting in the latrine, won't take off his clothes. You wanna gimme a hand with him?"

"All right," Garvey said. He was fully awake now, moistening his lips. "Be right in." Coyne hurried off and Garvey sat up painfully, holding his head. He found his glasses on the bed stand and fumbled on the floor for his slippers.

The latrine lights shocked his eyes, but in a moment he made out Lynch, slumped on one of the chairs in his blue suit, and Coyne hovering over him. Lynch looked terrible. His face shone bright red, the mouth loose and wet and the eyes filmed over. "Come on, boy," Coyne was saying. "Lemme take your coat off."

"Ah, lea' me alone, lea' me alone, will ya?" Lynch tossed his head and pushed Coyne's hand away from his shoulder. "There's old Frank. Wha'ya say, Frank? Listen, Frank, tell this sunvabish to lea' me alone, will ya?"

"Okay, Tom," Garvey said. "Take it easy now."

Coyne took one lapel of Lynch's coat and Garvey the other, but Lynch tightened his arms. "Lea' me alone, gah damn it! Both you bastards, lea' me alone!"

"Keep your voice down, Tom," Garvey said. They managed to work the coat down around his elbows when suddenly he stopped resisting, his eyes fixed glitteringly on the latrine door. Garvey looked up. Cianci, the night attendant, had just come in, blinking under the lights. The linen mask hung loose under his chin, revealing a childish mouth.

"Well," Lynch said. "Speaka the devil."

"Somebody speaking of me?" Cianci asked in mock concern, and then he smiled knowingly at Garvey. "Look, do you gentlemen want some help?"

"No thanks," Garvey said. "We can handle him."

Lynch glared at the attendant. "Thought I tol' you keep outa my way."

"Oh, he's really *blind*, isn't he?" Cianci said, smiling. He looked very small, very blond and pale in his white duck uniform.

"Thought I tol' you keep outa my *way*."

Coyne told Lynch to take it easy, and Garvey said, "You better leave, Cianci," but Cianci didn't move.

Lynch's eyes were slits. "Get that gah damn smile off your face and get *outa* here! Get *outa* here, you fairy bastard!"

"Oh, now, Lynch," Cianci said, taking a step forward, "you don't mean that."

Before they could grab his arms Lynch whipped out of the coat sleeves, sprang across the floor and drove his big right fist into Cianci's neck, just under the ear. Cianci crumpled quickly but Lynch's left caught him in the face before he sprawled to the floor. Coyne had one of Lynch's arms now and Garvey seized the other, pulling back on it with all his strength. In the unfamiliar shock of effort, Garvey's arms and shoulders burned; the muscles fluttered in his thin, invalid's legs. Lynch's voice was a high child's whimper: "Lemme go, lemme go—I'll kill 'im, I'll kill 'im—"

Cianci groped to his feet, holding his red-blotched face, just as the blood began to course from his nose and dribble on his uniform. "For Christ's sake, get *out*!" Garvey yelled, but he stood there, absurdly smiling through the blood, and said, "Let him go. It's all right." It couldn't have been that he wanted to fight—it seemed almost that he wanted to be hurt. Lynch advanced on him with a terrible struggling slowness, locked against Garvey and Coyne but pulling them along, while Garvey's slippers slid and scrabbled on the tiles.

"Let him go," Cianci said again.

Lynch broke from Garvey first, freeing his arm with a lunge that sent Garvey's glasses flying, and then he twisted away from Coyne. Whimpering and sobbing for breath, he seized Cianci's arm, wrenched it, swung him around like a flail and sent him crashing against the wall. Then he fell on him, sank one knee into his belly and both blunt thumbs into his throat. They had just hauled him off when Mrs. Fosdick burst in, wide-eyed, and said, "What's going on here?"

For an instant they all froze under her shocked eyes, Cianci half-risen against the tile wall, Lynch squatting spread-eagle in the arms of Garvey and Coyne. Then Coyne sat down, Garvey picked up his broken glasses, and Lynch stumbled over to one of the toilets and began to vomit. "I've got to have a doctor," Cianci said in a tight, breathless voice. "I think my arm is broken."

It was all over, then. The rest of the night, or morning, fell into the inevitable sequence of aftermath: the attendants taking Cianci away to the emergency ward; Mrs. Fosdick stumping around with her flashlight, ordering them to bed and then hurrying back to put it all into the Report; the hours of lying there in the dark—Lynch, lying quietly with a Kleenex wrapped around his raw knuckles and the red coal of a cigarette illuminating his eyes: "I'm sorry about the glasses, Frank"—and finally the turning on of the ward lights at seven o'clock, and Costello, scrubbing his eyes and looking around with a sleepy grin: "Jesus, what was all that commotion last night?" Breakfast, then, and the fresh starch, the early-morning efficiency of Miss Baldridge: "Lynch, that was the most disgusting exhibition I've ever heard of. You'd better start packing your things, because you can be sure the doctor will want you out of here and on the bus before noon."

But Lynch was not kicked out, to everyone's surprise. The doctor gave him a severe dressing-down, that was all, and then went into a conference with the other doctors, after which Lynch was removed from the ward and placed in one of the quiet-rooms—single-bed cubicles reserved for the very sick—to spend the remaining weeks until he would be taken to surgery. Miss Baldridge was plainly dumbfounded, and assured everyone that Lynch had been inordinately lucky, that it was only because his case was of unusual interest to the surgeons, which was probably true. For days there were conflicting rumors on what had become of Cianci, the most authoritative being that his arm had been sprained, not broken, and that after treatment he had been returned to duty on a different ward. Coyne and Garvey were cleared from the Report by Lynch's testimony that both had come into the latrine only after the trouble began, though Coyne made sure that everyone in the ward knew the real story, which he told with relish long after the men had stopped asking to hear about it.

Soon, except for the fact that Lynch was gone, everything seemed just about the same in the ward. At least that was the way Garvey described it to Lynch whenever he went to the quiet-room to visit him.

"How's everything in the ward?" Lynch would ask, lying very flat and still. He seemed to lie like that for hours in his tiny room, reading nothing, looking at nothing, talking to no one except during these brief, awkward visits. All he apparently did was finger the cord of the venetian blind that dangled near his pillow; it was stained a sweaty gray from handling.

"Oh, just the same, Tom," Garvey would say. "Same dull business. Got a new man in your bed, an elderly guy. Coyne's going out a lot lately; three nights so far this week."

"How about Costello? Still got that shack job of his? Car still come around for him all the time?"

"Seems that way. Nothing's really changed since you left."

And that, broadly, was the truth, since no one but Garvey could see any connection between Lynch's departure and the fact that Costello had begun hogging the portable telephone again. Only Garvey, lying across the aisle and listening, could find it significant that he began each call by reciting a New Jersey telephone number ending in *J*, and that his half of the ensuing conversation, more careless and confident than before, contained sentences like "Be around tonight, honey?" and "Sure I do, baby; you know I do." Lover Boy, they called him.

Bells in the Morning

AT FIRST THEY were grotesque shapes, nothing more. Then they became drops of acid, cutting the scum of his thick, dreamless sleep. Finally he knew they were words, but they carried no meaning.

"Cramer," Murphy was saying. "Let's go, Cramer, wake up. Let's go, Cramer."

Through sleepy paste in his mouth he swore at Murphy. Then the wind hit him, blue-cold as Murphy pulled the raincoat away from his face and chest.

"You sure like to sleep, don't you, kid." Murphy was looking at him in that faintly derisive way.

Cramer was awake, moistening the roof of his mouth. "All right," he said. "All right, I'm all right now." Squirming, he sat up against the dirt wall of the hole slowly, like an old man. His cold legs sprawled out, cramped in their mud-caked pants. He pressed his eyes, then lifted the helmet and scratched his scalp, and the roots of his matted hair were sore. Everything was blue and gray. Cramer dug for a cigarette, embarrassed at having been hard to wake up again. "Go ahead and get some sleep, Murphy," he said. "I'm awake now."

"No, I'll stay awake too," Murphy said. "Six o'clock. Light."

Cramer wanted to say, "All right, then, you stay awake and I'll go back to sleep." Instead he let his shivering come out in a shuddering noise and said, "Christ, it's cold."

It was in Germany, in the Ruhr. It was spring, and warm enough to make you sweat as you walked in the afternoon, but still cold at night and in the early morning. Still too cold for a raincoat in a hole.

They stared toward where the enemy was supposed to be. Nothing to see; only a dark area that was the plowed field and then a light one that was the mist.

"They threw in a couple about a half hour ago," Murphy was saying. "Way the hell off, over to the left. Ours have been going over right along; don't know why they've quit now. You slept through the whole works." Then he said, "Don't you ever clean that?" and he was looking, in the pale light, at Cramer's rifle. "Bet the son of a bitch won't fire."

Cramer said he would clean it, and he almost said for Christ's sake lay off. It was better that he didn't, for Murphy would have answered something about only trying to help you, kid. And anyway, Murphy was right.

"Might as well make some coffee," Murphy said, cramming dirty hands into his pockets. "Smoke won't show in this mist."

Cramer found a can of coffee powder, and they both fumbled with clammy web-equipment for their cups and canteens. Murphy scraped out a hollow in the dirt between his boots and put a K-ration box there. He lit it, and they held their cups over the slow, crawling flame.

In a little while they were comfortable, swallowing coffee and smoking, shivering when fingers of the first yellow sunlight caressed their shoulders and necks. The grayness had gone now; things had color. Trees were pencil sketches on the lavender mist. Murphy said he hoped they wouldn't have to move out right away, and Cramer agreed. That was when they heard the bells; church bells, thin and feminine in tone, quavering as the wind changed. A mile, maybe two miles to the rear.

"Listen," Murphy said quietly. "Don't that sound nice?" That was the word. Nice. Round and dirty, Murphy's face was relaxed now. His lips bore two black parallel lines, marking the place where the mouth closed when Murphy made it firm. Between the lines the skin was pink and moist; and these inner lips, Cramer had noticed, were the only part of a face that always stayed clean. Except the eyes.

"My brother and me used to pull the bells every Sunday at home," Murphy said. "When we was kids, I mean. Used to get half a dollar apiece for it. Son of a bitch, if that don't sound just the same."

Listening, they sat smiling shyly at each other. Church bells on misty mornings were things you forgot sometimes, like fragile china cups and women's hands. When you remembered them you smiled shyly, mostly because you didn't know what else to do.

"Must be back in that town we came through yesterday," Cramer said. "Seems funny they'd be ringing church bells there."

Murphy said it did seem funny, and then it happened. The eyes got big, and when the voice came it was small, intense, not Murphy's voice at all. "Reckon the war's over?" Something fluttered down Cramer's spine. "By God, Murphy. By God, it makes sense. It makes sense, all right."

"Damned if it don't," Murphy said, and they gaped at each other, starting to grin; wanting to laugh and shout, to get out and run.

"Son of a bitch," Murphy said.

Cramer heard his own voice, high and babbling: "That could be why the artillery stopped."

Could it be this easy? Could it happen this way? Would the message come down from headquarters? Would Battalion get it from Regiment? Would Francetti, the platoon runner, come stumbling out across this plowed field with the news? Francetti, waving his pudgy arms and screaming, "Hey, you guys! Come on back! It's all over! It's all over, you guys!" Crazy. Crazy. But why not?

"By God, Murphy, do you think so?"

"Watch for flares," Murphy said. "They might shoot flares."

"Yeah, that's an idea, they might shoot flares."

They could see nothing, hear nothing except the faint, silver monotony of the bells. Remember this. Remember every second of it. Remember Murphy's face and the hole and the canteens and the mist. Keep it all.

Watch for flares.

Remember the date. March something. No, April. April something, 1945. What did Meyers say the other day? Day before yesterday? Meyers told you the date then. He said, "What do you know, this is Good—"

Cramer swallowed, then looked at Murphy quickly. "Wait a minute wait a minute. We're wrong." He watched Murphy's smile grow limp as he told him. "Meyers. Remember what Meyers said about Good Friday? This is Easter Sunday, Murph."

Murphy eased himself back against the side of the hole. "Oh yeah," he said. "Oh yeah, sure. That's right."

Cramer swallowed again and said, "Kraut civilians probably going to church back there."

Murphy's lips came together in a single black line, and he was quiet for a while. Then, stubbing his cigarette in the dirt, he said, "Son of a bitch. Easter Sunday."

Evening on the Côte d'Azur

WHEN SHE'D PACKED up the remains of the picnic lunch and got the twins settled in their carriage, Betty Meyers looked around for Bobby, her five-year-old. Squinting against the sun, she finally saw him way up the beach, playing with some French kids. "Bobby!" she yelled, but he pretended not to hear and she started off to get him, slow with weariness, feeling the alien stares of men and girls who lay all but naked on the sand.

When Bobby saw her coming he took off, and she had to run clumsily after him, knowing she must look a sight with the heavy flesh wobbling in her playsuit. Finally she caught him and gave him a couple of good hard smacks. He set up an awful howl but he came along nicely enough, once she had a grip on his wrist. The French kids he'd been playing with backed away shyly, holding their hands to their mouths. She hated to hit him—it always made her feel like hell afterwards—but he'd been asking for it all afternoon. He stopped crying by the time they got back on the promenade—still snuffling, but she could tell the worst was over. "All right, now listen," she said. "Do you have to go? Because if you do, speak up now. I don't want you bothering me all the way home. *Do* you?"

"No, Ma."

"All right then. Come on." Pushing the twins' carriage, with Bobby walking beside her, she began the long trip back to the apartment, past the palm trees and sidewalk cafés, past the little bars around the yacht basin with their signs saying WELCOME U.S. NAVY AND MARINES.

As far as Betty Meyers was concerned the French could keep their

Riviera. They could take their whole lousy country and turn it over to the Communists tomorrow, for that matter, and she'd say "good riddance." All she wanted was to be back in Bayonne, New Jersey, where she belonged. Oh, she knew the Sixth Fleet was supposed to be a good deal, and everything. Some of the other Navy wives made her sick the way they carried on about it—"You mean you don't *like* it here? Don't you think it's *beautiful*?"—but you could always be sure the ones who talked that way were the ones that didn't have any kids. They could lie around rubbing sun lotion all over themselves in those sexy little bikini bathing suits, sucking up to the officers' wives and having a high old time. They could even learn French and at least be able to *talk* to people, maybe keep from getting cheated every time they went into a store, but what could she do?

"Hey Ma, buy me an ice cream," Bobby said. He sure got over his grief in a hurry. "Buy me an ice cream, Ma."

"Come on," she told him. "Come on. We can't stop now."

They went around the Hôtel de Ville and cut across the intersection where you always took your life in your hands, what with the way these people tore around with their damn motorcycles and their funny little cars. When they climbed the hill through the slummy part of town and came out on the highway, loud with trucks and buses, that was the last leg of the journey. She always had to steer the carriage with one hand here, and hang on to Bobby with the other, because once he had run ahead, gone off the sidewalk when trucks were coming and practically given her heart failure.

"Hey Ma, you're hurtin' my arm."

"I'll hurt it a lot worse if you don't start acting your age. Get your hands off that carriage."

"Hey Ma?"

"What is it now?"

"I have to go, Ma." And then the twins started to yell.

At last she turned off into the quiet garden of the apartment house. It was a big white slab of a house, set back from the road in a grove of royal palms. It was supposed to have been a luxury hotel before the war, but Betty didn't care if it had been the castle of the king of France—she hated the place. For one thing her apartment was too small—even now, with Eddie at sea—and for another thing she'd never met such snooty people in her life as the people who lived in that house. Even the concierge (and who the hell did she think *she* was?) acted like it was costing her money every time she said hello. It didn't seem to be anything personal, because Marylou Smith, the other Navy wife who lived there, got the same treatment. They just had some grudge against Americans, and they sure didn't care who knew it.

There was the usual trouble with Bobby in the elevator—he always wanted to stick his fingers through the cage when it was moving—and by the time Betty got the carriage wheeled into the apartment, she was just about ready to sit down and cry. It wasn't until she'd slammed the door that she noticed somebody had shoved a piece of paper underneath it. The handwriting looked so foreign that at first she thought it was written in French; then she made out the words.

> Make your infants be more quiet if you please. I receive many complains.
>
> Concierge.

Well, that did it. The hot tears ran down her nose as she bent over the stove to fix the twins' bottles, and she had to turn away so Bobby wouldn't see the puckering of her face. These damn, damn, damn people—this damn, damn, damn country. She had never been so lonely in her life.

"Hey Ma, whaddya *cryin'* about?"

"I'm not. None of your business. Go *away* now, willya please, Bobby?"

The doorbell rang and she wiped her face quickly, hurrying to answer it.

"Hi, Betty," Marylou Smith said in her sleepy Southern way. She came in all dressed up, as usual, dragging Brenda, her six-year-old.

"Boy, am I glad to see *you*," Betty said, and the funny part was it was true. She didn't even like Marylou much, but their husbands were shipmates and Marylou was about the closest thing to a friend she'd had since she came overseas. "Honestly, I'm gonna go nuts if I have to stay in this country one more *minute. Look* at this! Look what that damn little lowlife concierge had the nerve to stick under my door!"

Marylou read the note slowly, aloud, and dropped it on a table. "Oh, that. This the first one of them y'all got? We get 'em all the time. I just don't pay no 'tention any more."

That was something, anyway. At least she wasn't the only one.

Marylou strolled to a mirror and touched up her hair. "Where y'all been all day, Betty? Been looking all over for ya."

"Oh, down to the beach."

"Yeah? You shoulda *tole* me you was goin' down. I'da come along. Don't much like goin' down there by myself." Marylou didn't much like doing anything by herself, as a matter of fact—that was one of the annoying things about her. She was like a helpless kid; had to have somebody with her all the time. "Listen, Betty, let's us have supper together tonight, okay? I got this big old roast pork, and we can cook it in your place. Okay?"

"Okay," Betty said. Another time she might have thought up an excuse, but tonight it seemed like a good idea. At least she'd have somebody to talk to.

"I'll go get all the stuff then," Marylou said, and started for the door, trailing perfume. Betty couldn't understand why she always dressed up like that—nylons, heels, a tight skirt—just for sitting around the house. Maybe Southern girls were different, but it seemed funny. "Now you stay here and play, Brenda," Marylou said, shaking her finger, "and don't you get inta no trouble while I'm gone, hear?" But Brenda was already in trouble. She had picked up one of Bobby's toys, a broken sailboat, and when Bobby grabbed for it she gave him a shove that sat him on the floor. She was a mean one, that Brenda. "You watch your manners, hear?" Marylou said. She swung at her, missing, awkwardly stooping in the tight skirt.

Brenda skittered away out of reach, still holding the sailboat, and started acting up. "I'm gonna tell Daddy on you," she told her mother, fresh as you please.

"*What* you gonna tell him?" Marylou demanded, hands on her hips. It was funny to watch them together—they were like two little kids. "You're so smart, *what* you gonna tell him?"

"'Bout your boyfriend," Brenda said, and this time Marylou didn't miss. In two quick high-heeled steps she bore down on the little girl and hit her so hard the sailboat fell on the floor. "Don't you tell no lies, you little liar!" she yelled over Brenda's howling. "I'll teach you to go telling lies!"

Well, *really*, Betty thought, and it was hard to keep from staring. This would be one to tell Eddie when he came home—he always did say Marylou looked like a little tramp. Not that Betty had anything *against* the girl—and she was no prude or anything—but still, when a person's own kid said something like that, it really made you think.

"Don't know what gets *inta* that little head of hers, makes her talk that way to her own mother," Marylou said. "Now you hush your cryin', Brenda, and see if you can't act nice. Hear?"

The way it worked out, Betty did all the cooking. Marylou just sat around the kitchen smoking cigarettes, not even offering to help set the table, but Betty didn't really mind; at least by doing everything herself she could be sure it was done right. The dinner itself was a rat race, what with the kids throwing bread and gravy at each other, and yelling all the time, and afterwards there were a million dishes to wash. Marylou did the drying, which was some help, even though Betty had to keep stopping to show her where the various plates went. But finally they were through and the kids were all put to bed—they put Brenda in the twins' bed and let the twins sleep in their carriage—and they could relax over a cup of coffee in the living room, looking out at the evening sea through the tall trunks of the royal palms.

"You got a right pretty view from here," Marylou said, squirming contentedly on the couch. "I like it a whole lot better'n the one we got."

"Yeah, it's nice," Betty said, "but I dunno. I'm so used to it now I don't hardly notice it any more. Might just as well be *wall*paper or something." When Eddie was home his carrier was anchored within sight of the windows; it had been sort of nice to lie here and see its big silhouette out there on the water—reassuring, as if it were there to watch over her. Now a different part of the fleet was in, and the bay was crowded with smaller, funny-looking ships—minesweepers, she thought. "Six more weeks," she said. "Right?"

"Is that all it is, six weeks? I thought it was seven. No, lemme see"— Marylou counted her red fingernails —"yeah, you're right, six weeks."

"God, I can hardly wait, can you?" But even as she said it Betty knew it was only partly true. Lonely or not she was no fool, and she remembered the last leave well enough—Eddie complaining ("Can't'cha keep this place *clean*?") and worrying about the kids messing up his damn precious dress blues. And the evenings: play cards and quarrel, quarrel and play cards. "Listen, Marylou, this time when they're home, whaddya say we go out more, the four of us, instead of sitting around playing canasta every night. Eddie and I only went out twice the whole time he was here last time. And I mean you *need* to get out once in a while—get dressed up and go to one of those night-clubs in town, maybe just take a walk along the promenade or something—at least get out of the apartment and feel like a human being."

Marylou gave a little glancing smile that made her look just like Brenda. "Don't you like just goin' out with a girlfriend? Because I was just gonna say, why don't you and me go out tonight?"

"Ah, I dunno. Just the two of us, alone?"

Marylou shrugged, her eyes wide and bland. "Why not?" she said. "Lotta good places to go. There's this one real cute little place called the Hollywood Bar, you probably seen it, and inside it's just like the States, everybody's so friendly and all. Lot of the sailors take their wives there, and I mean it ain't like *some* of those places you see around. You don't see no whores in there, what they call business girls, or anything like that—"

"Ah, I dunno," Betty said. "Look, I don't want to sound like a prude or anything, Marylou, but I mean I got three kids and I got a lot of responsibilities. I'd feel kind of funny going out like that."

Marylou shrugged again and brushed a cigarette ash from her shapely thigh, looking a little hurt. "Okay," she said, "but it don't seem to me like there's any harm just sittin' around havin' a drink, maybe *talkin'* to a boy or somethin'. I know *my* husband wouldn't mind."

"Well no, mine prob'ly wouldn't either. It's just that I'd feel funny about it, is all."

"Why?"

"Well, just because—oh, I guess it's all right if all you do is *talk*. I mean—" She felt foolish, afraid she was blushing. "I mean, I hope that didn't sound like I thought *you*—" But anything she said now would only make it worse. She laughed. "Ah, don't mind me, I guess I sound like an old prude or something. I'm sorry. Sure, you're right."

This time Marylou's shrug was elaborate. "Don't make no difference to *me*, honey. You wanna go out? Okay. You don't? That's okay too." And all at once Betty knew she would go. It was as if she'd had it in the back of her mind all along—all evening, all day. "Okay, let's," she said. "But listen, we won't stay out long, because I don't like leaving the kids alone, okay? And we'll have to wait till we're sure they're asleep before we go."

"Sure," Marylou said. "I ain't in no hurry." She settled back and smiled. "You ain't gonna wear that, are you, honey?"

Betty laughed, looking down at her wrinkled shorts. "God no, wouldn't I look a sight? I oughta take a bath too, if we're going out. Listen, help me decide what to wear, Marylou, okay? C'mon over here to the closet."

Lazily Marylou got to her feet and watched as Betty went through her dresses, jangling the wire hangers. "I like that one there," she said. "That's real cute."

"This?" Betty said. "Don't you think it's a little too—I don't know—too formal or something?" But already she had decided to wear it. It was her best dress, an expensive black satin that Eddie liked, and she hadn't worn it since the last leave, the night he took her to see a Cary Grant picture that was playing in town. (They'd planned it for days, and they'd already paid and sat down in the theater before they discovered the sound track was in French—they couldn't understand a word of the whole picture, and she was so disappointed she almost cried.) "Okay," she said, taking it out. "I'll wear this one, then."

She bathed quickly and put on fresh underwear and nylons (she hadn't worn nylons since the last leave either, and they felt funny on her legs). Then she brushed up her suede pumps, put on the dress and fixed her face and hair, and when she was ready she stood posing in the mirror. "How do I look?"

"Real cute," Marylou told her, but Betty knew it wasn't true—especially when Marylou came to stand beside her. Betty would be the first to admit she wasn't much for looks. She was only thirty but she looked a lot older, especially in the body—she never had gotten her figure back after the twins. Her teeth were funny too, and now her forehead was peeling from a new sunburn, and the powder had only made it worse. She tucked in a few stray hairs and turned away, resigned. "Okay. Now let's check the kids and then we'll leave."

Marylou was right about the Hollywood Bar—it certainly did take you back to the States. It was long and dark, with leather seats and black mirrors, and it even had a jukebox. The man at the cash register greeted Marylou by name when they came in, friendly as anything, and though his accent was more English than American there wasn't anything French about him. They sat down at a little table against the wall, ordered beer and looked around. The place was loaded with American sailors. Right across the aisle there were four of them—two bored-looking chief petty officers and a couple of very young kids—and the others were crowded at the bar. There were hardly any other women. Marylou seemed content to just sit there quietly, but Betty felt she *had* to talk—just make conversation to keep from staring around the room. So she talked, hardly listening to Marylou's replies, turning her glass nervously. An odd feeling came over her that was strangely familiar—tight in the chest, warm, about to giggle—and then she remembered. It was exactly the way she used to feel in Miller's Drug Store back in Bayonne, years ago, when she and her girlfriends used to stop in there after school to fool around with boys. The thought startled her, and the next thing that happened made it worse: the two young sailors from across the aisle got up to go to the men's room, and as they passed they stared down at her and then at Marylou with a funny look in their eyes—sort of tough and scared at the same time. She didn't like it. "Marylou, you know what I think?" she whispered. "I think they think we're a couple of French whores or something. Business girls, or whatever you called them."

"Don't be silly, honey. Why'd they think that?"

She supposed it was silly, after all, and when she looked up a minute later she knew it was. The two chief petty officers were standing there with the kindliest, most reassuring smiles in the world. "Part of the States you girls from?"

Betty grinned. "How'd you know we were Americans?"

They both laughed, and their laughter was kindly too. "Aw, listen," the first one said, "I can spot a Navy wife a block away. You're Navy wives, right? I knew it. Part of the States you from?"

He put the question to Marylou this time, and when she said, "Raleigh, No'th Ca'lina," he burst out laughing. "Sho 'nuff? Well, shet me mouf!" Through it all the other man just stood there smiling, and Betty decided she would probably like him better. He was less handsome than the talkative one, but gentler looking, and shy men appealed to her.

"Listen," the talkative one said. "My name's Al and this here's Tom. You girls don't mind if we sit down, do you? Long as we're all old married people here?"

Betty and Marylou squeezed close together, making room for the men on either side, and it wasn't until he had settled himself beside Betty that Tom, the quiet one, finally spoke. "You from the South too? You didn't tell us yet." His voice was very low, and his lips curled in a bashful smile around the words. He had a big plain face and a little sandy mustache.

"No," she told him, "I'm from Bayonne, New Jersey. My name's Betty, by the way. Betty Meyers."

"Glad to know you, Betty. Mine's Tom Taylor. Bayonne, huh? I been through Bayonne a couple times, never stopped there. My home's in Baltimore."

"Is your wife over here with the fleet too, or is she staying home?"

"Oh, no, she's home. We got the three kids, you see, and she figured it'd be kinda tough for her over here."

"Now there's a smart girl," Betty said. "Your wife is really smart. Me, I got three kids too, but my husband told me all about how wonderful it'd be, with the beach and all, and how he'd be home a lot of the time and we'd have a lot of friends, and like a big sucker I said yes. Now if there was a boat going home tomorrow I'd be on it, believe me. How old are your kids?"

His wallet flipped open in the dim, smoky light, and she bent to look at snapshots. There was a heavyset woman of about thirty-five in a print dress, smiling pleasantly—Tom's wife—and a couple of tow-headed little boys in T-shirts, grimacing into the sun. "The big one's Tom junior, he's ten now, and the little one's Barry, he's six. Then we got a little girl fifteen months old—here, I'll show you. There. I took that when she was only about six months."

"Aw!" Betty said. "Isn't she a darling!"

"C'mon, c'mon, break it up!" Al was reaching across Marylou and snapping his fingers in front of their eyes. "Break it up, you two. Whaddya gonna drink?"

So they ordered another round, and Marylou and Al left the table to dance, on the small patch of cleared floor by the jukebox. "Care to dance?" Tom asked, and as they got up she noticed that the two young sailors were watching them, grinning and nudging each other. It annoyed her, and when they got to the dance floor she said, "Are they friends of yours? Those two?"

Tom laughed. "Them? Nah, they're just a couple kids from the ship; we were just talking to them." He laughed again in his soft, easy way, and slipped his hand around her for dancing. "These damn young kids you get in the Navy nowadays, they're all the same. You talk to them on liberty, buy 'em a beer or something, and right away they think they're in, you know what I mean? They think they're some kind of a big deal because the Chief buys 'em a beer." He held her stiffly at first, well away from his body, hardly touching her back with his hand. "I get kind of a kick outa that one on the right," he went on, "the redheaded one with the big ears? We call him Junior on the ship, and oh Jesus, does it make him mad. So tonight I called him Red once or twice, and I practically thought he was gonna lick my hand or something, like a puppy."

She laughed and glanced over at the redheaded one. The boy lowered his eyes blushing, looking about fourteen years old.

"No, but it's funny," Tom said, "when I talk to him it's almost like talking to my own kid—he don't seem no older'n that. I mean it, the *kids* you get in the Navy nowadays! It's like back in the war."

She let him draw her closer and relaxed, turning with the music, thinking: Isn't he nice? I'll bet they *do* think it's a big deal when he's nice to them. And wasn't I silly to worry about the way they looked at me! They're only kids.

Marylou and Al went back to the table when the tune ended, but Betty wanted to stay and dance some more. She hadn't danced in a long time, and Tom was a good dancer. The songs were all French, but that didn't matter—they were slow and rich, sung by girls with low, tearful voices, and they were nice to dance to.

When they finally went back to the table Betty found little shot glasses of whiskey beside their beer. "Hey, what's this? We didn't order this."

"Sh-sh-sh!" Al said, peering around Marylou. "Santy Claus brought it."

"Well, I don't know," Betty said. "Is it okay to drink it after all this beer?"

Al held up one finger and quoted solemnly: "Beer on whiskey—pretty risky. Whiskey on beer"— he wagged the finger —"never fear."

After that things got confused. They must have stayed in the Hollywood Bar for another hour, maybe longer, dancing and drinking and talking. She wasn't drunk—she knew she wasn't drunk—but everything blurred together because she was having such a good time. Afterwards it was hard to remember exactly what happened, except that when they left Al got a taxi from somewhere—a big square taxi—and she and Tom rode on the jump seats. They drove along the promenade: on one side the brilliant hotel fronts, some of them with tables outside, and orchestras in white dinner jackets and girls with beautiful shoulders in beautiful evening clothes; and on the other side palms and shrubs with colored floodlights hidden in the grass around them, and beyond them the dark sea. "Gee," Betty said, "isn't it nice the way they fix it up at night? It's really beautiful." She turned around to ask Marylou if she didn't think so too, but Marylou and Al were a single shape in the backseat—all she could see was the big blur of Al's back, with one of Marylou's white arms slanting across it.

Then they were back in the apartment and everybody was laughing, and Al was setting up glasses for a bottle of scotch he'd picked up somewhere. She turned on all the living-room lights, but somebody turned most of them off again and got some dance music on the radio.

"Sh-sh-sh!" she said, "turn it *down*, willya? I gotta check the kids." She tiptoed into the dark bedroom and looked at them, one by one: the twins dead to the world in their carriage, Bobby stirring a little as she tucked him in, Brenda buried in her pillow.

When she got back to the living room only Tom was there. "What happened to Marylou?" she asked him. "And Al?"

He stood up from the couch with a drink in his hand, smiling. "I think they went up to her place, to check her kid."

"But her kid's *here*."

"Well," Tom said with a little laugh. "I guess they just went up to—take a look at her apartment or something. C'mon, sit down."

She knew it was going to happen, then. Her throat tightened as she walked over to the couch, and the room seemed to roll like a ship in a slow ground swell.

"Here," Tom said. "Your drink's getting stale." His face was red and the corners of his bashful mouth twitched a little under the mustache as he handed her the glass. "That's a real pretty dress you got, Betty."

"Do you like it?" She smoothed the satin skirt over her thighs, sitting down beside him. "This is the first time I've worn it since Eddie—that's my husband—was home. We went to the movies."

"Oh yeah?" His eyes glittered at her.

"We went to see this big Cary Grant picture that was in town, I forget the name of it. Only we didn't find out till we got there that the sound track was all in French." Her voice sounded high and choked, and she had trouble getting her breath.

"Oh yeah?"

"The whole sound track was in French, and we couldn't understand a word of the whole picture."

"Oh yeah?" A muted piano waltz came from the radio, and the palms rustled outside. They both put their drinks down at the same time, and she knew it was going to happen. His hands were shy at first, and then they began to be sure—gentle but sure. "Don't, Tom," she said, turning her mouth away. "Don't. Please." But nothing in the world could stop it from happening now. "They'll come *back*," she whispered.

"No they won't," he mumbled against her mouth. "Not if I know old Al they won't." But she didn't really give in—couldn't—until she heard him say: "And anyway, I locked the door."

Then she gave in, surprised at the whimpering animal gasps of her breath between kisses, locking her arms around the warm strength of his neck and giving in, giving in, not caring about anything else in the world.

When it was all over they lay silent for a long time until their breathing was normal again, and she waited for a rush of guilt to overtake her. But it didn't come. Even when she forced herself to think of Eddie—to picture his face—it didn't bother her. This didn't have anything to do with Eddie at all. With her finger she traced the line of Tom's cheek, his smiling mustache, his rough chin. "Tom," she said. "Oh, Tom." She was beginning to feel breathless again. "I've just been lying here thinking about my husband, and you know what? I don't care. I just don't care about anything but us, Tom."

"Yeah, I know," he said. "That's the way it is, all right. I don't care either."

"Do you mean it? Do you mean it? Well, but Tom—what're we going to do?"

He sighed. "It's just something we'll have to think about, honey. We'll just have to figure it out. Gonna miss me?"

"You're not *going*—"

"I got to, Betty. I really got to. But I'll come back real soon. Soon as I possibly can."

"Oh don't go yet. Please stay a little while."

But he got up, and in a few minutes he was ready, buttoning his trim tan blouse, straightening it, combing his hair. Then they finished their drinks and had another cigarette, and they both wrote out their full names and addresses, very carefully, and gave them to each other. He kissed her and played around a little, and she did everything she knew how to make him stay, but it was no use. He kept saying he had to go, whispering, fondling her, reassuring her, backing toward the door. "Soon as I possibly can, honey, and we'll talk about it. Now let's see a smile." And after a final kiss she was alone. The important thing was to keep busy. She gathered all the glasses and ashtrays and rinsed them out, and straightened up the room. She turned the radio off, then turned it on again. She got into her pajamas and robe and spent a long time brushing her hair—a hundred strokes on each side—the way she used to do before she was married. If she was going to regret it, this was the time to start. And if she wasn't, well then, she wasn't. It was as simple as that. She tiptoed in to check the kids again. They were all covered. The soft light from the door fell on Bobby's face, sweet and babylike in sleep, and it made her smile to think how different it had been this afternoon: dirty and loud and wide-awake. ("Hey Ma, whaddya *cryin'* about?") Her eyes stung a little as she bent over the bed, very gently, and kissed him. She strolled back into the living room, moving gracefully, feeling loved and secure. She could write him tonight—"My darling Tom:"—but she was too tired. Tomorrow night would do, and maybe the next morning there would be a letter from him—maybe that night he would come back. She stood at the tall windows for a long time, looking out. The moon made a wide silver stripe on the sea, irregularly broken by the ships (which one was Tom's?), and the slick tops of the palm leaves glistened, almost as if they were coated with ice. The word "peace" ran through her mind. Everything was at peace.

Tom stopped for a cup of coffee in one of the late cafés near the pier. Looking into the bar mirror, the first thing he did was scrub the lipstick off his mouth with his handkerchief. He couldn't get it all off; it would take soap and water to get rid of the lingering pink glow. Then he saw in the mirror that the two kids were there at a table—Junior and his friend. They had their little white hats shoved down into their eyebrows, trying to look salty, and they were grinning and getting up to come over.

"Look who's here," Junior said. "Whaddya say, Chief?" He was eager as a young bride. Tom looked around without smiling. "What the hell you kids doing out so late? Too late for nice kids to be out."

"What happened to your buddy?" Junior asked, grinning. "He find a home?"

Tom looked narrowly at the boy and picked up his coffee. Any kid ought to know better than to talk to a chief that way. What happened to your buddy, for God's sake. But never mind; he'd get squared away quick enough, back on the ship. "How the hell should I know?" he said. "Don't act wise, Junior."

That shut him up, but the other kid moved right in. "So how'd it go, Chief? You make it?"

Tom put the cup down in its little saucer. "Son," he said, "any man couldn't make that oughta turn in his uniform."

They both howled and slapped their thighs. Tom spread out the slip of paper Betty had given him and got out his address book. "One a you kids got a pen?"

Two fountain pens were thrust upon him, opened for action. He selected one and carefully transcribed the address into the book. *Mrs. Betty Meyers* . . . Then he handed the pen back, dropped the paper on the floor and waved the book in the air a few times before closing it, to dry the ink.

"Well, I see you're keepin' her address, anyway," Junior said. "Couldn't of been too bad, if you're keepin' her address."

"Sure," Tom said. "Why not?"

"She got *your* address?"

It was such a stupid question that Tom played it along. "Sure," he said softly, looking at the kid with a slow smile, raising the cup to his lips. "Why not?"

The boy exploded. "Oh-ho-ho-*ho*! You wanna *watch* that, Chief—you wanna look *out* for stuff like that! Her *hus*band'll be in town one of these days!"

Still smiling, Tom put the cup down and shook his head from side to side. It was hard to believe. The *kids* you got in the Navy nowadays. "Oh, Jesus Christ, Junior. When're you gonna grow up? Whaddya think—I told her my real name?"

Thieves

"TALENT," ROBERT BLAINE said in his slow, invalid's voice, "is simply a matter of knowing how to handle yourself." He relaxed on his pillow, eyes gleaming, and shifted his skinny legs under the sheet. "That answer your question?"

"Well, now, wait a minute, Bob," Jones said. His wheelchair was drawn up respectfully beside the bed and he looked absorbed but dissatisfied, begging to differ. "I wouldn't define it as knowing how to *handle* yourself, exactly. I mean, doesn't it depend a lot on the particular kind of talent you're talking about, the particular line of work?"

"Oh, line of work my ass," Blaine said. "Talent is talent."

That was how the evening's talk began at Blaine's bed. There was always a lull in the tuberculosis ward after the wheeling-out of supper trays, when the sun threw long yellow stripes on the floor below the west windows and dazzled the silver spokes of wheelchairs in its path; it was a time when most of the thirty men who lived in the ward convened in little groups to talk or play cards. Jones usually came over to Blaine's bed. He thought Blaine the most learned man and the best conversationalist in the building, and if there was one thing Jones loved, he said, it was a good gabfest. Tonight they were joined by young O'Grady, a husky newcomer to the ward who sat hunched at the foot of Blaine's bed, his eyes darting from one speaker to the other. What was talent? Blaine had used the word, Jones had demanded a definition and now the lines were drawn—as clearly, at least, as they ever were.

"Best definition I can give you," Blaine said. "Only definition there is. Knowing how to handle yourself. And the ultimate of talent is genius, which is what puts men like Louis Armstrong and Dostoyevsky in a class by themselves among horn players and novelists. Plenty of people know more about music than Armstrong; it's the way he handles himself that makes the difference. Same thing's true of a first-rate ballplayer or a first-rate doctor or a historian like Gibbon. Very simple."

"Sure, that's right," O'Grady said solemnly. "Take a guy like Branch Rickey, he knows everything there is about baseball, but that don't mean he'd of made a top ballplayer."

"That's right," Blaine told him, "that's the idea." And O'Grady nodded, pleased.

"Oh-ho, but *wait* a minute now, Bob—" Jones squirmed eagerly in his wheelchair, charged with the cleverness of the point he was about to make. "I think I got you there. Branch Rickey is *very* talented—but as a baseball *executive*. His talent is in *that* field; he's not supposed to be a player."

"Oh, Jones." Blaine's face twisted in exasperation. "Go on back to bed and read your comic books, for Christ's sake."

Jones howled triumphantly and slapped his thigh, giggling, and for an instant O'Grady looked undecided whether to laugh at him or at Blaine. He picked Jones, and Jones's smile sickened under the attack. "No, all I meant is that you can't very well hold Branch Rickey up as an example of—"

"I'm not holding anybody up as an example of anything," Blaine said. "If you'd only *listen*, instead of using your stupid mouth all the time, you might find out what we're talking about." He turned his head away in disgust, and O'Grady, still smiling, stared at his thick hands. Jones mumbled a small, blurred word of deference that could have been "all right" or "sorry."

Finally Blaine turned back. "All I'm saying," he began, with the elaborate patience of a man who has pulled himself together, "is the very simple fact that some persons are endowed with an ability to handle themselves well, and that we call this ability talent, and that it need have nothing whatever to do with accumulated knowledge, and that a vast majority of persons lack this ability. Now, is that clear?" His eyes bulged, making the rest of his face look even more sunken than usual. One meager hand was thrust out, palm up, fingers curled in a tortured appeal for reason.

"All right," Jones said, "for purposes of argument, I'll accept that."

Blaine's hand dropped dead on the counterpane. "Doesn't make any difference whether you accept it or not, you silly bastard. Happens to be true. Persons with talent make things happen, put it that way. Persons without talent let things happen to them. Talent, get it? Cuts through all your barriers of convention, all your goddamned middle-class morality. Your talented man can accomplish anything, get away with anything. Ask anybody whose business is sizing people up—any of your qualified psychologists—or for that matter your con men and your gamblers—any reasonably astute person who deals with the public. They'll all tell you the same thing. Some have it, that's all, and some don't. Hell, I'll give you an example. You familiar with those small, expensive men's clothing stores up around Madison Avenue in the city?" They both shook their heads. "Well, doesn't make any difference. Point is, those stores are the best in town. Very conservative, good English tailoring. Probably the top men's stores in the country."

"Oh, yeah," O'Grady said, "I think I know the neighborhood." But Jones giggled: "All I know is Macy's and Gimbel's."

"Anyway," Blaine went on, "I walked into one of those places one day when I first came to New York—oh, back around 'thirty-nine or 'forty."

All the stories whose purpose was to show Robert Blaine as a seasoned man of the world were laid in 'thirty-nine or 'forty, when he had first come to New York, just as those intended to show him as an irrepressible youth took place in Chicago, "back in the Depression." Rarely were there any stories about the Army, in which he had performed some drab office job, or about the series of veterans' hospitals like this one that had been his life since the war.

"Just happened to be walking by—I don't know; on my way to see some blonde, I guess, and I saw this coat in the window, beautiful imported English coat. Well, I decided I wanted it right on the spot, probably even decided I *needed* it; that was the way I used to do things. Strolled into the place and told the guy I wanted to try it on. Well, the coat didn't hang right on me, too tight across the shoulders or something, and the guy asked me if I'd like to try something of better quality. Said he'd just gotten a few coats in from England. I said sure, and he brought out this *really* beautiful coat—" The word *coat* was all but lost in a sudden paroxysm of coughing that brought one of his hands up to clutch at the place where his last operation had been, while the other groped for a sputum cup. O'Grady glanced uneasily at Jones during the attack, but finally Blaine's crumpled chest stopped heaving under the pajamas and the swollen vein shrank again in his temple. He lay back, regaining his breath. It was impossible to picture him swinging along Madison Avenue on his way to see some blonde; impossible that any coat could ever have been too tight across his shoulders. When he spoke again his voice was very strained and slow.

"He brought out this really beautiful coat. You know, the kind that never goes out of style; full cut, beautiful tailoring detail, rich material. Well, the minute I put the coat on, it was mine, that's all there was to it. Good fit, harmonized well with the suit I was wearing. I told him I'd take it, even before I'd looked at the price tag. I think it was something over two hundred bucks; I'd probably have taken it if it'd been five hundred. But here I am, pulling the tag off the coat when I remembered I didn't have my checkbook with me."

"Oh Jesus," Jones said.

"Well, by that time the guy and I are chatting about clothes and everything—you know; big friends—so I decided I'd just bluff it through. Started walking toward the door, wearing the coat, and he said, 'Oh, Mr. Blaine, would you mind jotting down your address?' I said, 'Oh, yes, of course; stupid of me,' and laughed—you know—and he laughed, and I wrote down the name of the hotel where I was living then, and we chatted a little more. He said, 'You must drop in again, Mr. Blaine,' and I took off. Next day I got the bill in the mail and sent him a check. In other words, he didn't know who I was—I could have given him a phony address, anything. But just by the way I was dressed, way I walked, way I didn't look at the price tag until after I'd agreed to buy the coat, he figured it'd be safe to handle it that way."

Jones and O'Grady shook their heads appreciatively, and O'Grady said, "I'll be damned."

Robert Blaine lay back breathing hard, a smile hovering on his dry lips. The story had exhausted him.

"Really shows you what a man can get away with just by acting nonchalant," Jones said. "Like when I was a kid, and we used to lift stuff out of the dimestore down home. Hell, I bet between the gang of us we must of cleaned that dimestore out of"— his lips worked, smiling, as he cast about for a suitable figure —"well, a lot of money, anyway."

Blaine opened his mouth to explain that Jones had missed the whole point—he hadn't meant *shoplifting*, for God's sake—but he closed it again without speaking, reluctant to waste the breath. It was no use trying to explain anything to Jones; besides, Jones had settled back in the wheelchair now, twisted his mouth to one side and sniffed sharply through one nostril, which meant he was off on a story of his own.

"I remember one time when I was about fifteen years of age—no, must have been sixteen, because it was the year before I joined the Navy. Well, the other kids and I'd pretty well perfected that technique of acting nonchalant, and one day I got to feeling good, and I decided the dimestore was too tame. Decided I'd try my luck in this big Montgomery Ward store we had down home, which naturally was a lot harder. Thought I'd go it alone, see if I could get away with it, have something to brag about to the gang—you know how kids are. So in I walked, taking my time, circulating around . . ." His voice prattled on, almost effeminate in its preciseness, its Tennessee accent all but bleached out by the ten years he had spent away from home (five in the Navy, he would explain, holding up five fingers, and five in the hospital). Once he paused to cough into a neatly folded Kleenex, which he dropped into Blaine's waste bag. All the nurses agreed that Jones was an ideal patient; he never complained, never broke rules, and kept his belongings spick-and-span.

"I remember each item as if it were yesterday," he said, and spread his fingers to count them off. "One small monkey wrench; one of those jacknives with the five-inch blades; three or maybe four boxes of .22 caliber ammunition; two little sixteen-millimeter Mickey Mouse films—don't ask me why I got *those*—and a stainless-steel padlock. Well, they had this store detective there, and he saw me take the padlock. Let me get all the way to the door and then came over and put the arm on me. Took me upstairs to the manager's office with all that stuff in my jacket and pants pockets. Scared? Brother, I was scared half to death. But the thing was, he'd only seen me take the *padlock*, and neither he nor the manager stopped to think I might have other stuff too. The manager took the padlock and sat there chewing me out for about ten minutes, took my mom's name and address and everything, and all the time I'm standing there wondering if they'll frisk me before they let me go, and find those cartridges and the other stuff. But they never did; I walked out of there with all that stuff in my pockets, and went home. My mom never heard anything from the manager either. But brother, that was the last time I ever tried anything in *that* store!"

"Well, but don't you see, you're talking about *stealing*," Robert Blaine said. "What I meant was—"

But O'Grady interrupted him, and O'Grady's voice was stronger. "Reminds me one time in the Army, when we first hit Le Havre." O'Grady folded his big arms across his bathrobe. He loved to talk about times in the Army. "You guys ever been to Le Havre? Well, ask anybody that was there, they'll tell you it was one lousy town. I mean it was all bombed to hell, for one thing, and most of the part that wasn't bombed was off-limits, but the main thing was the way the people treated you. I mean, they just didn't have no damn use for GIs, I don't care *how* nice you treated them. So anyway, these three of my buddies and me go into this little gin mill, a real beat-up little place, and hell, we're just off the boat; *we* don't know how the people are. So we order a couple cognacs and the bartender gives us this real dirty look, just like this—" and O'Grady made an unpleasant face. O'Grady had hit Le Havre a year after the war, on his way to the Army of Occupation, and this had been his first night overseas, a burly adolescent with PX overseas cap cocked to the eyebrow, his eyes narrowed at foreigners. (Maybe the war *was* over, but weren't they headed for sure trouble with the Russians in Germany? Hadn't the captain said, "You men are still soldiers in every sense of the word"?)

"Well, he brings the drinks, puts 'em down, grabs our dough and takes off to the rear of the bar where these other frogs were sitting. So, you know, what the hell, we got kind of sore. I mean, we couldn't see no goddamn frog bartender treating us like shit, you know what I mean? So this buddy of mine, guy named Sitko, he says, 'Come over here, Jack.'" O'Grady's eyes grew cold, recalling Sitko's face. "He says, 'You compree English?' Guy says yes, a little, and old Sitko says, 'Whadda you got against Americans?' Guy says he don't understand—you know, 'no compree' or some damn thing—and old Sitko says, 'You compree all right, Buster, don't gimme that. Whadda you got against Americans?' Guy still makes out like he don't understand, see, and Sitko's really getting sore, but we tell him, 'Forget it, Sitko. The guy don't understand, leave him alone.' So we go on drinking, you know, couple more rounds, and old Sitko don't say anything, but he's getting madder all the time. Drunker he gets the madder he gets. So finally we're ready to leave, and Sitko says let's buy a bottle, take it back to camp. So we call the bartender back and ask him how much for a bottle. He shakes his head, says no, he can't sell no bottles. Well, that did it, far as old Sitko's concerned. He waits until the bartender goes away again, and then he ducks under the bar—there's this little gate like in the top of the bar, see, right where we're standing—and he grabs a bottle off the shelf and hands it out to this other guy, Hawkins, and says, 'Hold this for me, Hawk.' Then he hands one out to me and comes out with a couple more in his hands—clean as a whistle; those frogs never saw a thing. So we each of us had a bottle—oh Jesus, I forget what-all we had; cognac, we had that, and what's the name of that other stuff? Calvados—we had some of that too, and some other kind of stuff besides. So we shoved the bottles up inside our battle jackets and we're just leaving, almost to the door, when one of the frogs catches on. He starts yelling and pointing, and then they all come after us, but by that time we're out in the street, going like hell."

Jones giggled, rubbing his palms together and pressing them between his thighs. "You get away?"

"Oh, yeah, we got away all right—finally." O'Grady's face showed he had suddenly decided to amend the story—either because a full retreat seemed unmanly in the telling, or simply to make it last longer. "But just outside the door I dropped my damn bottle—didn't break, just fell on the sidewalk, and I hadda stop and pick it up."

"Oh Jesus," Jones said.

"So here I am bending over, picking up the damn bottle, and this big frog comes up behind me. I just straightened up and swung around, holding the bottle by the neck, and let him have it right across the side of the head. Didn't break that time either—don't ask me *what* it did to that bastard's head, but I think he was out cold—and I took off again. Never ran so fast in my life."

"Ha-ha *goddamn*," Jones said. "I bet you guys had a party *that* night, huh?"

"Boy, you ain't kidding," O'Grady said.

Robert Blaine had squirmed fretfully throughout the story, clearly annoyed. Now he propped himself up on one elbow and glowered at them. "Hell," he said, "you guys are talking about *stealing*. Hell, if you want to talk about stealing, that's different. *I'll* tell you a story. *I'll* tell you a story about stealing. In Chicago, back in the Depression. Lost my job on the *Tribune* just before Christmas. Little woman sitting at home with the kid—I was married then, see. Didn't work at it very hard, but I was; had a three- or four-year-old kid—and here I am out of a job at Christmas. Went off on about a four-day drunk, ended up in some hotel with this model I used to run around with, girl named Irene. Beautiful girl. Tall, long legs, looked like a million dollars."

O'Grady's eyes flicked at Jones in a quick smile of disbelief, but Jones was listening attentively, and Blaine didn't stop his flat-voiced monotone long enough to notice it. It seemed almost that he couldn't stop, that the talking was a kind of convulsion, a bloodless hemorrhage.

"She said, 'Robert, you've got to pull yourself together; do you know what day this is?' Turns out it was Christmas Eve. I said, 'Don't worry, honey.' Said, 'Come on, we got some shopping to do.' Checked out of the hotel—she had to pay the bill; I was flat broke by that time—and I grabbed a cab and took her to Marshall Field's. She kept saying, 'I don't understand, Robert. What's the idea?' Got to Marshall Field's, took her inside and started walking around the women's accessories department, pulling her along by the hand. Found a nice woman's handbag—I don't know, lizard-skin or something, about twenty-five bucks. Said to Irene, 'Think the little woman'd like this?' She said, 'Well certainly, but you can't afford anything like that.' I said, 'Here, hold on to it.' Handed her the bag and pulled her along through the crowd. Went to the toy department, picked up this big teddy bear, said, 'Irene, think Bobby'd like this?' She said, 'You can't *do* this, Robert.' Said, 'Why not? Doing it, aren't I?' Handed her the teddy bear and we took off. Teddy bear was small enough so she could hold it under her coat, see, she had this big fur coat—and we went all over the store that way. Got a couple more things for my kid, and then she said, 'We've got to get out of here, Robert.' Said, 'Not until we buy something for *you*, baby.' Took her to the blouse department, got this beautiful pure-silk blouse off the counter, just her size, and then we walked out the front door and into a cab. Took Irene back to her place, borrowed a couple bucks from her so I could pay off the driver, and then I rode home. Irene couldn't get over it. Kept saying, 'Nobody but you could do a thing like that, Robert.'" He began to laugh noiselessly, his eyes gleaming.

"Well," Jones said chuckling, twisting his fingers. "Just shows you what a man can get away with."

But Blaine was not finished. "Dutiful husband and father," he said. "Coming home with gifts the day before Christmas. In a taxicab—" He laughed again, and it was an effort for him to pull his lips back over the grin of his yellow teeth in order to speak. "That's the way I used to do things." He sank back on his pillow and fell silent, breathing hard, while Jones and O'Grady tried to think of something to say.

At last O'Grady said, "Well—"

Blaine interrupted him. "And that's not all I stole," he said. "That's not all I stole. Stole damn near everything I had in those days." His face was sober again now, his eyes glazed, and as he spoke his fingers crept inside the pajama top to explore the scars. "Christ, I even stole Irene! Her husband made better than fifty thousand a year; she took off to New York with me and we lived off his dough for six months. Me, I didn't have anything. Only she thought I had everything. Probably still does. Took a big wad of his dough and came to New York with me. I didn't have anything. She thought I had everything. Thought I was a genius. Thought I was going to be another Sherwood Anderson. Probably still does."

"Well, that's life, I guess," Jones said vaguely, and then both he and O'Grady became aware that Blaine was in some difficulty. His eyes had closed, and he was swallowing repeatedly—they could tell it by the bobbing of his sharp Adam's apple—and they could see the flannel of his pajama top move with each beat of his heart. His breathing was shallow and irregular.

For some moments O'Grady stared at him, wide-eyed, until Jones signaled it was time to leave by backing his wheelchair up and turning it around. Anxiously, O'Grady slipped off the bed and came over to wheel the chair for him.

"See you later, Bob," Jones called as they moved away, but Blaine made no reply. He didn't even open his eyes.

"Christ almighty," O'Grady said in a hushed voice as soon as they had left the bed. "What's the *matter* with him?"

"Nerves," Jones said with authority. "Happens to him quite often. Push me over to the nurse's office, will you, O'Grady? I'll just tell her about it; she'll probably want to check his pulse and whatnot."

"Okay," O'Grady said. "Whaddya mean by nerves, exactly?"

"Well, you know. He's pretty high-strung."

Miss Berger was the nurse on duty, and she was laying out the evening medications when they stopped at the office door. She looked up, annoyed. "What do you want, Jones?"

"Just wanted to tell you Bob Blaine isn't feeling too good, Miss Berger. Thought you might want to have a look at him."

"Who?"

"Blaine. Nerves are kind of acting up again. You know."

She shook her head over the medications tray, clicking her tongue. "Oh, honestly, that Blaine. *Nerves*, for God's sake. Big baby, that's all he is."

"I just thought I'd tell you."

"All right, all right," she said, without looking up. "I can't come now. He'll have to wait."

Jones and O'Grady shrugged in unison, and O'Grady started the wheelchair up again.

"Where to now?"

"Oh, I don't know," Jones said. "Might as well go lay down, I guess, take it easy for a while. What time's the movie tonight?"

A Private Possession

EILEEN PUSHES THE puff sleeve higher on her skinny arm but it slips down almost to her elbow again; the elastic cannot hold it. Aunt Billie buys all the dresses too big so she'll get more wear out of them. If Eileen pushes up both sleeves so that the cloth blouses properly, she can hold them there by keeping her arms pressed firmly against her sides. But as soon as she relaxes, the sleeves ease down again and hang limply, almost to her elbows. And the skirt, of course, is too long.

"Goodnight, Sister" . . . . "Goodnight, Sister."

The girls are filing out of the classroom and Eileen is near the end of the line. The nun, pale and rather sinister in her black robes, stands at the door with one of her white hands holding the other loosely at her waist. Eileen counts to herself: four more, three more, two more.

"Goodnight, Sister."

"Goodnight, Frances."

Now it is her turn. "Goodnight, Sister."

"Goodnight, Eileen."

And she hurries into the cool hallway that smells of pencils, threading her way between groups of little girls. She is taller than anyone in the fourth grade and has no friends. Some of the girls are afraid of her, and she accepts this with pride although she would rather be liked. But now she thinks only of getting outside and meeting her brother. The sun is blinding in the concrete school yard and she squints and makes a visor with both hands. Roger's group of boys is bunched by the corner of the building, and she picks him out. He is laughing and when he sees her he looks embarrassed. She starts toward the road, walking slowly so he can catch up. Above the chattering and shouting she hears him say, "See you guys," and then she hears his shoes scuffling up behind her.

"Leen, will you take it easy? Why d'ya always have to be in such a big rush?"

"We'll miss the trolley."

"Oh, miss the trolley. That ain't the only trolley."

"Don't say 'ain't.'"

"Why?"

"Because you know better, that's why."

"Aw, shut up."

She probes the pocket of her dress, feels the warm, hard fifty-cent piece she found in the playground that morning. "Roger?"

"What."

"Look what I found at recess."

"Hey! Where'd ya find it?"

She senses the quick envy in his voice and decides to make the most of it. "Wouldn't you like to know?"

"Come *on*. Where'd ya find it?"

But she raises her eyebrows coyly and smiles a secret smile. They are waiting at the trolley stop now, and Roger lapses into sullenness. After a moment he says, "Know what Whitey an' Clark an' them were saying?"

There is a tightening in her chest. It will be something about her.

"They said you had so many freckles you couldn't hardly see the skin between 'em, and you might just as well be a darkie."

"Think I care?" Then, after a pause, "I could tell you about some things *I* heard." But she sees the flicker of worry in his face vanish as he becomes confident she is making it up. And she can't think of anything mean enough so she doesn't carry it through except to say, "But I won't, because it's not polite."

"You didn't hear anything. I know you."

From the streetcar they watch yellow weeds streak by on the side of the road, look idly beyond them at the trim white houses and flat greenness of the Florida suburb. She decides to tell him about the half-dollar now. "Roger?"

"Yeah."

"I found it by the wire fence. Over there on the other side of the swings, you know?" The excitement of finding it returns and she can tell he is interested even though he says, "What do I care?"

When they walk up the driveway he kicks up small clouds of dust with his feet. "What're ya gonna buy with it?"

"I haven't decided. Maybe I won't buy anything, and just save it instead." She has almost forgotten to tell him the most important part. "Roger, don't tell Aunt Billie, all right? Promise?"

"Why?"

She isn't sure, exactly. It is mostly because she wants something of her own, something Aunt Billie can't touch. "Just because, that's why."

"Okay." And she looks at him, wondering if he understands.

Aunt Billie, in her room upstairs, is writing her weekly letter to their mother. She is a neat woman with a small, pretty mouth.

> The school is doing wonders for your offspring, Monica. They were a pair of wild Indians all summer, you know, and this discipline is *such* a relief. Roger seems to be doing splendidly at his studies and it's fine for him to be with other boys. Eileen, of course, is still a problem. One Sister tells me they simply *cannot* get her to take an interest, and heaven knows *I* can't handle the child. But she has quieted down a good deal. We haven't had a real tantrum for several months now.

Through the screened window she sees them starting up the driveway. She adds: "But they're really swell kids. I've grown quite enslaved by them." Then she puts the blue monogrammed page back in the stationery box. "Roger!" she calls through the window. "You'll ruin your new shoes doing that." She gets up and goes downstairs to let them in. "Now hurry and change your clothes if you want to, and wash carefully. Food's on the table."

Eileen feels better when she has put on khaki shorts and a pullover jersey. There is a good smell of sea and sand in the old clothes. She transfers the half-dollar from the dress to the pocket of the shorts.

"Eileen!"

"Coming."

On the enameled kitchen table there are two big glasses of milk and a plate of cream cheese and jelly sandwiches. Roger has already started. He is talking with his mouth full and has a milk mustache. Aunt Billie leans against the spotless white refrigerator, arms folded, smoking a cigarette. "Well, we'll see," she says to Roger.

He has been asking about the turtles again. There is a place down the road where you can buy a small live turtle with your name painted on its shell. They are forbidden at school and so have become a fad in Roger's class. The game is to see if you can keep one all day without getting caught.

Eileen bites into a sandwich and reaches for her milk. She decides she would like a turtle too, but not just for school purposes. She could play with it for hours and take care of it, let it crawl wetly across her arm. And it would have "Eileen" written gracefully on its back, with perhaps a rose or a coconut palm. It would be alive and hers. They cost sixty cents. Why, she could buy one tomorrow if she felt like it, and Aunt Billie couldn't do anything. Only it might be more fun to keep the money for something else. Or just for itself, as a secret.

"You mustn't *slump* so, Eileen."

"Roger's slumping."

"Well, Roger mustn't either. But it's more important for you to learn those things, dear. In a few years you'll be very grateful if you've learned to keep your back straight. A good posture is one of the most valuable things a lovely young girl can have."

This is an old theme of Aunt Billie's. Eileen thinks it inconsistent with other things she has heard, or rather overheard, Aunt Billie say. ("Of course, Eileen will never be a really pretty girl.")

No, Eileen decides, she'll keep the fifty cents just the way it is. She chews the sandwich methodically for a long time without swallowing, staring at the refrigerator. So many you can't see between them. Might as well be a darkie. She wonders if they really did say that. It doesn't matter. He said it, anyway.

Roger is anxious to go on talking about the turtles. "They only cost sixty cents, Aunt Billie. And they last forever, almost."

"I said we'll see, Roger, but we won't discuss it any further now. Eileen would probably want one too, and two times sixty cents is a dollar twenty."

Eileen is afraid Roger is going to mention the half-dollar; his face shows he has thought of a new approach.

"Well, yeah, Aunt Billie, but Leen has fifty—"

She has cut him off with a sharp glare that says, "You promised!"

"—cents already," he finishes lamely, and then he blushes and looks away. Eileen feels her mouth growing tight with anger as she looks at him.

Aunt Billie says, "All right, dear," hardly paying attention, but there is a long silence after this, and when Eileen glances up she is startled by the look of concern—no, curiosity—that has come into Aunt Billie's eyes.

"Why, Eileen, dear. Whatever is the matter? Roger, what did you say that upset her so? Something about fifty cents?" Kindly but shrewd.

"Nothing," Roger mumbles, making it worse.

The eyes are turned on Eileen again. "Dear, what is this about fifty cents? Do you have fifty cents?" Inquisitive, now, sensing something unpleasant.

The lie is automatic. "No." But it is also obvious.

"Eileen, dear. It doesn't matter to me whether you have fifty cents or not. It does matter whether or not you're telling the truth." And now it is an authoritative, confident voice.

"I am telling the truth, Aunt Billie. I don't have fifty cents. Roger just said that." And Roger looks shocked. Oh, he'd understand if he had to wear those dresses, if he had to—

"Eileen!"

Waves of dread and fear come over her. She begins to wonder if she should show the fifty cents after all.

"Come here."

Slowly she puts down her sandwich and rises from the table.

"Now either show me this fifty cents or tell me where it is. I've heard quite enough of this storytelling."

Dumbly, then, she produces the warm coin. Aunt Billie looks at it with wide, worried eyes. "But why were you so—" Eileen can see the accusation forming in Aunt Billie. "Where did you get that money, Eileen?"

And in slow terror, now, she realizes that saying "I found it" will sound like another lie.

"I—I found it."

"Tell me the truth."

"I did. I found it."

Roger is white-faced across the table. He is nervously fingering a sandwich, watching. "That's right, Aunt Billie, she found it," he says.

"Were you with her when she found it?"

And then the worst thing happens. Roger says "no, but—" and Eileen says "yes," at the same instant. Then they look at each other quickly, both shaking their heads.

Aunt Billie is looking steadily at Eileen. "I've heard quite enough of this. Go change your clothes, Eileen. We're going back to school."

She is unable to speak or move.

"Now. Go change your clothes. And wipe the milk off your face first."

With the back of her hand Eileen removes the milk mustache. Then she turns and walks out of the kitchen. She hears Roger say, "But she—" And Aunt Billie, sternly: "Never mind, Roger. This is between Eileen and me. It doesn't concern you at all."

Eileen puts on the flapping cotton dress and changes her sneakers for shoes. There is a drab nausea in her chest, like the first stage of car sickness. With the half-dollar in her pocket she goes to the front door. Aunt Billie is waiting for her; she has put on a hat and powdered her face. They are silent as they walk down the drive, and not until they are waiting for the trolley is Eileen able to say, "Aunt Billie, it's true. I did find it. At recess in the school yard."

"Dear, if you found it why on earth would you have been so afraid to tell me? Now don't make it worse. I'm sure one lie is bad enough."

On the streetcar a constriction of her throat is added to the nausea. Milk rides heavily in her stomach and the tastes of cream cheese and jelly cloy in her mouth. None of what is happening seems real. Beside her, Aunt Billie's profile is raised defiantly. The school yard is clean and deserted in the afternoon light. The nun who lets them in leads them slowly down the long, pencil-smelling corridor to Sister Katherine's office, and then they are inside and it is too late, and there is nothing to do but stand there.

Sister Katherine's face is warm and smiling at first. "Why, good afternoon, Mrs. Taylor." But when she looks at them closely her face begins to get like Aunt Billie's.

"I believe my niece has something to tell you, Sister. Go ahead, Eileen."

But if she tried to speak she would burst into tears, and there is nothing to say. Everything is purple and brown and black in the room. There are wide, washed boards in the floor, and a wrinkled black shoe peeks from the hem of Sister Katherine's robe.

"What is it, child?"

Sister Katherine's face is the color of a dead pig Eileen saw once on a farm.

"Perhaps you'd better explain, Mrs. Taylor."

"I think Eileen is quite capable of telling you herself. Go on, dear."

"I—" The floorboards blur and shift before her.

Aunt Billie sighs tiredly. "Well, Sister, it's simply this. It seems Eileen has stolen fifty cents; I presume it was from one of the other children, and I've brought her here to return it to you."

"Well, child?"

There is nothing to do but hand her the half-dollar. Eileen's throat is on fire and she thinks, It's a dream and I'll wake up.

And now Sister Katherine's face is opening and closing and there is a quiet voice: "You know this is a very wrong thing you've done, Eileen. I don't believe I have to tell you that when we do a very wrong thing we must expect to suffer for it. . . ."

The pig had been dead for three days in the rain. In a sudden panic Eileen wants to scream, "I didn't steal it! I found it! I found it!" Instead she stands there, waiting for it to be over.

And later Sister Katherine and Aunt Billie are shaking hands. "I can't *tell* you how badly I feel about this, Sister."

And soon they are in the gray school yard again, then at the trolley stop. On the streetcar, silent, she watches the lavender blur of passing weeds. (I hate her, I hate her, I hate her, I hate her.)

Roger is standing by the house, hands in pockets, when they come up the driveway. His eyes are round and his lips look small and pale. Aunt Billie goes inside and Eileen stands there with Roger for a minute. But there is nothing to say. You can't throw yourself into a boy's arms and cry, and she doesn't want to anyway. She doesn't want anybody's arms. She doesn't want— All she wants is to—

She walks erectly around the side of the house. There is a place out in back, a kind of toolshed, where she can be alone.

Upstairs, Aunt Billie has opened the stationery box again and started a new paragraph.

A *most* distressing thing just happened, Monica . . .

Eileen stands in the shed and stares at a plank shelf that holds two half-gallon cans of paint.

Sherwin-Williams: White Lead.
Sherwin-Williams: Forest Green.

And when the sobs finally begin they are long, scalding ones, the kind that come again and again.

The Comptroller and the Wild Wind

THE MORNING AFTER his wife left him, George Pollock, comptroller of the American Bearing Company, had breakfast at a counter for the first time in twenty years. He destroyed three paper napkins trying to remove one, whole, from the tight grip of the dispenser, and nearly upset a glass of water in an effort to keep his briefcase from sliding off his lap. And the breakfast itself was all wrong; the fat countergirl had put milk in his coffee before he had a chance to stop her, and the egg, whose timing he had specified at two and a half minutes, was entirely liquid.

"Miss," Pollock said, but she was hurrying past, calling "Scramble two, side of french," and paid no attention. "Miss," he said again, more sharply, and she turned around, lifting her eyebrows in a silent "yeah?"

"Look at this egg." He let some of it run from his spoon. "Does that look like two and a half minutes?"

"What is there, something wrong with it?" There were drops of sweat on her upper lip and a few strands of hair lay pasted on her cheek.

"It's raw," Pollock said. "I can't eat that."

She shrugged sullenly. "I'm sorry, Mister, I gave the order like you said." And she began to rinse glasses in the tub beneath the counter, not looking at him. He wanted to shout at her but controlled himself, aware that the other customers were watching. There was certainly no point in making a scene before the sallow office boys on his left or the heavy-faced man on his right who stared half smiling, his lips powdered white from a jelly doughnut. Instead he pushed the eggcup away and sipped at his milky, inadequate coffee. It would be good to get to the office, where everything was normal.

Once outside the steamy lunchroom door he squared his hat, settled the shoulders of his topcoat and set out briskly, enjoying the ring of his heels on the pavement.

A long time ago, he had married a girl with splendid long legs and a face that was described as pert (in the blue half-light of dawn she whispered, "darling, darling, darling," and the legs were strong, the face was wild and lovely). The girl had borne his child ("Oh, George, don't look, I'm so ungainly," she said, and, "George, I'm going to hate him if he doesn't look like you, or if he's a girl"), but the child had died. Everyone agreed she took it very well, and nothing between them was changed. The girl continued to worry about him and listen to his plans and keep house for him, first on West Tenth Street, where they had a cat, and then in Englewood, where they had a car and a garage. (It was once during the Englewood days that J. C. Farling, the general manager of American Bearing, said, "I want to tell you, George, you got a regular peach of a wife." And when he told her she laughed. "Oh, aren't they funny, those big, bald, half-articulate men with their terrible neckties? A regular peach of a wife. Imagine what *his* wife must be like. And imagine his being your boss." And he said: "Well, I'd hardly call John Farling half-articulate, Alice, whether you like his ties or not. You've got to learn to judge people for what they are, and Farling is a first-rate businessman." And she said: "That's not what I meant, dear; I'm not *judging* anybody.")

A little later the girl, or rather the woman, the wife who was becoming heavier and more nervous, began to keep house for him in Bronxville, and their lives became more ordered. ("But there's no *reason* for you to take a job, Alice," he said once, "and there's so much you wanted to do with the house. At Englewood you couldn't wait to get started on it." And she said: "Oh, George, it *is* a lovely house and I *am* happy here, but *look* at me—I'm getting fat and I sit around all day and I'm damned if I want to be like Mrs. Whiting and Mrs. Clark, with their luncheon clubs.")

The second year in Bronxville she began buying books of poetry all the time and wearing clothes that were thought a little strange for Westchester, and the third year they went through what he later thought of as their quarreling phase—a series of fights so frequent and bitter that when it ended, in the inevitability of mutual exhaustion, they decided they had reached a new maturity, had learned at last to live together as adults. And for the rest of the decade that changed them from nearly forty to nearly fifty they rarely quarreled at all. Perhaps they had not spent as much time together, perhaps they had fewer common interests, but at least they had not quarreled. And at least he had tried; he had always been gentle with her and tried to understand her. Once he had even bought and read, in private, one of those sensible books on menopause, feeling a little foolish about it afterwards, but reassured, because all the cases it described were real neurotic types and none of its clinical dogma could possibly have applied to Alice. And all along, right up until last night, he would have said they had a settled, well-adjusted marriage, imperfect as all marriages, but basically sound. And then quite suddenly it had all fallen away. She was standing in the middle of the living room when he came in, her face strangely white, and her suitcases were standing beside her. "George, I'm all packed. I wanted to be out before you came home because I wanted to avoid a scene. I was going to leave a note." He sat down on the couch and looked at her, still wearing his hat and holding his briefcase. "Oh, George, you're *not* shocked. Please don't pretend you're shocked. You know *exactly* what kind of a marriage we've had for the past five—my God, the past *ten* years."

"But where are you going? I just don't understand it, Alice."

"All right, then, I'll make it very simple so you can understand it. First I'm going into town to meet Max and then we're going to drive west."

"Max? Who's Max? You mean Max *Werner*? You mean you and he have been—"

She sat down on a suitcase and squeezed her hands together, looking at him, and then she broke into a shrill, short laugh. "Oh, George you *can't* tell me you didn't know about it!" And it was hard to tell whether she was being cruel or simply embarrassed. Werner was a tousled, intense man who taught history or something at some high school and used to drive her to lectures at some local poetry society. He had come to dinner once or twice, about a year ago. Had it started then? He sat there feeling stunned, that was all, and finally he said, "Well, I suppose there's very little I can say." After that, for a long while, they talked of legalities: arrangements to be made for a divorce and for the disposal of the house, which was in her name, agreeing several times on the vague statement that there was really plenty of time to take care of these things later, and it was all absurdly unemotional, even when she went to the hall, excusing herself, and telephoned to Werner in some New York hotel to say she would be late. But about seven she said, "You must be hungry, George," and they moved into the kitchen, where she began to make some coffee and a sandwich for him. And there, while he sat stiffly at the enameled table and watched her familiar movements with the Silex, watched the careful way she measured tablespoons of coffee, blood pumped into his throat in a sudden fury of jealousy and grief and he cried, "But I *love* you! You know I've always loved you!" That started it; for an hour they shouted at each other, dizzy with the release and impact of their terrible words, carried around the kitchen in the stalking, circling ritual of caged tigers, and afterwards he could remember only fragments of what they said.

Once, backed against the refrigerator with her eyes flashing up and down him and her mouth curled for hissing, she said, "Oh, how can anyone hate you; you're not hateful—you're just a pompous, posturing, *fussy* little man!" And another time, when he had turned away from her after saying something long and bitter about Werner, and stood hunched dramatically over the back of a chair, she came up behind him and said, very quietly, "I've never *felt* unfaithful to you, George, don't you see? What was there to be unfaithful *to*?"

It caught him off guard, and for a moment his mind seemed as clear, as grimly logical as her words. Did she really think that? Was it really that simple? He thought of his evenings at the club, playing cards. And he thought, fleetingly, of a pretty Irish waitress at the restaurant where he had lunch every day, the one who called him "Mr. Pollock," and whom he had watched with a foolish wistfulness only last week. But the moment was brief; as meaningless, probably, as all the things they were saying to each other, and he turned on Alice again. "This is what I get," he shouted, "after all I've—"

"Oh, yes, tell me, please! Tell me exactly how much you've given me. Give me an itemized goddamned account!" And the mindless ritual of the quarrel was resumed.

Finally she cried, which was a tremendous relief, and then they were both worn out. They drank coffee without talking much, and then she went upstairs to make up her face again. When she came down she telephoned for a cab, and then they were standing in the doorway with strange faces, muttering that they were sorry, and then she was gone. There was nothing to do but walk around the living room, wondering if the neighbors had heard them and seen the cab, wondering how to handle the business of the packing, the storage company, and the hotel.

Now, crossing Forty-second Street, Pollock tried to put his feelings in order. The rankling thought of Werner, the question of whether she would ever come back and the other question of whether he *wanted* her back—these, which had tortured his nerves all night, were now, if not dormant, at least mercifully assimilated in his mind; their shock was gone; he could deal with them later. He pushed through the revolving door into the lobby, where the jaunty young elevator starter made a harsh, annoying *crick-crack* with the gadget in his hand. All that possessed him now was a sense of being alarmingly alone, robbed of security; he knew the fear that grips the bowels of a child lost in a crowd. This was ridiculous, he decided, and as if to prove it he gave the brim of his homburg a curt yank, setting it lower on his forehead as he strode into the elevator. ("I love you in a homburg," she said once, years ago, when he had first started wearing one and felt self-conscious about it. "It's just right for your face—so neat, sort of, and urbane.")

"Morning, Mr. Pollock— Hey, the *Journal* really did it up brown, didn't they?" It was young Merton at his elbow in the elevator.

"What? Oh, good morning, Stan. What did you say?"

"*The Accountants' Journal.* Didn't you get yours?"

"Oh, it's out, is it? No, I didn't have a chance to see the mail this morning."

"Well, look. You even got a spot on the cover." He handed the magazine to Pollock as they got out, and they stopped on the way to the men's cloakroom while Pollock examined the cover and Merton beamed at him. There it was, about halfway down the index of feature articles, in the tiny black type of the *Journal*'s conservative format: "A Few Pointers on the Annual Report," by G. J. Pollock, page 19.

"How *about* that?" Merton said. He was the younger of Pollock's two assistant comptrollers, less than thirty, tense in his anxiety to please.

"Well," Pollock said, "I certainly never expected a place on the cover," although of course he had. Writing the article several months ago, at the request of the publicity department, had been a keen pleasure for him. They had wanted to let one of the publicity boys ghostwrite it, but he insisted on doing it himself and spent a week of evenings on the manuscript. Alice had helped him with the final draft, the day he stayed home with a cold, and she said it was very well written and read certain sentences aloud to show how nicely they were put together. The only thing she changed was the title; he had called it "Streamline Your Annual Report," and she said it sounded brash and that "streamline" was a commercial cliché. She had always liked essay titles to be dignified and reserved, she said, like "Aspects of the Novel" and "Notes Toward the Definition of Culture."

"Wait'll you see the inside," Merton said as they shed their coats and hats. "They gave you a two-page layout and they used both those chart illustrations."

"Fine," Pollock said, "fine," and they walked through the clattering bustle of the accounting department, with its daily barrage of "good morning's," to the partitioned executive offices in the rear. Old Snyder, the other assistant comptroller, was already at his desk in the outer office, gray and scrawny in his shirtsleeves and wearing his green eyeshade. He had been fifteen minutes early to work every day for as long as anybody could remember. Snyder did not subscribe to the *Journal*, and he clambered eagerly to his feet when he saw it. "Is it out? Let me see."

"Wait a minute," Pollock said, holding it back from him. "Haven't even seen it yet myself. Come on inside and we'll look it over together." They moved into Pollock's private office, where he sat at the desk while Snyder and Merton craned over each shoulder in an unconscious parody of assistantship. "Well, now, that's a very nice layout," Pollock said. They were all reading the part called "About the Author" that was set off in a neat little box on the title page:

> George J. Pollock has served as comptroller of The American Bearing Company for the past 15 years. Prior to his association with that company, which began in 1935, he was active in both public and private accounting in Providence, R.I., and New York.
>
> For helping to develop much of the information put forth in this article, Mr. Pollock writes, he is indebted to two of American

Bearing's other accounting executives, Albert T. Snyder and Stanley J. Merton, Assistant Comptrollers.

"Well," Snyder said with a nervous laugh. "You gave us a nice little plug there, that's fine."

"What? Oh, yes, Snyder. Thought you and Stan deserved *some* sort of recognition in this thing." Pollock's habit of calling Merton by his first name and Snyder by his last had been unconscious at first, when Merton first came to the office, but it had proved to be a nice piece of diplomacy. Merton, encouraged by this hint of conspiratorial recognition between himself and boss, could afford to be kindly if patronizing to the colorless old Snyder. And Snyder could feel that Pollock's use of his last name implied an old-line, professional dignity; office boys, after all, were called "Stan." It kept their rivalry constant but muted and worked out very well. They both called him "Mr. Pollock." "Stan," Pollock said, "if I may borrow this from you I'll give you my copy when it comes." He pressed a buzzer on his desk and Mrs. Halbak came in, a gray, businesslike secretary. "First," he told her, pulling out the writing board, "I want to get a note off before I forget it." In an instant she was ready, settled beside him with her pencil poised. "Interoffice letter to Mr. J. C. Farling, General Manager," he said, leaning back in his leather-backed chair. "Subject: Article in *Accountants' Journal,* parenthesis, attached. Paragraph. Thought you might want to look this over, period. A little publicity never hurts, comma, and this magazine is read by some twenty thousand accountants, comma, who are a notoriously talkative breed. Period. Paragraph." This drew appreciative snickers from Snyder and Merton, who were sidling toward the door. "I guess that's all, Mrs. Halbak. Sign it GJP and attach this." With a stout blue crayon-pencil he drew a check mark on the cover of the magazine, beside the title of his article.

The rest of the morning went easily enough, checking over some trial balance figures with Merton, and soon it was time for lunch. He went out with Merton (he lunched with Merton quite often lately, and almost never with Snyder) and as they went through the silent foolishness of gesturing for each other to enter the restaurant first, he wondered if the little Irish waitress would be there today. When they sat down, he caught a glimpse of her, slipping through the door marked "In" at the back of the crowded room, and he fingered his menu idly, waiting for her to reappear at the door marked "Out."

"Boy, I'm sure glad you found that snag before we had to run the whole trial balance over again," Merton was saying, peering over the bent back of a busboy who was clearing their table. "Would've had to waste the whole day."

Then she came out, walking quickly with a heavy tray, a small, copper-haired girl whose face was very young and serious. She stopped at the next table to serve a chattering party of women, and he watched her precise, graceful movements as she set a dish down, took two steps around a woman's chair, almost like a dance, and leaned forward again to put another dish in its place. When her tray was empty she slid it under her arm and drew her order pad from the waistband of her tiny apron, moving toward them. The seriousness, no more than tiredness, really, vanished from her face in a brilliant, simple smile. "How are *you* today, Mr. Pollock?—Hello." The added greeting and a fraction of the smile were for Merton, who was studying his menu and hardly seemed to notice.

"Very well, thank you, and you? You're *looking* very well."

"Oh, I'm so *tired* today; honestly, it's terrible. And six o'clock seems so far away."

"Well, you may certainly take as long as you like with us," Pollock said, and she smiled again. "I'd like a very dry martini to start with—will you join me, Stan?"

Merton looked up, surprised. "Why, yes, sure—what's the occasion?"

"Come, now, Stan," he said. "I'd hate to think I'm old enough to need an occasion, and I'm sure you're not." Merton laughed self-consciously, the girl politely. "We'll have two, then, Miss—what *is* your name, anyway?"

"Miss Hennessy, Mr. Pollock. Mary Hennessy."

"Miss Hennessy, then. Fine. Two very dry ones."

"All right, sir, and what would you like to eat? The lamb is very nice today."

They both ordered the lamb, asking that their coffee be brought with it, and Miss Hennessy moved off toward the bar. Pollock felt tense and exhilarated, afraid his face must be red. When the cocktails arrived he said, "Well, Stan, here's luck," and the first cold, wonderfully sour sip began to calm him. Soon he was pleasantly relaxed, and as Merton talked about the trial balance, his young face eager and respectful, Pollock watched him with a certain affection. A good lad, Merton, a very promising young accountant. Still had a few rough edges, but he had matured remarkably in his two years on the job, not only in his work but in his *attitude*, which was the important thing. Clothes, for instance; Pollock remembered the big-shouldered suits and garish neckties the boy had worn at first, and regarded with satisfaction the new Merton across the table: a good conservative tweed, oxford shirt and quiet tie. Pollock felt a sense of personal achievement in Merton, for while it would never have done to advise the boy directly on these matters, he had tried to impart, by his own example and by a phrase dropped here and there, something of his own convictions. It was all right for Farling and his sales executives to dress the way they did and to talk and act the way they did, for they lived in a different world, but an accountant was a professional man, like a lawyer, with a separate set of standards to uphold. Qualities that would be death to a salesman—dignity, reserve, even aloofness—were not only expected of an accountant but important to his success. It was a point old Snyder could never grasp; Merton had grasped it perfectly.

"Stan," he said, when Merton had finished talking, "you've done a lot of first-rate work for us at American Bearing, but I'm sure I don't have to tell you that."

"Well, that's very nice of you to say, sir, I appreciate—"

Pollock held up his hand. "Now, never mind, Stan, never mind that. We're out of the office now and I'd like to talk to you as, well, simply as a friend, if I may." Merton was smiling, a little flushed. "The point is, Stan, I know perfectly well that in a year or so, or maybe sooner, you'll be wanting to leave us for a job with a little more future—perhaps some smaller firm in a new, expanding field, and that's just as it should be." The girl was putting plates of food before them; he had not even noticed her approaching. "The lamb looks splendid, Miss Hennessy, but suppose you bring us two more martinis. You're with me, aren't you, Stan?" Merton nodded and the girl gave them her smile again.

"I just want you to know, Stan, that I wouldn't stand in your way for anything, and when the time comes for you to consider another offer, I hope you'll feel free to call on me for whatever advice I may be able to give you."

"Well, that's certainly a nice attitude for you to take, Mr. Pollock. Truth is, I have nothing else in mind at the present time, but if and when an opportunity does present itself it's nice to know that, well, that you feel the way you do, and that I can come to you for advice on it. My wife'll be glad too—" he grinned boyishly. "Otherwise, no matter *who* the offer came from, she'd be skeptical—you know, afraid I might get mixed up in something fly-by-night."

"Good, Stan," Pollock said, lifting his fresh cocktail. "I'm glad we had this little talk." Merton nodded, chewing, and Pollock watched him. His wife would be skeptical; what was she like? Pollock had met her once, a small, not very lively girl with thin lips. Probably the kind they described as cute; in ten years she would be dumpy. Finishing his drink, he watched Miss Hennessy putting dessert dishes before the women at the next table. The uniform was just right for her; a trim black dress with white collar and cuffs, and the small apron—no more than a few inches of starched white cloth. Facing his way, almost as if to pose for him, she stood erect, holding the tray high beside one shoulder, and handed a dish down to the table with a sweep of her other arm, stretching the dress tight across her small breasts. Then she whirled and walked off toward the door marked "In," a remarkably graceful, remarkably lovely girl.

His food was getting cold. "This little article of mine," he said, picking up his fork. "In a way I had this—what we've been talking about—in mind when I tacked on that little acknowledgment to Mr. Snyder and yourself. A small thing, of course, but perhaps it might be of some service to you—a trifle of added prestige."

"Oh, of course it will, sir," Merton said and grinned. "I'd already planned to make use of it in my résumé."

"Good, good," Pollock said, poking at the cold meat and mashed potatoes. He wanted another drink but was afraid Merton might think it strange. "And of course," he said after a moment, pushing the plate aside and reaching for his coffee, "it's useful to old Snyder too, in a different way. He can take it home and show his wife what an important man he is."

Merton's sudden, loud laughter startled him. He looked up and saw the boy convulsed, his eyes glittering, as if a shared secret joke had been released. "Jesus," he said, "can't you *picture* that? Maybe she'll buy him a new eyeshade!"

Pollock laughed too, rather hesitantly, and then looked at his plate, sorry. It was the first time he had ever confided in Merton that way, and he knew it was bad policy. He drank his coffee in silence and when he looked up again the girl was coming back, bringing their check.

"Why you hardly touched your lamb, Mr. Pollock. Anything wrong with it?"

"Nothing at all," he smiled at her. "I just wasn't very hungry today." She was adding up the bill, pursing her lips over the figures. Her lipstick was an off-red shade, almost orange, a perfect selection for her glistening red-brown hair. She did not have Alice's long thighs, but her own looked solid and nicely rounded under the shifting black skirt. When she had gone with a smiled "good afternoon," leaving them to divide the check and fumble in their pockets for money, Merton looked after her and turned back with a smile that was almost a leer. "Not bad, is she?"

Pollock stood up abruptly and threw his coins on the tablecloth, offended, and as they walked back to the office he talked very little to Merton, and on business matters only. The afternoon was intolerably long. He sat at his desk staring out the window, glad that Merton and Snyder were busy in the outer office. From time to time he felt guilty about his idleness and tried to concentrate on his work, but there was a dull ache in the back of his head, probably from the martinis, and before long he would find himself staring out the window again. At twenty minutes to five the telephone rang, and the voice of J. C. Farling's secretary said, "I have Mr. Farling on the wire, Mr. Pollock." Then there was a click and Farling came on: "George? Listen, that's a regular peach of an article."

"Well, thanks, John," he said, feeling the corners of his mouth curl into a tight smile.

"Why, *damn*, boy, *you* never told me you were a talented writer—stuff makes better sense than half the crap I buy from these advertising geniuses of mine! I mean it, George, you missed your calling—you want a transfer?" He laughed, making the telephone's diaphragm vibrate painfully, and Pollock managed to laugh with him. "—'Course, I'm only kidding, George. Don't any of us know where we'd be at today without you down there in Accounting. No, but listen, in all seriousness, George, it's a crackerjack."

"Well, I'm very glad you liked it, John. You had no objection to my using your name in that context, then, in the third or fourth paragraph? They approved it at Publicity, of course, but I'm delighted if it meets with your personal approval as well."

"Well, tell you the truth, George, I've just given it a quick once-over; got it here on my desk now, kind of glancing through, and Christ knows *when* the hell I'll get a chance to really sit down and read it, but listen, anything you want to say in there about me is fine and dandy as far as I'm concerned, so don't you worry."

"Well, I wasn't *worried*, John, it's just that I—"

"Okay, swell. Tell you, George, I got somebody here in the office and I got to run. Just wanted to tell you it's perfectly swell, all the way down the line."

"Appreciate that very much, John."

"Fine, fine, George; okay, then."

"Right," Pollock said, "thanks for calling, John." And before he was quite through there was a click and Farling was gone. He put down the telephone and saw that it was wet; his hands were sweating. He dried them on his handkerchief as he got up and walked to the window. The streets below were pale with early dusk, and he began to be very sure what he would do this evening. He would go back to the restaurant and wait for her. He would sit at the bar, have a cocktail and chat with her as she worked, and when the time came for her to leave—she said she left at six—he would say something charming: "I wonder if I might see you home?" Or perhaps, with a flourish of his hat and a half-clowning, courtly bow: "Look here, Miss Hennessy, I'd like to buy you a drink, and if that's against the rules I'd like to see you home. I'm sure *that* isn't against the rules."

Through the office partitions he heard the chatter and banging of desks that meant it was five o'clock. He stood over his own desk and put the papers in order, wanting to wait until the crowd was gone, and especially anxious to give Snyder and Merton a chance to leave. He usually walked to Grand Central with one or both of them, and it would be difficult to shake them tonight. Finally, when the noise had subsided, he took his briefcase and left. Snyder had gone home—the ridiculous eyeshade was the only thing left on his desk—but Merton had not. He was out in the nearly empty main office, still in his shirtsleeves, huddled over some papers with one of the bookkeepers.

Pollock waved goodnight, got his hat and coat and hurried to catch the elevator. But before he reached the ground floor it struck him as pointless to be carrying his briefcase, and, hoping Merton would still be busy, he stayed on the elevator to take it back upstairs. As the doors opened again he saw Merton disappearing into the cloakroom. The bookkeeper had been dismissed and there was no one left in the strangely hushed room.

Pollock hurried to his office; if he wanted to avoid Merton now the only thing to do was wait there with the door closed until he heard him leave. It seemed a long time, and he began to feel foolish for hiding, but finally he heard Merton's footsteps come out of the cloakroom and go toward the elevators. Midway they stopped, and Pollock heard him pick up a telephone and dial a number.

"Hello, honey," the boy said, "listen, I had to work late and I'm just now leaving, so I guess I won't make it to the store before it closes."

Annoyed, Pollock leaned against his desk, waiting.

"Huh?—Well, okay, then.—Sure.—What?—No, I feel all right, but I got a lousy headache. Had some drinks at lunch and I guess I'm not used to it.—No, with old *Pollock,* believe it or not. Can you beat that? Jesus, it was a riot too; the old bastard got half looped on two martinis and started giving me this big Lionel Barrymore routine. 'Son, you'll be leaving us soon for greater things, because youth must be served, and yackety, yackety, yack'—*Yeah*, I'm not kidding; and listen, then he says, 'I want you to know that I won't stand in your way—' What the hell's he think, I'm going to ask his *permission* before I quit or something?—Yeah, that's what I *felt* like telling him. Well, listen, honey, I want to get out of here. Tell you more about it when I get home, okay?—Okay, then. 'Bye now."

Pollock waited until the footsteps reached the elevators, and until the elevator doors opened and closed, before he left his hiding place.

The restaurant was almost empty but the bar was crowded. Pollock was relieved to see that no one from American Bearing was there. He took the end stool nearest the restaurant, and saw that she was serving tea or something at a table not far away, with her back to him. He looked away before she turned around, for it would be better if she saw him that way first, it would look less planned.

He drank the first martini a little too fast, and then looked over just in time to catch her eye. She smiled, raising her eyebrows in surprise, and went on with her work. He ordered another and gave his full attention to watching it being made; the bartender's casually careful measuring of ingredients into a mixing glass, the clamping of the glass mouth-in-mouth with the aluminum shaker, the vigorous pumping ritual that made the bartender's cheeks tremble, and finally the pouring of the drink into its frail stemmed glass.

"You're quite a stranger here in the afternoon, Mr. Pollock," the girl said. She was standing right beside him.

"Why, hello there," he said, "still tired? You know, you don't look any more tired now than you did at noon."

"Guess I've got my second wind." At first he thought she had come over just to talk to him, but then she said, "Two Manhattans, Harry," and he realized she was filling an order.

"Well, your day's nearly over now, isn't it?"

"Thirty-one more minutes," she laughed, her eyes shining. "I count 'em."

What lovely skin, he was thinking, lovely soft young skin. "Do you live far from work?"

"Brooklyn. Takes me about an hour."

He wanted to slide his hand around her waist as she stood there. Such a slim, straight little waist. "That must be quite a job, riding the subway so far every day."

"You get used to it," she said. "Just like everything else. Thanks, Harry." She picked up her tray and turned around, careful to keep the drinks from spilling, and then she was gone again.

Emptying his glass, Pollock let the olive roll into his mouth and chewed it slowly. She might not come back until quitting time, but it was all right. He would smile at her a few more times, and it would be only natural for her to stop again on her way out. And then it would happen, easily and casually. She would say, "Why yes, thank you, Mr. Pollock, that's awfully sweet of you," and they would get a cab, and on the way he would say, "Look, why don't you telephone your home and come to dinner with me," or something like that. It would be easy in the cab, enclosed with her, with the excitement of early evening rushing by and her body only inches away.

"Care for another, sir?"

"Yes, please." He shifted his position slightly, angling for a place in the bar mirror that wasn't blocked by rows of bottles, but when he found the reflection of his craning, solemn face, fingers fumbling at his tie, it made him feel absurd: a middle-aged cuckolded man, sprucing up for a planned seduction.

He settled back on the stool, depressed, and drank off part of the new cocktail. Alice and Werner, driving west—had they started yet? Was she laughing and excited? The blood started in his throat. The only thing to do was put it out of his mind.

Young Merton, two-faced and flip, an undeserving, crude young man. He decided to put Merton out of his mind too, and found that putting things out of his mind was surprisingly easy. He concentrated on looking out the plate-glass window at the endless succession of faces that passed, momentarily bright in the darkening street, windblown and tense with hurrying: a crowd of giggling office girls, a young couple talking eagerly with puffs of mist whipping from their mouths. Then for a while he concentrated on two quarters, a dime and three nickels that lay on the bar beside his glass. With a finger he arranged them in a straight line, pushed them into disorder and arranged them again. And then he concentrated on Miss Hennessy across the room as she walked toward the "In" door, hips swaying, skirt floating around the legs, hair bouncing lightly on the shoulders. There was a poem about returning no more. How did it go? Something about watching the boats go by.

"Fill it up, sir?"

"Yes, please." A poem by James Joyce: Alice had said, "Oh, look, George, read this one. I think it's lovely," and she handed him the book. They were in one of those little bookstores on Eighth Street that Alice liked, the ones with the creaking wooden floors. They were Christmas shopping and he was dead tired, his feet hot and sore in their tight shoes. (When was it? Not last Christmas; Christmas before last? Had it really been that long since they'd shopped together?) "Watching the Needleboats at San Sabba"—or San something-or-other. He read the poem over a few times before he understood it, and then he looked at her, and her eyes were shining. "Isn't that lovely?" she said. "Isn't that perfectly lovely?"

I heard their young hearts crying
Loveward above the glancing oar
And heard the prairie grasses sighing:
No more, return no more.

O hearts, O sighing grasses,
Vainly your loveblown bannerets mourn!
No more will the wild wind that passes
Return, no more return.

Suddenly it was five minutes after six. The clock had startled him; he checked it with his watch and swung around on the stool to look for her. Two new waitresses were moving among the tables. Had she gone? He watched the "Out" door and waited, his chest tight, and then she came, looking even younger in her street clothes. She glanced at her watch and began to hurry, almost running through the restaurant. He slid off the stool and started toward her. "Say, Miss Hennessy!"

She turned her head, startled, and smiled at him but didn't stop. "Goodnight, Mr. Pollock."

"Just a minute, Miss Hennessy, I—" She was almost to the door and he hurried to head her off, nearly colliding with a group of people coming in. "Look—" he began, and then he remembered about the hat and the little flourish he had planned, but it came off badly. "I'd like to buy you a drink, Miss Hennessy—Mary—but I suppose that's against the rules."

"Yes it is, Mr. Pollock. That's very nice of you but I'm late and I've got to hurry."

"Precisely," he said, stepping around her to block the door and touching her sleeve. "I know you're late and that's why I thought perhaps you'd allow me to see you home." She smiled and drew her sleeve away. "No, I'm sorry, Mr. Pollock, that's against the rules too. Now, why don't you go back and finish your—"

His hand slid around her arm and squeezed, tight, and his voice was nearly a shout: "*What* rules?"

Her eyebrows jumped and the smile was gone. He dropped his hand quickly and said, "I'm sorry, I didn't mean to startle you. It's just that I don't see why you should object when I'm only trying to be pleasant."

"Well, I do object." Her eyes were narrow now, darting first at him and then toward the bar, as if looking for help. "I don't like to be grabbed that way."

"But I wasn't *grabbing*, don't you understand? I was simply—"

"All right, Mr. Pollock, let's just forget it, all right? Goodnight."

And with a tentative half smile she slipped around him and out of the plate-glass door, closing it behind her and walking quickly away. For an instant he stood there uncertainly, and then he lunged out after her, cramming on his hat, aware as he passed the window that faces at the bar were laughing at him. She was twenty feet away, headed for a subway entrance, and he walked as fast as he could, then ran a few steps. "Wait a minute—I'm not drunk, don't you understand?" He was at her shoulder now, half running, the unbuttoned topcoat flapping behind him. "Look, you don't understand. If I made a scene back there I'm sorry—if you'd just let me explain—"

She stopped at the head of the subway stairs and faced him. "All right, Mr. Pollock, say whatever it is you want to say and get it over with. Don't *yell* like that and run after me. Everybody's *looking*."

"I'm awfully sorry, I don't know what gave you the idea that—well, I suppose a girl in your position does have a lot of trouble with men trying to pick you up—"

"Is that all you wanted to say?"

"Well, no, actually I"—he felt his mouth leap into a ridiculous grin—"simply wanted to take you to dinner and—"

"Let go of my arm."

"—get to know you a little better. I don't see any reason why—"

"Let go of my arm."

"—we couldn't have a pleasant—"

"Let go of my *arm*!" She squirmed away and ran down the steps, and he clattered after her, pushing past another man. At the landing she looked back, then fled down the second flight and through the crowd at the change booth.

"Wait a minute!" he called, clearing the last of the steps. "Wait a minute!" She was out on the platform now, and a train was there, and its doors were sliding open. "Wait!" A sharp blow caught him in the groin and doubled him over—the turnstile. In a rage he whipped back the skirt of his topcoat and jammed a hand in his pocket for a dime. He sprang free just as the doors closed, ran into the chest of a man in a leather jacket and reeled off to the side.

"Why the hell don't you watch out?" the leather jacket said.

The train was moving now and Pollock stood there watching it. Flatbush Avenue, Flatbush Avenue, Flatbush Avenue, and then it was gone.

"Hey *you*. I said why don't you watch out?"

"I'm sorry."

"Well, take it easy next time, for Christ's sakes, huh?"

"Of course. I'm sorry."

He went out and up the stairs, carefully buttoning his coat and righting his hat. And he walked four or five blocks before he realized, coming to a halt and looking around, that he had absolutely no idea where he was going.

A Last Fling, Like

HONESTLY, GRACE, IT really is good to be home. I mean it was a wonderful trip, seeing all those different places and everything, and I wouldn't of missed it for the world, but I don't know, it's funny. When I walked into the office today and saw all you girls working at the same old desks and you all acted so glad to see me, and when Mr. Willis came out with that real cute grin and says, "Well, look at the globe-trotter," you know what I felt like doing? I almost felt like crying.

And I mean, I never thought I'd feel that way about the office, you know it? Oh, I mean, I like all you kids a whole lot and everything, I don't mean it that way, but gee, after working there six years for those lousy two-dollar raises, getting so mad at Mr. Willis I could scream half the time, and always saving up for my trip—I mean, you'd think that when I finally quit and *took* the trip, I wouldn't care if I ever laid eyes on the place again. But I guess a person gets used to having things a certain way, and after that no matter what they do or where they go, they always like to come back. You know what I mean? Well, listen, Grace, I could sit here talking all night—I mean, it's like old times, coming here to Child's for coffee after work and everything—but honestly, I got to get home or my mother'll kill me. I told her I was just going to drop in at the office to say hello; she says, "Ah, I know you—you'll be there all day." So she was right, as usual. And also, Marty's coming over tonight and I got to pick up my dress from the cleaners before they close. So listen, Grace, I'll just give you the high points of the trip now, and we can talk about it some more when you're over at the house Friday night, okay? Because honestly, there's so much to tell I hardly know where to begin.

Well, first of all there was the boat trip, of course. Honestly, I'll never forget the way all you kids came down to see me off that day, and all those swell presents, and me bawling like a baby all over the place; it was really swell. Well, anyway, remember that real cute fella that got up and offered you his deck chair, and you all kidded me about him and I got so embarrassed? Well, the first day it turned out he was married—honestly, I was so mad—but his wife was real nice too, she was French, and we had the same table in the dining room.

There was this other fella at the table that was all right, a single fella. We sort of went around together on the boat until he started bothering me. I mean I liked him and everything, but he wanted to make dates with me in Paris, and dates with me on the Riviera, and dates with me in Venice and Rome—he was going to all the exact same places I was going, and it was really a problem. So I told him, "Look, Walter"—Walter Meltzer was his name, from Milwaukee—I told him, "Look, just because a girl's traveling alone doesn't mean she wants to spend all her time with the first fella she meets." And I guess he got the point, because I didn't see a thing of him after the boat docked. Except one time in Rome; I'll tell you about that later.

So anyway, I also met these two real nice girls on the boat, the ones I wrote you about, remember? Pat and Georgine? They were from Baltimore, both secretaries there, and honestly, they had so much fun together it made me homesick for the times you and I used to have. Well, Pat started going around with this real nice English fella on the boat, and Georgine was mad because she didn't have a date. I introduced her to Walter, kind of hoping I could get rid of him that way, but she said he wasn't her type. I don't think he cared for her much either. I mean, Georgine wasn't a homely girl, and she was very intelligent and had a real good figure and everything, but she was—I don't know, sort of quiet and too serious about everything. I liked Pat better, myself. But I got along real good with both of them, and later we all decided to stick together in Paris—I mean we had the same hotel and everything.

So we finally got to Le Havre, and that's where Pat had to say goodbye to her English fella, because he was staying on to Southampton. Well, she took so long to say goodbye to him that we almost missed the boat train, or anyway Georgine thought we almost missed it, and she got real mad at Pat. They weren't speaking all the way to Paris. But they made up as soon as we got there, and from then on we had a wonderful time. I mean, Paris was really wonderful.

The first day we went crazy buying clothes; I'm still kicking myself for spending so much money. That was when I got this dress I'm wearing—honestly, I could scream about this coffee stain down the front; my mother'll kill me when she sees it. And I got some others too; you'll see them when you come over Friday night.

When we went to the American Express was when I got all those letters from you kids at the office—honestly, they made me feel so good. And there was the cutest letter from Mr. Willis—did he tell you about it at the time? Oh, it was adorable—he says, "We've lowered all the venetian blinds to half-mast in your honor." Honestly, I thought I'd die laughing.

And that was where—the American Express, I mean—that was where we met these three real nice fellas I wrote you about. The GIs? We didn't know they were GIs at first because they were on furlough and they had on civilian clothes. We got to talking to them while we were waiting for our mail, and we went out with them about three times in all, I guess, before they had to go back to Germany. Pat's fella was the cutest, but I think mine was the nicest, in personality and everything. His name was Ike Archer, I guess I wrote you that, and he really was a nice person. Only thing was, he had these big pimples all over his face, you know, a real condition, like, and when he first tried to kiss me I pushed him away, sort of. I felt real bad about it afterwards, and later I let him kiss me goodnight, but I never did get so I enjoyed it. Anyway, we all had a lot of fun together.

They were the fellas that took us to Pigalle, and honestly, Grace, I never would of believed all those stories about Pigalle if I didn't see it with my own two eyes. I mean, they have all these cabarets where the girls don't wear any clothes—you know, not like a striptease, they go through their whole *act* naked. And of course all over Paris they have these prostitutes. You see them everywhere; the railroad stations, everywhere, honestly, you see them come right up to a fella and take him by the arm.

Anyway, these fellas also took us to a real cute place called Harry's New York Bar—it's a regular little American bar, like, you know? You'd never know you were in Paris. Afterwards we always used to go there when we didn't have dates; I mean, the three of us could have a real good time there by ourselves, and we didn't feel funny about going in alone, like we would of at a regular French bar. And then later we met these three airlines pilots—or I guess only one of them was a pilot, the others worked in the office or something. We got to talking to them there in Harry's, and they were the ones that took us to the artists' quarter, over on the Left Bank! Honestly, Grace, you sit in one of those sidewalk cafés and in five minutes you see the funniest-looking people you ever saw in your life walking by. Sort of like down in the Village, only much, much more so. All the girls wear these black sweaters and black slacks, it's like a uniform, and all the fellas either grow a beard or grow their hair down to their shoulders or *some* darn thing.

Oh yeah, I was going to tell you about the airlines pilots or whatever they were. We only went out with them that one time. The one I had was all right, except he was married. His friend told Georgine and Georgine told me, when we went to the ladies' room, and after that I felt kind of funny about it, you know what I mean? I mean, I wasn't a prude about it, but just the same I was glad when the evening was over. Besides, he wasn't really my type at all. He wasn't bad-looking, looked a little bit like Richard Widmark, but he was sort of on the plump side and his hands were always wet. You know those fellas with the wet hands? Another thing, he kept laughing all the time, whether anybody said anything funny or not. Just laughing, the way girls do, you know? Giggling, like. Anyway, Georgine wasn't too crazy about her date either, so we both stopped dating them after that first night, but Pat kept right on with hers. Personally, I couldn't see what she saw in him, but I figured that was her business. Georgine got real mad about it, though; she told Pat she was letting him go too far with her, and they had another big fight, but it didn't last long.

Anyway, on the whole we had a wonderful time in Paris, seeing all the sights and everything—Notre Dame, the Sacré-Coeur, the Eiffel Tower, everything. The Eiffel Tower was where the Frenchman tried to pick Pat up—I wrote you about that; wasn't that a scream? I mean he must of been fifty if he was a day, and there was the wedding ring right on his finger and everything. We finally had to take Pat into a taxi and drive away to get rid of him. And the Sacré-Coeur was where we took a lot of pictures—they're all terrible of me, as usual; my coat makes me look fat or something. You'll see them when you're over at the house Friday.

Oh, and of course we bought a lot of things, besides clothes, I mean. At the cafés, they have these little men—Arabs, I guess they are—and they come around and sell all these handworked leather things: wallets, handbags, everything like that. I bought this great big cushion case—I mean it's a leather case for a hassock, like, and you stuff it yourself?—I thought it'd look good in the alcove at home. And I bought your perfume. And listen, Grace, if you don't like it, when you're over Friday, I'll tell you what, maybe you could trade with my mother. I mean I think the bottle I bought her may be a little bit more your type than hers. See what you think, anyway.

So I stayed in Paris about three weeks, and then I was on my own again. Pat and Georgine stayed on at the hotel a while longer; they were going to visit Pat's brother in Germany and then go home. But I left, and that's when I went down to Cannes, on the Riviera? Honestly, Grace, it's really wonderful down there. First of all, the hotel was really nice; I mean the food was out of this world, and they were all so courteous and polite and everything. I was a little lonesome at first, but right away I met this real nice girl Norma—I wrote you a lot about her, remember? The one that was a schoolteacher in Rhode Island?

So we went swimming down there every day, Norma and me. At first I was scared to wear either of the bikini bathing suits I'd bought in Paris even though almost all the other girls wear them down there, and when I finally did wear one out to the beach Norma kidded me about it and I felt so self-conscious—honestly, it was terrible—so after that I went back to my old suit. Now I don't know *when* I'll ever get a chance to wear them. Probably they'd be all right for sunbathing or something, up on the roof.

Anyway, there was this real cute French fella there—he was what they call the physical culturist on the beach; gives people lessons in calisthenics, you know, and all like that?—and believe me, Grace, you never saw such a build in your life. Arms? My God, he had arms like that. And tan? I'm telling you, he was a real handsome specimen. But let me tell you what happened—it was really a scream. Well, I got to talking to him, he spoke a little English, and I thought he was going to ask for a date or something, you know? I mean, he seemed to like me a whole lot and everything, but he never did. So one time I happened to mention him to Norma, and she says something about how Jeanne must consider herself a very lucky girl. So I says, "Who's Jeanne?" And she says, "Why, the girl over there, didn't you know?" And she pointed to this real cute little blonde who worked at a counter there on the beach, selling soda and stuff. I says, "You mean she's his wife or something?" And Norma gives me this big wink and says, "Well, not exactly his *wife*." So it turned out she was his mistress, like, and everybody knew it, and here I am flirting with the guy to beat the band. And the funny part was, the girl didn't seem to mind at all—I mean, she always smiled at me and acted real sweet; she didn't seem to care *who* the guy made eyes at.

Well, so anyway, then Norma and I went to Nice together, but we didn't care for it much and we only stayed about a day before we took the train for Venice. Well, Venice was where we really went sight-seeing. Norma was a great one for sight-seeing anyway and she'd really read up on Italy. I'll show you some of the pictures we took when you're over Friday. There's one of Norma and me in a gondola—it's terrible of me, though; I'm like a mole, you can't see my eyes. We bought a few things there in Venice too. That's where I bought this silver brooch I'm wearing, and also this cigarette lighter. We didn't meet any fellas in Venice either, but I really think we had just as good a time by ourselves, and we probably got to see a lot more of the sights and everything than if we'd been going out on dates every night. But when we left Venice was when the only really bad thing of the whole trip happened.

Our last day there, before we went to Rome, Norma said why didn't we try eating at this little restaurant she'd seen, this real picturesque little place. We'd eaten all our other meals at the hotel, see, where the food was real good, and I said okay, so we did. Well, I thought there was something funny about the food the minute we started eating, or maybe it was the wine, but Norma says, "Ah, it's just your imagination." Anyway, we ate this big meal and then got right on the train, and my God, half an hour later we were both sick as a dog. Honestly, all I remember about that trip to Rome was running up and down to the lavatory on that train. I mean, it must of been ptomaine or something; I've never been so sick in my life. And when we got to Rome it was all we could do to get into a taxi and go to the hotel and lay down, for two solid days. And after that, whenever I saw a bottle of that red Italian wine, or any of the things we ate that night, I could feel it all coming back.

But after that was over—and I mean, we were really lucky, because it was the only bad thing that happened on the whole trip—after that we got out and saw the town, went to the Vatican and all. Norma only had a few days left before she had to go to Sicily, so we had to do some fast and furious sight-seeing. Norma was a big help; I mean, she spoke a little Italian, and like I said she'd really read up on the subject, so she could explain all about these old Roman ruins and things as we went along.

Anyway, after Norma left I didn't feel much like sight-seeing any more, and my money was running low anyway, so I stayed pretty close to the hotel for a couple of days. And then one night about three days before I had to go back to Le Havre to catch the boat, I went down to the lobby to buy some American magazines, and that's when I ran smack into Walter Meltzer, the fella I'd met on the boat? I mean, it was really a coincidence, staying at the same hotel and everything. So we ate dinner there in the hotel and then went to this nightclub, like, where they had this real good music. We had a pretty good time, and in a way I was a little sorry I gave him that brush-off on the boat, but still—I don't know, he wasn't my type. More your type, I think, Grace; you would of probably liked him a whole lot.

So anyway, that's about all there was. I hung around Rome a few more days and then started back to Le Havre. I stayed a day in Paris, tried to look up Pat and Georgine but they'd already gone to Germany. Oh, and I saw the most adorable dress that day, but I didn't have the money to buy it—honestly, I could of kicked myself. So, the next day I went to Le Havre, and that was that. There was a fella on the boat coming home, kind of an elderly man, who kept making eyes at me and trying to get me into a conversation and everything, but I didn't give him a tumble.

Oh, my God, Grace, look what time it is. My mother'll really kill me—oh, and look, you went and ordered me another cup of coffee while I was gabbing away. Well, long as it's here I guess I'll have to drink it, huh. I'm so late now another ten minutes isn't going to hurt—it's too late to get to the cleaner's now anyway. Besides, if Marty comes early he can wait; it won't kill him.

So here I've been talking a blue streak and I didn't even let you get a word in edgeways. But honestly, this is like old times, isn't it? Remember all the times we sat here planning my trip, with the maps and all? And now here we are again, and it's all over, and all that money's spent and everything. But I still don't think I could of used the money for any better purpose, you know it? I mean, it was something I'll always remember. Boy, is that coffee ever good—let me tell you, the only place in the world you'll ever get coffee like that is right here in New York.

Gee, it seems funny, though, you know? I mean, here I am home again, and in another two months I'll be getting married and everything—Mrs. Martin Krom. Can you imagine? Oh, and honestly, Grace, Marty's been acting so funny since I got back. He never did like the idea of the trip, you know, even though he never tried to talk me out of it or anything. I mean, we always had that understanding, right from the start, even before we got engaged. I always told him, "Look, I've been saving up and planning for this trip a long time, and I still have every intention of taking it." I mean, you know how I felt about it; it was going to be a last fling, like, before I settled down.

But anyway, I guess the fellas in Marty's office must of been kidding him about it or something, because listen, you know what he asked me the first night I was home? He asked me did I wear my engagement ring while I was gone. Well, I mean, I didn't mind him asking me, but something about the way he said it made me mad, you know? So I says, "Whaddya think I'd wear that for? Whaddya think I'm going to do, spoil the whole trip for myself? Keep myself from having any fun?"

He says, "Well, that seems like a funny way for an engaged girl to act." So I says, "Listen, don't give me that." I says, "A man never *has* to wear an engagement ring, so it's all right for you to talk. A man's supposed to be some kind of a privileged character, everybody lets him do what he likes." I says, "Listen, I seen plenty of *men* take a last fling before they get married, but just because a girl does it you give me this stuff about a funny way to act."

He says, "Well, you don't see *me* doing it, do you?"

I had to laugh at him; I says, "Listen, brother, don't kid yourself." I says, "You'd do it quick enough, if you had the money."

A Convalescent Ego

"ONE THING YOU might do while I'm gone," Jean said, "is rinse out those new teacups. Did you hear me, Bill?"

Her husband looked up from a magazine. "Sure I heard you. Wash the teacups." And he could tell by the shape of her shoulders and back as she bent to zip up little Mike's jacket that this was one of her days for feeling overworked and unappreciated. "Anything else you want me to do?" he asked.

She straightened up and turned around, sweeping back her hair with a tired hand. "Oh, no, I don't think so, Bill. You just—rest, or whatever it is you're doing."

"Park!" Mike demanded. "Park, park!"

"Yes darling, we're *going* to the park. Now, let's see," she said vaguely, "have I got everything? Keys, money, grocery list . . . yes. All right, then, come on, Mike. Say 'Bye-bye Daddy.'"

"Bye-bye Daddy," the little boy said, and she led him out of the apartment and slammed the door.

Bill settled back on the couch and picked up the magazine again, but the rankling memory of her words made it impossible to read. "Rest, or whatever it is you're doing." And just what did she *expect* him to be doing, two weeks out of the hospital? He was on doctor's *orders* to rest, wasn't he? Angrily he shut the magazine and flipped it toward the coffee table. It missed and splayed out on the rug, calling his attention to a number of cigarette ashes—his—that had fallen there too. Well, maybe she *was* overworked, but what did she expect? She was pretty lucky not to be a widow, wasn't she, after an operation like that? Using the magazine as a dustpan he scraped up most of the ashes and dropped them in an ashtray, and then rubbed the remnants into the carpet with his slipper. It wasn't until he went to the kitchen for a glass of milk (he was on doctor's orders to drink a lot of milk too) that he remembered about the teacups. She had lined them up on the side of the sink for washing—four plain little cups and saucers that she'd brought home the night before. "I couldn't resist them, Bill," she'd said, "and we do *need* new cups. You don't think it was terribly extravagant, do you?" He smiled as he lathered up the sink brush. This was her idea of a big extravagance now—four cups—when last year she'd have put them on the charge account without even thinking about it. A long illness certainly did change your attitude about money. But in another month he'd be on his feet again, bringing home a man-sized check every payday, and *then* she could begin to relax. They could do the kind of things they'd almost forgotten about—buy clothes they didn't need and go to the theater and throw parties and stay up late when they felt like it. Then maybe she'd get over this dreary business of watching every nickel. Then maybe she'd— Suddenly there was a sharp noise and a little mess of broken china in the sink. It was all over so fast that it took him a full minute, standing there with trembling hands, to figure out what had happened. The porcelain soap dish had given way under his brush, dropped from the wall and smashed, breaking the cup and saucer he'd just washed. He picked up the broken soap dish and scrutinized the place on the wall from which it had fallen, and his first consecutive thought was, Well it certainly wasn't *my* fault. The stupid thing had been hanging there by two little rusty hooks—almost any pressure would have broken it, and the remarkable thing was that it hadn't broken long ago. It certainly wasn't *my* fault, he told himself again. He gathered all the pieces and put them in the garbage. Then very carefully he washed the other cups and saucers, dried them and put them away. But his hands were still trembling as he hung up the dish towel, and his knees were weak when he went back into the living room. He sat down and lit a cigarette, turning the defiant little phrase over and over in his mind—wasn't *my* fault, wasn't *my* fault—with less and less conviction. Things like this had been happening nearly every day since he came home from the hospital. First there had been the discovery that he'd left his silver fountain pen behind, in the locker beside his hospital bed, and Jean had to make a special trip back to get it from the nurses. Then on the second or third day, when he'd insisted on helping with the housework, he had shaken the dust mop out the window so hard that the head of the thing fell off, five stories down into the courtyard, and left him absurdly shaking the naked stick over the windowsill. And there was the time he'd let the bathroom sink overflow, and the time he'd split the side of Mike's wagon wide open trying to nail the wheel back in place, and the terrible morning when he'd not only cut his thumb on the unwinding strip of a coffee can but spilled the coffee all over the floor. At first Jean had laughed about it ("Poor darling, you're just out of *touch* with things, aren't you?") but lately her reactions had alternated between elaborate kindliness and tight-lipped silence, and he didn't know which was worse. How, exactly, could he tell her about this? A pleasant little apology was out of the question; he absolutely could not say "Sorry, darling, I broke one of the cups," and expect to retain a shred of dignity. But what else was there to say?

Sweat prickled his scalp, and his fingers drummed convulsively on the table. He stamped out his cigarette decisively, smoothed his hair and forced himself to sit back and relax. You could drive yourself crazy taking little things so hard; he would have to pull himself together. The soap dish hadn't been fastened securely, it could have happened to anybody, and there was nothing to apologize for. And there was certainly no point in trying to tell her about it all at once, the minute she came in. Obviously, the only way was to let her discover it herself, and then give her the explanation sensibly and calmly, when she asked for it. He pictured the scene.

She would come in with her load of groceries, and Mike would probably be whimpering. He'd get up from the couch to take the bundles from her, of course, but she'd say, "No, that's all right, Bill. You sit still. Mike, stop that, now." He would try to take the bundles anyway, and she'd say, "No, Bill, don't be silly. Do you want to get sick again?" So he would sit down and watch her go into the kitchen with Mike tagging along. She might discover it right away, but more likely she'd be too busy at first. It wouldn't happen until after she'd gotten the food put away and Mike attended to, perhaps not until she'd started to make lunch. Then there would be an abrupt silence from the kitchen, and he would hear her polite, questioning voice: "Bill?"

"Yes, honey?"

"What happened to the soap dish?"

"It wasn't put up properly."

"It wasn't *what*?"

"Well, I can't shout," he would say, with dignity. "You'll have to come in if you want to hear me." And when she came to the kitchen door, with her expression of sorely tried patience, he would say, judiciously, "The soap dish wasn't put up properly, Jean. Didn't you ever notice that before? I don't see how you could've *helped* noticing it. There were only these two little rusty hooks, and—"

"You mean you broke it?"

"*No*, I didn't break it. I mean it wasn't my *fault*. Now look, do you want to hear what happened or don't you?"

She would sigh, perhaps even roll her eyes and then sit down with a great display of attention. "Well," he would begin, "I was washing the cups, you see, and when I lathered up the brush—just using the soap dish the way it's intended to be used—these two little rusty hooks gave way and the whole thing fell into the sink. And there was this cup and saucer that I'd just finished washing, you see, and—"

"Oh, no," she would say, closing her eyes. "Bill, did you break one of the new cups too?"

"*I* didn't break it! It was an accident, don't you understand? I didn't break it any more than you did!"

"Don't shout!"

"I'm *not* shouting!" And by that time Mike would probably be in tears again.

Bill sprang from the couch and stalked the floor, wrenching the sash of his bathrobe into angry knots. That would be exactly the *wrong* way to go about it. Why did he always play the fool? Why should he always set himself up for little humiliations like this? Oh, and she'd love every minute of it, wouldn't she, with that endless act she put on about bearing her burden with a smile. He'd had just about as much of that as he could take—that and all her little wisecracks about "resting." It was time she found out once and for all who *did* wear the pants in this family, bathrobe or no bathrobe.

Suddenly he stopped, breathless, poised on the brink of a new idea. With a grin he tore off the robe and strode into the bathroom to shave. At first, the idea was only a reckless blur in his mind, but in the slow process of shaving he developed it into an orderly, perfect plan of action. When he had finished shaving he would get fully dressed, in real clothes, and leave the apartment. She couldn't be back for another hour, and that gave him plenty of time. He'd take a taxi to the store where she'd bought the cups (luckily he knew which store it was) and buy a cup and saucer to replace the broken ones. Then he'd buy a soap dish with a decent, sturdy wall attachment, and on the way home he'd pick up a dozen long-stemmed roses—and a bottle of wine. He smiled as the extra idea of the wine leaped into his mind. That would be perfect—a bottle of really good wine, maybe even champagne, to celebrate. Then he would hurry home in time to get everything set, and this was how it would happen.

She would come in tired, loaded down with groceries, with Mike bawling and pulling at her skirt. "Mike, *stop* that!" she'd say, and as she bent to detach him from her legs a couple of grapefruit would probably topple from an overstuffed paper bag. "Oh—" she'd say, but before she could say anything else the load of bundles would be swept out of her arms, the rolling grapefruit snatched from the floor. "Bill!" she'd say, aghast, "what're you *doing*?"

"That should be obvious," he would say smiling, perhaps even bowing, controlling all the bundles in one arm while he pulled Mike off her with the other. "Won't you come in?" Then he would turn to Mike. "Go to your room, son, and cut out that sniveling. I won't have it." The boy's eyes would widen with respect as he sidled off toward his room. "Hurry up!" Bill would command, and Mike would disappear. "Now," he would say to his wife, "will you excuse me a moment, darling? Just make yourself comfortable."

"But Bill, you're *dressed*."

He would stop on his way to the kitchen, turn, and make another little bow. "Obviously." He'd stay in the kitchen only a second, just long enough to put the bundles down, and then he'd return, wheeling the tea cart on which he would have previously arranged the box of roses, the bottle of champagne in its ice bucket, two stemmed glasses and perhaps a little dish of salted nuts.

"Bill," she would say, "have you gone out of your *mind*?"

"On the contrary, darling." He would laugh softly. "One might almost say I've regained my sanity. Oh, here—these are for you." And when he had her sitting on the couch with the roses in her lap and a glass in her hand, he would dry the bottle with a flourish, pop the cork and serve it up. "Now," he would say. "May I propose a toast? To the noble memory of your courage and sacrifice throughout my illness; to the celebration of my complete recovery, which occurred today; and to the continuation of my excellent health"— here he would smile winningly— "and yours."

But before she drank she would certainly say, with fear in her voice: "Bill, how much did all this *cost*?"

"Cost?" he'd say. "Cost? Don't be absurd, darling. All that's over now. Drink!"

Exultant, he gave the razor a final sweep across his cheek and cut himself badly, just above the lip. His thoughts were interrupted by the business of washing the soap away and fixing a piece of tissue on the wound, and by the time he returned to the plan it had lost much of its luster. He persisted doggedly anyway, like a man trying to return to sleep for the completion of a dream.

"I'll explain it all from the beginning," he would tell her, "but not until you drink some of this."

Stunned, suspicious, she would take a tiny sip.

"Now. When you left here this morning, darling, I became very fed up with this stupid convalescence of mine—this 'resting,' as you chose so appropriately to call it. So fed up, in fact, that I got clumsy, and the very first thing I did was break one of your new cups. Yes! Smashed it to pieces, and I wouldn't blame you a bit if you're angry. But listen. Breaking that cup had a remarkable, therapeutic effect on me. Made me realize all at once that if I went on much longer that way I'd *really* be sick. Yes, and you'd be plenty sick too, of living with a man like that. So I decided to declare the whole thing over and done with, as of today. Go back to work and everything. And right away I began to feel like a million dollars. Never been so well in my life. Drink!"

"Now wait a minute," she would say. "Just try to calm down and let me—"

"I *am* calmed down."

"All right. Just let me get this straight. You broke a cup and so you steamed out of here and bought all these crazy things—spent more money than I've spent on food in the past two weeks. Right?"

"Darling," he would say, "I'll have earned it all back by tomorrow at this time. One half-day at the office will cover everything, and I have every intention of spending all my days—full days—at the office from now on."

"Oh, don't be a fool. You know perfectly well you're not allowed to work for another month."

"I know nothing of the sort. All I know is—"

"All *I* know," she would say, "is that I come home and find my budget ruined for weeks to come, you carrying on like a madman, *and* one of the new cups broken."

"The cup," he would say icily, "needn't bother you any more. It's been replaced. *And* so has the soap dish."

"Oh, no," she would say, closing her eyes. "You mean you broke the soap dish *too*?"

"Listen," he'd say, or probably shout. "I'm going to the office tomorrow, is that clear?"

"You're going to bed," she would say, getting to her feet. "Is that clear? And I'm going to make lunch, and then I'm going to see if the florist will take these roses back. That'll recover some of the loss, anyway. And I think I'll call the doctor too, and have him look at you. You've probably done yourself a great deal of damage this morning. You're hysterical, Bill."

By the time the scene had played itself out in his mind he was staring fiercely into the mirror, breathing hard. That was how she'd win, all right, as easily as that. She always won. And even if he did go to work in the morning the whole thing would be ruined, the whole point lost. He was blocked every way he turned. He slouched out of the bathroom and began absently putting on the robe as he walked around the carpet. But wait a minute, he thought, stopping in his tracks again. What if he wasn't *here* when she came home? What if he went to the office now, before she had a chance to stop him? It was only a little after eleven—he could leave now, get in a full half-day's work and *then* come home with the new cup and the soap dish, the flowers and champagne. What could she say to that? How could there be any argument when he confronted her with the accomplished fact? The beautiful logic of the thing was suddenly clear, and he nearly laughed as he tore the robe off for the second time and headed for his dresser. He yanked the pins out of a clean shirt and began dressing with brisk efficiency—dressing to go to work like any normal man, just as he'd once done every morning of his life. It was as if there had never been any illness, any hospital, any operation or any convalescence. Everything seemed in order for the first time in many months. He still felt a little weak in the knees, but that would go away as soon as he'd had a decent lunch. When he straightened up from tying his shoes, he almost blacked out in a rush of dizziness. He blinked and sat down on the bed, shaking his head. He was probably a little overexcited; he'd have to get a grip on himself, so that when he walked into the office he would look fit and rested. Already he could picture their faces when he got off the elevator. "Bill!" his boss would say, looking as if he'd seen a ghost, and Bill would grin at him and shake hands—"Hi, George"—and sit casually on the edge of his desk.

"But your wife said you wouldn't be back for another month at *least.*"

"Oh," he would say, "you know women, George. She exaggerates everything. Anyway, here I am. Cigarette?"

"Well, it's certainly great to see you, boy, but how do you feel?"

"Like a million dollars, George. Never better in my life. How's everything here in the shop?" It would be as simple as that. Then as soon as he'd straightened up his desk and shaken hands with everybody and answered all their questions he'd be back in commission again; doing a job and on the payroll.

But he'd have to hurry now, if he wanted to get out of here before she came home. Knotting his tie in the mirror, he planned the note he would leave for her: something short and to the point. "Decided to stop fooling around. Gone to the office. Feeling great. See you later. What kind of champagne do you like?" Or maybe it would be better to let the champagne be a complete surprise, when he made his triumphal return. He hurried over to the desk and wrote it out, omitting the part about the champagne, making the whole thing look very casual. Inspired, he finished it off with "P.S.—Cup, soap dish broken. Sorry. Will replace both on way home tonight." Then he propped it on the coffee table where she couldn't miss it, and chuckled.

She would come in loaded down with clumsy bundles, exhausted, with Mike howling and dirty and hanging on her skirt. "Mike, *stop* that! Stop it this instant! Bill?" she would call plaintively, "would you mind getting up for just a minute and giving me a hand? Bill, do you hear me?" And she'd stagger into the living room, enraged, dragging Mike and spilling half her groceries. "Look, Bill, I *hate* to tear you away from your—" But then she would stop, amazed, finding him gone and the apartment empty, and the little note propped on the table.

She probably wouldn't be able to do anything for an hour or so, until after she'd made Mike's lunch and gotten him settled for his nap, but after that the first thing she'd do would be to call him frantically on the telephone. He would take the call at his desk, leaning back in the swivel chair and answering the phone in a crisp, businesslike way.

"Bill?" she'd say. "Is that *you*?"

He would feign surprise. "Oh, hi, baby. What's on your mind?"

"Bill, have you gone *mad*? Are you all right?"

"Never better, honey. Say, I'm sorry about that cup, and the other thing, the soap dish. That what you called about?"

"Listen to me, Bill. I don't know what this is all about, but you're going to get right on the bus and come home. Do you hear me? No, better take a taxi. This instant. Do you hear me?"

"But *baby*," he'd say, "you know I can't quit work in the middle of the day. Want me to get fired?"

He laughed aloud—the line about getting fired was a hot one. He was all ready to go now, except for the piece of tissue on his lip. He pulled it off carefully, but the cut was still fresh and started to bleed again. Cursing, he dabbed at it with his handkerchief and stood by the door, waiting for it to heal. What would she say next, after the line about getting fired? Probably something like "Look. Just what is all this supposed to prove? Would you mind telling me?"

"Sure," he'd say. "Proves I'm well, that's all. Well man's got no business moping around the house all day making work for his wife. Ought to be out earning a living, providing a little security for her. Anything wrong in that?"

"Oh, nothing at all," she would say. "That's just lovely. You stay right there and make yourself ill, and come home tonight and collapse, and go to work tomorrow and come home in an *ambulance*. That's just *fine*, isn't it. That'll give me lots and *lots* of security, won't it?"

"Aw, now, honey, you're all excited about nothing. You've just got this stubborn idea in your head that I'm—" But probably about this point George would walk into his office, the way he always used to do when Jean was on the phone. "Say, Bill, here's a couple of reports you might want to look—oh, sorry." And he'd sit down, well within earshot, to wait until Bill was free.

"All right, Bill," Jean's voice would say coldly in the receiver. "I'll put it this way; either you come home right now—"

"Okay," he'd say, cheerily, trying to convey by the false tone that he was no longer alone, "okay, then, honey, I'll see you at six o'clock."

"Either you come home right now—"

"Right, honey. Six o'clock."

"—Or don't expect to find me here when you *do* come home. I'll be on the train for Mother's, and so will Mike. I've had just about enough of your kind of security." And there would be a little dry click as she hung up the phone.

Bill rubbed his head, sweating, looking at the note. He had never felt more thoroughly beaten in his life. He walked over to the table, crumpled the note and threw it into the wastebasket. That was that. And suddenly he stopped caring about the whole thing. Let her say or do whatever she wanted. Let anything happen. He was through. He surrendered. All he wanted was to go out and sit down in a bar and have a drink. Or two drinks or three. He grabbed his hat out of the hall closet, wrenched open the front door and stopped short. There she was, just coming in, about to put her key in the door he had flung open, looking up startled into his face. She was carrying only a few light packages, and Mike was neither crying nor pulling her skirt—he was grinning, in fact, and eating an apple.

"Well!" she said. "Where are *you* going?"

He jammed on his hat and brushed past them. "Out for a drink."

"Like that? With your suspenders hanging down?"

One sickening glance confirmed the fact: the suspenders hung in loops against his trouser legs. He spun around and glared at her, then started back toward her at a slow and menacing gait. "Listen. It's a good thing you came back before I left, because I've got a few things to tell you."

"Is it necessary to tell the neighbors too?" she inquired.

Grimly, controlling himself with a supreme effort of will, he followed her back into the apartment, took off his hat and followed her around while she disposed of the groceries and shooed Mike off to his room. Then she confronted him with a prim smile. "Now."

He planted his fists on his hips, rocked on his heels a few times and grinned evilly at her. "You know that soap dish? Well, it's broken."

"Oh." Annoyance flickered briefly on her face; then she resumed her thin little smile. "So *that's* what it is."

"Whaddya *mean* that's what it is? Another thing. You know those new cups? One of *them's* broken too! And the *saucer* too!"

She closed her eyes for an instant and sighed. "Well," she said. "I guess we don't need to discuss it. I'm sure you feel bad enough about it already."

"Feel *bad*? Feel *bad*? Why the hell should I feel *bad*? It wasn't my *fault*!"

"Oh," she said.

"Whatsa matter, don'tcha believe me? Don'tcha believe me? Huh? No, of *course* you don't. You're like a Communist *court*, aren'tcha? Everybody's guilty until proved innocent, aren't they? Huh? Oh no, not everybody, I forgot. Just me, right? Just poor stupid old Bill who drops ashes on the rug all day, right? Who's always 'resting,' right? Pretending to be sick while you bear your burdens with a smile, right? Oh, you *like* that, don'tcha? Love every minute of it, don'tcha? Huh? Don'tcha?"

"I will *not* take this, Bill," she said, her eyes blazing. "I will *not* take—"

"*Is that so? Is that so?* Because there's a couple things *I'm* not gonna take any more, and you better get 'em straight right now. I'm not gonna take any more of your wisecracks about 'resting,' understand? That's one thing. And I'm not gonna take any more of your—" His voice failed; he was out of breath. "Ah, never mind," he said at last. "You wouldn't understand." He took off his jacket, flung it on the couch and started to fix his suspenders; then with a gesture of disgust he let them fall again and plunged his hands in his pockets, staring out the window. He didn't even want a drink, now. He just wanted to stand here and look out the window and wait for the storm to pass.

"I certainly *wouldn't* understand," she said. "I'm afraid I *don't* understand why I should have to come home and find everything broken, and then get all this raging abuse from you *too*. Really, Bill, you *do* expect a lot."

The only thing to do was stand there and let her get it out of her system. He was spent now, unable to strike back or even to defend himself, a fighter hanging groggy on the ropes.

"What *does* go on in that mind of yours, anyway?" she demanded. "You're just like a child! A big, spoiled, stubborn child . . ."

It went on and on, but her voice lacked the shrill, nagging quality he had expected—instead it sounded hurt and almost tearful, which was worse. In the small part of his mind that remained clear he decided grimly that this quarrel would probably be a long one, the kind that lasted two or three days. The shouting and recriminations would stop soon, but there would be a long interval of cold silence, of polite little questions and answers over meals, of going to sleep without even saying goodnight, before he could decently go to her and say the big, simple thing that might have averted it all in the first place: "I'm sorry, darling."

Her tirade came to an end, and he heard her flounce off into the kitchen. Then there was a series of curt, businesslike kitchen noises—the refrigerator opened and shut, pots rattled, carrots scraped—and in a little while she came back again and started briskly straightening a slipcover right behind the place where he stood. What would she do, he wondered tensely, if I turned around and said it right now?

But at that moment a remarkable thing happened behind his back. Her fingers took hold of the dangling suspenders, pulled them up and deftly slipped them over his shoulders, and her voice—a new voice with laughter in it—said, "Fix your suspenders, mister?" Then her arms went around him and squeezed, tight, and her face pressed warm between his shoulder blades. "Oh Bill, I *have* been awful since you came home, haven't I? I'm so busy being tired and heroic I haven't given you a *chance* to get well—I haven't even let you know how terribly glad I am to have you *back*. Oh Bill, you ought to break *all* the dishes, right over my dumb head."

He didn't trust himself to speak, but he turned around and took her in his arms, and there was nothing sick and nothing tired about the way they kissed. This was the one thing he hadn't figured on, in all his plans—the one slim chance he had overlooked completely.

About the Author

RICHARD YATES was born on February 3, 1926, in Yonkers, New York. His parents divorced when he was two, and he grew up with his mother, a frustrated sculptor, and his older sister, Ruth.

Yates was a scholarship student at Avon Old Farms School. Upon graduation he served in the infantry in Europe during the last months of World War II. Soon after discharge he was diagnosed with tuberculosis, and spent a year and a half in a VA sanatorium. After leaving the hospital, he and his first wife, Sheila, moved to the south of France. While they were there, Yates's work came to the attention of Seymour Lawrence, then an editor at *The Atlantic Monthly*, who published "Jody Rolled the Bones" as an *Atlantic* First.

When he returned to the United States in 1953, Yates wrote freelance ad copy for Remington Rand and worked on *Revolutionary Road*. During this time, he drank heavily and had his first mental breakdown, beginning a lifelong battle with alcoholism and manic depression. He was divorced in 1959. The astonishing critical success of *Revolutionary Road* in 1961 led to a post as speechwriter for Attorney General Robert Kennedy, which was cut short by his brother John's assassination in 1963. Yates then moved to Hollywood and wrote many screenplays, including an adaptation of William Styron's *Lie Down in Darkness* for director John Frankenheimer, though none was ever produced.

Yates spent seven years teaching at the Iowa Writers' Workshop, where he met his second wife, Martha, and struggled to complete *A Special Providence*. After Iowa denied him tenure, Yates taught at several universities around the Midwest and finally relocated to New York City and wrote *Disturbing the Peace* as his second marriage disintegrated. Seymour Lawrence, now a book publisher with his own imprint, offered Yates a contract, and would publish him for the remainder of his career. Yates spent the next eight years in Boston, a productive period that saw publication of his last four books.

A second stint in Hollywood was followed by a Visiting Writer position at the University of Alabama in Tuscaloosa in 1991. When his teaching duties were completed, however, Yates was in too poor health to leave Tuscaloosa. A lifetime of smoking four packs of cigarettes a day had resulted in emphysema. Despite his flagging powers of concentration, he worked every day on a novel about his Kennedy speechwriting experiences entitled *Uncertain Times*. He was unable to finish it. He died on November 7, 1992, at the VA hospital in Birmingham, Alabama, of complications following hernia surgery.